READER'S DIGEST
BOOKS

www.readersdigest.co.uk

The Reader's Digest Association Limited 11 Westferry Circus Canary Wharf London E14 4HE

For information as to ownership of copyright in the material of this book, and acknowledgments, see last page.

Printed in France
ISBN 0 276 42868 4

READER'S DIGEST
BOOKS

*Selected and condensed
by Reader's Digest*

THE READER'S DIGEST ASSOCIATION LIMITED, LONDON

CONTENTS

THE ZERO GAME

Brad Meltzer

page 9

Matthew Mercer and Harris Sandler work on Capitol Hill in Washington. To inject some fun into their working lives, they join an undercover game that is being played by staff at all levels. The excitement of the betting system is so addictive that neither friend questions the rules—until one day Matthew realises that things are not what they seem. A lively and original best seller from a young writer who is winning fans worldwide.

PUBLISHED BY
HODDER & STOUGHTON

THE FIRE BABY

Jim Kelly

page 157

Freelance reporter Philip Dryden is better placed than most to know what's happening on his patch in the East Anglian Fens. But a series of incidents, starting with a missing girl and the discovery of some incriminating photographs, leaves him as baffled as the police. Together with his friend and driver, Humph, Philip travels the flat and seemingly endless landscape in search of answers to a tangle of questions, past and present.

PUBLISHED BY MICHAEL JOSEPH

THE PROMISE OF A LIE page 295

Howard Roughan

Late one night, Dr David Remler, a New York
psychologist, receives a disturbing phone call
from his intriguing new patient, Samantha
Kent. Anxious to help, Dr Remler rushes to
her aid, hoping to prevent a shocking act of
violence from spinning further out of control.
He has no idea what awaits him—or that he
is being artfully manoeuvred into a terrible
trap. A twisting, seductive tale of suspense
from a wonderful new talent.

PUBLISHED BY WARNER BOOKS, USA

THE DEATH AND LIFE
OF CHARLIE ST CLOUD page 437

Ben Sherwood

When Charlie St Cloud crashes his
neighbour's car and his little brother Sam
is killed, he swears he will never forget him.
Thirteen years later, while working in the
cemetery where Sam is buried, Charlie
meets Tess Carroll, a captivating yachts-
woman. As their relationship grows, he
is forced to make an almost impossible
choice. A delightfully different novel that
is both tender and uplifting.

PUBLISHED BY PICADOR

THE
ZERO
GAME

BRAD MELTZER

It's a game with its own set of rules. Played by staff and lobbyists in Washington's Capitol building. In secret.

Matthew Mercer is about to place a new bet—unaware that this time there may be much more than just money at stake . . .

ONE

I don't belong here. I haven't for years. When I first came to Capitol Hill to work for Congressman Nelson Cordell, it was different. But even Mario Andretti eventually gets bored driving two hundred miles an hour every single day. Especially when you're going in a circle. I've been going in circles for eight years. Time to finally leave the loop.

'We shouldn't be here,' I insist as I stand at the urinal.

'What are you talking about?' Harris asks, unzipping his fly at the next urinal. 'C'mon, Matthew, no one cares about the sign out front.'

He thinks I'm worried about the sign on the door that says MEMBERS ONLY—as in Members of Congress . . . as in *them* . . . as in *not us*—but after all this time here, I'm well aware that even the most formal Members won't stop two staffers from taking a whiz.

'I'm talking about the Capitol itself,' I say. 'We don't belong any more. I mean, last week I celebrated eight years here. What do I have to show for it? I'm thirty-two years old—it's just not fun any more.'

'Fun? You think this is about fun, Matthew? What would the Lorax say if he heard that?' he asks, motioning with his chin to the Dr Seuss Lorax pin on the lapel of my navy blue suit. As usual, he knows just where the pressure points are. When I started doing environmental work for Congressman Cordell, my five-year-old nephew gave me the pin to let me know how proud he was. 'I am the Lorax—I speak for the trees,' he kept saying, reciting from the Dr Seuss book I used to read to him. When I look at the tiny orange

9

Lorax with the fluffy blond moustache . . . some things still matter.

'The Lorax always fights the good fight,' Harris says. 'He speaks for the trees. Even when it's not fun.' He turns to the black man who's permanently stationed at the shoeshine chair right behind us, and says, 'Isn't that right, LaRue?'

'Never heard of the Lorax,' LaRue responds, his eyes locked on the small TV tuned to C-SPAN above the door. 'Always been a *Horton Hears a Who* guy myself.'

The doors to the rest room bang open, and a man in a grey suit with a red bow tie storms inside. I recognise him instantly: Congressman William E. Enemark from Colorado—Congress's longest-serving Member. But as he hangs his jacket on the coat rack and rushes towards the wooden stall at the back, he doesn't see us. And as we zip up our flies, Harris and I barely make an attempt to see *him*.

'That's my point,' I whisper to Harris.

'What? Him?' he whispers back, motioning to Enemark's stall.

'The guy's a living legend, Harris. Y'know how jaded we must be to let him walk by without saying hello?'

Harris makes a face, then gestures to LaRue, who raises the volume on C-SPAN. Whatever Harris is about to say, he doesn't want it heard. 'Matthew, I hate to break it to you, but the only reason you didn't throw him a "Hi, Congressman" is because you think his environmental record is crap.'

It's hard to argue with that. Last year, Enemark was the number one recipient of campaign money from the timber, oil *and* nuclear power industries. He'd hang billboards in the Grand Canyon if he thought it'd get him some cash. 'But even so, if I were just out of college, I would've stuck my hand out for a quick "Hi, Congressman". I'm telling you, eight years is enough—the fun's long gone.'

Harris's green eyes narrow, and he studies me with a mischievous look. 'C'mon, this is Washington, DC—fun and games are played everywhere,' he teases. 'You just have to know where to find them.'

Before I can react, his hand springs out and grabs the Lorax pin from my lapel. He glances at LaRue, then over to the Congressman's jacket on the coat rack. 'How much will you give me if I put it on his lapel?' he whispers, holding up the Lorax.

'Harris, don't . . .' I hiss. 'He'll kill you.'

'Wanna bet?'

There's a hollow rumble of spinning toilet paper from within the stall. Enemark's almost finished.

As Harris shoots me a smile, I reach for his arm, but he sidesteps my grip with his usual perfect grace. It's how he operates in every political fight. Once he's focused on a goal, the man's unstoppable.

'I am the Lorax, Matthew. *I speak for the trees!*' He laughs as he says the words. Watching him tiptoe towards Enemark's jacket, I can't help but laugh too. It's a dumb stunt, but if he pulls it off . . .

I take that back. Harris doesn't fail at anything. That's why, at twenty-nine years old, he was one of the youngest chiefs of staff ever hired by a senator. And why, at thirty-five, no one can touch him.

'How's the weather look, LaRue?' Harris calls to Mr Shoeshine, who, from his seat near the tiled floor, has a better view of what's happening under the stall door.

If it were anyone else, LaRue would tattle and run. But it isn't anyone else. It's Harris. 'Bright and sunny,' LaRue says as he ducks his head down towards the stall. 'Though a storm's approaching . . .'

Harris nods a thankyou and straightens his red tie. 'By the way, LaRue, what happened to your moustache?'

'Wife didn't like it—said it was too Burt Reynolds.'

'I told you, you can't have the moustache *and* the Pontiac Trans Am—it's one or the other,' Harris says.

LaRue laughs, and I shake my head. When the Founding Fathers set up the government, they split the legislative branch into the House of Representatives and the Senate. I'm here in the House; Harris works in the Senate, over on the northern half of the Capitol. It's a different world over there, but somehow, Harris still remembers the latest update on *our* shoeshine guy's facial hair. He's got the gift of the gab, and people love him for it. That's why, when he walks into a room, senators casually flock round him, and when he walks into the cafeteria, the lunch lady gives him extra chicken in his burrito.

Harris pulls Enemark's grey suit jacket from the coat rack and fishes for the lapel. The toilet flushes behind us. We all spin back towards the stall. The door swings open.

If we were brand-new staffers, this is where we'd panic. Instead, I take a deep gulp of Harris's calm and step in front of the Congressman as he leaves the stall. All I have to do is buy Harris a few seconds. But Enemark, someone who avoids people for a living, sidesteps me without even looking up and heads straight for the coat rack.

'Congressman . . . !' I call out, but he doesn't slow down. I turn to follow, but as I spin round I'm surprised to see Enemark's grey jacket hanging lifelessly on the coat rack. There's a sound of running water on the right side of the room. Harris is washing his hands. Across from him, LaRue rests his chin in his palm, studying C-SPAN.

'Excuse me,' Enemark says, taking his coat from the rack.

The way it's draped over his arm, I can't see the lapel. I glance over at Harris, who's wearing a calm on his face that's almost hypnotic.

'Son, did you say something?' Enemark asks.

'We just wanted to say hello, sir,' Harris interrupts, leaping to my aid. 'Really, it's an honour to meet you. Isn't that right, Matthew?'

'A-absolutely,' I say.

Enemark's chest rises at the compliment. 'Much appreciated.'

Harris steps towards him. 'I'm Harris Sandler,' he says. 'And this is Matthew Mercer. He does Interior Approps for Congressman Cordell.'

'Sorry to hear that.' Enemark gives a fake laugh as he pumps my hand. He opens his coat and slides an arm into the sleeve. A tiny flash of light catches my eye. There, on his lapel, is a tiny American flag pin, a little triangle with an oil well on it . . . and the Lorax.

I glance at Harris; he grins. When I was a freshman at Duke, Harris was a senior. He got me into the fraternity and, years later, got me my first job here on the Hill. Mentor then, hero now.

'Look at that,' Harris says to Enemark. 'I see you're wearing the logging mascot.'

LaRue is staring at the ground to keep himself from laughing.

'Yeah . . . I guess,' Enemark barks, anxious to be done with the small talk, and heads across the hallway to the House Floor. None of us moves until the door closes.

'The *logging* mascot?' I finally blurt.

'I told you there's still fun going on,' Harris says, looking up at the small TV and checking out C-SPAN. Just another day at work.

'I gotta tell Rosey this one . . .' LaRue says, rushing out of the room. 'Harris, they're gonna catch you sooner or later.'

'Only if they outthink us,' Harris replies.

I continue to laugh. Harris continues to study C-SPAN. 'Here we go . . .' He points at the screen as Enemark approaches the podium with his old-cowboy swagger. If you look real close—when the light hits him just right—the Lorax shines like a tiny star on his chest.

'I'm Congressman William Enemark, and I speak for the people of Colorado,' he announces through the television.

'That's funny,' I say. 'I thought he spoke for the trees . . .'

To my surprise, Harris doesn't smile. 'Feeling better? he asks.

'Of course—why?'

He leans against the inlaid mahogany wall and never takes his eyes off the TV. 'I meant what I said before. There really are some great games being played here.'

I give him a long, hard look and rub the back of my sandy-blond hair. At six feet four, I'm built like a palm tree and a full head taller than him. But he's still the only person I look up to in this place. 'What are you saying, Harris?'

'You wanted to bring the fun back, right?'

'Depends what kinda fun you're talking about.'

Pushing himself off the wall, Harris grins and heads for the door. 'Trust me—it'll be more fun than you've had in your entire life. No lie.'

TWO

SIX MONTHS LATER

I usually hate September. With the end of the August recess, the halls are crowded again, and with the October 1 deadline that's imposed on all Appropriations bills, we're clocking gruelling hours.

Leaving the polished hallways of the Rayburn House Office Building, I shove open the door to room B-308, call out to our receptionist, 'Here you go, Roxanne—lunch is served,' and drop two wrapped hot dogs onto her desk. As a professional staffer for the Appropriations Committee, I'm one of four people assigned to the Interior subcommittee. And the only one, besides Roxanne, who eats meat.

'Where d'you get these?' she asks.

'Meat Association event. Didn't you say you were hungry?'

She looks down at the dogs, then up at me. 'What's up with you lately? You on *nice* pills or something?'

I shrug my shoulders and stare at the small TV behind her desk. Like most TVs in the building, it's on C-SPAN for a vote on the House Floor. My eyes check the tally. Too early. No yeas, no nays.

Following my gaze, Roxanne turns round to the TV. I stop right there. No . . . there's no way. She can't possibly know.

'You OK?' she asks, reading my pale complexion.

'With all this dead cow in my gut? Absolutely,' I say, patting my stomach. 'So, is Trish here yet?'

'In the hearing room,' Roxanne says. 'But before you go in, some-one's at your desk.'

Confused, I hurry into the large suite that houses four separate desks. Roxanne knows the rules. With all the paperwork lying around, no one's allowed in the back office, especially when we're in pre-Conference . . . Which means whoever's here is someone big . . .

'Matthew?' a voice calls out with a salty North Carolina tinge.

Or someone I know.

'Come give your favourite lobbyist a juicy hug,' Barry Holcomb says from the chair next to my desk. As always, his blond hair is as perfectly cut as his pinstripe suit—both of which come courtesy of big-shot clients like the music industry and the big telecom boys and, if I remember correctly, the Meat Association.

'I smell hot dogs,' Barry teases, already one step ahead. 'I'm telling you, free food always works.'

Barry and I went to the same college and tend to see each other for a beer at least once a month. Although, since he's a few years older, Barry's always been more Harris's friend than mine—which means this call is more business than social.

'So what's happening?' he asks. There it is. As a lobbyist at Pasternak & Associates, Barry knows he's got two things to offer his clients: access and information. Access is why he's sitting here. Now he's focused on the latter.

'Everything's fine,' I tell him.

'Any idea when you'll have the bill done?'

I look around at the three other desks in the room. All empty. It's a good thing. My office mates already have their own reasons to hate me—ever since Cordell took over the Interior Approps subcommittee and replaced their former colleague with me, I've been the odd man out. I don't need to add to it by letting them catch me back here with a lobbyist.

Sitting just below the Grand Canyon lithograph that hangs on my wall, Barry leans an elbow on my desk, which is packed with volca-noes of paperwork, including my notes on the projects we've funded so far. Barry's clients would pay thousands, maybe millions, to see those papers. But Barry doesn't see them. He doesn't see anything. Justice is blind. And due to a case of congenital glaucoma, so is one of Capitol Hill's best-known young lobbyists.

As I move round to my desk, Barry's vacant blue eyes stare into the distance, but his head turns as he traces my steps, absorbing the sounds. If it weren't for the white cane, he'd be just another guy in a snazzy suit. Or, as Barry likes to put it, 'Political vision has nothing to do with eyesight.'

'We're hoping October first,' I tell him.

So why's Barry so interested? Because the Appropriations Committee writes the cheques for all discretionary money spent by the government. At last count, the Interior bill had a budget of $21 *billion*. There are four of us sharing this office, which means that each of us is in charge of spending over $5 billion. We control the purse strings.

It's one of the dirtiest little secrets on Capitol Hill: congressmen can pass a bill, but if it needs funding it's not going anywhere without an Appropriator. Case in point: last year, the President signed a bill that allows free immunisations for low-income children. But unless Appropriations sets aside money to pay for the vaccines, no one's getting a single shot.

'So everyone's good?' Barry asks.

'Why complain, right?'

Realising the clock's ticking, I flip on the TV that sits on my filing cabinet. As C-SPAN blooms into view, Barry turns at the sound.

'What's the tally?' he asks as I check the vote count.

I spin round at the question. '*What did you say?*'

Barry pauses. His left eye is glass; his right one is pale blue and completely foggy. The combination makes it near impossible to read his expression. 'The tally,' he repeats. 'What's the vote count?'

I smile to myself, watching him closely. It wouldn't surprise me if he were playing the game, too. I take that back. I would be. Harris said you can only invite one other person in. Harris invited me. If Barry's in, someone else invited him.

I check the totals on C-SPAN. 'It's thirty-one to eight,' I tell Barry. 'Only thirteen minutes left. It'll be a slaughter.'

'No surprise,' he says. 'Even a blind man could've seen that.'

I laugh at the joke—one of Barry's old favourites. But I can't stop thinking about what Harris said. *It's the best part of the game—not knowing who else is playing.*

'Listen, Barry, can we catch up later?' I ask as I grab my notes. 'I've got Trish waiting . . .'

'No stress,' he says, never wanting to be seen to push. Good lobbyists know better than that. 'I'll call you in an hour or so.'

'That's fine—though I may still be in the meeting.'

'Let's make it two hours, then. Does three o'clock work?'

I take it back. Even when he doesn't want to, Barry can't help but push. It was the same in college. Every time we'd get ready to go to a party, we'd get two calls from Barry. The first was to check what time we were leaving. The second was to recheck what time we were leaving. Harris always called it overcompensation for the blindness; I called it insecurity. Whatever the real reason, Barry's always had to work a little harder to make sure he's not left out.

'So I'll speak to you at three,' he says, hopping up and heading out. I tuck my notebooks under my arm and plough towards the door that connects with the adjoining hearing room. Inside, my eyes skip past the enormous conference table to the small TV at the back and—

'You're late,' Trish snaps from the conference table.

I spin midstep, almost forgetting why I'm here. 'Would it help if I brought hot dogs?' I stutter.

'I'm a vegetarian.'

Harris would have a great comeback. I offer an awkward grin.

Leaning back in her chair, Trish Brennan has her arms crossed, completely uncharmed. Thirty-six years old, with reddish hair and freckles, she's the type of person who says you're late when she's early.

As I pull out the chair directly across from her at the conference table, the main door of the hearing room swings open and the last two staffers finally arrive. Georgia Rudd and Ezra Ben-Shmuel. Ezra has a sparse beard and a blue shirt rolled up to his elbows. Georgia is quiet, wears a standard navy suit, and is happy to follow Trish's lead. Each is armed with an oversized accordion file and they head to different sides of the table. Ezra on my side, Georgia next to Trish. I represent the House majority, Ezra the House minority. Across the table, Trish and Georgia do the respective same for the Senate. And regardless of the fact that Ezra and I are in different political parties, even House Republicans and Democrats can set aside their differences in the face of our common enemy: the Senate.

My pager vibrates in my pocket and I pull it out to check the message. It's from Harris. YOU WATCHING? he asks in digital black letters.

I glance at the TV. Eighty-four yeas, forty-one nays.

Damn. I need the nays to stay under 110. If they're at forty-one this early in the vote, we've got problems.

WHAT DO WE DO? I type back on the pager's tiny keyboard, hiding my hands under the desk so the Senate folks can't see.

DON'T PANIC JUST YET, Harris replies. He knows me too well.

'Can we please get this going?' Trish asks. It's the sixth day in a row we've been trying to stomp each other into the ground, and Trish knows there's still a way to go. 'Now, where did we leave off?'

'Cape Cod,' Ezra says, and all four of us flip through the hundred-page documents in front of us that show the spending difference between the House and Senate bills. Last month, when the House passed its version of the bill, we allocated $700,000 to rehabilitate the Cape Cod seashore; a week later, the Senate passed its version, which didn't allocate a dime. That's the point of Conference: reaching a compromise—item by item by item. When the two bills are merged, they go back to the House and Senate for final passage. When both bodies pass the same bill, it goes to the White House to be signed into law.

'I'll give you three hundred and fifty thousand,' Trish offers.

'Done,' I tell her, grinning to myself. If she'd pushed, I'd have settled for an even $200,000.

'The Chesapeake in Maryland,' Trish says, moving to the next item. I look down at the spreadsheet. Senate gave it $6 million; we gave it nothing.

Trish smiles. That's why she was a pushover on the last one. The $6 million for Chesapeake was put there by her boss, Senator Ted Apelbaum, who happens to be the Chairman of the subcommittee—the Senate equivalent of my boss, Cordell. In local slang, the chairmen are known as Cardinals. What Cardinals want, Cardinals get.

In quiet rooms around the Capitol, the scene is the same. Forget the image of fat-cat congressmen horse-trading in cigar-smoke-filled back rooms. *This* is how America's bank account is actually spent: by four staffers sitting round a table without a congressman in sight.

My pager vibrates again. Harris's message is simple: PANIC.

I take another look at the TV. One hundred and seventy-two yeas, sixty-four nays. I don't believe it. They're over halfway there.

For the next two minutes, Trish lectures about why $7 million is far too much to spend on Yellowstone National Park. I barely register a word as the nays go from sixty-four to eighty-one.

'Don't you agree, Matthew?' Trish asks.

'Wha—?' I say, turning towards her.

Tracing my gaze back to its last location, Trish looks over her shoulder and spots the TV. 'That's what you're so caught up in?' she asks. 'Some lame vote for baseball?'

She doesn't get it. It isn't just any vote. It actually dates back to 1922, when the Supreme Court ruled that baseball was a sport—not a business—and therefore was allowed a special exemption from antitrust rules. Today, Congress is trying to strengthen that exemption, giving owners more control over how big the league gets. For Congress, it's a relatively simple vote: if you're from a state with a baseball team, you vote *for* baseball; if you're from a state without a team you vote against it. When you do the maths—that gives a clear majority voting for the bill, and a maximum of 100 Members voting against it—105 if they're lucky. But right now, there's someone in the Capitol who thinks he can get 110 nays. There's no way, Harris and I decided. So we bet against it.

Trish ploughs her way through the list. In the next ten minutes, we allocate $3 million to repair the sea wall on Ellis Island, $2.5 million to renovate the steps on the Jefferson Memorial, and $13 million to upgrade the bicycle trail next to the Golden Gate Bridge.

My pager once again dances in my pocket. Like before, I read it under the table. Harris's message says: 97.

I can't believe they're getting this far. Of course, that's the fun of playing the game. In fact, as Harris explained when he first extended the invitation, the game itself started years ago as a practical joke. As the story goes, a junior Senate staffer was bitching about having to pick up a senator's dry cleaning so, to make him feel better, his buddy snuck the words *dry cleaning* into a draft of the senator's next speech: '. . . although sometimes regarded as dry, cleaning our environment should clearly be a top priority . . .' It was always meant to be a cheap gag, to be taken out before the speech was given. Then one of the staffers dared the other to keep it in.

'I'll do it,' the staffer threatened.

'No, you won't,' his friend shot back.

'Wanna bet?'

Right there, the game was born. And that afternoon, the senator told the entire nation about the importance of 'dry, cleaning'.

In the beginning, they always kept it to small stuff: hidden phrases or an acronym in a commencement speech. Then it got bigger. Can you get twelve more votes for a bill? Can you get the Vermont Congressmen to vote against it? Can you get the nays up to 110, even when 100 is all that's reasonably possible? Politics has always been called a game for grown-ups, so why is anyone surprised people would gamble on it?

The rules are simple: the bills we bet on are ones where the outcome's clearly decided. A few months back, the Clean Diamond Act passed by a vote of 408 to 6; last week, the Hurricane Shelters Act passed by 401 to 10; and, today, the Baseball for America Act is expected to pass by approximately 300 to 100. A clear landslide. The perfect bill to play on.

Naturally, I was sceptical at first, but then I realised just how innocent it really was. It's like sitting in a meeting and betting how many times the annoying guy in your office uses the word 'I'. We don't change the laws or pass bad legislation, or overthrow democracy as we know it. We play at the margins where it's safe—and fun.

My pager once again shudders in my fist: 103, Harris sends.

'OK, what about the White House?' Trish asks, still working her list. This is the one she's been waiting for. In the House, we allocated $7 million for structural improvements to the White House complex. The Senate—thanks to Trish's boss—zeroed the programme out.

'C'mon, Trish,' Ezra begs. 'You can't just give 'em goose egg.'

Trish raises an eyebrow. 'We'll see . . .'

'Let's just split the difference,' Ezra says. 'Give it three and a half million, and ask the President to bring his library card next time.'

'Listen,' Trish warns. 'He's not getting a single muddy peso.'

It says 107 on my pager.

I have to smile as it inches closer. Whoever the organisers are—or, as we call them, the *dungeon masters*—these guys know what they're doing. The bets can go from twice a week to once every few months but when they identify an issue they always set the game at the perfect level of difficulty. Here I am, glued to a vote that was decided by a majority almost ten minutes ago. Even the baseball lobbyists have turned off their TVs. But I can't take my eyes off it. It's not the seventy-five dollars I've got riding on the outcome. It's the challenge. When Harris and I put our money down, we figured they'd never get near 110 votes. Whoever's on the other side obviously thinks they can. Right now they're at 107. Impressive . . . but the last three are going to be like shoving a mountain.

A buzzer rings through the air. One minute left on the clock.

'So what's the count at?' Trish asks, swivelling towards the TV.

'Hundred and eight,' I say as the C-SPAN number clicks up.

'I'm impressed,' she admits. 'I didn't think they'd get this far.'

The grin on my face widens. Could Trish be playing? Six months ago, Harris invited me in—and one day, I'll invite someone else. All you know are the two people you're directly connected to, one above, one below, so if word gets out you can't finger anyone else.

My pager says 109.

On TV, Ezra's boss, Congressman Witt from Louisiana, rushes across the screen.

Under the desk, I type in one last question: HOW DID WITT VOTE? NAY, comes Harris's answer.

Before I can respond, the pager vibrates one last time: 110.

Game over.

I laugh out loud. Seventy-five bucks in the toilet.

'What?' Georgia asks.

'Nothing,' I say. 'Just a stupid email.'

'Actually, that reminds me . . .' Trish begins, pulling out her own pager and checking a quick message.

'Is anyone here *not* completely distracted?' Ezra asks. 'We've got a serious issue—if the White House gets zilched, you know they'll threaten a veto.'

'No, they won't,' Trish insists, clicking away on her pager without looking up. 'Not this close to the election. They veto now and it'll look like they're holding up funding for the entire government just so they can get their driveway repaved.'

Knowing she's right, Ezra falls silent. I stare him down, searching for telltale signs. Nothing. If he is playing the game, the guy's a grand master.

'You OK?' he asks, catching my glance.

'Absolutely,' I tell him. 'Perfect.' And for the past six months, it's been exactly that. Blood's pumping, adrenaline's raging, and I've got an in on the best secret in town. And lucky for me, they're about to do it again. Any minute now. I check the clock on the wall. Two o'clock. Now that the vote's over, the camera pans back to the Speaker's rostrum and I focus on the small mahogany oval table just in front of it. Every day, the House stenographers sit there, clicking away. And every day, the only objects on it are two empty water glasses and the two white coasters they rest on. Today, however, is different. Today, there's just one. One glass and one coaster.

That's the signal. One empty water glass, broadcast all day long for the entire world to see.

There's a soft knock on the door and all four of us turn. A young kid wearing grey slacks, a cheap navy blazer and a blue-and-red-striped tie enters the room. On his lapel he wears a rectangular name tag that reads: HOUSE OF REPRESENTATIVES PAGE, NATHAN LAGAHIT.

He's one of a few dozen high-school pages who deliver mail and fetch water. The only person on the totem pole lower than an intern. 'I . . . I'm sorry . . .' he begins, realising he's interrupting. 'I'm looking for Matthew Mercer.'

'That's me,' I say with a wave.

Rushing over, he hands me the sealed envelope.

'Thanks,' I tell him, but he's already out of the room.

House and Senate pages barely leave a footprint. Ghosts in blue blazers. No one sees them come; no one sees them go. And best of all, since they get their instructions verbally, there's no physical record of where a particular package goes. An empty water glass tells me to be at my desk. A sealed envelope carried by a page tells me what I'm doing next. Welcome to game day.

'Trish, can't you just meet us in the middle?' Ezra begs as Trish shakes her head.

I angle my chair away from the group and examine the envelope. As always, it's blank. If I'd asked the page where he got it, he'd have said that someone asked him to do a favour. After six months, I'm done trying to figure out the game's inner workings.

I tear the envelope open. Inside, as usual, is a single sheet of paper with the royal blue letterhead of the CAG, the Coalition Against Gambling. The letterhead's an obvious joke, a reminder that this is purely for fun. Underneath, the letter begins, 'Here are some issues we'd like to focus on . . .' Just below that is a numbered list of fifteen items but, as usual, I go straight to the last on the list. All the rest are bullshit—a way to throw people off in case a stranger gets his hands on it. My mouth tips open as I read the words. I don't believe it.

'Everything all right?' Trish asks.

'Y-yeah,' I say with a laugh. 'Just a note from Cordell.'

My three colleagues instantly leap back to their verbal fist fight. I look down at the letter, trying to contain my grin.

(15) Insert Congressman Richard Grayson's land sale project into the Interior House Appropriations Bill.

I can feel the blood rushing to my cheeks. This isn't just any issue. It's *my* issue.

For once in my life, I can't possibly lose.

'So what do you think?' I ask as I rush into Harris's office in the Russell Senate Office Building. With its arched windows and tall ceilings, it's nicer than the best office on the House side.

'You tell me,' Harris says, looking up from some paperwork. 'Think you can really put the land sale into the bill?'

'Harris, it's what I do every day. We're talking a tiny request for a project no one would ever look at. Even Congressman Grayson, who made the original request, couldn't care less about it.'

'Unless he's playing the game.'

I roll my eyes. 'If you're a Member of Congress, you're not risking your credibility and entire political career for a few hundred bucks and a game. Besides, Grayson's project isn't a four-star priority that reaches the Member level—it's grunt work. And since it's my jurisdiction, it's not getting in there unless I see it. I promise you Harris— I already checked it out. We're talking a teeny piece of land in the middle of South Dakota. Land rights belong to Uncle Sam; mineral rights below used to be owned by some defunct mining company.'

'It's a coal mine?'

'This ain't Pennsylvania, bro. In South Dakota they dig for gold— or at least they used to, but when the gold ran out the company went bankrupt and the government's still dealing with the environmental problems of shutting the place down. Then a few years back, a company called Wendell Mining decided it could find more gold using newer technologies, so they bought the old company's claims out of bankruptcy, contacted the Bureau of Land Management and arranged to buy the land. The problem is, even though BLM has approved the sale, the Interior Department has them so buried in red tape, it'll take years to finalise unless they get a friendly congressional push.'

'So Wendell Mining donated some money to local Congressman Grayson and asked him for a bump to the front of the line,' Harris says.

'That's how it works.'

'And we're sure about the land? I mean, we're not selling a nature preserve to some big company that wants to put a mall on it, are we?'

'Suddenly you're back to being an idealist?'

'I never left, Matthew.'

He believes it. Growing up outside Gibsonia, Pennsylvania, Harris wasn't just the first in his family to go to college—he was the first in his town. As silly as it sounds, he came to Washington to change the world. But a decade later the world changed him. As a result, he's the worst kind of cynic—the kind who doesn't know he's a cynic.

'If it makes you feel better, I vetted it last year,' I tell him. 'The gold mine's abandoned. The town's dying for Wendell Mining to take over. The town gets jobs, the company gets gold and, most important,

Wendell becomes responsible for the environmental cleanup. Win, win, win, all around.'

For the first time since I entered his office, I see the quiet, charismatic grin in Harris's eyes. He knows we've got a winner here. A huge winner if we play it smart.

'OK . . .' he says. 'How much you got in your bank account?'

AT EXACTLY 9.35 the following morning, I'm sitting alone at my desk, wondering why my delivery hasn't arrived. On C-SPAN, the two water glasses are back on the stenographers' table. Everything's back to normal—or as normal as a day like this gets.

Ten minutes later, the door opens and a young female page sticks her head in. 'I'm looking for—'

'That's me,' I blurt.

Stepping into the room with her blue blazer and grey slacks, she hands me the sealed manila envelope and leaves. I look down at the envelope. Yesterday was spent dealing the cards. Today it's time to bet.

Ripping open the flap, I shake the envelope and two dozen squares of paper rain down on my desk. TAXI RECEIPT, it reads in black letters across the top of each one. I shuffle the pile into a neat stack and make sure every one of them is blank. So far, so good.

Grabbing a pen, I eye the section marked CAB NUMBER and quickly scribble the number *727* into the blank box. Cab 727. That's my ID. After that, I put a single tick in the top right-hand corner of the receipt. There's the ante: twenty-five dollars if you want to play. I don't just want to play, though. I want to win, which is why I start with a serious bet.

In the blank box marked FARE, I write *$10.00.* To the untrained eye, it's not much. But to those of us playing, well . . . mentally we add a zero. That's why they call it the Zero Game. In this case, ten bucks is actually one hundred.

Reaching into my top drawer, I pull out a fresh manila envelope and sweep the taxi receipts inside. On the front I write *Harris Sandler—427 Russell Bldg.* Next to the address, I add the word *Private,* just to be safe. Of course, even if Harris's assistant opens it, all they'd see is a ten-dollar taxi receipt—nothing to look twice at.

Stepping into our reception area, I toss the envelope into the metal basket we use as an out-tray. Roxanne does most of our interoffice mail herself. 'Roxanne, can you make sure to take this out in the next batch?'

She nods as I turn back to my desk. Just another day.

'Is it there yet?' I ask down the phone twenty minutes later.

'Been and gone,' Harris answers. 'The courier just left.'

'You left it blank, right?' I ask.

'No, I ignored everything we discussed. Goodbye, Matthew. Call me when you have news.'

With a slam, Harris is gone. And so are the taxi receipts. From me to my mentor, from Harris to his. Leaning back in my rolling chair, I can't help but wonder who it is. If Harris is an expert at anything, it's making connections. That narrows the list to a tidy few thousand. But if he's using a courier, he's going off campus. Former staffers are everywhere in this town. Law firms, PR firms, and most of all . . .

My phone rings, and I check the digital screen for caller ID.

. . . lobbying shops.

'Hi, Barry,' I say as I pick up. 'What can I help you with?'

'Tickets. This Sunday. Wanna see the Redskins get trounced from insanely overpriced seats? I got the recording industry's private box. Me, you, Harris—we'll have ourselves a little reunion.'

Barry hates football, and he can't see a single play, but that doesn't mean he doesn't like the private catering that comes with those seats.

'That sounds great, Barry. Did you tell Harris?'

'Already done.' Barry's closer to Harris so he always calls him first. But that doesn't mean the reverse is true. In fact, when Harris needs a lobbyist, he sidesteps Barry and goes directly to the man on top.

'So how's Pasternak treating you?' I ask, referring to Barry's boss.

'How do you think I got the tickets?' Barry teases.

As the founding partner of Pasternak & Associates, Bud Pasternak is respected, connected and one of the kindest guys on Capitol Hill. He's also Harris's first boss and the person who gave him his first big break: an early draft of a speech for the senator's re-election bid. Harris never looked back.

I study the arched windows on the side of the Capitol. Pasternak invited Harris; Harris invited me. It's gotta be, right?

I chat with Barry for another fifteen minutes to see if I hear a courier arrive in the background. His office is only a few blocks away. The courier never comes.

An hour and a half later, there's another knock on my door. The instant I see the blue blazer and grey slacks, I'm out of my seat.

'I take it you're Matthew,' a page with an awkward underbite says.

'You got it,' I say as he hands me the envelope.

As I rip it open, I take a quick survey of my three office mates, who are now sitting at their respective desks. Roy and Connor are on my left. Dinah's on my right. All three of them are over forty, professional staffers hired for their budget expertise. Congressmen come and go, but these three stay for ever. It's the same on all the Appropriations subcommittees. No matter which party's in charge, someone has to know how to run the government.

Dumping the expected pile of taxi receipts on my desk, I spot the one that's filled in. The fare's listed at fifty bucks. Unreal. One round and we're already up to $500. Fine by me.

Harris calls it the Congressional Pissing Contest. All across the Capitol, pages deliver blank taxi receipts. We all put in our bids and pass them up to whoever invited us into the game, who then passes them to their sponsor, and so on.

We've never figured out how far it goes, or how many branches exist: there could be four; there could be forty. But at some point, the bets make their way back to the dungeon masters, who collect, coalesce and start the process again.

Last round, I bid $100. Right now, the top bid is $500. In the end, whoever bids the most has to make the proposition happen, whether it's getting 110 votes on the baseball bill or inserting a tiny land project into Interior Approps. If you pull it off, you get the entire pot (minus a small percentage to the dungeon masters). If you fail, the money gets split among everyone who was working against you.

I study the cab number on the five hundred dollar receipt: 326. Doesn't tell me squat. But whoever 326 is, they clearly think they've got the inside track. They're wrong.

I've got my pen poised. Next to CAB NUMBER, I write the number *727*. Next to FARE, I put *$60.00*. That's $600 now, plus the $125 I put in before. If the bet gets too high, I can always drop out. But this isn't the time to fold. Stuffing all the receipts into a new envelope, I seal it up, address it to Harris, and carry it out to the front. Interoffice mail won't take long.

IT'S NOT UNTIL one thirty that the next envelope hits my desk. The receipt I'm looking for has the same cab number as before: 326. The fare is *$100.00*. An even grand.

I close my eyes and work the maths. If I go too fast, I'll scare 326 off. Better to go slow and drag him along. With a flourish, I fill in a fare of *$150.00*. Fifteen hundred. And still counting.

By a quarter past three, my stomach's rumbling and I'm starting to get cranky—but I don't go to lunch. We're too close to gift-wrapping this up.

'Matthew Mercer?' a page with cropped blond hair asks from the door. I wave the kid inside, and take the envelope.

'You're popular today,' Dinah says, hanging up her phone.

Turning my chair just enough so Dinah can't see, I open the envelope and peer inside. I feel my muscles tighten. It's not the amount, which is now up to $3,000. It's the brand-new cab number: 189. There's another player in the game. And he's clearly not afraid to spend some cash.

Scribbling fast, I up the bet to $4,000 and slide the receipt into the envelope. Then I head for the metal out-tray.

THE ENVELOPE COMES BACK within an hour, and I ask the page to wait so he can take it directly to Harris. Roxanne's done enough inter-office delivery service. Better not let her get suspicious.

I search inside the envelope for the signal that we've got the top bid. Instead, I find another receipt. Cab number 189. Fare of $500. *Five grand—plus everything else we already put in.* I hesitate for a nanosecond, wondering if it's time to fold. Then I remind myself we're holding all the aces. And the jokers. Cab number 189 may have the cash, but we've got the whole damn deck. He's not scaring us off.

I grab a blank receipt and write in my cab number. In the box next to FARE, I jot *$600.00.* That's a pretty pricey cab ride.

Exactly twelve minutes after the page leaves my office, my phone rings. Harris just got his delivery.

'You sure this is smart?' he asks the instant I pick up.

'Don't worry, we're fine.'

'I'm serious, Matthew. This isn't Monopoly money we're playing with. If you add up the separate bets, we're already in for over six thousand. And now you wanna add another six grand on top of that?'

When we were talking about limits last night, I told Harris I had a little over $8,000 in the bank. He said he had $4,000 at the most.

'We can still cover it,' I tell him.

'That doesn't mean we should put it all on black. Maybe it's time to walk away. No reason to risk all our money.'

'If you want to ease the stakes, maybe we can invite someone else in,' I suggest.

Right there, Harris stops. 'What are you saying?'

He thinks I'm trying to find out who's above him on the list.

'You think it's Barry, don't you?' he asks.

'Actually, I think it's Pasternak.'

He doesn't reply, and I grin to myself. He can't lie to an old friend.

'I'm not saying you're right,' Harris says eventually. 'But either way, my guy's not gonna go for it. Especially this late. I mean, even assuming 189 is teaming up with his own mentor, that's still a tractorful of cash.'

'And it'll be two tractorfuls when we win. There's gotta be over twenty-five grand in the pot.'

There's a pause at the other end. 'Just tell me one thing, Matthew—can you really make this happen?'

I'm silent, working every possibility. For once, I'm all confidence; he's concern. 'I think so,' I tell him.

'No, no, no, no, no . . . Forget "think so". I can't afford "think so". I'm asking you honestly. *Can you pull this off?*'

'This baby's mine,' I tell him. 'Only Cordell himself is closer.'

The silence tells me he's unconvinced.

'Harris, you know what the golden rule of Appropriations is? He who has the gold makes the rule,' I say. 'And we got the gold. Now, are you in?'

'You already filled out the slip, didn't you?'

'But you're the one who has to send it on.'

There's a pause. I hear him call to his assistant. 'Cheese, I need you to deliver a package.'

There we go. Back in business.

THE CLOCK HITS seven thirty and there's a light knock on my office door. 'All clear?' Harris asks, sticking his head inside.

'C'mon in,' I say, motioning him towards my desk. With everyone gone, we might as well speed things along.

As he enters, he lowers his chin and flashes a thin grin. It's a look I don't recognise. New-found trust? Respect? Before I can speak, there's a knock on my door.

'Matthew Mercer?' a female page with brown curls asks as she approaches with an envelope.

Harris and I share a glance. This is it.

She hands me the envelope, and I struggle to play it cool.

'Wait . . . aren't you Harris?' she blurts.

He doesn't flinch. 'I'm sorry. Have we met?'

'At orientation . . . you gave that speech.'

I roll my eyes, not surprised. Every year, Harris is one of four staffers asked to speak at the orientation for the pages. To most, it's a dull job. Not to Harris. The other three speakers drone on about the value of government. Harris tells them they'll be writing the future. Every year, the fan club grows.

'That was really amazing what you said,' she adds, unable to take her eyes off him. His square shoulders, dimpled chin, deep green eyes, strong black eyebrows—he's always had a classic look, like someone you see in an old black and white photograph from the 1930s. Never had to work it.

I can't take my eyes off the envelope. 'Harris we should really . . .'

'Listen, you have a great one,' the page says as she leaves.

'You, too,' Harris says.

The door slams with a bang, and Harris yanks the envelope from my hands and casually flips it open. He peeks inside and stays silent. If the bet's been raised, there'll be a new receipt inside. If we're top dog, our old slip of paper is the only thing we'll find. I try to read his face. I don't have a prayer. He's been in politics too long.

'What?' I demand. 'He raised it, didn't he?'

He looks up, lifting an eyebrow. He flashes the taxi receipt in his hand like a police badge. It's my handwriting. Our old bet. For $6,000.

'It's payday, Matthew. Now, you ready to name that tune . . . ?'

THREE

Next morning I'm the last to arrive in the hearing room. It's intentional. Let 'em think I'm not anxious about the agenda. As usual, Ezra's on my side of the table; Trish and Georgia are on the other. On the right-hand wall, there's a photograph of Yosemite National Park, showing the glassy surface of the Merced River dominated by the snow-covered mountain peak of Half Dome. Like the Grand Canyon picture in my office, the image brings instant calm.

'So, anything new?' Trish asks.

'Nope,' I reply, wondering the same about her. We both know the pre-Conference tango. Every day, there's a new project that one of our bosses 'forgot' to put in the bill. Last week, I gave her $300,000 for manatee protection in Florida; she returned the favour by giving me $400,000 to fund a University of Michigan study of toxic mould. As a result, the Senator from Florida and the Congressman from Michigan now have something to brag about during the elections.

I've got a mental list of every project—including the gold mine—that I need to squeeze in by the time pre-Conference is done. Trish has the same. Neither of us wants to show our hand first. So for two hours, we stick to the script.

By noon, Trish is looking at her watch, ready for lunch. If she's got a project up her sleeve, she's playing it cool—which is why I start wondering if I should put mine out there first.

'Meet back here at one?' she asks. I nod and slam my three-ring binder shut. 'By the way,' she adds as I head back to my office, 'there's one other thing I almost forgot . . .'

I spin round. It takes every muscle in my face to hide my grin.

'It's this sewer project in Marblehead, Mass.,' Trish begins. 'Senator Schreck's home town.'

'Oh, hell,' I shoot back. 'That reminds me—I almost forgot about this land sale I was supposed to ask you about for Grayson.'

Trish cocks her head like she believes me. I do the same for her. Professional courtesy.

'How much is the sewer?' I ask.

'Hundred and twenty thousand. What about the land sale?'

'Doesn't cost a thing—they're trying to buy it from us.'

'What's on the land now?' she asks.

'Dust, rabbit turds . . . What they want is the gold mine underneath.'

'They taking cleanup responsibility?'

'Absolutely. And since they're buying the land, we'll actually be *getting* money on this one. I'm telling you, it's a good deal.'

Trish knows I'm right. Standing behind the oval table, she shifts her jaw off-centre, trying to put a dollar value on my request. 'Let me call my office,' she says finally.

'There's a telephone in the meeting room,' I say, pointing her and Georgia next door.

As the side door slams behind them, Ezra packs up his own notebooks. 'Think they'll go for it?' he asks.

'Depends how bad she wants her sewer, right?'

Ezra nods, and I gaze at the Yosemite photo, waiting for the side door to open. It stays shut and I already feel drips of sweat trickling down my rib cage. I try to ignore the numbers floating through my brain. Twelve thousand dollars. Every nickel I've saved for the past few years. Or the twenty-five-grand reward. It all comes down to this.

Trish re-enters the room, cradling her three-ring binder like a girl in junior high. 'I'll trade you the sewer for the gold mine,' she blurts.

'Done,' I shoot back.

We both nod to consummate the deal. Trish marches off to lunch. I march back to my office.

And just like that, we're standing in the winner's circle.

'THAT'S IT?' HARRIS ASKS, his voice squawking through my receiver.

'That's it,' I repeat from my almost empty office. Everyone's at lunch but Dinah, who's on a call with someone else. I still watch what I say. 'When the Members vote for the bill—which they always do since it's filled with goodies for themselves—we're all done.'

'And you're sure you don't have any uptight Members who'll read through the bill and take the gold mine out?' Harris asks.

'Are you kidding? These people don't read. Last year, one bill was over eleven hundred pages long. I barely read it, and that's my job.'

'OK. And you have everything else?'

Reaching into the jacket pocket of my suit, I pull out a white envelope. Checking it for the seventh time today, I open the flap and stare at the two cashier's cheques inside. One's for $4,000.00. The other's for $8,225.00. One from Harris, the other from me. Both are made out to cash. Completely untraceable.

'Right here in front of me,' I say as I seal the envelope and slide it into a bigger manila mailer.

'They still haven't picked it up?' Harris asks.

'Don't stress yourself—they'll be here . . .'

There's a polite cough as the door peeks open. 'I'm looking for Matt?' an African-American page says as he steps inside.

' . . . any second,' I tell Harris. 'Gotta run—business calls.'

I hang up the phone and wave the page inside. 'I'm Matthew. C'mon in.'

As the page approaches my desk, I notice he's wearing a blue suit instead of the standard blazer and grey slacks. This guy isn't a House page; he's from the Senate. Even the pages dress nicer over there.

I seal the envelope, jot the word *Private* across the back, and put it in his hands. 'You know where this is going?' I ask.

'Back to the cloakroom,' he says. 'They take it from there.'

As he grabs the package, I notice a silver ring on his first finger. I didn't think they let pages wear jewellery. He smiles with a big, toothy grin. I smile right back. But it's not until that moment that I realise I'm about to hand $12,225 to a complete stranger.

'Be safe now,' he sings as he pivots towards reception.

He disappears through the door and I'm left staring at the back of someone's head. It's not a good feeling, and not just because he's carrying every dollar I own and all the savings of my best friend. It's more primal than that—something I feel in the last vertebra of my spine. Like nothing's necessarily wrong, but it's also not quite right.

I glance at Dinah, who's still haggling on the phone. I've got another half hour before I have to resume the battle with Trish. Plenty of time for a quick run to the Senate cloakroom to check things out. I hop from my seat and race out through reception. The page can't have more than a thirty-second head start.

Darting into the hallway, I turn a corner and make a right at the elevators. I spot him about a hundred feet ahead. His arms are swinging at his side. Not a worry in the world. I assume he's headed for the underground tram that'll take him back to the Capitol. To my surprise, he makes a sharp right and disappears down a short flight of stairs. Why's he going outside?

But as I shove my way through the door and race down the outdoor steps, it makes a bit more sense. The September day is overcast, but the weather's still warm. If he's walking the halls all day, maybe he's just after some fresh air. At the corner of Independence and South Capitol, all he has to do is make a left and cut across the street. Instead, he pauses—and makes a right. *Away* from the Capitol.

My Adam's apple swells in my throat. What the hell is going on?

I race towards the corner. When I reach it, the page is halfway down South Capitol. I whip out my phone and dial Harris's number. I get voice mail, which means he's either on the line or out to lunch.

I try to tell myself it still makes sense. Maybe this is how the dungeon masters play it—the last transfer gets dropped off campus. The more I think about it, the more it makes sense. But that doesn't make the reality pill any easier to swallow. He's got our money. I want to know where it's going.

At the end of the block, the page makes a left on C Street and disappears round another corner. I take off after him.

As he turns right on New Jersey Avenue, I'm at least fifty yards behind him. He's still moving fast, and now he's yakking away on his cellphone. We've entered the residential section of Capitol Hill—

brick town house squeezed next to brick town house. I walk on the other side of the pothole-filled street, pretending I'm looking for my parked car. It's a lame excuse, but if he spins round at least he won't notice me. The further we go, the more the neighbourhood shape-shifts around us. Within two minutes, the tree-lined streets give way to chain-link fences and broken bottles scattered across the concrete.

The page still has his phone pressed against his ear. There's a new glide in his walk. His body bounces with each step. The kid who quietly coughed his way into my office barely five blocks ago is long gone. Instead, the page moves without a hint of hesitation, tapping the envelope—filled with our money—against his thigh. To me, this is a rough neighbourhood. To the page, this is home.

Up ahead, the street rises slightly, then levels off just below the overpass for I-395 that runs overhead. As the page nears the overpass, he glances back to see if anyone's following. I duck down behind a black Acura. I count to ten and stand up straight again. Last I saw him, he was diagonally up the street. Now there's no one there. The page is gone. And so's our money.

In full panic, I'm tempted to run towards the overpass, but I've seen enough movies to know that the moment you rush in blindly, there's always someone lying in wait. My heart's punching against my chest and my throat's so dry I can barely swallow. I crouch down and chicken-walk slowly up the block. There are enough parked cars along the street to keep me hidden all the way up to the overpass. The closer I get, the more I hear the droning hum of traffic along 395— and the less I hear what's right in front of me.

I step out from behind a maroon Cutlass, the last of my hiding spots. As I enter the underpass, I look into the shadows and tell myself no one's there. The buzz of traffic whizzes by overhead. I look back down the block. No one's there. No one but me. Without anyone knowing where I am. What am I, insane? I spin round and walk away. He can keep the money, for all I care; it's not worth my li—

There's a muffled clacking in the distance. I twist back to follow the sound. It's coming from the other side of the overpass. I dart behind one of the enormous concrete pillars that hold the highway overpass in place. Angling my head round the column, I take my first full look. Beyond the overpass, up the block and off to the left, a dip in the side-walk leads to a gravel driveway. In the driveway, there's a rusted old industrial Dumpster. And right next to it is the source of the noise. Tiny stones being kicked by someone's feet. The page is making his way up the gravel driveway—and in one quick movement, takes off his suit jacket, yanks off his tie, and skyhooks both items into the open Dumpster. Without a pause, he heads back to the sidewalk, looking happy to be free of the suit. It doesn't make sense.

My Adam's apple now feels like a softball in my throat. As the page steps out of the driveway and fades up the block, he's still tapping the envelope against his thigh. And for the first time, I wonder if I'm even looking at a page.

How could I be so stupid? I didn't even get his name . . . tag. His name tag. On his jacket.

My eyes zip towards the Dumpster, then back to the page. At the end of the block, he makes a hard left and vanishes. That's my cue. I spring out from behind the pillar, dash down the sidewalk and head for the Dumpster. It's too tall to see inside. Even for me. But on the side, there's a groove that's just deep enough to get a toehold.

With a sharp yank, I tug myself up to the top of the Dumpster. Swivelling round, I let my feet dangle inside. There's a nauseating acidic stench. I stare down at the black plastic bags and push off with a soft nudge.

My feet pound through the plastic and I'm waist-deep in garbage. Wading towards the back corner of the Dumpster, I snag the page's navy suit jacket and go straight for the blue name tag.

SENATE PAGE, VIV PARKER

What's a girl's name doing on a guy's jacket?

Tyres screech in the distance, a car door slams. I turn at the noise. But I can't see anything except the mouldy interior walls of the Dumpster. Time to get out. Holding the name tag in one hand, I leap for the ledge, my feet scratching and sliding against the wall as I fight for traction. With one final thrust, I press my stomach over the ledge, twist myself over and plummet feet first towards the ground, still facing the Dumpster. As my shoes collide with the gravel, I hear an engine revving behind me, back towards the driveway entrance. Tyres screech once again and I spin at the sound. Out of the corner of my eye, I see the car's grille coming my way. Straight at me.

The black Toyota ploughs into my legs and smashes me into the Dumpster. My face flies forwards, slamming into the hood of the car. There's an unearthly crackle. Bone turns to dust. Oh, God. I scream out in pain. My legs . . . m-my pelvis is on fire.

'What's wrong wit you?' a male voice shouts from the car.

The blood pours from my mouth. *Please, God. Don't let me pass out* . . . In my left eye, I see nothing but red.

'All you hadda do was sit there!' the page screams, pounding the wheel with his fist. He yells something else, but it's muffled . . . all garbled . . . like someone shouting when you're underwater.

I try to wipe the blood from my mouth, but my arm's limp at my side. I stare through the windshield at the page, unsure how long he's been yelling. Around me, everything goes silent. All I hear is my own panting—a wet wheeze in my throat.

The page throws the car into reverse, sending me sliding off the hood. My back crashes against the Dumpster. I try to stand but my legs collapse beneath me and my whole body crumples in the dirt.

Straight ahead, the car bucks to a stop. But he doesn't leave. With my one good eye, I see the page shake his head angrily. There's a soft mechanical clunk. He shifts it back into drive. Oh, God. He punches the gas, the engine howls and the rusted grille of the black Toyota comes galloping straight at me. I beg for him to stop, but nothing comes out. The car thunders forwards. Sorry I got you into this, Harris . . . Mouthing a silent prayer, I shut my eyes tight and try to picture the Merced River in Yosemite.

'WATTYA MEAN, DEAD? How can he be dead?' Sinking down in his seat, Sauls felt a sharp contraction round his lungs. 'You said no one would get hurt,' he stuttered, cradling the phone to his chin.

'Don't blame me,' Martin Janos insisted on the other line. 'He followed our guy outside the Capitol. At that point, the kid panicked.'

'That didn't mean he had to kill him!'

'Really?' Janos asked. 'So you'd rather Matthew Mercer made his way to *your* office?'

Sauls didn't answer.

'Exactly,' Janos said.

'Does Harris know?' Sauls asked.

'I just got the call myself—I'm on my way down there right now. I'll have to sort out the kid first.'

'What about the bet?'

'Matthew already slipped it in the bill—last smart thing the guy ever did.'

'Don't make fun of him, Janos.'

'Oh, now you're having regrets?'

Sauls knew he'd regret this one for the rest of his life.

FOUR

'Harris, you sure this is right?' Senator Stevens asks me. I check the call sheet myself.

'Positive,' I reply. 'Edward—not Ed—Gursten . . . wife is Catherine. From River Hills. You met him flying first class last year.'

'And is he a Proud American?'

Proud American is the Senator's code for a donor who raises over ten grand.

'Extremely proud,' I say. 'You ready?'

Stevens nods.

I dial the number and grab the receiver. If I were a novice, I'd say, *Hi, Mr Gursten, I'm Harris Sandler . . . Senator Stevens's chief of staff. I have the Senator here for you . . .* Instead, I hand the phone to the Senator just as Gursten picks up. It's perfectly timed and a beautiful touch. The donor thinks the Senator himself called, instantly making them feel like old buddies.

'So, Ed . . .' Stevens sings. 'Where've you been my last dozen flights? You back in the cheap seats?' His pitch is off, but it still works like a dream. Personal calls from a senator always hit home.

There's not a congressman on the Hill who doesn't make these calls. Some do three hours a day; others do three a week. Stevens is the former. He likes his job. And the perks. And he's not about to lose them. It's the first rule of politics: you can do anything you want, but if you don't raise the cash, you won't be doing it for long.

As Stevens makes his pitch, my cellphone vibrates in my pocket. I reach for it. 'Harris,' I say.

'Harris, it's Cheese,' my assistant says, his voice shaking. 'I don't know how to . . . It's Matthew . . . he . . .'

'Matthew what?'

'He got hit by a car,' Cheese says. 'He's dead. Matthew's dead.'

Every muscle in my body goes limp, and it feels as if my head's floating away from my shoulders. '*What?*'

'I'm just telling you what I heard.'

'From who?'

'Joel Westman, who got it from his cousin in the Capitol Police. Apparently, someone found the bodies out by stripperland—'

'There was more than one?'

'Looks as if the scumbag who hit him took off in a panic. The car smacked into a telephone pole and the scumbag died instantly.'

Shooting to my feet, I run my hand through my hair. 'Why didn't . . .? I can't believe this . . . When did it happen?'

'No idea,' Cheese stutters. 'I just . . . I just got the call.'

The Senator looks my way, wondering what's wrong. Pretending not to notice, I do the one thing you never do to a senator. I turn my back to him. I don't care. This is Matthew . . . my friend . . .

'Everything all right?' the Senator calls out as I stumble for the door. Without answering, I rush from the room. Straight to the stairwell.

'The weird part is, some guy from the FBI was here looking for you,' Cheese's voice says in my ear. 'Said he wanted to talk to you as soon as possible.'

The walls of the stairway close in from every side. I tear at my tie, unable to breathe. I stumble down the stairs and shove my way outside, gasping for fresh air. It doesn't help. Not when my friend's dead. My eyes well up with tears, and the words ricochet through my skull. My friend's dead—

'Harris, are you there?' Cheese asks.

I tighten my jaw and try to bury the tears in my throat. I scout the street for a cab. Nothing's in sight. I start jogging up the block.

'Harris, talk to me . . .' Cheese begs.

'Just tell me where it happened.'

'D-Down on New Jersey. By the strip club. Listen, don't do anything rash—'

'Cheese, listen to me. Don't tell anyone what happened. This isn't office gossip; it's a friend. Understand?'

Before he can answer, I shut my phone, turn the corner and accelerate into a full-on sprint, my tie flapping over my shoulder.

RUSHING TOWARDS the overpass on New Jersey Avenue, I see flashing lights in the distance. But the moment I realise they're yellow instead of red, I know I'm too late. Up by a gravel driveway, the door of a flatbed tow truck slams shut, and the engine coughs itself awake. On the back of the flatbed is a black Toyota with a smashed-in front. The driver hits the gas, and the truck rumbles deeper into southeast DC.

'Wait!' I shout, chasing it up the block. '*Please, wait!*' On the back of the truck, the Toyota is still facing me, taunting me with its jack-o'-lantern grin. It's a twisted smile, with a deep indentation on the driver's side. Like it hit something. Then I catch the dark smudge towards the bottom of the grille. Not just something. Someone.

Matthew . . .

'*Wait . . . waaaait!*' I scream until my throat begins to burn. It still doesn't bury the pain. Nothing does.

The tow truck kicks back a cloud of exhaust and fades up the block. I scan up and down the street. There's not a strand of police tape in sight. Whoever worked this scene, whoever cleaned it up, found all the answers they needed right here. No suspects. No loose ends.

I kick a loose pebble from the street. It skips across and clinks against the sidewalk. Just shy of the telephone pole. There's some glass from the headlights scattered at the base and some torn-up grass where they dragged the car out. Otherwise, the pole's untouched. I crane my neck up. Maybe off by ten degrees.

Tracing it back, it's not hard to follow. Tyre tracks in the gravel show me where the Toyota's wheels started to spin. From there, the trail goes straight up the driveway. Dead-ending at the Dumpster.

There's a dent in the base of the Dumpster, and a dark puddle right below it. A black stain. All that remains.

My stomach cartwheels, and a snakebite of acid slithers up my throat. I stagger backwards, grasping for balance. It doesn't come. My back slams against the gravel driveway, my hands slicing across the stones. I'm not sure why I came here. I thought it'd make me feel better. It doesn't. I squint into the thin crawl space below the Dumpster. If I were small enough, I'd hide underneath, behind the gum wrappers, empty beer bottles, and . . . and the one thing that's clearly out of place. I see it because the sun hits it just right . . .

Cocking my head sideways, I slide my arm under the Dumpster and pull out the bright blue plastic name tag with the white writing:

SENATE PAGE, VIV PARKER

My mouth sags open. There was only one reason for Matthew to interact with a Senate page today. Our bet . . . If they were both out here, maybe someone—

My phone rings in my pocket.

'Harris,' I answer, flipping it open.

'Harris, it's Barry. Where are you?'

I look around the empty lot, wondering the same thing myself.

'Just heard about Matthew,' Barry says. 'I can't believe it. I'm . . . I'm so sorry.'

'Who told you?'

'Cheese. Why?'

I shut my eyes and curse my assistant.

'Harris, where are you?'

It's the second time Barry's asked that question. For that reason alone, he's not getting an answer. Climbing to my feet, I brush the dust from my pants. My head's still spinning, but I need to find out who else knows. 'Barry, have you told anyone else about this?'

'No one. Almost no one. Why?'

He knows me too well. 'Nothing,' I tell him. 'What about Matthew's office mates—they heard yet?'

'Actually, that's who I just hung up with. I called to pass the word, but Dinah . . . Trish from the Senate . . . they already knew.'

I look down at the page's name tag in the palm of my hand. In all the time we were playing the game, it was never important who we were betting against. But right now I've got a bad feeling it's the only thing that matters.

'Barry, I gotta go.'

I press the END button and dial a new number. But before I can finish, there's a soft crunch of gravel behind the Dumpster. I race round to the back of it, but no one's there.

I take a deep breath and let it wash down to my abdomen. My finger once again dives for the keypad. Time to go to the source, the person who brought me into the game. Barry's boss. My mentor.

'Bud Pasternak's office. How can I help you?' says a female voice.

'Melinda, it's me. Is he in?'

'Sorry, Harris. Conference call with a big client.'

Behind me, there's another crunch of gravel. I spin round to follow the sound. Further up the driveway, behind some bushes. That's it. I'm gone.

'Wanna leave a message?' Melinda asks.

Not about this. Matthew . . . the FBI . . . It's like a tidal wave, arched above me, ready to crash down. 'Tell him I'm coming by.'

'NICE TO SEE YOU,' Janos said, throwing a quick wave to the female security guard in the lobby of Pasternak & Associates.

'Can I have you sign in for me?' the guard asked, tapping her finger on the binder that was open on her desk.

Janos stopped midstep. This wasn't the time to make a scene. Better to play it quiet. 'Absolutely,' he replied as he approached the desk. With a flick of his pen, he scribbled the name *Matthew Mercer* on the sheet.

The guard stared at the letters on Janos's blue and yellow FBI windcheater. A few years back, the Justice Department announced that nearly 450 of the FBI's pistols, revolvers and assault rifles were missing. Whoever stole the guns clearly thought they were valuable. But they were not nearly as valuable, Janos thought, as a single windcheater, nabbed during an Orioles game. Even the Capitol Police won't stop a friendly neighbourhood FBI agent. To seal the deal, Janos quickly flashed a shined up sheriff's badge he got in an old Army-Navy store.

When Janos made eye contact, the guard looked away. 'Nice day outside, huh?' she said, staring out through the lobby's enormous plate-glass window.

'Absolutely,' Janos repeated as he headed for the elevators. 'Pretty as a peach.'

'NICE TO SEE YOU, Barb,' I say, ploughing through the lobby of Pasternak & Associates and blowing a kiss to the security guard.

'How's Stevens?' she asks.

'Old and rich. How's . . . how's your hubby?'

'You forgot his name, didn't you?'

'Sorry,' I stutter. 'Just one of those afternoons.'

'Everybody has 'em.'

It doesn't make me feel any better.

I step inside the waiting elevator and hit the button marked 4. The moment the doors close, I slump against the back wall. My smile's gone, my shoulders sag. In my pocket, I fiddle with the page's name tag.

With a ping, the doors slide open on the third floor, and I squeeze outside into the modern hallway with recessed lighting. There's a receptionist on my right—she'll never buzz me through. I go left. The hallway ends at a frosted-glass door with a numeric keypad. I punch in the code I've seen Barry enter a hundred times, the lock clicks and I shove my way inside. Just another lobbyist making the rounds. If I'm lucky, Pasternak will still be in the conference room—

'Harris?' a voice calls out behind me.

I spin round. To my surprise, I don't recognise the face.

'Harris Sandler, right?' he asks again, clearly surprised. His voice creaks like a loose floorboard, and his hangdog green eyes lock onto me like a bear trap. Still, the only thing I'm concerned with is the blue and yellow FBI windcheater he's wearing.

'Can I talk to you a moment?' the man asks as he points me back towards the conference room. 'I promise . . . it'll only take a second.'

'Do I know you?' I ask, searching for info.

The man puts on a fake smile and rubs his hand along his buzz-cut salt-and-pepper hair. I know that move. Stevens does it when he meets constituents. A poor attempt to warm things up. 'Harris, maybe we should find a place to talk.'

'I . . . I'm supposed to see Pasternak.'

'I know. Sounds like he's been a good friend to you.' His body language switches almost imperceptibly. He's smiling, but his chin pitches towards me. I make my living in politics. Most people wouldn't see it. I do. 'Now, do you want to have this discussion in the conference room, or would you rather discuss it in front of the whole firm?' he asks.

'If this is about Matthew—'

'It's about more than Matthew,' the man interrupts. 'What surprises me is Pasternak trying to keep your name out of it.'

'I don't know what you're talking about.'

'Please, Harris—even a nongambling man would bet against that.'

He doesn't just know about Matthew. He knows about the game. And he wants me to know it.

I stare at him coldly. 'Pasternak's in the conference room?'

'After you . . .' he says, motioning up the hallway.

I lead. He falls in right behind me.

I glance over my shoulder and give him a quick once-over. Windcheater, grey slacks and chocolate-brown calfskin shoes. The pewter logo says they're Ferragamo. I turn back towards the hallway. Nice shoes for government pay.

'Right in here,' he says, pointing to a door on my right. Like the one by the elevators, it's frosted glass, which shows me only the blurry outline of Pasternak as he sits in his favourite black leather chair at the centre of the long conference table.

I grab the doorknob and give it a twist. As the door swings open, I am surprised to find that the lights are off. Except for the fading sunlight from the large bay windows, Pasternak's sitting in the dark.

The door slams behind me, followed by a slight electrical hum. Like a transistor radio being turned on. I spin around just in time to see the man with the hangdog eyes lunging at me. In his hand is a small black box. At the last second I raise my arm as a shield. The box slams into my forearm and burns with a sharp bite. Son of a bitch. Did he just electrocute me?

He expects me to pull away. Instead, I grab the hand holding the box and tug him even closer. As he tumbles towards me, off balance, I punch him square in his eye. His head snaps back and he stumbles, crashing into the closed frosted-glass door. The black box flies from his hand and shatters on the floor, scattering batteries along the carpet. The man doesn't go down as easy. He looks up at me with an admiring grin, licks the corner of his mouth and sends me the message: if I plan on doing any damage, I have to do better than that.

'Who taught you how to punch?' he says as he scoops the pieces of the black box into his pocket. 'Your dad or your uncle?'

He's trying to show off some knowledge . . . to get me emotional. No chance. I've spent over a dozen years on Capitol Hill. When it comes to mental boxing, I've taken on a congressful of Muhammad Alis. But that doesn't mean I'm going to risk it all in a fist fight.

He climbs to his feet, and I look around for help. 'Buddy,' I call out to Pasternak. He doesn't move. Back by the conference table he's leaning back, one arm dangling over the armrest of his chair. His eyes are wide open. The world blurs as the tears swell in my eyes. I race towards him, then quickly stop short. Don't touch the body.

Behind me, I hear the hiss of the blue and yellow windcheater as Hangdog slowly moves towards me. FBI, my ass. I turn to face him, and he tosses out another cocky grin, convinced he's blocking my only way out. I spin back towards the bay window and the door that leads to the patio behind it.

I dart like a jack rabbit for the glass door. Like before, there's a numeric keypad. My hands are shaking as they tap out Barry's code. 'C'mon . . .' I beg, waiting for the magnetic click. Hangdog races round the conference table. The lock pops. I shove the door open, then spin around, trying to slam it shut.

He jams his hand into the doorway just as it's about to close. There's a sharp crunch. He grits his teeth at the pain but doesn't let go, glaring at me through the glass. He wedges his shoe in the door and starts to push.

I look over my shoulder at the rest of the patio, which is filled with teak Adirondack chairs. Straight ahead is a stunning view of the Capitol dome—and, more importantly, the other four-storey building that sits directly next door. The only thing between the buildings is the seven-foot alley that separates them.

41

The man winds up for a final burst. As his shoulder pounds into the door, I step away and let it swing wide. He falls to the floor, and I run straight for the edge of the roof.

'You'll never make it!' he calls out.

Again the mental game. I don't listen. I just sprint across the terra-cotta pavers. Straight for the edge. I tell myself not to look at the gap, but as I barrel towards it I don't see anything else.

I clear the seven-foot canyon, and hit the roof of the adjacent build-ing on the heels of my feet, skidding forwards until I fall back on my tail bone. A hot lightning-bolt of pain shoots up my spine. But there's no time to stop. I look back. Hangdog is racing at me, about to match my jump.

Scrambling to my feet, I look around for a doorway or stairwell. Nothing in sight. Except the metal tendrils of a fire escape that creep over the parapet like the legs of a spider. Making a dash for it, I hop over the ledge, slide down the rusted ladder and hit the top landing of the fire escape with a clang. Holding the railing and circling down-wards, I leap down the stairs half a flight at a time. By the time I'm on the first floor, I feel the whole fire escape vibrate. Up above, the man hits the top landing. I've got a three-floor head start.

With a kick, I unhinge the metal ladder, sending it sliding down towards the sidewalk. I clamber down it till my shoes smack the con-crete. As I look up at Hangdog, who's just reached the first-floor landing, I hear the jingling of keys behind me. I turn my head. A twenty-year-old kid with a pair of headphones is opening the back door to his apartment building.

Hangdog leaps down the ladder. I leap towards Headphones.

''Scuse me, kid—sorry,' I say, cutting in front of him. I grab his keys from the lock and slide into the building, slamming the door shut and leaving him outside with Hangdog. I can already hear Hangdog pounding his shoulder against the door.

Behind me, the grey industrial stairwell can take me up or down. From the view at the banister, up leads to the rest of the building. Down goes down a flight and dead-ends at a bike rack. Logic says to go up. It's the clear way out. Which is exactly why I go down.

Descending towards the dead end, I find two empty mop buckets and seven bikes, one with training wheels. Hopping over the metal grating of the bike rack, I curl down into a tight ball and glance up towards the banister. From this angle, I'm as hidden as I can get.

Up above, the door crashes into the concrete wall, and he enters.

I hold my breath while he makes his decision. His fingernail taps quietly against the banister. He's peering over the edge.

Two seconds later, he races for the stairs . . . but with each step the sound gets fainter. In the distance, another metal door slams into a wall. Then silence. He's gone. But as I raise my head and take a breath, I quickly realise my problems are just beginning.

I try to stand up, but vertigo hits fast. I can barely keep my balance—adrenaline has long since disappeared. As I sink back into the corner, my arms sag like rubber bands at my side. Like Pasternak. And as for Matthew. *God* . . . I shut my eyes. They both stare back at me. They're all I see. Matthew's soft smile and gawky stride . . . the way Pasternak always cracked his middle knuckle . . .

I lick my upper lip, and the taste of salt stings my tongue. It's the first time I notice the tears running down my face.

It was a game. Just a stupid game. But like any other game, all it took was a single dumb move to stop play and remind everyone how easy it is for people to get hurt. Whatever Matthew saw . . . whatever he did . . . that creepy nut chasing me is clearly trying to keep it quiet. At any cost.

I shake my head. The way he set it all up . . . and that black box with the two needles on the base, whatever the hell it was. He may not be FBI, but the guy's clearly a professional. And it doesn't take a genius to spot the trend. Pasternak brought me in, and I brought in Matthew. Two down, one to go.

One thing's for sure: I can't get out of this myself—not without help. I stand up, and race up the stairs and out of the back door. I run five blocks without stopping. Though I'm still not sure it's far enough, I flip open my phone and dial a number.

'It's Harris,' I say. 'I need some help.'

'Just tell me where and when. I'm on my way . . .'

'CAN I GET YOU ANYTHING?' the waitress asks.

'Yeah . . . yeah,' I say, looking up from the menu, which she thinks I've been reading for far too long. She's only partially right. I *have* been sitting here for fifteen minutes, but the only reason the menu's up is to hide my face.

'I'll take a Stan's Famous,' I tell her. 'Rare. No cheese.'

Stan's Restaurant is located one block down from the *Washington Post*, so there are always a few reporters and editors lurking around. If something goes wrong, I want witnesses with access to lots of ink.

I glance at my wrist and study the front door. I asked him to meet me at nine; now it's almost nine thirty. I pick up my phone just to—

The door swings open, and he strolls inside. He keeps his head down, hoping to keep a low profile, but at least four people turn and pretend to look away. Now I know who the reporters are.

When I first met Lowell Nash, I was a second-year staffer and he was the chief of staff who wrote my recommendation for Georgetown Law's night division. At forty-two, Lowell's now the youngest black man ever to hold the position of Deputy Attorney General. THE NEXT COLIN POWELL? read one headline in *Legal Times*. Playing to the article, Lowell keeps his hair cut short and always sits at perfect attention. He knows the value of looking the part.

'You look like crap,' he says, folding his black overcoat across the back of the chair and tossing his keys next to my cellphone.

I look up. 'Lowell, I need your help.'

He folds his hands on the table. 'How bad is it?' he asks.

'Pasternak's dead.'

He nods. News travels fast. 'I heard it was a heart attack.'

'That's what they're saying?'

This time, he's the one to stay quiet. He takes a quick scan of the restaurant, then twists back to me. 'Tell me about Matthew.'

I start to explain but cut myself off. It doesn't make sense. He doesn't know Matthew.

Lowell and I lock eyes. He quickly looks away.

'Lowell, what's going on?'

'Burger—rare,' the waitress interrupts, plopping my plate down in front of me with a clang. 'Anything for you?' she asks Lowell.

'I'm great . . . thanks.'

When she's gone I whisper, 'Lowell, enough with the anxious silent-guy act. This is my life. If you know something . . .'

He won't face me. He's fidgeting with his keys. 'They marked you.'

'What?'

'You're marked, Harris. If they find you, you're dead.'

'What are you talking about? Who's *they?*'

Lowell looks over his shoulder. I thought he was studying the reporters. He's not. He's studying the door. 'You should get out of here.'

'I . . . I don't understand. Aren't you gonna help me?'

'Listen to me, Harris. These people are animals.' His eyes drop back to his key ring, which has a small photograph of his wife and four-year-old daughter in a plastic frame attached to it. 'We're not all perfect, Harris,' he eventually says. 'Sometimes, our mistakes hurt more than just ourselves.'

My eyes stay glued to the key ring. Whatever they have on Lowell . . . I don't even want to know.

'You should leave,' he says for the second time.

The hamburger in front of me goes uneaten. My appetite is gone. 'Do you know the guy who killed Matthew and Pasternak?'

'Janos,' he says as his voice cracks. 'The man should be in a cage.'

'Who does he work for? Are they law enforcement?'

His hands begin to shake. 'Don't ask me any more,' he begs. He's staring at his watch. 'Go now. *Now.*'

Standing, I ignore the trembling in my legs and take a step towards the door. Lowell grabs me by the wrist. 'Not out the front,' he whispers, motioning towards the back.

I pause, unsure whether to trust him. It's not like I have a choice. I dart for the kitchen and push my way through the swinging door.

'You can't go back there,' the waitress snips at me.

I ignore her. Sure enough, beyond the sinks there's an open door. I sprint outside, hurtle up concrete steps and keep running, making a sharp right down a poorly lit alley. Whoever these people are—how the hell could they move so fast? From Lowell's reaction, it's clear to me that, whoever Janos is working for, they're drilling through my life. And if they can get to someone as big as Lowell . . .

Instinctively I reach for my phone. I pat all my pockets. Damn! Don't tell me I left it in the restaurant? I stop and turn round.

No. I can't go back.

Double-checking to be sure, I stuff my hand inside my breast pocket. There's actually something there, but it's not a phone.

I open my palm and reread the name on the blue plastic name tag:

SENATE PAGE, VIV PARKER

The white letters glow. It's going to be a long night, but as I turn the corner up Vermont Avenue, I know exactly where I'm going.

OUTSIDE STAN'S RESTAURANT, Lowell Nash scanned the sidewalk, stared at the shadows in the doorways of every storefront. But as he turned the corner onto L Street and hurried towards his car, he didn't spot a twitch of movement.

With one last glance at his surroundings, he unlocked the door of his silver Audi and slipped inside.

'Where the hell is he?' Janos asked from the passenger seat.

Lowell yelled, jumping so fast he banged his funny bone against the car door.

'Where's Harris?' Janos demanded.

'I was . . .' He grabbed his funny bone, holding it in pain. 'Aaah . . . I was wondering the same about you.'

'What are you talking about?'

'I've been waiting for almost an hour. He finally got up and left. Where were you?'

Janos's forehead wrinkled in anger. 'You said ten o'clock.'

'I said nine.'

'Don't bullshit me.'

'I swear, I said nine.'

'I heard you say—' Janos cut himself off. He studied Lowell carefully. He was crouched over, refusing to make eye contact.

'Don't fuck with me,' Janos warned.

Lowell looked up, his eyes wide with fear. 'I'd never do that . . .'

Janos narrowed his glance. A second passed. Then two.

Janos's arm sprang out like a wildcat, slamming Lowell's head into the driver's-side window. Refusing to let go, Janos pulled back and smashed him against the glass again. The window cracked from the impact, leaving a jagged vein zigzagging across the glass. Lowell felt a trickle of blood skating down the back of his neck.

Without saying a word, Janos opened the door and stepped out into the warm night air.

FIVE

'There—he's doing it again,' Viv Parker said on Monday afternoon, pointing to an elderly senator from Illinois.

'Where?' Devin whispered.

'Right *there* . . .'

Across the Floor of the Senate, in the third row of antique desks, the Senator from Illinois was staring at Viv.

As pages for the US Senate, Viv and Devin sat on the small carpeted steps on the side of the rostrum, waiting for the phone to blink. It never took long. Within a minute, a low buzz erupted from the handset.

The head page shot to his feet. 'Floor, this is Thomas,' he answered in a Virginia twang. 'Yep—I'm on it.' He turned to Viv as he hung up the phone. 'They need you.'

Nodding, Viv stood up, but stared down at the blue-carpeted floor in a final attempt to avoid the glance of the Senator from Illinois. Fiddling with the Senate ID round her neck, she wondered what he was staring at. Maybe it was her cheap navy suit . . . or the fact that she was black. Or that she was taller than most pages, including the boys. Five feet ten and a half inches—and that was without her beat-up shoes and the close-cropped Afro that she wore just like her mom's. Her skin colour, she could handle. Same with her height—like her mom taught, don't apologise for what God gave you. But if it was her suit, as stupid as it sounded, well . . . some things hit home. Since the day they had started, all twenty-nine of her fellow pages loved to complain about the uniform requirement. Everyone but Viv. As she knew from her school back in Michigan, the only people who moan about obligatory uniforms are the ones who can compete in the fashion show.

'Move it, Viv—they need someone now,' the head page called out from the rostrum.

Viv rushed to the cloakroom in the back of the chamber.

'Got one for you, Viv,' Ron Blutter announced as she pulled open the glass-paned door and smelt the familiar stale air of the cloakroom. Originally designed to store senators' coats when they had business on the Floor, the cloakroom was now where the pages got their instructions.

'Is it close?' Viv asked, already exhausted.

'S-414-D,' Blutter said from his seat behind the desk. Of the four young full-time staffers who answered phones in the cloakroom, Ron Blutter, the twenty-two year old in charge of the page programme, knew it was a crap job—keeping track of his party's puberty-ridden teenagers—but at least it was better than being a page.

'They asked for you personally,' Blutter added. 'Something to do with your sponsor Senator Kalo's office.'

Viv nodded. The only way to get a job as a page was to be sponsored by a senator. And as the only black page in the entire programme, she was accustomed to the fact that there were other requirements of the job besides delivering packages. 'Another photo op?'

'I'm guessing.' Blutter shrugged as Viv signed herself out and headed for the door.

S-414-B . . . S-414-C . . . S-414-D . . . Viv recited to herself as she followed the room numbers on the fourth floor of the Capitol. She hadn't realised that Senator Kalo had offices up here, but that was typical Capitol—everyone scattered all over the place. She stopped at the heavy oak door and gave it a sharp knock.

Waiting for a response, she was surprised not to find one.

She knocked again, then opened the door a tiny crack. 'Senate page,' she announced. 'Anyone here . . .?'

Still no response. Viv didn't think twice. If a staffer was tracking down the Senator for a photo op, they'd want her just to take a seat by the desk. But as she entered the dark office, there wasn't a seat. In fact, there wasn't even a desk. Instead, at the centre of the room were two large mahogany tables, pushed together so they could hold the dozen or so outdated computer monitors piled on top. The walls were bare. No pictures . . . no diplomas . . . nothing personal. This wasn't an office. More like storage. From the layer of dust that covered the half-lowered blinds, the place was clearly deserted. In fact, the only evidence that anyone had been in there was the handwritten note on the edge of the table:

Please pick up the phone.

At the bottom of the note was an arrow pointing to the right, where a telephone sat on a filing cabinet.

Confused, Viv raised an eyebrow, unsure why someone would—

The phone rang, and Viv jumped. She picked up the receiver. 'H-hello,' she answered cautiously. 'Who's this?'

'Andy,' a warm voice answered. 'Andy Defresne. Now, who's this?'

'Viv . . . Viv Parker. Is this some kinda joke? Thomas, is that you?'

There was a click. The phone went dead.

Viv hung up the receiver and looked up to check the corners of the ceiling. She'd seen something like this on *Bloopers and Practical Jokes* once. But there wasn't a camera anywhere. And the longer Viv stood there, the more she knew she'd been there too long, already.

She rushed to the door and turned the knob. But as the door swung open, she stopped in her tracks. A man with messy black hair was blocking her way.

'Viv, huh?' the man asked.

'I swear, you touch me, I'll scream so loud . . .'

'Relax,' Harris said, stepping inside. 'I only want to talk to you.'

I SEARCH FOR A NAME TAG on the girl's lapel. It's not there. Reading my reaction, she's obviously scared.

'Stay back,' she threatens. Stepping backwards into the room, she takes a deep breath, winding up to scream. I raise my hand to cut her off; then, out of nowhere, she tilts her head to the side.

'What a minute . . .' she says, raising an eyebrow. 'I *know* you.'

I match her raised eyebrow with one of my own. 'Excuse me?'

'From that . . . from the speech you gave. To the pages.' She bumps back into the edge of the table and looks at me. 'You were . . . you were really good. That bit about making the right enemies. I thought about that for a week.'

She's trying to sweet-talk. My guard's already up.

'And then that thing you did with the Lorax . . .'

'I don't know what you're talking about.'

'Nu-uh . . . c'mon—you put that pin on Congressman Enemark. That was . . . that was the coolest thing ever.'

Like I said, my guard's up. But as I spot the wide-eyed smile on her face, I'm already starting to relax a little. At first glance, she's slightly imposing, and it's not just the dark navy suit that adds another year or two to her age. It's her height—she's taller than me. But the longer she stands there, the more I see the rest of the picture. The frayed stitching on her suit, the worn creases in her white shirt. She's definitely not from money, and the way she's fidgeting and trying to hide a loose button, it's still an issue for her. Still, although she's must be only seventeen, her mocha brown eyes have a real maturity to them. I'm guessing early independence forged from a lack of cash—either that or she's getting Oscar for best actress.

'Who told you about the Lorax?' I ask.

She shyly turns away at the question. 'You can't tell him I told you, OK? Please promise . . .' She's truly embarrassed.

'You have my word.'

'It was LaRue . . . from the bathroom.'

'The shoeshine guy?'

'Nikki and I saw him in the elevator and he was laughing. We asked what was so funny and he told us. But he swore us to secrecy . . .' The words tumble from her mouth. 'Can I just say . . . putting that Lorax on him . . . that's easily the best prank of all time! And Enemark's the perfect member to do it to.' Her voice picks up steam. She's all gush and idealism. 'My grandad . . . He was one of the last Pullman porters and he used to tell us if we didn't pick the right fights—'

'Do you have any idea how much trouble you're in?' I blurt.

She finally hits the brakes. 'Wha—?'

I've forgotten what it is like to be seventeen. Zero to sixty, and sixty to zero, all in one breath.

'You know what I'm talking about,' I say.

Her mouth gapes open. 'Wait,' she stutters. 'Is this about the pens Chloë stole? I told her not to touch 'em, but she kept saying—'

'Lose anything lately?' I ask, pulling her blue name tag from my pocket and holding it out between us.

She's definitely surprised. 'How'd you get that?'

'How'd you lose it?'

'I have . . . I have no idea. It disappeared last week—they just ordered me a new one.' She's not stupid. If she's really in trouble, she wants to know how much. 'Why? Where'd you find it?'

I bluff hard. 'Toolie Williams gave it to me,' I say, referring to the young black kid who, according to the newspapers, drove his car into Matthew. Who was found dead in the same street.

'Who?'

I have to clench my jaw to keep myself calm. I reach once more into my pocket and pull out a picture of Toolie from this morning's Metro section. 'Ever seen him before?' I ask, handing her the photo.

She shakes her head. 'I don't think so . . . Why? Who is he?'

There are forty-three muscular movements that the human face is capable of making. I have friends, senators and congressmen, who lie to me every day. Pull the bottom lip in, raise the upper eyelids, lower the chin. I know all the tricks. But, as I stare up at this tall black girl I can't find a single twitch that shows me anything but innocence.

No make-up, no trendy jewellery, no fancy haircut—none of the totems of popularity. There's a girl like her in every school—the outsider. In five years she'll kick off her shell and her classmates will wonder why they never noticed her.

'Toolie,' I say 'is just someone who knew a friend of mine.'

Now she's confused. 'So what's it have to do with my name tag?'

Leaning forward, she takes a look at the name tag. Around her neck, her ID badge begins to twirl. I spot a photo of a black woman Scotch-taped to the back. I'm guessing Mom or an aunt. Someone who keeps her strong—or at least is trying to.

No way this girl's a killer.

'Actually, I'm trying to figure that out myself.'

'Well, what's the name of your friend?'

I decide to give it one last shot. 'Matthew Mercer.'

'Matthew Mercer? Isn't that the guy who got hit by a car?'

I reach out and snatch the newspaper photo from her hands.

Now she's the one studying me. 'Did *he* have my name tag?'

I don't answer.

'Why would he—?' She stops herself, noticing my stare. 'If it makes you feel better, I don't know how he got it. I mean, I understand you're upset about your friend's accident . . .'

I look up as she says the word *accident* and she locks right on me. Her mouth hangs open, but her eyes show shrewdness. She's got depth in her gaze.

'What? she asks. It was it an accident, wasn't it?'

'OK, calm down,' I say, forcing a laugh. 'Listen, you should really get going, Viv. That's your name, right? Viv? Viv, I'm Harris.' I extend a soft handshake and put my other hand on her shoulder. 'Of course it was an accident. I'm sure it was. Positive. I just . . . when Matthew was hit by the car, your name tag happened to be in a Dumpster near the scene. No big deal—I just figured if you saw anything . . . I promised his family I'd ask around. Now we at least know it was just something in the nearby trash.'

She nods, relieved. 'So you're OK? You got everything you need?'

In the ten minutes since I've met her, it's the hardest question she's asked. When I woke up this morning, I thought Viv would have all the answers. Instead, I'm back to another blank slate—and right now, the only way to fill it is to figure out who else is playing the game. I've got notes in my desk . . . The thing is, Janos isn't stupid. The moment I try to step back into my life, he'll stab his little shock box straight into my chest, where it'll really do some damage. I don't have a chance. Not unless I figure out how to get some help.

'Thanks again for finding the name tag,' Viv says. 'Let me know if I can ever return the favour.'

I replay the words in my head. It's not the safest bet I've ever made, but right now, with my life on the line, I don't think I've got much of a choice. 'Listen, Viv, I hate to be a pain, but . . . are you really serious about that favour?'

'S-sure . . .'

'It's just a quick errand—for an upcoming hearing we're working on. All you have to do is grab some briefing books and an electronic organiser. Sound OK?'

Viv scans the room around us. It's the one flaw in my story. If everything were kosher, why are we talking in a storage room? 'Harris, I don't know . . . We're not supposed to do pick-ups unless they come through the cloakroom.'

'Please, Viv—'

'I'm sorry,' she says, her voice breaking slightly. 'I can't.'

Knowing better than to beg, I wave it off and force a smile. 'No, I understand. I'll just call the cloakroom—it'll be done in no time.'

She stares right through me. 'I really am sorry about your friend.'

I nod a thankyou. 'And if you ever need anything, just call my office,' I say, forcing a smile.

She likes that one. 'And don't forget,' she adds, lowering her voice in her best impression of me, 'the best thing you can do in life is make the right enemies . . .'

'No doubt about that,' I call out as the door closes. She's gone. My voice tumbles to a whisper. 'No doubt about it.'

HEADING UP the fourth-floor corridor towards the elevator, Viv told herself not to look back. The desperate look on Harris's face was all she needed to see to know where this was headed. When she saw him speak to the pages, he'd glided through the room so smoothly that she was tempted to look at his feet to see if they touched the ground. Yet today, Harris was shaken . . . on edge. It didn't take a lifetime in politics to see the hurricane coming, and the last thing she needed now was to step inside the whirlwind. Not your problem, she told herself as she pressed the call button.

A rumble broke the silence and the door to the elevator slid open, revealing the operator, a grey-haired black woman sitting on a wooden stool, reading a newspaper. Viv stepped inside.

'Home base?' the operator asked from behind the paper.

'Sure,' Viv answered with a shrug. Leaning against the back railing of the elevator, she glanced at the newspaper over the woman's shoulder. Her eyes went right to the headline: HIT-AND-RUN DRIVER'S IDENTITY RELEASED. Below it was the photo that Harris had just shown her. The young black man. Toolie Williams. Viv couldn't take her eyes off him. For some reason, her name tag was found near a dead man. Even the very best reason couldn't be good.

'Here you go,' the elevator operator announced as the elevator bucked to a halt and the door creaked open. 'Second floor . . .'

The moment Viv had avoided the Senator from Illinois and his leering glare, she had heard her mother's insistent scolding in the back of her brain. *Stand up for yourself. Always stand up for yourself.* That was part of the reason Momma had wanted her to come to Capitol Hill. But right now, as Viv looked down at the grainy photo in the newspaper, she realised that Mom had only part of the picture. It's not just about standing up for yourself—it's also about standing up for those who need help.

'This your stop or not?' the operator asked.

'Actually, I forgot something upstairs,' Viv replied.

'You're the boss lady. Fourth floor it is . . .'

VIV KNOCKED on the door. No answer.

'Harris, it's Viv. You in there?'

There was a click. The doorknob turned, the door opened and Harris stuck his head out, cautiously checking the corridor. 'You OK?'

Viv stared Harris straight in the eye and said, 'You still need help with that pick-up?'

He tried to hide his grin, but wasn't good enough to pull it off. 'It's not gonna be easy. Are you sure you can—?'

'Harris, I'm one of two black girls in an all-white school. One year, they broke into my locker and wrote *nigger* across the back of my gym shirt. How much harder can it get? Now tell me where to go before I get all skeezed out and change my mind.'

WHILE I WAIT for Viv to do the pick-up, I grab the phone in the storage room and dial a number.

'Congressman Grayson's office,' a young man answers.

I grip the receiver and give the receptionist just enough of a pause to make him think I'm busy. 'Hi, I'm looking for your Appropriations person,' I finally say. 'Somehow, I think I misplaced his info.'

'And who should I say is calling?'

I'm tempted to use Matthew's name, but the news has probably already travelled. 'I'm calling from Interior Approps. I need to—'

Cutting me off, he puts me on hold. A few seconds later, a gruff voice is on the line. 'This is Perry.'

'Hey, Perry, I'm calling from Interior Approps, filling in on Matthew's issues after—'

'Yeah . . . I heard. Really sorry. Matthew was a sweetheart.'

He says the word *was*, and I close my eyes. It still hits like a sock full of quarters.

'So what can I do for you?' Perry asks.

I think back to the original bet. Whatever Matthew saw—the reason he and Pasternak were killed—it started with a gold mine sale in South Dakota that needed to be slipped into the Appropriations bill. Grayson made the initial request. I don't have much information beyond that. This guy can give me more.

'Actually, we're just re-examining all the different requests,' I explain. 'With Matthew gone, we want to make sure we know everyone's priorities.'

'Of course . . . happy to help.'

'OK,' I begin. 'I'm looking at your list, and, obviously, I know you're not shocked to hear you can't have everything on it. So we'd just like to know which projects are your must-gets?'

'The sewer system,' he shoots back, barely taking a breath. 'If you can do that . . . that's the one that wins us the district.'

He's smart. He knows how low his Congressman is on the ladder. If he asks for every toy on the Christmas list, he'll be lucky if he gets a single one. Better just to focus on the Barbie Dream House.

'So everything else on this list . . .'

'Is all second-tier.'

'What about this gold mine thing?' I ask, teeing up my bluff. 'I thought Grayson was really hot for it.'

'Hot for it? No. We put that in for a donor as a pure try-our-best.'

Matthew had told me exactly the same thing.

'Weird,' I say, digging. 'I thought Matthew got some calls on it.'

'If he did, it's only because Wendell Mining lobbied up.'

I write the words *Wendell Mining* on a sheet of paper, then ask, 'What about the rest of the delegation from South Dakota. Anyone gonna scream if we kill the mining request?'

He thinks I'm covering my ass before I cut the gold mine loose, but what I really want to know is, who else in Congress has any interest in the project?

'No one,' he says. 'It's a dump in a town so small it doesn't even have a stoplight.'

Three nights ago, someone bid $1,000 on the chances of putting this gold mine in the bill. Someone else bid $5,000. That means there's at least two people out there watching what is going on. But right now, I can't find them.

'So how we looking on our sewer system?' Perry asks.

'I'll do my best,' I tell him, looking down at the words *Wendell Mining* on my sheet of paper.

Slowly I feel the chessboard expand. Of course. I didn't even think about it . . .

'I gotta run now, Perry,' I say, already feeling the sharp bite of adrenaline. 'I just remembered a call I have to make.'

'HI, I'M HERE for a pick-up,' Viv announced as she stepped into Room 2406 of the Rayburn Building, home office of Matthew's boss, Congressman Nelson Cordell from Arizona.

The young man behind the front desk began searching his desk for outgoing mail. 'I didn't call for a page,' he said.

'Well, someone did,' Viv said. 'It was a package for the Floor. You have a phone I can use?'

He pointed to the handset on the side table. 'I'll go and see if anyone else called it in.'

'Great . . . thanks,' Viv said as the young man disappeared through a door on the right. The instant he was gone, she picked up the phone and dialled the five-digit extension Harris had given her.

'This is Dinah,' a female voice answered. As head clerk for the House Appropriations Interior subcommittee, Dinah had incredible access and a staggering amount of power. More importantly, she had caller ID on her phone extension, which was why Harris said the call had to be made from Cordell's office.

'Hey, Dinah,' Viv began, keeping her voice low and smooth, 'this is Sandy over in Congressman Cordell's office. I'm sorry to bother you, but we wanted to take a look at some of Matthew's briefing books, just to make sure we're up to speed for Conference . . .'

'I don't think that's such a good idea,' Dinah blurted. 'It's not smart to let that information outside the office.'

Harris had warned Viv this might happen. That was why he gave her the ultimate comeback.

'The Congressman wants them,' Viv insisted.

There was a short pause. 'I'll get them ready,' Dinah said.

Over Viv's shoulder, the door opened, and the young receptionist re-entered the room.

'Great,' Viv stuttered. 'I'll send someone down to pick 'em up.'

She hung up and turned to the receptionist. 'Oops—wrong room.'

'Don't worry,' he replied. 'No harm done.'

Viv headed for the door.

Refusing to wait for the elevator, she ran down the four flights of stairs, jumping down the last two steps and landing with a smack on the polished floor of the basement of the Rayburn Building. Viv hadn't felt this excited since her first day as a Senate page. She was done shuffling mail and finally doing what the page programme had originally promised—making an actual difference in someone's life.

Sliding to a stop in front of room B-308, she felt her heart jab against her chest. This was Matthew's office—and if she wasn't careful, she'd never be able to pull it off. She checked the corridor, then twisted the brass knob and entered the room. She was hit by a sudden sense of relief when she saw that the receptionist was black.

Without a word, Roxanne glanced up at Viv, studied her ID, and gave her a warm smile. 'Whatcha need, doll?'

'Just here to pick up some briefing books.'

'Right through there,' Roxanne said, pointing to the back.

Viv headed for the door, and Roxanne turned back to the current vote on C-SPAN. Viv couldn't help but grin. On Capitol Hill, even the support staff were political junkies.

'So where are we now?' a male voice was asking as Viv entered the back room.

'I told you, we're working on it,' Dinah replied. 'He's only been gone for two—' She cut herself off. 'Can I help you?' she barked at Viv.

Before Viv could answer, the man in front of Dinah's desk turned. Viv looked him straight in the eye, but something was off. He stared too high, like he was . . . Then she spotted the white cane.

'I said, can I help you?' Dinah repeated.

'Yeah,' Viv stuttered, 'I'm here for the briefing books.'

'On the chair,' Dinah said, pointing towards the desk across from her own.

Viv slipped behind the desk and saw two enormous three-ring notebooks sitting on the chair. She also noticed a pile of picture frames stacked face up on the desk. Like someone was packing up . . . or someone was *being* packed up. Time froze as she caught a glance of the top photo, a tall, gawky man with sandy-blond hair standing in front of a sapphire-blue lake. Viv had never met Matthew, but once she saw his photo, she couldn't take her eyes off him.

Behind her, she felt a strong hand on her shoulder. 'You OK?' Barry asked. 'Need any help?'

Viv yanked the notebooks from the chair and, forcing an awkward grin, stumbled back around the desk to the door.

'Just make sure we get them back,' Dinah called out.

'Soon as the Congressman's done, they're all yours,' Viv said.

SIX

'What about his house?' Marcus Sauls's voice squawked down the cellphone.

'He's got a loft on the outskirts,' Janos said, keeping his voice down as he hurried along a marble hallway in the Russell Senate Office Building. 'He doesn't own the place, though—or much of anything else. No car, no stocks, nothing in his bank account. Anything else you want to know?' he added.

'Family and friends?'

'The boy's smart. He's been in Congress ten years. Know how ruthless that makes you? Even though he's well connected, the job alone keeps him from reaching out to coworkers. And after we tagged his buddy at the US Attorney's Office. . . I don't think Harris gets fooled twice.'

'Bullshit. No one survives alone. There's someone out there he trusts. You think you can find him?'

Stopping in front of a tall mahogany door, Janos gripped the doorknob and gave it a hard twist. 'That's my job,' he said. He clicked the END button on his phone and stuffed it into the pocket of his FBI windcheater.

Inside, the office was exactly the same as last time he had been there. Harris's desk was untouched behind the glass divider, and Harris's assistant still sat at the desk out front.

'Agent Graves,' Cheese called out as he saw Janos. 'What can I help you with today?'

'LEGISLATIVE RESOURCE CENTER,' a man answers. 'You're speaking with Gary Naftalis. How can I assist?'

'Hey, Gary—I'm calling from Senator Stevens's office. I'm hoping you can help me out. We've got a company that's been calling us about this bill, and we're trying to figure out which lobbyists they're working with. You guys still cover that?'

'Only if we want to keep the lobbyists honest, sir.' He laughs.

It's a bad joke, but a valid point. Every year, over 17,000 lobbyists descend on Capitol Hill, each one armed with a Tommy gun of special requests. Combine that with the boatloads of bills that are submitted and voted on every day and it's overwhelming. As anyone on the Hill knows, there's too much work for a staffer to be an expert on it all. So if you need some research? Call the lobbyists. Want some talking points? Call the lobbyists. If what they give you is good, you'll keep coming back. And that's how influence is peddled. Quietly, quickly, and without leaving fingerprints.

The thing is, right now I need those fingerprints. If Pasternak was playing the game, other lobbyists played as well. Fortunately, all lobbyists are required to register with the Legislative Resource Center and list the names of their clients.

'Can I ask you a huge favour?' I pitch. 'My Senator's about to rip my head off . . . So if I gave you the name of a particular company right now, would you mind looking it up for me, Gary?'

He pauses, then asks, 'What's the name of the company, sir?'

'It's Wendell Mining,' I tell him.

I hear the clicking of his keyboard, and I stop pacing back and forth across the storage room. Staring out through the vertical blinds, I have a clear view of the narrow path and marble railing that run along the west front of the building. The morning sun's beating down on the copper roof, but it pales against the heat I'm feeling right now.

'Sorry,' Gary says. 'They're not coming up.'

'Whattya mean, they're not coming up? I thought every lobbyist had to disclose their clients . . .'

'They do. But we're barely halfway through the pile of disclosure forms. We get over seventeen thousand each registration period. Do you know how long it takes to scan in and update our data base?'

'Weeks?'

'Months. The last deadline was just a few weeks ago in August. So your best bet is to give us a call later in the week, and we can check if it's in there.'

I remember that this is the second year Wendell Mining made the request. 'What about last year?' I ask.

'Like I said, nothing came up—which means they either didn't have a lobbyist, or that person didn't register.'

That part actually makes sense. When it comes to getting earmarks, the smaller companies try to do it by themselves. Then, when they fail, they cough up the beans for a pro. 'Listen, I appreciate th—'

There's a loud knock on the door. I go silent.

'Sir, are you there?' Gary asks through the receiver.

Another knock. 'It's me,' Viv calls out. 'Open up.'

I leap for the door and undo the lock.

'Mission accomplished, Mr Bond. Onto the next?' Viv sings, sliding past me with a frenetic new bounce in her step and the two notebooks cradled under her arm.

Gary's voice crackles through the receiver. 'Sir, are you—?'

'I'm here . . . sorry,' I say, turning back to the phone. 'Thanks for the help. I'll give you a call next week.'

As I hang up, Viv dumps the two notebooks on the desk.

'I guess you didn't have any problems,' I say.

'You should've seen me, Harris. You woulda been proud.'

'Did Dinah say anything?'

'You kidding? She was blinder than the blind guy.'

'The blind guy?'

'All I need now is a code name . . .'

'Barry was there?'

'Something cool—like Senate Grrl . . .'

'Viv . . .'

'Or Sweet Mocha. How 'bout that? Sweet Mocha. Ooh, yeah!'

'*Dammit, Viv, shut up already!*'

She stops mid-syllable.

'You sure it was Barry?' I ask.

'I don't know his name. He's a blind guy with a cane.'

'What did he say?'

'Nothing—though he was slightly off . . . like he was trying to prove he wasn't that blind, y'know?'

I lunge for the phone and dial his cell. No. I hang up and start again. Go through the operator. Especially now.

Five digits later, the Capitol operator transfers me to Interior, and Roxanne answers.

'Hey, Roxanne, it's Harris. Listen, I'm sorry to bother you, but it's kind of an emergency. Is Barry still floating around back there?'

Viv waves for my attention, slowly moving towards the door. 'I'll be right back,' she whispers. 'Just one more stop.'

'Wait,' I call out.

She doesn't listen. She's having too much fun to sit around for a scolding. The door slams, and she's gone.

'Harris?' a voice asks in my ear. I'd know it anywhere. Barry. 'How are you? You OK?' he asks.

'Why wouldn't I be?' I shoot back.

'With Matthew . . . I just figured . . . Where are you, anyway?'

'I'm home,' I tell him. 'I just needed to take some time.'

'I left you four messages.'

'I know . . . and I appreciate it—I just needed the time.'

He doesn't buy it for a second. But that's the way he is. When it comes to personal interactions, the only thing Barry ever sees is himself, sitting alone in the dark.

Of course, when it comes to Hill gossip, his radar's still better than most. 'So I assume you heard about Pasternak?' he asks.

I stay quiet. He's not the only one with radar. There's a slight rise in his pitch. He's got something to tell.

'Can you believe it? A heart attack. Guy runs five miles every morning and wham—it stops pumping in a . . . in a heartbeat Carol is heartbroken . . . his whole family.'

'Can I ask you a question?' I say. 'Do you have a dog in this race?'

'What?'

'Wendell Mining, the request Matthew was working on . . . Are you lobbying it?'

'Of course not. You know I don't do that.'

'I don't know anything, Barry.'

He offers a playful laugh. I don't laugh back.

'Let me say it again for you, Harris—I've never once worked on Matthew's issues.'

'Then what are you doing in his office?'

'Harris, I know you've had two huge losses this week—'

'What the hell is wrong with you, Barry? Stop with the mental massage and answer the fucking question!'

There's a long pause on the other line. He's either panicking or in shock. I need to know which.

'Harris,' he eventually begins. 'I want to come see you. Just tell me where you really are.'

I stare at the phone. 'I gotta run. I'll talk to you later, Barry. Goodbye.' Slamming the receiver in its cradle, I turn again towards the window and study the sunlight as it ricochets off the roof.

TOWERING OVER Cheese's desk, Janos painted on a semifriendly grin.

'You think he's OK?' he asked in his best concerned tone.

'He sounded OK in his message,' Cheese replied. 'More tired than anything else. He's had a rough week, y'know, which is why he's taking the week off. Now tell me why you need to speak to him.'

'We're just following up on Matthew Mercer's death. They wanted us to talk to a few of his friends. Just standard follow-up . . .'

The front door to the office opened, and a young black girl in a navy suit stuck her head inside. 'Senate page,' Viv announced, balancing three small red, white and blue boxes. 'Flag delivery?'

'What?' Cheese asked.

'Flags,' she repeated. 'American flags . . . y'know, the ones they sell to people just because it went up a flagpole on the roof. Anyway, I've got three here for a'—she read the words from the top box—'Harris Sandler.'

'Just leave 'em here,' Cheese said, pointing to his own desk.

'And mess up your stuff?' Viv asked. She motioned through the glass partition at Harris's messy work space. 'That your boss's pigpen?' Before Cheese could answer, Viv headed through the door in the partition. 'He wants the flags . . . let him deal with them.'

Janos eyed the girl carefully. She had her back to him, and her body blocked most of what she was doing, but it looked like a routine drop-off. Without a word, she cleared a space for the boxes, set them on Harris's desk, and spun back to leave. She jumped when she saw Janos staring right at her.

'H-hey,' she said, smiling, as their eyes locked. 'Everything OK?'

'Of course,' Janos replied dryly. 'Everything's perfect.'

Viv moved towards the door.

Janos looked again at Harris's desk, where the flag boxes were neatly stacked. Even then, he didn't think much of it. But as he turned back to watch Viv, he saw the last glance that she aimed his way. Not at *him*. At his windcheater. *FBI*.

The door slammed, and she was gone.

'So what were we saying?' Cheese asked.

Eyes still locked on the door, Janos didn't answer. It wasn't that unusual for someone to check out an FBI jacket . . . but add that to the way she walked in, going straight for Harris's office . . .

'Have you ever seen her before?' he asked.

'The page? No, not that I—'

'I have to go,' Janos said as he calmly turned towards the door.

'Just let me know if you need more help,' Cheese called out.

Flipping open the first of the two notebooks, I thumb to the Gs and continue to turn the pages until I reach the tab marked *Grayson*, where there is an analysis of every project the Congressman has ever asked for—including the transfer of a gold mine to a company called

Wendell Mining. The analysis, to Matthew's credit, is exactly what he originally told me. The Homestead gold mine is one of the oldest in South Dakota, and both the town and state would benefit if Wendell Mining took it over. To drive the point home, there are three photocopied letters clipped into the notebook: one from the Bureau of Land Management, one from the Wendell Mining CEO, and a final, gushing recommendation from the Mayor of Leed, South Dakota, where the mine is located. Three letters. Three letterheads. Three new phone numbers to call.

The first call, to BLM, gets me voice mail. Same with the call to the CEO. That leaves only the mayor. I dial the number, and as the phone rings I glance down at my watch. Viv should be back any—

'L-and-L Luncheonette,' a man with a cigarette-burned voice and Hollywood-cowboy drawl answers.

'I'm sorry,' I stutter, 'I was calling Mayor Regan's office.'

'And who should I say is calling?' the man asks.

'Andy Defresne,' I say. 'From the House of Representatives.'

'Well, why didn't you say?' the man adds with a throaty laugh. 'This is Mayor Regan. What c'n I do for you?' he asks.

'To be honest—'

'Wouldn't expect anything but,' he interrupts, laughing wildly.

'Well, sir, I'm working on Congressman Grayson's request for the land sale at the Homestead mine, and I'm just trying to make sure we do the right thing and put local interests first. We're trying to think who else we should go to for support, so would you mind walking me through how the town might benefit from the sale of the mine?'

The mayor laughs again. 'Son, to be honest, you got as much chance sucking bricks through a hose as you do finding someone who'll benefit from this one.'

'I'm not sure I understand.'

'Maybe I don't, either,' the mayor admits. 'But if I were putting up money for a gold mine, I'd at least want one that had some gold. The Homestead mine is empty. The last ounce of gold was mined almost twenty years ago. Since then, seven different companies have tried to prove everyone wrong, and the last one went bust so ugly they took most of the town with 'em.'

'I'm sorry, Mr Mayor—maybe I'm just dense, but if there's no chance of finding gold, then why d'you write that letter?'

'What letter?'

My eyes drop to the desk, where Matthew's old notebook holds a letter endorsing the land transfer to Wendell Mining. It's signed by the Mayor of Leed, South Dakota. 'You are Mayor Tom Regan, right?'

'Yep. Only one.'

I study the signature at the bottom of the letter. There's a slight smudge on the *R* in *Regan* that makes it look just messy enough that it'd never get a second glance. And right there, for the first time since all this started, I start to see the ripple in the mirror.

'You still there, son?' the mayor asks.

'Yeah . . . no . . . I'm here,' I say. 'I just . . . Wendell Mining . . .'

'Let me tell you about Wendell Mining. When they first came sniffing here, I personally called MSHA to—'

'Em-sha?'

'Mine Safety and Health Administration—the safety boys. When you're mayor, you gotta know who's coming to your town. So when I talked to my buddy there, he said these guys at Wendell may've bought the mining claims to the land and even put enough money in someone's pocket to get a favourable mineral report—but, so help me, when we looked up their track record, these boys've never operated a single mine in their lives.'

A sharp pain burns in my stomach. 'You sure about that?'

'Son, did Elvis love bacon? So when those trucks showed up—'

'Trucks?' I interrupt.

'The trucks that showed up last month. Isn't that what you're calling about?'

'Y-yeah. Of course.' Matthew transferred the mine sale into the bill barely three days ago. 'So they're already mining?' I ask, confused.

'God knows what they're doing . . . I went up there myself—y'know, just to make sure they're doing things right with the union—and they don't have a single piece of mining equipment up there. Not even a pelican pick. And when I asked them about it, those boys shooed me away like a fly on the wrong end of a horse.'

My hand holds tight to the receiver. 'You think they're doing something other than mining?'

'I don't know what they're doing, but if it were up to me . . .'

Behind me, someone pounds on the door. 'It's me,' Viv calls out. I stretch the phone cord and undo the lock. Viv steps inside. The bounce in her step is gone.

'What's wrong?' I ask. 'Did you get the—?'

She pulls my electronic organiser from the waist of her pants and tosses it straight at me. 'There—you happy?' she asks.

'What happened? Was it not where I said it was?'

'I saw an FBI agent,' she blurts, 'talking to your assistant.'

'What?' I slam down the phone. 'What did he look like?'

'I didn't see him that long . . . buzzed salt-and-pepper hair . . . a creepy smile . . . and eyes that kinda, well . . . kinda look like a hound dog if that makes any sense . . .'

'*Janos*.' My eyes flash over to the door. It's unlocked.

I dart full speed at it, ready to twist the lock shut. But just as I'm about to grab it, the door bursts towards me, slamming into my shoulder. Viv screams, and a thick hand slides through the crack.

Luckily, momentum's on my side. My full weight collides with the door, pinching Janos's fingers in the doorjamb. As he yanks his hand free, he barely grunts. As the door slams shut, I dive for the lock and click it into place. The door thunders as Janos rams himself against it. The hinges shudder. We're not going to last long.

'Window!' I say, turning to Viv, who's frozen in shock. Her eyes look like they're about to explode. I grab her hand and twirl her towards a small window that's high on the wall.

There's another thunderclap against the door.

Viv turns and panics. 'He's—'

'*Just go!*' I shout, pulling one of the chairs towards the window.

Hopping up on the chair, Viv tries to unhook the window latch. 'I think they're painted shut!' she shouts, pounding on the frame with the base of her palm. She gives it one final shove and the left window swings outwards. I give her a boost up. There's another loud bang against the door. The lock buckles. Two screws look like they're about to come loose.

Viv is already halfway out of the window.

A screw flies from the lock and clinks against the floor as Viv crashes against the balcony outside. Behind me, I spot Matthew's notebooks sitting on the nearby table. I need that info. I scramble back towards the desk, and tear the Grayson section from one binder.

The door flies open and crashes to the ground. In a mad dash, I leap on the chair and dive towards the open window. My pelvis jars against the sill, but I get through and tumble onto the balcony floor.

'Which way?' Viv asks, slamming the window shut.

I clamber to my feet. Rolling up the stack of papers and shoving them in my pocket, I grab Viv's wrist and tug her to the left, along the three-foot-wide balcony that runs the length of the Senate wing towards the enormous Capitol dome.

I glance over my shoulder just as the window bursts open behind us. When Janos sticks his head out, it only makes us run harder.

The sun beats down, reflecting off the white marble railing so brightly I have to squint to see. Good thing I know where I'm going. Up ahead, the balcony forks as we approach the base of the Capitol dome. We can go straight on round the dome, or make a sharp left into a nook round the corner. Last time I was running from Janos, he caught me off guard. This time, we're on my turf.

'Left,' I say, yanking the shoulder of Viv's suit. As I tug her round the corner, there's a rusted metal staircase dead ahead. It leads up to the roof directly on top of the room we were just in. 'Keep going,' I say, pointing her towards it.

Viv keeps running. I stay where I am. By my feet, a trio of thin steel wires runs along the balcony, just outside the windows. During the winter, the maintenance division sends a small electric current through the wiring to melt the snow. Squatting down, I grab them and pull as hard as I can. The staples that hold them in place pop through the air. The metal wiring goes taut as I lift it a few inches from the ground. Perfect ankle height.

Just as Janos turns the corner, his legs slam into the wiring and he yells out in pain as the metal slices into his shins. Tumbling forwards, he skids face first along the ground. The sound alone is worth it.

Before he can get up, I leap towards him, gripping him by the back of his head and pressing his face against the green copper floor which is burning hot in the sun. He finally screams—a guttural rumble that vibrates against my chest. It's like trying to pin a bull. Even as I grab the back of his neck, he's already on his knees, lashing out, swiping a meaty paw at my face. I duck, and his knuckles barely connect with a spot below my shoulder. It doesn't hurt—but as my entire right arm tingles and goes numb, I realise that's where he was aiming all along.

'*Harris, run!*' Viv shouts from the top step of the metal staircase.

She's right about that. I can't beat him one-on-one. I sprint as fast as I can, my arm flapping lifelessly at my side. Behind me, Janos is still on the ground, clawing at the wires. He'll be loose in seconds.

'*C'mon!*' Viv yells, waving me up.

Using my good arm to hold the railing, I scutter up the stairs to the catwalk that zigzags across the Senate wing roof. From here, with the dome at my back, I weave through a maze of electrical wiring and air ducts.

'You sure you know where you're—?'

'*Here*,' I say, cutting to the left, down a metal stairway that takes us off the catwalk and back down to a different section of the balcony. Thank God neoclassical architecture is symmetrical. There's even a corresponding window that'll take us back into the building.

I kick the window frame as hard as I can. The glass shatters but the frame holds. Wood splinters in my hands as I yank on the frame, and the window flies open. The pounding of Janos's feet on the catwalk is getting closer.

'Go!' I say, helping Viv climb inside. I'm right behind her, landing hard as I hit the grey-carpeted floor. I'm in someone's office.

A worker comes rushing in. 'You can't be in here—'

Viv shoves him aside, and I fall in right behind her. As a page, Viv knows the inside of this place as well as anyone.

We cut through the welcoming area of the office and fly down a narrow curving staircase that echoes as we run. We duck out on the third floor of the Capitol, where the closed door in front of us is marked SENATE CHAPLAIN. Viv tries the doorknob.

'It's locked,' she says.

There's a loud thud from above. Viv jack-rabbits to her left, up the corridor and towards another flight of stairs. I head for the elevator, which is a bit further, just around the corner.

'Elevator's faster . . .' I tell her.

I hit the call button and hear a high-pitched ping. Viv quickly catches up. As the doors slide open, we hear footsteps lumbering down the stairs. Shoving Viv in the elevator, I follow her inside, and jab wildly at the DOOR CLOSE button. 'C'mon, c'mon . . .'

Janos is a few feet away. I see the tips of his outstretched fingers.

'Get ready to pull the alarm!' I shout at Viv.

Janos lunges forwards, and our eyes lock. He jabs his hand towards us just as the door clicks, thunks and slides shut.

The elevator rumbles downwards, and I can barely catch my breath.

'My . . . my hand . . .' Viv whispers, picking something from her palm, which is bright red with blood. She pulls out a piece of glass from one of the broken windows

'You OK?' I ask, reaching out.

She doesn't answer. She's in shock. But she's still sharp enough to know she's got far more important things to worry about. 'Why's the FBI chasing you?' she asks at last.

'He's not FBI.'

'Then who the hell is he?'

This isn't the time to explain. 'Just get ready to run,' I tell her.

'What are you talking about?'

'You think he's not sprinting down the stairs right now?'

She shakes her head. 'It's not a continuous staircase—he'll have to stop and cross the hallway at one of the landings. There's no way he'll beat us down.'

The elevator bobs to a stop in the basement, and the door slides open. I barely take two steps before I hear a loud click-clack on the metal treads of the staircase directly in front of us. I look up to see Janos whipping round the corner onto the top step. The smallest of grins spreads across his lips.

Son of a bitch.

Viv takes off to the left, and I'm right behind her. We've got nothing more than a thirty-step head start on Janos. Viv makes a sharp left so we're not in his direct line of sight, then a quick right. Down here in the basement we're like rats in a maze, twisting and turning as the cat licks his chops behind us.

Dead ahead, the long corridor widens. At the end, sunlight glows through double glass doors. There's our way out: the west exit, the door the President uses as he steps out for his inauguration.

Behind us, the gap is closing. Viv is slowly losing steam. *C'mon, Viv . . .* Only a few feet to go.

He reaches out, raising his hand for the final grab. The door's straight ahead. But just as he lunges forward, I grip Viv's shoulder and make a sharp right, whipping us both round the corner.

Janos skids across the polished floor, struggling to follow. It's too late. By the time he's back in pursuit, Viv and I have shoved our way through a set of black vinyl double doors that look like they lead to a kitchen.

But as the doors swing shut, we find fourteen armed policemen milling around. This is the internal HQ of the Capitol Police.

'There's a guy back there muttering to himself,' I announce. 'He started following us for no reason, saying we were the enemy.'

'I think he snuck off a tour,' Viv adds. 'He doesn't have an ID.'

Janos shoves open the doors. Three Capitol policemen move in.

'Can I help you?' one of them asks. He's unimpressed with the FBI windcheater, which he knows can be bought in the gift shop.

Before Janos can even make up a lame excuse, Viv and I continue further up the hallway in front of us.

'Stop them!' Janos shouts, taking off after us.

The first officer grabs him by the windcheater, pulling him back. 'Now let's see some ID.'

Twisting and turning back through the maze of the basement, we eventually push our way outside to the east front of the Capitol, where groups of tourists are taking pictures in front of the dome.

We race towards First Street, looking for a cab.

'Taxi!' Viv and I shout simultaneously as one slows down.

We both slide inside. While Viv is still catching her breath, she glares at me and says, 'Now what the hell is going on?'

RIDING THE ESCALATOR DOWN to the lower floors of the Smithsonian's Museum of American History, I keep my eyes on the crowds and my hands on Viv's shoulders to keep her calm. After what happened in the Capitol, she doesn't trust anyone—including me—which is why she jerks her shoulders and shoos me away.

The museum's not the ideal place to change her mind, but it's enough of a public place to make it unlikely that Janos will start hunting. We step off the escalator and she turns to face me.

'I sorry,' I begin. 'I never meant for it to happen like this.'

'I don't want your apologies, Harris. Just tell me why Matthew was killed.'

As we walk through an exhibit that tracks America's progress in manufacturing, it takes me almost fifteen minutes to tell her the truth. About Matthew . . . and Pasternak . . . and even about my attempt to go to the Deputy Attorney General. Amazingly, she doesn't show a hint of reaction—that is, until I tell her what set all the dominoes tumbling. The game . . . and the bet.

Her mouth drops open. She's primed to explode. 'You were betting?' she asks. Gambling on Congress?'

'I swear, it was just a stupid game. Just on the small issues—nothing that ever mattered . . .'

'*It all matters!*'

'Viv, please . . .' I beg.

She lowers her voice. 'How could you do that? You told us we should—' She cuts herself off as her voice cracks. 'That entire speech you gave . . . Everything you said was crap.' Her shoulders sag as her disappointment turns into sadness. No matter when it happens, idealism always dies hard. 'That's it—I'm out,' she announces, shoving me aside.

'Where are you going?'

'To deliver some senator's mail . . . and gossip with friends . . . and check on our running tally of senators with bad hair.'

'Viv, wait,' I call out, chasing after her. I put a hand on her shoulder, and again she tries to yank herself free.

'Get. *Off!*' she shouts. Shoving me away, she marches off through the exhibit hall. She's not a small girl. I forget how strong she is.

'You can't do this,' I beg, racing after her.

She stops. 'Don't you *ever* tell me what to do.'

'Viv, they'll kill you.'

Her finger's frozen in midair. 'What?'

'They'll snap your neck and make it look like you tripped down some stairs. Just like they did with Matthew.' She's silent as I say the words. 'You know I'm right. Now that Janos knows who you are, you think he's just gonna let you go back to refilling senators' water glasses?'

Her brow unfurrows, and her hands start to shake.

'I'm sorry, Viv.' It's the second time I've said those words. But this time, she needs them.

'I was just doing you a favour,' she stutters, her voice breaking.

'I shouldn't have asked you, Viv—I never thought . . .'

She looks down at the photo on the back of her ID. 'I . . . I need to make a call—'

'Don't call your mom, Viv. You mustn't put your family at risk.'

'*I* shouldn't put them at risk? How could . . . How could you do this to me?' She stumbles back. 'You wrecked my life.'

'Viv . . .'

'Don't *Viv* me. You wrecked it, Harris, and then you—oh, God . . . Do you have any idea what you've done?'

'I swear, if I thought this would happen . . .'

'Please don't say you didn't know . . .'

She's absolutely right. I should've known. I spend everyday calculating political permutations but when I came to this, the only thing I was worried about was myself.

'Viv, I swear, if I could undo it—'

'But you can't!' She's still in shock, struggling to process everything that's happened. 'We should call the police . . .' she stutters.

'They've already got to the number two person at Justice—the Deputy Attorney General. All paths to law enforcement take us straight back to him.'

Viv's quick enough to see the big picture instantly. 'What about going to someone else . . .? What about any of the other pages?' she asks. 'Maybe they can tell us who they made drop-offs to . . . y'know, who else was playing the game.'

'There are no delivery records from the cloakroom. All the instructions are verbal. And anyway, the pages weren't used for the gold mine bets. That kid who hit Matthew—Toolie Williams—he had your name tag. He wasn't a page. Janos must have paid him to dress like one to do the collection. . . I'm guessing that Janos is acting on behalf of someone who has a vested interest in the outcome.'

'You think it goes back to the gold mine?'

'Hard to say, but they're the only ones who benefit.'

'I still don't understand,' Viv says. 'How does Wendell Mining benefit if there's supposedly no gold in the mine?'

As I pull the rolled-up pages from Matthew's briefing book out of my pocket, I tell her what the mayor told me—Wendell was already getting to work, but there wasn't a piece of mining equipment in sight. 'And if there's no gold, what are they doing down there?'

'Why don't you just call the mayor back and—?'

'And what? Ask him to take a little snoop around and then put his life in danger? Besides, even if he did, would you trust the answer?'

Viv again goes silent. 'So what do we do?' she finally asks.

All this time, I've been looking for a lead. I reread the name of the town on the sheet of paper in my hands. *Leed, South Dakota.* The only place that has the answer.

SEVEN

Two hours later, we're climbing out of a taxi at Piedmont-Hawthorne's Corporate Aviation Terminal in Dulles, Virginia.

I pay the cabbie, and he gives us a wave.

'You sure this is legal?' Viv asks as she follows me towards the squat, modern building.

'I didn't say anything about legal; all I'm looking for is smart.'

'And this is smart?'

'You'd rather fly commercial?'

Viv goes back to her silence. We went through this on the ride over here. There aren't many places you can get a private plane in less than two hours. Thankfully, Congress is one of them. And this way, the authorities won't even ask for ID.

All it took was a phone call. According to the rules, a senator can use a private jet as long as he reimburses the government for the price of a first-class commercial ticket, which we can repay later. It's a genius loophole—and Viv and I just jumped headfirst right through it.

As we're about to enter the building, an automatic door slides open, revealing a room that reminds me of a fancy hotel lobby.

'Can I help you find your aircraft?' a woman in a business suit asks as she leans over the reception desk on our right.

'Senator Stevens,' I say.

'Here you go,' a deep voice calls out just past the reception desk. I look over as a pilot with blond hair nods our way.

'Tom Heidenberger,' he says, introducing himself. He reaches over and shakes Viv's hand as well. 'Senator on his way?' he asks.

'Actually, he's not gonna make it. I'm speaking in his place.'

'Lucky you,' he says with a grin.

'And this is Catherine, our new legislative assistant,' I say, introducing Viv.

The pilot leads us towards the back of the building, Viv purposely walks a few steps behind. She still hasn't forgiven me.

I take one last look at the reception area behind me and notice a thin man in a pinstripe suit sitting in one of the upholstered chairs. It's like he appeared out of nowhere. I try to get a better look at him, but he averts his eyes, flipping open his cellphone.

'Everything OK?' the pilot asks.

'Yeah . . . of course,' I insist as we reach two locked security doors. The woman at the reception desk hits a button, and there's a loud magnetic *thunk*. The doors unlock, and the pilot shoves them open, ushering us outside. No metal detector . . . no screening . . . no hassle. Fifty feet in front of us, sitting on the runway, is a brand-new Gulfstream G400. I try to act unimpressed. Our chariot awaits.

As we climb the carpeted stairs to the plane, I glance back at the terminal, trying to get another look at the thin man inside. He's nowhere in sight.

Ducking down and stepping into the cabin, we find nine leather club chairs, a buttery tan leather sofa, and a waiting flight attendant.

'Let me know if there's anything you need,' she offers. 'Champagne . . . orange juice . . . anything at all.'

A second pilot is already in the cockpit. When they're both on board, the flight attendant shuts the door, and we're on our way. I take the first chair in the front. Viv takes the one right at the back.

The flight attendant doesn't make us put on our seat belts or read a list of rules. 'The seats recline all the way,' she offers. 'You can sleep the whole flight if you want.'

The sweetness in her voice is at fairy godmother levels, but it doesn't make me feel any better. The only person I trust now is a seventeen-year-old who hates me. And even though I'm sitting on a $38-million private airplane, it doesn't change the fact that two of my closest friends are gone for ever, and some hired killer is ready to make sure we join them. There's nothing to celebrate.

The plane rumbles forward, and I sink down in my seat. Outside the window, a man salutes us as we leave. Over his shoulder, back in the hangar, I notice sudden movement as the thin man appears. He presses his open palms against the plate-glass window and watches us leave.

'Any idea who that is?' I ask the flight attendant, noticing that she's staring at him, too.

'No idea,' she says. 'I figured he was with you.'

'THEY'RE ON A PLANE,' Janos said into his phone as he stormed out of his hotel, signalling for a cab.

'How do you know?' Sauls asked at the other end of the line.

'Redial on Harris's phone said he was talking to the mayor.'

'You think he's going to Dakota?' Sauls moaned. 'I don't believe it. I got an embassy dinner tonight, and they're—' He cut himself off. 'You better get your ass to South Dakota before they—'

Janos hit the END button and slapped his phone shut. After his run-in with the Capitol Police, he already had one headache. He didn't need another. He slid inside the cab and slammed the door.

'Where to?' the cabbie asked.

'National Airport,' he replied.

THE SOUTH DAKOTA SKY is pitch-black by the time our rented Chevy Suburban turns west onto Interstate 90.

Viv is staring out of the front window, arms crossed. After four hours of similar treatment on the plane, I'm used to the silence, but the further we get from the lights of Rapid City the more disconcerting it gets. And not just because of Viv. Once we passed the exit for Mount Rushmore, the lamps on the highway started appearing less frequently. Now I haven't seen one for miles. Same with other cars. It's barely nine o'clock local time, but there's not a soul in sight.

'You sure this is right?' Viv asks anxiously, turning towards me for the first time in five hours.

'We're doing fine,' I reply, forcing confidence into my voice.

She smiles faintly. I'm not sure if she believes it, but at this point—after travelling this long—she'll take anything she can get.

Up ahead, the road swerves to the right, then back to the left. As my headlights bounce off enormous cliff faces on either side of us, I realise we're weaving our way through a canyon.

Viv leans forward, craning her neck to look up through the windshield in pure amazement. 'Are those the Black Hills?'

In the distance, the walls of the cliff rise dramatically—at least 400 feet straight towards the clouds. If it weren't for the moonlight, I wouldn't even be able to see where they end.

'I take it they don't have mountains where you're from?'

She shakes her head, still dumbfounded. There's only one other person who looked at mountains like that. Matthew. He always said they were one of the only things that ever made him feel small.

'You OK there?' Viv asks.

Snapped back to reality, I'm surprised to find her staring straight at me. 'O-of course,' I say, turning back to the road.

She raises an eyebrow. 'You're really not as great a liar as you think.'

'I'm fine,' I insist. 'It's just . . . being out here. Matthew would've liked it. He really . . . He would've liked it.'

Viv watches me carefully. I stay focused on the road. I've been in this awkward silence before. It's like the thirty-second period right after I brief the Senator on a tough issue. Perfect quiet. Where decisions get made.

'Y'know, I saw Matthew's photo in his office,' she eventually says. I stare at the road, picturing it myself. 'The one with the lake?'

'Yeah, that's the one,' she nods. 'He looked . . . He looked nice.'

'He was.'

This time the silence is longer than before.

'Michigan,' she quietly whispers.

'Excuse me?'

'You said, *they don't have mountains where you're from.* Well, that's where I'm from. Michigan.'

'Detroit?'

'Birmingham.'

I tap my thumbs against the steering wheel as a kamikaze bug splats against the windshield.

'That still doesn't mean I forgive you,' Viv adds.

'I wouldn't expect you to.' Up ahead, the walls of the cliff disappear as we leave the canyon behind. 'So do you like Birmingham?' I ask.

'It's high school,' she replies, making me feel every year of my age.

'We used to go up for basketball games in Ann Arbor,' I tell her.

'Really? So you know Birmingham? You've been there?'

'Just once. A guy in our fraternity let us crash at his parents'.'

She looks out of her window at the side mirror. The canyon's long gone—lost in the black horizon.

'Y'know, I lied,' she says, her tone flat and lifeless. 'About being one of only two black girls in the school . . . There are actually fourteen of us. I just wanted to convince you I could handle myself.'

'Viv . . .'

'I thought you'd think I was strong and tough and—'

'*It doesn't matter*,' I interrupt. 'I mean, fourteen . . . out of how many? Four hundred? Five hundred? That's still pretty outnumbered.'

The smallest of smiles creeps up her cheeks. She likes that one. But from the way her hands grip the seat belt across her chest, it's clearly still an issue for her.

'It's OK to smile,' I tell her.

She shakes her head. 'That's what my mom always says. Right after *"Rinse and spit"*.'

'Your Mom's a dentist?'

'No, she's a . . .' Viv pauses. 'She's a dental hygienist.'

And right there I spot it. That's where her hesitation comes from. It's not that she's not proud of her mom . . . but she knows what it feels like to be the one kid who's different.

Again, I don't remember much from when I was seventeen, but I do know what it's like to have Career Day at school when you secretly hope your dad's not invited. And in the world of Ivy League Washington, I also know what it's like to feel second class.

'Y'know, my dad was a barber,' I offer.

She shyly glances my way. 'You serious? Really?'

'Really,' I say. 'Cut all my friends' hair for seven bucks apiece. Even the bad bowl cuts.' She gives me an even bigger grin.

'Just so you know—I'm not embarrassed about my parents,' she insists.

'I never thought you were.'

'The thing is . . . they wanted so bad to get me in the school district, but the only way to afford it was by buying this tiny little house that's literally the last one on the district boundary. Y'know what that's like? I mean, when that's your starting point . . .'

'You can't help but feel like the last man in the race,' I say, nodding. 'Let me tell you something,' I add. 'There's something else that goes along with feeling like you're last in the race—and that's a hunger in your gut no one else'll ever comprehend. They couldn't buy it with all their money. Know what that hunger gives you?'

'Besides my big butt?'

'Success, Viv. No matter where you go, or what you do. Hunger feeds success.'

As my words fade beneath the hum of the engine, Viv studies the long road in front of us and, to her credit, never lets me know what she's thinking. She's gonna be a ruthless negotiator one day.

'How much farther till we get there?' she finally asks.

'Fifteen miles until we hit Deadwood . . . then it's at least a good hour or so after that. Why?'

'No reason,' she says, pulling her legs up so she's sitting Indian-style in the passenger seat.

'If you want, I bet we can grab a bite to eat in Deadwood. Even out here, they can't mess up grilled cheese.'

'Grilled cheese in Deadwood sounds great.'

JANOS HAD TAKEN two different planes, and still he hadn't reached his destination.

'Minneapolis?' Sauls asked through the cellphone. 'What are you doing in Minneapolis?'

'I heard they have a great Foot Locker at the Mall of America,' Janos growled, pulling his bag from the conveyor belt. 'Getting stuck in the airport just wasn't enough fun for one night.'

'They cancelled your flight?'

'Let's just say South Dakota isn't the top priority on the airlines' flight plans. But don't worry,' he said. 'There's a flight to Rapid City first thing tomorrow. As soon as they wake up, I'll be standing on their chests.'

THERE ARE FEW THINGS more instantly depressing than the stale smell of an old motel room. The sour, mossy whiff is still in the air as I wake up. The digital lights on the alarm clock tell me it's 7 a.m.

When we checked in last night, after midnight, I made Viv wait in the car as I told the woman at the front desk that I needed one room for myself and one for my kids. I don't care how mature Viv looks. A white guy in his thirties checking into a motel with a younger black girl and no luggage—even in a *big* town, that'll get people chatting.

On my left, the seventies-era flower-patterned curtains are closed, but I can still see a sliver of the dark sky outside. I plug in the iron I borrowed from the front desk. With all the running around, our suits look like we played baseball in them. If we plan on pulling this off, we're gonna have to look the part.

As the iron heats up, I turn to the phone on the nightstand and dial Viv's room. It rings over and over. No answer. I'm not surprised. After what we've been through, she has to be exhausted. I hang up.

Putting on my slacks, I again check my watch. Even the earliest flight won't get Janos in for another ten minutes, not including the two hour drive to get here. We're OK. Just go knock and get her up.

Undoing the chain lock, I tug the door open. A puff of fresh air shoves back at the mustiness—but as I step out and head to my right, I feel something smack into my ankles. I plummet face first towards the concrete breezeway.

It's impossible. He can't be here yet . . .

Then I hear the voice behind me. 'Sorry . . . sorry,' Viv says, sitting on the floor of the concrete breezeway, tucking her long legs out of the way. 'You all right?'

'What are you doing out here?'

'My room stinks. Literally. Like a geriatric barn.'

I climb to my feet. 'So you're always up this early?'

'Page school starts at six fifteen. The woman at the front desk . . . she's all talky, but in a cool way, y'know? I've been chatting with her for the past half hour. Can you believe there were only two people in her graduating class? This town's in trouble.'

'What are you—? I told you not to speak to anyone.'

Viv shrinks down, but not by much. 'Don't worry—I told her I'm the au pair . . . taking care of the kids.'

'In a blue business suit?' I ask, pointing to her outfit.

'I didn't wear the jacket. Don't worry—she believed it. Besides, I was hungry. She gave me an orange,' she explains. She pulls a piece of fruit from her pocket and hands it to me. 'One for you, too.'

'So she's the one who gave you the brochures?'

She looks down at a faded pamphlet in her lap entitled *The*

Homestead Mine—Staking a Claim in Our Future. 'I just thought I should read up on it. That's OK, right . . . ?'

There's a faint noise by the stairwell at the far end of the breezeway. Like a crash.

'What was—?'

'Shh,' I say.

We both check the breezeway, following the sound. No one's there. There's another crashing sound. That's when we see the source of the noise. An ice machine dumping ice. Just ice, I tell myself. It doesn't make me feel any calmer. 'We should—'

'—get out of here,' Viv agrees.

We head for our respective doors. Four minutes of ironing later, I'm dressed to go. Viv's already waiting outside, her head once again buried in the tourist pamphlet.

'All set?' I ask.

'Harris, you really gotta look at this place—you've never seen anything like it.'

I don't need to read the pamphlet to realise that she's right. We have no idea what we're getting into, but there's no slowing us down. Whatever Wendell's digging for, we need to know what's going on.

THE GOLD HOUSE MOTEL'S main lobby is emptier than I expected. Beside the vacant desk I spot a metal display rack filled with tourist brochures like the one Viv picked up. SEE HOW A REAL GOLD BAR IS MADE! EXPLORE THE MINING MUSEUM! But from the faded, yellowed paper, we already know the museum's closed, and the gold bars haven't been seen in years.

'Pretty sad, huh?' a female voice asks.

I spin round, and a young woman with short black hair emerges from a back room and steps behind the front desk.

'Hiya, Viv,' she calls out, wiping some sleep from her eyes.

I shoot Viv a look. *You gave her your name?*

Viv shrugs and steps back. 'I'll go check on the kids,' she says, moving for the front door.

'They're fine,' I say, refusing to let her out of my sight. She's already said enough.

'Can you tell us how to get to the Homestead mine?' I add.

'So they're reopening it again?' she asks.

'I have no idea,' I counter, leaning an elbow on the front desk and fishing for info. 'Everyone seems to have a different answer.'

'Well, that's what I hear—though Dad says they still haven't talked to the union.'

'Have they at least been throwing some business your way?' I ask, wondering if she's seen anybody in the motel.

'You'd think they would, but they got it all in trailers up there. Kitchens, sleeping quarters . . . everything. I'm telling you, they get an F in making friends.'

'They're probably just mad they couldn't find a Holiday Inn,' I say. She smiles. Everyone hates the chains.

'Listen, about those directions . . .' I prompt.

'Of course. Directions. Left outta the driveway, then a sharp right up the hill. All you gotta do is follow the road.'

With a quick hop, she boosts herself over the front counter, grabs my arm, and leads me to the door. 'See that building . . . looks like a giant metal teepee?' she asks, pointing up the mountain. 'That's the head-frame.' She reads the confused look on my face. 'It protects the mine shaft from bad weather. That's where you'll find the cage.'

'The cage?'

'The elevator,' she says. 'I mean, assuming you wanna go down . . .'

Viv and I share a glance. Up until this point, I didn't even think that was an option.

'Just follow signs for the Homestead,' the woman adds. 'Won't take you five minutes.'

We thank her and head for our Suburban.

As we weave our way up the hill, we're focused on the two-storey triangular building that sits on top. Turning the final corner, the trees disappear, the paved road ends, and a dirt space the size of a football field spreads out in front of us. It's as if they've shaved off the top of the mountain.

'So you have any idea what we're even looking for?' Viv asks, studying the terrain.

It's a fair question—and one I've been asking myself since the moment we stepped off the plane.

'I think we'll know it when we see it,' I tell her.

'But you really think Wendell Mining were the ones who had Matthew killed?'

'All I know is, for the past two years, Wendell has been trying to buy this old mine. Last year, they failed. This year, they tried to cut through the red tape by sliding it into the Appropriations bill, and according to Matthew would've never gotten anywhere had it not showed up as the newest item up for bid in our little game.'

'That doesn't mean Wendell Mining had him killed.'

'You're right. But once I started digging around, I found out that Wendell not only forged at least one of the letters endorsing the transfer, but that this wonderful gold mine they supposedly want doesn't have enough gold in it to make an anklet for a Barbie doll. And they're so anxious to get inside, they've already started moving in. Add that to the fact that two of my friends were killed for it and, well . . . you better believe I want to see this thing for myself.'

We pull towards the edge of the gravel-covered parking lot, which is filled with at least a dozen other cars. Off to the left are three construction trailers, with guys in overalls busily going in and out, while two separate dump trucks back up towards the teepee-shaped building. According to Matthew's report, the place is supposed to be abandoned and empty. Instead, we're staring at a beehive.

Viv motions to the side of the building, where another man in overalls is using a fork-lift to unload a huge piece of computer equipment from the back of an eighteen-wheeler.

'Why do you need a computer system to dig a giant hole in the ground?' Viv asks.

I nod. 'That's the hundred-thousand-dollar question, isn't—?'

There's a sharp tap as a knuckle raps against my window. I turn and spot a man with the filthiest construction hat I've ever seen. He puts on a smile; I hesitantly roll down the window.

'Hiya,' he says. 'You guys from Wendell?'

'Yeah . . . we're from Wendell,' I say.

'Shelley, you there?' a voice squawks through the two-way radio on his belt.

''Scuse me,' he says, grabbing the radio.

While Shelley listens on the radio, I motion to one of the few open parking spaces. 'Listen, should we . . . ?'

'Uh—ya . . . right there's perfect,' Shelley says as the guy on his two-way continues talking. 'There's gear in the dry,' Shelley adds, pointing at the large red-brick building just behind the metal teepee. 'And here . . .' He pulls a bunch of round metal tags from his pocket and drops four of them in my hand. Two are imprinted with the number 27; the other two have the number 15. 'Don't forget to tag in,' he explains. 'One in your pocket, one on the wall.'

With a quick thanks, we're headed for our parking spot.

'You sure you know what you're doing?' Viv asks.

'Viv, this place doesn't have a drop of gold in it, but they're setting up shop like that scene from *E.T.* when the government shows up. I'm not saying I want to go down the mine, but you have any better ideas for figuring out what's going on around here? My father was a barber, but my friends' dads used to mine. Believe me, even if we do go in, it's like a cave—we're talking a few hundred feet down, max . . .'

'Try eight thousand,' she blurts.

'What?'

'Th-that's what it says. In here . . .' She looks down at the brochure in her lap. 'Before it was closed down, this place was the oldest operating mine in all of North America.'

I snatch the brochure from her. 'Since 1876', it says on the cover.

'*Eight thousand feet,*' she continues. Can you imagine? That's six Empire State Buildings straight into the ground . . .'

I flip the brochure over and confirm the facts: fifty-seven levels . . . two and a half miles wide . . . and 350 *miles* of underground passageways. I glance out of the window. Forget the beehive. We're standing on an entire ant farm.

'Maybe I should stay up here,' Viv says. 'Sorta keep lookout . . .'

She glances anxiously behind us, as a silver Ford pick-up pulls into the parking lot. Viv checks to see if the driver looks familiar. I know what she's thinking. Janos can't be far behind.

'You really think it's safer to be up here by yourself?' I ask.

She doesn't answer. She's still watching the pick-up.

'Please just promise me we'll be fast,' she begs.

'Don't worry,' I say, swinging my door open and hopping outside. 'We'll be in and out before anyone even knows it.'

LIGHTLY TAPPING the side of his thumb against the top of the Hertz rental car counter in the Rapid City airport, Janos made no attempt to hide his frustration.

'What's taking so long?' he asked the young employee with the Mount Rushmore tie.

'Sorry . . . just been one of those busy mornings,' the man behind the counter replied, shuffling through a pile of paperwork. 'OK, here we are. Now, when will you be returning the car?'

'Hopefully, tonight,' Janos shot back.

'And will you be needing any insurance on the—?'

Janos's hand shot out like a dart, gripping the man's wrist and swiping the key from his hand. 'We done?' he growled.

'It's a blue Ford Explorer . . . in spot fifteen,' the man said as Janos ripped a map from the pad on the counter and stormed towards the exit. 'You have a good day, now, Mr . . .' The man looked down at the photocopy of the New Jersey driver's license Janos had given him. Robert Franklin. 'You have a good day, now, Mr Franklin.'

WALKING FAST with my briefing book in hand, I keep up my senator-like stride as we head for the red-brick building. The book is actually the owner's manual from the glove compartment of the Suburban, but no one'll ever get a good look. On my right, Viv completes the picture, looking like the faithful aide to my Wendell executive.

'You think they're underground?' Viv asks, noticing the sudden decrease in population the closer we get to the brick building.

'Hard to say; I counted sixteen cars in the parking lot. Maybe all the work's being done back by the trailers.'

As we turn the corner of the building, there's a door in front of us and a metal staircase that heads down and into an entrance on the side of the building. We go for the stairs. As we step down, little bits of rock slide from our shoes through the grating and down to a concrete alley twenty feet below. Staring through the steps, Viv starts slowing down.

'Viv . . .'

'I'm fine,' she calls out, even though I never asked the question.

Inside the red-brick building, we cross through a dark tiled hallway and go through a door that's hanging off its hinges. Surrounding us are rows of open industrial showers, the nozzles just pipes sticking out of the wall. And when I think of the miners washing away yet another gruelling day of work, it's truly one of the most depressing sights I've ever seen.

'Harris, I got it!' Viv says, calling me back to the hallway, where she taps a sign that says THE RAMP. Below the words, there's a tiny arrow pointing down another set of stairs.

'You sure that's the—?'

She motions to an old metal punch clock next to the sign. No question about it. This is where the miners used to start their day.

The stairway narrows until we dead-end at a rusted blue metal door that reminds me of the door of an industrial freezer. I give it a sharp push, the door cracks open slightly, and a sharp, hot gust of air bursts out. It's a wind tunnel down there.

'Smells like rocks,' Viv says, covering her mouth.

I shove harder, and the door swings open. Reminding myself that the man in the parking lot told us to come this way, I will myself to step through into the narrow concrete corridor beyond.

As the door shuts behind us, the wind dies down, but I can taste the bitter air on my tongue.

The corridor curves to the right. There are some full mop buckets along the floor, and a fluorescent light in the ceiling. Finally, a sign of life.

The corridor straightens out and we get our second sign of life.

'What is it?' Viv asks, hesitantly moving forwards.

Up ahead, the right and left sides of the hall are covered from floor to ceiling with shallow metal storage racks filled with gear: dozens of rubber boots, thick nylon tool belts, mine lights and white construction helmets.

'Is this gonna fit?' Viv asks, forcing a laugh as she pulls a helmet onto her short-cropped Afro. 'What's this?' she adds, tapping the clip on the front of her helmet.

'For the light,' I say, pulling one of the mine lights off the shelf. But as I do so, I notice that it's connected by a black wire to a paperback-sized battery, which is connected to some clips on the shelf. This is a charging station.

Unlatching the clips, I pull the battery from the shelf and slide it onto one of the nearby tool belts. As Viv fastens it round her waist, I thread the wire over the back of her shoulder and hook the light onto the front of her helmet. Now she's all set.

She flips a switch, and the light turns on. Twenty-four hours ago, she would've bobbed her head back and forth, teasing me by shining the light in my face. Now the excitement's long gone.

'How do we know which ones are charged?' she asks. 'For all we know, this came back ten minutes ago.'

I look at the shelves. 'Yours is from the left, I'll take mine from the right,' I say. 'Either way, we'll at least have one that works.'

She nods at the logic as I grab two orange mesh construction vests. 'Put this on,' I tell her, tossing one of them her way.

Sceptically examining herself as she tightens the Velcro straps on the vest, she says, 'I look like I should be doing roadwork.'

'Really? I was thinking more crossing guard.'

She laughs at the joke—it's exactly what she needed.

'Feeling better?' I ask.

'No,' she says. 'But I'll get there.'

AT THE FAR END of the hall, the basement walls are lined with wooden benches that stretch for at least a few hundred feet. During the mine's heyday, miners must have lined up here every morning, waiting for their ride to work.

'What's that noise . . . ?' Viv asks.

Straight ahead, the corridor opens into a room with a thirty-foot ceiling, and we hear a deafening rumble. The wooden benches vibrate slightly, and the lights begin to flicker—but our eyes are glued to the elevator shaft that slices from floor to ceiling through the centre of the tall room. Like a vertical freight train, the elevator rockets up through the floor and disappears through the ceiling. Unlike a normal elevator, however, this one is only enclosed on three sides. Sure, there's a yellow steel door that prevents us from peeking into the shaft and having our heads chopped off, but above the door we can see straight into the empty elevator as it flies by.

Stepping further into the room, we crane our necks up at the elevator shaft. There's water running down its wooden walls. As a result, they are dark, slick and slowly rotting. The closer we get the more we feel the draft of cold air emanating from the shaft.

'Think that's the teepee up there?' Viv asks, pointing with her chin at the sliver of sunlight that creeps through the very top of the shaft.

'I think so—the woman in the motel said that's where the—'

A dull thud echoes down the shaft from the room above. It's followed by another . . . and another, soft and even—like footsteps. Viv and I both freeze.

'Frannie, it's Garth. Cage is at station,' a man's voice announces in in a flat South Dakota accent. His voice reverberates through the shaft—it's coming from the room above us.

'Stop cage,' a female voice replies, crackling through an intercom.

There's a loud shriek of metal as the steel safety gate on the front of the cage is thrown open. The footsteps clunk as they enter the cage. 'Stop cage,' the man says. The door slides shut with another shriek. 'Going to thirteen-two,' he adds. 'Lower cage.'

'Thirteen-two,' the woman repeats. 'Lowering cage.'

A second later, there's a soft rumble, and the benches behind us again start to vibrate.

'Oh, shit . . .' Viv mutters, and we both race to opposite sides of the shaft. Viv goes left; I go right. The elevator screeches past us like a free-fall ride in an amusement park, but within seconds, the thundering sound is muffled as it fades down the rabbit hole. Six Empire

State Buildings straight down. And then . . . deep below us, the metal of the cage lets out one final gasp.

Next to the yellow door there's a short wall with a break-glass-in-emergency fire alarm. Next to that is a phone receiver and a matching rusty keypad. There's our way in.

I glance back at Viv, who's got her hands up on her head and a dumbfounded look on her face as she studies the elevator shaft. 'Nuh-uh-uh,' she says. 'Nuh-uh. No *way* you're gettin' me in that . . .'

'Viv, you knew we were going down . . .'

'Not in that rusty old thing, I didn't. Forget it, Harris. Momma don't let me get on buses that run inta *that bad* a neighbourhood.'

'So where are you gonna hide?'

'Plenty of places. Lots of 'em . . .' She looks around at the wooden benches . . . the narrow hallway . . . The rest of the room is bare.

I cross my arms and stare her down.

'C'mon, Harris, *stop* . . .'

'Viv, trust me on this: we need to stay together.'

She studies my eyes, then glances at the intercom. Just behind us, leaning against the wall, is a blue sign with white stencilled letters:

Level	Station Code
Top	1-1
Ramp	1-3
200	2-2
300	2-3
800	3-3

The list continues through all fifty-seven levels. Right now, we're on the Ramp. At the very bottom, the list ends with:

7700	12-5
7850	13-1
8000	13-2

The 8,000-foot level. Station code: 13-2. That's the code the guy with the flat accent yelled into the intercom to take the elevator down, which means that's where the action is. I turn back to Viv. She's still glaring at the blue sign and the number 8000.

'Hurry up and call it in,' she mutters. 'But if we get stuck down there,' she threatens, 'you're gonna pray God gets you before I do.'

Wasting no time, I pick up the receiver and dial the four-digit number that's printed on the base of the rusty keypad: 4881.

'Hoist . . .' a female voice answers.

'Hey, it's Mike,' I announce, playing the odds. 'I need a ride down to thirteen-two.'

'Mike who?' she shoots back, unimpressed. From her accent, I know she's a local. From my accent, she knows I'm not.

'Mike,' I insist, pretending to be annoyed. 'From Wendell.' If the Wendell folks are just moving in, she's been having conversations like this all week. There's a short pause.

'Where are you?' she asks.

'The Ramp,' I say.

'Wait right there.'

There's a giant rumble in the distance—like a train pulling into a station. The floor starts to vibrate, and I can feel it against my chest. The lights flicker ever so slightly, and there's a sharp screech as the brakes kick in and the cage rattles towards us. But unlike last time, instead of continuing through the ceiling, it stops right in front of us.

I glance through the cut-out window in the steel door, but there's no light inside the cage. It's going to be a dark ride down.

'OK, get yerself in and hit the intercom,' the hoist operator says. 'And don't forget to tag in before you go.' Before I can ask, she explains, 'The board behind the phone.'

Hanging up the receiver, I cross behind the short wall that holds the phone and fire alarm. On the other side of the wall, short nails are hammered into a square plank of wood and numbered 1 to 52. From my pocket I pull out my own two tags—both numbered 27. *One in your pocket, one on the wall*, the guy out front said.

'You sure that's smart?' Viv asks as I put one of my tags on the nail labelled 27.

'If something happens, it's the only proof we're down there.'

Tentatively she pulls out her own tag and hooks it on the nail labelled 15. 'Harris . . .'

Before she can say it, I cross back to the front of the cage. 'It's just insurance—we'll be up and down in half an hour.' With a sharp yank, I pull the lever on the steel door. The lock unhooks with a thunk, but the door weighs a ton. As I finally tug it open, a mist of cold water sprays against my face and a drumbeat of water droplets bangs against the top of my helmet. It's like standing under the edge of an awning during a rainstorm.

'Let's go,' I say to Viv, reaching down and twisting the latch at the bottom of the inner gate. With one last pull and a final metal shriek, the gate rolls open, revealing an interior that is all rusted metal, slick with water and covered in dirt and grease.

I motion to Viv, and she hesitantly follows me inside. 'It's a steel coffin,' she whispers, her voice echoing off the metal. I can't argue with the analogy. Built to carry as many as thirty men standing shoulder to shoulder and to withstand any blasting, the space is as cold and bare as an abandoned boxcar.

Flipping a switch on the front of her helmet, Viv turns on her mine light and takes from her pocket a metal device that looks like a thin calculator. She holds it up. Below the screen is a button marked $O_2\%$.

'Oxygen detector?' I ask, and she nods. 'Where d'you get that?'

'On the shelves.'

The black digital numbers on the screen read 20.9. While I wonder if that is good or bad, I flip on my own light and approach the intercom. I press the large red button and, remembering the protocol, say into the speaker, 'Stop cage.'

'You close the safety gate?' the woman's voice buzzes through.

'Doing it right now . . .' Reaching up, I drag the gate back into place. It screeches against the rollers and slams with a metal clang. Viv jumps at the sound. No turning back.

'Going to thirteen-two,' I say into the intercom, using the same code from before. 'Lower cage.'

'Thirteen-two,' the woman repeats. 'Lowering cage.'

There's a grinding of metal and one of those never-ending pauses you get on a roller coaster. Right before the big drop.

'Don't look,' the woman teases through the intercom. 'It's a long way down . . .'

My stomach leaps into my chest as the cage plummets. For the first few feet, it's no different from an elevator ride, but as we pick up speed and plunge down the shaft, my stomach sails up towards my oesophagus. Jerking back and forth, the cage bangs wildly against the walls of the shaft, almost knocking us off our feet.

'Harris, tell her to slow down before—!'

'Lean against the wall—it makes it easier!' I call out.

'*What?*' she shouts, though I can barely hear her. Everything's drowned out by a never-ending screeching roar.

'*Lean against the wall!*' I yell.

Taking my own advice, I lean back and fight to keep my balance. It's the first time I take a glance outside the cage. Through the grating of the safety gate the subterranean world rushes by: a blur of brown dirt . . . another tunnel. Every eight seconds, a different level whizzes by. We've got to be going at forty miles an hour.

'*You feel that?*' Viv calls out, pointing to her ears.

My ears pop, and I nod. I swallow hard, and they pop again.

It's been over three minutes since we left, and we're still headed down what's easily becoming the longest elevator ride of my life. On my right, the entrances to the tunnels whip by at their regular blurred pace . . . and then, to my surprise, they start to slow down.

'We there?' Viv asks.

'I think so,' I say. 'How we doing on air?'

She looks down at her oxygen detector. 'Twenty-one per cent is normal—and we're at twenty point four,' she says, flipping to the instructions on the back. She's doing her best to mask her fear. 'Says here you need sixteen per cent to breathe normally . . . nine per cent before you go unconscious. At six per cent, you wave bye-bye.'

'But we're at twenty point four?' I say, trying to reassure her.

'We were twenty point nine up top,' she shoots back.

The cage bucks to a final halt. 'Stop cage?' the woman asks through the intercom.

'Stop cage,' I say, pressing the red button.

As I take my first peek through the metal safety gate, I look up at the ceiling, and the beam from my mine light bounces off a bright orange stencilled sign dangling from two wires: 4850 LEVEL.

'You gotta be kidding me,' Viv mumbles. 'We're only *halfway*?'

I press the intercom button. 'Hello . . . ?'

'What's wrong?' the hoist operator barks back.

'We wanted to go to the eight thousa—'

'Cross the drift and you'll see the Number Six Elevator. The cage is waiting for you there. Now, step outside, and tell me when you're in.'

I tug on the safety gate, and it rolls out of the way. A downpour of water from the shaft forms a wet wall that partially blocks us from seeing out. Darting straight through the waterfall, I dash out into the mine, where the floor, walls and ceiling are all made of tightly packed brown dirt. No different from a cave, I tell myself, stepping ankle-deep in a puddle of mud. On both sides of the tunnel in front of us are another twenty feet of end-to-end benches like the ones up top. If I close my eyes, I swear I can see the ghostly afterimages of hundreds of miners—heads hung low, elbows resting on their knees—as they wait in the dark, beaten from another day spent underground.

Crossing the drift, we head straight for the door marked ELEVATOR NO. 6. As we enter the new cage and I pull the safety gate down, I can practically smell Viv's claustrophobia setting in. The lower ceiling makes this coffin feel even smaller.

'This is Number Six Hoist,' the woman announces through the intercom. 'All set?'

I glance at Viv. She won't even look up. 'All set,' I say into the intercom. 'Lower cage.'

'Lower cage,' the woman repeats as the metal coffin starts to rumble.

Next stop: 8,000 feet below the earth's surface.

EIGHT

'You there yet?' Sauls asked, his voice breaking up as it came through Janos's cellphone.

'Almost,' Janos replied as his Ford Explorer blew past yet another thicket of pine, spruce and birch as he made his way towards Leed.

'What's *almost*?' Sauls asked. 'You an hour away? Half hour? Ten minutes? What's the story?'

Gripping the steering wheel, Janos stayed silent. He didn't need to listen to this nagging. Flipping on the radio, he turned the dial until he found static.

'You're breaking up,' he said to Sauls. 'Can't hear you . . .'

'Janos . . .'

Slapping his phone shut, Janos tossed it onto the empty passenger seat and focused back on the road.

WELCOME TO LEED—HOME OF THE HOMESTEAD MINE, the billboard on the side of the road said.

Janos breezed right by it, recalculating the timeline in his head. Even if their jet took off immediately, they couldn't have arrived before midnight. And if they didn't get in until midnight they had to sleep somewhere.

Making a sharp left turn into a parking lot, he pulled up and eyed the neon VACANCY sign in front of one of the squat buildings. It was clear that the Gold House Motel was still open.

He opened his door and headed inside. On his left he noticed a rack of tourist brochures. All of them were faded by the sun, every single one—except for the one entitled 'The Homestead Mine'. The sun hadn't faded it a bit—almost as if . . . as if it had just been exposed in the last hour or so.

THE CAGE PLUNGES straight down as my ears once again pop and a sharp pain corkscrews through my forehead. As I fight for balance something tells me my headache isn't just from the pressure.

'How's our oxygen?' I call out to Viv, who's cradling the detector in both hands as we're jarred back and forth.

She cocks her head. 'Why are you suddenly worried?' she asks, studying my face. For the past 5,000-plus feet, Viv's anchored herself to my own emotional state: the confidence that snuck us in here, the stubbornness and the desperation that got us on the first cage. But the moment she gets her first whiff of my fear, she's floundering. She looks down at the detector, her forehead covered in sweat. The cold breeze that whipped through the top of the shaft is long gone. The deeper we go underground, the hotter it gets.

'Nineteen . . . we're down to nineteen,' she stutters, coughing and holding her throat. Nineteen per cent is still within normal range, but her chest rises and falls quickly and she slumps against the wall. I'm still breathing fine.

Her body starts to tremble, and as the shaking gets faster she can barely stand up. A loud, empty gasp echoes from deep within her chest. Oh, no. If she's hyperventilating . . .

Viv looks across at me, her eyes begging for help. 'Hhhh . . .' Gripping her chest, she gives a long gasp and crumples to a sitting position on the the floor.

'Viv!'

I leap towards her just as the cage is slammed to the right. Off balance, I crash into the left wall, shoulder-first. A jolting pain runs down my arm. Viv's still gasping, and the sudden jolt sends her falling forward. I dive at her, catching her just as she's about to hit the floor. I turn her round and cradle her body in my arms. Her eyes dance wildly back and forth. She's in full panic. 'I got you, Viv . . . I got you,' I tell her, over and over. I lick a puddle of sweat from the dimple of my top lip. It's easily over ninety degrees down here.

'W-what's happening?' Viv asks. As she looks up at me, her tears run back towards her temples and are swallowed by her hair.

'The heat's normal. It's just the pressure from the rocks above us . . . plus we're getting closer to the earth's core.'

'What about oxygen?' she stutters.

I turn to the detector, which has tumbled to the floor beside her. As my light shines across the digital screen, it goes from 19.6 to 19.4 per cent. 'Holding steady,' I tell her. 'We're gonna be fine, Viv. Just keep taking deep breaths.'

Following my own instructions, I suck in a chestful of steamy, hot air. It burns my lungs like a deep breath in a sauna. As another tunnel whizzes by, my ears pop once more and I swear my head's about to explode. But just as I clench my teeth and shut my eyes, there's a screech and a sudden tug of forward momentum that reminds me of a plane coming to a sharp stop. We're finally slowing down, and Viv's breathing does the same.

'There you go . . . just like that . . .' I say, holding the back of her neck. Her huffing and puffing is smooth and steady as the cage jerks to its final stop. For a full minute, we dangle there, not moving.

I pull away, climbing to my feet. It takes Viv a moment, but she eventually turns round and offers an appreciative grin. She's trying to be strong, but I can see she's still freaked.

'Stop cage?' the hoist operator asks through the intercom.

Ignoring the question, I turn to Viv. 'How you doing?'

'OK,' she replies, sitting up straight, trying to convince me she's fine. 'Now tell her you're all right before she starts to worry.'

'Sorry, Hoist,' I say into the intercom. 'Just wanted to readjust some gear. All's well. Stop cage.'

'Stop cage,' the operator repeats.

I tug open the safety gate and give the outer door a shove. A hot wind seeps through the opening—and this time, the heat's almost unbearable. Blinking the dust from my eyes, I step through the water that drips from above the door and out onto the dirt floor. In front of me, the ceiling lowers to about nine feet and the walls narrow like a wormhole. Along the muddy floor, I follow some ancient metal train tracks. They're in good enough shape to tell me how the miners are moving all that computer equipment through the mine.

After a few yards the tracks branch out like spokes on a wheel—into different tunnels. I eye each one, noticing that the mud on most of the tracks is caked and dried. But in the far left tunnel, it's soaking wet, complete with a recent bootprint. It's not much of a lead, but it's all we've got.

'You ready?' I call back to Viv, who's now sitting on a plank of wood outside the cage.

She doesn't budge. 'I'm sorry, Harris. I can't . . .'

'Whattya mean, *you can't?*'

'I just . . . can't,' she insists, curling her knees towards her chin.

'You said you were OK.'

'I didn't want to be upstairs all by myself.' She faces me. 'You should go,' she blurts. 'Please, Harris. Just go . . .'

'But if we split up—'

'*Go!*' she insists, fighting back tears. 'Find what they're doing.'

With everything we've been through in the past forty-eight hours, it's the first time I've ever seen Viv Parker completely paralysed. As she buries her face in her knees, I'm reminded that the worst beatings we take are the ones we give ourselves.

I turn to leave, sloshing through the wet mud.

'Take this,' she calls out. She holds up the oxygen detector and wings it through the air, directly at me. As I catch it, there's a loud screeching noise behind her. The cage rumbles back to life, disappearing up the elevator shaft. Last plane out.

'If you want to leave,' I tell her, 'just dial the—'

'I'm not going anywhere,' she insists. Even now she won't completely give up. 'Just find what they're doing,' she says again.

I nod, and my helmet light draws an imaginary line up and down her face. Then I turn back towards the tunnels.

'So can I get you a room?' the dark-haired woman behind the motel's front desk asked.

'Actually, I'm just looking for my friends,' Janos replied. 'Have you seen a white guy and a young black girl?'

The woman cocked her head. 'They're your friends?'

'Yeah, my friends from work. We were supposed to fly in together last night, but I got delayed and—' Janos cut himself off. 'Listen, I got up at four o'clock for my flight this morning. Now are they upstairs or not? We've got a big day ahead of us.'

'Sorry,' the woman said. 'They checked out over an hour ago.'

TEN MINUTES LATER, I'm ankle-deep in runny mud that, as my light hits it, shines with a metallic rust colour. All around me, the walls of the rocky cave are a patchwork of colours—brown, grey, rust and mossy green. Above me are the rustiest pipes I've ever seen in my entire life. Like the walls and the rest of the ceiling, they are slick with water. At this depth, the air is so hot and humid that the cave itself sweats. And so do I. Every minute or so, a new wave of heat ploughs through the tunnel, then dissipates. In . . . and out. In . . . and out. It's like the mine is breathing.

I glance down at the oxygen detector: 18.8 per cent. The footprints ahead of me tell me at least two others have made the trek. For now, that's good enough for me.

Wiping the sweat from my face, I follow the curve of the railroad tracks along the tunnel until I reach a fork in the road with five different choices. Shining the light on each one, I see that, like before, four of them are caked in dried mud, while one's wet and fresh. There's a sign spray-painted directly onto the rock wall in this tunnel: DANGER—BLASTING. Damn.

I open my wallet, pull out my bright pink California Tortilla Burrito Club card, and wedge it under a rock by the entrance of the tunnel I'm about to leave—the equivalent of leaving breadcrumbs.

I make a sharp right into the wet tunnel, which I quickly realise is slightly wider than the rest. From there, I stick with the train tracks, following the soupy mud through a fork that goes left, and another that goes right. Spray-painted signs point to LIFT and 7850 RAMP, but the arrows are now pointing in different directions. To be safe, I put down more breadcrumbs at each turn: my Triple-A card at the first left, the scrap of paper that holds my list of movies to rent at the next right. The distances aren't far, but the jagged walls, the muddy train tracks . . . everything looks alike. Without the breadcrumbs, I'd be lost in this labyrinth.

I make a left and wedge my gym membership card under a rock. Further along, I come across a shallow hole dug into the wall on my left. My light shines directly into it, casting deep shadows along its jagged edge. The light's almost yellow in colour. And as I pass the hole and continue even further into the tunnel, I'm surprised to see that the yellow tint is still there.

Oh, no . . . don't tell me—

A high-pitched buzz erupts above my forehead and it doesn't take long to realise the sound's coming from my helmet. In front of me the light fades to brown. Before, I could see at least fifty feet in front of me. Now it's down to thirty. I don't believe it. My hands start shaking, and I stare down at the battery pack on my tool belt. Viv was right about the charging station . . . The problem is, it's becoming increasingly clear I picked the wrong side.

Spinning round as quickly as I can, I tell myself not to panic—but

I can already feel the tightening in my chest and my breathing speeds up. I look up . . . down . . . side to side . . . The world's starting to shrink. Along the walls and floor, the shadows creep in closer. If I don't get out of here fast . . .

I sprint back the way I came, but the rocks underfoot make it hard to run. My ankles bend and turn with every step and the helmet light jerks wildly in front of me. I focus on the white gym membership card that's dead ahead. If I can get there, I can at least get one last look at the other breadcrumbs so I know where to turn. The light flickers, and it takes everything I have to ignore the burning pain in my chest. Almost there . . . *Don't let it go. Don't lose it.* As the light shrivels and I lean forward and reach out for the archway in front of me, the entire cave and everything in it goes completely . . . and utterly . . . black.

As THE DARKNESS HITS, I keep my arm outstretched in front of me to stop myself from ramming into the wall. I never get there. My foot sinks into a hole, and I lurch off balance. My knees tear across the rocky floor as I crash into the ground. I put my hands out to break my fall, but the momentum's too much. Sliding headfirst, I face-plant across the gravel.

Lying there until my breathing settles, I open my eyes. I hold my hand to my face, but nothing's in front of me. This isn't like turning up the lights in your bedroom and waiting for your eyes to adjust.

'Viv!' I call out through the tunnels. 'Viv, can you hear me?'

The question goes unanswered. For all I know, she took the elevator back to the top.

'*Is anyone here?*' I scream as loud as I can.

The only sound I hear is my own laboured breathing and the grinding of rocks as I shift my weight. I've never heard the world as silent as it is right now, 8,000 feet below the earth. I start to stand up, but quickly change my mind and decided to crawl on all fours, patting the ground ahead of me like I'm looking for a lost contact lens.

I palm my way to my right until I find the jagged wall, then follow a sharp right turn through the archway. As my right hand stays with the wall, my left hand sweeps the ground like a human metal detector, making sure I don't hit another hole.

Twenty-five feet later, my knees are aching, and an opening on my right leads to a parallel tunnel where I can go right or left. There are openings like this in every direction, but I'm pretty sure this is the one where I left the scrap of paper. I search the muddy ground. The list of movies I want to rent is somewhere along the floor. Using just my fingertips, I systematically sift through the pebbles at the base of the wall, working from the right to the left. It's nowhere to be found. Still, I don't need a scrap of paper to tell me I made a right-hand turn into this section of the tunnel. Feeling my way, I find the edge of the wall and follow it out to the left.

Heading further up the tunnel and crawling diagonally across the train tracks, I reach out in the darkness for the right-hand wall. It should be right in front of me . . . I stretch out my arm all the way . . . reaching . . . reaching . . . But for some reason, the wall isn't there. I stop midcrawl and grip the train tracks. If I took a wrong turn . . .

'*Viv!*' I call out. No one answers.

Refusing to panic, I swivel around on my butt and slowly extend my leg out as far as it goes. If the wall's really here—and I'm pretty sure it is—it'll . . . *Thunk.*

There we go.

Keeping my foot pressed against the wall, but still sitting, I let go of the train track, stretch forwards, and hug the wetness of the wall with my hands. I keep patting it just to make sure it's there.

Back on my knees, it takes me two minutes to crawl along the rubble, my right hand patting the wall again, my left hand tracing the ground. Finally I feel the rounded curve of another archway as the cave tunnel opens up on my right. I search for my Triple-A card. Like before, I don't have a prayer. But I remember making a left here, so this time I go right.

The tunnel soon opens up again. I'm now in the cavern with five different tunnels to choose from. This time, if I pick the wrong one, this place really will be my coffin.

'*Viv!*' I call out. '*Viv—are you there?*'

I hold my breath and listen as my plea echoes down each of the tunnels. It reverberates everywhere at once. The original surround sound. Holding my breath, I wait for a response. But I'm once again buried in underground silence.

I look around, but the view doesn't change. There's no up, down, left or right. The world teeters sideways as dizziness flips to vertigo. I'm on all fours but still can't hold my balance. With a crash, I fall on my side. My cheek rolls into the rocks. It's the only thing that tells me where the ground is. There's nothing but ink in every direction— and then, out of the corner of my eye, I spot tiny, tiny flashes of silver light. They only last a second—bursts of sparkles, like when you shut your eyes too tight. But even as I turn my head to follow the glow, I know it's just my imagination. I've heard of this before . . . Miner mirages.

'Harris . . . ?' a voice whispers in the distance.

I assume it's another trick of my imagination. That is, until it starts talking back.

'*Harris, I can't hear you!*' it shouts.

'Viv, is that you?'

'Keep talking. Where are you?'

'In the dark—my light went out! I need you to come get me!' There's a pause. 'I can't!' she yells. 'Just follow the light!'

'There is no light! I turned too many corners—I can't see!'

'Then follow my voice!'

'Viv! Are you listening?! It's bouncing through every tunnel!' I pause, keeping my sentences short, so the echo doesn't interfere. 'It's too dark! If I take the wrong turn, you'll never find me!'

'You really need me to come there?' she asks, her voice shaking.

'You have a light! I can't move,' I call back. 'Viv . . . Please . . .'

As I lie in the darkness, the cave once again goes silent. Just the thought of heading into the darkness . . . especially by herself . . . I saw the pain in her eyes before. She's terrified.

'Which of these tunnels do I take?' she shouts, her voice booming through the caves.

I sit up straight. 'You're the greatest, Viv Parker!'

'I'm not joking, Harris! Which way do I go?'

There's no mistaking her desperate tone. This isn't easy for her.

'The one with the freshest mud! Look for my footprints!' My voice echoes through the chamber, fading into nothing.

'You have tiny feet!' she calls back.

I try to smile, but we both know she's got a long way to go.

'You can do it, Viv! Pretend you're in a fun-house!'

'I hate fun-houses! They scare me! Harris, it's too dark! I can barely see . . . !' The cave goes quiet.

I give her a second, then call out. 'Viv, everything OK?'

No response.

'Viv . . . ? Are you there?!'

Dead silence. My jaw tightens, and for the first time I start wondering if we're not the only ones down here. If that guy who chased us caught a different flight—

'Just keep talking, Harris!' her voice finally rings through the air.

She must've entered the main stretch of tunnel. Her voice is clearer. 'Just keep talking!' she shouts, stuttering slightly. 'Tell me about work . . . your parents . . . anything . . .' she begs. She needs something to take her mind off what's going on.

It's a simple request, but I'm surprised how long it takes me to come up with an answer.

'Senator Stevens is so insecure, he makes me walk him to every vote on the Floor, just in case he's cornered by another Member. And he's so cheap, he doesn't even go to dinner any more without bringing a lobbyist. That way, he doesn't have to pick up the bill . . .'

'You serious?' Viv asks. She's still wavering, but I hear the laughter in the back of her throat.

'When I finished college, I was such an idealist, I started and quickly dropped out of a graduate theological programme. Even Matthew didn't know that. I wanted to help people, but the God part kept getting in the way . . .'

From the silence, I know I've got her attention. I just have to bring her in. 'I helped redraft the bankruptcy law, but since I'm still paying back my Duke loans, I have five different MasterCards,' I tell her. 'My most distinctive memory from childhood is catching my dad crying in the boys' department of Kmart because he couldn't afford to buy me a three-pack of white Fruit of the Loom undershirts and had to buy the Kmart label instead . . .'

My voice starts to sag. 'I spend too much time worrying what other people think of me . . .'

'Everyone does,' Viv calls back.

'When I was in college, I worked in an ice-cream store, and when customers snapped their fingers to get my attention I'd break off the bottom of their cone, so when they were a block or two away their ice cream would drip all over them . . .'

'Harris . . .'

'My real name is Harold. In high school they called me Harry, but when I got to college I changed it to Harris because I thought it'd make me sound more like a leader . . . And for the past week, despite my best efforts to ignore it, I've really felt that with Matthew and Pasternak gone, after ten years on Capitol Hill, I don't have any real friends . . .'

As I say the words, I'm on my knees, curling down towards the floor. I can feel the tips of the rocks press against my forehead, but there's no pain. There's no anything. As the realisation hits, I'm completely numb—as hollow as I've been since the day they unveiled my mom's headstone. Right next to my dad's.

'Harris . . .' Viv calls out.

'I'm sorry, Viv—that's all I've got,' I reply. 'Just follow the sound.'

'I'm trying,' she insists. But unlike before, her voice doesn't boomerang through the cavern. It's coming directly from my right. Picking up my head, I trace the noise just as the darkness evaporates. Up ahead, the neck of the tunnel blinks into existence in a faint glow of light. I have to squint to adjust.

I look away just long enough to collect my thoughts. By the time I turn back, I've got a smile pressed into place.

'Harris, I'm really sorry . . .'

'I'm fine,' I insist.

'I didn't ask how you were.' Her tone is soft and reassuring.

I look up at her. The light's glowing from the top of her head.

'What, you ain't never seen a guardian angel with an Afro before? There's like, fourteen of us up in Heaven.'

I can't help but grin. 'Sweet Mocha . . .'

'To the rescue,' she says, completing my thought. Standing over me, she lifts her arms, flexing her muscles. Her shoulders are square. Her feet are planted deep. I couldn't knock her over with a wrecking ball. Extending a hand, she offers to pull me up. On the Hill, an offer of help is always about something else. I look up at Viv's open hand. Not any more.

Without hesitation, I reach upwards. Viv grabs my hand in her own and gives me a hard tug to get me back on my feet.

'I'll never tell anyone, Harris.'

'I didn't think you would.'

She thinks about it for a moment. 'Did you really do that thing with the ice-cream cones?'

I nod, continuing to hold her hand. There's only one light between us, but as long as we stay together, it's more than enough. 'Now are you ready to see what they're digging for down here?' I ask.

As she shoves her shoulders back, there's a new confidence in her silhouette. Not from what she did for me—what she did for herself.

'Just hurry up before I change my mind.'

I plough forwards along the rocks, deeper into the cavern. 'Thank you, Viv—I mean it . . . thanks.'

'Yeah, yeah and more yeah.'

'I'm serious,' I add.

KICKING THROUGH THE GRAVEL of the Homestead mine's parking lot, Janos counted two motorcycles and a total of seventeen cars and pick-up trucks. Out of the whole lot, only two looked like they had ever met a car wash: the Explorer that Janos drove . . . and the jet-black Suburban parked in the far corner.

Janos slowly made his way towards the Suburban. South Dakota plates like everyone else's . . . He lightly put his hand on the driver's door, watching his reflection bounce back at him. Behind him, he heard a crush of loose gravel and, in an eye blink, spun to follow the sound.

'Whoa, sorry—didn't mean to surprise you,' the man in a Spring Break '94 T-shirt said. 'Just wanted to know if you needed any help.'

'I'm looking for my coworkers,' Janos said. 'One's about my height—'

'With the black girl. Yeah, of course—I sent 'em inside,' Spring Break said. 'So you're from Wendell, too?'

'Inside where?' Janos asked, his voice as calm as ever.

'The dry,' the man said, pointing with his chin at the red-brick building. 'Follow the path—you can't miss it.'

Waving goodbye, the man headed back towards the construction trailers. And Janos marched straight to the red-brick building.

VIV AND I CONTINUE to weave slowly through the darkness, retracing my steps. Now the ground slants slightly downwards, and as the never-ending hole takes us even deeper, the temperature keeps getting hotter. Viv is once again breathing heavily.

'You sure you're—?'

'Just keep going,' she insists.

After two hundred or so feet, there is a sign marked LIFT, with an arrow pointing to a tunnel on our right.

'You sure we're not going in circles?' Viv asks.

'Can't be—the ground keeps going down,' I tell her. 'I think most of these places are required to have a second elevator as a precaution—so, if something goes wrong with one, no one gets trapped down here.'

Suddenly, an ear-splitting chirping rips through the air, like a nuclear assault warning. I freeze and look around. If we tripped an alarm . . .

Deeper down the tunnel, a bright headlight ignites, and an engine rumbles to life. It was down here all along, hidden in the dark. Before we can even react, it barrels towards us like an oncoming freight train.

Viv tries to take off. I tug her back by the wrist. The thing's moving so fast, we'll never outrun it. Better that we not look guilty.

The engine grinds to a halt a few feet in front of us. I follow Viv's light as it shines across the side of the banged-up open yellow truck. Behind the wheel is a bearded, middle-aged man in an old pair of overalls. He shuts down the engine. 'Sorry about the heat—we'll have it fixed up in the next few hours,' he offers.

'Fixed?'

'You think we like it like this?' he asks, using his mine light to circle the walls and ceiling. 'We're a belch shy of a hundred and thirty degrees . . .' He laughs to himself. 'Even for eight thousand, that's hot.'

I quickly recognise the flat South Dakota accent of the man who came down in the cage before us. But what catches my attention is his tone of voice. He's not attacking. He's apologising.

'Thanks,' I laugh back, anxious to change the subject.

'No, *thank you*. If it weren't for you guys, this place woulda still been boarded up.'

'Yeah, well . . . happy to help. How's it looking?' I ask.

'You'll see when you get down there. Everything's in place,' he explains. 'I should really get back, though . . . We got another shipment coming in.' With a wave, he starts the engine and the shrill scream of the chirping pierces the entire tunnel. Just a warning system as he drives through the dark—like the beeping sound when a big truck goes in reverse.

I stay watching the train, making sure it's gone.

'Hey, Harris . . .' Viv says.

'Hold on, I want to make sure he's—'

'Harris, I think you should take a look at this *now* . . .'

I turn round. If she's still worried about the—

Up ahead, we've now got a clear view of the very end of the tunnel—the truck was blocking it before. Two brand-new, shiny steel doors gleam in the distance. There's a circular glass window cut into each one, and while we're too far away to see through them, there's no mistaking the bright white glow that seeps out through the glass.

This is what we came for. The light at the end of the tunnel.

THE SIGN on the polished steel doors says: WARNING: AUTHORIZED PERSONNEL ONLY. I stand on my tiptoes to get a look through the windows, but the glass is opaque. We can't see inside.

'What about ringing the doorbell?' Viv asks.

On my right, built into the rock, is a metal plate with a thick black button. Viv reaches out to push it.

'Don't—' I call out.

I'm too late. She rams her palm into the button.

The double doors shudder, and we both jump back. There's a tremendous hiss, and two pneumatic air cylinders unfold their arms. The doors open towards us.

I crane my head to get a better look. 'Viv . . .'

'I'm on it,' she says, pointing her light inside. But the only thing that's there—about ten feet ahead—is another set of double doors. And another black button. Which Viv once again presses.

Behind us, there's another loud hiss as the original steel doors begin to close. Viv spins around, about to run.

'It's OK,' I say.

'What are you talking about?' she asks, panicking. The doors are about to squeeze shut. This is our last chance to get out.

I scan the walls. A tiny sign on the top left-hand corner of the door says: VAPOR-TIGHT DOOR. There we go.

'It's an air lock.' I say

With a heavy *thunk*, the outer doors slam shut and the cylinders lock into place. We're now stuck between the two sets of doors. Twisting back to the black button, Viv pounds it as hard as she can.

There's an even louder mechanical hiss as the doors in front of us slowly churn open. A burst of bright light and a gust of cold wind come whipping through the opening. It blows my hair back, and we both shut our eyes.

The wind dies fast as the two zones equalise. I can already taste the difference in the air. Sweeter . . . almost sharp on my tongue. As I finally open my eyes, it takes me a few seconds to adjust. The light is too bright.

We're in a wide-open, stark white room that's bigger than an ice-skating rink. The ceiling rises to at least twenty feet. Along the floor, hundreds of red, black and green wires are bundled together in braids as thick as my neck. On my left, there's an open alcove labelled CHANGING STATION, complete with cubbies for dirty boots and mine helmets. Right now, though, the alcove's filled with lab tables, half a dozen bubble-wrapped computer hubs and routers, and two state-of-the-art computer servers. Whatever Wendell Mining is doing down here, they're still setting up.

'What the hell's going on?' Viv asks.

I shake my head, replaying the question over and over in my head: what's a multimillion-dollar laboratory doing 8,000 feet below the surface of the earth?

NINE

Down in the basement of the red-brick building, Janos stopped at the charging station for the mine lights. He'd been there once before—right after Sauls hired him. In the six months since, nothing had changed.

Taking a closer look, he counted two gaps in the charging station— one on each side. Thinking they were playing the odds, they had gambled, he realised. Everybody gambles. That's how it always is.

He stepped past the wooden benches and entered the large room with the elevator shaft. He headed straight for the phone.

'Hey, there—was hoping you could help me out,' Janos said into the receiver. 'I'm looking for some friends . . . two of them . . . and was just wondering if you sent them down in the cage?'

'From Ramp Level, I sent one guy down, but I'm pretty sure he was alone.'

'You positive? He should've definitely been with someone . . .'

'Honey, all I do is move 'em up and down. Maybe his friend went in up top.'

Janos looked up through the elevator shaft to the level directly above. That's where most people came in, but Harris and Viv . . . they'd be looking to keep it quiet. That's why they would've followed the tunnel down here.

Janos slid around to the other side of the short wall, where a square piece of wood held fifty-two nails. He focused on two metal tags labelled 15 and 27. Two tags. They were still together.

Everybody gambles, he said to himself—but what's most important to remember is that, at some point, everybody also loses.

'THINK THEY KNOW we're here?' Viv asks, shutting off her light.

I look around the laboratory. The brackets are attached to the wall, but the surveillance cameras aren't up yet. 'I think we're clear.'

Stepping deeper into the lab, I point to a trail of muddy footprints leading towards the far left corner of the room.

'I thought you said Matthew put the land transfer to Wendell in the bill a few days ago?' Viv points out as we follow the trail. 'How'd they get all this built so quick?'

'They've been working on the request since last year. My guess is that the authorisation was just a formality. I bet they figured no one would mind the sale of a dilapidated mine. And as far as I can tell, there's nothing illegal about what Wendell's done.'

'That depends on what they're building down here,' she says.

We head down a corridor, and there's a room off to our right. Inside, a large wipe-off board leans against a four-drawer filing cabinet. There's also a brand-new metal desk.

'Ever see one of those desks before?' I ask.

'I don't know . . . they're kinda standard.'

'They just redid some of our staff offices. We got the same ones for all our legislative assistants . . . They're government issue.'

She looks back at the desk. 'So now you think the government built all this?'

'Viv, take a look around. Wendell said they wanted this place to mine gold, and there's no gold. They said they're a small South Dakota company, and they've got the entire Batcave down here. Why would you possibly believe that they're who they say they are?'

'That doesn't mean they're a front for the government.'

'I'm not saying that,' I reply, heading back into the corridor. 'But whoever Wendell really is, they're clearly hunting for something bigger than a few gold nuggets.'

'So what do you think they're after?' Viv says, chasing behind me.

'Maybe they're not after anything. Look—they've got everything they need right here.' I point to the boxes and tall gas canisters that line both sides of the corridor. The first few dozen canisters are marked MERCURY; the rest are labelled TETRACHLOROETHYLENE.

I go straight for the boxes that are stacked up to the ceiling. There are hundreds of them—each one tagged with a small sticker and barcode. I tear one off for a closer look.

Under the barcode, the word PHOTOMULTIPLIER is printed. But as I open a box to see what a photomultiplier actually is, I'm surprised to find that it's empty. I kick a nearby box just to be sure. All the same—empty.

'Harris, maybe we should get out of here . . .'

'Not yet,' I say, rushing past the boxes to where the corridor dead-ends at a single steel door. It's heavy, like a bank vault, and latched tightly shut. Next to the door is a biometric handprint scanner. To judge from the loose wires that are everywhere, it's still not hooked up, so I give the latch a sharp pull. It opens with a pop. The frame of the door is lined with black rubber to keep it airtight.

Inside, the room is long and narrow like a two-lane bowling alley. In the centre, on a lab table, are three red boxes covered with wires. Whatever they're building, they're still not finished. A huge crate in the corner is labelled TUNGSTEN, and on our right there's a ten-foot metal O. The sign on the top reads: DANGER—DO NOT APPROACH WHEN MAGNET IS ON.

'What do they need a magnet for?' Viv asks.

'What do they need this tunnel for?' I counter, pointing to the metal piping that runs down the length of the room, past the magnet.

Searching for answers, I spot a tall oval door, the kind they have on a submarine, and a second biometric scanner. Again, wires are everywhere.

As I fly towards the door, Viv grabs my sleeve and tugs me back. 'What if it's not safe in there? Look at the door. It could be radio-active or something.'

'Without a warning sign out front? These guys aren't that stupid.'

'So what do you think they're building?'

I ignore her. I'm not sure she wants to know my answer.

'You think it's bad, don't you?' Viv says.

Yanking free of her grip, I head for the door.

'You think they're building a weapon, don't you?' Viv calls out.

I stop right there. 'Viv, they could be doing anything from nano-tech to bringing dinosaurs back to life. But whatever's in there, Matthew and Pasternak were both killed for it, and now they're sizing the nooses for our necks. Unless you plan on living in a car for the rest of your life, we need to figure out what the hell is going on.'

I grab the lock on the submarine door and give it a sharp turn. It spins easily and there's a loud *thunk* as the wheel stops and the door pops open. As it swings inwards, we're hit by a sharp, sour smell.

'Oh, man,' Viv says. 'What is that? Smells like a . . .'

'Dry cleaner's,' I say, and she nods.

Stepping over the threshold, we scan around for the answer. The room is even more spotless than the one we came from. And straight in front of us, a fifty-yard-wide crater is dug into the floor. Inside it is a huge, round metal bowl the size of a hot-air balloon cut in half. The walls of the bowl are lined with thousands of what look like camera lenses, one right next to the other, each one peering inwards towards the centre of the sphere. The thousands of perfectly aligned lenses form their own glass layer within the sphere. Hanging from the ceiling by steel wires is another bowl, inverted. When the two identical halves are put together, it'll be a perfect spherical chamber.

'What in hell?' Viv asks.

'No idea, but I'm guessing those things are the photomultipliers—'

'What do you think you're doing?' someone yells from our left.

I turn towards the sound. Rushing straight at us is a man in a bright orange hazardous-materials suit, complete with its own Plexiglas face plate and gas mask. If he's wearing that . . .

'We're in trouble . . .' Viv mutters.

I want to run, but my legs won't move. I can't believe I led us into this—even the smallest amount of radiation could . . .

The man reaches towards the back of his neck and yanks the radiation hood off his head, tossing it to the ground. 'You have any idea what you've done?' he yells. 'These are supposed to be clean-room conditions. You know how much time and money you just cost us?' If I had to guess his accent, I'd go with eastern European, but something's off. He's got sunken dark eyes, a black moustache and silver, wire-rimmed glasses.

'How'd you get down here?' the man continues. 'You're not even mining people, are you?' He reaches for an intercom with a red button.

'Harris . . .' Viv warns.

I'm already on it. The man dives for the alarm. I grab him by the wrist and shove him back. He's stronger than I expected. Using my own weight against me, he whips me round, slamming me into the wall. My head jerks back, and my helmet hits the wall so hard I actually see stars. He adds a rabbit punch to my gut, hoping it'll take the fight out of me. But *his* head's exposed; *I'm* wearing an unbreakable mine helmet. Grabbing him by the shoulders, I ram my head forward and headbutt him. As he staggers back, I look over at Viv.

'Get out of here!' I tell her.

'They'll kill you for this!' the man with the moustache yells.

Holding him tight, I grip his shoulder with one hand and wind up to hit him again. Thrashing wildly, he digs his fingers into my wrist. As I let go, he tries to make a run for it, but I grab him by the back of his containment suit and yank him back as hard as I can. He may not have been the one to kill Matthew and Pasternak, but right now he's the only punchbag I've got. As he stumbles off balance, I give him one last shove—straight for the edge of the crater.

'No . . . !' he screams. 'It'll all—!'

There's a loud, shattering crash as he clears the ledge and slides headfirst down the inside of the bowl, smashing through every photomultiplier tube he hits, clearing a path all the way to the bottom. The tubes crack easily, barely slowing him down . . . that is, until his collarbone smacks into the thick metal pylon at the base of the bowl. There's a muted crunch. Bone against metal.

'Time to go!' Viv says, tugging me back towards the entrance.

I look around the rest of the room. Beyond the sphere, there are two more submarine doors. They're both shut.

'Harris, c'mon!' Viv begs. 'The moment he gets up, he's gonna howl at the moon! We gotta get out of here, now!'

Knowing she's right, I turn round and leap back out through the submarine door. We run back through the lab, past the lab tables, past the canisters and computer servers. Just behind the servers, I notice a small bookshelf filled with empty clipboards and a black ring binder with a label that reads: THE MIDAS PROJECT. Pulling it off the shelf, I flip to the first page. It's filled with meaningless numbers and dates, but in the top right-hand corner of every page is the word 'Neutrino'. I tuck the book under my arm and follow Viv to the first door of the air lock.

She punches the black button that's just beside the door, and we wait for the hydraulic hiss. As the doors swing open, we step into the air lock and Viv pounds the second black button.

'Put your mine light on,' I tell her.

She flips a switch, and the light blinks on. Behind us, the doors to the lab ease shut and the doors in front of us wheeze open.

'Let's go . . .' I call out, darting into the black tunnel.

THE INSTANT HE HEARD the steel cage start moving, Janos pounced for the nearby phone on the wall.

'Hoist . . .' the female operator answered.

'This cage that's coming up right now—can you make sure its next stop is at the Ramp?' Janos asked, reading his location from the sign.

'Sure, but why do you—?'

'Listen, we got an emergency up here. Just bring the cage as fast as you can. You get that?'

'I got it . . . the Ramp.'

Shoving his hands in the side pockets of his jean jacket, Janos felt for the black box and flicked the switch. All he had to do was wait.

Over his shoulder, the wooden benches started to rattle and the fluorescent lights began to flicker. The elevator was on its way.

With a final wheeze, the metal cage popped up from the abyss. Yanking on the lock, Janos whipped the corroded yellow door open. As it crashed into the wall, his jaw stiffened. 'Sons of bitches . . .'

Inside the cage, drips of water slithered down the greasy metal walls. Other than that, it was empty.

'HURRY . . . RUN . . . !' I yell at Viv as I shove open the door to the cage and sprint through the wide room in front of us. According to the sign on the wall, we're at level 1-3—the same level we came in on. The only difference is, we used a different shaft to get out. Wasn't hard to find—all we had to do was follow the spray-painted LIFT signs. Eight thousand feet later, we're back on top.

'I still don't see why we had to take the other shaft,' Viv says.

'Because Janos has had plenty of time to catch up with us.'

Like the tunnels down below, the room up here has metal rail tracks running along the floor. There are at least half a dozen empty train cars, two mud-soaked Bobcat diggers and a small swarm of three-wheel ATVs. This is clearly the vehicle entrance, but right now all I care about is the exit.

'There!' Viv yells, pointing to her right, just past all the diggers.

I follow her as she runs to a narrow wooden door that looks like a closet. Finally I see what's got her so excited—not just the small door but the sliver of light that's peeking through underneath.

Daylight.

As Viv throws the door open, it's like coming out of a dark movie theatre and stepping into the sun. The whole world lights up with fall colours—orange and red leaves, the baby blue sky—that seem neon when compared with the mud below.

Viv stops to sniff the sweet smell of plum bushes that fills the air, but I grab her by the wrist.

'Don't stop now,' I say. 'Not until we're out of here.'

Two hundred yards away the triangular outline of the main building slices towards the sky. From what I can tell, we're on the opposite side of the parking lot from where we first started.

A loud siren bursts through the air. It's coming from a bullhorn up on the metal teepee building.

'Don't run,' Viv says, slowing.

She's right about that. As a half-dozen men run towards the main mining entrance, we head in the opposite direction, letting the road lead us back to the parking lot. Everything's just as we left it. Tons of cruddy old pick-up trucks, two classic Harleys and—

Wait . . . something's new . . . One shiny Ford Explorer. There's a map with a Hertz logo on the passenger seat.

'HOIST . . .' the female operator answered.

'You were supposed to bring the cage straight here!' Janos shouted into the receiver.

'I did. There was no one in it. Why would I make it stop anywhere?'

'If there was no one in it, why was it even *moving*?' Janos roared.

'He . . . He asked me to bring both cages to the top. He said it was important.'

Janos clamped his eyes shut as the woman said the words. How could he possibly have missed it? 'There are *two* cages?'

'Sure, one for each shaft. You have to have two—for safety. He said he had stuff to move from one to the other . . .'

With a loud slam, Janos rammed the receiver back in its cradle and took off for the stairs. A shrill alarm screamed through the room, echoing up and down the open shaft. Rushing up the stairs two at a time, he burst out of the red-brick building and tore back towards the parking lot.

On the concrete path in front of him, the man in the Spring Break T-shirt was the only thing blocking his way. 'Can I help you with something?' the man asked, motioning with his clipboard.

Janos ignored him.

The man stepped closer, trying to cut him off. 'Did you hear—?'

Janos whipped the clipboard from the man's hands and jammed it hard against his windpipe. As Spring Break doubled over, clutching his throat, Janos raced for the lot—but just as he got there, the Suburban peeled out, kicking a spray of gravel through the air.

Undeterred, Janos went straight to his own Explorer. They had barely a ten-second head start. But when he reached the Explorer, he could see something was wrong. The tyres. They were all flat.

'*Damn!*' Janos screamed, punching the side mirror and shattering it with his fist.

Behind him, there was a loud crunch in the gravel.

'That's him,' someone said.

Spinning round, Janos turned to see four miners who now had him cornered between the two cars.

Grinning darkly, they moved in towards Janos.

He grinned right back.

WITH MY EYES on the rearview mirror, I pull off the highway and follow the signs for Rapid City airport. Next to me, Viv is looking through the Midas Project notebook.

'And . . . ?'

'Nothing,' she says. 'Two hundred pages of nothing but dates and ten-digit numbers. I'm guessing it's just a delivery schedule.'

'What's the earliest date in there?' I ask.

Viv flips to the first page. 'Almost six months ago. April the 4th, seven thirty-six a.m.—item number 1015321410. I guess they did figure that getting the authorisation in the bill was just a formality.'

'Yeah, well . . . thanks to me and Matthew, they almost got it.' Pointing back to the notebook, I add, 'So there's no master list to help decipher the codes?'

'That's why they call 'em codes. 1015321410 . . . 1116225727 . . . 1525161210 . . .'

'Those are the photomultiplier tubes,' I interrupt.

She looks up from the book. 'Wha—?'

'That last one was a barcode on those photomultiplier boxes.'

'And you remember that?'

From my pocket, I pull out the sticker I ripped off earlier and slap it on the dashboard. 'Am I right?' I ask as Viv rechecks the number.

She nods, then looks down, falling silent. Her hand snakes into her slacks, where I spot the rectangular outline of her Senate ID badge. She pulls it out and steals a glance at her mom. I pretend not to see.

Avoiding the main entrance for the airport, I head for the private air terminal and turn into the parking lot. We get out of the car in silence and follow the signs marked *Lobby*.

'Senator Stevens's party?' a short-haired blonde woman asks from behind the reception desk.

'That's us,' I reply. Pointing over my shoulder, I add, 'I didn't know where to return the car . . .'

'There is fine. I'll let the pilot know you're here,' she says, picking up the phone. 'Shouldn't be more than a few minutes.'

I look over at Viv, then down at the notebook in her hands. We need to figure out what's going on—and there's one place that might be able to help. 'Do you have a phone I can use?' I ask the woman at the reception desk. 'Preferably somewhere private?'

'Of course, sir—upstairs and to the right is our conference room. Please help yourself.'

'So whattya think that sphere in the lab is for?' Viv says as we head up the stairs.

'No idea. But it's clearly got something to do with neutrinos.'

She nods. 'And a neutrino is . . .?'

'I think it's some type of subatomic particle.'

'Like a proton or electron?'

'I guess,' I say. 'Beyond that, you're already out of my league.'

The conference room has an octagonal table and a matching credenza that holds a saltwater aquarium. I go to the window, which overlooks the parking lot. All's clear, for now.

'For all we know it could be good, though, right?' says Viv. 'Maybe they're trying to turn stuff into gold. The project *is* called "Midas".'

I shake my head. 'Forget mythology—we should talk to someone who knows their science. Or who can at least tell us why people would bury a neutrino lab in a giant hole below the earth. But first I must make one other call.' I pick up the phone and dial.

As I wait for my call to be answered, I look back out of the window for Janos's car. We're still alone.

'Legislative Resource Center,' a woman answers.

'Hi, I'm looking for Gary.'

There's a short pause, then a man's voice: 'Gary Naftalis.'

'Hey, Gary, this is Harris from Senator Stevens's office. You said to give you a call about the lobbying forms for—'

'Wendell Mining,' he interrupts. 'I remember. Let me take a look.'

He puts me on hold, and my eyes float over to the aquarium. There are a few tiny black fish and one big purple and orange one.

'I'll give you one guess which ones we are,' Viv says.

Before I can reply, I hear Gary's voice through the receiver. 'Today's your birthday,' he says.

'You found it?'

Viv turns my way.

'Right here,' Gary says. 'Must've just got scanned in.'

'What's the name of the lobbyist?'

'I'm checking,' he offers. 'OK . . . according to the records we have here, starting in February of this past year, Wendell Mining has been working with a firm called Pasternak and Associates.'

'Excuse me?'

'And the lobbyist on record—man, his name's everywhere these days. . . ' My stomach turns as the words burn through the telephone. 'Ever hear of a guy named Barry Holcomb?'

'EVERYBODY SMILE,' Congressman Cordell said, as he stretched a grin into place and put his arms round the eighth-graders who flanked him on both sides of his desk. 'On three, say, "President Cordell" . . .'

'*President Cordell* . . .' All thirty-five eighth-graders laughed as the flashbulb popped.

'Thank you so much for doing this—it means more than you know,' Ms Spicer said, shaking the Congressman's hand. Like any other eighth-grade social studies teacher, she knew this was the highlight of her entire school year—a private meeting with a congressman. What better way to make government come alive?

'They got a place where we can get T-shirts?' one of the students called out as they made their way to the door.

'You're leaving so soon?' Cordell asked. Turning to Dinah, who was just making her way into the office, he asked, 'Can we push our meeting back?'

Dinah shook her head, knowing full well that Cordell didn't mean it. 'Sorry, Congressman . . .' she began. 'We have to—'

'You've already been incredible,' Ms Spicer interrupted. 'Thank you again. For everything,' she added, her eyes locked on Cordell.

'If you need tickets to the House Gallery, just ask my assistant,' Cordell added, grinning, as the group filed out. Even when the door slammed shut, the smile lingered. It was pure instinct.

'So how do we look?' Cordell asked Dinah, collapsing into his seat. 'Just tell me what they're gonna bust our nuts on.'

'Actually, not much,' Dinah began, handing him the final memo on the Interior Appropriations bill. Now that the pre-Conference hagglings with Trish were over, the Final Four—a senator and a House Member from each party—would spend the next two days hammering out the last loose ends so the bill could go to the Floor.

'The only speed bump will be the White House structural improvements,' Dinah explained. 'Apelbaum zeroed them out, which truthfully doesn't matter—but if the White House gets miffed . . .'

'. . . they'll shine the spotlight on all our other projects as well. I'll take care of it.' Looking down at the memo, Cordell asked, 'Any other problems?'

'Nothing big. By the way, we also got that South Dakota land transfer—the old gold mine. I think it was the last thing Matthew grabbed from the goody bag.'

Cordell gave a silent nod, an indication to Dinah that he had no idea what she was talking about. But by pairing the mine with Matthew's name, she knew that Cordell would never give it away during Conference.

'Meanwhile,' Cordell began, 'about Matthew . . . His parents asked me to speak at his funeral.'

'I'll write up a eulogy, sir.'

'That'd be great. I thought you'd want to take the first draft.' Turning back to the memo, he added, 'So, we got what we wanted?'

Dinah smiled. All teeth. 'We got everything and more, sir.'

Cutting back through the welcome area of her boss's personal office, Dinah said a quick hello to the young receptionist then bounded out into the marble hallway.

'So we done?' Barry asked her, stepping out from behind a tall Arizona state flag.

'All done.'

Neither of them said another word until they turned the corner and stepped into an empty elevator.

'Thanks again for helping me out with this,' Barry began.

'If it's important to you . . .'

'It was actually important to Matthew. That's why I'm involved.'

'Either way—if it's important to you, it's important to me,' Dinah insisted as the elevator doors slid shut.

With a single sweep of his cane, Barry looked around, listening. 'We're alone, aren't we?'

'That we are,' she said, stepping closer.

'Then let me say a proper thankyou,' he said and, sliding his hand through her short blonde hair, leaned forward and gave her a long, deep kiss.

'FINAL BOARDING CALL for Northwest Airlines flight 1168 to Minneapolis–St Paul,' a female voice announced through the Rapid City airport terminal. 'All passengers should now be on board.'

As Janos handed the gate attendant his boarding pass, his cellphone vibrated in his jacket pocket. As he pulled the phone out, the gate attendant smiled and said, 'Hope it's a quick call—we're about to push back . . .'

Shooting her a dark glare, he headed up the boarding bridge. He didn't need to check caller ID to know who it was.

'Do you have any conception how much money your sloppiness just cost me?' Sauls asked calmly through the phone. 'He threw our technician into the sphere. Sixty-four photomultiplier tubes completely shattered. You know how much each of those costs? You blew it, Janos.'

'I'll take care of it.'

Sauls went silent. 'That's the third time you've said that,' he finally growled. 'But let me promise you right now—if you don't take care of it soon, we'll be hiring someone to take care of you.'

With a soft click, the phone went dead.

TEN

'**D**addy's going to work now,' Lowell Nash called out to his four-year-old daughter early the following morning.

Never taking her eyes off the videotaped glow of *Sesame Street*, Cassie Nash sucked the tip of one of her pigtails and waved her hand. 'Bye, Daddy . . .'

Lowell smiled and waved goodbye to his wife, who was sitting right next to Cassie in the living room of their Maryland home.

At a few minutes past seven, Deputy Attorney General Nash locked the door behind himself, then twisted the doorknob and checked it three times. By the time he reached the driveway his smile was gone. As he'd done every day for the past week, he checked every tree and shrub in sight. He checked the cars that were parked on the street. Most importantly, as he unlocked the doors on his silver Audi, he checked his own front seat. The lightning-shaped fracture was still fresh in the side window, but Janos was gone. For now.

Since the day he graduated from Columbia Law School, Lowell had always been careful with his professional life. He told his accountant not to be greedy on his taxes, and reported every gift he ever got from a lobbyist. No drugs . . . no outrageous drinking . . . nothing stupid at any of the social events he'd attended over the years.

Too bad the same couldn't be said of his wife. It was just one dumb night—even for the college kid she was back then. A few too many drinks . . . A cab would take too long . . . If she got behind the wheel, she'd be home in minutes instead of an hour. By the time she was done, a boy was paralysed, his pelvis shattered. Through some expensive legal manoeuvres, the lawyers expunged her record. But somehow Janos found it. THE NEXT COLIN POWELL? the *Legal Times* headline had asked, referring to Lowell. Not if this gets out, Janos warned the first night he showed up.

Lowell didn't care. He didn't get to be number two at Justice by running and hiding at every threat. Sooner or later, the news about his wife would come out. There's no way he'd hurt Harris for that.

That's when Janos started showing up at Lowell's daughter's preschool. And at the playground where they took her at weekends. For Lowell, that was it. Family was a different story.

Janos didn't ask for much: to keep him informed when Harris called—and stay the hell out of it. Lowell had thought it would be easy. It was harder than he ever imagined. Every night, the tossing and turning increased. Last night he was up so late, he heard the paper hit his doorstep at 5 a.m.

No doubt about it, Lowell had been careful. Careful with his money, with his career and with his future. But now, as a droplet of rain splattered against his windshield, he realised there was a fine line between *careful* and *cowardly*. He couldn't just sit there any longer. Picking up his cellphone, he dialled the number for his office.

'Deputy Attorney General's office. This is William Joseph Williams,' his assistant answered.

'William, it's me. I need a favour. In my top left-hand drawer, there's a set of fingerprints I got off my car door last week.'

'The kids that cracked your window, right? I thought you already ran those.'

'I decided not to,' Lowell said. 'But I've changed my mind. Put 'em in the system; do a full scan—every data base we've got. And tell Pilchick I'm gonna need some detail to watch my family.'

'HARRIS, SLOW DOWN,' Viv begs, chasing behind me as I cross First Street and wipe the rain from my face.

'Harris, I'm talking to you!'

I'm barely listening as I whip open the glass doors and charge into the lobby of Pasternak & Associates. It's just a hair past seven. Morning security shift hasn't started yet so Barb's not in.

'Can I help you?' a guard with some acne scars asks.

'I work here,' I insist forcefully enough that he doesn't ask twice. He looks at Viv.

'Nice to see you again,' she adds, not slowing down. She's never seen him before in her life. He waves back. I'm impressed. She's getting better every day.

By the time we reach the elevator, she's ready to tear my head off. The good news is, she's smart enough to wait until the doors close.

I pre-empt her. 'Viv, I don't want to hear it.' Early this morning, I picked up a new suit from the locker at my gym. Last night, after throwing our shirts in the plane's washer-dryer and using the onboard shower, we spent the entire flight back using the plane's satellite phones to track people down at the National Science Foundation. Thanks to a promise that we'd be bringing along Congressman Cordell himself, we were able wrangle a meeting. But the NSF can wait. Right now, this is more important.

The doors open on the second floor, and I head for the frosted glass doorway with the numeric keypad. I quickly punch the four-digit code, shove open the door, and weave my way through the maze of cubicles and offices. It's still too early for support staff to be in, so the whole place is silent.

'You sure you even know where you're—?'

Two steps past a black and white photo of the White House, I make a sharp right into an open office. On the black lacquered desk, there's a keyboard with a braille display. If there were any doubt, the Duke diploma on the wall tells me I've got it right: Barrett W. Holcomb. Where the hell are you, Barry?

He wasn't home when we went by his apartment last night—but I figured if we came here early enough . . .

There's a tapping sound behind us. We both turn.

'Harris?' Barry asks as he steps through the door. 'Is that you?'

'You scheming piece of shit!' I yell, lunging forward.

Barry hears me coming and instinctively tries to sidestep. He's too late. I'm already on him.

'They were our friends! You've known Matthew since college!' I shout, forcing him backwards.

'What are you talking about?'

'Was it because some business deal with Pasternak went wrong? Or did he just pass you up for partner, and this was your revenge?' I shove his shoulder, and he stumbles off balance. 'How much did they pay you?' I yell, staying right behind him.

'Harris, please . . .' he begs. 'I'd never do anything to hurt them.'

'Then why was your name in the damn lobbying disclosure form for Wendell Mining?' I explode with one final shove.

Staggering sideways, Barry slams into the wall. Slowly, he picks his chin up to face me. 'You think that was me?'

'Your name's on it, Barry!'

'My name's on all of them—every single client in the entire office. It's part of being the last guppy in the food chain. Those forms—filling them out—it's grunt work, Harris. Support staff fill them out. But ever since we got fined ten grand because a partner didn't fill his out a few years back, they decided to put someone in charge. Lucky me.'

'You're telling me Wendell Mining isn't your client?'

'Not a chance.'

'But all those times I called—you were always there with Dinah . . .'

'Why shouldn't I be? She's my girlfriend.'

'You're dating Dinah?'

'Just starting—it's been less than two weeks.'

'Why didn't you tell us?'

'You kidding? A lobbyist dating the head clerk in Appropriations? She's supposed to judge every project on its merits. If this got out, Harris, they'd string us up just for the fun of it.'

'I . . . I can't believe you're dating her.'

'What? Now I can't be happy?'

Even now, that's all he sees. Perceived slights. 'So the help you've been giving to Wendell . . .'

'Dinah said it was one of the last things Matthew was pushing for. I just . . . I just thought it'd be nice if he got his last wish.'

I stare at Barry, searching his eyes. One is made of glass, the other's all cloudy but locked on me.

'Then whose client are they?' Viv speaks for the first time.

'Wendell Mining?' Barry asks. 'They've only been with us a year, but as far as I know, they only worked with one person: Pasternak.'

The words hit like a cannonball in my gut. If Pasternak was in on it from the start . . . 'He knew all along,' I whisper.

'Knew what?' Barry asks.

'Hold on,' Viv says. 'You think he set you up?'

'M-maybe . . . I don't know . . .'

'Harris, what's going on?' Barry asks.

Still reeling, I look through Barry's door into the rest of the office. It's still empty—but it won't be for long.

'Barry, where does the firm keep its billing records?' I ask. 'Or time sheets—anything that shows Pasternak was working with Wendell.'

'Why would you—?'

'Listen to me, Barry. I don't think Matthew was hit by that car accidentally. Now please . . . where are the billing records?'

Barry's frozen. He turns his head slightly, listening to the fear in my voice. 'They're online,' he mumbles.

'Can you get them for us?'

'Harris, we should call the—'

'Just get them, Barry. Please.'

He pats the air, feeling for his desk chair. As he slides into place, his hands leap for his keyboard.

'JAWS for Windows is ready,' a computerised female voice says, indicating that the screen-reading function is in place. 'Log-in user name? Edit,' the computer asks.

Barry types in his password and logs in. A few quick keystrokes take him directly where he's going.

'Billing Records,' the voice says. 'Use F4 to maximise all windows.'

I stand behind Barry, watching over his shoulder, though the monitor's switched off. Viv's by the door, staring up the hallway.

When Barry types in Wendell Mining, his fingers are moving so fast that the voice comes out 'Wen— Mining'.

The computer beeps, like something's wrong.

'Client not found,' the computer says. 'New search? Edit.'

'This doesn't make sense.' Barry's hands are a blur of movement.

The female voice can't keep up. 'Ne— Sys— Wen— Min— Searching data base . . .'

He's widening the search. I stare intensely at the blank computer screen. It's better than watching Viv panic by the door.

'Harris, you still there?' Barry asks.

'Right here,' I reply as the computer whirs.

'Client not found in system,' the voice replies. 'End of record.'

'I don't understand,' Barry says. His hands move faster than ever.

'Full— Sys— Searching . . .'

'Barry, what the hell is going on?'

'Search error,' the mechanised voice interrupts. 'Client name not in system.'

Barry stares down at his keyboard. 'They're gone,' he says. 'Someone must have deleted the file. I checked through the entire data base. It's like they were never clients.'

'What about hard copies?' I ask. 'Is there anything else that might show that Pasternak worked with Wendell?'

'I . . . I guess there's Pasternak's client files . . .'

A loud chirp screeches through the air. All three of us wince at the sharpness of the sound. It's the fire alarm.

Viv and I exchange glances. The alarm continues to scream. If our FBI guy is here, it's a perfect way to empty the building.

'Are Pasternak's files still in his office?' I ask Barry.

'Yeah . . . why?'

That's all I need. 'Let's go,' I call to Viv.

We rush out, make our way back to the bank of elevators and see that this isn't just a drill. There's a chorus of three elevator alarms competing with the main fire alarm, and when a middle-aged man shoves open the metal emergency door to the stairs, a wisp of dark grey smoke swims into the hall. Something's definitely burning.

Viv looks at me over her shoulder. 'You don't think—'

'C'mon,' I insist, pushing past her to the stairs. I'm not leaving without Pasternak's records.

'Harris, I'm not doing this any more . . .'

Leaping up the stairs two at a time, I quickly reach the top. I head down the hallway towards Pasternak's office and a thick dark cloud of smoke. As I make a sharp right round the last corner, a wave of heat punches me hard in the face—but not nearly as hard as the hand that reaches out and clutches my arm.

'Sir, this area's closed. I need you to make your way to the stairs,' he says over the screaming alarm.

On his chest is a gold and blue SECURITY badge. He's just a guard.

'Sir, did you hear what I said?'

I nod, barely paying attention. I'm too busy staring over his shoulder at the source of the fire. As I watch, there's a loud crash, and the oak door to Pasternak's office collapses off its hinges, revealing the three tall filing cabinets that run along the wall just behind it. From the looks of it, all of them are fireproof. The problem is, all of them have their drawers pulled wide open. The papers inside crackle and burn. Every few seconds, a few singed black scraps somersault through the air. I can barely breathe through all the smoke. The world blurs through the flames. All that's left are the ashes.

'Now please, sir, head down the stairs.'

I still don't move, but I feel a soft hand on the small of my back. 'C'mon Harris,' Viv tells me.

My body's in shock, and as I turn to look at her she reads my face in an instant. Pasternak was my mentor; I've known him since my first days on the Hill. 'Maybe it's not what you think,' she says, tugging me back towards the stairs.

The tears run down my face, and I tell myself it's from the smoke. Sirens howl in the distance. I try to run, but I can't. My legs feel like they're filled with Jell-O. I slow to a lumbering walk.

'What? Now you're just giving up?' Viv asks.

I can barely look her in the eye. 'I'm sorry, Viv . . .'

'That's not good enough! You think that takes the guilt off your plate? You got me into this, Harris—you and your dumb I-own-the-world-so-let's-play-with-it egoism! I'm sorry your mentor tricked you, and that your Capitol Hill existence is all you have, but I've got an entire life in front of me, and I want it back! So get your rear end moving, and let's get out of here. We've got an appointment with a scientist that you're making me late for!'

Stunned by the outburst, I can barely move. 'Viv, you know I'd never—'

'I don't want to hear it.'

'But I—'

'You did it, Harris. It's done. Now, you gonna make it right or not?'

Outside the building, someone barks instructions through a bullhorn. The police are here. If I want to give up, this is the place to do it.

Viv heads up the hallway.

'Hold on,' I call out, chasing after her. 'That's not the best way.'

Stopping midstep, she doesn't smile or make it easy. And she shouldn't. It has taken a seventeen-year-old girl to make me act like an adult.

'HOW'S IT LOOK?' Lowell asked as his assistant stepped into his office in the main Justice building on Pennsylvania Avenue.

'Let me put it like this,' William began. 'On a scale of one to ten, it's Watergate.'

Lowell forced a laugh. He was trying to keep it light, but the red folder already told him this was only getting worse. Red meant FBI.

'The fingerprints belong to Robert Franklin of Hoboken, New Jersey,' William began, reading from the folder.

Lowell made a face, wondering if the name Janos was fake. 'So he's got a record?' he asked.

'Nosiree.'

'Then how'd they have his fingerprints?'

'They got 'em internally. From their staffing unit. Apparently, this guy applied for a job with the FBI a few years back.'

'So why didn't they hire him?'

'They're not saying. It's too high up for me. But when I begged for a hint, my buddy over there said they thought the application was sour.'

'They thought he was trying to infiltrate . . . We should run him outside the system, see if he—'

'Whattya think I've been doing for the last hour?'

Lowell gripped the armrests of his leather chair. 'Just tell me what you found,' he insisted.

'I ran it through a few of our foreign connections, and according to their systems the prints belong to someone named Martin Janos, a.k.a. Janos Szasz, a.k.a.—'

'Robert Franklin,' Lowell said.

'One and the same.'

'So why'd they have his prints over there?'

'That's the cherry on top. Apparently the guy used to work at Britain's Secret Intelligence Service, MI5.'

Lowell closed his eyes, trying to remember Janos's voice. If he was British, the accent was long gone. Or well hidden.

'After two years in Her Majesty's Service, Janos is fired for insubordination. Then he's gone for almost five years, reappears one day over here, applies to the FBI under a new ID, gets rejected for trying to infiltrate, then steps back into the abyss, never to be heard from again—that is, until a few days ago, when he apparently uses all his hard-trained skills to . . . uh . . . smash the window on your car.' William stared hard at his boss. 'Sir, if there's anything you need me to—'

'I appreciate it, William. I truly do. But before I get you knee-deep in this, let's just see what else we can find.'

'Absolutely, sir,' William said with a grin. 'That's what I'm doing right now. I ran all of Janos's identities through the guys at the Financial Crimes Enforcement Network. They came up with an offshore account that bounces back through Antigua.'

'I thought we couldn't get to those . . .'

'Yeah, well, since nine-eleven, some countries have been a little more cooperative. According to the guys at FinCEN, the account has four-million-dollars'-worth of transfers from something called the Wendell Group. So far, all we know is that it's a shelf company with a fake board of directors.'

'Think you can trace ownership?'

'That's the goal,' William said. 'And I've seen these guys work before. If I gave them your last name, they'd find the twelve-dollar savings account your mom opened for you when you were six.'

'I appreciate what you're doing William,' Lowell said. 'I owe you for this.'

VIV STEPS OUT of the cab in downtown Arlington, Virginia, and cranes her neck to study the twelve-storey office building towering over us.

Approaching the front entrance, I pull open one of the heavy glass doors and check the street one last time.

'Morning. How can I help you today?' the receptionist asks.

'We're here to see Dr Minsky,' I say. 'Congressman Cordell . . .' I add, using the name of Matthew's boss.

'IDs, please?'

Viv shoots me a look. We're trying to avoid using our real names.

'No worries, Teri, they're with me,' a female voice interrupts.

Back by the elevators, a tall woman in a designer suit waves at us like we're old friends.

'Marilyn Freitas—from the director's office,' she announces, pumping my hand and smiling. The ID badge round her neck tells me she's Director of Legislative and Public Affairs. They're already pulling out the big guns—and I know why. The National Science Foundation gets over $5 billion annually from the Appropriations Committee. If I'm bringing one of their appropriators here, they're going to roll out the brightest red carpet they can find.

'So is the Congressman here?' she asks, smile still in place.

'He should be joining us shortly—though he said we should start without him,' I explain. 'Just in case.'

Her smile sinks a bit, but not by much. 'Whenever he gets here is good by us,' she says as she leads us back to the elevators.

We ascend to the ninth floor and Marilyn walks us to a sitting area that has all the charm of a hospital waiting room.

'Dr Minsky?' she calls out, knocking lightly and turning the knob of the door marked 1005.09. Only the National Science Foundation assigns rooms a decimal designation.

As the door opens, a distinguished older man with puffy cheeks and a beard is already out of his seat, shaking my hand and looking over my shoulder. He's searching for Cordell.

'The Congressman should be here shortly,' Marilyn explains.

'Andy Defresne,' I say, introducing myself. 'And this is—'

'Catherine,' Viv says, refusing my aid.

'One of our interns,' I jump in.

'Dr Arnold Minsky,' he says, shaking Viv's hand. 'My cat's name was Catherine.'

I hate meeting with academics. Social skills are always slightly off. But Viv nods as pleasantly as possible, checking out his office in an attempt to avoid further conversation.

Minsky goes to his desk and, as I take the seat directly across from him, Viv slides into the chair that's next to the window. It's got a perfect view of the street out front. If we can find the leading expert on neutrinos, so can Janos.

'So what can I help you with?' Minsky asks.

'We were wondering if we could ask you a few questions about neutrinos . . .' I begin.

'YOU SAW THEM?' Janos asked, holding his cellphone in one hand and gripping the steering wheel of the black sedan with the other. The morning traffic wasn't bad, even for Washington, but at this point any delay was enough to get him raging. 'How'd they look?'

'Harris could barely get a sentence out, and the girl was ready to take his head off.'

'So you took care of everything in the office?'

'Everything you asked.'

'And they believed it? What you told them?'

'Even the Dinah stuff. Unlike Pasternak, I see things through to the end.'

'You're a real hero,' Janos said wryly.

'Yeah, well . . . don't forget to tell your boss that. Between the loans, the surgery and all my other debts . . .'

'I'm well aware of your financial situation. That's why—'

'It's more than the money. They asked for this. The snubs . . . the shrug-offs . . . People think it goes unnoticed.'

'Did they say where they were going next?' Janos asked.

'No, but I have an idea . . .'

'So do I,' Janos said, making a sharp right and pulling into an underground parking garage. 'Just focus on Harris. If he calls back, we need you to keep your eyes and ears wide open.'

'Ears I can help you with,' Barry said. 'It's the eyes that have always been a bit of a problem.'

'NEUTRINOS, EH?' Dr Minsky says, unbending a paperclip and tapping it lightly on the edge of his desk. He's clearly excited. If there's some new data out there, he wants to play with the toys first.

'It's actually a friend of the Congressman's who's looking at the project,' I say. 'It's not for public consumption.'

He gets the hint. Congressmen do favours for friends every day. Minsky knows that if he wants favours from us in future, he has to help us with this.

'Let me do it like this,' he says, shifting into professor mode. 'In the subatomic world, there are three kinds of particles that have mass. The heaviest are quarks, which make up protons and neutrons. Then, there are electrons and their relatives, which are lighter. And finally come neutrinos, which are so incredibly lightweight there are still some doubters out there who argue they don't have mass at all.'

I nod, but he knows I'm lost.

'Here's the significance,' he adds. 'You can calculate the mass of everything you see in a telescope, but when you add it up it's still only ten per cent of what makes up the universe. That leaves ninety per cent unaccounted for. So where, as physicists have asked for decades, is the missing ninety per cent?'

'Neutrinos?' Viv whispers, accustomed to being a student.

'Neutrinos,' Minsky says, pointing the paperclip her way. 'Of course, it probably isn't the full ninety per cent, but a portion of it.'

'So if someone's studying neutrinos, they're trying to . . .'

'. . . crack open the ultimate treasure chest,' Minsky says. 'Neutrinos were produced at the Big Bang, at supernovas, and even, during fusion, at the heart of the sun. Unlock neutrinos and you potentially unlock the nature of matter and the evolution of the universe.'

It's a nice answer, but it doesn't get me any closer to my real question. Time to be blunt. 'Could they be used to build a weapon?'

Minsky cocks his head slightly, analysing me with his scientist's eyes. 'Why would someone use it as a weapon?' he asks.

'I'm not saying they are, we just want to know if they can.

Minsky drops his paperclip and puts his hands flat against his desk. 'Exactly what type of project is this for again, Mr Defresne?'

'Maybe I should leave that for the Congressman,' I say, trying to defuse the tension. All it does is shorten the fuse.

'Maybe it'd be best if you showed me the actual proposal.'

'I'd love to—but right now it's confidential.'

The fuse is on its last hairs. Minsky doesn't move.

'Listen, can I be honest with you?' I ask.

'What a novel idea.'

I purposely twist in my chair and pretend he's got control. He may have twenty years on me, but I've played this game with the world's best manipulators. Minsky's just someone who got an A in science.

'OK,' I begin. 'Four days ago, our office got a preliminary proposal for a state-of-the-art neutrino research facility. It was delivered to the Congressman at his home address.' Minsky picks up his paperclip, thinking he's getting the inside track.

'Who did the proposal? Government or military?' he asks.

'What makes you say that?'

'No one else can afford it. You have any idea how much these things cost? Private companies can't pull that kind of weight.'

Viv and I exchange a glance, once again rethinking Wendell, or whoever they really are.

'What can you tell me about the project?' Minsky asks.

'Apparently, it's purely for research purposes, but when someone builds a brand-new lab a mile and a half below the earth, it tends to get people's attention. Because of the parties involved, we want to make sure that this won't be coming back to haunt us ten years from now. That's why we need to know the worst-case scenario.'

'So I'll bet they're going with an old mine, huh?' Minsky mutters.

'How'd you know?' I reply.

'If you don't use a mine, you're adding years to the project, plus billions of dollars.'

'Why do you have to be down there in the first place?' Viv asks.

'It's the only way to shield the experiments from cosmic rays.'

'Cosmic rays?' I ask sceptically.

'Yes, I realise it must sound a little sci-fi,' Minsky says, 'but up here, even the dial in your wristwatch is giving off radium—there's interference everywhere. Down below the earth's surface, all the radioactive noise is shut out.'

'Location, location, location,' Viv mutters, glancing my way. For the first time in three days, things are finally starting to make sense. We thought they wanted the mine to hide the project, but they need the mine to get the project going. That's why they needed Matthew to slip the mine in the bill. Without it they have nothing.

'Of course, what really matters is what they're doing down there,' Minsky points out. 'Do you have a schematic?'

'I do . . . it's just . . . it's with the Congressman,' I say. 'But I remember most of it: there was this huge metal sphere filled with these things called photomultiplier tubes—'

'A neutrino detector,' Minsky says. 'You fill it with heavy water so you can stop, and therefore detect, the neutrinos. You can't see neutrinos under a microscope; the only way to see them is to watch their interactions with other particles. When a neutrino hits an atom, it generates a certain type of radiation, like an optical sonic boom. All we can see is the boom, which tells us that the neutrino was there.'

'So you measure the reaction when the two collide,' Viv says.

'Exactly. And as neutrinos interact with other particles, they actually change identity. It's a Jekyll–Hyde type affair. That's what makes them so hard to detect.'

'So the tubes are for observation purposes?'

'Think of it as a big enclosed microscope. It's an expensive endeavour. Only a few exist in the world.'

'What about the magnet?'

'What magnet?'

'There's a huge magnet in a long, narrow room.'

'They have an accelerator down there?' Minsky asks, confused.

'No idea. The only other thing is a big crate of TUNGSTEN.'

'A tungsten block. That definitely sounds like an accelerator. But if you have a detector, you don't usually have an accelerator. The noise from one . . . it'd interfere with the other.'

'So what happens if you put a detector and an accelerator together?'

'I don't know,' Minsky says. 'I've never heard of anyone doing it. There are certainly some potential defence applications. If you want to know if a particular country has nuclear weapons, you can fly a drone over the country, get an air sample, and then use the "quiet" of the mine to measure the radioactivity in the air sample.'

If it were that simple, Wendell would've just requested the mine from the Defence subcommittee. Trying to sneak it through Matthew and the Interior subcommittee was playing dirty—which means they've got their hands on something they don't want made public.

'What about weaponry . . . or making money?' I ask.

Lost in thought, Minsky twirls the tip of his paperclip through his beard. Then to our surprise, he grins. 'Ever hear of transmutation?'

'Alchemy?' I ask. 'Like King Midas?'

'Alchemy,' Minsky replies, 'is a medieval philosophy. Transmutation is a science—transforming one element into another through a subatomic reaction.'

'I don't understand. How do neutrinos . . .?'

'Think back. Jekyll and Hyde. Neutrinos start as one flavour, then become another. Here . . .' He opens a drawer in his desk and pulls out a laminated sheet of paper. The periodic table. 'I assume you've seen this before,' he says, pointing to the numbered elements. 'One—hydrogen; two—helium; three—lithium . . .'

'I know how it works,' I insist.

'Oh, you do?' He smiles. 'Find chlorine.'

Viv and I lean forwards in our seats, searching the chart. Viv's closer to tenth-grade science. She jabs her finger at the letters Cl.

'That's right. Atomic number seventeen,' Minsky says. 'Well, years back, in one of the original neutrino detectors, they filled a hundred-thousand-gallon tank with it. The smell was horrific.'

'Like a dry cleaner's,' Viv says.

'Exactly,' Minsky says, pleasantly surprised. 'Now, remember, you only see neutrinos when they collide with other atoms—that's the magic moment. But when the neutrinos ploughed into a chlorine atom just right, the physicists suddenly started finding . . .' Minsky presses his paperclip against the next box in the periodic table. Atomic number eighteen. Argon.

'Wait, so you're saying when the neutrino collided with the chlorine atoms, they all changed to argon?' I ask.

'All? We should be so lucky . . . No, no, no—this was one little argon atom. One. Every four days. It was an amazing moment—and completely random, God bless chaos. And if the atoms were isolated in an accelerator, and the accelerator shielded deep enough below the ground . . . well, think about what would happen if you could control it. You pick the element you want to work with; you bump it one box to the right on the periodic table. If you could do that . . .'

My stomach twists. 'You could turn lead to gold.'

Minsky shakes his head—and then starts laughing. 'Gold? Why would you ever make gold?'

'I thought Midas . . .'

'Midas is a children's story. Think of reality. Gold costs what? Three hundred . . . four hundred dollars an ounce? No if you truly had the power to transmute, you'd be a fool to make gold. In today's world, there are far more valuable elements. For instance,' Minsky again stabs the periodic table with his paperclip, 'neptunium.'

'Neptunium? What's that?' I ask.

'Ah, but you're missing the point,' Minsky says. 'The concern isn't

What's that? The concern is *What could that be?'* With one final jab, he moves his paperclip to the nearest element. Pu.

'Pu?'

'Plutonium,' Minsky says, his laugh long gone. 'In today's world, arguably the most valuable element on the chart.'

'Hold on,' I say. 'You're telling me that people could smash some neutrinos against some neptunium and create a batch of plutonium?'

'I wouldn't be surprised if someone was working along those lines, at least on paper.' He's speaking with the calmness of someone who thinks it's still theoretical. Viv and I know better. We saw with our own eyes the sphere . . . the accelerator.

'And is neptunium hard to find?' I ask.

'Now that's the vital question,' Minsky says, knighting me with his paperclip. 'For the most part, it's a rare earth metal, but neptunium-237 is a by-product from nuclear reactors. Global monitoring of neptunium only began in 1999. That leaves decades of neptunium unaccounted for. Who knows what happened to it?'

'So it's out there?'

'Absolutely,' Minsky says. 'If you know where to look.'

As the consequences hit, I squirm in my seat. Whatever branch of the government Wendell Mining is, the news isn't going to be good.

'Can I just ask one question?' Viv says. 'There can only be a handful of people who are capable of putting something like this together . . . Wouldn't you know if something like this were going on in the neutrino community?'

Minsky scratches his beard. 'It's a big world out there. I can't possibly account for everyone in my field.'

'We should get going,' I say, hopping to my feet.

'I thought the Congressman was on his way?' Minsky asks as we head for the door.

'We've got what we wanted. I'll be sure to tell him how helpful you were,' I reply, whipping the door open and motioning Viv outside.

'Please send him my best,' Minsky calls out.

As we run for the elevators, Viv asks, 'So where are we going?'

The one place Janos thinks we'll never go. 'The Capitol.'

'YOU NEED TO READ THIS.' Lowell's assistant shoved a red folder onto his boss's desk.

Lowell reached for it, flipped it open and scanned the cover sheet. His eyes went wide, and within thirty seconds he was racing down the circular stairwell to the basement garage, with William a few yards behind.

'Where are we going? Shouldn't we tell someone?'

'Tell them what? That we know who really owns Wendell? That they're not who they say they are? Sure, they're linked to Janos, but until we get the rest, there's nothing to tell.'

'So where does that leave us?'

'Not *us*,' Lowell said. '*Me*.' He leapt down the last few steps and shoved open the door to the parking garage. He didn't have to go far. Deputy Attorney General gets a spot right in front.

Lowell unlocked the silver Audi and slid inside.

'What are you doing?' William asked.

'I'm going to see a friend,' Lowell said, starting the engine.

It wasn't a lie. He'd known Harris for ten years. That was why Janos came to him in the first place.

He'd already tried Harris at work, at home and on his cellphone. If he was in hiding, there was only one place he'd be—the one place he knew best. And right now, finding Harris was the only way to get the rest of the story.

'Why don't you at least bring some back-up?' William asked.

'I know how Harris thinks. We want him to talk, not panic.'

'But, sir . . .'

'Goodbye, William.' With a hard tug, Lowell slammed the door. As he pulled out of the garage and into the daylight, he missed the black sedan that was trailing a few hundred feet behind.

ELEVEN

'Next group, please! Next group!' the policeman calls out, waving us towards the visitor's entrance on the west front of the Capitol. Lost amid the tour groups, Viv and I keep our heads down. We're in the one place where no one checks our ID or looks at us for more than a second. On average, the west front handles 4 million visitors a year. We blend in.

'Put all cameras and phones on the X-ray,' one of the guards says to the group. As the high-school students in our group make their usual fuss, Viv and I slip through the metal detector.

We stay with the group as it makes its way under the grand domed ceiling of the Rotunda and directly below to the Crypt, the circular room that now serves as an exhibition area for historical documents. The guide explains that the rounded shape of the Crypt supports not only the Rotunda but also the Capitol dome directly above it. On cue, the group members all crane their necks up to the ceiling—and Viv and I slip out to the right, through the doorway next to the Samuel Adams statue. A freestanding sign reads NO TOURS BEYOND THIS POINT, but I've been here before—it's open to staff. The hallway dead-ends at a black wrought-iron gate. Behind it, under a rectangular glass case, a long black cloth is draped over what looks like a coffin. The plaque on our right tells us it's the wooden catafalque that supported the bodies of Lincoln, Kennedy, LBJ, and everyone else who has ever lain in state in the Capitol.

Over my shoulder, the click-clack of boots on the floor lets me know that the Capitol cops are just about to pass. Trying to look like staffers but feeling like prisoners, Viv and I stare into the tiny concrete cell, which was originally designed to be a tomb for George and Martha Washington.

'Isn't it amazing?' I ask Viv, shoving some pep into my voice.

'Incredible,' she says, following my lead.

Back in the hallway, the footsteps are right behind us. They stop. There's a crackle through a radio.

'Yeah, we'll be right there,' one of the cops says.

The footsteps pick up—then, just like that, they're gone.

Viv and I follow a hallway to the right, which leads us even deeper into the sand-coloured corridors of the basement. Unlike the rest of the Capitol, the halls down here are narrow and cramped. A labyrinth of turns has taken us past garbage rooms, paint storage, HVAC equipment and every type of repair shop.

'You swear this looks familiar?' Viv asks as the ceiling gets lower.

'Absolutely,' I tell her. I don't blame her for being nervous. We haven't seen a sign or another human being for at least three minutes.

'I really don't think this is right,' she insists.

'You're not supposed to.'

She thinks I'm being glib. I'm not.

We pass half a dozen closed doors, most of which have nameplates that tell you what's inside. I go for a nondescript, unlabelled door on my left—room ST-56. I reach into my pocket, pull out a set of keys and stab one into the lock. As the door opens, I jab the light switch.

Viv looks at the long, spacious room, then asks, 'Hideaway?'

I nod and grin.

There's a chocolate-brown leather couch, flanked by matching mahogany dressers. Above the couch, a collection of antique toy sailboats is mounted on the wall. Adding to the men's-club feel, there's also a twelve-foot fish—I'm guessing a marlin—up on the left-hand wall, and a bag of golf clubs just inside the door.

Hideaways are the best-kept secret in the Capitol: private sanctuaries where senators get away from staff, lobbyists and the dreaded tour groups who want just-one-quick-photo-please-we-came-all-this-way. How private are they? Even the architect who manages the entire Capitol building doesn't have a full list of who's in each one. Most aren't even on the floor plan.

'So how do you know Stevens won't come down here any minute?'

'He doesn't use this one any more—not since he got the one with the fireplace.'

'Wait. He has more than one hideaway?' Viv asks, disgusted.

'C'mon, you really think they keep this stuff fair? LBJ had seven.' My eyes stop on the hand-carved coffee table. A set of keys with a familiar key ring sits on top.

There's a loud flush of a toilet. Before either of us can run, the bathroom door swings open.

'Don't look so surprised,' Lowell says, stepping into the room. 'Now, do you want to know what you've got yourselves into or not?'

'How DID YOU get in here?' I ask.

'Same as you. When I was Chief of Staff, they gave me a key.'

'You're supposed to give it back when you leave.'

'Only if they ask for it,' Lowell says, pretending to be playful.

It doesn't work. He may've been a great friend, but that disappeared the moment he sent me running out of that restaurant.

'I know what you're thinking, Harris, but you don't understand the position I was in. Janos threatened my family . . . came to my daughter's playground . . . smashed my head when I tipped you off that night,' he says, showing me the Band-Aid.

Now he's going for sympathy. 'The only reason Janos was there, Lowell, was because you *set it up!*'

'Harris, please. I swear to you—I'm not working with him.'

'And I'm supposed to believe you now? Do you even realise how stupid it was to come here? You think Janos didn't follow you?'

'If he did, he'd be standing here right now. Can't you just listen for a second?' Lowell begs.

I point him towards the door. 'Get out, Lowell.'

'Harris, I know who they are,' he blurts. 'I know about the Wendell Group. I had them put through the system. At first glance, they seem as solid as Sears—registered in Delaware, a furniture-importing business—but when you dig deeper, you see they're a subsidiary of a corporation in Idaho, which is part of a holding company that's registered in Antigua . . . Layer upon layer. The whole thing's a front.'

'For the government, right?'

'How did you know?'

'You could see it in the lab. Only a government would have that kind of cash.'

'What lab?' Lowell asks.

'In the mine.' From the look on his face, this is all brand-new. 'In South Dakota . . . They've got an entire lab hidden in a mine,' I explain. 'You could tell from the machinery that the experiments—'

'Were they building something?'

I look at Viv. She knows we don't have a choice. If Lowell were in on it, he wouldn't be asking the question.

'Plutonium,' I say. 'We think they're creating plutonium.'

Lowell stands there, frozen. His face goes pale. I've seen him nervous before, but never like this. 'We have to call someone . . .' he stutters, scanning the office for a phone.

'On the dresser,' I say.

Lowell's fingers pound across the digits, dialling his assistant. 'William, it's me . . . Yeah,' he says, pausing a moment. 'Just listen. I need you to call the Attorney General. Tell him I'll be there in ten minutes.' He slams down the phone and races for the door.

'It still doesn't make sense,' Viv calls out. 'Why would the US government build plutonium when we already have plenty? All it can do is get in the wrong hands . . .'

Lowell turns. 'What makes you think it's *our* government?'

Viv's confused. 'I thought you said . . .'

'You have no idea who owns Wendell, do you?' Lowell asks.

The room's so silent, I hear the blood flowing through my ears. 'Lowell, what the hell is going on?' I ask.

'We traced it back, Harris. It was well hidden: after Antigua, it bounced to a fake board of directors in the Turks and Caicos, who had a registered agent with an address in Belize. Naturally, the address was fake, but the name was traced back to the owner of a government-owned concrete company in Sana'a, capital city of Yemen.'

'Yemen? You're telling me Wendell Mining is a front for Yemen?'

He nods. 'And do you have any idea what happens if they start making plutonium and selling it to whoever's got the fattest money clip? Know how many lunatics would line up for that?'

'All of them.'

'All of them,' Lowell repeats.

'But it's impossible . . . they gave money . . . someone would have noticed . . .'

'Believe me, I've been searching for a single Arabic name on the list. These guys usually only hire their own, but the way they're hidden . . . I'm guessing they brought in someone over here to put on a public face and grease the right pockets. Some CEO-type so it all looks clean. We're looking at this guy Andre Saulson, whose name is on one of Wendell's bank accounts. One of our boys noticed the address matches an old listing we had for someone named Sauls. It'll take some time to confirm, but he fits the mould. London School of Economics . . . Sophia University in Tokyo. We looked at him a few years back for art fraud—he was supposedly trying to move the Vase of Warka when it was snatched from Iraq's National Museum, which is probably how the Yemenis found him. Very high-end scams. Yemen bring him in on the Wendell project for credibility, then Sauls hires Janos to flatten out the speed bumps, and maybe even another guy to help them manoeuvre through the system . . .'

'Pasternak . . . That's how they got into the game.'

'Exactly. They bring in Pasternak—he may not even know who they really are—and now they've got one of the best players in town. All they have to do is get their gold mine. You have to give them credit. Why risk the wrath of inspectors in the Middle East when you can build your bomb right in our own back yard? Set it up right and Congress will even give you the land for free.'

My stomach plummets. I can barely stand up.

'W-what do we do now?' Viv asks.

Lowell's already in rescue mode. 'Lock the doors behind me. Time to ring the king.'

I've heard the term before. Once he gets to the Attorney General, they're calling the White House.

As Lowell disappears out of the door, Viv notices his keys on the coffee table. 'Lowell, wait!' She grabs the key ring and follows him.

'Viv, don't!' I shout. Too late.

As I run for the door, I hear Viv scream. I step out into the corridor just as she backs into me. Up the hallway, Janos has his forearm pressed against Lowell's neck, pinning him to the wall. As he pulls his black box away, Lowell's body convulses slightly, then drops lifelessly to the floor. I look down at my friend. His eyes are still open, staring blankly at us. Janos doesn't say a word. He just lunges forward.

'*Run!*' I shout to Viv, yanking her by the shoulder and pushing her up the corridor, away from Janos.

Janos smirks as he barrels towards me, trying to intimidate. He expects me to run. That's why I stay put. This lunatic's killed three of my friends. He's not getting a fourth.

'Keep going!' I call to Viv, making sure she has enough of a lead.

From Janos's angle, he can't see what I'm looking at through the open doorway: the Senator's leather golf bag leaning against the wall. I reach for the clubs, but just as my hand grabs a nine iron, Janos ploughs into me, slamming me back against the doorjamb. Pinning me there, he stabs the black box at my chest. I knock his arm aside with the club and ram my head forwards, headbutting him hard in the nose. His hound-dog eyes widen the slightest bit. He's actually surprised. Time to take advantage.

'Get . . . off!' I shout, shoving him backwards. Before he can get his balance, I hold up the golf club like a baseball bat and rush at him. As I swing the club, he protects the black box, cradling it close to his chest. He thinks I'm going high. That's why I go low, arcing the club downwards and smashing him hard in the side of his knee.

There's a loud crack, and the club vibrates in my hands. It's enough to send his leg buckling beneath him, but at the last second he rolls with the impact. I move in closer for another swing. That's my mistake. As he falls to the ground, he yanks the nine iron from my hands. He's so fast, I barely see it happen. It's a quick reminder that I can't beat him one-on-one. Still, I got what I wanted. Behind me, Viv's turned the corner. We've got a head start.

I turn and sprint as hard as I can up the hallway. As I turn the corner, I practically plough into Viv.

'What are you doing?' I ask. 'I said to run.'

'I wanted to make sure you were OK.'

Behind us, the golf club scrapes against the concrete floor. Janos is getting up. As he starts running, the echoes of his footsteps are off beat. He's definitely limping.

Frantically, I search the hallway for help, but most of the doors down here are locked and unmarked.

'What about that one?' Viv asks, pointing to a door that's marked SERGEANT AT ARMS. I lunge for the doorknob. It doesn't twist. Locked. Damn. We're running out of corridor, and this time the Capitol police are too far away. We must do something quick.

Up ahead, on our left, there's a loud mechanical hum. It's the only door that's open. The sign on it reads: *DANGER:* MECHANICAL EQUIPMENT—AUTHORIZED PERSONNEL ONLY.

I look over my shoulder to see how we're doing just as Janos tears round the corner like a wounded tiger. He's got the golf club in one hand and the black box in the other.

'Move . . .' I say, tugging Viv towards the open door.

Inside, the concrete room is narrow but deep—I can't even see the end of it—filled with row after row of buzzing ten-foot-tall industrial exhaust fans and air compressors, interconnected by a jungle of ductwork. By the door, there's a wall full of glass pressure gauges that haven't been used in years, as well as two garbage cans and a bucket with tools in it. Behind the garbage cans, a dark green army blanket is crumpled on the floor.

'C'mere . . .' I whisper to Viv, tugging her towards the garbage cans.

'What are you—?'

'Shhhh. Just duck.' Shoving her down, I grab the blanket and drape it over her head.

'Harris, this isn't—'

'*Dammit, Viv—for once, listen*,' I scold. 'Wait till he runs past. When he's gone, go get help.'

'But then you're . . . You can't beat him, Harris. He'll kill you.'

'Please, Viv, just get help.' Our eyes lock. When Viv first saw me speaking to her page class, she thought I was invincible. So did I. Now I know better. And so does she. Tears start to fill her eyes. After everything we've been through, she doesn't want me to leave.

Kneeling down, I give her a tiny kiss on her forehead. 'You're an amazing person, Vivian. And you're gonna make a great senator one day.'

'Yeah, well . . . I'm still gonna need a great chief of staff.'

It's a sweet joke, but it doesn't make it any easier. I haven't felt this bad since my dad died. I feel a lump in my throat. 'I'll be fine,' I promise, forcing a smile. Before Viv can argue, I pull the blanket over her head, and she disappears from sight.

Convincing myself she's safe, I go for the tools, searching for a weapon. I grab a pair of needle-nose pliers and dart deeper into the room, clanging the pliers against every metal machine I pass to make as much noise as possible. Anything to keep Janos moving past Viv. As I turn the corner behind an enormous air-conditioning unit, there's a scraping sound. Italian shoes skid to a stop.

Janos is here. I pound on the metal grille. Janos starts running. *C'mon, Viv*, I say to myself. *Now's your chance . . .*

THE STAINED ARMY BLANKET reeked of a mixture of sawdust and kerosene, but that was the last of Viv's worries. She could hear the scratching of Janos's shoes as he entered the room. From the noise Harris was making—banging on what sounded like sheet metal in the distance—she figured Janos would run after him. And for a few steps, he did. Then he stopped. Right in front of her.

Holding her breath, Viv did her best to remain motionless. The only thing she could see was the tip of her right foot sticking out from underneath the blanket. *Was that what Janos was looking at? Don't move an eyebrow until he's gone.*

Eventually, Janos's footsteps moved away and faded into silence. Viv waited another few seconds before scurrying for the door.

'Help!' she cried, once she had burst into the hallway. 'Someone . . . we need help!' Piles of discarded office furniture were the only things to hear her call. Heading back to the Capitol Police, she raced towards the staircase—but just as she turned a corner, she smacked flat into the chest of a tall man in a crisp, pinstripe suit.

'Help . . . I need help,' Viv said, her voice racing.

'Take it easy,' Barry replied, his glass eye staring just off to the left as he put a hand on her arm. 'Now tell me what's going on.'

FOLLOWING AN AISLE between two air compressors, I listen carefully for Janos, but the churning of the equipment drowns out every other noise. The only good part is, if I can't hear him, he can't hear me.

At the end of the aisle, I turn right. To my surprise, the room keeps going, a labyrinth of ductwork and ventilation machinery that never seems to end. I crouch under a section of ductwork and follow an adjacent aisle even deeper into the dark room, which is looking more and more like a cellar. Mildewed brick walls . . . damp, mud-caked floors . . . and not a window in sight. The further I go, the more the machinery thins out, and the quieter it gets.

A cool draught blows against my face. I glance up at the dark arches of the ceiling and a high-pitched whistle sounds overhead. I thought the air tunnels were running above and below me. But as I look at the curves of the walls, I realise this entire room is one giant tunnel. When the Capitol was first built, air conditioning didn't exist, so an elaborate system of tunnels was built underground to bring air up into the building. While it's obviously been updated, the system is still in place. And that's why all the air-conditioning units are here.

I can now hear the pounding of heavy footsteps. Janos is getting closer. The sound echoes on my right, then my left. It doesn't make sense. He can't be in two places at once.

As I spin round to follow the noise, my elbow crashes into one of the ducts, sending a metallic gurgle reverberating through the room. I duck down and hear the rumble echo behind me. Way behind me. I flick a finger against a duct. There's a light ping on impact, followed by an echo of the ping about thirty feet over my shoulder.

'Capitol Police are on their way!' I shout, heading towards the left side of the room. With the help of the echo, Janos should hear it from the right. It's not the greatest trick in the world, but it'll buy some time and let Viv ride in for the rescue.

'Did you hear what I said, Janos? They're on their way!'

He's too smart to answer. That's why I decide to get personal.

'You don't strike me as a fanatic, Janos, so how did they get you to sign up? Something against the US, or was it purely financial? C'mon, Janos—I mean, even for a guy like you, there's gotta be some limits. Just because a man has to eat, doesn't mean you lick every piece of gum off the sidewalk.'

The footsteps get louder, then softer as he second-guesses and backtracks.

'Don't get me wrong,' I continue, hiding behind an oval water heater, 'I understand life is about picking sides, but these guys . . . You're not exactly from their nest. They may want *us* dead now, but you're not too far down the list.'

The footsteps get slower.

'You think I'm wrong? They'll not only put a knife in your spine, they'll know exactly which two vertebrae to stick it between to make sure you feel every single inch of the blade. C'mon, Janos, think of who we're talking about . . . This is Yemen—'

The footsteps stop.

I lift my head. 'They didn't tell you, did they?'

Again, silence.

'What, you think I'm making it up? It's Yemen, Janos. You're working for Yemen!' I sneak out from behind the water heater and curve back in Janos's direction, still crouching low. 'How'd they hide it from you, anyway?'

I don't hear a footstep anywhere. He's either taking it in or trying to follow the sound of my voice. Either way, there's not a chance he's thinking straight.

Silently, I weave behind a ten-foot-tall blower fan encased in a dusty metal grille. Connected to the grille is a long aluminium duct that runs a good twenty feet across the room, back towards the door. From where I'm crouched, I have a clear view that runs along the underside of the duct. There's no mistaking the Ferragamo shoes on the other end. Janos is dead ahead, and from the way he's standing there, frozen in frustration, he has no idea I'm behind him.

Gripping the needle-nose pliers, I slowly chicken-walk forward. In his right hand Janos has the black box; in his left is the Senator's nine iron. If I'm right, those are the only weapons he's got. Anything else—a knife or a gun—he'd never get through the metal detector.

He's just a few feet away. I'm so close now, I can see the overgrown stubble on the back of his neck. I tighten my jaw and raise the pliers. On three: *one . . . two . . .*

Springing upwards, I aim the pliers at the back of his neck. In a blur, Janos spins round and swats the pliers from my hand with the club. Before I can even react, he's got his other arm up in the air—and the black box stabs directly at my chest.

'Hurry. We have to get help!' Viv insisted, tugging on Barry's sleeve.

'Relax, I already did,' Barry said, scanning the hallway. 'They should be here any second. Now where's Harris?'

'In there,' she said, pointing back to the machinery room.

'Take me there.' He grabbed Viv's elbow.

'Are you nuts?' she asked.

'I thought you said he was in there with Janos.'

'I did, but—'

'So would you rather stay out here and wait for the Capitol cops, or get in there and save his life? He's alone against Janos . . .'

'But . . . but you're blind!'

'So? Janos is smart; if two people walk in, he's not risking a confrontation. He'll run. Now you coming or not?'

Viv looked over her shoulder, and once again checked for the Capitol Police. Barry was right. They were running out of time. She quickly led him forward. She wasn't leaving Harris alone.

Halfway up the corridor, they passed Lowell's lifeless body, still sprawled on the ground. Viv glanced up at Barry. He couldn't see it.

'Lowell's dead,' she said.

'Are you sure?'

She looked back at the frozen body. 'I'm sure.' Turning back to Barry, she added, 'Was he the one who called you?'

'What?'

'Lowell. Did he call you? Is that how you knew to come?'

'Yeah,' Barry said. 'Lowell called.'

Barry's cane collided with the base of the door. Viv reached out and pushed it open. 'How's it look?' Barry whispered.

Nothing had changed. The mop bucket. The garbage cans. Further back in the room, though, she heard a deep, guttural grunt. Like someone in pain.

'Harris!' she cried, tugging Barry into the room. As fast as she moved, he held tight to her elbow. 'You sure you can keep up?' she asked as they rushed forwards.

'Absolutely,' Barry said. 'I'm right behind you.'

As she turned away from him and focused back on the room, she felt his grip tighten. 'Barry, that hurts.' She tried to pull her arm free, but he didn't let go. 'Barry, did you hear what I—?'

She spun towards him, and he backhanded her across the face. The punch caught her just above the mouth, her top lip split open, and as she fell off balance to the floor she could taste blood. Crash-landing on her knees, Viv scurried on all fours to get away. Barry was right behind her. She tried to scream, but before she could get her words out, Barry wrapped his arm round her neck and pulled tight. Viv coughed uncontrollably, unable to breathe.

'I'm sorry—did you say something?' he asked. 'Sometimes I don't hear so well.'

MY EYES ARE FOCUSED on the two fangs on the end of Janos's black box. They're going straight for my heart. Twisting, I try my best to slide out of the way, but Janos is ruthlessly fast. The needles miss my chest, but they punch through my sleeve, sinking into my biceps.

Pins and needles shoot down my arm and ripple across my finger-tips. In seconds, my flesh is burning and a rancid stench fills the air.

Janos is so focused on protecting the black box, he almost doesn't notice me snatch the golf club from his other hand. Enraged, he raises the box for another pass. I swing wildly, hoping to keep him back. To my surprise, the tip of the club catches the edge of the box, sending it crashing to the ground, where it cracks open. Wires, needles and batteries scatter across the floor. I glance back at Janos. His unforgiving eyes tear me apart. He's had enough.

I once again raise the golf club and take a swing at his head. He sidesteps it neatly and hammers the knuckle of his middle finger into the bone on the inside of my wrist. A jolt of pain seizes my hand, and my fist involuntarily springs open, dropping the club.

Like a precision boxer, Janos jabs his knuckle straight into the dimple on my upper lip. The hot burst of pain is unlike anything I've ever felt, and my eyes flood. I can barely see, but I lash out with a sharp punch. Janos leans left and grabs my wrist as it passes his chin. Taking full advantage of my momentum, he pulls me towards him and, in one quick movement, lifts my arm up and digs two fingers deep into my armpit. There's a bee sting of pain, but before it even registers, my whole arm goes limp. Still not letting up, Janos lets out a throaty grunt and spears me with another jab that hits me between my groin and belly button and sends me stumbling backwards. I trip over some vents and crash flat on my ass behind an enormous air-conditioning unit. But as Janos thunders towards me, leaping over the vents and landing with a thump, his eyes aren't on me. He's looking directly over my shoulder. I follow his gaze.

Less than twenty feet away is a dark open hole that's wider than an elevator shaft, and from the looks of it, just as deep. I've heard about these but never seen one for myself. Here's where the fresh air comes in from beneath the Capitol. Some people say the holes run down hundreds of feet and, from the echo that whistles past me with a burst of fresh air, that doesn't sound too far off.

Next to the hole, a rectangular metal grate is propped upright against the wall. Usually, the grate serves as a protective cover, but right now, the only thing on top of the hole is a thin strip of yellow and black police tape with the word CAUTION on it. The tape couldn't keep out a sneeze.

Janos grabs my shirt collar and lifts me to my feet, then shoves me back towards the hole.

'D-don't do this . . .' I beg, fighting for my footing.

As always, he's silent. I try my best to stay on my feet. He again slams me in the chest. The impact feels like a sonic boom. I fight to hold on to his shirt, but I can't get a grip . . . Stumbling backwards, I fly towards the hole.

WITH BARRY'S ARM locked tight round her neck, Viv squirmed and thrashed in every direction. Her nails dug into his forearm. It only made him pull tighter, tugging her close. But as he did, Viv reached over her shoulder and clawed at his eyes.

Protecting his face, Barry turned his head to the side. That's all Viv needed. Reaching back, she grabbed a clump of his hair and pulled with everything she had.

'Aaahh!' he roared, leaning forward to stop the pain. 'Son of a—!'

Viv pulled even further, until finally he was off balance. Then, throwing her weight backwards, she felt him crash onto an exposed pipe, which drilled into his back. Howling in pain, Barry fell to his knees. He could hear Viv's shoes scuff against the concrete. She scrambled deeper into the room. Not far. Just enough to hide.

Rubbing his back, Barry swallowed the pain and looked around. There wasn't much light, making most of the shadows seem like muddy blobs floating in front of him. To his left, there was a scraping sound. Viv was moving again. Barry turned his head, but nothing flashed by. It was the same muddy blob as before. Had it moved? No . . . stay focused, he told himself.

A second later, he heard a high-pitched clink behind him. He turned to chase the sound, but the pitch was too high. Like a pebble against metal. She'd thrown something.

'Now you're testing me?' he shouted, trying to sound strong. He scanned the room—left to right, up and down—but nothing moved. All around him, machines hummed their flat, droning symphony. On his left, a compressor finished its cycle, clicking into oblivion. The wind whistled straight at him. Barry isolated each sound—every clink, hiss, sputter, creak and wheeze. But still no sign of Viv.

'Don't be stupid,' he warned, his voice cracking. 'You really think I can't see you?'

The room was dead silent. For a moment, Barry felt a tightening at the centre of his chest, but he quickly reminded himself there was no reason to panic. Viv was too scared to take a chance by trying something—

Shoes clunked at full gallop across the floor. Behind him, Viv was running for the door. Barry spun round. There was a sharp grinding of metal against concrete as she picked up an empty propane tank. He assumed she was moving it to get to the door, but by the time he caught sight of her, he was surprised that her shadow wasn't getting smaller. It was getting larger. She was coming right at him.

'Take a good look at this, asshole!' Viv shouted, swinging the propane tank with all her strength. She held tight as it collided with the side of Barry's head. 'Did you see that? That bright enough for you?' she shouted as he fell to the floor.

Barry reached for her leg, but his world was already spinning. Viv dropped the propane tank on his chest, knocking the wind out of him.

'You really thought you had a chance?' she screamed. 'What d'you think—you could beat me because I'm a girl?'

Looking up, Barry could see Viv's long shadow standing over him. It was the last thing he saw as the world went dark.

STUMBLING BACK towards the open hole, I spin to the side and try to turn myself round. By the time I can see into the pit, I'm only a few steps from the rim. But at least I'm moving fast. My foot touches the edge of the hole, and I use the speed to take a huge diagonal leap to my right. I just clear the corner of the hole—which is good—but now I'm headed straight for a brick wall—which is bad.

Putting my palms out, I slam into the wall at full speed. My arms take most of the impact, but as my full weight hits, my elbow gives way and I collapse to the floor in pain. I roll over onto my back, and look up just as Janos yanks me up by the front of my shirt. He back-hands me across the forehead. The impact knocks me into the side of an air conditioner where it meets the wall. I'm all out of running space.

'You don't have to do this,' I tell him.

Janos gives a thin sneer. Gripping my ear, he squeezes hard and twists it back. I can't help but lift my chin. He tightens his grip, and I'm staring at the ceiling. My neck's completely exposed. Winding up for the final blow, he . . .

. . . snaps his head to the left and staggers off balance. Something clipped him in the back of the head.

Gripping the nine iron I dropped earlier, Viv readies the club in perfect batting stance. 'Get the hell away from my friend,' she warns.

Janos looks over in disbelief. It doesn't last long. His fists constrict in rage, and he lunges at Viv like a rabid dog. She swings the club with clenched teeth, hoping to put another dent in his head. I tried the same thing earlier. She doesn't have a chance.

Catching the club in midswing, Janos twists it sharply, then jabs it forward like a pool cue towards her face. The blunt end of the club stabs her right in the throat. She clutches her neck, unable to breathe. The club drops to the floor. Janos doesn't need it. As Viv violently coughs, he moves in for the kill.

'S-stay back,' she gasps.

Janos grips the front of her shirt, pulls her towards him, and swipes his elbow into her face, again and again.

'*Don't touch her!*' I shout, hurtling forward. My legs are shaking, barely able to hold me up. I don't care. He's not taking her, too.

Ignoring the pain, I slam him from behind and wrap my arm round his neck. He swipes his hand back over his shoulder, trying to take my head off.

Viv goes to scratch at his cheek, but Janos is ready. He kicks her in the face. As she flies backwards, slamming into the air conditioner, Janos whips his head back, smashing me in the nose.

The loud pop tells me it's broken. Letting go of Janos, I stumble backwards, my face a bloody mess.

Janos marches right at me . . . a walking tank. Glancing at the open hole, he shoves me back, and I crash to the ground. He tugs me to my feet and pulls me in for one last shove.

'You can't win,' I stutter. 'No matter what you do . . . it's over.'

Janos stops. His eyes narrow with his smirk. 'I agree,' he says.

Last time, I made the mistake of trying to grab his shirt. This time, I go for the man himself. Stealing his own trick, I reach out, grip Janos's ear, and hold tight.

'*What are you—?*' Before he can even get the question out, we're both heading for the hole.

My foot slides over the edge. I still don't let go. Janos's head jerks forward. As I slip down, sliding off the edge, Janos grabs my arm, trying to ease his own pain. It slows our descent but I'm moving fast, and he's following me, head first. As we fall, he lets go of my arm with one hand and claws at the concrete; I kick at the inside walls of the hole, searching for a foothold. Janos shuts his eyes, digging in with everything he has. And then . . . out of nowhere . . . we stop.

I'm dangling by my left arm, which is the only part of me not in the hole. My elbow's on the edge, holding part of my weight, but my hand grips Janos's ear with whatever strength I have left. It's the only reason he's holding my wrist. Flat on his stomach, one shoulder over the edge, he continues to hold tight. If he lets go, I'll plunge down the hole, but I'll be taking part—if not all—of him with me.

'Janos, you drop him and you'll race him to the bottom,' a familiar female voice warns. I look over Janos's shoulder. Viv's on her feet, the golf club cocked in the air. She puts a foot on his hip, threatening to shove him down.

Janos freezes . . . and grabs my arm. My weight's no longer on his ear, but I still hold tight to it. He doesn't even try to turn his head towards the voice. I don't blame him. As close as he is to the edge, one wrong move, and we're both going down.

'Drop the club, Vivian,' he barks.

'Pardon?' In Viv's mind, he's in no position to make demands.

'Drop the golf club,' he repeats. 'Put it down, or I let Harris go. You'll hear him scream all the way down. Think you can handle that?'

Her mouth opens slightly. For anyone, this is tough. For a seventeen-year-old . . .

'Viv, listen to me!' I shout. 'Hit him while you have the chance!'

'Not so smart, Vivian,' Janos warns, his voice unflinchingly calm. 'You do that and Harris plummets with me.'

'Viv, don't let him get into your head! No matter what you do, I go down. He's gonna drop me anyway. Do you understand?'

My voice cracks as I say the words. She knows it's true—and she's smart enough to catch the consequences: if she doesn't take him out now, he'll be all over her in an instant.

I feel Janos's grip tightening round my wrist. He's ready to dump me and make a jump for Viv.

'Do it now!' I shout.

With the nine iron poised in the air, Viv stares from Janos to me, then back to Janos. Her hands begin to shake, and the tears roll down her cheeks. She doesn't want to do it, but the longer she stands there, the more she realises there's no choice.

'*Hit him, Viv! Hit him now!*' I shout.

'Harris . . .' she calls out. 'I don't want to—'

'You can do it,' I tell her. 'It's OK . . . I promise . . .'

With one last stab, Janos jams his finger into my wrist. My grip pops open, but he doesn't let me fall. Instead, he grabs my hand, crushing my fingers together. He likes being in control.

'Please, Viv . . . please do it!' I beg.

Janos turns towards her, and lets out a small, almost inaudible laugh. He doesn't think she has it in her.

He's wrong.

Viv sniffs up a final noseful of tears, puts all her weight behind the club and swings away. Janos immediately lets go of my hand and turns to pounce on her.

Janos expects me to drop to my death. But he doesn't see the tiny foothold I've been balancing on for the past few minutes—a two-inch ledge in the interior wall of the hole. I flex my leg, and leap upwards just enough to grab Janos by the back of his shirt. Lunging at Viv, he's totally off balance. Barely able to hold the edge of the hole with my right hand, I yank him back with my left. I give him a sharp tug towards the hole, duck down, and let gravity do the rest.

'What are you—?' He never gets the rest of words out. Tumbling out of control, he plummets backwards into the mouth of the hole. As he passes, he clutches at my shoulders . . . my waist . . . my legs . . . even the sides of my shoes. He's moving too fast to get a handhold.

'Nooo . . . !' Janos screams as he disappears into the darkness. I hear him bounce off one of the interior walls . . . then another. The screaming never stops. Not until there's a muted thud at the bottom.

TWELVE

They still haven't found him. They never will.

I'm not surprised. Like any great magician, Janos knew the value of a good disappearing act. He must have done himself some damage. It was a forty-foot drop. And they found bloodstains down there. But he managed to rip the grating off the safety gate at the bottom and get away.

It's been seven hours since we left the depths of the Capitol basement and air tunnels. To check that the air system wasn't compromised, they evacuated the entire building. If the Capitol is under a full-on terrorist assault, the bigwigs get relocated to a top-secret off-site location. If the attack is minor and containable, they come here, right across the street, to the Library of Congress.

Waiting outside the closed doors of the European Reading Room on the second floor, I sit on the marble floor, my shoulder resting on the leg of one of the enormous glass display cases filled with historical artefacts that line the hallway.

'Sir—please don't sit there,' a nearby FBI agent says.

'What's it make a difference, huh?' my lawyer, Dan Cohen, says as he rubs a hand over his shaved head. 'Let the poor guy take a seat.' An old friend from my Georgetown Law days, Dan's a half-Jewish, half-Italian meatball of a guy stuffed into a cheap suit. After graduation, while most of us went to firms or to the Hill, Dan went back to his old neighbourhood in Baltimore and took the cases most lawyers laugh at. Dan always liked a good fight. But by his own admission, he no longer has any connections in Washington. That's exactly why I called him. I've had enough of this town.

'Harris, we should go,' Dan says. 'You're falling apart, bro.'

'I'm fine,' I insist.

'C'mon . . . don't be a jackass. You've been through five and a half hours of interrogation—and it's almost midnight. You need to get your nose set.'

'You know what they're doing in there?' I say, pointing to the closed doors.

'It doesn't matter . . .'

'It *does* matter! To me it does. In fact, after everything I've been through, this is the one thing I care about right now.'

Forty minutes later, the doors to the reading room open and Viv walks out with a bandage over her eyebrow. Her bottom lip is cut and swollen, and she's holding a baby-blue ice pack to her other eye.

I climb to my feet and try to make contact, but a double-breasted suit quickly steps between us.

'Why don't you leave her alone for a bit,' her lawyer says, putting his palm against my chest. 'She's had a long night.' He's a tall African-American with a bushy moustache. When we were first taken in, I told Viv she could use Dan, but her parents quickly brought in their own attorney. I don't blame them. Since then, the FBI and the lawyer have made sure Viv and I haven't spoken to each other.

'Mr Thornell, it's OK,' Viv says, nudging him aside. 'I can . . . I'll be fine.'

Checking to be sure, Thornell decides to relent. He steps over to where Dan and the FBI agent are. For now, we've got a corner of the gilded hallway all to ourselves.

Viv avoids my gaze. 'Y'know, you didn't have to do what you did in there,' she finally says.

'I don't know what you're talking about.'

'They told me what you said. That you forced me into this . . . that when Matthew died, you threatened me into helping you . . . that you said you'd "break my face" if I didn't get on the private jet and tell everyone I was your assistant.'

My answer's a whisper. 'I didn't want you to follow the ship down.'

'What?'

'You know how these things go—who cares if we saved the day? I made bets on legislation, misappropriated a corporate jet, and arguably contributed to the death of my best friend . . . Even if you were there for the very best reasons—and believe me, you were the only innocent in the whole crowd—they'll take your head off just because you were standing next to me. Assassination by association.'

'So you just twist the truth and take the fall for everything?'

'Believe me, Viv, after what I sucked you into, I deserve far worse than that.'

'Don't be such a martyr.'

'Then don't be so naive,' I shoot back. 'The moment they think you were acting on your own is the exact same moment they put you on the catapult and fire you.'

'They did fire me,' she says nonchalantly.

'What? How could they—?'

'Don't look at me like that. So what if I lost my job? Big deal. I'm a seventeen-year-old page who lost her internship. I don't quite consider it the end of my professional career. Besides, you really thought they'd believe all that crap?'

'When I told it, it was flawless.'

'Flawless, huh? *Break my face?*'

I can't help but laugh.

'Exactly,' she says, finally taking the ice pack off her face. 'I appreciate you trying, though, Harris. You didn't have to.'

'No. I did.'

She stands there, refusing to argue. 'Can I ask you one last thing? When we were down there with Janos, and you were stuck in the hole . . . were you standing on that little ledge the entire time?'

'Just towards the end . . . my foot stumbled on it.'

She's silent for a moment. I know what she's after.

'So when you asked me to swing the golf club . . . ?'

There we go. She wants to know if I was really willing to sacrifice myself, or if I just did it to distract Janos.

'If it makes you feel any better, I'd have asked you to swing, either way.'

'That's easy to say now.'

'Sure is, but I didn't find the foothold till the last second, when he broke my grip.'

She stops as the consequences sink in. It's no lie. I would've done whatever it took to save her. Foothold or not.

'Take it as a compliment,' I add. 'You're worth it, Viv Parker.'

She has no idea what to say.

Up the hallway, a cellphone starts chirping. Viv's lawyer picks it up and puts it to his ear. Nodding a few times, he closes it and looks our way. 'Viv, your parents just checked into their hotel. Time to go.'

'In a sec,' she says. Sticking with me, she adds, 'So still no word about Janos?'

I shake my head.

'They're not gonna find him, are they?'

'Not a chance.'

'Think he'll come hunting for us?'

'I don't think so. Security cameras got pictures of him entering the Capitol. It's not like they need us as witnesses or to identify him. So there's nothing to be gained by putting bullets in our heads.'

'I'll remember that as I check behind every closed shower curtain for the rest of my life.'

'We've been sitting here for eight hours. If he wanted us dead, it already would've happened.'

It's not much of a guarantee, but it's the best we've got.

'So that's it? We're done?'

I look back to my lawyer as she asks the question. After a decade on Capitol Hill, the only person standing in my corner is someone who's paid to be there. 'Yeah . . . we're done.'

'So where do you go from here?' she asks me.

'Depends what type of deal Dan cuts with the government. Right now, the only thing I'm worried about is Matthew's funeral. His mom asked me to give one of the eulogies. Me and Congressman Cordell.'

'I wouldn't sweat it—I've seen you speak. You'll do him justice.'

It's the only thing that anyone's said in the last eight hours that's actually made me feel good. 'I'm sorry again for getting you into—'

'Don't say it, Harris.'

'But being a page . . .'

'It paled beside what we did these last few days. Just paled. The running around . . . finding that lab . . . even taking a shower in a private jet! You think I'd trade all that so I could refill some senator's seltzer? Didn't you hear what they said at page orientation? Life is school. It's *all* school. And if anyone wants to give me crap about being fired, well . . . well, when's the last time they jumped off a cliff to help a friend? God didn't put me here to back down.'

'That's a good speech. I'm serious about what I said before: you're gonna make a great senator one day.'

'Senator? You got a problem with a giant, black woman president?' I laugh out loud.

'I meant what I said, too,' she adds. 'I'll still need a good chief of staff.'

'You got a deal. Even I'll come back to Washington for that one.'

'Oh, so now you're leaving us all behind? What are you gonna do then—write a book? Or just kick back on a beach somewhere like at the end of all those thrillers?'

'I don't know . . . Dan was saying there's a junior high school in Baltimore that could use a good civics teacher.'

'Hold on a second . . . you're gonna teach?'

'And that's so bad?'

She thinks about it a moment. A week ago she would've said there were bigger things to do with my life. Now we both know better. Her smile is huge. 'Actually, that sounds perfect.'

'Thank you, Viv.'

'Though you know those kids'll eat you alive.'

I grin. 'I hope so.'

'Ms Parker—your parents!' her lawyer calls out.

'Be right there . . . Listen, I should run,' she tells me, offering a quick hug.

'Knock 'em dead, Viv.'

'Who, my parents?'

'No . . . the world.'

She pulls away with that same toothy grin she had when we first met. 'Y'know, Harris,' she says. 'When you originally asked me for help . . . I had such a crush on you.'

'And now?'

'Now . . . I don't know,' she teases. 'I kinda think I should get a suit that fits.' Walking backwards up the hallway, she adds, 'I'm serious about that chief of staff job, Harold,' she calls out as her voice echoes down the long hallway. 'Only eighteen years until I reach the age requirement. I'll expect you there bright and early.'

'Whatever you say, Madame President—I wouldn't miss it for the world.'

THIRTEEN

'Have a nice evening, Mr Sauls,' the driver said, opening the back door of the black Jaguar.

'You, too, Ethan,' Sauls replied, climbing out of the car and heading to the front door of the exclusive six-storey building on central London's Park Lane.

Stepping into his well-appointed apartment, Sauls went straight to the kitchen and headed for the shiny black-panelled refrigerator. Grabbing a glass from the counter, he pulled the fridge open and poured himself some cranberry juice. As the door shut, he could see his own reflection in it and there was someone standing behind him.

'Nice address,' Janos said.

Sauls spun round so fast he almost dropped his glass. 'Don't scare me like that!' he shouted, setting the glass on the counter. 'God . . . I thought you were dead!'

'Why would you think that?' Janos asked. He stepped in closer, one hand in the pocket of his black overcoat, the other clenching an aluminium cane. He lifted his chin, highlighting the cuts and bruises on his face. His left eye was bloodshot, a fresh scar was stitched across his chin, and his left femur was shattered into so many pieces, they had to insert a titanium rod into his leg to stabilise the bones.

'I've been trying to contact you; there's been no answer for a week,' Sauls said, stepping back. 'Do you even know what's going on? The FBI seized it all. They took every last thing from the mine.'

'I know. I read the papers,' Janos said, limping forwards. 'By the way, since when did you get a driver?'

'What are you—? You followed me?'

'Don't be paranoid, Sauls. Some things you can spot from your bedroom window.'

'What do you want, Janos? If it's money, we paid you just like we said . . .' Backed up against the kitchen counter, Sauls stopped.

One hand still in his pocket, Janos fixed his eyes on his partner. 'You lied to me, Marcus.'

'I . . . I didn't! I swear!' Sauls insisted.

'Answer the question,' Janos warned. 'Was it Yemen, or not?'

'It's not what you think . . . When we started—'

'When we started, you told me Wendell was a private company with no government ties.'

'It's the same result either way!'

'No, it's not! One's speculation; the other's suicide! You have any idea how long they'll hunt us for this? Now who signed the damned cheque—was it Yemen or not?'

'Janos, please calm down and—'

Janos pulled out a gun and shoved it against Sauls's forehead, digging the barrel against his skin. 'Was. It. Yemen. Or. Not?'

'Yemen!' Sauls stuttered, his face scrunched up as he shut his eyes. 'It was Yemen . . . Please don't kill me . . . !'

Without a word, Janos lowered the gun.

'I'm sorry, Janos . . . I'm so sorry . . .' Sauls continued to beg.

'Catch your breath,' Janos demanded, handing Sauls the glass of cranberry juice.

Sauls desperately downed the drink, but it didn't bring the calm he was searching for. His hands were trembling as he lowered the glass, which clinked against the counter.

Shaking his head, Janos turned to leave. 'Goodbye, Sauls,' he said.

'S-so you're not gonna kill me?' Sauls asked, forcing a smile.

Janos turned and held Sauls with a stare. 'Who said that?'

Sauls started to cough. Slightly at first. Then harder. Within seconds, his throat exploded into a hacking wheeze. He grasped at his neck. It felt like his windpipe had collapsed.

Janos didn't say a thing. He left before the convulsions started.

EPILOGUE

'Here he comes,' the guard by the door calls out to me. With both his arms and legs in shackles, Barry shuffles forward, guided by the prison guard towards the orange plastic seat on the other side of the glass partition.

'Who?' Barry asks as I read his lips. His guard mouths my name.

The moment Barry hears it, he pauses, then quickly covers it up with a perfect grin. It's a classic lobbying trick: pretend you're happy to see everyone. Even when you can't see.

The guard lowers Barry into the seat and hands him the receiver that's hanging on the glass. Crossing one leg over the other, Barry tugs on the leg of his orange jumpsuit like it's his regular $2,000 suit.

I lift the chipped receiver to my ear. I've been waiting two weeks for this, but it doesn't mean I'm looking forward to it.

'Hey,' I whisper into the mouthpiece.

'Man, you sound like crap,' Barry sings back, already trying to act like he's inside my brain. 'Like someone kicked you in the face.'

'Someone did,' I say, staring straight at him.

'I don't know how you can complain,' he adds. 'The way the press is reading it, you're coming through just fine.'

'That'll change when the gambling part gets released.'

'Maybe yes, maybe no. Sure, you won't get another government job, and you'll probably be a pariah for a few years, but that'll pass. I mean, look at it this way—at least you have your shoelaces.' He twirls an ankle and I notice there are no shoelaces in his sneakers. He's trying to play it cool, but he's picking at his wristband. 'By the way, did you see the piece in today's *Post*?' he adds. He smiles wider, but he's scratching even harder at the wristband. 'They actually called me a *terrorist*.'

I stay quiet. He's definitely taking the public fall. Even though Lowell's office was able to trail Sauls's name back to Wendell, it took weeks to prove what really went on. Today, with Sauls dead and Janos missing, they need a neck for the noose—and Barry's it.

'I heard you hired Richie Rubin. He's a good lawyer,' I point out.

Barry smells the small talk a mile away—he used to be in the business of it. Now he's annoyed. The smile disappears fast. 'What do you want, Harris? Let me guess. You're dying to know why I did it.'

'I know why you did it,' I shoot back. 'When you have no loyalty, and you're so damn paranoid you think the world's against you—'

'The world *is* against me!' he shouts. 'Look where I'm sitting! Not all of us are lucky enough to lead your charmed life, Harris.'

'So now it's my fault?'

'Just tell me why you're here.'

'Pasternak,' I blurt.

A wide smile creeps up his cheeks. 'It's gnawing at you, isn't it? Pasternak was supposed to be your mentor. The one person you turned to when you had an emergency. And now you're wondering how your personal radar could be so completely wrong?'

'I just want to know why he did it.'

'Of course. It's the curse of being an overachiever: you can't handle a problem that can't be solved. If it makes you feel better, I don't think Pasternak knew who was driving the train. Sure, he took advantage of you, but that was just to get the mining request in the bill.'

'I don't understand.'

'What's to understand?' Barry asks. 'It was an unimportant request for a defunct gold mine in South Dakota. But he knew Matthew would never say yes to it—not unless he had a good enough reason. From there, Pasternak just took the game and put in the fix.'

'So Pasternak was one of the dungeon masters?'

'The what?'

'The dungeon masters—the guys who pick the bets and collect the cash. Is that how the mine request got in the game?'

'How else would it get there?' Barry asks.

'I don't know . . . all those months we were playing . . . the people we were betting against—Pasternak and I tried to figure out who else was in on it. He even made a list of people who were working on particular issues . . . But if he was a dungeon master—' I cut myself off as the consequences sink in. Barry's cloudy eye's staring straight at me; his glass eye's off to the left. Out of nowhere, he starts to laugh.

'You're kidding me, right? You did figure it out, didn't you?'

I try my best to act informed. 'Of course—I got most of it . . . Which part are you talking about?'

His foggy eye looks right at me. 'There is no game. There never was one. It was all bullshit. Smoke and mirrors. The only people actually playing the game were you and Matthew.' As his words creep into my ear, my body goes numb. I feel like my personal gravity's just doubled, like I'm sinking through the seat of my orange plastic chair.

'Two minutes,' the guard behind Barry announces.

'It's brilliant when you think about it,' Barry adds. 'Pasternak talks it up, you believe him, then they fill in a few taxi receipts and you guys think you're in on the biggest secret Capitol Hill has to offer.'

I force a laugh, my body still frozen.

'Man, just the thought of it,' Barry adds. 'Dozens of staffers placing bets on unimportant legislation without anyone knowing? Please, what a dream. Like anyone here could even keep their mouth shut for longer than ten seconds. Gotta give Pasternak his credit, though. You thought you were playing a great joke on the system, and the entire time, he's playing the joke on you.'

'Yeah . . . no . . . it's definitely amazing.'

'It was humming like clockwork, too—until everything with Matthew. Once that happened, Pasternak wanted out. I mean, he didn't want to hurt anyone.'

'That's . . . That's not what I heard,' I bluff.

'Then you heard wrong. The reason he put this together was the exact same reason anyone does anything in this town. Pasternak's billings were down thirty-six per cent this year alone. After the first year of failing to get the gold mine transferred, he decided to go with the more inventive back door. Say hello to the Game—the most harmless way ever to sneak an earmark into a bill. But then Matthew got curious, and Janos came in, and, well . . . that's when the train jackknifed off the tracks . . . You gotta love the name, too—the Zero Game—so melodramatic. But it *is* true: in any equation, when you multiply by zero, you always wind up with nothing, right?'

I nod, dumbfounded.

'So who told you anyway?' he asks. 'FBI, or did you figure it out yourself?'

'No . . . myself. I . . . got it myself.'

'Good for you, Harris. Good man.'

Stuck in my seat, I just sit there, looking at him. It's like finding out a year of your life has been a staged production number. And I'm the only putz still in costume.

'Time,' the guard says.

Barry keeps talking. 'I'm so glad you—'

'I said, *time*,' the guard interrupts. He pulls the receiver from Barry's ear, but I still hear his final words.

'I knew you'd appreciate it, Harris! I knew it! Even Pasternak would be happy for that!'

There's a loud click in my ear as the guard slaps the phone in its cradle. He pinches the back of Barry's neck and yanks him from his seat. Stumbling across the room, Barry heads back to the steel door.

As I sit alone at the glass partition, staring through to the other side, there's no question Barry has it right. Pasternak said it the first day he hired me. It's the first rule of politics: the only time you get hurt is when you forget it's all a game.

BRAD MELTZER

Like one of the ambitious characters in his novels, Brad Meltzer, at twenty, thought he had his life mapped out. Newly graduated from the University of Michigan, he was about to go to law school, but decided to have a year out. He took a job at *Games* magazine in Boston, which turned out to be a fiasco. He soon left and remembers thinking, 'I have one year and I can either watch a lot of television or I can try to write a novel.'

Like many before him, he failed the first time, receiving twenty-four rejection letters for a coming-of-age novel titled *Fraternity*. But Meltzer was hooked and, during his first year at Columbia law school, he completed *The Tenth Justice*, persuading his tutor that it should count as an exam credit. In 1997 it soared into the *New York Times* bestseller lists and, one year later, *Dead Even* met with similar success. Now Meltzer's thrillers are routinely translated into over a dozen languages.

The Zero Game grew out of stories that Brad Meltzer heard when he was a nineteen-year-old intern on Capitol Hill. 'Two different government employees have told me they've seen a smaller variation of the game being played, e.g., people betting on how many votes will be cast for a certain bill. That's scary. Also, I'm honestly amazed by how many staffers on the Hill, when they hear the plot, say, "I wouldn't be surprised if someone was doing that right now!"'

To research the gripping mine scenes, Meltzer took his life in his hands and descended into an abandoned gold mine. 'Two weeks after I did that, a group of miners got trapped in a Pennsylvania mine. They were two hundred and forty feet down; I was eight thousand. I'm a moron for doing it, but I think it makes for one of the scariest scenes I've ever written. My wife wanted to kill me—but for my readers, I'll risk my life!'

So how does Brad Meltzer, who now lives in Florida with his wife Cori and their baby son, get new ideas? 'Research, research, research. You can invent all the stuff you want, but if it doesn't smell real, readers will know in a nanosecond. To me, fiction is at its best when it has one foot in reality.'

THE FIRE BABY

JIM KELLY

When Black Bank Farm was hit by an
American plane in the summer of
1976, only two people emerged from
the flames alive—Maggie Beck and
the tiny baby she was clutching.

Twenty-seven years later, lying on her
deathbed, Maggie finally decides to
tell the truth about what really
happened that night . . .

Tuesday, June 1, 1976

The Great Drought

East of Ely, above the bone-dry peatfields, a great red dust storm drifts across the moon, throwing an amber shadow on the old cathedral. Overhead a single, winking plane crosses the star-spangled sky. Flight MH336, just airborne from the US military base at Mildenhall, flies into the tumbling cauldron of dust.

The diamond-hard sand begins to shred the turning turbines. The fuselage dips as the engine suffocates and begins a descent of such violence that the passengers float, despite their seat belts, in a weightless fall towards their deaths.

At precisely 11.08 p.m., according to the pilot's watch recovered at the scene, the fuselage buries itself in the soft earth. The distant cathedral rocks with the impact and the crows, roosting on the Octagon Tower, rise in a single cloud.

A fireball marks the point of impact at Black Bank Farm. At the heart of the fire a cold white eye burns where 50,000 gallons of kerosene converts to gas in a single second.

At the foot of the vast white pillar of rising smoke the air crackles with the heat. And in the ashes of what had been Black Bank Farm she stands alone. Her, and the baby.

They are the only ones alive. Her, and the baby.

The family died at the table: her mother, her father. His last words will stay with her till her deathbed: 'The cellar, Maggie. A celebration.' She'd gone to get the bottle, leaving Matty in his cot by the empty fireplace. Celebration: a family christening to come, now that Matty had a father.

In the damp of the cellar she heard it coming, the final wail of the failing engines, the ripping metal and the blow of the impact. Sometimes she wished she had died then, as she should have. Instead, she found the stairs and climbed up to count the dead, hung like game from the burning rafters. Then the real horror, in the tiny swaddled bundle with the blackened limbs.

Outside, with her secret in her arms, she felt him kicking and nudging, with the jerky half-conscious movements only a child can make. Even here, in what had been the kitchen garden, she felt the heat prickling her skin. She smelled her hair singe, as the black hanging threads turned to ash-white corkscrews. A lock ignited and burned into her cheek. She had a lifetime to feel the pain but even now it terrified her with the slow insidious intimation that the worst was yet to come.

A fire in her blood. And the baby's.

She took a limping step towards the coolness of the night. These ashes weren't cold like the ones in the grate at Black Bank. These were white with heat, an ivory crust beneath which breathed the cherry embers. She smelled flesh burn and knew, with the clarity of shock, that it was hers.

And then she saw him. A hundred yards from the house, shielding his face from the heat with an out-turned palm.

He'd been waiting to join the celebration. Her father had been confident Maggie would change her mind that night. 'Come at eleven. She'll come round for Matty's sake. It's the baby. She'll come round.'

And with the intuition of a lover Maggie knew where he'd been, knew where he'd been waiting in the night. The old pillbox. Their pillbox; the concrete hexagonal space where they'd made Matty.

She'd heard a siren then. The first. From the base. They'd be at Black Bank soon, but not soon enough to save him. Not soon enough to save him from the life she planned for him in those few seconds. It was the best decision of her life. And the quickest.

Then they were together. So she smiled as she trembled. The yellow-blue light of the kerosene was in his eyes and briefly she remembered why she had loved him once. But she saw that he looked only down, at the baby. His finger turned back the fold in the blanket. He saw the face for the first time. And the fool smiled too.

'Our boy,' he said, wishing it was so. 'He's safe. Our boy?'

'Dead,' she said, and pulled the blankets back to let him see the stencilled blue capitals on the soft linen: USAF: AIR CONVOY.

He looked at the farmhouse. 'Dead? You can't be sure.'

He looked at the blanket again. 'I'll get him,' he said. 'Stay here.' She watched him run into the flames, until they closed behind him, like the hushed velvet curtains of a crematorium.

Saturday, June 14, 2003

27 Years Later

The glass of water stood like an exhibit on the pillbox shelf. When the sun reached the western horizon it shone directly into the hexagonal room through the gunslit and caught the liquid, sending a shifting rainbow of incredible beauty across the drab concrete walls.

Its cool limpid form was held for ever in his memory: but then he knew that for ever, for him, was not a long time. As the heat rose towards midday he could see the level of water drop, and he sucked in air to catch the memory of the moisture.

It was his life now, trying to reach the glass. But he knew, even as he stretched and felt the handcuffs cut into his wrist, that he would never touch it. On the first day he'd stretched out and left a line in the sand, three feet short of the far wall. By the third day he'd stretched until he heard his joints crack. The next day he'd won six inches in a single panic-stricken lunge, the pain of which had made him swoon. When he came to, the blood had dried and the cut at his wrist showed the glint of a bone. That night the fox came for the first time, circling, sniffing death.

His jailer noted his efforts to reach the glass with satisfaction, smoothed clean the sand and refilled the glass with the bright water from the sparkling plastic bottle. Then he took the carved knife from its place, sticking out of the door jamb, and held it to his victim's throat. A minute, sometimes two, then he returned it, unblooded.

There was something familiar about the jailer. Something in the way he leaned against the concrete wall by the glass and smoked. Something in the downcast eyes.

He yearned to hear his voice, but the jailer hadn't spoken.

The routine was silently the same. He'd hear first his footsteps on the tinder-dry twigs beneath the pines. The iron door pushed open, the glass refilled. Then he'd stand and smoke. A packet sometimes. How long does that take? An hour? Two?

Sometimes he came twice a day, the sound of his car suddenly loud as it parked beyond the trees he could see through the gunslit. But he'd always go without answering the questions. And then once at night. He was afraid then, for the first time, that the jailer would kill him before the thirst did. His tormentor was drunk and the storm lantern put tiny red flashes in his eyes. But still he said nothing.

He'd speak before the end. He felt sure of that. But he wanted to know now. Know now for which of his crimes he was being punished.

Thursday, June 5—Nine Days Earlier

1

Philip Dryden looked down on the taxi cab parked on the neat shingle forecourt of The Tower Hospital. In the front seat was a large sleeping figure encircled by the Ipswich Town sweatshirt. The driver's delicate hands were clasped neatly over an ample tummy. The slumbering cabbie's tiny mouth formed a perfect O.

'How can he stand it?' Dryden asked, turning to the figure laid out under a single white linen sheet on the hospital bed. 'It's eighty-four degrees. He's parked in full sun. Fast asleep. All that meat. Cooking.'

The figure on the bed didn't move. Its immobility was a constant in his life, like the heat of that summer. Heat. Inescapable heat, like a giant duvet over the Fens. He felt a rivulet of sweat set out from his jet-black hair and begin a zigzag journey across his face. His features were architectural. Precisely, Early Norman. The head of a knight, perhaps, from a cathedral nave, or illuminated on a medieval parchment. Illuminated but impassive, a dramatic irony that nicely summed him up.

The Tower was on Ely's only hill. A precious hundred feet above the expanse of the Black Fens that stretched in a parched panorama to the distant wavy line of the horizon.

He looked down at Laura. His wife had been in The Tower nearly four years since the accident at Harrimere Drain. Dryden had met the other driver on a lonely fen road head-on, swerved over the verge, and the two-door Corsa had plunged into twenty feet of water in the roadside dyke. Harrimere Drain.

He'd been dragged to safety, but Laura, unseen on the back seat, had been left behind. He tried never to imagine what she must have thought when she regained consciousness. Alone in the dark, in pain, and gasping for breath in the diminishing pocket of damp air.

Three hours later the emergency services got her out. She was in the coma then. Locked In Syndrome: LIS. Locked away from the horror of those 180 minutes of total isolation; locked away from the knowledge that she'd been abandoned; locked away from him.

The bedside clock flipped over a number: 11.58. Dryden fingered the gold chain round his neck. He pulled on it until the single brass Chubb-lock key came out into his hand. The crash had been two days before his thirty-third birthday and he hadn't got back to their flat in London until a month later. That's when he found his present. A white envelope, a card showing a black and white shot of the Fens near Ely, and a newly cut key. The inscription on the card read *Love, Laura*; nothing else.

He'd tried the locks in the flat first, then her parents' café and flat. He'd tried the local locksmiths in north London where they lived, but none could recall a visit from the Italian girl with the copper hair. He'd tried the two cottages out on Adventurer's Fen, which they'd inspected during their long debates about moving out and starting a family. But the doors were rotten and the keyholes rusted. Ivy obscured the sign engraved in the bricks: Flightpath Cottages.

How many other locks had he tried since Laura's accident? A thousand? Two? But nothing. Only Laura knew which door the key opened, and she hadn't spoken since the night of the crash.

Eleven fifty-nine and one minute to the news on the radio. He flipped open his mobile and rang Humph's business number: Humphrey H. Holt, licensed minicabs for all occasions. Not quite all occasions. In fact, hardly any occasions at all. Humph's cab, a battered Ford Capri, looked as though it had been retrieved from a dump on the outskirts of Detroit.

Dryden's face, normally stonily impassive, creased with pleasure as he watched the cabbie start awake and fumble for his mobile.

'It's me,' he said, unnecessarily. They knew each other's voices better than they knew their own. 'Put the local radio on. Last item. I need to hear.'

They zoomed dizzily over the wavebands until Humph picked up the signal. 'The headlines at noon on Radio Littleport.'

Dryden, for a decade one of Fleet Street's sharpest reporters, listened with complete indifference to the usual tales of political intrigue, international violence and lurid show business, before the station moved on to the local items.

'And now the time is four minutes past twelve on Radio Littleport, the Voice of the Fens. Here is an urgent message from East Cambridgeshire County Police Force. Will Estelle Beck, the only daughter of Maggie Beck of Black Bank Farm, please go immediately to The Tower Hospital, Ely, where her mother is gravely ill.'

Dryden clicked off the mobile without thanking Humph. Then he walked across the large, carpeted room and folded his six-foot-two-inch frame into the hospital chair beside the room's only other bed. In it lay the wheezing body of Maggie Beck.

He hoped her daughter would come soon. He had seen very few people dying, but the signs seemed shockingly clear. Her hair was matted to her skull. She seemed to draw her breath up from a pit beneath her, each breath a labour that threatened to kill her. Her skin was dry and without tension—except for the single mark of a livid burn that cut across one side of her face in the shape of a corkscrew.

'They'll come,' he said, hoping she'd hear.

In the oddly detached way in which he expressed almost all his emotions, Dryden had come to love Maggie Beck. When his father died in the floods of '77, Maggie, still a teenager and newly married, had moved in to look after his mother. Dryden had been eleven. Maggie had taken the spare room and helped his mother through the weeks before the coroner's inquest, and then the excruciating absence of a burial. His father had been presumed drowned, swept off the bank at Welch's Dam, and the body never found. For his mother this had been the final burden, which Maggie helped her to bear. The heartache of grief without a corpse to cry over.

Maggie had her own tragedy to carry—the air crash at Black Bank that had killed her parents and her infant son. They shouldered their grief together, farmers' wives who didn't want to subside under the weight of their misfortunes. They'd travelled together—day trips and weekends that took them far from the memory of their lives. He'd met her many times at Burnt Fen in his mother's kitchen, a big woman with farmyard bones as familiar and comforting as the Aga.

Maggie knew she had cancer. Dryden had gone out to Black Bank to see her and knew that she expected to die. The specialists had suggested it might be good therapy for Laura if she shared her room. Maggie said yes without a pause and raided her savings to afford The

Tower's substantial fees. She would spend her last few months in comfort, for she had a task to complete before the cancer took her life. She wanted to tell her story. Dryden gave her a tape recorder so that each day she could spill her tale to a silent audience.

She'd been in The Tower a month and each day Estelle had come to sit with her mother—until now. But the best days for Maggie were when Estelle brought the American. Dryden had met him twice, by Laura's bedside. 'Friend of the family,' Maggie said. A pilot, tall and slightly wasted, with the drawn features of a victim. Every day they had come—until this last weekend. The doctors assured them the end was months away, if not years. Maggie had agreed to a break, to let her daughter go. Let them both go.

The moment they left, Maggie's health had rapidly collapsed. She had felt the change within her, the subtle beginning of the process of death. She had to get Estelle back, she had something to tell her. About the secrets that had consumed her life.

'Promise me you'll find them in time,' she said. Dryden noted the plural.

He didn't like telling lies. 'I can't,' he said. 'The police are trying; what more can I do?'

Her eyes pleaded with him. 'Then promise you'll forgive me too.'

'Forgive you for what?'

Her hand fluttered, searching on the bedside table where the tape recorder stood. 'I've said it here. But I must tell them too.'

'I promise.'

She cried. The first time he'd seen her buckle after all the months of pain.

He was doing all he could. The police appeals, ads in the papers along the coast where Estelle and the American had gone touring. Why didn't Estelle ring? Why didn't she answer her mobile phone?

He walked back to his wife and touched her shoulder. 'Laura?'

Her eyes were open. Seemingly sightless, but open. He imagined she slept—why not? So she needed waking like everyone else. And he liked using her name, now that he knew for certain that on some level, however deep and however distant, she could hear him.

The caretaker walked by in the corridor outside, dragging laundry bags and whistling 'Ode To Joy', each note perfectly pitched.

Humph beeped from the cab. They had a job. Dryden had to go but he knew there was no real hurry. *The Crow*, the paper for which he was chief reporter, had a final deadline of 3 p.m. The handful of stories he had yet to file would take him an hour or so to knock out.

He sat on the bed and took Laura's hand.

They'd made the breakthrough three months ago. The heatwave had just begun and Dryden, unable to sleep, had spent the night on the deck of his boat at Barham's Dock. The sunrise had driven him to walk and a pack of foxes had dogged his tracks into town, scavenging across fields of sunburnt crops. The Tower had slept, the night nurse looking up from her studies to wave him through. He'd tried the routine a thousand times: taking her hand and beginning the endless repetition of the letters. Waiting for the tiny movement that would signal intelligent life, like a radio blip across the galaxy.

That first time she'd done it perfectly, L-A-U-R-A. No mistakes. He'd sat on her bed and wept for her. Wept for joy that she was somewhere. But wept most for himself, doomed perhaps to spend his life beside a hospital bed, waiting for messages from another world.

Humph beeped again. Dryden placed the smallest finger of Laura's right hand in his palm so that it barely touched his skin. The neurologist had shown him how. They had a machine, too, the COMPASS, but Dryden liked doing it this way—the way they'd first done it. The communication was intensely personal, as though he were a lightning rod, channelling her energy back to earth.

'OK. Let's concentrate.' The specialist had told him to give her a warning. 'OK. We're starting. A, B, C, D, E . . .' and on, a full two seconds for each. He felt the familiar tingle of excitement as he got nearer: 'J, K, L'—and there it was, the tiny double movement.

It didn't always happen. One out of five, six perhaps. They'd always got the next bit wrong until Dryden had hit upon the idea of beginning at M and running through the alphabet rather than starting at A. He moved on, with the two second gaps, but she missed it. Two tiny movements—but on the B.

He felt irritation, then guilt. The neurologist had explained how difficult it must be. 'It's about as easy as playing chess in your head. She's learned to combine certain muscle movements, small tremors in the tissue, to produce this timed response. We have no way of knowing how much time she needs for each letter.'

He did the rest. L-B-U-S-A. Three letters right, two just a place away in the alphabet.

He felt a fierce pride and love burn, briefly, at her achievement. The specialist had told him to be patient—a word that always prompted in Dryden an internal scream. Laura's messages were halting, disjointed, sometimes surreal. He must wait to see if she would ever emerge from the confused penumbra of coma.

'Patience,' he said out loud. A virtue of which he had no trace.

HUMPH PARKED in the lay-by three miles east of Ely. It was a lay-by like all lay-bys, distinguished by nothing. The A14 east–west trunk roads linking the port of Felixstowe with the industrial cities of the Midlands was punctuated by them. At this hour—lunchtime—it was a canyon of heavy goods vehicles ticking over and spewing carbon monoxide into hot air already laced with grease from the Ritz T-Bar.

'Coffee. Four sugars,' said the cabbie, unfolding a copy of the *Financial Times* with casual familiarity. He played the stock market the way many people played the horses. He lost a lot, but when he ran out of things to read the *FT* made a snug, pink blanket.

Humph was Dryden's chauffeur. There was no other way to describe it. They had shared a life of aimless motion for nearly four years since Laura's accident. Humph had a few regular customers who paid well—early-morning school runs, and late-night pick-ups for club bouncers in Newmarket and Cambridge. The rest of the time he was on call for Dryden. *The Crow*, Dryden's newspaper, was happy to pick up the modest bills as it made up for the fact that they appeared to have forgotten to pay their chief reporter a salary. Humph's home-life was as non-existent as Dryden's, due to an acrimonious divorce. He had a picture of his two girls stuck on the dashboard.

The Ritz T-Bar was a regular meeting place for Dryden and the crew of stragglers he counted as his 'contacts'. He noted that Inspector Andy Newman's car was already parked at the end of the lay-by. The detective drove a clapped-out Citroën with a sticker in the window for the Welney Wildfowl Trust. Andy 'Last Case' Newman, as he was known to his fellows, was more interested in sighting a sparrowhawk than a crook. Mentally he had been on the allotment for a decade. He had twenty-three days to run to statutory retirement age.

Dryden queued for a cup of tea. The Ritz was standard issue in the mobile tea-bar world: sugar bowl with one teaspoon and several lumps of coagulated glucose; one copy of the *Sun*—tied to the counter with a piece of string; a hotplate with a row of sausages sizzling in six-point harmony. And one oddity: a bird cage in which sat a moth-eaten parrot.

The proprietor was tall, with blond hair tinged nicotine-yellow. His conversational powers, which Dryden had tested before, were strictly limited to Premier League football, female lorry drivers and the weather. As he pushed the styrofoam cup of tea across the counter, Dryden noticed the livid raised mark of a skin graft on his hand.

'Johnnie,' said Dryden, putting his change on the Formica top.

'Steamin' again,' said Johnnie, shuffling coins between the lines of five-, ten-, twenty- and fifty-pence pieces he had on the counter-top.

Dryden left it at that. He got into Newman's car and sat pretending to sip the tea. Newman, binoculars pressed to his face, was scanning the field opposite. Eventually he placed them on his lap with a sigh. 'Herring gull,' he said.

Dryden produced a piece of paper. It was a story put out by the Press Association that morning. *The Crow* paid for the wire service PA provided—a regular series of news stories churned out online to the terminal on the news editor's desk. Dryden had a search mechanism on his screen that alerted him when a story came up with a headline containing the key words TWITCHER(S), BIRD(S), RARE or EGG(S).

He'd rung Newman that morning as soon as the story had appeared on the wire. RARE SIBERIAN GULL SPOTTED, ran the headline. The bird had been blown onto the bird reserve at Holme on the north Norfolk coast. Once the news hit the papers thousands of twitchers would descend on the spot. This way, Andy Newman got there first.

'Thanks,' he said stuffing the paper in the glove compartment. They had long since dispensed with any pretence that their relationship was anything other than cynical. Newman got his tips and Dryden got a story. It was as simple as that. Newman retrieved a large brown envelope that had been stashed in the glove compartment. Dryden extracted some photographs from the envelope.

'They're X-rated,' said Newman, as he raised his binoculars to watch a flock of flamingos rising from the distant waters of Wicken Fen Nature Reserve.

And so they were. Twenty prints, black and white. Two bodies. One female. Her face was to the camera in a few, the eyes glazed. Dryden guessed she'd been drugged. The man's face was crueller. A professional. A porn star's body. Hairless and smooth. But ugly. They were always ugly in these pictures, whatever they looked like.

She'd have been beautiful anywhere else. Blonde, bright eyes, leggy. Dryden guessed twenty—perhaps younger. The stud was older, late twenties; the cynical smile added another couple of decades. But it was the room that left Dryden uneasy. Walls, but no right angles. Bare concrete. Graffiti: layers of it, decades of it.

The camera angle never changed. It was outside looking in, through a narrow horizontal slit. Night time.

'It's a pillbox,' said Newman, lowering the binoculars. 'There were thirty thousand built in the late thirties, forties. There are probably ten thousand left. The pictures turned up in a house in Nottingham. A raid—illegal immigrants.'

One of the HGVs shuddered past, drowning out the whine of the cars on the A14.

'Operation Ironside,' Newman said. 'April 1940. They thought the Germans were going to invade on the east coast. So they built pill-boxes. About a hundred and fifty of them across the region.' Newman handed Dryden the binoculars and pointed north across a field of dry peat to a windbreak of poplars.

It took Dryden a minute to find it with the binoculars. One of its sides caught the sun, the narrow machine-gun slit a jet-black shadow.

'That one?'

'Nope. Roof's collapsed.'

Dryden looked again. The roof did indeed sit at an angle.

'And there's this,' added Newman.

One of the prints Dryden had ignored was a blow-up part of the wall. He'd thought it was just a duff picture, but now he could see faintly stencilled letters neatly set out by a wall bracket.

'It probably held a phone,' said Newman. 'The number identifies the pillbox. At least it would if we had records. Which we haven't.'

'But?' There had to be more.

'The first three numbers give the area: one-zero-three. Isle of Ely.'

'So what's the story? More to the point, what's the crime?'

'We're looking for anyone who's seen anything unusual around a pillbox. Cars at night. Lights. Clothing left in them. Kids might have seen something. The crime? My guess is the girl's drugged. She's somebody's daughter. Somebody's girlfriend.'

Dryden thought about the girl in the pictures and the look of bewildered fear in her eyes. 'Could she be missing?'

'It's possible. You can say we've got the national police computer on the job and the missing persons' files are being scoured.'

THE CROW'S OFFICES stood in Market Street between a seed wholesaler's and the old jail. It had a door to the street that boasted a cat flap and one of those flip-over plastic signs that reads OPEN or CLOSED. Inside, the floorboards were bare and behind a counter sat

Jean, *The Crow*'s half-deaf receptionist and switchboard operator. As a front lobby it hardly compared to that of the *News*, Dryden's one-time Fleet Street employer, which had been manned by two jobs-worths in quasi-military uniforms, contained a fountain, and enough seating for a planeload of waiting holidaymakers.

The Crow. Established 1846. Circulation 17,000 and steady. The *News*, circulation 3.6 million and rising. Dryden breezed through the door, checked his watch at 1.30 p.m., and flipped the sign to CLOSED. Ely was still a member of that sleepy band of towns where some of the shops close for lunch. Besides, Thursday was early closing.

He took the stairs three at a time and pushed open the door at the top marked NEWSROOM. The room on the other side wouldn't have qualified as a cupboard on Fleet Street. Dryden had left the *News* after Laura's crash. *The Crow* paid the bills for his floating home and gave him plenty of time to be at Laura's bedside. The insurance company paid for The Tower, an arrangement from which they were, at present, unable to renege. Laura's accident had resulted in a media blitz and the story had taken up the front pages of the tabloids, on and off, for a month. At the time she had been one of the principal characters in the TV soap opera *Clyde Circus*. Her condition, once diagnosed, had kept the story going. Locked In Syndrome—or LIS—was news. Victims appeared to be in a deep coma but could, at times, be entirely conscious despite the lack of movement.

Dryden had met the onslaught of Fleet Street with resignation—after all, he'd been on their side for the best part of a decade. At every opportunity during interviews he'd dropped the name of the Mid-Anglian Mutual Insurance Company into the story, praising the way they had paid up instantly for Laura to be cared for at The Tower and for treatment by some of the world's leading coma experts. They had little choice but to go on footing the bills. But he knew it wouldn't last. One day soon, a polite letter would inform him that less expensive care would be appropriate. It was a corrosive anxiety.

But for now he needed only an income to pay his bills, to be near enough to visit Laura, and to have something else to fill his days other than the image of his wife laid out beneath a single sheet. The position of chief reporter on *The Crow*, offered after a month of casual shifts, had been an admirable solution to all three problems.

Dryden tried the coffee machine. It took a variety of foreign coins that *The Crow*'s staff collected on holiday. The editor, Septimus Henry Kew, always referred to this as a principal staff benefit. It was probably the only one. Thursday was press day, so by 3 p.m. the newsroom would be as full as it ever got. Three subs, the news editor, the editor and Splash the office cat. *The Crow* had two reporters— Dryden and his junior sidekick, Garry Pymoor.

Garry thudded through the front door, plodded up the stairs, and flopped into his desk. The junior reporter made sure the editor was not behind his smoked-glass partition, then lit up a cigarette. The newsroom was officially nonsmoking. He flipped open his notebook. 'What's a Fen Blow?' he asked.

'It's a dust storm. In dry weather the fields in the Black Fen can lose their topsoil. Dry peat is effectively weightless. If a strong wind hits during a period when there's no crop cover, a field can literally take off, and once airborne the dust cloud can travel for miles.'

Garry nodded. 'There's one coming. I did police calls from the magistrates' court. They said they'd got one near Manea, coming east.'

'Great. Phone Mitch. I've got a job that way—I'll keep an eye out.' Mitch was *The Crow*'s photographer. He was a miniature Scotsman with a passion for tam-o'-shanters. Fen Blows made good pics but poor stories. Unless they hit town the only damage they did was to farmers' incomes, which, even for a paper like *The Crow,* was a minority interest, given that automation and chronically low wages had taken thousands of farm workers out of the fields.

'And there was more on the Beck appeal,' added Garry. 'They've had nothing from the radio appeals. Apparently the police think the daughter is away on holiday—north Norfolk coast. So they've contacted the tourist boards, RNLI, b and bs—the lot.'

'Fine,' said Dryden. 'Knock out two paragraphs for the front page.'

'According to someone at Black Bank—one of the farm hands— she's travelling with some Yank.'

'Name?'

Garry leafed through his notebook. 'Koskinski. Lyndon. Apparently he's based at Mildenhall on temporary leave or something.'

Dryden saw again the tall pilot standing by Maggie's bed. 'Knock it out,' he said, and booted up his own PC. His phone rang.

'Hell-oo . . .' Inspector Newman's voice always sounded ten feet away from the phone. 'A bit more. The stud. His face. It's on the records. West Midlands police have picked him up. Couple of hours ago, at his flat. Few hundred videos in the spare room—Vice Squad are checking them out.'

Dryden scratched a note as Newman spoke. 'The girl?'

'Says he can't remember. Said it was all consensual. Blah, blah.'

'So he knew the cameras were running?'

'Looks like it. Not surprised to see his bum in the frame anyway.'

'Occupation?'

'Long-distance lorry driver. Surprised he had the time. And, Dryden, nothing sensational, OK? Just an appeal for information.'

'Would I?' It was one of Dryden's favourite questions. The answer was 'yes'. There was a pause on the end of the line.

'Hold on,' said Dryden, pulling up the PA wire online. Newman's extra information warranted an update.

Dryden found a second take on the rare-bird story, which had run at 1.16 p.m. 'Rare gull finds love on the beach'.

'There's an extra paragraph on your gull: "Ornithologists at Holme Nature Reserve on the north Norfolk coast made a further plea for twitchers not to descend on the remote spot after news leaked out that a rare Siberian gull had been spotted yesterday. They said that two of the birds, which normally spend the summer in Scandinavia, had now been sighted and appeared to be a breeding pair."'

'Thanks,' said Newman. 'I might go and do some crowd control.'

THE SACRED HEART of Jesus was about as spiritual as a drive-in McDonald's and twice as ugly. This was brutally apparent because that is exactly what it was built next to. The two shrines crouched against the wire perimeter fence surrounding the United States Air Force Base at RAF Mildenhall.

Dryden hardly ever went to church, but he was prepared to make an exception to keep his promise to Maggie Beck. The police appeals might not work. He needed to do something else.

Inside the church, Major August Sondheim was sitting in the front pew. August and Dryden had two meeting places: the church, or Mickey's Bar by the other public gate to the base. The church meant August was sober, which was a sacrifice of supreme proportions because August was a major league drunk. His CV, however, was decked with glittering prizes: degree from Stanford, West Point, Purple Heart in Korea, Pentagon in the Gulf War. August was head of public relations at USAF Mildenhall, with oversight of Lakenheath and Feltwell, the two other US bases on the flat expanse of Breckland.

Dryden had met August a year before when Fleet Street had got hold of a story that the US military were stockpiling nuclear weapons on the base in case they needed to be shipped quickly to war zones in

Iraq, Afghanistan or North Korea. A couple of the quality broadsheet newspapers rang Dryden and asked him to check it out. As a reporter, Dryden had always put more store in trusting his contacts than diligent research. In the long run, his copy had turned out to be more accurate that way and he delivered it quicker. And he could tell when someone told him a lie. He was pretty sure August was honest. The major might not tell him something that was true, but Dryden liked to think he would never tell him something false.

Dryden had killed the story. August said they'd had a shipment on the base for twenty-four hours and now they were clean. Dryden had charged the papers three days' money for research and surveillance. Then he had rung them and told them the base was clean. Only time, or a very nasty accident, would prove him wrong.

'Well?' said August. He was tanned with silver-grey hair swept back as though his days as a pilot had shaped his body for speed.

Dryden said: 'I need some help. A woman's dying. She wants to see her daughter. She's on a break. A holiday. But her mother's fading fast, faster than anyone thought. The daughter is called Estelle Beck and she's travelling with a family friend—a relative of some kind, I think. Lyndon Koskinski. He's a US pilot here at Mildenhall.'

August nodded, trying not to think about families. His wife had left him ten years earlier. He'd come home to their clapboard house in Georgetown to find she'd flown to Hawaii with the family accountant. She'd remembered to take two things with her, their twelve-year-old daughter and her chequebook. The girl was called April and she must be a woman now, but whenever August thought her image might pop into his mind he conjured up a glass of Bourbon instead.

Now he stood up and stretched. 'So there's a story in this, is there? Deathbed plea from dying mum—that kinda thing?'

'I guess. But she asked me to do this. There may be a story, sure. It's not the only reason I do things. I am capable of independent action. I'm bound,' said Dryden. It was an odd phrase, but he meant it. They walked to the entrance door, their shoes slapping on the cheap wooden parquet flooring.

Dryden had spotted a locked door beside a utilitarian concrete font. August looked the other way as Dryden retrieved the brass key round his neck and tried it in the lock.

'No go,' said Dryden, genuinely surprised as he always was not to have unlocked Laura's secret.

'You're mad,' said August, with envy.

2

Dryden had been turning the microfiche for several minutes before he caught sight of the black and white picture for which he had been searching. It was from the *Cambridge Evening News* of June 2, 1976. A front-page picture showed a pall of smoke shrouding a distant line of poplars, while in the foreground the tail fin of a plane stuck up from a field of wreckage. The fuselage lay twisted, melted like the cellophane from a packet of cigarettes incinerated in an ashtray. A house, clearly demolished by the impact of the aircraft, was blackened stone, with a few tortured beams exposed to the sky.

The caption was in the best traditions of stark news reporting: 'The scene yesterday of the Black Bank air disaster in which 12 died.'

Dryden looked up from the microfiche as the cathedral bell tolled four o'clock. He had decided to refresh his memory about the crash at Black Bank Farm. Maggie Beck's life had been unremarkable but for this tragedy, which had swept away her parents and her only son.

PLANE CRASH KILLS 12. The headline was set above the picture of the scene. Below it a strapline aimed at pathos: MOTHER SAVES BABY FROM FLAMES BUT SEES HER OWN SON DIE.

Dryden turned the knob on the side of the microfiche reader and the page slid down. Most of the nationals were agreed on the main facts by the second day. The coverage was objective and largely avoided criticism of the US Air Force. It was still the height of the Cold War and the US was a trusted ally. Nonetheless the facts spoke for themselves. The Met Office at Norwich had issued warnings that night that dust storms would crisscross the Fens. Light aircraft at Cambridge were grounded, but the tower at USAF Mildenhall let MH336 begin its journey on schedule.

The tabloids put the issue of blame to one side and concentrated instead on the personal tragedies of those who died. Dryden chose the *Daily Mirror* for an in-depth account, and had read it twice before he identified exactly what was tugging at his memory. On board that night was the pilot, Captain Jack Rigby, his copilot and three servicemen travelling home with their wives and children. One couple, Captain Jim Koskinski and his wife Marlene, were travelling with their two-week-old baby son, Lyndon. Marlene's father had died two days earlier in Antonio. The USAF had a transport flight booked and they owed young Jim a favour after fifty straight bombing missions over North Vietnam and Laos. The transporter had limited passenger capacity, but the USAF offered to fly the family home.

'Koskinski,' said Dryden, out loud. The librarian, a stunning redhead looked up and scowled. Dryden scowled back.

'Lyndon Koskinski,' he said, louder still. The Becks' family friend, the man now travelling with Estelle. The man he had to find.

Dryden discovered a sausage roll in his jacket pocket and munched it, remembering he'd had nothing since the ritual egg sandwich with Humph this morning, Overhead he heard the familiar rumble of a transatlantic air tanker flying into Mildenhall. The aerodrome had opened as an RAF base in 1934 but by the fifties the Americans had moved in in force, so that at the time of the Black Bank crash the base was already the US 'gateway to Europe'. Today, with 100,000 passengers a year, and billions of gallons of fuel ferried in to support US operations in the former Yugoslavia, the Mediterranean and the Near East, it was an exotic American township of nearly 7,500 people.

Dryden refocused on the microfiche. The only survivor among the air passengers had been Lyndon Koskinski, aged thirteen days. Maggie Beck had found him in the remains of the farmhouse, still secure in a travelling cradle strapped into his seat. She'd walked out of the flames with him wrapped in a USAF blanket, having seen her own child trapped, and clearly dead, in the farmhouse. She'd saved Lyndon's life, thought Dryden, and now he was here to see hers end.

The next day—June 3, 1976—the *Cambridge Evening News* had a picture of Maggie Beck coming out of the mortuary at Cherry Hinton. The caption caught the horror of the moment: 'Maggie Beck leaves the city mortuary after identifying the bodies of her parents, William and Celia Beck, and her 15-day-old son Matthew John.'

The good news came two days later. Redmond Koskinski, Snr, and his wife Gale were shown holding their grandson at a photocall at USAF Mildenhall. They had flown the Atlantic to take custody of the child. 'We have met Miss Beck and extended our thanks to her courage in saving Lyndon's life,' said Koskinski, according to the *Daily Telegraph*. They flew home with their grandson, and two coffins.

Inquests on all those killed were held the same day. *The Crow*'s reports were the most detailed but, given the cataclysmic forces involved in the disaster the verdicts—of accidental death—were a foregone conclusion. The heat of the crash had made most of the post-mortem examinations on the passengers impossible. Dental records were required for all formal IDs on the crew and passengers.

Maggie's parents were buried at the church on Black Bank Fen. It had been their last wish, according to an interview with William Beck's sister, Constance, shortly before the funeral. Matthew John, known as 'Matty', was cremated at his mother's request.

DRYDEN LOWERED the window of the Capri and let the breeze buffet his ear. It was evening but the heat of the day still made the cab stink. Hot plastic, socks and sump oil merged in an odour that Humph liked to call 'Home'. The promise Dryden had made to Maggie Beck weighed on him, but he felt he had done everything he could, short of touring the north Norfolk coast himself on the off-chance he could spot her missing daughter. In the meantime he had a job to do, which meant finding a decent story for the next edition of the *Ely Express*, *The Crow*'s downmarket tabloid sister paper.

Dryden had spent many hours that summer scanning the national papers for stories to follow up in the Fens. He'd begun to spot the pattern in early May. The odd paragraph here and there but, essentially, the same story. Police raids on lorry parks on the motorways. Illegal immigrants in small groups. Mainly sub-Saharan West African in origin. They probably crossed the Med from the North African coast to the ports of the South of France. Then north to the Channel and via container ship to Felixstowe, where they could be shipped across country by lorry. Some had got out en route for the West Midlands. At night, in roadside lay-bys, welcomed by silence and fear.

And the same promise. Jobs. Pickers in the fields. An idyllic picture, laughably misplaced. Dryden scanned the horizon. Miles of empty dry peat. Thousands of acres and not a single living thing except the wheeling birds. No pickers. Even at harvest time you couldn't see them in the fields. They shuffled along in the shade of the picking machines. Then they disappeared inside the sheds for the rest of the summer. Sorting, cleaning and packing, but always hidden.

He knew that several police forces were tracking the illegal trade. 'Operation Sardine', as it was called, had been coordinated by East Cambridgeshire and the East and West Midlands forces with help from Norfolk and Suffolk. He'd been given a briefing in Coventry at the regional crime squad's HQ by the detective leading the operation. Dryden had been on several raids, but little of substance had been found so far. So he'd started to make his own enquiries, which was why he was going to try his luck at Wilkinson's celery plant.

'Appointment's at six o'clock,' said Dryden, checking his watch.

Humph grunted and pressed the tape button on the dashboard. All the cabbie's copious spare time was devoted to taped language courses. Each Christmas he would take a holiday in the country of choice, neatly avoiding the necessity to endure the festive season alone. Greece this year, Poland last year. Only France was taboo. He and his ex-wife had gone there for their honeymoon. That was before she'd run off with the postman. Humph had seen him once, loitering outside the divorce courts in London. He'd been balding, with sloping shoulders and a paunch, and Humph's daughters had held his hands with, he judged, obvious distaste. So not France.

On the tape, Andreas, his imaginary friend from Thessaloniki, asked him the time. Humph repeated the question and answered in Greek. Then he asked Dryden a question, a rare enough occurrence in itself. 'Why Wilkinson's?'

It was a processing and packaging plant for celery, one of several small-time businesses that had sprung up on the Black Fen. They employed a silent work force several thousand strong. The big operators, like Shropshire's outside Ely, had multi-million-pound works and a work force recruited from agricultural colleges across Europe. To compete, Wilkinson's had to cut corners. That meant cheap labour and health regulations stretched to breaking point.

'Illegal immigrants,' said Dryden, reaching into his pocket and extracting two-thirds of a pork pie gently dusted with fluff.

Humph was steering with his elbows as he tore the cellophane off a diet sandwich. He loved diet sandwiches. 'Who says?'

Dryden was guessing. He'd recognised long ago that his interest in people smugglers went beyond a story. Claustrophobia was one of the things that terrified him. The thought of being entombed in a container lorry was a cliché of hell, but no less real for that.

He flipped down the sunshade as the car turned due west on the road by the Forty Foot Drain, a drove road known with affection by the locals as the Fen Motorway.

To the south a farmstead stood about a mile back from the road. The only way to get to it by car was over a private cast-iron bridge across the Forty Foot Drain. It was the kind of place he and Laura had talked about the last time they'd talked at all. Since then it had been four years of monologue. He'd talked for both of them as she lay in her coma. Sometimes he would imagine her part of the conversation, and when the messages started he would say the words out loud, trying to recall the exact inflection of her voice, the subtle combination of a Neapolitan childhood and a north London adolescence.

The last time they'd talked, really talked, they'd been on their favourite walk, along the bank-top by Little Ouse, past the old Victorian grain silos at Sedge Fen, then over the iron bridge to the north side and the wide desolation of Adventurer's Fen. It had been the day before the crash in Harrimere Drain. It was their spot, the place they'd daydream about. But there were only two houses—pathetic brick semis built for farm workers in the 1920s. Both were crisscrossed with cracks in the brickwork, the peat beneath their flimsy foundations shrinking as the new, electrical fenland pumps sucked the moisture out of the peat below.

'A house,' said Dryden. 'We should decide. Move out of London and start a family.' He'd kissed her hair but she hadn't answered.

He'd wanted to walk on, towards Adventurer's Wood, but she had pulled him back. Something was wrong. He knew it then, and he knew it now. But what? A house and a family was what they wanted but only after: after she'd done one last series of *Clyde Circus*. After he'd done one more year at the *News*. After—the word he hated most now—after Harrimere Drain.

It wasn't as if money was a barrier to fulfilling their dream. One of the many aunts from Campania, who had emigrated with Laura's parents to help run the family restaurant in north London, had left her a nest egg: £80,000. It was all they needed out on the fen. It sat in Laura's trust account, getting fatter, and it sat there still, administered by the solicitors and her parents. None of Laura's family had mentioned the bequest since shortly after the accident, an act of faith which signalled their belief that one day he and Laura would buy the house, start the family and begin again.

Humph flipped open the glove compartment and fished out two bottles of vodka. He collected miniatures on runs to Stansted Airport. He handed one to Dryden, sensing his friend was descending into a rare bout of depression.

'Cheers,' said Humph, repeating a few random phrases in Greek.

They'd reached Manea. Wilkinson's stood on the edge of the town. A triple set of mammoth MFI-style blocks with a windswept car park full of the kind of cars that spend half their life up on bricks. Most of the work force, which had to support a twenty-four-hour production line, were picked up by the company coach on bleak corners in the middle of the night. They parked underneath the Wilkinson's sign.

The staircase was steel and ran in a zigzag tower up the outside of the main block. At the top was a door with an entryphone, so he pressed the button and after ten seconds of crackle heard the lock turn. He pushed the door open and walked down a long neon-lit corridor to another door. There was a strong smell of disinfectant and his shoes stuck to the featureless cream lino.

He knocked once and walked in before anyone could stop him. A man in a shabby suit stood up from the only desk. He was a bit like a stick of celery himself. About six feet six, with white hair and narrow shoulders. 'Mr Dryden? Ashley Wilkinson. Don't think I can help you any more than I did on the phone. But do sit down.'

Behind his desk was a plate-glass window, a good ten feet long and five feet high, looking down on the shop floor. It was the celery shed. Tractors brought the crop in off the fields and dumped it down chutes at the far end from Ashley Wilkinson's office, where it tumbled onto conveyor belts. By the time it got to the other end it was cleaned, trimmed and neatly packaged. Radio One blared from a crackly tannoy system and the workers, each with a white plastic hairnet, moved with that odd combination of listlessness and physical economy born of the production line.

Dryden decided to be nice, a rare tactic in his repertoire, and invariably unsuccessful. 'I understand West Midlands police have been making enquiries. Illegal immigrants. I'm told two men have been arrested and removed to the Home Office detention centre outside Cambridge.' Dryden flicked open his notebook until he reached a page that contained a shorthand note of three tips for the weekend's race meeting at Newmarket. 'Two West Africans, I understand.'

'*Sub judice*,' said Wilkinson. 'And your information is wrong. They had papers. There's no suggestion we knew they'd come through Felixstowe. We'll check the references next time,' said Wilkinson.

Dryden noticed the disguised admission. 'Good workers?'

'Fine. Darn sight better than the locals.' Wilkinson looked down through the plate glass at his work force. 'Lazy bastards most of 'em.'

British management at its motivational best, thought Dryden.

The tannoy muzak cut out and a voice cut in: 'Mr Wilkinson to the loading bay. Mr Wilkinson to the loading bay.'

'I'll show you out.'

Dryden noted relief in his voice. He shut his notebook. 'Ever been done before for employing illegal immigrants?'

But Wilkinson was already hitting numbers on his mobile phone. Interview over.

A door led out of the back of the office onto an observation balcony, from which a stairway dropped down onto the shop floor. They made their way between the production lines, watched by every worker in the shed. For a whites-only fastness like the Fens, the work force looked like an outpost of the Notting Hill Carnival. Cheap labour, thought Dryden. But he said, 'Mind if I have a chat with one of the workers?'

Wilkinson hesitated. Dryden pushed his luck. 'I could always just hang around by the gate and catch them on the way home.'

'This is Jimmy Kabazo,' said Wilkinson, leading him over to a half-partitioned office at the side of one of the production lines. 'He's the day-shift foreman. Talk to him if you like. He'll show you out too.'

Jimmy was black. Night black. Dryden guessed he was Nigerian.

'Follow me, sir,' he said, the voice pitched high and sing-song. Jimmy was short and wiry with tight-curled hair and the kind of smile that could hide any emotion. He wore the regulation Wilkinson's white overalls with a laminated badge: FOREMAN.

Dryden told him what he'd heard about the police raid. The smile never flickered: 'Yeah. Bad news for the rest of us.'

'Police?'

Jimmy nodded, still beaming. 'They bin round, yeah. Everyone upset now. We're legal. We got the papers.'

'How d'you hear about Wilkinson's?'

'Good news travels fast.' He must have been joking, but it was difficult to tell.

They talked about life in the shed. The six o'clock start, the mindless work, the wages. 'The worst thing is the windows,' said Kabazo, meaning the lack of them. 'The summer goes, the winter comes, we don't know. We just work. Always the same.'

They shook hands. 'See you again,' said Dryden, somehow knowing he would.

Outside, Humph was asleep in the cab. Dryden leaned on the roof and ate a packet of mushrooms he'd sneaked into the glove compartment and followed that with some small but perfectly formed Scotch eggs. He chased them down with a miniature Grand Marnier.

About a mile away an HGV cut the landscape as it powered its way towards the Midlands. Dryden imagined the dark, fetid interior of the container and wondered what, or who, was on board.

DRYDEN DRANK some more on the way back to Ely while Humph, enthused by the general air of gaiety, made a spirited attempt to knock a random postman off his bike on the edge of town on the off-chance it might be his ex-wife's lover. The cabbie wound down the window as the postman's bike mounted the pavement and embedded itself in a hawthorn fence: 'Bastard!'

'It wasn't him, was it?' asked Dryden.

'Nope,' said Humph happily.

They parked at The Tower. Dryden's life was largely marked by random motion, but at the end of each day he came back to Laura. He grinned at the nurse at reception, making a half-hearted attempt to hide the effects of the alcohol, and tried not to skip to the lifts.

He walked to Laura's bed, touched her arm briefly, as he always did, and checked Maggie. She was asleep, curled in the same tortured ball as before. Then he stood over the COMPASS machine. The specialists had brought it in two months ago. It consisted of a computer PC and keyboard. On the screen was an alphabet grid.

ABCD
EFGH
IJKLMN
OPQRST
UVWXYZ

The concept was simple. A small electronic trigger was placed in Laura's hand, which she could use to navigate and highlight individual letters. Clicking on a highlighted letter printed it on a ticker tape that chugged out of the COMPASS.

The first problem was random erratic movements and mishits on the trigger. These distorted the printout record. The second problem was much bigger. Laura was not 'conscious' in any accepted understanding of the word, though she could clearly see the COMPASS screen, if only intermittently. She drifted in and out of Dryden's world to bring an occasional message; few made sense. On one level she was 'back', back from the coma that had so completely enveloped her after the crash. But her visits were swift, unannounced, and often cryptic. A long line of ticker tape lay folded in a neat concertina at Dryden's feet, ready to be deciphered.

He'd met Laura while working for the *News* on Fleet Street. Her father owned a north London Italian café, Napoli, where the regular clientele squeezed themselves down a long corridor from the café counter to a small room with six tables decked out in checked table-cloths. The food was simple but sublime: fresh figs, golden balls of mozzarella, piquant ragu, and pungent Parma ham, all washed down with the Vesuvio her father prized. One evening Dryden had found himself in the suburbs on a job, doorstepping a politician who'd had to resign over allegations of fraud. He'd sneaked into the Napoli while the police were inside the house taking a statement. Hurrying, he'd spilt the pasta course into his lap. Laura had helped him mop up the mess in an oddly erotic dance of embarrassment. Love, as Dryden liked to recall it, at first fumble. Despite Laura's long apprenticeship in food she had kept her figure, and avoided the fate of her plump aunts. While her mother helped to run the business, she had brought up three younger brothers and cooked most of their meals.

So each evening Dryden tried to fill her room with aromas of the past. It was a ritual he found deeply satisfying. Beside Laura's bed stood a bottle of the same Vesuvio, the cork drawn and replaced. On a plate he put fresh fruit, cutting the figs to let them breath. He poured out a glass of wine and set it down beside her. Then he would chat for half an hour. About his day, about Humph's planned Greek holiday, about what he'd seen in the world outside The Tower. Then he'd tear off the ticker tape, and take it out to Humph's cab.

SGDFDYFYJF FLIGHTPATI SGD PK ABI YCND

He ran his finger along it, enjoying again the thrill of deciphering this opening message. The first time she had used the COMPASS to say anything other than her name. But for the missed H at the end the single word was perfect. Flightpath. Flightpath Cottages; the now derelict houses they'd discovered together on Adventurer's Fen. A vision of where the future could be, if Laura recovered. A home, a family, and everything they'd wanted before the accident.

SHSHFT ROSA SDGDU

Rosa was her mother. He'd photocopied the ticker tape and sent it to Turin, where her parents had retired. He could only imagine the tears that had flowed. And he'd taken a copy to the family restaurant in north London, which was now run by Laura's three brothers.

Dryden's favourite was the simplest. Its straightforwardness an echo of the life they had lost.

SGDHFYU MYHAIR SHDSIDK

He had then, and he did it now, because he was lost for words. He raised her head and ran the brush back through the auburn hair, feeling the warmth of her body through the nape of the neck. He kissed her once and left.

Humph was waiting in the Capri in the midst of an Athenian street wedding. Three tiny empty bottles of ouzo were lined up on the dashboard. Humph wasn't a drunk driver, which meant they were going to be parked for a long time.

Dryden got in the cab but left the door open. Humph gave him a miniature bottle of Greek brandy and went back to the wedding. Dryden read the ticker tape and spotted the four attempts at LAURA. The ticker tape had a digital time check along one side. All four had come just after seven o'clock that night.

Then he saw it. At 8.08. A burst of nonsense with those two words. His hair stood on end despite the fact that he told himself it must be a bizarre, random chance.

PDGUT WLGHJKOR T HISKFOT HJKKDHGSI
THGYUS GHJYOU JNKOWFGH THEY
WHISPERKKJTNFMR
AEWGHCMI GKIAKA JEJUOIFK

But even as Dryden tried to dismiss it he had to ask himself: did she mean the nurses? Visitors? And what, he wondered, did they whisper about?

HE LED HER through the trees to the cast-iron door and even as the blood pumped in her ears she noticed that when he turned the key in the lock it clicked over with a barely audible, oily ease. She remembered later, on the park bench, thinking that he'd been there before. That he'd done it all before, with others. She knew that now, when it was too late.

That was the first time that night she'd felt like crying for help, and the last time she could have. She watched his body move ahead of her with a sinuous sexuality that had struck her dumb despite the fear. She'd never craved sex like that. And only now, looking back, did she understand that it was the drug that had made her blood run hot.

But before the drugs she'd seen him, she had to admit that, and called him over with her eyes. He'd breezed through the door of the Pine Tree pub that Monday night with an easy, athletic, grace. Mondays: the quietest night of the week, with a few locals and the quiz team. She was bored, and she must have radiated that, like a lighthouse seeking a ship.

She got closer, collecting the glasses, close enough to see the face. The face of a comic-book hero, her very own Action Man. Blond cropped hair and pale fingers with spotless nails. She wondered then: how could someone so beautiful, so clean, so perfect, be interested in her?

She should have known when he made the call, on his mobile, walking away from the bar. He winked then, something that normally made her laugh at men. But she just beamed, stupidly, knowing already that something wasn't right, but not caring, now she sensed that his body could be hers.

She washed the glasses, served the locals, and watched him at the end of the bar. She hated the Pine Tree, she told him, but needed it to pay the university bills.

'University?' he'd said, smiling.

'Yeah. East London. It's great,' she said.

'The heat,' he'd said, his smile confined to his red lips. 'You want a drink?'

She'd taken for a vodka and tonic and left the drink on the bar beside him as she worked, returning, sipping, feeling lots of things that should have made her run. She'd been confused then, getting the change wrong a couple of times with the locals. And she dropped a glass: 'Sack the juggler,' they'd all laughed. She felt her legs buckle but thought it was the vodka and the heat of the night.

She sipped another drink and heard her laughter, over loud, in between the CD tracks. She never really drank much, which is why she didn't taste the metallic edge that laced the vodka.

She asked Mike, the landlord, to lock up and do the ashtrays. He was a friend of her dad's from way back when they were in the army together in the Far East. But he'd been upstairs all night with his feet up in front of the telly. So he hadn't seen, hadn't sensed, as he surely would have, her disorientation.

'Date,' she whispered, and brushed a kiss across his cheek. He'd smelt it then, and kicked himself later for not stopping her. Not the vodka but something else, the drug sweating out through her skin.

The moon hung over the Pine Tree like a giant sunlamp. The car suited him, she thought, opening the silver-grey door and catching the sickly scent of the air freshener. Alfa Romeo? Perhaps, she told the police later, but she couldn't be sure.

She got into the car aware of her long legs, the tight jeans around her bum, and the tight T-shirt that tucked under her breasts.

'I know a place,' he'd said and she imagined a flat, with sophisticated lighting and a bed a mile wide.

They drove into the night. By the time they turned down The Breach she didn't care where they were. The stars seemed to be darting across the sky and she felt her heart racing. They parked and she stumbled through the ditch grass by the moonlight, laughing as he tugged her forward. And then she'd seen it for a second between the trees and she felt the grip of his fingers tearing into her wrist.

The pillbox.

Friday, June 6

3

He'd first seen the Mollies dancing by moonlight on the water's edge one evening soon after Laura's accident. He'd wandered aimlessly for hours during those first weeks, trying to throw off the depression that clung to Laura's room at The Tower.

It was past midnight when he'd come upon them first, in the water meadows beyond the town quay. The Mollies danced, laughing, and collapsed by their narrow boat to drink and smoke. He'd written stories about them for *The Crow*, but had never thought of them as embodying a way of life, a style of escape, a glimpse of freedom. A largely female band of singers and dancers, their black and white costumes reflected the darker side of rural life in the Fens. They spent winter nights preparing the muscular routines they would perform in spring and summer. To the rhythmic thud of a drum they danced, knees brought high and suspended for a beat, before descending with crack of boot on gravel or stone.

He'd sat with them that night round their fire. He'd even talked about the accident and Laura. They'd talked about the New Age, about living on the boat, about the river and its life. And he'd seen Etty's eyes in the firelight, a forthright promise he could have another life.

They danced now in front of the Cutter Inn, a sunbaked audience of shoppers and mums with pushchairs arranged in a dutiful semicircle, with the river a backdrop to the high-stepping Mollies.

Dryden raised his beer glass to Humph, parked by the riverside twenty yards away. The cabbie waved a small orange juice back. Humph had a headache. The cabbie avoided the word hangover, as if this made it impossible for him to have one, but there was no doubt his fragile state was associated with five small bottles of ouzo consumed during an imaginary celebration in Nicos's taverna.

'Mollies,' said Dryden to himself. 'The military wing of the morris men,' and drained his pint. He listened to the rhythmic thud of the drum and thought about Maggie and his promise. There had been no news from the police—he'd checked that morning—and he'd left another message for Major August Sondheim at Mildenhall air base. If there was nothing by nightfall, a tour of the north Norfolk coast in Humph's cab loomed.

In the meantime, Dryden had time to kill and a story to stand up. He had enough to run something on Wilkinson's celery plant and the people smugglers, but it needed some colourful background to bring the story alive. The Mollies were among his best contacts. By turns anarchic, naive, streetwise and mundane, they provided a vivid view of Fen life. Once he'd got the job at *The Crow*, he'd tapped into the knowledge they collected pursuing their unconventional lifestyle. Often asleep during the day, roaming at night, working out in the fields when they needed the money, they knew more about the real life beyond the town than a Panda car full of detectives.

The lead Molly, with a black hood and the hangman's noose round her neck, stood, blindly watching, as the others danced. Decked out in coloured rags with black and white painted faces they paced out metrical steps to the thud of the drum.

Mitch was taking pictures for the *Express*. 'Bunch o' dykes if you ask me,' he whispered in his bleak Glaswegian accent, missing his own Fen pun.

Something about the motionless girl with the black hood and the noose caught his eye. Even he jumped when she moved. Some kids in the crowd squealed as her dance began, threading its way between the rest of the Mollies who stood still, only their chests rising and falling as they fought to recover their breath. It was an eerie but a simple trick. The black hood, made of flimsy gauze, let the dancer see her way in the bright sun as she danced up to the crowd, right to their faces, her knees brought to waist height, before backing off.

She stopped when she got to Dryden. The drumbeat climaxed and stopped dead as she raised the noose with a jolt and let her head loll on the broken neck. Snap!

It was a finale guaranteed to kill any applause. The crowed moved away with indecent haste. The Mollies were associated in local legend with what the locals called the Water Gypsies—dropouts who lived in a line of dilapidated narrow boats on the edge of town and grew illegal substances in gaily painted decktop pots. According to whispers they indulged in pagan rituals, including naked moonlight dancing and group sex. The Water Gypsies struggled hard to live up to this reputation, but still spent more time playing Scrabble than dancing under the stars.

Dryden sipped his beer. 'Hi,' he said. The girl whipped the hood off and a bun of blonde hair dropped to her shoulders. She had several beautiful features, dominated by the hair, and the kind of brown eyes you can swim in. She was tanned by her work—crop picking— and her figure was full like Laura's. Etty, always just Etty, for all the Mollies who lived on the narrow boat, had forgotten their surnames.

'Dryden,' she said, taking a gulp from his pint. 'You got my text message then. Nothing like a throbbing pocket, is there?' She smiled, revealing too many teeth and extravagant laughter lines.

She flopped into a seat while Dryden went and got her a pint of cider from the bar. When it arrived, she downed a third of it in a single gulp.

'The people smugglers. We saw them,' she said. She eyed Dryden with thinly disguised lust. 'What's it worth?' she asked, putting her hand on Dryden's knee.

Dryden pretended not to notice. He'd been a journalist long enough never to show interest when a good story surfaced. It simply upped the price, even if it was being measured in pints of cider.

'Last Friday night. We were out in the van,' said Etty, filling the silence.

Etty and the rest of the crew from the *Middle Earth*, one of the narrow boats, ran a VW caravanette. It had curtains, which, considering what went on inside it, was a blessing for everyone.

'There were two lorries parked in the lay-by on the A14 where the tea bar is. They let some men out of one of them. They were black.'

'Time?'

She jiggled her empty glass. Dryden completed another bar run, aware as always with Etty that the more they drank the lower his defences fell. But for Humph's brooding presence, they were defences that might well have been breached some time ago.

Refilled, she took a glug. 'One o'clock. The tea bar was closed, but that creepy bloke was there who's usually behind the counter. It looked like a drop. There were other people to meet the lorry, a group of them—all black, 'cept one. The driver was a white guy. Shaved head, really mean-looking. We buggered off in the van.'

'Were they putting them back in the lorry?'

Etty nodded. 'Last thing we saw they were all back on except a group of them—half a dozen maybe. They went off overland. East from the lay-by, across Black Bank Fen. Like a chain gang.'

THE PHONE WAS BLACK, Bakelite, and bang in the middle of the newsdesk. When it rang everyone jumped. Luckily it rang very rarely. It had been installed nearly fifty years earlier by Sextus Henry Kew, the present editor's father, then sole proprietor of *The Crow*. It had no dial, and its twin sat on a shelf on the public side of the counter below. When Dryden first arrived, a small metal label sat beneath the phone marked 'Complaints'. He had snipped the wire one evening after a drinking bout with Humph, and then stolen the label, which had then reappeared in Dryden's boat, neatly screwed to the panel above the toilet roll in the loo.

The editor had spotted the fault within a week. Thereafter Septimus Henry Kew would pick up the receiver, every Friday, and check the dialling tone as he opened up the office. Dryden had suggested that mice were gnawing through the cable. Henry sent Garry Pymoor out for a trap and called an electrician. 'The readers,' said Henry, recalling an aphorism of his father's, 'must be heard.'

When the black phone rang, it was every man for himself.

It rang.

Garry, confidence buoyed by his Friday lunchtime diet of four pints of pale ale, picked up his own phone immediately and dialled an imaginary outside number, leaning back in his seat and closing his eyes as if steeling himself for a particularly difficult interview. Charlie Bracken, the news editor, had his coat on in seconds and was heading for the stairs. 'Ciggies,' he said, patting a pocket.

The phone rang again. Dryden failed to move, befuddled by the effects of a liquid lunch of his own at the Cutter. It rang again. If it rang four times Henry would be out of his office. Dryden, who liked nothing but a quiet life, walked over and picked up the receiver.

'Hi. Newsroom. Philip Dryden speaking.' He always hit a confident tone. That way he had plenty of room for what was, inevitably, an occasion for abject apology.

'Hello now. I didnae think this thing would actually work,' said a voice dipped daily in nicotine. 'The name's Sutton. Bob. It's no' really a complaint about yon paper. It's the polis I'm after complaining about.'

'I'll be right down,' said Dryden, who loved nothing better than landing a well-judged boot into the idle body of the local constabulary. He clattered down the newsroom steps with enthusiasm. Bob Sutton turned out to be human incarnation of the Tate & Lyle sugar man: a cube of muscle with arms and legs hung from the corners of a barrel chest. He wore a cheap security man's jacket in black. He was in his forties, with sandy thinning hair and an accent that Dryden guessed originated somewhere on the Clyde. He would have looked menacing if he hadn't clearly spent most of the last twenty-four hours crying. He rubbed butcher's fingers into reddened eye sockets.

'It's my dau'ta. Alice. She's gone missing. I've had the police round. Bloody useless, man. They seem to think she's run off. It's crazy. She'd not go with a fella like that. She's a good girl,' he added, taking a cigarette from behind his ear and gripping it between his teeth.

Dryden reflected that it was every father's lament, that his own daughter could not fail but be a grown-up extrapolation of an innocent five-year-old. But he took a note. Alice, aged twenty-one, had last been seen leaving her job as a barmaid at the Pine Tree pub, three miles west of Ely, five days ago shortly after closing time. The landlord had told her father and the police that she had spent most of the evening chatting with a young man in a white T-shirt, jeans, and a pair of wraparound reflective sunglasses that were held in his short blond hair. He had described the man as perhaps late twenties, with an athletic build and a confident manner. The landlord's wife, who had seen him briefly, said he looked like a male model.

Later, said the landlord, Alice had asked to go early, explaining that she had a date. He'd watched her getting into a silver sports car beside the Pine Tree. She'd been seen sitting in the front with the bloke: kissing, he said, trying to find euphemisms for what he'd seen.

'He chatted her up,' said Bob Sutton. 'No way she'd just be going after someone. It was him that made the first move—no question.' He produced a box of matches and moved to light the cigarette. Dryden pointed timidly at the 'No Smoking' sign. Sutton glowered.

'Done it before?' asked Dryden, judging the moment badly.

'Never,' said Sutton, thumping a fist on the counter, which jumped on the rebound. 'Can you do owt?'

Dryden shrugged. Missing girls were two a penny. He could do something for the *Express*, but that didn't publish for four days. And a freelance paragraph on the missing girl would sell nowhere on Fleet Street. Alice was probably having the time of her life with her dream man, either that or he'd dumped her and she was making her way home, pausing only to delay the inevitable humiliation.

Sutton searched his jacket pockets and flipped a portrait-sized snapshot over the counter.

Dryden felt the hairs rise on his neck. The last time he'd seen those eyes they'd been glazed and staring out of one of Inspector Newman's X-rated snaps. It was the girl in the pillbox, but this version was quite different: college scarf, excited smile, and the sheepish grin that said: 'Daddy's Girl'.

He calculated rapidly and decided Inspector Newman needed to hear first. 'I can try to find her, Mr Sutton. Perhaps use the pic? Would that be OK?'

'Sure, laddie. You do that. Anything comes up ring me.'

The card said: *Bob Sutton. Head of Security. The Smeeth, Wisbech.*

Sutton paused in the doorway. 'Meanwhile, I'm lookin' too.'

Dryden wondered what Bob Sutton would do if he knew that the place to start looking for innocent Alice was under the counter at the local back-street video shop.

HUMPH SWUNG the Capri through the gates of The Tower and grinned as the tyres screeched on the loose chippings. Dryden gave him a long-suffering look. 'Do you have to do that every time?'

They parked where they always parked, beneath a monkey-puzzle tree. Dryden eyed the forecourt of the hospital. Most nights he delayed his visit by sitting on a wrought-iron bench on the edge of the lawn. Tonight there was someone there already.

Humph slipped his tape into the deck. The imaginary Greek village was celebrating: a new taverna was opening and Nicos was looking forward to the food. '*Methedes*,' said Humph, spraying the dashboard with a light raincloud of spit.

Dryden pushed open the door. He was almost past the bench when the man on it spoke. 'Philip Dryden?' The man stood up, stepping into the pool of neon light shed by The Tower's foyer. It was Lyndon Koskinski. Dryden felt a surge of relief that he'd managed, at least in part, to fulfil Maggie's wishes.

Koskinski brushed down the creases on his uniform, that of a major in the US Air Force. He radiated a shy intelligence and a civilised reserve that made Dryden wary.

'Hi,' said Dryden, walking back.

The pilot's face was handsome in the light, spare of flesh and still with a desert tan. He was bare-headed with his forage cap folded and held under one epaulette. The hair was brown-blond and longer than military regulations normally allowed; the eyes were hooded and held a permanent squint. Dryden felt himself in the presence of a personality that radiated an almost tangible sense of calm and self-possession. But the air of complete physical control was undermined by his hands, which fluttered awkwardly at his pockets.

'Hi, Lyndon,' said Dryden, the tone light. They shook hands.

'Major Sondheim got the message to me. About Maggie. We're both back. Estelle's up in the room.'

Dryden saw again the newspaper picture of the baby saved from the crash at Black Bank being held up by his grandparents for the *Evening News*'s photographer. He'd be twenty-seven now. The only survivor, with Maggie Beck, of the 1976 air crash.

Koskinski looked up at the half-moon Victorian window. 'I phoned the base to see if I could get my treatment in the UK extended. The medics said Major Sondheim had left a message. So we came back.'

Nobody seemed to be in a hurry to go up to Maggie's bedside. Dryden sat down. 'I was reading, yesterday, about the crash. The crash in '76. She saved your life, that night. Bringing you out of the fire.'

Lyndon, not answering, took out a Zippo lighter; standard issue for GIs since Vietnam. This one was worn to a golden sheen by years of use. Koskinski flicked the top up, sparked it. Dryden noted a pronounced shake in the pilot's hand.

'This was Dad's,' said Koskinski, gazing into the flame.

'They found it?' said Dryden. 'At Black Bank?'

Koskinski shook his head: 'They didn't find anything at Black Bank. Not even a body. The coffin just carried his medals and a dress uniform. Grandpa told me that, later, I never forgave him. No, their luggage went separately from the air convoy. Clothes, some furniture, stuff from 'Nam. This was in a trouser pocket. Not much else.'

'What happened to you?' Dryden was pleased with the ambiguity of this question.

'Nerves got shot,' he said, examining the shaking hands.

Dryden nodded and let him fill the silence. 'I spent some time in Al Rasheid. Baghdad Hilton. The war. Four weeks in a cell.'

'Solitary?' asked Dryden, imagining it would be better if it was.

Lyndon shook his head. 'Nah. I was with Freeman, Freeman White. We came down together—engine failure. Freeman was bad. But we stayed together.'

'Where's Freeman?'

'Mildenhall. Medical treatment like me, then home, I guess. Ejector seat made a mess of his head.'

Dryden winced. 'You kept in touch with Maggie Beck. It's been nearly thirty years.'

'*She* kept in touch. She lost her kid. It must've hurt plenty. I guess I'm a consolation. I don't have to do anything. I just seem to help.'

'Why now?' said Dryden, relaxing visibly, trying to put his interviewee at ease. 'Why visit now? Did you know Maggie was ill?'

'No. They knew at home but, I guess, they felt—my folks—I had enough to deal with. I was just going home. To Austin, to Texas.'

'Folks?'

'My grandparents. They brought me up after the crash. We've talked about Maggie and they think I should stay too, hang around while she needs me. We all owe her. I was flying back to the States but they've got the medical teams here. I had some treatment to wait for—that's when I ran out to Black Bank. I didn't plan to. It just kinda happened. I'd never been. Weird.' He shook his head.

'Why weird?'

'Coming back through Mildenhall like that. Just like Dad did in '76. I'm glad. I'm glad I'm here.' He smiled again, and Dryden sensed a real joy, even excitement.

Lyndon flicked the lighter again, then pocketed it and looked at his watch. 'We'd better go. She's out cold but the doc said I should be there when she comes out of it. If she comes out of it.'

'We,' said Dryden, standing up reluctantly. 'Why we?'

'She asked. She asked both of us—Estelle and me—to make sure you were here too. She's got something to say—to all of us.'

A CURTAIN HAD been drawn round Maggie's bed. Lyndon slipped inside while Dryden sat beside Laura's bed, holding her hand with a pulsing grip, watching the shadow-show. Spasmodically a brief flame flared, seen through the gauzy material of the mobile screen.

Dryden looked into Laura's eyes. Did she know what was happening? 'They've come,' he said, gripping the fingers still harder. 'August found them. Trust August. She'll be fine now.'

One of the shadows stood and parted the curtain. Lyndon Koskinski stood over Laura's bed. 'I've wondered, you know, about her,' he said. 'When we've been visiting, we've often sat here, talking, and thought about her. I'm sorry.'

Dryden, confused by kindness, shrugged. 'She's getting better. That's what they say, anyway.'

'Maggie wants you now,' said Lyndon simply, turning back towards the screen. Dryden stood up, feeling uneasy, aware he was about to be asked to play some role other than sceptical observer.

Estelle Beck sat at her mother's bedside. Her slim, athletic body squeezed into a pair of stone-washed jeans and a white T-shirt. Her hair was a trendy blond bob cut asymmetrically. The bedside lamp showed a face younger than her twenty-five years. The unmarked, olive skin held a bloom in both cheeks: the eyes a sensational lichen-green. She could have been looking out of a sixth-form end-of-term picture. Dryden had met her at visiting time, and once out at Black Bank. Maggie had told Dryden her daughter was a teacher, in a primary school out on the Fens. Barrowby Drove.

She smiled now, seeing him. 'Hi. Thanks for everything. I feel so guilty we were away . . .' Her hand sought out her mother's on the counterpane.

Estelle leaned forwards and stretched out a hand towards Maggie's face. Her mother's eyes opened slowly and she raised her head from the pillows with surprising force.

'Estelle?' Maggie said, taking her daughter's hand. She smiled.

'I'm here,' said Estelle. 'And Lyndon. And Dryden, as you asked.'

Dryden felt uncomfortable, like an interloper.

Lyndon crouched down beside Estelle and the three held hands together. Maggie's other hand covered her mouth, afraid perhaps to tell a secret she had vowed to keep. Suddenly exhausted, she slumped back and let her hand fall, the eyes closing and rolling back. Lyndon stood up, retreating to the shadows. In the long silence that followed he retrieved the lighter from his pocket and sat, rhythmically flicking the flame on and off. On and off.

They all jumped at Maggie's voice, suddenly loud in the hushed space around the deathbed. Her eyes remained closed and still but the tendons in her neck flexed visibly with the effort of speech. 'I lied,' she said, and Dryden was astonished to see tears running in a beaded stream from one eye.

They waited. Maggie's eyes opened again, but this time she saw nobody, at least nobody there. 'Dryden. My witness. I lied.' She raised a hand. 'Lyndon?'

He came forwards from the shadows and folded long tanned fingers around hers. 'We all lie,' he said, and Dryden noticed a glance of complicity with Estelle.

'I'm sorry, Lyndon,' Maggie said. 'It was your life. I stole your life and ended it. Matty didn't die, Lyndon. He's never died. I lied. I lied to the coroner. To the police. To . . .' She fought for breath and Lyndon made to get help. 'No. Please stay. This is all I have left to do. I lied to give you a different life. You're Matty . . . You're my son . . .'

There was silence as Lyndon knelt again at the bedside. Estelle sank back into the shadows, regrouping as the fixed points of her life were scattered by a single confession. She had a brother now, not a yard away, while she'd been putting flowers on the grave of a stranger for twenty years. And Lyndon? He'd gained a mother, on her deathbed, and lost a father he'd loved as a hero.

Maggie struggled to say more. She turned to Estelle and offered a hand. Dryden watched her daughter's arm rise up, as if from under water, to clasp the fingers. And Dryden saw fear in Maggie's eyes. The whites of her eyes were oddly vibrant in a dying face as she scanned their circled faces, pleading, searching. She had more to say, more she had to say, but she couldn't say it. Like a scream for help in a nightmare, the sound wouldn't come. Estelle kissed her mother's head and held her tight. But still there were no words.

Lyndon went for the doctor and a nurse gave Maggie morphine.

'She'll sleep now,' said the nurse, so they all went outside to take in lungfuls of cool air. Then Lyndon and Estelle went back and sat by the bedside again. But when Maggie spoke it was only with the echo of a whisper, so they didn't hear. There were just two words, spoken as she died that morning at 3.30 a.m.

'The tapes,' she said.

DAWN GREYED the hospital's Gothic tower as two orderlies carried Maggie Beck's body out of the foyer on a sealed stretcher. Dryden got out of the cab and stood, shivering, as the ambulance crept past.

Lyndon Koskinski walked behind it to the gates and then stood watching it until the curve in the road took it finally out of sight. They were twenty feet apart but in the stillness of dawn they could almost whisper.

'I'm sorry,' said Dryden.

Koskinski's shoulders sloped and his hands fluttered to his face, pushing back hair and rubbing eyes. 'She should have told us. Before. She should have told us,' he said, walking closer.

'It was her secret.'

'It was my secret,' said Koskinski, his voice suddenly angry. 'She should have told me. At least. What can I do now?' he asked.

'Look after Estelle,' said Dryden.

He laughed then, the sound of a cynical lover rather than a grieving son, and Dryden's skin crept.

Koskinski pulled a letter from his pocket. 'Maggie left this for you. I must go back,' he said, looking up at Laura's room with dread.

Dryden took the letter. 'Can I do anything?' he said.

Koskinski laughed again. 'No one can do anything. Believe me.'

Dryden sat on the iron bench and opened the letter. It was in Maggie's elegant copperplate.

My dear Philip,

When you read this I shall be dead, a thought which I'm forced to admit is not entirely repugnant to me. I have made a dreadful mess of things, as you must now know.

There were many things I wanted to say in person before I died to the people whose lives I have disfigured. I am conscious that I have done many wrongs, to many people. I have tried to deal with each. I have discharged my two secrets. They have weighed me down, Philip, and I shall be glad to be free of them.

This letter concerns Lyndon's father. I am talking about his natural father. I know that this man, who I once loved, has never been far away. I have not seen him since 1976. Indeed I have made sure of that. But I have watched his life, at first with some satisfaction, later with misgivings and a growing sense of my own guilt.

At first his identity was well known, at least within the family, although I doubt if they ever uttered his name after Matty was born. I certainly never did. We expunged him from history. I will not name him here, but for more complex reasons than shame and anger. I feel now that he deserves his anonymity if he wishes to keep it. He is a victim too. The only person who can rightly name him is himself.

Whatever his faults, and believe me they were grievous, I have robbed this man of his son. I want to give him a chance to recover some of the life he could have had if I had not done what I did. I admit, freely, that I do this more for Lyndon than his father. But never mind. Both will benefit.

Philip, I want you to do something for me. I want you to tell my story. Tell everyone I lied. That Matty did not die in the air-crash at Black Bank. I believe his father will come forward. He loved Matty and I know that, if it was as strong as mine, this love will have endured and even deepened over the years. So I want you to say, Philip, in the newspaper, that if he comes forward he will be eligible for a portion of my estate. In many ways I cheated him out of it in 1976. I have set aside the sum of £5,000 for him alone. It is not much, but in his present circumstances I think it is enough. The solicitors dealing with my will—Gillies & Wright—are in a position to confirm his identity. They will hand over the money only in the presence of my son, and only in person.

I know these requests are onerous and may seem baffling to you, but please carry them out without change or delay. I would wish the story you write to appear after my funeral.

And one final request. The memorial stone marking the site of the 1976 crash carries Matty's name. I have no wish for it to be removed, but please see to it that Lyndon Koskinski's is added. My solicitors will find the sum of £100 in my will to cover the costs of the stonemason. I shall lie in the same graveyard as that child, who I wronged so completely.

Your loving friend, who will always be in your debt.
Margaret Alexandra Beck

OUTSIDE TWENTY-NINE Wissey Way, Humph parked by his own front gate and, flipping open the glove compartment of the cab, exhibited no desire to travel the last three yards to his own front door.

Dryden was equally overcome by the need to go nowhere. Humph passed him a bottle of Bell's whisky and then switched off the interior light. He tried to weigh up whether Dryden's silence was due to Maggie Beck's death, but as he was silent most nights it was a difficult call. 'Nice old girl then,' he said eventually.

'Yeah,' said Dryden, swigging the tiny bottle and accepting a refill. He shrugged as if it didn't matter. He told Humph about Maggie's confession. 'But there was more I think, something else . . . '

'Perhaps it's on the tapes,' said Humph.

'The tapes,' said Dryden. 'I guess they're Estelle's. Yes. You're right. It must be on the tapes.'

He stretched out his legs and took out the letter, handing it to Humph. Then he took out that night's section of ticker tape torn off the COMPASS machine. He read the first take and passed it over, wordlessly, to the cabbie.

DHFVIUROIF SUFJJ SUFT DKJOO JJ INDIGA FGJGF SHFDUTH ABABYGHTUKDN FHGFHFO SHOSJ

Dryden searched in his jacket pocket for the chocolate bar he had bought earlier that day.

Humph squirmed in his seat. 'A baby?'

'Maggie said she swapped the kids on the night of the Black Bank air crash. The one that survived—the Yank pilot—is her son.'

'Jesus!' said Humph, actually turning in his seat. 'How does Laura know?'

Dryden considered this: 'I guess she heard Maggie using the tape recorder. If that's the baby Laura means.'

THE LAST TORCH *had faded three hours ago and Emmanuel had wanted to cry then. Others did. He heard them when the lorry stopped and killed its engines. But the fear had shut them up.*

No one talked now. The blackness was total. But that wasn't why they were afraid. They were afraid because of the heat, and the way it seemed to be stealing away the oxygen they craved. Emmanuel's chest hurt as he breathed, and he had to suck the air just to stop the screaming pain in his lungs. He pressed his forehead against the coolness of the metal walls and he tried to do what his father always said: 'Emmy. Act your age.'

Sixteen. He was proud of that. A man at last in the village. Just in time to leave. He felt the self-pity well up as he thought about home: his touchstone. Almost thirty-one days now, counted out and marked up in his diary. He'd written down what he'd missed most; the way the dogs barked at night and the cool, overwhelming presence of the great river. Their lives depended on the river because his grandfather's boat meant they could all eat. He ferried the foreigners to the mine and back. But it hadn't been enough. First his father had left and sent money. Now he too must send money home.

He reached out a hand and touched an arm. It jerked away. None of them were friends now. He felt the indignation swell into tears. They were supposed to look after him. There was Kunte, Josh and Abraham from the village. His guardians, his grandfather had said, in front of everyone. The village would never forget what had hap-pened to Emmy, but then he thought they might never know. Could that really happen? Could he die and no one would know?

He'd seen England for the first time that day, sometime before dawn in a lay-by on a busy road. In the lay-by the driver's torch beam blinded them. A few had been let out, but something was wrong.

'There's no choice,' the driver said, pushing most of the men back inside and crashing the tailgate back down. They'd driven on and then Emmy had heard the sound of gates opening. Then silence. The driver got out and a car started up. Then nothing.

The night had gone. Emmanuel knew. Now the sun was rising. Just beyond the thin aluminium curtain that kept him from the air.

He wasn't the first to panic. Even in the dark he knew it was Abraham: he'd known him all his life. He heard his fists hit the walls. Then everyone moved. Blindly in the dark. And Emmanuel felt the pain across his chest, and as he panicked too he knew, with the true insight of the living nightmare, that this was the beginning of the end.

Monday, June 16: Ten Days Later

4

Aboard *PK 129* Philip Dryden had not slept. That was the lie he lived with: the truth was that he had slept, but could not face the nightmares that proved he had. He went up on deck with a mug of coffee to watch the sunrise. When he'd bought *PK 129,* shortly after their accident, it was chiefly for the unspeakable romance of the small teak plaque in the wheelhouse that read: DUNKIRK: 1940.

Dryden liked his floating home: it combined permanence with mobility and a pleasing sense of the temporary. If he ever got bored with the view he could just pay for a new mooring. She was a steel-built inshore naval patrol boat for which Dryden had paid £16,000.

He made a fresh batch of coffee in the galley. Through the porthole he spotted Humph's Ford Capri parked at Barham's Farm. He laughed out loud at Humph's biggest joke: the only cabbie in Britain with a two-door taxi; a triumph of indifference over reality.

Dryden checked his watch: 8.10 a.m. He'd arranged to get to Black Bank early. The call had been difficult. They were busy, said Estelle Beck, arranging for the next day's funeral. He sensed animosity in her voice, even fear. Getting up early suited him. It was press day for the *Express* and he wanted to run Maggie Beck's deathbed confession and the plea for Matty's father to come forward. He was happy to follow Maggie's stipulation that his story should run after the funeral—but he still needed an interview, and a family picture, to make sure it got the space it deserved.

'Have you listened to the tapes?' he'd asked Estelle.

'At nine then,' she said, by way of reply. 'At Black Bank.'

Dryden knocked on the cab bonnet and held up the cup of coffee. Peace offering. Normally Humph's working hours began at 9 a.m.

Humph was chatting to Nicos again about the village olive festival. Reluctantly he sipped the coffee. 'No egg?'

'No egg,' said Dryden. 'Full English at the Bridge after the interview.' The Bridge was a greasy spoon in town that specialised in fried everything on fried bread. For Humph they did a drive-in-service complete with an improvised in-cab food tray.

Humph wiggled in his seat by way of indicating mounting excitement at the prospect of such a feast. They pulled out into the busy A10, already nose-to-tail with sleepy drivers heading for Cambridge, seventeen miles to the south.

Dryden flipped down the vanity mirror on the passenger side and looked himself in the face. He was fingering the sallow skin beneath his eyes when he saw the motorbike in the rearview mirror. The bike was black, with cow-horn handlebars. The rider was in oxblood-red leathers with a matching helmet and a black tinted visor. A flag flew from the aerial, which Dryden failed to recognise. A white star on a blue background took up one-third, the others were red and white.

'Easy Rider's a bit close,' said Dryden.

Humph made a point of never consulting his rearview mirror. It was angled to provide a squint view of his own face. He felt too much information was confusing and a curse of modern life.

The motorbike trailed them at varying distances along the A10. Dryden guessed from the size of the air ducts to the front of the engine cowling that it was a 2,000cc at least. 'Why the hell doesn't he just breeze past?' he asked.

But then Humph swung the cab off the main road and onto a drove. Originally cattle tracks, the network of drove roads provided the Fens with a latticework of short cuts and dead ends that did not exist on any map. Dryden skewed round in his seat but couldn't see the biker.

The road to Black Bank was the loneliest road Dryden knew in a landscape disfigured by solitude. It ran for seven straight miles through the fen. The drought had killed the crops and the soil had been left to the sun. Even a light breeze raised clouds of red dust. As Humph's cab bumped along the drove it left in its wake a series of miniature crimson whirlwinds.

A mile into the fen Dryden saw the tail fins of the transatlantic fuel tankers parked on the apron of the main runway at Mildenhall US Air Base. It must have been six miles away but airport flotsam littered the landscape. Nissen huts from the war held hay and sugar beet, and just short of Black Bank they saw their first Stars and Stripes flying from a bungalow. And the Mildenhall Stadium. A dog track boasting US fast-food outlets, a bar with draught Schlitz, and popcorn stalls. Six days a week it was deserted, but its car park was big enough to take an incoming B-52 bomber.

Black Bank Farm stood on a plain of fen peat that stretched to the edge of sight. Some of the farm's façade had survived the aircrash that had killed Maggie Beck's family, but the stone had been burnt carbon black. Foursquare, with a central doorway and Georgian windows, it faced south across a kitchen garden. A new kitchen block stood to the west, an unadorned example of seventies utility, and beyond that a large steel-framed barn. A line of poplars grew in a natural shield at the rear of the house, protecting it against the north winds.

Humph pulled up short of a cattle grid by a sign: BLACK BANK FARM LTD: SALAD CROPS.

'I'll walk from here,' said Dryden, throwing open his door.

Inside the gate was a granite memorial stone listing the victims of the 1976 crash: the three UK civilians first, then the nine US citizens.

WILLIAM VINCENT BECK
MARY MAUD BECK
MATTHEW 'MATTY' BECK

CAPT. JACK RIGBY
MAJOR WILLIAM H. HOROWITZ
MAJOR JIM KOSKINSKI
MARLENE MARY-JANE KOSKINSKI
CAPT. MILO FEUKSWANGER
LT. RENE FEUKSWANGER
AIRMAN JOHN DWIGHT MURPHY
KYLIE PATRICIA MURPHY
JOHN MURPHY, JNR.

IN MEMORIAM, it said simply, followed by the date.

Dryden walked on to the front door of Black Bank Farm and knocked, praying it wouldn't open.

But it did. Estelle Beck leant against the jamb in US combat fatigues. Her T-shirt carried a single Stars and Stripes across her bust.

She held a large Alsatian by the collar while eating a tomato.

'He won't hurt you,' she said, with a smile that never touched the lichen-green eyes. She looked as if she hadn't slept for a week. Her knuckles were white as she gripped the dog's collar.

'Then I won't hurt him,' said Dryden. 'What's he called?'

'Texas,' she said, a laugh dying in her throat.

Pitch, thought Dryden. The difficult bit. He took a half-step backwards. 'Maggie asked me to be a witness for a reason. She wants me to find Lyndon's father. I sent you a copy of the letter?'

She nodded. He looked beyond her to the dark interior of the house and saw a foot poised on the staircase. A trainer, Nike, new and still shop-white below a pair of jogging pants.

'It's what she wanted,' he said. Experience told him that if he had to say anything more she wouldn't let him in.

Estelle dropped the dog's collar and it padded nonchalantly past. In the darkness beyond her Dryden saw a lighter flare, then snap out.

'Come in. It's a mess.'

He met Lyndon in the hall. He was putting a large bottle of mineral water into a rucksack. He didn't have to explain why he was there. He was home, but he didn't look like he was staying. Lyndon twisted a basketball in his slender hands. 'Excuse me,' he said to Dryden, and fled into the shadows of the house.

Estelle turned right into the front room. An upright piano supported a clutch of family photos, a mockery of the truth they now knew. The newest showed Maggie in bed at The Tower with Lyndon on one side and Estelle on the other.

Dryden picked it up. 'Could I borrow it? We'll need a picture.'

Estelle shrugged. Dryden thudded down into an armchair. 'I'll keep it short.' Like most of the phrases he loved, it meant nothing.

Estelle sat at the dining-room table sorting through some papers.

'So. Where to start?' said Dryden. Clearly she didn't know. There was a long silence while somewhere music played. Folk.

'You were born after the crash?'

'In 1978. Two years,' she said. Dryden sensed she wanted to go on but was diverted by a greater truth.

'And your father . . .?' He knew much of the story himself, largely retold by his mother. But Fen gossip had clouded the detail.

'Donald. Donald McGuire. Mum went back to the Beck family name after Dad died. They married in 1976. A few months after the crash. He was much older. She talks about it on the tapes—we've been listening together. It's such a help, hearing her voice. Thank you—it was your idea, wasn't it? It must have done Mum so much good in those final months, to talk about her life. She felt very guilty about what she did but she had a very noble life in a way. Steadfast. That's the word Lyndon uses. It's painful—very painful for him.

'We left the tape recorder in Laura's room. We've cleared out the rest of her stuff—but we thought you should have it back.' She shuffled some of the papers on the table. 'I don't think she ever regretted marrying Dad. But I got the feeling she did it to get away from here, from the memory. I think she fell in love with the idea of a new life. Away from Black Bank. He had a farm on Thetford Chase—Forest Farm. Mum moved there and that's where I was born. He died in 1982. We sold the farm. There'd been a manager here and it had made money. Black Gold, Mum called it, the peat . . . you can grow anything ten times a year. Mum wanted to come back.' She looked out over the kitchen garden. 'God knows why.'

From somewhere to the rear of the farmhouse came the rhythmic thudding of a basketball hitting a wall. Dryden heaved a sigh and decided it was time to ask the only question that really mattered: 'Any idea why she gave her son away?'

Estelle rose. 'Drink?' He followed her into the kitchen. By the door a notice board held snapshots covered by a clear plastic sheet. Most were of Lyndon, from the naked baby in the paddling pool with the sunburnt arms to the proud airman by his warplane on a windswept New Mexico airstrip. In several of the shots a grey-haired couple in expensive leisure clothes hovered in the background.

Estelle offered Dryden black coffee from a filter machine, while she got herself a Pepsi from the fridge. She studied the pictures.

'Mum always made a point of keeping in touch. She'd not met Lyndon since the crash until this summer. There was a real spark—I guess now we know why,' she said.

Dryden sipped the coffee and said, 'Jealous?'

She laughed. 'Of Lyndon! No way. It was dead exciting. An American cousin. And the family—the grandparents—sent presents. Toys and stuff. Clothes. It was great. He couldn't be a threat—he was an ocean away. And it gave me an identity at school—the American kid. Least I wasn't the Fen kid like the rest. That counts. No, I never resented Lyndon.'

'And then he just turned up?'

'He knew Mum was ill. We'd written. I'd even telephoned—we always did at Christmas. But he was in Iraq and then he got shot down and we didn't hear until the Koskinskis—the grandparents— sent Mum a letter. About Al Rasheid—the prison. Some US personnel were taken there—for interrogation. But Lyndon had nothing to tell them, so they let him rot. That was how lucky he was.'

She turned her back on the kitchen table, put her palms down flat on the top and jumped up to perch on the edge. 'I'd never seen her cry like that. When she got the letter. She wept for days. I guess he'd died twice for her. It must have turned her inside out—and nobody to tell.'

They heard the unmistakable sound of a limousine creeping sedately over gravel. Estelle grabbed at her throat. 'It's the undertakers. They want to run through the details.' She looked at the rear of the house with something which looked closer to fear than anxiety.

Dryden made for the back door: 'I can tell Lyndon,' he said.

Relief flooded over her. 'Thanks. We should both see them. She's his mother too.'

LYNDON LOPED across the farmyard and thrust the basketball with surprising force at Dryden's midriff. He pushed his black wraparound pilot's glasses up into his hair and leaned against the bar wall with the grace of a natural athlete. He flashed a smile that was a testament to the efficiency of Texan dentistry and an affluent childhood.

'This must have been a difficult time,' said Dryden.

'Difficult? Hell, no. I've just found out that the life I had was someone else's, and that my life never got lived. I've visited my own graveside. Confused? Cheated? Pissed angry? You said it.'

He grabbed the ball and shot at the hoop, twanging the metal and sending the ball on a zigzag course round the farmyard until it rolled into one of the sheds.

'What sort of life was it—Lyndon's?' asked Dryden.

The US ace pilot walked towards him with the hint of a military swagger and slipped the glasses down again, cloaking his eyes. 'Great. Texas. The big country. I'm always near folks here. Kinda gets ya. It looks like a wilderness but it ain't.'

Dryden shrugged. 'There are places. Go north. The fen gets deeper.

You can lose yourself there. Adventurer's Fen. That was . . . is our place.'

'Yeah?' said Lyndon.

Dryden got back to Lyndon's past. 'So the life you had. In the States—there was money?' he asked.

'Yeah. Loads. Pa Koskinski was US Navy. Big shot. Pentagon. We had three cars, a pool, tennis court. A maid, a gardener, and an air-conditioning system big enough to cool an English county.'

'Happy childhood?' tried Dryden.

Lyndon squatted down on his haunches in the dust. He took out the Zippo lighter from his trouser pocket, flicked it open and lit it once, before holding the cool chrome case to his forehead.

'You can't miss what you don't know—that's what they say here, yeah? Well, I missed 'em. I thought they died here,' he said. 'Mum and Dad. Jim and Marlene. I know their faces better than I know my own. But they're always the same age. Twenty-seven years ago, right here. But guess what—they're total strangers. I might as well have your picture in my wallet.'

'Maggie had kept in touch?' asked Dryden, sensing a tailspin into depression.

'Yeah. Christmas, birthdays, pictures of Estelle, that kind of thing. I think my grandparents were grateful and they felt some compassion for her. They felt . . . implicated in some way.'

'But this visit. This was the first time you'd met your mother?'

He nodded.

Dryden should have thought longer about the next question. 'And your sister?'

'Half-sister,' he said, too quickly. 'Different dads.'

'You know about Maggie's letter? About your father?'

He nodded. 'Sure. Means nothing. Nothing means nothing. Brother, sister, father, mother. You tell me. Who can I trust?'

He flicked the Zippo one last time and, standing, pocketed it. 'I've had enough of the past, Mr Dryden. I'll leave the rest of the questions for Estelle. And why the questions?'

'Maggie wanted me to write her story. You saw the letter. I just want to get things right. But no more questions . . . Except one,' he nodded at the Zippo lighter. 'Ex-smoker?'

'Ex most of the time,' he said. 'Not always.' Lyndon walked towards the barn to fetch the basketball. Dryden followed. Inside, out of the blinding light, something crouched in the shadows.

It was a Land Rover. Dryden knew nothing about cars but this looked expensive: a 1970s gem, lovingly restored. The leather seats showed a lifetime's wear. The paintwork was creamy white, the blue letters 'UN' emblazoned on the bonnet and side doors.

Lyndon took off the dark glasses. 'It's a 1973 model. In great shape. I got her off a guy on the base who couldn't afford to take her home. They'd used it for the peacekeepers in Bosnia.'

'It's beautiful,' Dryden said, noting that the bonnet was still hot and the red dust of the Fens lay in a film over the paintwork.

He changed tack. 'I passed the memorial to the Black Bank victims. I guess they'll have to make some changes.'

Lyndon smiled then, and flipped the Zippo open to watch the flame. 'And I used to think, you know, that I could have died here in the crash with my folks. I used to think that would have been better. And now look—I did.'

'But they weren't your parents.'

'It wasn't my life. That's the real point, isn't it? If she hadn't given me away I'd have had another life. A life that didn't have three garages, a college education, West Point, and a cell in Al Rasheid.'

'But what would it have had? Your other life?'

'Her.' He looked back towards the farmhouse. 'But she chose differently. Which is something I have to live with.'

'The hearse has arrived,' Dryden said. 'Estelle said to say.'

Lyndon slipped the glasses into a pocket and held out his hand. 'Do you have family, Dryden? Brothers, sisters?'

'Only child,' said Dryden.

'Me too. I guess I always will be—despite what Maggie said. You can't change a life with a few words, Dryden. It shouldn't change things. I'm the same person. She's the same person—Estelle. What does it change?'

Dryden didn't answer. But he thought: Everything.

HUMPH DROPPED Dryden in Market Street and he took the steps into the newsroom three at a time. He felt a sense of elation now that he was able to discharge his debt to Maggie Beck. The story had hung over him for the ten days since her death at The Tower.

Through the door marked NEWSROOM he found the *Express* in full flow—the deadline was an hour away at noon. Copies would be on the street at going-home time and delivered with the evening newspapers to homes in Ely and the surrounding villages.

Charlie Bracken looked pathetically pleased to see his chief reporter back in time. 'You got it?'

Dryden nodded at the news editor and chucked the family picture he'd got from Black Bank into the darkroom, where Mitch was printing up a landscape shot of another Fen Blow for the front page.

'Picture too,' he told him.

'Great. It's the splash. Human interest stuff, eh?' Charlie picked up his jacket and headed for the door. 'Ciggies,' he told nobody.

Dryden sat at his PC and knocked out the story in ten minutes.

A deathbed confession by an Ely woman has rewritten the history of one of the Fens' most famous disasters.

The crash of a US Air Force transporter onto a farmhouse at Black Bank, near Ely, in 1976 left 12 dead and only two survivors. Until now they were thought to be the farmer's daughter, Maggie Beck, and a newborn child being flown home with its parents to Texas.

Ms Beck, then 16, walked out of the wreckage of the farm, carrying the baby. She said her own two-week-old son Matty had died with the rest of her family. But on Friday night at The Tower Hospital, Ely, Mrs Beck told relatives, shortly before her death, that she had swapped the children.

After the crash her son was flown to the US and brought up by the parents of a US pilot who died in the crash—Major Jim Koskinski. The boy—Lyndon Koskinski—became a pilot in the US Air Force and, having kept in touch since the 1976 crash, was visiting the Beck family home when his mother fell seriously ill with cancer. He was at her bedside when she died.

Major Koskinski is on leave from the USAF after active service in Iraq where he was forced to bail out of his aircraft and spent a month in a Baghdad jail before coalition forces liberated the city.

He spoke exclusively to the *Express* about his feelings.

'I'm a US pilot. That's my life. This doesn't change anything, shouldn't change anything. I do feel cheated, and angry and lost. I can't imagine why she did it. We never had a chance to speak.

'Yes, I'm confused. Who wouldn't be? I've just visited my own grave,' he said. It now appears the grave marked Matty Beck at St Matthew's Church, Black Bank, is that of Lyndon Koskinski.

Dryden, who'd decided to leave his notebook in his pocket during his visit to Black Bank, made the quotes up. He didn't so much rely on his own memory as the poor memories of others.

Military police at USAF Mildenhall will be investigating the original crash records to see how Mrs Beck was able to fool doctors and officials at the time.

Ely police will be informed of the confession and will have to re-open the inquest into the reported death of Matty Beck in 1976. But detectives indicated that they are unlikely to take the case any further given the length of time involved and the death of Mrs Beck.

Before her death Mrs Beck left instructions that the father of Matty Beck be allowed to contact his son now that the truth has been told about the events at Black Bank in 1976.

She has made provision for him to inherit a sum of £5,000 if he contacts solicitors Gillies & Wright of Ely. They are in a position to verify his claim.

Dryden filed it to the newsdesk computer basket. Now that he had written it he saw how clearly one question still hung over Black Bank Farm. Why did Maggie Beck give her son away?

He checked his watch: nearly noon. He picked up the phone and ran through the usual litany of last deadline calls to the emergency services. The fire brigade had two fires, less than average in that incendiary summer. The first had started in a lock-up garage on the edge of town and gutted two council houses.

'Anyone hurt?'

'Nah,' said the control-room operator. 'It was mid-morning. Mum at work, kids at school, Dad's a travelling salesman.'

'Cause?' asked Dryden.

'Kids. Mucking about in the garages. The other one's different.'

Dryden heard the inexpert two-finger tapping of a PC keyboard. 'Here we are, register office—at Chatteris. Someone broke in, smashed the place up, set fire to the filing cabinets—destroyed all the records. Every last one.'

'Bloody hell. Someone's honeymoon went wrong.' Dryden took the details for a paragraph in the Stop Press. The phone rang again as he put it down. It was Jean, the receptionist. 'Dryden? There's a girl here to see you.' Jean had taken up a voluntary unpaid job as Dryden's chaperone. 'Shall I tell her to go away?'

Dryden took the stairs four at a time on the way down, missed the last one and went flying. The girl helped him to get up.

'Hi,' said Dryden. She was tall, leggy, with blue eyes and dyed blonde hair. She didn't look eighteen, but the last time Dryden had seen her she'd been posing in Inspector Andy Newman's illicit porn shots. Alice Sutton was holding a cutting from last week's edition of the *Express*. It was Dryden's story on her: FATHER'S PLEA OVER MISSING GIRL. He'd run it straight without any link to Newman's pillbox porn story, which he'd got into *The Crow*. But he'd left Newman a message telling him the ID of his snapshot star.

'It's about this,' she said.

Dryden nodded. He took her over to an alcove where they did interviews. 'You turned up?'

She nodded. 'I've been to the police. OK. It's all over. I told them everything. I want to leave it at that.'

Dryden shrugged. 'Sure. And your dad?'

Which is when the tears started to flow. Dryden put his arm round the girl and he felt Jean's eyes boring into the back of his head.

She appeared beside them. 'Tea?' she asked. And Dryden nodded.

'We can't find him,' said Alice, as soon as Jean was out of earshot.

'We?'

'Mum. I got back last night. She said he'd gone out a couple of days ago, at night—on the Saturday. Said he knew what was going on. Who'd done those things to me, and taken the pictures. Jesus,' she said, burying her face in her hands. 'The pictures.'

'How did he get to see them? The police normally keep that kind of thing pretty much under wraps.'

'He had friends, didn't he? He has friends everywhere, that's how he does his job. He got an attachment by e-mail. That made it worse. He said they'd be all over the net, just like real porn.'

'How'd he take it?' asked Dryden, wishing he hadn't.

'Mum said he sparked out. Broke some furniture. Then he drank some whisky on his own. All night, Mum said.'

'Do the police know he's gone?'

She nodded, snuffling. Jean appeared with a cup of tea.

'Any idea where he'd been looking? Did he say anything?'

'Nothing. He just said it was something to do with the lorries.' She slurped tea noisily from the cup. 'He works in transport security. HGVs—so he's always talking to the drivers. I guess it's his job. He told Mum someone had said something. About . . . the pictures.'

'What happened that night? The night in the pillbox . . .'

'You tell me.' Tears welled up and plopped into Alice's tea. 'This bloke started chatting to me at the pub where I work—the Pine Tree. The police said he put something in my drink—but they couldn't prove that. The dishwasher took all the traces off the glass.

Anyway, it's a drug, OK . . . makes you feel sexy.'

'Do you think he'd done this before?'

'Yeah.' The embarrassment flooded back. 'Jesus. How could I? Look—you ain't gonna put this in the paper, are you?'

'No,' said Dryden. 'But I should write about your dad, yes? See if anyone has seen him.'

She could have left it there but she needed to tell the whole story. 'He took me to the pillbox. I must have slept . . . afterwards. I woke up on a park bench, on the river bank by the Cutter. There was a fiver in my purse that hadn't been there the night before. I guess it was to get home. Thoughtful, eh? But I couldn't. They'd left me a picture. In the purse with the fiver. One of the snaps. I just sat there looking at it and thinking what they'd think, at home, if they ever saw it. I guess it was a threat. To make me keep quiet. So I ran. Friends in London. I'm at East London University—Docklands. I should have phoned but I was scared, scared Mum and Dad had found out . . .'

Dryden nodded. 'And you can't recall anything else your mum said about your father? About the lorries?'

Then she remembered. Dryden saw it in her eyes.

'Mum said something about a lay-by. He spends a lot of time in them, watching, you know. It's his job to make sure the drivers aren't flogging the stuff or carrying cargo for other companies. Greasy spoons, that's what he calls them. He said . . .' and she bowed her head. 'He told Mum that was where you could buy the pictures.'

'The police will find him,' said Dryden.

'That's what we're afraid of,' she said, pushing her chair away.

5

Humph pulled into the Ritz lay-by and stopped the Capri in a cloud of red dust. Disturbed in the middle of his afternoon nap to make the run, he moodily flicked through his language tapes. 'I need my sleep,' he said.

'Well, take a nap now. Be my guest. I'm paying.' Dryden turned to face him but Humph had the earphones on for his tapes—not those little plug ones you tuck inside the ear, but the big ones, like rubber dustbin lids.

Dryden had wanted to visit the Ritz T-Bar ever since Etty had told him about the 'people smugglers' using the lay-by as a drop-off point. Now Alice Sutton had given him another good reason to get a cup of tea and a carbon monoxide sandwich. If Bob Sutton had been checking lorries passing through the Fens he'd have got to the Ritz eventually. But the tea bar was closed. The shutters were down and a note was stuck on them in childish capital letters three inches high: SHUT 'TIL FURTHER NOTICE.

Dryden noted the apostrophe and the motorbike that had pulled up on the opposite side of the road. It was black, and the rider wore oxblood-red leathers. He thought about walking over to confront his uninvited shadow, but an HGV rolled into the lay-by and obscured the view. The driver got out and walked over to read the note.

'Bastard,' he said, kicking one of the wheels of the kiosk.

'Closed then?' said Dryden.

The driver read the note again. Up close. 'Never closes, Johnnie, not while it's light. Never.'

Dryden tried to modify his personality to suit that of his prospective interviewee: a professional trick made considerably more difficult by the need to look like a shifty, man-of-the-world. 'Johnnie runs quite a business,' he said, offering the lorry driver a jelly bean.

Nothing. Lights out. The driver looked at the sweets as if Dryden was peddling ecstasy tablets to nuns.

'Worth a fortune.' Dryden stepped closer. 'And what about the immigrants, eh? People smuggling must pay,' he added. 'Bloke told me those poor bastards pay six hundred quid a time. He runs the lorries through,' he said, tilting his head towards the empty tea bar. 'Gets 'em jobs. Amazing, eh? Wonder what 'is cut is?'

'Should drown the blighters,' the driver said.

Dryden hesitated before executing his next tactic, sensing at some subliminal level that he may have already stepped outside the strict etiquette laid down by the Road Hauliers Association. 'Then there's the dirty pics, of course. Hmm? You had any of them, have you? Apparently they get stowed away with the immigrants. Sort of reverse trade. I'd be interested. You know, to get a cut too.'

Dryden leered and tried a wink, which, in the circumstances, was a bonus. It meant he got to see the fist that hit him with just the one eye. The pain came a second later. A red-hot electric pulse that collapsed his spine and knees with frightening efficiency.

Then the guy picked him up by the shirt and pushed him hard up against the metallic side of the Ritz. Dryden's vision blurred.

'Who told you that?' his assailant said, surprisingly quietly. Over his shoulder Dryden could see Humph in the Capri, eyes closed, headphones still on. The motorbike had moved on. Cars swept past like they always do, innocent of any crime.

'Just heard it,' he said, and the guy laughed in a friendly way that made Dryden's heart freeze. Then he took Dryden's arm, twisted it round his back, and began to apply his weight. The elbow joint began to give with a series of plastic pops. Dryden screamed but the passing cars drowned him out. The bloke was whispering in his ear now: 'Let's keep that to ourselves, yeah?'

'OK,' said Dryden, pathetically eager to comply. The vicelike grip was released, so he sank to his knees and threw up. He kept his eyes down until he heard the lorry rumble back out on to the A14. He knelt there some time while he waited for his breathing to return to normal, and for his fingers to stop vibrating like windscreen wipers.

Out of the hot dust of the road, Inspector Andy 'Last Case' Newman's battered Citroën appeared. He got out, walked over and rattled the shuttered front of the Ritz, before turning to Dryden. He gently opened the fast-closing left eye, looking for broken blood vessels. 'That's gonna be a corker. Care to tell me who did it?'

'A driver. I suggested he was after porn. He took exception.'

'We can put him down as a "No", I think, don't you?' said Newman.

Dryden wanted to laugh but still felt too sick. 'Bob Sutton, Alice's father, picked up something about the pornography racket in a lay-by, according to his wife. But I guess you know that already.'

Newman nodded, peering in through a gap between the door and metal frame. A green parrot lay silent in an ugly little bundle.

'Parrot's a stiff,' he said. 'Shame, he could have told us where the proprietor's gone.'

There was a whiff of putrid beefburger on the air so they moved upwind. Newman took out his notebook and flipped over the pages: 'Ex-wife of the Ritz owner came in yesterday. Substation at Shippea Hill. She hadn't seen him for a month—six weeks.'

'Why'd she wait so long?'

'They were separated. Ten years. But he paid her some cash, every month. He missed the date and she went looking for him.'

'It's like the Bermuda triangle around here,' said Dryden. 'Alice Sutton goes missing, then Bob Sutton goes missing, now this guy.'

'People lose themselves. It isn't a crime. Alice Sutton is back. I'd like to find her dad but my guess is he's still on her trail, and it led to London. When it goes cold he'll be back.'

'And this guy?' said Dryden, circling the Ritz, massaging his arm.

'Is more interesting,' said Newman. 'We've had him down for the illegal immigrants for some time. It's a drop-off point. We let him carry on so we could get an idea when the lorries were coming through. Try and spot the ones with the human cargo. Now it looks like he's mixed up in porn too. Perhaps he's stepped out of line. They wouldn't like that. These people are capable of anything.'

Dryden fingered his swelling eye and walked back to the tea bar. He pulled at the gold chain round his neck and tried Laura's key in the lock of the chipboard door. Nothing.

Newman watched with exaggerated patience of a nurse on a psychiatric ward. 'Johnnie Roe's the name,' he said. 'Villain. You should see his file at the nick. Takes up a whole drawer. Petty in every sense of the word plus two really black marks, a GBH five years ago. And procuring, that was ten years ago. Nottingham.'

'Procuring?'

Newman sighed. 'He was a pimp. He sold girls. Got it?'

They strolled back to the cars. Humph was just unscrewing the top of a glove-compartment gin bottle. He shared few pastimes with Dryden but baiting coppers was one. He waved the bottle at Newman and grinned hugely.

'I'll leave you two gentlemen to it, then,' said Newman, getting slowly into his car.

Humph waved him off with a feminine flutter of the fingers.

Dryden slumped into the passenger seat and checked his injury in the vanity mirror.

'Shit,' said Humph, noticing the blackening eye for the first time. 'Sorry. I was . . . ' and he weakly shook the earphones.

'Not your fault,' said Dryden 'Drink?'

Humph fished out two Bacardis.

Dryden looked for the maps in the passenger-side door compartment. He went for the Ordinance Survey four inch to the mile. The question was simple: where was Bob Sutton? Like Inspector Newman he must have been searching for the pillbox in which his daughter had been raped. He came to the Ritz because he'd heard this was where you could pick up the pictures. Newman had said that the pictures had turned up in Nottingham during a raid on illegal immigrants. So there was more than a circumstantial link with the people smugglers. And Etty had told him the Water Gypsies had seen illegal immigrants being decanted in the Ritz lay-by, and then setting off across Black Bank Fen.

Dryden found the lay-by on the map. Etty had said the immigrants were led east, which meant they were heading across Black Bank Fen. A single drove cut the fen in half and was marked on the map: The Breach. Halfway along, about three miles from the Ritz, a small plantation of pines was marked: Mons Wood. And at its heart there was a small hexagonal symbol. A pillbox. Dryden tapped his finger on it. 'There,' he said. He tried not to notice that it was less than a mile from Black Bank Farm. He didn't believe in coincidences, so he couldn't believe in this one.

DRYDEN NEEDED two things: a bag of ice and a copy of the *Express*. Humph rearranged the rearview mirror so that he could see the black eye burgeon. 'Corker,' he said, swinging the cab out onto the main road and heading for *The Crow*'s offices.

'Thanks for the bodyguard service,' said Dryden unkindly.

'If I'd known you were going to wink at a seventeen-stone HGV driver I'd have been keeping my eye out,' said Humph.

'I think his reaction points to more unsavoury motives than affronted feelings, don't you? I'd guess he had a cab full of hard porn. That's why he was looking for our mutual friend Johnnie Roe.'

In *The Crow*'s front office there was a pile of *Expresses* for sale, fresh off the presses. Dryden took one and jumped back into the cab. His story on Maggie Beck had made the splash—complete with the picture of Estelle and Lyndon with their mother. There was a chemist next door who advised him that he needed a cold compress for his eye.

Dryden knew exactly where he could get one. 'Five Miles from Anywhere,' he told Humph, getting back in the Capri.

The Five Miles from Anywhere was a pub at the confluence of the Ouse and the Cam rivers. It stood on a lonely promontory accessible only via a dispiriting three-mile drove road. Most of the clientele were families from the pleasure boats using the moorings by the pub.

They parked on the gravel forecourt with a satisfying screech of bald tyres. Humph killed the engine: 'G and T, please, and a packet of cashew nuts.' He began to fumble with the language tapes.

For once Dryden's infinite patience fled. 'No,' he said. 'You're coming with me. We're going to sit outside and have a drink and . . . and a chat.'

'Chat?' said Humph, horrified.

Dryden got out, but leaned back through the open passenger window. 'I'll see you at one of the picnic tables.'

The bar was empty, so Dryden rang a bell. He waited for a bleary-eyed barman to organise his trousers before ordering drinks, nuts, and a bar-towel packed with ice. Humph, astonishingly, had reached the picnic table by the time Dryden walked out with the drinks.

'I hope you're bloody satisfied,' said Humph, wiping a curtain of sweat from his forehead with a handkerchief the size of a pillowcase.

Dryden sat back and held the ice to his eye while sipping from a pint at the same time. The silence between them deepened like a grudge, until Dryden set the ice aside. 'So,' he said, heavily. 'How are you? Who's cleaning the house these days?'

Dryden had initiated several conversations that summer about the problems of finding someone to clean clothes and homes—a not-too-gentle hint that Humph had finally taken. The cabbie fumbled with the nuts. 'The woman who does,' he said.

'Does she indeed?' said Dryden, smirking.

'No, she doesn't,' said Humph, emphatically.

'And the kids?'

Humph's two daughters—Grace, six, and Naomi, three—lived in a nearby village, with their mother and the postman of doubtful parentage. Humph got to see them every other weekend for outings arranged, down to the smallest detail, by his ex-wife.

'Next Saturday. Pantomime, apparently, in Cambridge.'

'A pantomime in June?'

Humph shrugged. 'It's *avant garde.*'

'Oh no it isn't,' said Dryden.

'Yes it . . .' Humph stopped himself just in time, grunted and reached for the G&T. All the liquid disappeared as if inhaled. So Humph got to his feet and said words never otherwise uttered in Dryden's presence. 'Same again?'

He tottered off and returned with what looked suspiciously like a double G&T, a pint, and an astonishing array of bar snacks.

Humph took a big breath. 'So, Laura, how is she then?'

Retaliation, thought Dryden, brilliantly executed. Suddenly his insistence on a communication seemed ill-judged. 'I . . .' he said, and then he spotted the motorcyclist with the oxblood-red leathers. He was just getting out of Humph's Capri. Dryden could see that he was taking a hammer out of his pocket. Then he pulled it back over his shoulder and crashed it down on the cab's windscreen.

Dryden's jaw dropped and he pointed stupidly.

Humph turned to see what the reporter was pointing at and an emotion close to murderous anger crossed his features. His cab was a little peripatetic island of security, and now someone was defiling that sanctuary. So Humph was mad, and when he shouted 'Oi!' everyone on the Great West Fen heard—including the motorcyclist.

Dryden would recall afterwards the lack of panic in the rider's movements. He put on the helmet with the black visor and ambled to his motorbike. The engine was already purring, drizzling a stream of hot air out of the double exhaust pipes: and then he was gone, visible only as the invisible centre of a dwindling red dust storm.

Humph got to the cab first. The seats had been slashed with a knife and his beloved fluffy dice snipped off. The contents of the glove-compartment bar had been swept to the floor, with a few breakages, and the picture of Humph's daughters had been torn into pieces. A single scratched knife line crossed the bonnet in an ugly zigzag.

Dryden looked inside the Capri and decided to try for a laugh. 'It's the mark of Zorro,' he said.

Did Humph have tears in his eyes? He looked at Dryden now. 'You made me get out,' he said, by way of accusation.

The newspaper cutting was taped to the front windscreen with a piece of masking tape. It was Dryden's story about Maggie Beck.

DRYDEN SAT on the roof of *PK 129* long after sunset. He lolled back in a deckchair, cradling a cup of cold black coffee, and flicked on the heavy-duty torch he'd retrieved from the tackle room. The beam cut the night like a searchlight, catching moths in a holding pattern overhead. The wind had dropped and the temperature was still in the mid-eighties. He checked his pockets: mobile phone, Ordnance Survey maps, notebook, binoculars, and a quarter-pound of wine gums.

Monday night. Ten thirty. What did he think he was doing? One of his many vices was passivity, punctuated with sudden bouts of often ill-advised activity. He knew that such a bout was imminent.

So far nobody had acted on the information published in the *Ely Express*. He'd asked the solicitors, Gillies & Wright, to leave a message on his landline if Lyndon's father made contact. But it was still early. The *Express* was delivered to most homes that evening and would be read, piecemeal, over the coming days. According to Maggie Beck's last letter, Lyndon's father was likely to read the story.

Her letter had also suggested another mystery: she had planned to divulge two secrets on her deathbed. What remained unsaid? He knew the heart of the mystery was on Black Bank Fen and he planned to return. There was no doubt he was drawn to what he feared. Even before the accident in Harrimere Drain he'd been claustrophobic. Now it was the central anxiety of his life. So two images were pulling him back: Alice Sutton, drugged and abused in her pillbox nightmare, and the unseen hell of the smuggled people, crammed inside the black, swaying lorries. And a third, Lyndon Koskinski in his dark, stifling cell, cradling the salvation that was the Zippo lighter.

So tonight he would visit the pillbox on Black Bank Fen.

He heard the familiar clatter of the cab's exhaust pipe hitting the sleeping policeman on the lane running down to Barham's Dock. Humph's assaulted car coasted into view.

Dryden pulled open the passenger door and passed Humph a mug of bitumen-black coffee.

'Why?' Humph said. 'Where?' He was good at questions.

'Why? I'm haunted by a small hexagonal room,' said Dryden. 'Where? Black Bank Fen. Follow The Breach near the Ritz lay-by.'

They hit the drove road across Black Bank Fen twenty minutes later. The Breach was unsigned, unsurfaced and deserted. They hadn't passed another car in their entire journey.

Dryden used the torch to read the map and guided them east. The occasional light of a farm cottage twinkled like a passing yacht. Overhead a fuel transporter heaved itself towards Mildenhall.

After ten minutes Dryden spotted a stand of pine trees which stood out against the sky. 'Mons Wood,' he said. Humph parked and began to rummage among the language tapes.

As the dead engine ticked to silence, Humph repeated his question. 'Why here?'

Dryden sighed. 'Newman has a set of pornographic pictures taken in a wartime pillbox. At night. The girl's drugged. The pictures turned up in the Midlands in a police raid on a house used by illegal immigrants. They're dropping groups off in the Fens and finding them jobs as pickers. I talked to Etty. She's seen lines of them crossing the countryside. Immigrants, using The Breach, crossing Black Bank Fen. I checked the map. This is the only pillbox on the fen.'

Humph was asleep. Tiny snores popped like a coffee percolator. That was the great thing about Humph, he was always there for you. Right there, in his seat.

Dryden got out of the car and stood in the deafening silence that only a large open space can produce. He shivered in eighty degrees of heat, his anxieties crowding round like witnesses at an accident.

The woodland around the pillbox was dry and his footsteps crackled on broken twigs and dead grass. He sensed the presence of the box rather than saw it: a hard-edged blackness within the shifting shadows beneath the pines. He picked his way forwards along an animal track and met a fox coming the other way. The torchlight caught the eyes and the nose, and the shiny liquid around its snout.

Dryden could see the pillbox now, one wall catching the moonlight. He moved anticlockwise, tracing the hexagonal outline of the box, until he came to the door. He rattled it loudly, the sound helping to quell the panic rising in his throat. The door had a newish-looking deadlock, but stood slightly ajar. He pushed it open and sent a beam of light into the dark space within.

Out of the shadows came a figure, head down and running. Dryden's head met his assailant's with the kind of crack that is only muffled by two intervening layers of skin. A dagger of pure pain stabbed him in his black eye. What did he recall? An eyeball, white. A flash of ivory teeth beautifully arranged in tombstone order. Nothing more. Then he passed out. A curtain of cosy blackness fell before his eyes and he was no longer there to feel the fear. In the cab Humph dozed dreamlessly.

Dryden came to with a start. The torch lay beside his head illuminating the straw, its beam slightly yellow, the battery fading. Had he been out for hours? He would have run from the pillbox if he could have stood up. But his overriding feeling was of thirst, prompted by the taste of blood in his throat. Which is when he saw, by the torchlight, the glass. It was on the opposite wall, immediately below a rectangle of black, star-studded sky, which was the gunslit, on a shelf. It was exactly in the middle of the shelf, like a chalice left on an altar.

Dryden was panicking now, and trying to suppress the reason why. He knew the body was there. In the moonlight its pale form had begun to emerge, like secret writing, from the straw-lined confusion of the pillbox floor. He rolled the torch in the straw and let the light give the corpse all three dimensions. It cast a shadow now, low and lifeless across the straw, and it was the shadow of a man.

The body wore jeans, no socks, but the torso was naked. One arm was outstretched behind the torso, where it was manacled to the wall.

The rest of the body was in a ball, except for the other arm, which stretched out forwards along the floor, towards the shelf and the single, empty glass. Why reach out for an empty glass? Easy. It hadn't been empty once.

Dryden stood up and circled the body. He could see the top of the head now, tucked down into the straw, and the thinning blond hair tainted with the yellow of cigarette smoke.

Dryden's head swam and he knew he was about to pass out. The darkness came but he went into it carrying a single image: the victim's skin. It looked unnaturally dry and parched and across the outstretched arm and arched back it was streaked with livid patches of discoloured flesh. He recalled, instantly, his last visit to the Ritz T-Bar and the cup of tea placed on the counter by the owner—the hand that held the cup crossed with a raised purple skin graft.

THE BEAM OF LIGHT from the pillbox gunslit shone out across Black Bank Fen like the lantern beam of a landlocked lighthouse. Dryden had watched from the Capri as first the scene-of-crime team, and then the pathologist, had picked their way through the edge of Mons Wood towards the box. The body was still in situ, awaiting the medics who sat patiently in the ambulance drawn up on The Breach. Humph offered him a whisky and he took it thankfully.

There was a sharp tap on the near-side window, which made them both jump. Inspector Andy Newman's head appeared. 'OK. When you're ready, Philip?' The detective took him under the arm, partly to keep him on the narrow path marked out by the forensic team's white flags, and partly to hold him up. It was the first time Newman had used his first name and he was pathetically grateful for the kindness.

'I met the fox here,' said Dryden, and Newman gave him an old-fashioned look.

'Mr Toad, was it? Peter Rabbit not at home?' Their laughter drew resentful looks from the forensic team combing the woodland.

'No. Yes. Seriously—a fox. I couldn't be sure, but I thought it had blood on its snout.'

A man appeared at Newman's shoulder in a head-to-foot plastic shell suit. The policeman did the introductions. 'Dr Beaumont—Home Office pathologist—this is Philip Dryden, chief reporter on *The Crow*, Ely. He found the body, Doc. An hour ago.'

Beaumont had the eyes of the true professional: intelligent, alert, even excited, but inured to death by the sight of a thousand corpses before his thirtieth birthday. 'Mr Dryden is right, Inspector. There are signs of animal activity around, on, and to some extent in the body. Most of those injuries being inflicted after death,' he finished. 'Shall we?' he added, turning back towards the pillbox.

A scene-of-crime tent had been erected over the entrance to the pillbox, and here Newman and Dryden donned blue plastic suits. Dr Beaumont led them inside. The most striking feature of the victim's body was the tautness of the limbs. The chain that linked the manacled hand to the wall was still taking the weight of the corpse.

'Cut the chain,' said Beaumont, and a scene-of-crime officer stepped forwards with bolt-cutters. Beaumont put an arm under the corpse's chest and took the weight. 'OK—now.'

The chain sheered and bounded back to the wall while the torso of the corpse slumped forwards the last two inches to the straw floor.

Beaumont got close to the victim's face, still unseen and tucked beneath the shoulders, and examined it with a pencil torch and forensic scalpel. He filled several plastic bags with minute traces of hair, blood and skin.

Newman walked across the floor between two white chalk lines until he got to the shelf under the gunslit. 'And this was like this? Empty?' he said, tapping the glass with a ballpoint.

'Yup,' said Dryden, wishing he could drink some water now.

'Let's turn him over,' said Beaumont, and the room suddenly filled with the forensic team. They flipped the corpse over.

It was the owner of the Ritz T-Bar. His mouth was stretched open in a frozen scream, the eyes tinged pink with broken blood vessels. The skin was caked in what looked like salt, with rime around the thin, blotched lips. The nose had been destroyed by a violent blow.

Dryden knelt and examined the face. 'What are those?'

They directed one of the halogen lamps on the face. On each cheek and across the chin were a series of livid puncture marks, with blue bruising around each.

Beaumont didn't answer, but used a gloved finger to slightly massage the skin.

Newman lifted the chain that had secured the victim to the wall, using the ballpoint looped through one of the iron links. The manacle contained a single lock and was smeared with blood and skin tissue where the man had lunged forwards towards the glass and injured his wrist. The other end was looped through an iron ring in the wall and secured with a simple padlock.

'That's interesting,' said Newman, turning his torch on the manacle. A line of script had been stencilled into the metal.

Dryden shrugged. 'An African language? Indian? Arabic? It's not European, that's clear.'

The ambulance team arrived with a bright neon-yellow body bag.

'Any sign of the killer?' Dryden asked Newman, as they walked back to the Capri.

Newman shook his head. 'There are some tyre marks further down the drove. Looks like a four-wheel drive. You can't remember anything about him at all? The bloke who bowled you over.'

Dryden shrugged.

Beaumont came out, peeling off the white surgical gloves.

'The punctures in the face; any idea?' said Dryden.

The pathologist consulted his notes. He held out his right hand: 'Three puncture marks on the left cheek.' He held out his left hand: 'Four on the right.' He stepped forwards and held Dryden's face in a grip with his fingertips, gently applying pressure. 'My guess is someone held him like this, and then went on applying the force. Some of the nails dug in. The thumbs raised bigger welts, to the centre, the fingers less so, trailing off towards the neck.'

'Then he hit him?' said Dryden.

Beaumont nodded, releasing his grip. 'Yes. Hard.'

'Did it kill him?'

'No. No, I don't think so. I think he died of thirst.'

DRYDEN, RELEASED from police questioning at 12.30 a.m., got Humph to drive him to *The Crow*. He filed stop-press single paragraphs to all the broadsheets and most of the tabloids for the Tuesday morning's late editions. He'd agreed with Inspector Newman to withhold most of the details, but there was enough there to flog the story: wartime pillbox, semi-naked corpse. The discovery was attributed to a local farmer—name also withheld.

Having finished filing he woke Humph to drive him to The Tower. There was no way either of them would sleep so they shared what was left of Humph's Greek picnic and rammed that home with a couple of Metaxa 3-Star brandies. Dryden brought Humph up to speed on the investigation by reading out the copy he had filed. The cabbie whistled once, then settled down to sleep again.

Dryden decided it was visiting time. He, and the nursing staff, had long decided that her sleeping time should be respected, and despite her open eyes the room was darkened, and the COMPASS machine turned off, between 10 p.m. and 7 a.m.

Dryden sat for a minute, studying her face in the blazing moon-light, then went to the window. Below, the caretaker was sweeping the forecourt. Clearly an insomniac, he whistled happily. Beethoven, perhaps 'The Emperor', thought Dryden.

He turned back to the room. It had changed since his last visit. Estelle and Lyndon must have been in to ferry out Maggie's stuff. The cardboard box in which Dryden had stored Maggie's tapes had been emptied shortly after her death; the box pushed under the bed. The only thing left of Maggie's in the room was the tape recorder on the window ledge.

Dryden walked over to the COMPASS machine. For once his curiosity seemed dimmed. He stuffed the ticker tape in his pocket unread, and went back to the cab.

SHFYTJF SHDURIT DHEOFJO DJDO
GHGEIKOW WATCHWHITE KRUBBYO
ASAIUDSJ HD UCANSEETIERIVERGHHUJI

OVER THE WEEKS he'd learned the telltale signs. The tiny sounds which said the light was coming.

First there was the outer gate. A rusted hinge grated. Not like the others he could hear at dawn and dusk. The hundreds of iron doors opening and closing in the prison of Al Rasheid. This one had a note. He'd played cornet at High School. Was it a G?

He only had a few seconds then to prepare. He had to close his eyes, he must, because the pain would be sweeping, a burning poker of agony thrust into his eye sockets and down into his brain.

But he had to open his eyes to savour the light, to relieve the human inkwell of darkness that was his life. So to ready his eyes he pressed his fingers into the sockets, producing the dancing colours that helped prepare for the light.

After the rusted hinge came the keyhole. There must be a disc of metal covering the keyhole on the outside. The jailer flipped it up to insert the key and for a second a magical key-shaped beam crossed the cell and fell on the wall.

So he'd moved Freeman there, to catch the light. Freeman, who'd survived like he had, drifting down inert to the desert. Lyndon blamed himself for the injury. He'd panicked, hitting the button for the ejector seats before his copilot was ready. So he'd caught the cockpit canopy with his head, breaking the skin and the skull, and blackening his eyes. He held Freeman's head in his hands sometimes, tenderly, feeling for the fractures beneath the skin, and the sickening click of the cranial plates that had been dislodged by the canopy.

But when the keyhole light fell on Freeman's face his eyes never opened. For eighteen days they'd been in this solitary silence. And Freeman hadn't moved: even though Lyndon gave him most of his food and cleaned the head wound with the water he craved to drink. But Freeman lay still, stiller with each passing day. One day soon, Lyndon knew, the keyhole light would find his eyes forever open.

The door flew open with military swiftness. The light engulfed them. Direct sunlight. Lyndon's eyes hurt so much he always cried out. And then the jailer showed his pity, smoking a single cigarette in the doorway as Lyndon tried to see out on the world. Once he saw the leaves of a cedar tree over the far wall flickering from lime green to silver grey in a breeze.

And he always made the same plea for Freeman: 'Take him away, not me. Take him away. He needs a doctor. Look!' And Lyndon would draw back the bandage on the forehead to reveal the purple wound, with its iridescent greenish tinge. He'd take some of the water then, and bathe away the pus and the flies.

But the jailer smoked: not cruelly, but with his back turned. There was never ever any warning of the end of the light. Just the sudden diminution of the sunburst and the rocking percussion of the iron door crashing against the jambs. And then the darkness again, and the terror of the small space he knew so well.

Tuesday, June 17

6

Dryden held the cup of black coffee to his lips and watched the tiny tremor in his right hand translated into wavelets on the surface of the liquid. He gulped the caffeine with an addict's concentration, then picked up Humph's flask and confirmed it was empty. The events of the night before were still a cartoon strip of indelible, technicolour images, from the blue-spotted skin grafts on the victim's back to the bright yellow fluorescence of the body bag in which they'd taken him away. Had he slept? Humph had driven him back to

PK 129 but they'd drunk little bottles until dawn without speaking.

Dryden looked at the ceiling and remembered where he was: church. Precisely, St Matthew's Church on Black Bank Fen. Newman had fended off media enquiries by scheduling a press conference for 10 a.m., close to the site of the murder.

The church, and its tiny bell tower, had sagged with the years into the rich peat soil. For more than eighty years the building had limped on as a machine store, estate office, and finally a community centre. A single pool table stood on the altar, a razor-blade slash exposing the chipboard beneath the sun-bleached green baize.

Inspector Andy 'Last Case' Newman, arranging papers on a trestle table, looked up. 'That's them.'

They heard cars bumping along the drove road. Her Majesty's Press was on parade. There was plenty of interest. Dryden had filed early-morning paragraphs for the late editions of the Fleet Street papers, and a full story for the first editions of the local evening papers in Cambridge, Norwich and Peterborough. He'd left an answerphone message for Charlie Bracken, telling him he was at the press conference. Then he'd called Mitch and told him to get some scene-of-crime pics at the pillbox, if he could get near.

Newman had pinned the cuttings from the nationals to a large board by the church door marked: INCIDENT ROOM: PRESS.

There was a small room to the left of the church doors, where Newman's sergeant, Peter Crabbe, was making tea. Half a dozen uniformed coppers were trooping in, having spent the early hours combing the fields for evidence. A WPC was sticking photos and maps to the main incident-room board.

Dryden stood up. 'So why here?' he asked. 'Why not use the nick in Ely? It's a long way for the press to come.'

Newman parked an ample backside on what had been the altar rail. 'Exactly. Some peace and quiet—once I've got rid of you lot.'

The press shuffled in like extras from *One Flew Over The Cuckoo's Nest*. The man from the *East Anglian Daily News*, Joey Forward, was the best dressed, and he had his flies open. PA's man, Mark Yarr, appeared to have his pyjamas on under a jumper. The rest headed for the free coffee.

Dryden had one more chance for a private question. 'What about the porno shots? Is it the same pillbox?' He kicked himself for panicking the night before and not checking the walls before he'd gone back to the cab to phone the police.

'Too early, Dryden. Looks the same—but then most of 'em do.'

Dryden knew he was bluffing. The military code number on the pictures could be easily matched if it was the same pillbox.

'Are you looking for Bob Sutton?' He knew Sutton's search for his daughter's rapist must make him a leading suspect.

Newman's patience snapped. 'For Christ's sake, just wait, Dryden.' The press pack, fired up by mugs of Nescafé, took their places.

Newman opened a manila folder and adjusted reading glasses. 'The body of a white male was found last night in a pillbox about half a mile from this church. He was manacled to the wall.'

'We can read the papers. Tell us something we don't know.' It was Mike Yarr. 'Like an ID.'

'Enquiries are continuing into the identity of the victim. I can tell you he appears to be aged between forty to fifty years. Now, if I may continue . . . ' Newman pressed on. 'I am prepared to release details of this man's death, but one aspect must remain under embargo until you are otherwise directed to print it. Agreed?'

This was standard procedure in murder cases. The police often withheld details in order to weed out cranks who rang up to confess to the killing. Dryden had not been told to keep anything out of his reports except his own name—and the fact an empty glass had been found at the scene. The rest of the press pack nodded wearily.

'Fine,' said Newman. 'The cause of death is to be ascertained, but we are working on the theory that he was poisoned.'

'With?' asked Dryden, surprised. The pathologist at the scene had guessed that the man had died of thirst.

Newman flicked through some notes. 'Samples are at the lab but the stomach contained benomyl, carbendazim, and thiophanate-methyl. Fungicidal weedkiller to you lot. But this wasn't the garden variety. Industrial strength. Usually sold for crop spraying.'

'And he drank it, did he?' Mike Yarr asked.

'Yup,' said Newman, still reading. 'Which was hardly surprising, given his severely dehydrated condition. You can use all this, gentlemen.' Notebooks were flipped open. 'The pathologist who got to him first on site reckoned he hadn't had any fluid for a least six days. It was eighty-two degrees in the box at two this morning. In the day? A hundred and twenty, possibly more. In the pathologist's words, the victim's body tissue was about as moist as a Jacob's cracker.'

'But it didn't kill him?' asked Joey Forward.

'No. But it would have. I won't go into the specific details, but let's say it would have been a race between gagging on his own swollen tongue or drowning in his own stomach juices. His last meal had been taken even longer ago than his last drink.'

'When was his last drink—the poison cocktail—taken?' It was Mike Yarr again.

'About twenty-four hours before his body was found. Pathologist at the scene believed he would have died within an hour of drinking the poison. But in his case it would have been quite a long hour.'

'And the body—found by a farmer it says 'ere.' It was Mike Yarr, ostentatiously reading a copy of the *Mail*. 'No name given.'

'Those details we are withholding while investigations continue.'

The press corps examined Dryden, and he examined a wine gum he'd found in his pocket.

'Further points of interest. The victim was naked above the waist but fragments of clothes were found among ashes in the pillbox.'

'What kinda clothes?' said Forward.

'White linen. With traces of animal fat. Tomato ketchup.'

'Suggesting?' said Yarr.

'Anything you like. Now. There was also a lot of loose change on the floor, more than a tenner's worth in coppers and silver.'

Newman pinned a black and white photograph to the incident-room board. It showed a narrow-bladed seven-inch knife sticking horizontally out of a wooden door jamb. The hilt was gilded and carved with raised, geometrical patterns.

'And this. No traces of blood and no knife wounds on the victim. The designs are Arabic.'

'Fingerprints?' said a voice from the back.

Newman thought for a second. 'Yes. We're putting them through the computer now. I'll keep you up-to-date on any developments.'

'Plus,' he added, putting up another print. A plastic Tesco bag with its contents, presumably, laid out in military rows on the green baize of the pool table for the picture. Torch, pre-packed sandwich, apple, two motoring magazines, a small cassette player with ear phones, and two bottles of mineral water. And a cheap metallic picture frame. The quality wasn't good enough to see the subject of the photo that sat inside, slightly off-centre.

Dryden leaned forwards in his chair. 'The snap?'

Newman put a third print up on the board—it was the photograph blown up. A dog, a mongrel, with a piece of rope round its neck. There was a plastic water bowl at its feet. In the background was a sluggish river, mulligatawny-brown, and some tropical vegetation.

'Well, it ain't the Thames, is it?' said a voice at the back.

'Our guess is tropical Africa, south of the Sahara,' said Newman.

'So what do we think happened?' asked Yarr.

Newman shrugged. 'He was tied to the wall. Left. Tortured? His wrist was broken in the manacle. Skin very badly cut. And the pathologist says his vocal chords were in shreds.'

'Shouting?' said Dryden, knowing he was wrong.

'Possibly, but the pathologist said the damage was violent. Screaming more like,' said Newman.

Dryden closed his eyes and tried to imagine what that would have sounded like. A human voice, shredded, echoing across Black Bank Fen. And then he tried to imagine who would have heard it.

THE PRESS LEFT Black Bank in a caravan of cars, Humph leading the way along The Breach. Dryden watched the rest of the press turn south towards London and Norwich. The Capri turned north towards Ely, where the cathedral's distant image was already buckling in the heat of the day. A cloud was so unusual that summer that when a large shadow dashed across the landscape, Humph pulled the cab up by the side of the road. Dryden got out and scanned the horizon. The sun was behind them but it wasn't a cloud that had blotted it out. It was a column of smoke, rising from the fen just west of the city.

'Jesus,' Dryden said. It looked like an oil painting from hell.

Dryden rang Mitch, who was still at the scene of Johnnie Roe's murder. 'I guess it's a field fire. On the peat. But it's a biggy—get as close as you can, Mitch—I want to see the burn marks on that bloody hat of yours. The pics are for *The Crow* on Friday—so no rush.'

Humph slung the cab off the main road and headed south along a drove of concrete slabs; they traced a route around parched fields.

'It's the old airfield,' said Dryden, already tasting the smoke.

Witchford Aerodrome had been a Lancaster bomber base in the war. Dryden had done a piece the year before after a farmer had ploughed up the remains of a German Heinkel that had come down in a raid. It had buried itself in the soft peat of the winter of 1941.

But Witchford's days of glory were long gone. Now the old hangars and conning tower were derelict and deserted except on Saturdays and Tuesdays, when the grass runways were used for car-boot sales. As the cab got closer they could see the parked ranks of cars through a mirage of tumbling hot air at the base of the column of smoke. Heading towards them was a crowd of a couple of hundred bargain hunters pursued by the drifting, noxious cloud of straw smoke. And they were coming at quite a speed, most of them holding handkerchiefs to their mouths. Coughing, screaming, laughing and crying, the crowd swept past Humph's Capri and kept going. Humph pulled up and killed the engine.

Through the smoke Dryden could see two fire tenders working their way towards the seat of the fire in a field beyond the car boot sale. Through the purple-red flames Dryden could make out the shape of a bright yellow combine harvester. They were deathtraps in hot weather, with sparks flying and enough grease and oil caked to the machinery to make sure the chaff and straw caught fire with a satisfying *boom!* The top soil had caught alight as well, a common danger that summer. The peatfields of the Black Fen were essentially a huge open fireplace waiting for a light.

The fleeing crowd regrouped beyond the flimsy remains of the wartime perimeter fence. Dryden grabbed a rag from the cab boot, poured the contents of a bottle of mineral water over it, covered his face and set off for the parked cars. Humph sat happily watching the fire spread, munching a diet chicken sandwich.

Dryden walked 200 yards towards the blaze, his eyes streaming as the smoke swirled around him, before a fireman emerged from the gloom in full breathing gear and grabbed him by the arm muttering: 'Idiot. Follow me.' Dryden tried to say 'Press' but the breath of air he would have used turned out to be sixty per cent carbon monoxide. The fireman led him to a door in one of the vast 1930s aircraft hangars and pushed him in with enough force to leave him flat on his face. 'Stay in there,' he said, fading back into the smoke.

The open door faced west so the drifting smoke was slipping harmlessly round the building. He lay still, catching his breath. Then he stood up and surveyed the building, which must have been nearly eighty yards long and a hundred feet high.

Up against the vast closed hangar doors a white van was parked. Dryden walked over and put his hand on the bonnet.

'Still warm,' he said. The side of the van was painted a light green with a white-lettered sign: WILKINSON'S FOR CELERY. On the passenger seat there was a clipboard and mobile phone. He looked round the hangar again, but it was still empty.

Where was the driver? In the far wall there was a single door marked FLIGHT GROUP. Dryden pushed it open and looked down a long corridor. He could hear music; African, with a solid rock beat.

He inched open the second door to find a Nissen hut: a curved corrugated iron roof over a concrete floor. The windows were all skylights and high enough to give no view. Rows of iron bedsteads crowded against the side walls. The springs were rusted and shot. At the far end Jimmy Kabazo, the foreman from Wilkinson's celery plant, stood watching him.

Dryden walked in and decided to try easy informality. 'Hiya.'

Jimmy bent down and turned off a portable CD player. Dryden noticed that not all the beds were bare. Two or three on each side had sleeping-bags on them and fresh twenty-first-century rubbish under them, from sandwich wrappers, to cans and empty crisps packets.

Dryden picked one of the bare beds and sat where the pillow should have been, bringing his legs up off the floor. 'Looking for someone?' he asked, nodding to the sleeping-bag on the next bed.

Kabazo grinned. 'Nope. Just waiting.'

'Friend of mine saw them,' said Dryden, knowing he didn't need to spell it out. Evidence of the people smugglers was all around them. He guessed Kabazo was an illegal immigrant too, or at least mixed up in the trade.

'We safe?' Kabazo asked. Dryden couldn't be sure if he was referring to the fire, or to the likelihood that he would go to the police over what he'd found.

Dryden decided innocence was best. 'Just a peat fire—the combines start them. We're fine—it's mostly smoke.'

'Saw dem where?' said Kabazo.

'Black Bank Fen. Going across country—east. From the lay-by on the A14. That's where they took them out of the lorries.'

'Ritz,' said Kabazo, nodding, trying to calculate what Dryden knew and who he would tell.

'This is between us. OK? I'm not after anyone—just a story. No names. No need for names.'

Kabazo nodded but didn't move. 'I'm waiting,' he said again. 'My boy. Today maybe. Tomorrow. Police mustn't know.'

Dryden shrugged. 'Sure. Why should they?'

'Who you tellin' den?'

'Nobody. It's not my job. I'm interested in the story. I mean it; I don't need names.'

Kabazo nodded. 'He'll come. The skinhead said. Winston. He said last week, this week . . . maybe later. I don't trust him.'

'Winston?'

Kabazo stood at the foot of Dryden's bunk. 'The driver. Our people pay him, he does the dirty work. With the Ritz man—Johnnie.'

Suddenly sunlight blazed down through the skylights, indicating the runway fire was out.

'They've found a body. On Black Bank Fen,' said Dryden. 'A man. In his forties. I think it's Johnnie—but they won't say.'

Kabazo's eyes widened. 'How long?'

'A few days—perhaps. What would they have done if Johnnie hadn't been there? Where's the next drop?'

Kabazo shook his head. 'Nottingham. If the driver knew. Perhaps Winston doesn't come, then they don't know.'

'I can ring you with the ID on the body at Black Bank. OK?

'Yes,' Kabazo said. 'Ring the factory. Leave a message.'

They walked back to the main hangar in silence and stood in the sunlight at the door. Outside the crowd was being marshalled towards the cars. The bones of the combine harvester were black and crumpled, fire still licking around the driver's padded seat.

'Can you contact them? Get Winston?' asked Dryden.

'They don't like it. They got the money. And I left them a bag for Emmy. Food and his things. His music. I sit tight some days. Wait some more. Sensible boy, my boy. He's the first I send for with the money. Emmy's a good boy.'

Kabazo took a wallet from his jeans pocket and flipped it open to show a snap: a boy, maybe fourteen, stood grinning under an African sun. In the background a great river, too wide to offer a view of the far bank, swept past. But it was what the boy was holding that made Dryden's blood freeze: a mongrel dog with a rope collar.

DRYDEN STOOD ALONE in the graveyard of St Matthew's and, looking at his shoes in the dust, observed that he had no shadow. The sun beat down vertically on Black Bank Fen for Maggie Beck's burial.

The funeral cortège had left Black Bank Farm a few minutes earlier. He could see it now, zigzagging towards St Matthew's. A brief ceremony had been held on the farm first. Humph had parked the Capri by the churchyard gates and stood beside the cab, a mark of respect only Dryden could truly appreciate.

It was the first burial at St Matthew's since Maggie's husband Don more than twenty years earlier. The newly dug grave lay open next to Maggie's mother and father's which, according to the stone, also contained the small remains of Matty Beck, aged two weeks.

Estelle's limousine followed the hearse. Her shoulders were hunched in a silhouette of sadness. The second car carried a woman who had to be helped into a wheelchair. The rest of the funeral party walked behind the cars, led by a priest in black and white. A dozen farm workers followed in ill-fitting suits. But no Lyndon. Dryden considered his emotional state. The last time they'd talked the anger had been visible. Anger at Maggie for giving her son away. Bewilderment as to the reason for that betrayal. Determination to find some sort of justice amidst the mess that his life had become. And Estelle? What part did his half-sister have to play in the rest of his life? He'd felt a distance between them, a fracture opened up by Maggie's deathbed confession.

Estelle saw Dryden as she walked to the graveside and seemed to shrink further into herself at the sight. At their first meeting Dryden had detected anxiety and anger; now she radiated something else, something far more dangerous: defiance?

Dryden retreated to the shade of a lime tree as they gathered round the grave. The priest's vestments, which hung lifeless in the heat, drank in the light. Dryden looked away to rest his eyes on the horizon, where he found a lone figure standing in a group of pines. A white Land Rover was parked on its far side, the open tailgate just visible beyond the barn end. The figure, Dryden could now see, was dressed in USAF grey. Then someone touched Dryden's arm.

Estelle Beck's eyes were bloodshot but bright. 'Thank you for coming.' She gripped his arm. 'The police came, this morning,' she said, watching the funeral party shuffle out of the graveyard. 'About the man they found, in the pillbox. It's terrible. It feels so close,' she added. 'It's frightening—I'm frightened. Out here.'

'They'll find who did it,' said Dryden. 'Try to put it out of your mind—at least for today.'

'Out of my mind?' said Estelle, too loudly. 'God! The torture . . . how could anyone do that? Such an inhuman thing . . . ' She covered her mouth. 'Like Tantalus.'

Dryden considered the classical allusion and how perfect it was. The king chained to a pillar in a pool of water and left to die of thirst. The perfect torture.

The woman in the wheelchair was pushed towards them by the priest. Estelle stooped to kiss her. 'Come back to the farm, Connie.'

The woman shook her head: 'God bless, dear. I won't, forgive me.

But come and see me soon.' The priest pushed her on towards the waiting cars.

Dryden looked around. 'No Lyndon? I thought he'd be here.'

Estelle's features softened, but Dryden still struggled to see a shadow of Maggie's humanity in the bitter green eyes. 'Well, he's not. I told him he'd regret it—but he said one more regret wouldn't change his life.'

'Give him time. His life is in pieces,' he said.

She shivered despite the heat. 'Yes. Pieces.' She looked about.

'At least he has you. And a home.'

'Lyndon isn't comfortable at Black Bank, I'm afraid. He went soon after Mum's death. I don't know where. Perhaps back to the base. He won't tell me. Says he needs the space and the time.'

Dryden wondered why Lyndon Koskinski did not want to spend time with his newly found half-sister.

Estelle looked to the funeral cortège. 'I must go. Some of the hands are coming back for a drink. It's the least I could do. They've run this place for Mum.'

'Will you sell?' Dryden asked.

'It may not be mine to sell. Lyndon's the oldest child. And male.' She shrugged. 'I've been listening to the tapes Mum made. Her life.'

Dryden thought of the long hours Maggie had talked and Laura, perhaps, had listened. 'Does she say why she gave Matty away?'

She shook her head and looked north. Dryden saw that the white Land Rover had gone. 'Not a word,' she said. Dryden sensed the lie, and wondered if she'd listened to the tapes alone.

7

Mickey's Bar stood by one of the giant concrete blocks the Americans had used to block Mildenhall air base's residential roads from terrorist attack. Beyond the wire stretched the fen, but this side of Mildenhall was like any other small Midwestern town of 7,500 lost souls. Most of them needed a drink and a reminder of home. There were two other customers who sat at the long bar on high stools. One wore a lumberjack's checked shirt and was reading *USA Today*, the other smoked Lucky Strikes, with obvious enjoyment.

Dryden ordered a small draught Schlitz and sat watching the bubbles rise. One puzzle had brought him to Mickey's Bar. How could Maggie Beck swap two babies and get away with it? He'd promised to help her put right the damage her lie had done—but he couldn't go on without being sure he wasn't helping to construct a greater lie. And the good reporter in him told him he had to check the story out. At least then he would feel confident that only one question would remain: why had she swapped the babies?

Dryden checked the three clocks behind the bar: 13.30 GMT/ 08.30 NY/04.30 LA. He drank his cold beer and looked at himself in the bar mirror. He was unaware he was handsome, an oversight that had saved his character from vanity at least. What he didn't look like was a US serviceman. The jet-black stubble and the unruly hair was reason enough to mark him down as local civilian staff. The gleaming blue-black eye added to his eccentric appearance.

Major August Sondheim walked in briskly and took the next high stool. The barman needed no prompting: double Bourbon on ice minus the fancy umbrella.

'Philip. Good day,' said August, draining his drink and pushing the glass back across for the barman to refill. Dryden stuck a ten-pound note on the bar top and looked forward to the small change.

August ran a hand through his militarily trimmed white hair. 'Laura?'

That was the problem with Dryden's friends. They all asked the same question.

'Same. Better. I get messages. Sometimes they make sense.'

August slapped a twenty-dollar bill on the counter, but the bartender was way ahead of him.

Dryden started his second beer. He'd phoned August the day before to ask for details on the Black Bank air crash, 1976. For Maggie to successfully switch the babies she would have had to hoodwink the US military authorities into accepting that her own son, Matty, was in fact Lyndon Koskinski. How had that been possible?

August never wrote anything down but luckily he had a good memory before lunch. 'I read the file on the crash. Not much. Why would the woman lie after all? This kid, her kid, was about the same age as the Koskinski boy—a few days difference. Their colouring and weight were similar.'

'How did Maggie know that?' asked Dryden.

August shrugged. 'The dead child was found among the wreckage of the farmhouse. The body was clearly visible. The boy had died instantly from massive internal wounds caused by the impact. My guess is Maggie found him, quickly realised the similarity in age and saw her chance to swap the babies. It looks like Maggie removed the blanket the Koskinski kid was wrapped in, and used it to swaddle Matty Beck.'

Dryden paid for another round, feeling the room begin to gyrate.

'The child who survived was examined by the base medic on duty that night, a different one had delivered the child at the US clinic. By the time of the crash the original doctor was Stateside, his tour over.'

August downed a fourth drink, but Dryden wasn't counting. 'There was a problem they should've checked out,' said August. 'But hey, the grandparents had been told, they wanted the kid, the rush was understandable.'

'What kind of problem?' said Dryden, slurring his words.

'Blood. They gave the kid a transfusion because of a slight head injury. He'd lost some blood. Luckily they double-checked the type. It didn't match the records. They put it down to an error. Sounds incredible now, but remember, Dryden, this woman had given her own son away. Nobody could have imagined she was lying. All the Koskinski grandparents had seen were a few shots taken after his birth—and we all know what newborn kids look like, right? Walnuts. And don't forget Maggie Beck went on to identify the kid in the mortuary as her son. Who's gonna ask: "You sure about that, lady?"'

'What about the autopsy?'

'Not our jurisdiction. Local coroner. It'll be in the records. But apart from weight and vital statistics they had nothing else to go on. She identified him, for Christ's sake.' August sipped the bourbon. 'Any idea why she did it?'

'Nope. She left some tapes—recordings she'd made, setting out her life story. Perhaps the reason is in there.' Dryden burped. 'What do you know about Koskinski? What happened to him in the desert?'

August gave him a sidelong look. 'Let's sit down.'

They took a booth.

'He came down in Iraq. Engine failure. Captured and taken in for interrogation. He was held in Al Rasheid. I don't need to paint pictures, I'm sure, but every expense was spared. So when they did fly him out it was felt, understandably, that we owed him some R and R, and some time to recuperate. He's under medical treatment as well— base hospital unit are dealing with that. Enough?'

Dryden nodded but remembered his golden rule: there's always one more question. 'And he's back on the base?'

'He has a room. We don't keep tabs. As I said, we owe him. The base commander has requested an interview, as have the local police. Clearly there's the issue of the paternity—which affects nationality. I can't imagine it's an insuperable problem. But who knows? Bureaucracy can kill. He needs the passport checked—that kind of thing. There's the issue of the crime that Maggie committed. But there seems little to gain from anyone taking that any further.'

Dryden tried again. 'Medical treatment, you said. Anything specific?' August stood up, indicating that it was time to change bars.

'Claustrophobia,' he said, and gave Dryden a genuinely happy smile. Six bourbons, thought Dryden, that's all it takes.

DRYDEN WALKED to the Capri with the light steps of someone propelled by alcohol. Humph was holding his mobile, which had a text message from Inspector Andy Newman. It read simply: 'Sardine'. Dryden told Humph to head north to the coast to West Lynn, Gifford's Haulage Yard. The raid had been on the cards for weeks and Newman had promised Dryden the story once the police decided to go in. Codename, Operation Sardine. Dryden's expectations were low, he'd been on similar outings that had produced a string of dull down-page stories. The idea was to catch the people smugglers with their cargo on board, but so far all they'd found had been empty containers and parked cabs. But now, at least, Dryden's interest in this illicit trade had quickened.

They drove north in companionable silence. Humph was still sulking after the attack on his beloved cab. He'd put masking tape on the seats and the fluffy dice had been re-attached to the rearview mirror. The cabbie had acquired a tape of Greek balalaika music and he played it now, aware that it would drive Dryden to despair.

Gifford's lorry park was the size of six football pitches, acres of bleak concrete, enlivened by 200 HGV containers. A heat haze was already rising from the baking metal boxes. Dryden mistook a heavy sense of foreboding for the beginnings of a hangover. Pressing his face against the diamond-weave electric fence, he picked up an electric charge that made his watch run backwards for a week. Humph, sitting in the cab, was beginning a Greek conversation with Eleni.

'Claustrophobia,' said Dryden out loud to nobody, kicking the wire fencing. That's local journalism for you, he thought. Unbearable excitement in exotic locations. He felt tired and drained. The black eye throbbed and made him feel bilious. The pillbox murder had shocked him far more than he had admitted, even to himself. People smugglers and porn pushers made his flesh crawl. He had no interest in meeting them and a positive fear of them trying to meet him. The newspaper cutting left on the Capri windscreen was a clear warning to leave the story of Black Bank Fen to history. He felt threatened, confused, but most of all defeated by his inability to see clearly how events were linked. But he had little doubt that they were.

Then the dogs arrived. Three vans pulled up and half a dozen uniformed coppers spilled out. Inspector Andy Newman arrived in an unmarked police car. One of the uniformed PCs rolled up the backs of the three vans: Dryden counted fourteen dogs, every one an Alsatian.

The keyholder was in the second van. He was tall with the kind of fissured face reserved for those addicted to illegal substances in commercial quantities. The gates swung open on the sunlit maze of the container park and the dogs ran.

Viewed from above, the scene was bizarre: a laboratory maze with the role of the mice taken by fourteen skittering dogs. They were using their noses, but if they'd used their eyes they would have seen the gravid cloud of flies hanging, despite the onshore breeze, over a lime-green container marked ZKA—RAPIDE.

It took the dogs twenty minutes to find it. While waiting Dryden told Newman about the Nissen hut at the old airfield at Witchford. 'Looks like that's where they let them sleep—kind of depot, I guess.'

Newman, ill-tempered, was watching the dogs scrabble round the lime-green container. 'We'll check it out. But my guess is they've changed their routine. Johnnie Roe's death must have put the fear of God into them. They'll be finding a new route.'

Two PCs with bolt-cutters got to work on the tailgate restraints on the container. The bolts sheared and the container door swung open to emit an overpowering wall of stench.

Pork, thought Dryden, the smell of cloying grease unbearable. Dead pigs, about thirty of them, scattered the floor. The heat in the container drifted out. A slick of animal fat began to trickle over the tailgate. Between the pigs were the telltale signs that people had shared their final journey—but got off just in time. Ice-cream wrappers, burger-bar cartons, and human faeces.

'Unbelievable,' said Newman. Then he checked the ever-present clipboard. 'Nark told us there were two.'

The next container along was lime green as well. It still had a cab attached. Same markings: ZKA—RAPIDE.

The same two PCs got to work on the tailgate. But this time Dryden didn't watch. One of Inspector Newman's DCs had broken open the cab door, and he climbed up after him. On other jobs this had made the best copy, giving Dryden a chance to examine the detritus of the real villain—the driver who knew he had a human cargo. Maps, fags, sweets, and always the soiled copy of the *Sun*. He looked at the date: June 10, seven days old.

He knew something was wrong when he looked in the wing mirror. Newman was smoking. He'd given up a year earlier, but he was gulping in the nicotine now. And the change in the atmosphere was tangible, the squad of cynical coppers tautly alert. The dogs went berserk as Dryden jumped down and ran to the back.

Pork, he thought. But this time it wasn't pigs, this time it was people. All of them were black and soaked in sweat and urine. They blinked in the sun and cracked bent limbs. There was an almost complete lack of any human sound, except that of lungs sucking in air. Gradually Newman's team helped them out, while Dryden took a walk upwind, gulping in lungfuls of sea air.

When he got back there was only one person left in the back of the container. He knew immediately it was a corpse. One arm was flung behind the neck, which craned up for air, while the other stretched up towards the place where light would have been. He didn't want to see the face but he did. It was Emmy Kabazo.

DID JIMMY KABAZO kill Johnnie Roe? It was a thought Dryden could not dislodge as he sat in the Capri, the doors open, and drank in the big sky over the sea like some visual antidote to the image of Emmy Kabazo's tortured body. They'd parked by the beach at Old Hunstanton so that Dryden could phone over the story—single paragraphs for the tabloids, but more substantial stories for the white broadsheets. The spate of work helped him deal with the helplessness he felt. Jimmy had to be a suspect. When Dryden had talked to him at the old airfield he claimed to be waiting for Emmy's arrival. But what if his son was long overdue? Had Jimmy tried to track him down through the Ritz? Had he tortured Johnnie to find out where his son had gone? Had Johnnie died not knowing how to give him the answer he needed—the answer that could have saved his life?

'Gonna swim?' Humph said, scrabbling in the glove compartment for a miniature bottle of gin. He'd bought a large bottle of tonic and a lemon at a roadside service station. He produced two plastic cups and sliced the lemon with a Swiss Army knife. 'Sorry, no ice,' he said, trying to cheer Dryden up.

'What's Emmy short for?' asked Dryden.

Humph gave him the drink and sipped his own. 'Emmanuel?'

Dryden gulped the drink, failing to blot out the double image of Emmy's corpse and Johnnie Roe's skin grafts. Then he rooted in the Capri's boot for his swimming shorts and a towel. He wanted the North Sea to dilute whatever was left on his skin of the odour of rotting flesh. He walked off into the dunes to change, then ran towards the sea. The water was a Mediterranean blue but the temperature of meltwater off a snow-covered roof. Thankfully the fizzing white spume of the waves gave off a cleansing rush of ozone.

He sat in the sand and thought about being here with Laura four summers ago. They'd talked about the two cottages they'd seen, on Adventurer's Fen: Flightpath Cottages. Derelict and sodden with damp, they would cost less to knock down than restore. It had been a discouraging day and Laura had seemed distant. The cottages weren't right, they'd agreed that. But they shared a view that redefined the concept of panoramic. The wide snaking river running north, the reed beds to the east and west, and the deep cut of the Thirty Foot Drain providing the final defence against the outside world. And Laura's reticence seemed coupled with another emotion, just below the surface. Excitement? Perhaps. Dryden sensed a coiled spring of elation somewhere within her. He was growing impatient with their search and suspicious that Laura was avoiding the commitment the house would symbolise. She'd hugged her secret to herself.

The memory didn't improve his mood. He felt depression sweeping over him like a cold front over a trawler at sea. He took evasive action, retrieving a piece of white folded paper sticking out of his trouser pocket. It was the printout from Laura's COMPASS machine that he had failed to read the night before.

He saw the name but didn't recognise it, even though he felt his skin goosebump, despite the eighty-degree heat. Until now Laura's messages could have been just the product of her unique view on the world. A view of hospital visitors whispering and discussing family secrets around the deathbed of Maggie Beck. But this was a warning.

WATCH WHITE

Freeman White, Lyndon Koskinski's fellow prisoner in Al Rasheid jail. Koskinski had said he was stationed at Mildenhall, undergoing medical treatment.

They were back at The Tower within an hour. Dryden sensed now that Laura had been at the centre of what had happened to Maggie Beck in the last days of her life. The life she had recorded on tape.

He climbed the stairs to Laura's room. The COMPASS machine was silent but a length of ticker tape hung motionless in the room's fetid air. She was getting more expert at using the machine. Dryden could see that now. The jibberish was probably all involuntary movements. But when the message came it was separate and clear.

SHDUTUF F GKO GLDJUCN TAPESECORDER
FDHGFI FHGO SHSYGFKF DHDYWISJ SJSOSOJ

He felt the hair on his neck prickle. She was one letter out. He should have noticed before—the tape recorder Estelle and Lyndon had left on the window ledge was gone.

The nurse on duty at the desk in the foyer seemed mildly affronted that Dryden could suggest one of the staff was a thief.

'I can't imagine anyone here has taken it,' she said. 'Perhaps Mrs Beck's family took it?'

'They said they left it, it's mine. But I'll double check,' said Dryden. 'In the meantime, perhaps you could ask around? If it turns up, no questions will be asked. Otherwise, I guess it's the police.'

Then he told Humph to take him home. They drove in silence to Barham's Dock where *PK 129* lay motionless under a large moon.

'Drink?' asked Dryden, getting out, and not looking back.

He knew something was wrong before he reached the boat. It lay low in the water and he could see now that the bow was much lower than the aft. He heard Humph behind him: 'Shit.'

About three feet of black, stinking river water lay inside the main cabin. A crude siphon pump had been set up to draw the water up over the bulwarks and into the cabin well. He plucked one end of the pipe from the river and climbed aboard. He submerged the pipe in the water in the wheelhouse and then flipped one end of it overboard, reversing the flow and beginning the long task of draining the boat.

They edged on board, aware that *PK 129* had a dangerous list to port. Humph found the newspaper cutting—identical to the one left on the Capri's windscreen. It was pinned to the chart board in the galley. Pinned with a carving knife.

THE CHILDLESS HOUSE had mocked Maggie Beck from the first day: the day they'd driven through the military monotony of the Forestry Commission estates. The windows mocked her with their identical view of pine trees and sandy paths. And the ivory dress mocked her too, even now, from its crepe-paper package above the wardrobe. She longed for the view across Black Bank Fen, wondering at the same time how she could miss, so much, something she had hated so much. The memory of an amphitheatre sky haunted her claustrophobic life. She longed for a horizon, a distant view of miniature people, a cloud casting a shadow half a county away.

She'd married Don two years ago. He could have been her dad. She knew that's what everyone was saying behind their hands. Sometimes she wished he was. Then she could have shared the memory, the memory of the falling star that had taken Matty away.

Why had she married him? Children, security, kindness, decency. Four powerful reasons she knew now did not add up to love.

She went to the front room and touched Matty's picture: the one she'd taken when he was a week old. She loved this image, the one she saw every day, but she loved her secret more. So she ran upstairs to the laundry room where the chest was. She opened it and slipped her hand down beside the old clothes until she found the waxed wallet that held the airletters. They'd started to arrive last year on Lyndon's first birthday. She'd had to ask, by registered letter. She'd lost Matty, they knew that, she only asked to see how the boy she'd saved was growing. Her favourite showed him naked, just two, standing in a lake with a smile like a searchlight and a plastic Captain Hook cutlass.

She flipped it over but she knew the inscription, knew all the inscriptions: 'Tokebee, Michigan. Summer 78. Lyndon plays pirates.'

That's all she had until now: pictures of a memory. Until now. She'd checked her watch: 9.38.

Where was Don? He should be here, they'd agreed that, together. She ran to the nursery and checked the temperature: 74° F, just like the book had said. She rested her hand on the blanket in the cot and felt the familiar surge of grief, of loss, the almost overwhelming conviction that she could feel his body warmth even now, two years later.

She cried at the funeral. Cried openly for the little boy she didn't know, and secretly for the little boy she'd sent to live another life 5,000 miles away. Her lover's tears were real. They burst out of him like a spring and he'd knelt in the red dust and wept like a child who

*can find no logic in the world's cruelty. It was the only time she'd felt
like touching him since the night she'd seen the pictures. The pictures
of her. She could have reached out, told him even then, and ended
those tears. But she kept her secret, and bathed instead in his grief.*

*The doorbell rang. She clattered downstairs, fumbled with the
latch and threw it open, knowing it was Don. He was trying to smile,
trying to hide what he felt: 'There's something wrong. The boy's gone,
Maggie. We have to talk to them again.'*

*She hated his farmer's face then, with the cheeks nipped red by
the frost.*

Wednesday, June 18

8

Dawn: the sun broke on the eastern horizon and swung a searchlight beam over the landscape. From the observation platform
on which Dryden stood he looked down on the canopy of trees that
seemed to cover the earth. To the east a large freshwater lake broke
the sea of feathered, sunlit, green: motionless except for an excited
flock of flamingos, an impossibly pink blotch on the eggshell-blue
water. He was the only one in the tree hide forty feet above Wicken
Fen. He felt his spirit swell at the sheer scale of the landscape below
him, and the skyscape above.

He heard weary footsteps climbing the wooden ladder. He didn't
need to turn to know it was Andy Newman, climbing reluctantly to
their meeting, despite the promise of some on-duty birdwatching.

'I've got a paper to fill,' said Dryden. Wednesdays were tough on
The Crow, with three inside news pages to fill.

Newman fixed his binoculars on the distant flock of flamingos. 'I
would have thought one emaciated corpse in a pillbox would do.'

'Old news,' said Dryden, manufacturing a yawn which turned into
the real thing. He'd spent the night with Humph in the Capri and
sleep had eluded him. He'd been up at dawn to check out the damage
on *PK 129*. And he'd rung August and requested a background interview with Freeman White. 'How about confirming the ID?'

Newman dropped the glasses. 'Can't do. But you know anyway. It's
got to be Johnnie Roe—mobile tea-bar owner and general low-life.'

'Ex-wife?'

'She only reported him missing because the cheques stopped.'

Dryden nodded. 'You were watching the Ritz. Why?'

'Like I said, the immigrants. We'd got most of the staging posts nailed between Felixstowe and the Midlands. A necklace, every thirty miles, like Little Chef. They picked up food, gave 'em air, and unloaded a handful for the local labour market. Then the rest went on. Or, in the case of the shipment we opened yesterday, got dumped.'

'ID on the kid in the lorry?' Dryden tried to make the question sound as casual as possible.

Newman laughed. 'Nobody's talking. We haven't got names for the ones that survived yet. But we will.'

Dryden had promised Jimmy Kabazo he wouldn't go to the police. But that was before Kabazo's son had turned up dead. He told Newman about his meeting with Kabazo at Wilkinson's, and again at the old airfield, and the snapshot he'd shown him of Emmy.

'It's the same kid?' asked Newman.

'Pretty sure,' said Dryden.

Newman made two mobile phone calls: one to the station at Ely to get out and interview Kabazo at Wilkinson's; the second to a scene-of-crime unit to re-examine the Nissen hut the people smugglers had used as a dormitory. He'd visited it himself after Dryden had told him it was being used, but now he had a child's death on his hands. Any forensic link between the hut and the HGV could be crucial in tracking down the people responsible for Emmy Kabazo's death.

'The pictures,' Dryden said. 'Is it the same pillbox in which the pictures of Alice Sutton were taken? And if it is, where's her father?'

Newman sighed, tearing his eyes away from the pink splodges of the birds. 'It's the same box. I can tell you that detectives from the East Midlands force will be re-interviewing our friend the porn-star stud tomorrow morning. The fact that a corpse has been found on the film set may loosen his tongue—but I wouldn't bet on it.'

'Name yet for the stud?'

Newman slipped a notebook from his windcheater. 'Selby, Peter. Aged twenty-six. Address, Caddus Street, Rushden. Worked for a haulage company in the town: A. Ladd and Sons.'

'You found fingerprints at the pillbox?' Dryden asked.

'Yup. Bob Sutton. Don't tell his wife. In fact don't tell anyone until *The Crow* comes out on Friday. OK?'

Dryden was thinking fast. So Alice Sutton's father had gone looking for her and not come back. Now the body of Johnnie Roe had been found in the pillbox where the pornographic pictures had been taken. According to Alice, her father had been to the Ritz T-Bar and was probably aware of Johnnie Roe's role in running a depot for the people smugglers.

'Jesus! Did Sutton kill Roe?'

Newman shrugged. 'It's getting pretty crowded in this pillbox. Alice Sutton and the stud. Then Johnnie. Now Sutton looking for his daughter. If it had a turnstile they could have sold tickets.' He pocketed the binoculars. 'When you write the Bob Sutton story I'd like you to add an appeal for information. There's no body yet—we can't presume he's dead. Anything anyone knows about him, and his recent movements. And that goes for Johnnie Roe too. He's been a loner for ten years. Doesn't mean his life was empty. Any information dealt with sympathetically—you know the form.'

THE ONLY THINGS moving on the Tudor Hall Estate were the net curtains. The object of this twitching interest was obvious: Humph's cab was lowering the tone of the neighbourhood. Inside the cab Dryden slumped in the passenger seat and let the tune from 'Little Boxes' play in his head. It helped block the sound of a Greek street party on Humph's tape, for Nicos was celebrating and everyone in the village was invited. Even, apparently, Humph. Dryden hoped they'd ordered extra portions.

He eyed the front door of number thirty-six, the home, according to the telephone book, of Robert L. Sutton, avenging father of Alice. A Barratt-style semi, it was adorned with fake carriage lamps and a couple of equally dubious Doric columns. Dryden tried to look like an insurance salesman as he rang the bell and stood to attention.

He tried to remember what Bob Sutton had looked like when he'd come into *The Crow*'s offices. Squat, muscle-bound and industrial, the human cannonball. His house didn't suit him, but perhaps it had been chosen to suit someone else. Sure enough the someone else opened the door. It was 10.20 in the morning but she was dressed to kill: tall, dark and shaped like a model.

Elizabeth Jane Sutton put one high-heeled shoe ahead of the other and let her knees kiss in a classic photo-call pose. 'Sorry. Can I help?'

Her daughter Alice appeared behind her, wearing what Dryden guessed passed for nightwear in teenage-daughter-land. 'Oh God,' said Alice, recognising Dryden from her visit to *The Crow* and fled.

'It's Bob, isn't it?' said the mother. The make-up drooped.

'Philip Dryden. *The Crow.* There's no news,' he said, lying effort-lessly. 'I'm sorry to disturb you but it might help to get some more publicity in the paper. Five minutes?' Dryden felt a fraud. He had little choice but to claim ignorance about the fact the police had found Bob Sutton's prints inside the pillbox. The police would be round that afternoon to break the news. Either way events had taken a disturbing twist: the chances were that either Sutton was Johnnie's murderer, or another victim yet unfound. In the meantime Dryden needed an interview and a picture of the missing man.

Thirty seconds later he was sitting on a leather sofa.

Mrs Sutton sat herself down on a chair. 'Bob's gone,' she said, nervously playing with an earring.

'I know. He came to see me at *The Crow* about the pictures of Alice. But she came home, didn't she? What did your husband say?'

She looked away and lit a cigarette. 'He was gone. He hasn't seen Alice—I doubt he knows she's back. That's the bloody stupid . . .' She was either blinding herself with cigarette smoke or beginning to cry.

'I need to find him too,' he said. 'Did he say what he was doing exactly, how he was going to find Alice?'

On the wall hung a picture of Bob Sutton in uniform. Dryden guessed it was the military police. It was a sunny picture, with the white light bleaching out the edges, and a colonial mansion in the background fringed with palms. He nodded at it. 'Overseas?'

She lit up. 'Hong Kong. I was born there. My father was Royal Engineers. Bob was Military Police. It was a glamorous life—then.'

'May I borrow it? I'll bring it back within twenty-four hours, I promise. If we run a story appealing for witnesses, it would help.'

She nodded and he stood up and took the picture down.

As he sat down again, she came over to take the seat next to him. 'He found something,' she said at last. 'One night. He went out and when he came back he was . . . excited. But he wouldn't talk about it. He never wanted to talk about what had happened to Alice. I was angry about that, still am. It wasn't up to him to put it right. It was up to both of us.' She stubbed out the cigarette and lit a fresh one with surprising grace. 'One of his so-called mates in the force sent him the pictures of Alice,' she said. 'He couldn't take that. He sat on this sofa and cried like a child. Clutching the pictures. As if it mattered. At least it showed she was alive. I've never seen him cry before. I was frightened . . . frightened about what he'd do to make things right.'

'Frightened he'd hurt someone?'

She nodded twice. 'I begged him to tell me what he'd found out there,' she said, nodding out through the fake mullioned windows towards the fen. 'He said he would the next day . . . There was blood—all over his handkerchief. I found it later—after he'd gone. He'd chucked it in the bin in the kitchen so I wouldn't see. Lots of blood really. I checked his clothes, it was just the handkerchief.'

'So when was that? The first time he came home?'

'The police asked that,' she said, unblinking.

'And what was the answer?'

'Last Friday night. We were going out, that new Italian on Market Street. I'd dressed up. He dragged himself in at midnight. Sober.'

'What did he say?'

'Said he was near. Close to finding her. Her,' she flicked her chin upwards. 'And all the time she was in some bedsit in Camden Town.'

'She's OK?' asked Dryden.

'She can't remember. Not the pictures. So she ran away, and I don't blame her. What did anyone expect her to do—the police said she'd almost certainly been given that drug—the date-rape thing. She can't believe it's her in the pictures either.'

'And he went out again when?'

'Next night. The Saturday. He wasn't scared. I know when he's scared, it wasn't like he wasn't in control of whatever it was . . . '

'But he didn't come back . . .'

She lit a fresh cigarette. 'You could see his office . . . the police did,' she said, standing up. It was the spare room next to Alice's. There was a PC, a card-file box, and a telephone and fax. Dryden flicked through the card file. Each one was for a separate job—the client's details poorly spelt out in childish capital letters.

'Bob Sutton Security,' she said, and at last began to cry. 'The job was the best he could get after the army. He didn't have much of an education—no certificates. Nothing. It's tough when you're his age.' Alice came in and wrapped her arms round her mother's neck.

'In the blue folder,' she said, leading Alice away.

And they were. The same stud. Different girls, but all in the pill-box. But they weren't pristine like Alice's shots, they were dog-eared. They'd been through many grubby hands.

And police statements, photocopied transcripts of taped inter-views. Dryden guessed Sutton's police contacts had come in useful again. He'd used his contacts in the lorry trade to pick up the trail of the people smugglers who'd traded in the pornography at the same

242

time as illegal immigrants. He'd almost certainly identified the Ritz as a dropping-off point. Then he'd made contact with the police about the man they'd arrested in connection with the pictures of Alice—which in turn had led to other interviews, other raids. In the end he'd had enough information to act. He'd gone out and found something that Monday night. Was it the pillbox? Had he confronted Johnnie Roe and got a confession? Or had he dragged Johnnie there himself?

Dryden replaced the pictures in the folder with the statements and went downstairs. The two women were standing at the door. 'When your husband went out the second time, Mrs Sutton, what did he take?'

She shrugged. 'Torch, I think. It's one of the torches they give the military police. It's got a heavy rubber covering so it can double up as a Black Jack . . . and his nookie kit.'

'What?'

Alice and her mother laughed. 'His nookie kit,' said Alice. 'He did a lot of private detective work—mainly husbands cheating on their wives. He had to spend a lot of time sat in the car watching, with his cameras. So he had a nookie kit—chocolate bars, sandwiches, crisps, cake . . . a bit of a feast.'

Dryden was standing outside now in the sunshine. The temperature was rising. 'Anything to drink?'

'He always took a flask of tea. But that night he took water too. Two big bottles of Evian.'

A TEXT MESSAGE was waiting on Dryden's mobile when he got back in the cab outside Bob Sutton's home. He'd rung Garry straight back. *The Crow*'s junior reporter had been monitoring emergency calls and picked up a violent incident at the city mortuary, where Emmy Kabazo's body was waiting for an official ID.

They pulled off the main road at a sign that said MORTUARY. The building itself was a long, brick two-storey block in 1930s Fascist style. Two ambulances stood silently at a 'goods in'.

Jimmy Kabazo was standing outside the plate-glass entrance foyer with a crowbar in his hands. As Humph pulled the Capri up beside a police car, Jimmy ran at the doors of the main entrance and delivered a shattering blow with the iron bar. The reinforced glass splintered in a complex pattern, like expanding crystals.

Dryden got out of the cab, but left the door open so he could retreat. He understood Kabazo's rage. If he'd read the newspapers or listened to the local radio he'd know about the body found in the container lorry. He'd know it was the body of the only sixteen-year old in the human consignment abandoned by the people smugglers. In other words, he knew, almost certainly, that it was his son.

Kabazo waited for him as Dryden walked the fifty yards between them. 'I'm sorry. I'm sure they'll let you see him,' said Dryden.

Tears bathed Jimmy's face. 'They said I had to wait—talk to the policeman.'

Dryden knew that anger and despair were a high-octane emotional cocktail, so he kept a safe distance from the crowbar.

'I was there when they found him,' he said.

Kabazo dropped the crowbar and they listened to it roll away. Dryden noticed that it left a thin trail of arterial-red blood in its wake.

'It is him?' said Kabazo.

'I think so,' said Dryden. 'But you must see him. You will.'

Then they heard a car skid off the main road and head towards them across the tarmac. At the wheel was DS Peter Crabbe, Newman's sidekick.

Jimmy ignored him. 'You were there?'

Dryden nodded and held out his arms. 'We should talk. Inside?'

'I must see him,' said Jimmy simply, seeing DS Crabbe advancing, accompanied by the two uniformed policemen from the squad car. Some of the anger had washed out of him, and his shoulders sagged. Crabbe left the PCs to take Kabazo into custody and led the way towards the mortuary doors. He pushed a button to one side, which opened up an intercom to the desk inside. 'OK. Open up now please—the situation is under control. DS Peter Crabbe.' He held up his warrant card to the glass.

The doors slid open electronically, spilling shattered glass as they did so. One of the PCs from the squad car slipped handcuffs on Jimmy as they waited in the reception area. He didn't resist, his eyes set on the interior doors to the mortuary. One of the two medical orderlies behind the foyer counter held a bandage to his head, from which a thin trickle of blood had run down to his collar.

'I've radioed for medical,' said Crabbe, turning to Kabazo. 'While we're waiting, Mr Kabazo—I presume?'

Dryden nodded. 'Mr Kabazo wished to identify the body of his son,' he said.

Crabbe turned to him. 'Mr Kabazo. Are you responsible for this?' He gestured towards the orderly with the head wound.

'They wouldn't let me see him,' said Kabazo.

'We called at Wilkinson's, Mr Kabazo, to invite you to a formal ID. They said you were sick.'

'Perhaps. Why are we waiting, Detective Sergeant?'

Crabbe decided that he might as well press ahead with the ID while he had Kabazo in the building.

One of the mortuary assistants hit some security buttons and the interior set of doors swished open. Beyond that Crabbe led them through two sets of doors. There was a sweet, medicinal smell in the air, which Dryden could not identify. They stopped in front of a door marked: AUTOPSY UNIT. Inside, the room was lit by sunshine from skylights. A row of surgical tables stood in the centre of the room. There was a body on one and the sunshine fell on the zip-up hospital-green bag in which it was wrapped.

A woman in a white body-suit appeared and stood by the table with her hand on the zip. Crabbe took Kabazo's arm, marched him forwards to the table, and nodded briskly. The bag was unzipped to the chest of the boy. Dryden had waited too long. He felt, rather than heard, the breath leaving Kabazo's body, and only heard the scream of despair as he fled from the room.

HUMPH EDGED THE CAB forwards in the queue at the security gate. The air-base wire ran into the distance like the edge of a giant chicken run. A grey B-52 was coming in to the runway leaving a streak of lead half a mile wide hanging like a dirty washing-line in a blue sky. Dryden's request for an interview with Captain Freeman White had got a prompt response from August Sondheim by text message: INTERVIEW NOON. Dryden wondered what was in it for August.

'No wisecracks,' said Dryden, as they edged towards the heavily armed military guards.

The sentry ambled up to Humph's cab and made the mistake of tapping on Humph's window, a little military two-tap.

The cabbie wound it down. 'Wing Commander?' he said, beaming.

Dryden leaned across with his wallet open to show a press pass. 'Excuse me. Major Sondheim is expecting us.'

The barrier went up and the sentry barked. 'Follow the red lines, sir. To the red car park. Major Sondheim will meet you there, sir.'

Humph saluted as they sailed past.

The base was a town crowded round a single runway long enough to take the big transatlantic flights. Dryden shifted in his seat, aware that his claustrophobia had kicked in as they'd slipped inside the high-wire cordon. Military hardware dotted the horizon, from bristling communications masts to rocking radar dishes. They swept past one of the many on-base canteens that was built of blood-red brick and boasted a single, neon sign for McDonald's. At the traffic lights controlling the runway crossing, August thumped his hand on the roof and leaned in on Humph's side.

'Hiya. Over there.' He pointed to a group of prewar hangars. Humph parked and began to blow up the in-flight pillow he'd bought at Stansted Airport for just such occasions.

August took Dryden by the arm and led him to a US military Jeep. It was 11.45 and August was sober, but the strain was showing. His diction was as sharp as the crease on his trousers. In the back of the Jeep was one of his PR staff, a woman in fatigues with a clipboard.

'Meet the enemy, Sergeant DeWitt,' said August. She nodded into the rearview mirror. Even in a partial reflection Dryden could tell she was a woman of impressive credentials. Her uniform tried, but failed, to encompass a heart-stopping bust.

'Right,' said August, gunning the Jeep past two red lights and crossing the runway to a group of postwar three-storey dormitory buildings. Through the distant perimeter wire Dryden could see the tall pines that marked Mons Wood and the edge of Black Bank Fen.

'We have a problem,' said August, pulling up outside one of the buildings. 'Lyndon Koskinski has gone AWOL.'

'I thought he was on leave?' Dryden got out and, deserting the air conditioning in the US-built Jeep, felt the heat from the tarmac slap him in the face. Now he knew why August had agreed to his interview request: he needed help.

'He was. But if you live on base you have to report; daily. If you leave base you have to sign out. He's done neither for more than a week. The police—civilian at Ely—want to talk to him about his mother's death. More precisely about his own—reported—death. Procedure, nothing suspicious. There is also the issue of his passport. He's fought for America—nobody is going to block an application for citizenship, but he needs to make it. His current passport is invalid. And a British one would take months to issue.'

'Have you tried out at Black Bank?' asked Dryden.

'Ms Beck? She says she hasn't seen him since her mother's funeral.'

'So you want me to interview the room-mate. Run the story with an appeal for Lyndon to come forward and help the police clear up loose ends. Bit of heart-sob piece. That it?'

August didn't answer, but led the way. The block smelt of carbolic and old trainers. They climbed to the top floor.

August stopped in front of one of the dormitory doors marked:

R145
MAJOR LYNDON KOSKINSKI
CAPT FREEMAN WHITE——BASE FIRE TEAM

August knocked smartly. Lyndon's room-mate was black, heavily built, with grey curly hair. Dryden and August sat on one bunk, White opposite. His bed was covered in several layers of newspaper, in the middle of which was a jumble of oily machinery: cogs, cables and bolts. His fingers showed the grease where he'd been working.

And there was the wound. Lyndon Koskinski had said he'd been injured ejecting from their plane over Iraq. A welt about six inches long had healed on White's skull but could still be traced from his right cheekbone to the hairline. The right eye was cloudy and Dryden guessed from the way he held his head to one side that it was blind.

'Mechanic, eh?' asked Dryden.

'I ain't seen Lyndon for days,' White said, ignoring the question.

Dryden tried to recall the stature of the motorcyclist who had vandalise Humph's cab. The height was right.

'We weren't that close, you know . . .' He spread two huge hands on his knees. 'Guy's got a life to lead, yeah? He wanted time. Space.'

August folded a knee flat over the other. 'But you were in Iraq together. You had to ditch. That's right, isn't it?'

White glanced up at a picture pinned above Lyndon's pillow. An F-111 on a hot white runway somewhere sandy where the tide never came in. Lyndon had a high-tech flying helmet under his arm. White was next to him.

Dryden flipped open a notebook.

'Yeah. I was the pilot that day—he was navigating. We bailed out, got separated . . .'

'How come?' said Dryden standing and looking at the snapshots pinned to a cork board.

'We parachuted down a few miles from each other. I got picked up right off by a field patrol. Republican Guard. I'd hit the canopy on the way out when we ejected. Made a mess of my head. I don't remember much about it. Lyndon came down over the horizon. They sent a squad of the local militia after him—took 'em a week to find him. We both ended up in Al Rasheid. Some cell. It was grim, you can guess.'

'So you had that in common,' said August. 'Four weeks together in that cell. That was a bond. You must feel close, no?'

'Sure,' said White, beginning to rearrange the cogs and bolts on the newspaper. 'Lyndon saved my life in there. Fed me, gave me his water, kept the wounds clean. I really don't remember a lot—but I'd be dead otherwise.' Dryden sensed he hadn't wanted to say this, but couldn't help himself.

'So you owe him your life. That's a big debt,' said Dryden, probing.

White ignored him again. 'Three months ago he was great, when we got back. He was going Stateside once he'd got his weight back. Then he went out to the farm—Black Bank. You know . . .?' Dryden and August nodded.

'That seemed to go OK. He was kinda pleased. He loves his grand-parents. That's them.' He pointed at a colour snap of Lyndon on a beach. The grandparents stood stiffly on either side. 'Maggie was really pleased to see him. I guess she wanted to get close.'

'He saw a lot of her?' asked Dryden, looking out the window.

'Yeah. He stayed out there—she gave him a room. Food was good, that's what he wanted. It got him off the base. He looked great. Got a tan. This summer of yours is unreal.'

Dryden sat on the bunk beside him. 'It's a one-off. Even we don't believe it. So—then Maggie died.'

'Yeah. Then she died and he kinda collapsed.' They left the silence for him to fill. 'He came back the next morning. Brought his stuff.'

'Stuff?' August leaned back against the wall. Dryden appreciated the classic interview technique. Relax when things get interesting.

'Clothes. Books. Everything he'd taken. I asked him what was up. He said Maggie had died, that everything was different. Then he shut up. Packed a kitbag with his washing stuff and fresh clothes and went. Didn't say goodbye, didn't say anything.'

Dryden spoke from the window. 'Did he leave anything valuable— anything that you knew was precious to him?'

White shook his head. Dryden was looking out of the window when he saw the box. He guessed it was made from an exotic hard-wood, almost ruby red, and constructed in a carved fretwork.

'That's nice,' said Dryden, careful not to touch it. 'Middle Eastern?'

'Yup. Aden, the Souk—good for presents.' White looked at his watch. 'I'm due on duty, gentlemen. Flying a desk. Then physio.' Neither Dryden nor August believed him, but they stood up anyway.

Dryden thought, There's always one more question. 'And you've not had contact with Lyndon at all—phone, text, letter . . . nothing?'

'Like I said. Nothin'. Nothin' for days.'

'May I?' said August, pointing to the bathroom.

'Sure.' White busied himself collecting some papers while Dryden looked around. He waited until August pulled the chain and then he stepped in close and picked up one of the fly-wheel cogs on the bed.

'Motorcyle?' he asked.

White looked him in the eyes. 'Yup.'

'Thought so,' said Dryden, tossing the cog into White's hands. 'Dangerous things. You should be careful.'

August appeared, so he grabbed White's hand. 'Thanks. You've been really helpful.'

Back in the Jeep August set out the ground rules. 'There's no hiding the fact Koskinski's gone AWOL. I know that. But he deserves some sympathy too. A month in a cell can mess up anyone's head. Then he gets home and discovers he isn't who he thought he was. He gets a mother twenty-seven years after he was made an orphan.'

Dryden held his hands up. 'I hear you. No problem. I never planned to label him Most Wanted Man.'

'You can quote White, but no name, OK? Just a friend on the base. Pilot—you can say that in *The Crow*, this week. Yup?'

Dryden felt a line had been crossed. 'I can say what I bloody well like, when I like. But as it happens I won't name him, and yes, it will be in this week's paper, OK?'

'I owe you a drink,' said August, but really he owed it to himself, so they drove in silence to Mickey's Bar.

9

The primary school at Barrowby Drove was a postwar prefab. The heat outside was ninety degrees and rising. Inside, underneath a corrugated-iron roof, it must have been higher. As soon as Dryden went through the door the heat hit him, just before the smell did.

'Fen kids,' he said. Humph was in the cab outside baking, but at least he was pot-roast; this was cabbage and socks.

Dryden was standing in an anteroom full of pegs marked with names. He'd gone to a similar school himself on Burnt Fen, fifteen kids from six families, and he'd smelt of cabbage too. He peeked through a glass porthole into the single classroom. Estelle Beck was at the front of the class perched precariously on the teacher's desk, her legs up in the lotus position. She didn't look much like a teacher and she certainly didn't look like the teacher at Barrowby Drove. She was wearing sports gear and an array of pencils stuck out of her hair like punk spikes. On the blackboard were some mathematical symbols Dryden didn't dwell on. Every head in the class was down, tiny fists holding pencils in cack-handed grips.

Dryden knocked and every head turned except hers. The silence dissolved in excited whispers as Estelle beckoned him inside.

'OK, OK,' said Estelle, holding up a hand for silence: 'Let's try and remember our manners. Remember what we've learned about how to behave with visitors, Jonathan . . . ?'

Jonathan stood. 'Welcome to Barrowby Drove School,' he said, turning scarlet.

She then introduced Dryden to the class. 'This is Mr Dryden,' said Estelle. 'He's a reporter with *The Crow*.'

Jaws dropped universally, indicating that visitors to Barrowby Drove School were rarely as exotic.

'OK—little ones around the art table please with crayons and paper. Middle group please read the next chapter of *Harry Potter and the Chamber of Secrets*. Jonathan is in charge.'

Estelle lead the way through another door into a small playground.

'It's Lyndon,' said Dryden. He saw that the electric-green eyes were extremely bright, almost preternaturally alive.

'My brother,' she said. 'What about him?'

'Well, officially he's AWOL from Mildenhall. Have you any idea where he might be? Did he attend the reading of the will?'

She shook her head. 'No. He'd said from the start he wanted nothing. Which is a bit awkward as he got everything.'

'How do you feel about that?' said Dryden, cursing himself for a maladroit question.

'Mum knew I hated Black Bank. I hated it almost as much as she did. I think leaving it to Lyndon was a masterstroke. I feel free of it for the first time in my life. That answer your question?'

Dryden ignored the hostility. 'The last time you saw him, what was his mood?'

She looked out over the fen. 'He's very angry. Desperate. I worried about him when he was at Black Bank. Now he's gone, it's worse. I think he's gone away so he can't hurt anyone he likes. Loves.'

'Could he hurt himself?'

'Maybe.' She forced herself to go on. 'I think so. Yes. Don't you? He's an American, he fought for his country, and now that's been taken away from him. He spent nearly thirty years thinking he'd lost his mother when he was two weeks old—then, with almost her last breath, he discovers she's alive. How much grief can one person take? What would you feel?'

'I'd want to know why she'd done it, why she gave me away.'

'Which is exactly what we don't know. She was unhappy at Black Bank, she hated her life in many ways. The tapes are very clear about that. About what my mother suffered . . .'

'You've listened to all of them?'

She answered immediately, as if under cross-examination in a courtroom. 'Yes. All those we found under the bed. Each one. From her earliest memories on Black Bank to her final illness . . . '

'Forgive me,' said Dryden, stepping closer. 'Did you get the sense that she'd completed the story? Does the last tape end abruptly?'

'It just runs out. You think there's more?'

'Possibly. The tape recorder's gone—you didn't take it?'

She shook her head. 'No. I said, we left it for you.'

'And she gave no hint about why she gave Matty away?'

'She said she had no choice,' said Estelle. 'And that she'd never regretted what she'd done, even though she grieved for her son for nearly thirty years.' She walked off to tap a barometer mounted on the schoolhouse wall next to a thermometer. She had her back to him when she spoke. 'If you find him first, Mr Dryden, tell him to speak to me. Tell him to ring the mobile.' She touched her breast pocket to check the phone was still there.

Dryden walked back with her towards the classroom. 'One question. Did Lyndon take the Land Rover?'

'Yes, yes he did.'

Dryden spun on his heel, taking in the circular horizon of the Black Fen. 'That's going to be difficult to hide. You can see for ever.'

She considered the view: a shimmering expanse of tumbling hot air. 'Sometimes the truth's a lot closer.'

HUMPH DROVE him to Barham's Dock as the sun fell. He left Humph rummaging in the drinks compartment and rang his landline answerphone: still no word from Gillies & Wright. How could Maggie have miscalculated? She'd been convinced Lyndon's father would come forward. If there was no further news soon Dryden needed a new lead on the story to run the appeal again—this time in *The Crow*.

He checked his watch: 8.45 p.m.—time for night calls. Every evening he did the round of six: police HQ at Cambridge, local cop shop at Ely, fire station at Cambridge, county ambulance control at Histon, the coastguard at Cromer and the AA regional centre at Peterborough. Most nights it was six blanks, which was a good job as Dryden usually made the calls having taken a series of nightcaps with Humph. Tonight it was miniature crème de menthes. Sickly green bottles of alcoholic medicine.

Dryden hit the mobile. He knew something was wrong when he finally got through to the duty officer at the county police HQ.

'We've got two units on the perimeter wire at Mildenhall. Request from the base commander. Fire. No other details at this time.'

'Shit,' said Dryden, cutting to fire HQ. Humph carefully screwed the top back on to his second bottle and started the cab's engine.

'We've got three tenders on the airfield,' said the operator.

'From . . .' said Dryden, hoping his luck would hold.

'Mildenhall, Ely and Soham.'

The military at Mildenhall had three tenders of their own on the air base. If they'd called for assistance something had gone off with a big bang. He flicked through his contact book. He knew one of the Ely firemen whose wife was a nurse at The Tower. They'd met at a fund-raising barbecue, the summer before Laura's accident. He'd been on the *News* then but could never let a social occasion pass without ruining it by asking someone for their mobile telephone number. He rang it now, it picked up, but all he could hear was garbled shouting.

'. . . here. Darren Peake here. Darren . . .'

'Hi. Hi. It's Philip. Philip Dryden from *The Crow*. Sorry. We met at one of the fund-raisers. Are you at the Mildenhall fire?'

Generally firemen were press-friendly. They like seeing the pictures taken from the at-scene videos in the local paper and *The Crow* covered all their sports sponsorship events.

'Yeah,' said Peake. 'It's a sight. Fire-training facility has gone up, then a petrol tank. I'm officer in charge at the scene for the civil—give us a wave. The yellow hat. *Ciao*.'

Dryden checked the back seat for *The Crow*'s office cameras and a decent pair of binoculars. Humph already had the cab on the road going east, while overhead the sky was turning from blue to purple like a giant bruise as the sun set. They saw the single gout of fire ten miles short of the end of the runway; a vertical eruption of fuel-blue flame closely followed by the crump of exploding metal.

The approach roads to the base were closed by military police with mobile roadblocks but Humph swung the Capri off down an unlit drove road around the perimeter wire. They big-dippered along the rock-hard farm track until they bounced out into a field of unmown grass gone to seed. It was a campsite run by an enterprising local farmer exclusively for plane spotters to watch arrivals and departures at Mildenhall. The entire population of this dysfunctional holiday camp was up against the perimeter wire, including half-a-dozen kids in stripy pyjamas.

The fire was 200 yards beyond the wire. Dryden pressed his face against the diamond-webbed fence with all the rest. The guy next to him made Humph look like a bathing belle. He shielded his eyes by pulling down a cap peak slightly smaller than a garage door. A small boy at his knee looked up with adoring eyes. There was a lot to look up to. 'What happened?' said Dryden, hoping the guy wouldn't swing round and flatten him.

'The fire house went up.'

Dryden realised immediately that the big man didn't know he was not one of the brothers. 'Actually. I'm a reporter,' he said. 'Just driven out—what's a fire house?'

Dryden took an evasive step back as the big man swung round. He looked at Dryden as one would greet an alien life form, spitting effortlessly over Dryden's head and then cracking his knuckles.

'Fire house is where they practise fire-fighting. OK? It's just a brick shell—but with concrete floors. Only difference they have metal hatches over the windows, doors, chimney—all the outlets. That way they can control the fire. This one's got a fake fuselage attached, and a wing with an engine. They flood 'em with high-octane fuel and then—Bang!'

They returned to the mesh fence. 'So what went wrong?'

'Guess they didn't have this one under control.'

Dryden saw Darren Peake's yellow hat bobbing on the edge of the fire zone. He rang him on the mobile and waved, stupidly, from beyond the wire. Darren strolled over, removing the hat and the breathing gear and Dryden took some pictures through the fence as he approached with the fire in the background.

'There's a body in there,' he said, sucking water from a bottle attached to his protective suit. 'Guy's a crisp. Not a lot left, even the teeth are carbonised.'

'How?'

Darren replaced the yellow hat. 'Between you and me? There was a practice scheduled for tomorrow morning; they usually let us know just in case so we can stand by. There's a reservoir of aircraft fuel inside. Looks like someone dumped chummy and lit the fuel. There are ventilation grills on all four outside walls which provide the fire with air—they were all open. Some sparks got out and lit the runway grass. That heated up the waste oil tank, which exploded.'

They all looked back as a hissing sound overrode the screaming of the flames. Several jets of foam were being played on the flames, which fluttered before dying in a cauldron of steam. The fire house was instantly buried under a snowdrift.

'Send us some prints eh? Show's over,' said Darren, walking off.

Dryden woke Humph up. 'There's a body in there. This place will be crawling with police when they get the call. Let's go.'

Humph, horrified, fired the Capri into life.

'I'D LIKE YOU to come with me, OK?'

Humph studied the Capri's rearview mirror.

'I've never asked before. I won't again. Once.'

'Last time,' said Humph, fingering the retied ends of his beloved fluffy dice.

'Jesus,' said Dryden. 'He slashed the seats. It wasn't Pearl Harbor, This is important. I need your help.'

Dryden got out of the car, slammed the door and took the steps two at a time into the reception area of the hospital. Humph followed carefully, picking his way up each individual step, and when he got to the top he surveyed the plush carpet-muffled interior of The Tower. 'Is there a lift?'

They rode up to the third floor in a silence punctuated by the bronchial whistles of Humph's pulmonary system coping with the shock of physical effort.

Humph had never actually seen Laura. His partnership with Dryden had begun in the desolate weeks after her accident when the reporter needed ferrying from the hospital to his mother's house on Burnt Fen. Dryden's rare excursions into memory had given an impression of his wife characterised by an exuberance of warmth:

Latin temperament, Italian colouring, and ample curves. Humph had seen a picture reluctantly withdrawn from the zipped pocket of the wallet: a broad face blessed with perfect skin, brown eyes with a slight cast, and a jumble of auburn hair. The cabbie was not surprised to find the real Laura dramatically different. Her skin was ice-white and lifeless. The eyes open, brown, but blank; the arms laid straight at the sides, and the lips pale and parted by a centimetre. The teeth behind were perfect, linen white, and dry.

'She's beautiful,' said Humph, lying.

Dryden nodded, pleased at the lie, and oddly moved. 'Tear it off,' he said, pointing at the ticker tape from the COMPASS machine.

'Why?' said Humph, tearing off the sheet and sitting down on two bedside chairs.

'Tell me what it says. It's beginning to freak me out. She told me to watch Freeman White. I'm pretty sure he's responsible for the threats, the attempt to sink my boat. How the hell does she know?'

Humph shrugged and studied the jumbled letters.

SGARTFN FH F F DGFDHFYRND LOPQJFCYOID
SGSHSIIH SHSJOSD SDHFUTKG SHFDGFYTO GHLL

'Nothing,' said Humph.

'There's gotta be,' said Dryden, snatching the paper.

There was a long silence in which Dryden tried to force meaning from the jumble of letters.

Then the ticker-tape machine bashed out a single letter: T.

They both jumped, Humph's return to earth producing a perceptible after-tremor.

The COMPASS machine ticked and printed a second letter: TH.

'Tell me, Laura,' Dryden said, looking into her vacant brown eyes.

THE. Then she stopped. A minute passed.

THE WHISSLES

Dryden tore off the sheet and studied the letters again. 'Wait in the car,' he told Humph.

Dryden sat beside Laura's bed. 'I need help,' he said. 'Not this.'

He waited by the COMPASS machine for an hour in silence.

SHE KNEW THE MOMENT when she'd made the decision: the unilateral decision that she loved him. She'd always loved the idea of him, ever since she'd understood what America was. But that day at the track, she'd gone to get hot dogs and Cokes while he strolled round the cars before the first race. Running his fingers sensuously along the beaten metal, the way he'd run his fingers over her.

When she got back with the food the first race had begun. What she remembered was that he seemed to be the only thing that wasn't moving. The backdrop was chaotic. The stock cars raising dust even that early in the summer, the metal screeching as two clashed on a bend. The crowd, mostly US military, had run to the rail to view the wreckage, to cheer the two drivers emerging from the dust.

And he'd just stood there, on the grass with his leg up on the running board of the Land Rover, flicking the Zippo. His self-contained stillness made her want to be near him always. It was the antidote to her own life, which had never seemed to have a centre, let alone one which would always hold. Even as she approached with the food and the drinks he didn't turn.

She touched his arm. 'Lyndon?' And that was when he knew he'd fallen in love with her, the point when he knew he wanted to come back to the world he'd lost in Al Rasheid. He'd been lonely ever since, avoiding strangers because they could ask questions, and friends because they couldn't, because they felt that saying nothing was the kindest cure for what he knew they must call many things—his illness, his injuries, his imprisonment, his lifelessness.

In truth he'd always been lonely. His lifelessness was older than his imprisonment. His childhood had been oddly passionless, an orphan doted on, but never loved, not with the unconditional love of a parent. An orphan placated by money. A friendless boy who'd been lonely all his life: which is why he'd survived Al Rasheid.

Estelle had ended that loneliness because their shared history made her unique. She'd known him all his life, but he was a stranger. Ever since he could remember they'd sent her presents from Texas, dolls when she was a child, then clothes, CDs, pictures of the desert, and the city where they lived. And she'd sent pictures back, from the awkward Fen child in farm clothes clutching her American doll, to the blonde teenager with the all-American smile.

'Pretty kid,' said his grandfather, sourly. They'd resented the contact, his grandparents, he knew that now. He knew that it was Maggie who had kept them together, persisted, and used their guilt to keep the link alive.

And Estelle had envied him his family as well. The lack of parents, the doting grandparents, the freedom. Her father had died when she was four, long before her memory had been born. And her mother had loved her as her second child, precisely that and nothing more. A great love, but always, she sensed, short of its absolute potential.

And so they'd shared a childhood, an adolescence, despite the 5,000 miles that had always separated them. When he'd been stationed overseas he'd flown out via the Pacific—but they'd told Maggie he was posted in Iraq and that if he came back through the UK he'd visit. But after Al Rasheid he couldn't face them, despite the calls from home telling him Maggie was ill.

His depression had deepened, alone in his room at the base. He had to drive, anywhere. He'd seen the sign and felt the past pulling him towards the centre of his life: that moment when the plane had disintegrated in a fireball of aviation fuel. He'd never wanted to see the spot where his parents had died. But just after the sign came the memorial stone.

He'd left the car and walked to the house. There was no answer so he walked round to the yard. She had a towel out on the grass by the greenhouses. A bikini, in sky blue he remembered, contrasting with the butter-yellow hair. A CD player belting out country-and-western. She hadn't heard him so he stood and considered her, trying to recall what it was like to hold such a body. He couldn't remember the name of the last woman he'd made love to. But now he wanted to hold this woman.

So he'd said hello. She'd jumped up and removed her sunglasses. And that was the start of it, and now there was an end to it.

Thursday, June 19

10

Dryden checked the court list again. He was first up on the rota for the magistrates: Peter Selby, of Caddus Way, Rushden. The stud from the pillbox porn show.

In the main courtroom the press bench was empty except for Alf Walker, a veteran wireman who had the county magistrate circuit stitched up, making a decent living filing anything juicy to the nationals. He cut *The Crow* in for a nominal fee.

Normally Dryden would have left this one to Alf, but he had developed a strong personal interest in the pillbox on Black Bank Fen.

Alf's hobby was birdwatching, and his notebook pages alternated between beautifully inscribed shorthand verbatim notes and mildly gifted line drawings of British birds. He was halfway through a fine kestrel when Dryden slumped onto the bench next to him.

At that moment the court clerk entered and promptly called the court to order. 'All rise!' The magistrates trooped in.

'How's Andy?' Dryden whispered. Walker was a member of the same birdwatching society as Inspector Andy Newman. Dryden had noticed that he and Alf were occasionally blessed with the same inside information as a result.

'Chasing his arse. He's got two corpses and no idea. But I doubt he's losing any sleep over it.' Alf nodded at the dock: 'Hey up.'

It was Peter Selby, the stud from Newman's pornographic snaps. Dryden reckoned he was six feet two, blond lifeless hair cut short. He'd been given bail at his last appearance and was in a casual T-shirt that showed off the flawless muscles Alice Sutton had, at first, found so sexy. Even more so after she'd been slipped the date-rape drug.

But it was the face that was most forgettable. It was odd but true that a complete set of perfect features can make a face repellent: a hymn to symmetry without a trace of character.

His lawyer stood up, which was the first clue that Peter Selby had friends with wallets. This was no country circuit solicitor; the suit was navy-blue, pinstripe, and cut to perfection. Behind him sat two juniors armed with papers, mobile phones and bottles of Evian.

The prosecuting officer stood up slowly as two court ushers brought in four boxes and set them on the solicitor's bench.

For the first time Dryden noticed the group sitting behind the legal team. There were five men, four were black and smartly dressed, the fifth was white and, but for the company he was keeping, Dryden would have had him down as a member of the British National Party: a close-shaven head, military fatigues and an ugly botched attempt at a Union Jack tattoo on a bulging bicep.

'Sir,' said the solicitor, addressing the chairman of the bench. 'We are opposing the renewal of bail set on June the 10th at ten thousand pounds. We believe the accused may abscond.'

'What has changed since his last appearance?' The chairman of the magistrates was a local farmer.

The ushers opened the boxes and handed some of the contents to the court clerk, who passed them up to the magistrates. The skinhead leaned forwards to chat to the legals.

'These were found in a lock-up garage rented by the accused in

Melton Mowbray, sir. There are nearly twelve thousand separate items.'

The chairman looked like he might want to see all of them.

'As you can see, sir, the scale of this operation is far wider than first thought. Large amounts of similar material, some involving girls clearly below the age of consent, have been found in containers at both Hull and Felixstowe. They had been prepared for export. Senior officers of the Cambridgeshire constabulary are investigating what they believe to be a two-way trade: people smuggled in and this, er, literature, smuggled out. Interpol is cooperating with the enquiry, as is the Serious Crime Squad.'

The chairman of the bench nodded. 'I see. Mr Smith-fforbes?'

The expensive lawyer stood up slowly. 'Sir, I am afraid the Crown has put forward no facts to link the defendant to the mass production for export of this material. He is, if I may say so, a victim as much as these poor girls. It is his contention that he was unaware his, er, activities were being photographed and he intends to establish his innocence of the charges in the Crown Court. He has agreed bail and volunteered to meet very strict bail requirements.'

The prosecuting solicitor stood up. 'I think your worships will have noted that the defendant appears in many of the pictures I have shown the bench. Of the two thousand items recovered so far he appears in nearly six hundred. It is our belief he is a central figure in this illicit trade and we fear that those who have garnered considerable wealth from this traffic would find it convenient if he was to disappear. We believe they will see ten thousand pounds as a small price to pay.'

The skinhead said something to the legal team, who passed it on to Smith-fforbes. He stood up smartly. 'My client is willing to meet fresh bail conditions—including a considerably higher bail figure.'

The three magistrates conferred with the clerk. 'Very well,' said the chairman of the bench. 'We were minded to agree to remanding the defendant in custody. But am I right that the police do not think they will be able to move to a trial of this matter before Christmas?'

The prosecuting solicitor stood up slowly. 'That's correct, sir. The enquiries are extremely complex . . . and several other arrests are imminent,' he added, casting a glance back over the court.

'I see. Well, we do not think the defendant can be rightly held for that length of time. We therefore grant bail at a figure of fifty thousand pounds. Mr Selby will report to his local police station twice daily during that period.'

Selby's advocate was on his feet again. 'If I may just comment, sir. My client is, of course, a long-distance lorry driver. That condition of the bail was waived at the last hearing to allow him to continue in gainful employment.'

The chairman looked unimpressed. 'I know. But not this time. I'm afraid he will have to find other gainful employment.'

'Court rise,' said the clerk.

Outside, the WRVS ran a tea bar when the court was sitting. Dryden and Alf bought their drinks and sat down.

They watched as the four black men in suits from the back of the court got into two smart powder-blue Jags that pulled up at the court-house steps. The skinhead sat back in one of them, studying documents while he used a mobile phone.

'What do you reckon?' asked Dryden.

Alf shrugged. 'Well, it was about four grand's worth of lawyers. So I think we can rule out his Post Office savings, don't you? And it wasn't their only case of the day—they've earned their money twice.'

'Another case? I thought Selby was first up?'

Alf flicked back through his notebook. 'Nope. Remand. Jimmy Kabazo. Up on a GBH charge—cracked a mortuary attendant over the head with an iron bar. Our friends in suits argued that it was down to emotional distress. Police suggested they were also investigating the possibility that he was an illegal immigrant—but the bench kicked that out as they had no evidence to support it. Then they said—a bit belatedly if you ask me—he might be a suspect in that nasty killing out on the Fens—the bloke in the pillbox.'

'Jesus—so they freed him?'

'Yup. Bit of a cock-up. Police solicitor looked a bit sick. Anyway he was out—and into the waiting arms of that creepy skinhead and his mates. Bail of five thousand pounds agreed by the advocate. Passport had been withdrawn already for examination.'

'So he just walked off?' said Dryden, his patience draining away.

'Nope. There was a bit of a row outside the court. They tried to get him into one of the Jags to shut him up but he wasn't having it. He hung around the PC on duty for a bit and they got the hint—left him alone. Then he walked off—into town.'

Dryden walked back to *The Crow* wondering what Jimmy Kabazo would do next. If the death of his son had been an accident, someone had been reckless in dumping the van. If the van had been deliber-ately dumped then the driver had effectively left them all to die. Did

Jimmy know the truth? And did he know who was responsible?

Paying Jimmy's bail must have been a real quandary for the smugglers. They needed him out of police custody to make sure he didn't talk. But once freed he would be out to avenge Emmy's death. Dryden guessed the number one target was the skinhead driver Jimmy had described at the airfield. He was undoubtedly the tattooed yob who had sat through the stud's appearance and was now lolling in the back of the Jag. The only real question was whether the skinhead would be Jimmy's first victim or his last.

DRYDEN HAD BEEN at Barham's Dock supervising the raising of the *PK 129* when he'd taken the call from August. A press conference had been set up to deal with enquiries over the fire-house fatality. 'Is it linked to Black Bank?' asked Dryden, knowing it must be.

'Who knows?' said August. 'We may never know who chummy was. Anyway—one o'clock at the press centre at the old RAF huts.'

Dryden checked his watch: 12.50 p.m. Humph was parked in the cab about fifty yards away across the grassy overgrown runway. Dryden was sitting outside Hut B: Squadron A. The huts had been in use since the September 11 attacks on New York. Being outside the perimeter wire, they offered a convenient place for community and press liaison without testing the security on the main gates.

Dryden closed his eyes and again asked himself the pressing question: why did someone want him to stop writing about Maggie Beck? Was it Freeman White? And if it was, *why* was it? Freeman and Lyndon were close. Was Dryden a threat to Lyndon? Or were the attacks on Humph's cab and *PK 129* somehow linked to the murder of Johnnie Roe, or even to the people smugglers?

His brain swam, unable to compute the interlocking facets of three stories that had become fixed in a baffling embrace. Was there any way forward? He sensed that if he could find the last tape that Maggie made before her death he could begin to unravel the truth. He would visit The Tower that night and begin his own enquiries.

When he reopened his eyes it was to see a crocodile of walkers making its way across the runway from Gate B. Her Majesty's press had arrived en masse, and were being escorted by Sergeant DeWitt.

Inside, the old hut had been turned into a small conference centre. Seats with flip-down note tables were set in rows. A spread of sandwiches and nibbles had been laid on a table down one side of the room. A dozen bottles of wine had been provided. On the opposite side of the room a long table had six PCs linked up to the Internet.

August had invited Inspector Newman along to take questions too. Technically, the base was sovereign US soil while the 120-year lease ran its course. In practice, a suspicious death on a US air base had attracted the interest of the Home Office in London.

Joey Forward, the local man for the *East Anglian Daily News*, put forward his first question. 'So, this body that was burnt like a cinder. Nasty business. Any ideas, Sergeant?'

'Major. Major August Sondheim. The murder victim . . .'

'Murder?' cut in Dryden. 'Why so sure?'

'All the windows and doors on the fire house were locked from the outside. We don't know if the man died inside, or was dead before the fire was lit . . . we never will, I'm afraid. We'll be lucky to get an ID off the dental records. Not a piece of flesh left on him.'

'Any link with the Black Bank killing?' asked Mike Yarr, the PA wireman.

August shrugged. 'Local CID investigating, gentlemen. Inspector Andy Newman will take your questions on that.'

Newman stood up and pinned a large Ordnance Survey map on the board at the front of the conference room. Red circles marked the pillbox in Mons Wood and the fire house on the air base.

'Clearly, two such incidents within five miles of each other give us cause for concern, gentlemen. At the moment we will be operating two incident rooms and two enquiries—but I shall head both. If there are links, I can assure you we will not miss them.'

'Timing on the ID?' asked Dryden.

Newman consulted some notes. 'It has to be forty-eight hours. This is no ordinary medical examination. The inside of the fire house is essentially a crematorium. We are dealing with ashes.'

'Any clues at the site?' said Forward.

August shot the cuffs on his uniform. 'All I can say is, the victim was male. Lots of bridgework on the teeth, which might help with the ID. And a metal cylinder by the body could be the core of a heavy-duty torch.'

'Anyone missing on the base?' asked Forward.

Good question, thought Dryden.

August didn't miss a beat. 'No member of the base complement is unaccounted for. Nor outside civilian staff.'

Lyndon Koskinski, of course, was neither: a nice distinction.

August ploughed on before anyone could delve deeper. 'As to

timing. The last fire exercise was two weeks ago. The building was cleared then. So any time between then and now.'

Mike Yarr had been told by the news desk in London to get a terrorist line on the killings. That would ensure the copy was used nationwide. 'Clearly there are concerns about terrorist attacks, Major. Can you comment on that?' he asked.

August sighed. 'We are ever vigilant here at USAF . . . ' As August began to run through a tedious prepared line on the terrorist threat, Dryden stood up, stacked a plate with miniature pork pies and sat before one of the PC screens. He'd pulled the cork on a bottle of red wine and poured himself a large glass. The PC was logged on to the USAF Mildenhall site. He scrolled through the site to the notice-board section—an Internet message page.

B Block Stateside congrats to Jaynette and Mike on the arrival of Mike Jnr. Go Fella!

Friends of Michael J. Doherty, base medic 1975–2000 will want to know that he died peacefully in his sleep here at home in Salt Lake on June 5. A long illness bravely borne.

And then he saw it. He read it three times, before shutting the PC down to think. Then he booted it back up and took a verbatim note.

This is a long shot but it's a message for the lovebirds. I was really privileged to be the witness. And the snapshots are great, especially the ones in the white Land Rover, and I thought that maybe one day you might want to share the memory after all. So just email me and I'll send them online, if that's OK. The guy at the register office said I should do it this way coz you'd mentioned the base. So, no names! But if you want to remember Cromer—email me. I always will.

Dryden called up a fresh email form and hit REPLY. The PC automatically reprinted the sender's email: jon.cummings@norfolkconstab/cromer. He typed: It was great to hear from you. We'd still like to keep our secret here but we'd love the pictures. Please send them to the e-mail below—it's a friend who's online and he's got a colour printer. And thanks for being there! Dryden added: pdryden@hotmail.com, and poured himself another glass of red wine.

He wondered how many white Land Rovers there were in the Fens and was appalled by the consequences if there was only one.

11

If he hadn't tried to track down Johnnie Roe's wife he'd have never known the dog track was there. This was Thursday night out: Fen-style. The Billy Row International Greyhound Stadium was a cauldron of light in the wasteland beyond the Mildenhall wire.

Dryden sat on the cab roof eating a beefburger. The Capri's windows were open in the heat and he heard the seven pips on the radio. She'd said 7.45—after the first race on the card.

A couple of Fleet Street nationals were still interested in the bizarre pillbox killing—now they wanted family, friends, anything that could put a real life to a grisly death. He'd told Newman he wanted to do some more background work on Roe's life. Newman had given him the ex-wife's full name. Luckily, she was in the book. The call had been awkward but at least she'd agreed to meet. Her voice had been tough, distorted by suspicion.

Already the punters were arriving. The Fens were a celebration of Americana: Midwest variety. Most of the cars rolling in for the dog racing were playing one or other of Dryden's two least-favourite forms of music: country-and-western. Humph had his headphones on and was reading the book that went with his language tapes.

Dryden slid off the roof and landed lightly on the hot tarmac. By the turnstiles was The Greyhound 'Nite Spot'. He had a pint of imported Bud at the bar, then left at 7.29 precisely, but was still able to find an empty half-acre of terrace by the time the first race began. The dogs' speed and beauty thrilled him. By the time they crossed the finishing line after three laps, he was cheering with the rest.

She was beside him suddenly, with a tray of race cards and cigarettes. She was probably under fifty but she'd been given a double helping of wrinkles, and none of them were laughter lines. The hair was once blonde, but now it was grey and cut lifelessly short.

'Well?' she said, and sat down on the concrete terrace.

'Sally Roe?' asked Dryden. She nodded, looking at her hands.

'You were married to Johnnie Roe?' he asked, trying to think fast and talk slowly at the same time.

'In 1978.'

'Thanks for agreeing to meet.'

'Not a lot of choice once you had the number.' She smiled in half-apology for the aggressive tone.

Dryden smiled back. 'The police said you were divorced. Years.'

She nodded. 'Yeah. I got out in '93.'

'Any reason?'

'Loads. Best forgotten. But one thing Johnnie never forgot was that kid. When he'd had too much that was what it all came down to. Every argument. Every fight. We never had children. So he grieved for Matt. It brought it all back—what you wrote in the paper.'

Dryden was thinking fast, but he'd just been lapped.

She turned to face him. 'Johnnie and Maggie were quite an item. We all thought they'd stick together you know—not like the other teenage flings. He really wanted the kid—that's why he went back into the fire that night. That's how he got the burns—you should have seen his back.'

I have, thought Dryden. 'Johnnie Roe was the father of Maggie Beck's boy?' he said.

She nodded. 'Oh, yeah. It made Johnnie what he was.'

'And what was that?' said Dryden.

She found a packet of cigarettes in her breast pocket and lit up. 'A bastard, really. But he could have been something else. If he'd come out of that fire with that kid his life would have been worth something. As it was he didn't see the point in trying to be anything. He said he was a zero. Mr Zero. Which was nice for me of course, being Mrs Zero. But by the time I left him zero was an over-estimate.'

'But at the start?'

She laughed. The bell for the next race was rung and some of the crowd moved down to the rail.

'The heat was bad then as well,' she said. 'In 1976. I knew both of them. They broke up after the crash. I got the impression he'd offered to marry her. Anyway, the crash changed everything. We'd known each other before and we drifted back.' She watched the dogs being manhandled into the stalls. 'It was good at the beginning.'

The starting pistol cracked and a fresh set of dogs burst out of their traps. Dryden watched the dust the dogs kicked up drift across the floodlit sky.

She put her arms around her knees and drew them up. 'She must have hated him. To do that. Give his son away.'

'Any idea why?'

'No. Jack was local. Webbed feet, the lot. He was even glamorous, for the Fens. Blond. What passed for trendy. And nineteen, with a good job driving vans for the building company.'

'And the baby—Matty—was, what? Rebellion, passion, a mistake?'

She laughed again, this time for real. 'All three. Rebellion for her, passion for both of 'em. A mistake too: what a start in life.'

'They were a couple then. Everyone knew?'

'No way. Her just sixteen? They met on the QT. That's where Matty come from. She used to tell me, you know. Moonlight meeting in the woods. They had a secret place. So they made Matty. She was proud of that, it wasn't a problem for her. She'd have brought him up on her own if she had to, but they wouldn't have it at Black Bank. Her father was a tough man. Fen farmer. She brought the bruises to school sometimes. He wanted her to bring the father home. Any father.'

'But Maggie didn't want him?'

'God knows why. There were worse; most of 'em were worse. He turned out bad, but it didn't have to be that way.'

There was a break in the racing. Kiosks were selling hot dogs. Dryden bought two and they sat and ate in silence. He tried to imagine the scene that night: the smoking ruin out of which Maggie had walked. 'So she saw her chance, and gave the boy away. And she never said why? Even to you?'

'She never visited him in hospital afterwards. She was out in a few days but Johnnie was in and out of hospital for weeks. Skin grafts, stuff like that. She wouldn't go near him. So I visited him. I guess I knew what I was doing, but life isn't fair, is it? And if she didn't want him, why not? He was a charmer was Johnnie.

'Anyway she married the following year. At Black Bank she was lonely, haunted. So she found herself a husband and a new home. A Breckland farmer. He was in his fifties . . . a bachelor. Don. They moved away and got a manager in at Black Bank. Bit of a surprise when she came back with the baby—Estelle, wasn't it? Don died young, so she sold up and returned home. I never understood why. I think she liked being haunted. Perhaps the ghosts were all she had.'

She stood up, smoothing down the cheap blue uniform with the sprinting greyhound on the shoulder.

Dryden nodded. 'But they weren't all ghosts. She knew Matty was still alive. Perhaps she thought he'd come back one day. Why do you think she gave him away?' asked Dryden, rising. It was the only question without an answer. 'Did you ever hate Johnnie?'

'Constantly and with a passion at the end. But that was because of what he was. And he was what he was because of Matty.'

'He got into trouble . . . the police?'

She laughed. 'You could say that. After Maggie his life fell apart. I was there, otherwise it would have been worse. But he was into anything that would make money fast—petty theft, porn, all sorts. He went inside a couple of times . . . but I was long gone by then, although I guess I got a cut—he never missed on the divorce payments. Odd sense of duty, he never showed it when we were married.'

'Did anyone else live or work at Black Bank who might know why she gave Matty away?'

She lit up a fresh cigarette. 'Yeah. Early on. There was an aunt. The father's sister. Spinster. Constance. In her forties then, I think. She'd be seventy-odd now. She came to help on the farm, in the house. But she was gone by the time the crash happened. I guess it didn't work out . . . She was a lot smarter than Maggie's parents. She didn't fit in.'

'Constance. The surname?'

She shrugged. 'Tompkins, I think. Thompson? She left for a job—librarian? Possibly . . . But I've got it in my mind she emigrated. They had family in Canada, the north.'

'Canada?' he said. She was ready to go, so he tried a last question. 'Did you ever see her again?'

'Once. I was in Ely. It must have been five years after the crash, more. She was with the daughter and I remember thinking how lucky she was. That kid was beautiful. Maggie wasn't ugly you know, but she was a Fen farmer's daughter. Heavy bones and the skin—potato white we used to call it at school. But the little girl was perfect, like kids can be. Cute, that olive skin and the butter-yellow hair. Kids are a blessing,' she said, and left.

THE RIVER SLAPPED itself against the bank as the last of the pleasure cruisers swept past the quayside. Customers on the verandah of the Cutter Inn sat happily, oblivious of the fact they were being eaten alive by Fen mosquitoes. It was the end of another long summer's day, and a hint of a mist was hauling itself out of the river.

Dryden left Humph parked on the bank with his language tape, six diet chicken-and-mayonnaise sandwiches, and a miniature bottle of Metaxa 3-Star brandy. He cradled a bottle of decent whisky under one arm. He needed more information about Johnnie Roe's secret life, and the Water Gypsies traded in best single malt.

He set off south along the river bank, past the ghostly white forms of the floating gin palaces that made up eighty per cent of the summer traffic on the main river. Soon the bright lights of the Cutter disappeared round a bend in the river and the moorings were taken up with narrow boats.

From somewhere the distinct aroma of hash drifted with the mist off the river. Dryden treated himself to half a dozen lungfuls and pressed on. He found the *Middle Earth* at the end of the line. He put a foot on the narrow boat's back landing-stage and thumped hard on the roof of the *Middle Earth*.

A moth-eaten man with no clothes threw open the rear doors.

'Nice out,' said Dryden, grinning.

'Dryden. What do you want?'

Dryden held up the bottle of malt whisky. 'I've got this for Etty—and a tenner for information received.'

Etty appeared. 'Dryden. Welcome. Why the clothes?'

'Call me conventional. Can I . . .?'

Garments were being hastily donned. Dryden counted five girls and three men and tried not to work out what had been going on. Someone produced glasses and he poured out the malt.

Etty sniffed the tenner Dryden had given her and secreted it among the underclothes surrounding her. 'I was actually looking for some more information,' said Dryden, sipping his own malt.

The moth-eaten bloke and one of the girls shuffled off towards the forward cabin, presumably to conclude unfinished business.

But Etty had sharpened up, overcoming the effects of whatever she'd been smoking. 'About . . .'

'Johnnie Roe. The people smugglers. They used to use the Ritz T-Bar, but now that's closed down. And they had people living up at the old air base at Witchford. The police are on to that too. So they must be operating out of somewhere else. Any idea where?'

'There's some new pickers out for the harvest,' Etty said. 'They arrived the day before yesterday. My guess is their papers are phoney. They get dropped off by van for the night shifts. They don't know exactly where they're living and their English isn't great, but I heard them talking. There's a lot of languages but English is the only one they share. They call it the silos, where they're sleeping. They're pretty unhappy with it—no shops around, no nothing.'

'Silos?' said Dryden.

Etty finished her malt and licked her lips. 'A cluster of them. It has to be Sedge Fen. The old grain works.'

LAURA'S ROOM was silent and flooded with light. The COMPASS machine trailed a six-foot ticker tape. Dryden sat by the bed and studied the letters. Halfway down, still lost in the random signals, he took Laura's hand, knowing it was for his own comfort rather than hers. When he reached the foot of the ticker tape he kept his eyes down, folded it and kissed her once.

The messages had stopped, he knew that now. He stood by the window in flat, cheerless heat and thought about what it meant for him if she had finally retreated, back into the coma that had engulfed her after the crash in Harrimere Drain. It meant that the nightmare was coming true. A lifetime spent at the foot of a hospital bed pretending to talk to a comatose figure that used to be his wife. A dialogue of self-deception he felt he could neither face nor abandon.

'If you're not here, why do I have to be?' he asked out loud.

He waited for an answer, feeling the anger lift his pulse rate. The silence in The Tower was complete, until he heard the caretaker in the corridor outside. It was Ravel this time, *Bolero*.

'The whistler,' said Dryden, and kissed Laura's hand.

Out in the corridor he heard the sound of a pail of water being slopped onto a floor. Through a door he found his way onto a spiral staircase. When the door slammed behind him, the light fled. Looking down through the metal rungs of the steps he saw the faint glow of distant light. He edged down the narrow steps.

The light came from a series of bulbs strung along fifty yards of cellar corridor. Under the far light the caretaker was mopping.

Dryden watched from the shadows. The caretaker was perhaps sixty, tall, but with a spine bent into a curve by years of labour. A minute passed and then a kettle's whistle blew. The man straightened his back, took his mop and pail, and disappeared through a doorway. The whistle died. Then the music began. Bruch, the violin concerto, swelled to fill the damp air.

Under cover of the London Symphony Orchestra, Dryden walked to the door and looked in. It was a sitting room of sorts. A table, chair, and single bed were the only furniture. A bookcase, made of planks on bricks, filled one wall. On the other were narrow, vertical, wooden tape holders. There were hundreds, possibly thousands.

'Quite a collection' said Dryden, in a pause in the Bruch.

The caretaker wheeled round, the tin cup he held shaking instantly. Dryden could only imagine what kind of life had produced a face like that. In the cellar's half-light the deep lines were as sharp as knife wounds, the eyes hooded and cast down. Without looking at Dryden, he walked to the tape recorder and hit the STOP button. It was the recorder Dryden had bought Maggie. Its predecessor, a moulded seventies version three times as big, stood beside it still.

'I'm sorry, I thought they'd left it behind. I . . .'

Dryden held up his hand. 'Keep it. It's not important. Was there a tape inside?'

The caretaker looked puzzled. 'A tape? Yes, yes . . . I'm sorry. I didn't think . . . Again. I'm sorry. So sorry.' He rummaged in a kitchen drawer. He held up the tape, the fingers of his hand trembling, and Dryden took it, turning it like a diamond in his hand.

Dryden left and as he climbed the stairs he heard the Bruch swell out again. Outside, Inspector Newman had parked his Citroën next to Humph's cab. They were busy ignoring each other as Dryden appeared, flopping into the passenger seat beside the policeman. 'Anything new?'

'If you count an ID on the body in the fire house at Mildenhall, yes,' he said. 'This is unofficial, OK?' Dryden nodded. 'Bob Sutton. Teeth gave it away—military work. We got the X-rays from Hong Kong. Perfect match. Wife's upset.'

'Getaway. Some people, eh?'

Newman refused to take the bait. 'Which sort of cuts him out as number one suspect for torturing and killing Johnnie Roe.'

'Why does it rule him out? He had a great motive. His only daughter had been lured into that pillbox, raped, abused. He must have thought Johnnie Roe knew where she was. Perhaps he was trying to get it out of him.'

'So who killed Sutton?'

'You tell me,' said Dryden. 'But he's still my call on Roe's torturer.'

'Great,' said Newman. 'Two killers, not one.'

As he got out Dryden tried a last question before heading back to Humph's car: 'The bag in the pillbox. The picture, the food. It was Emmy Kabazo's?'

'Yup. Dad identified it for us during questioning before his release on bail. Doesn't put him in there though, does it? And it's Bob Sutton's prints on the knife anyway. Work that one out.'

JIMMY KABAZO hugged himself and thought of Emmy, his son. Then he lifted the rifle barrel to his lips and kissed the cool stock. He whispered 'Emmy' as he lowered his eye to the oval of the gunsight. The target crosshair swam slightly through a tear, and then cleared.

He swept the telescopic sight across the familiar contours of Sedge Fen. The main silos stood in a group, rising out of the black peat flatlands. At the foot of the silos clustered the little agricultural town that had been Sedge Fen. Storage sheds, machine shops, offices, canteens, a first-aid block and the charge hands' tied cottages.

He shivered, not because of the cool morning air, but because he knew he would use the gun today. It would be Emmy's last revenge: the skinhead.

He'd botched his first revenge. Jimmy sobbed with the memory, the tears welling again. He thought of Emmy, and the body in the mortuary that was all that was left of him, and the pain doubled him up. He clutched his arms around his chest and waited for the despair to subside. He looked around him, but the room was comfortless. Red brick stripped of plaster with a single window. It had provided him with the perfect eyrie. A lonely water-pumping station, long abandoned, far enough away to avoid perfunctory patrols, but within range.

'Cheated,' he said.

He'd waited by the Ritz, in the Wilkinson's van, half a mile along the main road by an emergency telephone. He'd waited all night for Emmy with the bag, so that he'd have something to eat while they took him to the old airfield. Something for comfort. An excuse really, to see his son after nearly eighteen long months of lonely exile. And just after midnight a lorry had swung into the lay-by and the driver killed the lights. But Jimmy didn't move. He knew the warnings the smugglers had given. That the police would run a lorry too one day, to catch the middle-men. So he waited for the driver to unload, for Johnnie Roe to appear from the Ritz. But the minutes had slipped by and nobody had come. And so the lorry had powered out.

So Jimmy left the bag with the presents behind the Ritz, hanging from the door handle, and went to work. The next evening the bag still hung here. So he switched to day shifts and watched each night from the van. He'd thought how much he loved his son and how stupid he had been to entrust his life to the people smugglers. To the skinhead.

Two days gone. On the Friday night the square man full of muscles had parked up and examined everything like a policeman. He'd held open the top of the Tesco bag with a pen, using a miniature spotlight to look inside. With a bunch of keys he'd worked on the Ritz's locks until the back door had opened and he'd searched inside. Outside, *he'd found something on the ground. Jimmy sensed the excitement, as the man squatted down on his haunches in the dust and then walked carefully eastwards towards the Fen. And then the square man had returned to his car. The next night he'd come again, and this time he'd brought a larger torch, and a rucksack, and he'd taken the bag. Emmy's bag, and walked off across Black Bank Fen.*

So Jimmy followed, taking the car jack from the boot to keep his courage hot. Across Black Bank Fen, behind the square man with the Tesco bag that held his son's life. Across Black Bank Fen until they reached Mons Wood, and the pillbox in the moonlight.

Was Emmy inside? Jimmy waited as the square man went in and he listened, hoping with such intensity to hear his son's voice that he conjured it up. He heard 'Papa'. He heard 'Help'; a hallucination more powerful than any sound he'd ever really heard. So he called out Emmy's name—but it was the square man who came out. And he had blood on his hands. He wouldn't have killed him if the muscled man hadn't been so strong. He hit him with the jack from the car, across the chest. But the fool ducked and took the blow across the forehead and just grunted, standing there. Even in the moonlight Jimmy saw the shock in his eyes. So Jimmy hit him again.

He left him in the grass and ran inside, but Emmy wasn't there. Only the man from the Ritz, strung out across the floor, reaching for the empty glass. He thought Jimmy had come to save him. So he begged for the glass. Begged for the water. There was blood round the man's mouth, which trickled as he spoke. Jimmy guessed the square man had hit him. A bruise, green in the moonlight, was rising over the man's cheek and eye, distorting his face.

The contents of the Tesco bag had been dumped on the floor. Jimmy looked down at them and the man from the Ritz saw his chance.

'I told him. I don't know whose they are. I missed the lorry. Tuesday. Perhaps it was for them?' Then his eyes turned again to the glass on the shelf and he almost whispered it this time. 'A drink.'

So Jimmy asked him where Emmy had gone. What was the plan if the drop was missed? Was there a plan? But he wouldn't say, or he didn't know. And then, when Jimmy didn't give him the water, he made something up, babbling rubbish to win himself the water. Jimmy had felt anger then, and humiliation. He felt a fool, manipulated always by the white men who ran his life, the men who had lost his son. A bargain they had failed to keep. They'd taken the money and his son.

So he left the glass on the ledge. And then he ran, hearing the man's screams diminish slowly, until he could only imagine them in the silence of the fields.

The humiliation came back now, fresh and powerful. He took up his post at the open window again, pulling the gunsight to his eye and training it on the loading bays. 'It's where he sleeps,' he said, out loud. The skinhead who had driven the lorry. The skinhead the black men paid to do the job. So he put the crosshairs of the gunsight over the red door they always used, and waited.

He thought of Emmy's body in the morgue, but this time there were no tears. He'd kissed him that one last time and although his skin had been cold, he'd made him a promise as the lips touched his cheek. The skinhead. Then the red door opened and he led them out, the metal in his teeth catching the sun. A truck must be coming. The skinhead blinked in the sunlight and spread his arms wide in an embrace of life, while the others went to flag the truck in off the drove road. Arms wide, his face to heaven; the skinhead grinned and rubbed his hands in his short, cropped hair. So Jimmy put the crosshairs on his neck, waited a second to make sure they were both still, pulled the trigger, and sent him to hell in a spurt of bright, arterial blood.

Friday, June 20

12

Dryden had considered playing Maggie's last tape on the Capri's deck. Did he have the right? Technically it was Maggie's testament, and it had been left for Estelle and Lyndon to hear. He'd try Estelle at Black Bank first, then he'd play it. Still, he had one other option to try to find his own answers to the mystery of Black Bank. What he needed was to talk to someone who had been there in 1976, but was prepared to tell the truth now about the Beck family.

Tracking Constance Tompkins down had been easy enough. He'd checked with a contact at County Hall and they'd traced her through the files on the county library service. She had emigrated, but she was back now and drawing a pension. They were happy to give Dryden the address once he explained that Maggie Beck's children wanted to contact their great-aunt.

Which had led him here to Fenlandia. The wooden sign on the

stone gate-post said: REST HOME. The house stood somewhere in a stand of pine trees at the end of a dreary, dead-end lane out of town.

Dryden left Humph ordering a bottle of make-believe Retsina at Nicos's taverna and crunched his way up the gravel drive until the building came into view. Wisteria drooped from the eaves in a splash of washed-out purple and ivory. A line of wicker chairs stood in firing-squad formation behind the glass of the conservatory. All were empty except one.

He'd rung ahead and the woman who had answered the phone said Mrs Constance Tompkins would love to see him. Now, she led Dryden past some residents in the TV lounge and through to the conservatory, where Mrs Tompkins was reading a novel with rapt concentration. She didn't look up when they arrived and, while she might have been deaf, Dryden suspected she was just ignoring him.

'I'll leave you alone for a few minutes,' said the proprietor, touching Mrs Tompkins's arm. 'This is the man I mentioned, Connie. From the newspaper.'

The old lady folded the book and put her reading glasses away. She looked sprightlier than she had at Maggie's funeral.

'Hello,' she said. 'You want to know about Maggie, don't you? I read the piece.' She pulled a copy of *The Crow* from the side of the cushions she sat on. 'It's got your name on it.'

Dryden sat down. 'Maggie died before she could tell Matty why she did what she did. I think she planned to tell him. She left some tapes—about her life. Estelle says she never explained, at the beginning at least, why she swapped the children. Matty should know—it's what Maggie would have wanted. Do you know, Mrs Tompkins?'

She smiled. 'I'm letting go of the past now, Mr Dryden.' She tapped his knee with her book. 'It's very therapeutic.'

'But you went to the funeral . . .' He had her then. He could tell she wasn't sure if he'd been there. 'Do you know? Why she did it?' he asked, and knew instantly that she did.

'Maggie was a sweet girl. I don't think Johnnie was all bad either. Rudderless sort of man, lost, and angry about something. I knew they were seeing each other. He'd once done some work on the farm as a picker. She'd been protected at Black Bank, perhaps over-protected. It was a very old-fashioned place. I found it stifling.'

Dryden watched Connie's bright eyes dancing over the lawn.

'I watched her several times that summer; she'd leave the house in the evening and set out across country. I don't think she thought I was a threat to her so she didn't seem to care that I knew. Assignations,' she added, hugging herself. 'Romantic, I thought then, so I said nothing. She told no one about the baby until she had to. She told me first—I think she wanted advice about how to break it to my brother. She was very matter-of-fact about it. I think she thought Johnnie would be her husband.'

A gong sounded discreetly from somewhere within Fenlandia.

'Morning coffee,' said Mrs Tompkins. A woman in a white nurse's uniform brought a tray. Dryden noted the superior biscuits.

'You like it here?' he said, taking one.

'As Maurice Chevalier said in a different context, Mr Dryden, it's better than the alternative.'

'Must be expensive though?'

'Very. I married late and well. Ideal.' She smiled. She slurped coffee and pressed on. 'Then something happened—to Maggie. She stopped seeing Johnnie.'

'This was when, exactly? Sorry—if you can remember.'

'Oh, I can remember all right. It was her birthday—Maggie's. It was 1976, she'd be sixteen then. February the 10th. There'd been a party at home. A bit half-hearted, I'm afraid. The baby was a cloud over her parents. Then Sally had called, that was her friend. She was quite different, very modern. She wore a low-cut blouse.' Dryden thought of the disappointed woman he'd met at the dog stadium. 'I think they'd gone dancing—the old Mecca in Broad Street. I got the impression they'd meet boys there. Anyway, I heard Maggie come home. Her parents had given me a room in the attic at Black Bank.' The old woman's eyes narrowed. 'Maggie was up there too— a teenager's room next to the old retainer.'

Connie looked into Dryden's eyes, making her decision. 'I found the photos on the stairs. I got up to see if she was all right. I went out of my room and the moon was pouring in through the skylight above the stairwell. And they were there; three photographs, one of them torn. At first I thought they were all of Maggie. I was shocked, of course. They were naked, both of them, making love. Tangled up together. I could see it was Johnnie. But then I looked at them again. The girls weren't her at all, they were other girls.

'Then I picked up the photograph she'd torn up. I knew, of course. I was putting the pieces together when she came back out. I knew it was her this time. Just like the others. Naked with Johnnie.'

'What did she say?' asked Dryden.

'Neither of us said anything. I just gave the photos to her and she took them and went back to her room.'

'And Johnnie didn't come back after that?'

'Apparently not for some time. I left within a few weeks. I'd got a job—library assistant in Peterborough. I wrote to Maggie. She wrote back. Guarded, of course, but she told me things. About how Bill—my brother—wanted her to bring Johnnie to Black Bank, to give the baby a father. I think she was in despair, actually. I even thought she might take her life. I told Bill not to push. But he was quite rude. Told me to leave family matters to the family. Very pointed.'

'What do you think the pictures meant?'

She pushed a bell button on the wall beside her. 'Does it matter? Johnnie was always decked out with a camera. He was a pornographer—that's clear, I think. Perhaps he thought the pictures were funny. Perhaps he sold them to his friends. Perhaps he thought it didn't matter. But it did, Mr Dryden. And Maggie made him pay for it in the end by giving away the one thing he really wanted—a son. I don't think she could have faced life with Johnnie, so she gave Matty away and there was no need to marry any more. She'd give Matty a life away from Johnnie, and herself a life away from him. It was very neat, but she paid a terrible price, didn't she?'

The proprietor came up behind them.

'Goodbye, Mrs Tompkins,' said Dryden, rising. 'One last question. Lyndon needs to know why. Perhaps, could you . . .'

She took his hand. 'You tell stories for a living, Mr Dryden. Tell this one for me.'

Back in Humph's cab Dryden sat and tried not to think. He looked again at the picture he had downloaded from his PC that morning: a happy wedding-day shot, confetti on the groom's smart pilot's uniform, brother kissing sister. The visceral age-old revulsion swept over him again, and he tried to imagine what it felt like for them.

He found Maggie's last tape in the glove compartment. 'Black Bank,' he said, and hoped it was for the last time.

'DRY LIGHTNING,' said Dryden, as Humph's cab bumped through the gates to Black Bank Farm. The bolt struck some trees at Mons Wood with a crack like an artillery shell. The tallest pine torched itself, a cracking suicide of sudden purple flame. The sight of fire seemed, incredibly, to deepen the heat. The featureless horizon appeared to pulse, the hot air on the fen boiling over the shadowless fields.

Humph's Capri skidded to a halt in the red dust before the old farmhouse. Estelle was at the door, one hand clutched to her throat. She looked very frightened.

Dryden produced the tape from his pocket and held it up like a trophy. 'I think we should listen to this. It's the last one. She said everything would be explained.'

'Everything is,' said Estelle, her voice crackling like the air.

She turned on her heels and disappeared inside the cool blackness of the farmhouse. He found her in the kitchen, up on the wooden worktop with her legs folded beneath her. Beside her was a portable tape recorder.

'Your husband?' said Dryden, leaning against the wall.

She flinched at the word. 'I told him you'd find out. He had some crazy idea we could just live in the States. Say we were married in the UK. Keep the other secret. But you can't keep a secret from yourself. And the passport was wrong. They'd have to change that. So we couldn't just go. Could we?'

'And the tapes . . . she did say why she gave Lyndon away?'

She nodded, not trusting herself to speak.

'I know too,' said Dryden. 'Constance Tompkins just told me.'

Estelle looked at him. 'We listened to the tapes after the funeral. Lyndon was there. Mum wasn't very explicit, I guess. But it's pretty clear. About Johnnie. Johnnie and the pictures. I think Mum was sick. Sick with anxiety. Sick that Lyndon—that Matty—would be abused, sucked into that life. How could she have married him? And in shock. She'd just seen her parents die, die horribly. And then she made that decision, almost instantly. I told Lyndon . . . he has to see it through the eyes of the girl, the girl Mum was.' Tears welled freely out of her eyes and down her chin. 'She loved Lyndon,' she said, as if insisting on a great truth that had been disputed.

'But Lyndon doesn't believe that?'

'I think he feels it's not the reason he wanted. He wanted something else . . . I don't know what. Just something that made it OK. This doesn't make it OK. I don't think anything could . . .'

'You knew who the father was, didn't you?'

She looked scared then. 'Mum never said. I think she wanted it forgotten. That's one of the reasons she went away. And Johnnie went away too for a bit. When he did come back he must've kept his distance. She never mentioned him. People forget, even in a place like this. But I knew. Kids, they talk. When we got back to Black Bank

I was twelve. I went to the secondary school and I was famous—
infamous. I came from the place where the plane had crashed. At the
time everyone knew Johnnie was the father. Why else would he have
run into the flames? But you can imagine the scandal. So I found out
pretty quickly. Sometimes, for a dare, we'd go to the Ritz T-Bar and
I'd buy a Coke. He never knew I hated him.'

'Did Lyndon know?'

'Not before Mum died. But I told him that night—and it was on the
tapes.' She bit her lip.

Dryden walked towards the tape deck. 'Maggie said that the tapes
would answer all the questions. We should give her that chance,' he
said. He took the last cassette and slipped it into the recorder. They
listened to Maggie's breath, laboured and intimate, unnaturally close.
It filled the kitchen with a tangible sense of her.

'Estelle?' The voice was an echo of the woman. 'My love, I lied to
you as well.'

Estelle covered her mouth and waited to see which way her life
would turn.

'We promised each other we'd tell you. But then each year came
and went and we wondered why. It made no difference to us . . .
Every Christmas. Every birthday. All those chances missed . . .'

The breathing interrupted her, the failing heart bruising her ribs.

'Then Don died and it was all down to me. I just couldn't. He loved
you too, Estelle. Loved you more than anything—more than his life.
He said that before he died—believe me. He didn't count for anything without you. He told me that for you. His daughter . . .'

She took a breath and held it.

'But you weren't, love. Or mine. We tried to have a family, but it
didn't happen. I think it was a punishment for me although the doctors said it was Don. But it was my punishment for giving Matty
away. For walking away from a child. And a punishment for both of
us for wanting a son. Only a son.'

The tape clicked off, then almost immediately back on. 'The adoption service promised us a son. It was easier then, even with Don's
age. But it went wrong, the family took the boy back at the last
minute and it broke my heart, Estelle, broke my heart again. So we
said we'd be happy to take the next child. We didn't mind then if it
was a boy or a girl. We just wanted it . . . wanted you. And when Don
brought you home I loved you from the minute I first saw you. I loved
you like my own . . . more than my own.'

Estelle was frozen. 'Mum,' she said, and began to cry again.

'A few people knew,' said Maggie. 'But Connie had gone, and I didn't really have anyone I could tell at Black Bank. So we thought it was best left. School: it worried us. That you might be teased. So we brought you back to Black Bank as our child. You are our child, love.'

Out on the fen seagulls wheeled, calling, sensing the long drought was about to break. The laboured breathing on the tape returned and slowly dwindled into sleep. Dryden switched it off.

'My God,' said Estelle, and Dryden knew instantly that she was thinking about Lyndon. About the consequences of another lie.

'Where is he?' said Dryden.

'My God,' she said again.

'Laura tried to tell me to watch out for Freeman White, Lyndon's room-mate.'

Estelle just said 'Laura', and cried again. 'We didn't know she could hear us. I'm sorry. We just used to talk. About us. About what to do after Mum died. We didn't do it in front of Mum because she could hear us, even, sometimes, when she slept. We couldn't be sure. We wanted to surprise Mum—about us, when she was better. We still thought that then—that she would get better. And after she died we went back to pick up her things. Laura must have heard. We talked about what to do. We thought she was in a coma. I'm sorry.'

Dryden nodded so that she could go on. 'We asked Freeman to follow you. We were desperate. You were asking questions, so many questions. I couldn't refuse because you were right, it was what Mum wanted. She wanted it all out. And you came out to see us. We thought you were close to finding out about the marriage.'

'And the fire at the register office? White too?'

She looked him in the eyes, a silent affirmation. 'We thought it would destroy the evidence. Give us some time to think. We told Freeman not to hurt you. But Freeman owes Lyndon everything, his life, really. So he agreed to help, when we told him we just needed to know if you'd got close. And if you had, we wanted to warn you off.'

'Where's Lyndon?' asked Dryden.

'I have to tell him,' she said. 'Before . . .'

In the silence thunder rolled. 'Has he ever talked about suicide?'

She nodded. 'Sometimes, since Mum died. He left, left here, the night before Mum's funeral.'

'And you've no idea where he is?' Dryden asked.

'He took the Land Rover and went. Said he'd find somewhere to think. He wanted space. He said he knew a place . . . out there.' She looked out over Black Bank Fen as a lightning bolt zigzagged down into a stand of trees. 'He said you'd told him of a place he could go.'

'Me?'

'To be on his own. That's what he said . . . a place you loved. Somewhere like Texas—somewhere he could be free.'

Dryden saw it then as he'd seen it last; the black peat of Adventurer's Fen stretching out to the reed beds by the river. 'Does he have a mobile?' he asked.

'Yes. But he never answers. Just listens to the messages.'

'Ring him. Tell him about the last tape. Tell him we're coming.'

THE JAILER CRIED, *that last time, when Johnnie asked him what he'd done to deserve the torture of the pillbox.*

'Just tell me,' said Johnnie, as though the answer marked the only difference between the real world and his hexagonal cell. 'I'm being punished. I know that. I'm going to die here. Tell me why.'

Lyndon took the decision then. He'd planned to stay silent, but the appeal was so direct, and he had such an overwhelming answer, he knelt before his victim and took his face in his hands. 'What do you see?' he asked, feeling his nails puncture Johnnie's bristled flesh.

Johnnie felt his life hinged here: in an airless pillbox where he'd once made love to Maggie Beck. His jailer's voice, he noticed, was American. It surprised him. 'I can't see the glass,' he said. Lyndon's head obscured the diamond-like beauty of the water on the shelf.

Lyndon dug his thumbs into the dehydrated flesh. 'What do you see?' he asked again, knowing now he would have to give his father the answer. And he knew why he'd avoided speaking until now, for he felt an urge to be tender, to cradle the head of the man who had run into the flames of Black Bank to save his son. He fought it back, and thought of his mother, tortured too, by the knowledge that to save her son she must give him away. 'Think of a mirror,' said Lyndon.

Johnnie tried to think. His mind screamed for water, for the glass beyond the jailer's eyes. His head swam and those eyes filled his world. 'My eyes?' he said, knowing instantly he was right, feeling his heart contract with dread.

'I'm your son,' said Lyndon, and let him fall to the ground.

Johnnie fainted then, the thirst beginning to destroy his brain, as it had ravaged his flesh. When he came to, the pain had gone. His mind floated free, and he could consider what he knew with shocking clarity.

'You can't be,' he said, angry that the jailer should torment him further. 'Matty died. In the fire.'

'Maggie switched us. Me and the American kid. She did it to cheat you. Because of what you were. You made her do it, and it's destroyed my life. Our lives.' He showed Johnnie the wedding ring on his finger, balled his fist, and hit him hard. The cartilage of Johnnie's nose collapsed and the blood flowed out in gouts.

But this time Johnnie didn't pass out. 'What was I?' he said, trying hard to remember how he'd lost Maggie, how he'd lost the life he could have had.

'You took pictures. Making love to Maggie. Was it in here? Or did that come later?'

Johnnie remembered then, and felt ashamed that he had forgotten this crime, rather than all the others. 'Later,' he said, looking at the water in the glass as the thirst returned.

Lyndon hated him then, not because of what he'd done to Maggie, but because he couldn't know what he'd done to him. So he wrapped his bleeding hand in his T-shirt, took the glass, stood before his father, and drank it dry.

THEY DROVE TOWARDS Adventurer's Fen under a rotting sky. The drought was dying, overblown with heat, and ants had invaded the dashboard of the Capri, in anticipation of the final storm. Dryden had the window down, and as they pulled past the memorial stone to the victims of the 1976 aircrash, he felt a wind on his cheek and, for the first time that summer, it carried the taste of rain.

In the rearview mirror Dryden watched Estelle. She'd left a message for Lyndon telling him about the last tape, about her adoption. 'We're OK. It's OK,' she'd said, but none of them, least of all her, believed it now. Her eyes told Dryden what she feared. That if they found Lyndon on Adventurer's Fen, they'd find him dead. That the real tragedy was that he'd risked so much for nothing. Had done so much that could not be undone.

Dryden's mobile rang, the signal splintered by the storm: 'Hi. Police have just issued a statement'—it was Garry—'they've found a body at Sedge Fen. At the old processing works under the silos. Gunshot to the head, high-calibre rifle. Newman is out there now.'

'Arrests?'

'Jimmy Kabazo. Gave himself up at the scene. Sergeant said he was as happy as Larry. They found him standing over the corpse.'

'Get out there. Ring Mitch. He needs to get out anyway, the drought's breaking. These lightning strikes will start fires—some will spread. And there's a wind. These fields are like moondust—there's bound to be a blow or two as well. Tell him to get some shots at Sedge Fen and then cruise round. Got that?'

Garry was gone, lost in a hail of static.

They drove north, then turned east beneath a sky beginning to boil with clouds. To the east, coming towards them, Dryden spotted the first Fen Blow—a dust storm a mile high and rolling forwards like a giant tumbleweed from an outsized Western.

Humph swung the Capri off the metalled road and hit the shingle of a drove road. A small copse of pines was a sheaf of fire in the middle of Adventurer's Fen. The rest lay before them as it had always done in Dryden's dreams: 300 acres of blissful solitude and beauty. To the north and west the Little Ouse was its boundary, edged by fields of reed marsh. To the east lay the razor-sharp edge of Thetford Forest, the ancient border between the black peat of the fen and the sandy brecklands.

A single drove road ran down to the river past Flightpath Cottages. A hogweed grew from an upstairs bedroom window and both doors had crumpled in the damp of the last winter. Two 'For Sale' boards stood at crazy angles in the peat.

'I guessed wrong,' said Dryden.

'There!' said Estelle, at the moment he saw it too. Leaning between Dryden and Humph, she pointed down the drove road to the edge of the reed marsh. It was a new house, despite the old reclaimed bricks. It was roofed in slate and an old-style wooden verandah surrounded it at ground level. At the southeast corner a tower rose above the first floor, a tiny folly. A kitchen garden had gone to seed on the south side. A gate stood, but no fence. Dryden's heartbeat quickened, but he kept at bay the knowledge that it was with recognition.

Humph rattled down the rutted track to within a hundred yards of the house and then pulled up as the Capri's suspension groaned and cracked under the strain. The white Land Rover, until now hidden behind the house, had come into view.

'Tell him I love him,' said Estelle, terrified, Dryden guessed, at what she would find inside the house. 'Tell him it's OK.'

Dryden swung the door out. He leaned back in through the open passenger window. 'I've got something to tell him. Something he still doesn't know,' she said. 'If he's alive, tell him that.'

Humph struggled out on the driver's side, sure testimony that he thought Dryden was about to do something stupid. Dryden nodded to the Capri. 'Stay with her.' Humph simply raised a finger and pointed east to where the forest edge had stood a minute earlier. Not now: the tumbling front of the dust storm rolled out from the trees towards them. Dryden felt his guts liquidise and in the panic of the moment his simply repeated himself. 'Stay with her.'

So Humph ducked back into the Capri and Dryden was alone when the dust fell. At first it merely shimmered over his skin, accompanied by a slight fall in the light levels. A hissing of minute particles of dry earth seemed to fill Adventurer's Fen. Then the light dipped again, the sun disappeared, and the wind began to drive the dust into his eyes, nose and ears. The house had disappeared but the path remained at his feet. Dryden staggered down it. He choked once, then stopped, doubled over, and filled his lungs with the air close to the ground. For a minute, less, he ran in a void of orange-brown dust. Then the façade of the house appeared, like cheap scenery, a one-dimensional grey, featureless outline. He threw himself against the door and tried the handle, knowing it was locked.

He began to skirt the house, cupping his hands at the first window to the right of the door to view a sitting room with rugs on the polished floorboards, job-lot pictures and unmatched lightshades. 'Rented,' he said, pressing his forehead against the window for coolness, and sucking in air by pressing his lips to the glass. He moved on, past another locked door and round the far corner.

French windows extended the length of the verandah at the back of the house. Lyndon Koskinski sat inside on a cheap white sofa. In one hand he held a mobile phone, in the other his Zippo lighter. Both hands rested on his lap and his eyes appeared to be closed. To one side of the French windows a door stood open. Dryden slipped through and into the kitchen, and closed the door behind him.

The next door was glazed and opened easily into the room with the white sofa. Lyndon didn't turn his head but Dryden saw that his eyes were open now, although they were empty of light.

'Lyndon,' said Dryden, and nothing moved.

He took a step forwards and caught the smell. He guessed it was petrol—but aircraft fuel was possible. The fumes were rising and billowing out from the sofa. Dryden could see now that it was soaked, the dark stain only lightening at the armrests and behind Lyndon's head. Dryden breathed in and felt a wave of fume-induced nausea.

'Things have changed,' he said, trying to control his voice.

Lyndon blinked again, slowly like a lizard, but did not turn from the view from the window. 'I know. Estelle told me everything.' He held up the mobile and let it drop in his lap. An empty spirit bottle lay in the folds of the sofa.

'It changes things,' Dryden said again.

'For Johnnie Roe? He's still dead.' Lyndon laughed then. 'The only thing that's changed is that he died for nothing.'

'And you killed him.' As Dryden said it he knew it must be true. The motives were compelling and multiple. Johnnie Roe was the father who had denied him a life, a mother, and finally a wife.

Lyndon smiled and fingered the Zippo lighter expertly at his chest. 'Yes. I suppose I did. I never planned to. At first I just wanted to hurt him. You know?' Dryden nodded stupidly. He didn't know.

'Hurt him bad. My life, everything—was down to him. So I thought I'd re-create it for him. Al Rasheid. My cell. I enjoyed that.'

'What did you want?'

'At the beginning I wanted him to confess. We'd listened to the tapes. Maggie told us why she'd given me away. But I wanted to hear him say it. Tell me what he'd done to make her do it.'

'You used the knife,' said Dryden, recalling the intricately carved and gilded knife.

Lyndon nodded. 'I got it in Aden—in the Souk, with Freeman.'

Dryden nodded. 'And the manacles? The chain you used?'

'Mine. The jailer at Al Rasheid gave me the key when the invasion of Baghdad began. They let all the prisoners go free.'

'So did he confess?'

'No. But then, I think now, he didn't know his crime. Or hadn't guessed. I wanted him to know. I wanted to punish him for making Mum do it. Telling the lie that's done all this, brought us here. He was dying from the thirst. I could see that. So I watched.'

'Why don't you give me the lighter?' asked Dryden.

Lyndon smiled again. 'Then I just found that guy's body—his head stoved in. Sutton? I read it in the paper—the name. And then I thought he must have told someone he'd gone to the pillbox. He had a family, people who cared. They'd come looking. And someone had killed him. So someone else knew Johnnie was there. They'd find out what I'd done to him. How I dragged him there, through the dust, and chained him up. I had to get rid of Sutton's body.'

Dryden tried to stem the fear that was constricting his throat. 'And

Freeman White took care of that. He's on the fire crew at the base—it says it on his door. Your door.'

Lyndon tipped his head by way of assent. 'Then Johnnie died. That was the Sunday. I just found him. Taut, like that, and reaching out for the glass.'

'I presume we met at the pillbox,' said Dryden, fingering the blue-black eye.

'Another five minutes and I'd have had the body out . . . I was shocked, you know—that he'd died so suddenly. I didn't expect that.'

Lyndon flipped open the top of the Zippo. Dryden tried to think. 'You can put it back together again. Your life. Lyndon's life. Estelle's in the car.' Lyndon looked up then, but outside there was now only the drifting pall of the dust, darkening by the second. 'She's got something to tell you. She said there was more,' said Dryden.

Lyndon shrugged. 'Murder. In Texas they give you the chair,' he said, fingering his throat. '"Burn." That's what they say: "Let 'em burn. Killed his own father." That's me.'

'But not here . . .' said Dryden.

'Civilised,' said Lyndon, sneering. 'But they might deport me. US citizen . . . but then again. The final laugh on me. Well, well, he ain't a Yank after all. So he can rot in one of our jails. Ten years . . . fifteen? Maybe more.'

'Estelle loves you. That's why she's here. She doesn't need to be.'

He held the Zippo at arm's length and lit it once. In the gloomy penumbra of the storm it was a brilliant flame: 'She wouldn't come with me. She wouldn't just leave. I knew it was right. She didn't trust me. Didn't believe. She knows that. We'll always know that.'

He flicked the ignition wheel on the Zippo lighter and held it to his chest. A cold blue flame spread over his sweatshirt. Then the flame jumped silently to his arm, and the doused sofa beneath him. Lyndon raised a fluttering hand, despite himself, to ward off the heat. Then the blue flames engulfed him in what looked like a cool shroud. The colder orange flames slipped down to the bare floorboards where the petrol ran in a river towards the kitchen.

Then Lyndon began to scream. He turned his head rapidly from side to side as the heat bit in, wanting to end his life with the dignity of self control. But the pain was too much and the scream broke through the blue shroud, and Dryden ran from it, ran anywhere, to escape the agony.

He closed the heavy wooden door behind him as the fire leapt across the room. He was in a corridor as familiar as a nightmare, at the end of which stood a front door like any other. He ran to it, his heart leaping, and turned the Yale lock to open it, but the door wouldn't move. There was a Chubb below it, locked fast, and no key. So he turned to face the fire, which he could hear buffeting the door he had closed. It was an odd place, he thought, to die.

'Not here,' he said, without conviction, as he considered the smoke slithering under the door, and then the tongues of flame beginning to curl under like searching fingers.

Then the door imploded with a silent percussion that popped his ears. In slow motion the wood became kindling as a tumbling fireball swept towards him. As he turned his back on it he was yelling— Humph said that later—yelling for water. Then he yelled for anything that would stop the pain which was eating into his back.

Which is when he thought of Laura. It was the coolness of her bed that called him. The lack of fire and warmth. The iciness he desperately craved now. He wanted to be by her bedside for ever.

'Please, God, let her see me again,' he said as, gagging on the gases, he dropped to his knees.

It wasn't his own death that scared him. It was the idea that she'd think he'd left her again, like he had in Harrimere Drain, in the flooded car. There were many things he had said since the crash, but only one thing had he repeated each night at The Tower: 'I'll be back.'

'Please, God,' he said, silently this time. 'Let her see me again.'

When he opened his eyes he was an inch from the lock. It was the Chubb: gold, and oddly icy. He put his lips to it and the kiss was as cold as Laura's skin. So he pulled the chain at his neck and he put the key in the lock and he heard it effortlessly tumbling, the locksmith's wheels falling nicely into their allotted slots.

Then he thanked God, shouted his name and, pulling the door towards him, fell out, back into the world that wasn't on fire, his arms flailing in a fiery semaphore.

WHEN HE CAME TO, Estelle was kneeling, holding him, with his back to the dust storm. Ahead the house burned, a single column now of cherry-red flame fifty feet high. The pain along his spine was distant, but he knew that it was shock that had dulled it, and that it was blossoming slowly, but relentlessly. The dust storm blew, and somewhere in the hiss of the cloud in which they existed he could hear Humph talking on a mobile. Estelle's eyes were locked on the burning house, while she held her sweatshirt to her mouth to block the fumes.

Dryden's chest heaved. 'You knew,' he said. 'Lyndon died thinking he'd killed Johnnie Roe. Thinking he died of thirst. But that's not right, is it?'

She didn't try to deny it. 'No.'

'You'd been there—to the pillbox. At Maggie's funeral you said Johnnie had been tortured like Tantalus. It was too perfect a description. None of the reports had the details. But you knew . . .'

Humph's voice floated into their world. 'They're coming.'

She coughed back the fumes. 'He disappeared—after the night Mum died. He knew about Johnnie then, from the tapes. He came past a couple of times and we met at the hospital—to clear away her things. Freeman came too. But I knew Lyndon was struggling, struggling, with all of it. We had to talk. He just wanted to go back home—as if nothing had happened. It was crazy. He was crazy. It wasn't something you could just forget. Then I saw the lights one night—out at Mons Wood. And the Land Rover, in the trees.'

'You found Johnnie?'

'Yes. In Mum's pillbox; she'd talked about it on the tapes. Where she'd met Johnnie. And I knew then that Lyndon had taken him there. I'd thought of revenge too. But what could I do? Then, suddenly, he was there. And I had that power, of life and death, given to me without asking. So I went back the next night with some of the chemicals they use for the fields. Weedkiller. Dad . . . Don, Don always said they were lethal, and to keep them away from kids because they were tasteless. Like water. And colourless. We kept supplies locked up at Black Bank. So I filled the glass with the poison and I gave it to him. He started screaming. Saying it burnt him inside. So I left.' She turned to Dryden and he sensed she'd taken a decision. She smiled. 'I don't regret it. I just wish I'd told Lyndon. Why didn't we talk? I wouldn't go back with him. We couldn't get past that.'

They watched the house burn. 'Now Lyndon's gone too,' said Dryden, shaking badly as the shock subsided. The pain was making it difficult for him to think.

'I had something to tell him,' said Estelle, and she let her hands drop to her stomach, where they cradled the flesh. Dryden knew then why Laura had told him there was another baby.

'A child,' he said, and she turned to him again.

'I wanted to tell him that I didn't go to the hospital. The last time we spoke we decided. I wouldn't go with him so he said that it would be best if the child wasn't born. I wanted to hurt him then, for being brutal. So I said OK. I said I would get rid of the child. He must have died thinking I had.'

The dust storm had vanished as quickly as it had descended on Adventurer's Fen. In the silence the house crackled like kindling.

'Lyndon. How did he die?' Estelle said.

'The lighter. Petrol, I think. It was over very quickly.'

She twisted her head back in despair. 'We never escaped, did we? Any of us. From that fire. From this.'

And she started to walk towards the flames. Dryden stood up, felt the fen sweep round him in a dizzy vision and lunged after her. He clutched at Estelle's arm and then his knees buckled and he brought her down into the dust with him.

'The child can escape,' he said, and blacked out.

POSTCRIPT

As the ambulance took Dryden away from Adventurer's Fen the rain fell. Fizzing droplets turned to tiny clouds of gas over the burning forest and dripped from the open rafters of the house that Laura had built. The house she had built for them.

It hadn't been her secret alone; she'd shared it with her parents. Six months before the accident at Harrimere Drain they'd come back from Italy, from retirement, on a visit. She wanted to take the money left to her in trust to build the house Dryden wanted, for the family they both wanted. She took them out to the spot and let them feel the thrill of the secret too. The secret she hugged to herself that last summer, even as she understood the shadow it cast over Dryden. But with her parents she agreed to keep the secret, at least for a few more weeks, until his birthday.

After Laura's accident her parents flew back to be at her side, and after the weeks in which she might have died had passed, they asked Dryden what he wanted to do with the money in the trust fund. They'd agreed a plan on the flight: if he said he wanted the money they'd tell him about the house on Adventurer's Fen. If not, they'd rent it, bank the money as an investment, and keep the secret in the hope that when Laura came out of the coma she, and Dryden, could enjoy the surprise—at last. It was a sound investment, and a clever compromise. Dryden had told them to invest the money safely. He carried the key she'd given him, and they carried Laura's secret.

Which is why Dryden's key was made to fit a lock in a house that should have existed only in a dream.

Andy 'Last Case' Newman retired a month after the deaths on Adventurer's Fen. All three killings, of Bob Sutton, Johnnie Roe and Winston, the people smuggler, appeared on his file as solved. Lyndon Koskinski was Johnnie Roe's presumed killer. Dryden and Estelle kept her secret to themselves. Newman was commended and moved to the north Norfolk coast, shortly afterwards identifying a new sub-species of Arctic tern: *Borealis Newmanii*.

Estelle gave birth to a baby girl on Christmas Day at Black Bank Farm. She was christened Margaret. Dryden was invited, and after the ceremony they went to the graveyard at St Matthew's and stood before Lyndon's grave. He'd been buried with Maggie and Don. Dryden, hospitalised after the burns he had received at Adventurer's Fen, had only just escaped a wheelchair.

Lyndon's one-time grandparents in Austin had sent a wreath, which carried a small flag: a white star on a blue background with broad stripes of white and red—the flag of the Lone Star State.

Estelle asked Dryden to ring them. They'd taken the call, listened to a factual account of what had happened, and thanked him. He sensed few emotions, except bitterness and loss.

Jimmy Kabazo pleaded guilty to the murder—reduced to manslaughter—of Winston Edgeley on the direction of the judge at Cambridge Crown Court. A similar plea was entered and accepted for the killing of Bob Sutton. The judge said the crimes were heinous, but the agonised mental state of the defendant was sufficient to warrant a plea in mitigation. Jimmy Kabazo didn't care. He was deported to Nigeria to serve his sentence: ten years, concurrent, on both charges. His son Emmy was buried in the corporation cemetery at King's Lynn.

Alice and Ellie Sutton buried Bob in the cemetery at Ely. The gravestone said: GAVE HIS LIFE FOR HIS DAUGHTER.

The memorial stone to the victims of the 1976 aircrash still stands: the name of Lyndon Koskinski has been added, as Maggie requested.

Major August Sondheim was diagnosed with cirrhosis of the liver. He took sick leave and flew home to see his daughter. After three months in a Vermont nursing home with Sergeant Rachel DeWitt at his side his health improved and he took early retirement. He is still an alcoholic, but hasn't taken a drink since his disease was diagnosed. He will be a father again in six months' time.

Peter Selby, eventually charged with aggravated rape and indecent assault, asked for eighty-three similar charges to be taken into account. He named five other defendants before his appearance at Peterborough Crown Court. All were found guilty. Selby got twelve years, the rest fourteen.

Captain Freeman White was released from police custody after being questioned about the death of Bob Sutton. Owing to insufficient evidence, no charges were ever brought. He was discharged from the US Air Force two months later. He cashed in his military pension for a lump sum and bought a motorcycle repair business in Austin, Texas.

Humph spent the following Christmas in Thessaloniki. He is now learning Walloon.

Dryden suffered third-degree burns to his upper back, left shoulder and left arm. Extensive skin grafts were needed. The operations were performed at The Tower. He took Maggie's bed to be near Laura, and told her the whole story. The COMPASS machine delivered no further messages.

When he was well enough to walk he stood at the foot of Laura's bed and told her what he was going to do. The insurance money had come through after the fire. He would rebuild Adventurer's Fen and rent it out again. It would be their home one day. One day soon. Then he went out and met a surveyor on the land.

While he was out the COMPASS machine chattered into life.

SAHDNF HGY DSPP DFHGI SIOOOOIFIWFOWEF
ADG S S HJGUT I LOVE YOU FGFKJSHJAO AAJA

JIM KELLY

Jim Kelly describes the brooding atmosphere of the Fens so evocatively in *The Fire Baby* that the landscape almost feels like a physical presence in the novel. He clearly finds much inspiration in the flat and seemingly infinite spaces surrounding his home, having set his first book, *The Water Clock*, there as well. 'We live in Ely, at the heart of the Black Fens, so-called because of the peat soil. I love the place. I am slightly claustrophobic and the Fens promise, and deliver, almost unlimited space. Yet despite being wide open, the landscape is mysterious. There are few good roads, endless miles of tracks, and lots of dead ends hemmed in by water. It is one of the few real wildernesses left in England.'

Both of Kelly's books feature his two series characters, journalist Philip Dryden and his sidekick, Humph. 'Dryden is a projection of what I would like to be,' Kelly says of his clever, tall, dark and handsome creation. Humph, on the other hand, is, 'an overweight taxi driver who never steps out of his fetid car. Many people who read my first book would say to me, "That Humph character is you, isn't it!" So perhaps I am a bit of both.' Kelly already has plans to feature the pair in at least two more books.

Like Dryden, Kelly is a journalist, and he writes mainly about education issues for national papers such as *The Guardian* and the *Financial Times*. 'But I was a provincial journalist for ten years before going to Fleet Street so I know how Dryden lives. It is an exciting job being a local reporter and one I missed a lot when I went to London. You are much more a part of the stories you write, and you have to keep your eyes and ears open all the time.'

At the heart of *The Fire Baby* is the idea that tremendous damage can be done by lies. 'I've always been fascinated by the power of lies,' Kelly says, 'especially small ones. When told, they are often dismissed as white lies. The problem is that if they are not corrected they can become extremely threatening. They are like unexploded bombs really, and once uncovered they can start to tick.'

howard roughan

the promise of a lie

Sometimes trust is everything.

A patient should be able to trust the
therapist in whom he confides his
innermost thoughts and feelings.

But shouldn't the therapist
also be able to trust his patient?

PART I

one

To be perfectly blunt and unprofessional, my line-up that day read like the maladjusted all-star team of Manhattan.

My nine o'clock was a bulimic, twice-divorced executive who was having an affair with her married boss. My ten o'clock was a guilt-ridden kleptomaniac who could never keep what he stole. He was always revisiting stores in order to put things back. Then came my eleven o'clock: a sexually compulsive cellist. A couple of hours for lunch and paperwork, and it was time to reload.

Two o'clock: a soap-opera actor who could no longer distinguish between himself and the character he played. Next up was my three o'clock. On second thought, don't get me started on my three o'clock. Finally, there was my last patient of the day. My four o'clock. The main reason I remember that day at all.

His name was Kevin Daniels. A struggling young writer who'd written seven screenplays and had yet to sell any of them. Kevin's frustration had manifested in a bitter hatred of the very people he wanted to impress. To Kevin, Hollywood was infested with, and I quote, *culturally retarded wayward whores destined to make feel-good-movie johns out of all of us*. I could only imagine how his screenplays read.

On this particular afternoon, an overcast Thursday in the middle of October, Kevin arrived at my office with an uncharacteristic smile. He professed to having significant news.

'I've had a moment of intense clarity, an epiphany,' he said. He lowered his voice to a whisper. 'I need to be in the belly of the beast. I'm moving, David. I'm going to Hollywood.'

'To fight the battle from within,' I said.

'Exactly,' he said. 'I flew out there last weekend and rented a place in Hollywood Hills. I'll be heading back there the day after tomorrow.'

'You're not wasting any time, are you?'

'Not if I can help it. Do you approve of my moving, David?'

I cautioned myself. Much about psychotherapy, or at least the way I approached it, was predicated on the belief that an opinion should never do more harm than good. My job was not to ferret out right from wrong in any absolute sense. Only what was right or wrong for a particular patient.

'Do I approve of your moving?' I said. 'I'm not sure my thoughts have anything to do with approving or disapproving. The important thing—and this is something you and I have been talking about for quite some time—is that no one has more control over your life than you do. While that won't guarantee you success, it will guarantee you the right to make your own decisions. For better or worse.'

He shrugged. 'I can live with that.'

After looking at each other in silence for a few seconds, we both realised that continuing to talk merely because we had time left in the hour would be silly. He told me I should charge him for a full session.

'No, this one's on the house,' I said. 'Buy two hundred, get one free.'

He laughed and we shook hands. I wished him luck.

That's why I remember that day so well. I'd told Kevin what I'd been telling him repeatedly over four years: that no one can have more control over your life than you do. It was pretty good advice, I thought. Too bad it was wrong. *Dead* wrong.

I know this because Kevin's leaving created an opening in my schedule . . . and the person who filled it was going to be all the proof I needed.

THE VERY NEXT night around eight o'clock Parker reached out and poked his index finger at the doorbell. As the three of us stood there waiting, I took the opportunity to complain one more time.

'I can't believe I let you two talk me into coming to this thing,' I muttered.

'Nonsense,' Parker replied. 'You wouldn't be here unless you wanted to be.'

'That's very shrink of you,' I said.

'And that's a *nondenial* denial,' said Parker.

I chuckled. 'There's the lawyer I know and love.'

Parker's wife, Stacy, gave him a nudge. 'Will the lawyer I also know and love ring the doorbell again,' she said. 'I don't think anyone heard us.'

Parker rang the bell again. The door opened almost immediately.

'*Omigod!* Will you look who's here,' she practically shrieked. Cassandra Nance, all ninety-eight pounds of her, stood before us with a bony hand slapped over her mouth in mock surprise. A little black dress draped her shoulders as if it were still on the hanger. The woman was thin. 'Come in, come in,' she said.

Air kisses, initial pleasantries, and the customary bottle-of-wine handover. A rented man in a tuxedo took our coats. Cassandra led us into the party. As she did, she locked her arm around mine and whispered in my ear, 'It's really great you could make it, David.'

By that point I was resigned to the situation. This was the appearance to keep up appearances, and I was prepared to put in the good effort. But before that could happen, I needed to say hello to Mr Bartender. After a brief, one-sided conversation with the guy, I was handed my bourbon and water. Two quick sips and I was ready.

I looked around. Seemingly every ethnicity, ideology and sexual orientation was represented—all happily conversing with one another and all somehow connected to our hostess.

My connection was originally through Parker and Stacy, who were friends of Cassandra's. Parker Mathis was my freshman-year roommate at Columbia. Over the course of four years, we became best of friends. That we'd each decided to remain in the city after graduation, practically made us brothers. I had even forgiven Parker for growing up to be a criminal defence attorney.

I had to hand it to him for his success in choosing a bride. Stacy Mathis was smart, witty, attractive, and the founder of a women's crisis centre in Harlem. The complete package topped off by a halo.

For the next couple of hours I made the rounds, shaking hands and trading anecdotes, happy to discover that my group social skills, while a bit rusty, hadn't completely deserted me.

Then, en route to another bourbon and water, I felt a sharp tug on my arm courtesy of Cassandra. She was standing with a few other people. 'David, you absolutely have to hear this!' she announced.

'Hear what?' I asked, obliging her.

'Nathan's theory, that's what. It's positively Neanderthal.'

'Oh, c'mon, Cassandra, you can't pretend to tell me you disagree,' said the man I presumed was Nathan. We hadn't met.

'Nathan Harris,' he said to me. We shook hands.

'David Remler,' I told him.

'Yes, I know. I read your book.'

Cassandra, ever the hostess, said: 'David, you've met Jane and Scott Wallace.'

'Yes,' I said, smiling at the other couple rounding out our circle.

'Good,' she said. 'So go on, Nathan, tell David what you were saying. I'm curious what our resident psychologist will make of it.'

Nathan was fortyish, thin, tan out of season, impeccably groomed. The word *dapper* came to mind. So did *pompous*. 'What I was saying,' he began, 'is that I have this theory about the true difference between men and women. Very simply, I believe men are superior to women when it comes to all things tangible—things that we can actually touch. For example, men are far better than women when it comes to building things. I don't just mean in terms of physical construction; I'd include the planning and design as well. All the great architects throughout history have been men. Consider the arts—all the great painters and sculptors have been men as well. The better surgeons? Men. The better chefs? Men. Even when it comes to making money—cold, hard cash—men are better at it than women.'

Nathan paused and took a sip of his drink. While he did, I glanced at his hands. Much to my surprise: a wedding band. He went on. 'Ah, but women,' he said, 'when it comes to the intangible—the things you can't touch—women have us men beat by a mile. When it comes to feelings and emotions, women rule and men are powerless. And don't think that women don't know this. They know it all too well and take full advantage; often luring us men into a serene sense of being in control, only to suddenly turn the tables.'

'So,' said Cassandra. 'What do you think of Nathan's theory?'

'I think it's very interesting,' I answered. 'You seem to be saying, Nathan, that while men are the hands of our collective culture, women represent the heart. Numerous exceptions notwithstanding, that's a pretty tenable idea. Take one thing you didn't mention. Sex. Not who's better at it, but the widely held belief that men view sex as a physical act, while women view it as an emotional one. I think that kind of supports what you're talking about.

'However, the notion that women use this difference as a way of tricking and deceiving—sort of like men are from Mars and women are Venus flytraps. I don't really buy that. To me that paints a rather unflattering and inaccurate picture of what I've always considered the more compassionate sex. Wouldn't you agree, Cassandra?'

She looked ready to kiss me. 'I couldn't agree more.'

'Sold!' I announced. I shook the empty glass in my hand. 'Now if you'll all excuse me, I seem to need a refill.'

Not so fast, David.

'Interesting,' Nathan Harris said, scratching his temple. 'Let me ask you something, though, David. Can you honestly say that you've never been taken advantage of emotionally by a woman?'

'I don't think so,' I answered. 'Of course, the night is still young.'

Everyone found that amusing except Nathan. 'I'm afraid I don't really buy *that*,' he said, throwing my words back at me. 'Somewhere along the line surely you've been the victim of a woman?'

'Nathan dear, don't you think we're getting a bit personal?' said Cassandra, coming to my rescue.

'I'm not asking him to name names or reveal intimate details,' said Nathan indignantly. 'I'm simply asking him to be honest.' He turned to me. 'You can be honest with us, David, can't you?'

That about did it. It was time to put Nathan in his place. I was about to say a few things I knew I'd later regret.

'Excuse me, do you mind if we borrow David for a moment?'

Parker, with Stacy by his side, had leaned in over my shoulder. I was being sprung.

'I'm afraid I've been summoned,' I told the group. It happened so fast that Nathan could do nothing except stare helplessly.

A safe distance later, I thanked Parker and Stacy for their timely appearance.

'We figured as much,' said Parker.

I performed an exaggerated deep sigh and kidded, 'Like I said, I don't know how I let you two talk me into coming to this thing.'

'Oh, c'mon, David,' said Stacy. 'You've had a good time tonight, admit it.'

'If I do admit it, can we leave?'

Soon after, the three of us shared a cab home. We discussed (read: gossiped about) some of the people we'd encountered that evening.

At Sixty-ninth and Third, the taxi pulled over to let me out. As I opened the door, I thanked Parker and Stacy for not taking no for an answer when they asked me to join them for the party.

Once out on the sidewalk, the autumn night air crisp and biting, I watched as their cab sped off, fully aware of the inevitable. Now it was I who'd be discussed by Parker and Stacy. They'd talk about me and continue to wonder, as they surely had since the day it happened: in missing her as I still did, would I also miss out on the rest of my life? At the time, I was kind of wondering that myself.

IT HAD BEEN nearly three years since my wife, Rebecca, died at the age of thirty-one. She was four months' pregnant at the time.

Rebecca and I owned an apartment in Manhattan. In addition, we owned a cottage out in Connecticut. Our weekend retreat.

Often, Rebecca would get a jump on the weekend with a Thursday-night drive out to the cottage. As a freelance writer, she made her own hours. I'd work a full day on Friday and join Rebecca that evening at the cottage after taking the train up to Danbury.

Such was the case that second weekend in November. But on that Friday evening, instead of Rebecca picking me up at the station as she usually did, a policeman was there waiting. His job was to take me to the county coroner's office.

Earlier that morning, a freezing rain had fallen all around the lake area. Rebecca had left the cottage during the worst of it to pick up groceries. It was a head-on collision. An eighteen-year-old kid behind the wheel of his parents' Lexus. He hadn't been drinking or smoking pot. The kid was just a kid, driving too fast. He lost control of the car and spun into the oncoming lane. Right into Rebecca.

Yes, in time I found I could deal with talking about her death. It was *thinking* about it that I couldn't handle. I could easily disengage from the concern and curiosity of others; the caring questions and the post-mortem rubbernecking merely disguised as caring questions. But I couldn't escape my own thoughts . . . and the frequency with which they'd turn to Rebecca. And our baby.

It was too early to know if we were having a boy or a girl. Rebecca had every intention of finding out the sex as soon as she could. Having no strong opinion either way, I left it up to her. In the meantime, we didn't discuss names. That was my suggestion. Waiting until we knew the sex meant 50 per cent less arguing, I joked. Agreeing not to discuss names, however, didn't mean we weren't thinking about them. I know I was. I was sure she was as well.

A few weeks after Rebecca died, I was looking through the closet when I found a baby name book. I never knew Rebecca had purchased one, and given the hiding place, I guess that's how she wanted it.

I sat down on the floor in front of the closet. I began flipping through the pages, glancing at a circled name here, a checked name there. Then I came across it. Tucked in the page that ended the Ss and began the Ts was a piece of white paper. On it was a list. Not of potential baby names, though. Rebecca had written a sentence near the top. It read, *Things we will teach our child* . . . Underneath, she'd jotted down the following:

> *To love.*
> *To laugh.*
> *To laugh some more.*
> *To listen and learn.*
> *To say please and thank you.*
> *To have opinions.*
> *To respect those of others.*
> *To be honest.*
> *To be a friend.*
> *To be yourself.*

How long I sat there I can't remember. I read what Rebecca had written over and over until I memorised it. I put the paper back in the book. The next day, I went to a bank and rented a safe deposit box. I placed the book in it. I told myself that if I ever forgot any part of Rebecca's list, I'd come and remind myself. I've yet to go back.

two

There was a brief message waiting for me when I arrived at my office Monday morning. It was from Mila, or *Mamka* (Czech for 'Mom') as I was fond of calling her. I think she was fond of my calling her that as well. She'd never had any kids.

Mamka, aka Mila Benninghoff, was my secretary, bookkeeper, insurance company liaison and all-around godsend. At seventy, she made it look easy. Having lived in Prague for both the Nazi and Soviet invasions, she knew from hard.

The set-up the two of us had was ideal, albeit a little unorthodox. Mila oversaw the scheduling of my appointments, my correspondence, my billing, and everything else in my day-to-day life. All from her apartment. Which was fine by her and exactly how I wanted it.

The workload didn't mandate someone's sitting out in my reception area full-time, particularly since I never took calls during a session.

So from her rent-controlled, one-bedroom apartment near Gramercy Park, Mila would call me in between my appointments to pass along any messages—those she fielded herself and those forwarded by my answering service. Mila's message that afternoon regarded the opening in my schedule created by Kevin Daniels's departure for Hollywood. I'd told her about it, and she was going to get back to me after checking the waiting list.

'David, it turns out there is someone on the list,' began Mila's message. 'His name is Sam Kent, and he'll be your Thursday, four o'clock.' I wrote it down in my calendar.

THAT AFTERNOON I was meeting Debra Walker Coyne, my esteemed literary agent for lunch at the Four Seasons to discuss the outline for my second book.

The reason there was going to be a second book was due to the surprise success of my first, *The Human Pendulum*. It spent eleven weeks on the *New York Times* nonfiction best-seller list. Though not without a lot of help from the gods of timing. It happened like this. Months before my book was published, a rabbi from the Upper West Side was arrested for murder. According to the district attorney's office, the rabbi, who was married, was supposedly having a sexual relationship with a female member of his congregation. When the affair went sour and the woman threatened to expose him, he allegedly went to her apartment and strangled her.

At first, the evidence seemed overwhelming. The rabbi's fingerprints were at the scene and a nosy neighbour had seen him leaving. On top of that, the woman was strangled with wire, the gauge of which matched that of a half-used spool found in the rabbi's home.

Finally, there was the diary. The woman had kept a detailed account of her relationship with the rabbi. Apparently, it was a creepy read. Particularly fascinating were the numerous references to the rabbi's threatening to harm the woman if she betrayed his trust. The last entry—the smoking entry, if you will—was dated the morning of the woman's death. It read, simply: *I think he's going to kill me today*.

The arrest of the rabbi and the ensuing trial were perfect fodder for every news outlet in the city. It was a whopping good story. It had murder, sex, religion. Then, before I knew it, it had me.

All thanks to one Ethan Greene. Ethan was an enterprising young prosecutor with the Manhattan D.A.'s office. He was also on the spot. His superiors were convinced they had their man, rabbi or not, and in Ethan, they believed they had the right prosecutor to nail him.

Ethan was intuitively smart, polished, and had no reservations about putting a rabbi away for life. Best of all he was Jewish. The image of Ethan fighting for not only justice but the sanctity of his own religion was deemed to be just the right touch—both in the courtroom and in the court of public opinion.

The rabbi claimed the woman was very unstable and had somehow decided the two of them were destined to be romantically involved.

The rabbi said he'd tried to counsel the woman, while also being quite clear about the impossibility of his ever being more to her than a spiritual adviser. As for his being at the woman's apartment, he was merely making a house call, trying one last time to help. It was no use, though. On that day, said the rabbi, he left the woman's apartment believing she needed psychiatric care. He called a hospital to enquire about a programme. Phone records indicated as much.

Was the rabbi telling the truth? Or lying to save himself?

No matter how the jury was digesting the rabbi's story, the defence would still have to address the question: Who, then, killed the woman? Simple. She killed herself.

It could've happened. Or so suggested a medical expert put on the stand by the rabbi's defence team. Suicide by self-garroting. Physically achievable, claimed the expert, a professor at Harvard Medical School. The expert went on to cite two other cases in which the same type of suicide was thought to have occurred.

The defence lawyers strutted as if they had it all figured out. The woman had strangled herself with a strip of picture wire common to a million households. She was despondent over being romantically rejected. She was also angry. Enough to want to make the suicide look like a murder. Suddenly, things were looking up for the rabbi.

That's when I got the call from Ethan Greene. The problem, he said, was the jury. He had to convince them it was OK to convict a rabbi. That they'd still be able to sleep at night, having put away a 'holy man'.

'Fair enough, but why me?' I asked.

Ethan explained. He'd first heard of me over dinner with a friend, discussing the dilemma presented by the rabbi. Ethan's friend, who himself was a budding psychologist, mentioned my book and how it might apply. Ethan purchased *The Human Pendulum* the following morning. He liked what he read. He loved one part in particular.

He reminded me of the woman who killed her children the same month she won a 'Teacher of the Year' award. Then there's that nice family man who raised millions of dollars for charity yet one day dragged a guy out of his car and kicked him to death—all because the guy had the temerity to honk at him after the traffic light turned green.

These are stories we hear from time to time and will continue to hear time and time again. They won't go away. Nonetheless, we persist in thinking of them as aberrations. Anomalies to the spectrum of human behaviour. Quickly, we try to ascertain the mitigating factors. Medication the person was taking. A suppressed trauma from childhood. Excessive stress, the playing of violent video games. Anything and everything. Just so long as we don't have to confront the disturbing reality head-on: *good people can do very bad things*. Because to accept that means we're all capable of doing the unspeakable.

It means that we're all at risk on the Human Pendulum.

Which is not to say that your friendly, law-abiding neighbour will be chopping up his entire family with an axe anytime soon. Only that out there somewhere, *somebody's* friendly, law-abiding neighbour will be. And right now he doesn't even know it. As troubling as that may sound, it could be worse. You could be that neighbour.

My initial response to Ethan's plea for help was a polite yet firm no. He persisted, though, pointing out that my testimony could be crucial in getting the jury to accept what they already knew—that the rabbi, like the rest of us, wasn't impervious to temptation.

Still, I continued to say no and Ethan continued to implore me. That's when the point was made clear. Ethan wasn't exactly *asking*.

'Dr Remler, you will be testifying in my case. I don't like subpoenas. They're a lot of paperwork, but if that's what it's going to take, so be it.' Well, when you put it that way . . .

Two days later I got called to the stand and nervously spoke of the unfortunate but undeniable reality that there's no tenured status for do-gooders. Human behaviour, I said, quoting from my book, is like the fine print of a mutual-fund prospectus: past performance doesn't guarantee future results.

I never once looked at the rabbi. I fixed my gaze on Ethan while intermittently acknowledging the jury. To my eyes they seemed as if they really didn't give a damn about Dr David Remler and his precious little book. When I stepped down from the stand, Ethan gave me a shrug that I took to mean 'Well, it was worth a shot.'

Closing arguments came the next day. The verdict three days after that. The smart money was on the rabbi. The legal pundits on cable were pretty much all in agreement. Not guilty. I was prone to agree.

Of course, I of all people should've known better than to try to predict human behaviour. *This just in*, announced the radio host of the jazz station I listened to when eating lunch in my office. I sat at my desk with a tuna sandwich, waiting to hear if it would be one word or two. It was one. Guilty.

Ethan Greene had prevailed. Later that night, I'd watched on the news as he stood in front of the courthouse after the verdict was read and spoke to reporters. He chose his words carefully. He praised the work of his department and the wisdom of the jury.

Then the footage of Ethan switched to footage of some older Hispanic woman. She looked familiar. Yes, she'd been in the first row, third from the right. In this age of the post-verdict juror interview, here was this woman, one of the jurors, telling the reporter what had really influenced her decision. 'I guess what really made the difference for me was that psychologist witness. The one with the book.'

Ditto, said the young man in a business suit standing next to her. He'd sat somewhere in the second row of the jury box. He claimed it was my testimony that helped him overcome what had been one of his main obstacles: believing a rabbi could ever do such a thing.

Ten seconds later, my phone was ringing. I picked it up to hear Parker. 'Congratulations,' he said. 'You're about to become a bestselling author.'

'What makes you say that?' I asked.

'Because you just demolished one of the oldest tenets of trial law: the character witness. Now every attorney and law prof in the land will have to read your book to see what all the fuss was about,' he said. 'You wait.'

I didn't have to wait long. Within a few days, my editor called to say that a second printing of the book had been ordered. My literary agent, Debra Walker Coyne, was fielding calls from a horde of news programmes, all wanting me to make an appearance. To Debra this meant more books sold and I agreed to do one show. Debra called to say she could get me on with Charlie Rose. By the time the show aired, Parker's prediction had come true. I was a *New York Times* bestselling author.

three

A t four on the nose, I double-checked my calendar for the correct
name of my new patient. Mr Sam Kent, according to Mila. I got
up from my desk and opened the door to the reception area. What I
saw wasn't quite what I expected. I hesitated.

'Is something wrong?' she asked.

Sitting on the couch against the wall was a woman, a black shoulder bag by her side. She was wearing a long raincoat with a high collar, and a soft grey Yankees baseball cap.

'I'm sorry,' I answered. 'You're not—'

'I am. Sam Kent. Short for Samantha.' She stood up and we shook hands.

'Dr Remler. But call me David.'

'OK, David.'

'My secretary told me you were *Mr* Sam Kent,' I said. 'The Sam name notwithstanding, I assume you spoke with her.'

'Emailed, actually. When I first called a few months back, I got your service. I gave them my email address because I was moving and my phone number would be changing.'

'Well, that explains it,' I said. 'Come on in.' I motioned with my arm, and Sam Kent stepped into my office. She removed her raincoat. She had on blue jeans and a red sweatshirt.

'Where should I sit?' she asked. They always did.

'Sofa or chair, whichever you prefer.'

She preferred the chair, a wingback opposite mine. We both sat. I looked at my new patient. She was now visibly upset.

'I'm sorry,' she said, wiping away a tear. 'I promised myself I wouldn't do it, but I still did. Right off the bat, no less.'

'You mean cry?'

'No,' she said. 'Lie.'

'What about?'

'You asked me whether I had talked to your secretary. I told you why I didn't give a phone number. I said it was because I was moving.' She wiped away another tear. 'I was never moving.'

I got up, grabbed a box of tissues off my desk, and walked it over to her. She took one and dabbed her eyes.

'OK,' I said, returning to my chair. 'I take it there was some reason you didn't want to give out your phone number.'

'It's the same reason that I'm here,' she said. 'My husband.'

Usually, a first session is nothing more than an extended introduction. The immediate concern is getting to know each other. Occasionally, a patient delves right into things. This was one such occasion.

'Your husband . . . what is it about him, Sam, that brings you here?'

She reached for another tissue. Wiped her eyes. Proceeded to look right into mine. 'I'm here because I want to kill him,' she said.

'When you say you want to kill him, are you speaking literally or figuratively?' I asked.

'Both,' she said. 'Though as you might imagine, it's the "literally" that has me worried.'

'That you might actually do it?'

'That, and how I could be so crazy even to think such a thing.'

'Believe it or not, that doesn't make you crazy,' I told her.

'I beg to differ.'

I continued: 'Let's put your murdering ways on the back burner for a moment. I'm still a little confused about how your husband has anything to do with not giving out your phone number.'

'That's easy,' she said. 'Say your office calls and he picks up or he hears a message. I couldn't have that. He can't find out I'm seeing a therapist.'

'Why's that?'

'Because he'd know I'd be talking about him.'

'He wouldn't like that, huh?'

'You have no idea.'

She was right. I had no idea. That would have to change. While there was no rush, I chose to seize the opportunity she was giving me. 'What does your husband do for a living?'

'He's a venture capitalist. He and a partner have a firm downtown.'

'Wall Street?'

'That's where the money is, as he likes to say.'

'Does he work a lot?' I asked.

'All the time.'

'Is the firm successful?'

'Very,' she said. The subtext being *very* very.

'What about children? Do you have any?'

'A little boy,' she said, her expression warming. 'He's two.'

'How is your husband with him?'

The warm expression disappeared. 'As I said, he works all the time.'

'And how many years have you been married?'

'Five.'

'Do you love him?'

'I told you I wanted to kill him. I don't love him.'

'Did you ever?'

She thought about it. 'I believe I did once. Early on.'

'Do you fight a lot?'

'Not any more,' she said. 'Fighting assumes you still care.'

'Which I guess begs the question: why haven't you left him?'

'Because if I did, he'd be the one killing me.'

Here we go again, I thought. 'Literally?' I asked.

'Figuratively,' she answered. 'He told me that if I tried to divorce him he'd make sure I'd never get custody of our son.'

'How would he accomplish that?'

'I think I just need a little time with that one.'

'Has he ever hit you?'

She shook her head. 'No. He's too smart for that. Any man can hit a woman. Only he knows how to render one helpless.'

'Which is how?'

'Condescension. Ridicule. He belittles my every move, questions my every motive. He's turned my family against me, as well as my friends. He tells me I'm not as pretty as I once was. Or as thin.'

'When he says these things, what do you say in return?'

'I wish I could say I gave it right back. I wish I was that strong. I'm not. It hurts too much. And he knows it. It's like he feeds off of it.'

With that, the timing seemed right. At some point during every first session I asked the same question. 'What do you want to gain by coming here?'

'The strength to stand up to him,' she said. 'Once and for all.'

She reached for another tissue, and I decided to keep the remainder of the session as light as possible. We talked about her background. She'd been raised in Larchmont, north of Manhattan. Only child. Parents retired in Tempe, Arizona. She graduated from Brown. Worked in fashion. Dreamed of being a designer. Ended up working as a buyer for Bergdorf's. Met her husband at a fashion show.

After fifty minutes, we agreed to meet once a week. Same day and time. Thursday, four o'clock. The subject turned to payment. She reiterated how important it was that her husband not know she was going to a therapist.

'He sees all my cheques and credit card charges,' she said. 'Can I pay you in cash?'

I told her I didn't see why not.

She reached into her bag and removed a bank envelope. Three crisp hundred-dollar bills were taken out and handed to me.

'Wouldn't your husband notice the bank withdrawal?'

'A girl has to have her walking-around money, doesn't she?' Sam put her raincoat back on and adjusted her Yankees cap.

'Are you a fan?' I asked.

'My uncle was a season ticket holder while I was growing up. He took my dad and me to a lot of games. Pretty good memories.'

We shook hands.

'So I'll see you next week,' she said. Sam Kent. Samantha Kent. Mrs Samantha Kent.

She left my office, and I sat behind my desk to jot down notes. I always wrote. Never typed. Even my book was written in longhand.

I recorded the bare essentials. A physical description of her: early thirties, attractive, affluent without pretence. A few facts about her background: places lived, jobs, anything else that could've shaped who she was. Finally, a summation of the issues touched on. In bullet-point fashion, I recounted the conversation about her husband.

I never once asked his name. If she'd offered it up, fine. My experience, however, was that it was harder for some patients to be as forthcoming about their problems when discussing others by name. Her husband, therefore, would remain 'the husband' as far as I was concerned. That little shred of privacy she could afford him would in turn afford her the opportunity to be more honest.

The mind works in mysterious ways. So must a psychologist.

'HELLO, DAVID.'

'Hi, Mamka,' I said. '*Rád te˘vozím.*'

Mila chuckled. 'You just told me it was good to drive me.'

'Damn. I thought I had that one. How do you say "Good to see you"?'

'*Rád te˘vidím,*' she replied, her accent kicking in perfectly.

She had come to my office for her regularly scheduled visit. Every other Tuesday at five o'clock. The main purpose of our meeting was for me to sign cheques she'd brought along. Utilities, the lease, and other things relating to the practice.

'By the way,' I said to Mila after signing the last of the cheques. 'My new patient, Mr Sam Kent? He's not a he. He's a she.'

'You mean he's a transvestite?'

Mila had perhaps lived in New York too long.

'No,' I said. 'What I mean is, Sam Kent is actually a woman. Sam is short for Samantha. Anyway, for reasons I can't go into—you know, patient privacy and all—she's going to be paying me in cash. So if you could deposit this with the rest of the cheques,' I said, handing her the $300 Sam had given me.

'Sure.' She put the cash in a folder she used for the cheques. 'Oh, one other thing,' she said. 'Don't forget, you've got the Kesper Society cocktail party this Friday.'

I frowned. 'Can't you write a note saying I'm too sick to attend?'

She frowned back. 'Now what kind of Mamka would I be if I did something like that?'

'The best kind.'

TWO DAYS LATER I welcomed Sam Kent back to my office. Her jeans and sweatshirt were replaced by a sharp-looking grey flannel suit. There was make-up and jewellery. Her blonde hair, which had last been tucked beneath a Yankees cap, was now straight down and long. A very polished look.

'I think you've exceeded the dress code,' I said.

'Fancy lunch with a girlfriend,' she explained, dropping into the wingback opposite mine. 'I confided in her about coming to see you, and she knew who you were. She read some article on you.'

'Is that right?'

'Yes. And she mentioned you lost your wife a few years back. Is that true?'

'Yes, it's true.'

'I'm so sorry. I was wondering . . .' Her voice trailed off.

'What is it?'

'Well, did it help or hurt more that you were a psychologist? What I mean is, given what you do for a living, I'd think you'd be almost too aware of your emotions to grieve as one normally would.'

A lot of patients did this. Assumed that because they were revealing their deepest, darkest, most intimate secrets they were entitled to know anything and everything about me. I couldn't tell them that my personal life was none of their business. That would jeopardise the trust and openness all therapy is based on. So, I'd throw out an honest titbit about me that related as much if not more to them. I was about to do exactly that when Sam caught herself.

'What am I *doing?*' she said with gasp. 'This is none of my business. I apologise. I don't know what I was thinking.'

'It's OK,' I said. Which it was. Also pretty refreshing.

'This is about me and let's keep it that way,' she said.

'OK,' I replied. 'You mentioned that if you tried to divorce your husband he'd make sure you'd never get custody of your son. How would he do that?'

'I tried to kill myself,' she said, her voice remaining calm.

I expected tears. There weren't any. Her face was expressionless.

'When did this happen?' I asked.

'A few years ago.'

'Before you were pregnant?'

'God, yes.'

'What is it you did?'

'I swallowed thirty Halcions with a bottle of wine,' she said.

'Yet, here you are today,' I said.

'My husband found me. He was supposed to be out to dinner with a client. The client called him to cancel—an emergency at home. Ironic, huh? My husband came back to our place and there I was.'

'Tell me, what did your husband do?'

'Well, let's see. He saw the empty bottle of pills near the bed and asked how long it had been since I took them. I told him it had been long enough, which it clearly hadn't because I was still pretty lucid. My husband went to the medicine cabinet and grabbed a bottle of Ipecac. He force-fed me a couple of ounces, and the next thing I knew I was puking my guts out.'

'What happened next?' I asked.

'I slept like a baby and woke up the next morning.'

'You didn't go to the hospital?'

'No. I knew I was going to be all right. At least physically,' she said. 'That night, a hospital wasn't going to do anything for me mentally. I assured my husband I didn't need to go.'

'He was OK with that?'

'More than OK, I think. I'm sure he felt relieved,' she said. 'Better to have a wife who committed suicide than a wife who's known to all his friends and associates as the one who'd *tried* to commit suicide. Going to the hospital meant there was a good chance the story would get out. Bad for business and really bad on the cocktail circuit.'

'So you never told anyone about that night?' I asked.

'Not until this moment, no.'

'And your husband?'

'Not a soul, *yet*. That's his leverage,' she said. 'If I ever file for divorce he swears he'll tell the court about my trying to kill myself. Which means there goes my son.' She crossed her legs. 'Courts don't award custody to suicidal mothers.'

'It's not as cut and dry as you think,' I said. 'Determinations have to be made. Usually by folks like me. In your case, you weren't a mother when this happened. It was a few years ago. People change. Ultimately, a court might trust that you pose no risk to yourself.'

'That's the problem. The word "might". There's too much at stake for me to put faith in a word like that.'

'So instead you've been living the alternative—a compromised life with your husband.'

'Because it meant being with my son, yes.'

'Now you see and feel the consequences. How it's no life at all.'

'That would be an understatement,' she said.

'It's strange, though, Sam. The more I listen to you, the less I understand your husband's motivations. What's in it for him?'

'The ultimate freedom, that's what,' she replied. 'He does whatever he wants, whenever he wants, *who*ever he wants.'

'You're saying he's had affairs?' She nodded. I continued, 'Have you confronted him about it?'

'He'd just deny it and accuse me of being paranoid.'

I had no follow-up to that. I simply sat there looking at Sam Kent, seeing a woman who needed out of her marriage, and fast. That's why she'd come to me. To give her the strength to walk away, she'd said. The question remaining was how I was going to accomplish that.

'What are you thinking, David?' she asked, breaking the silence.

'I'm thinking you deserve better,' I said.

four

It's good to have at least one friend who's a lawyer. I'd shared that observation with Parker as a segue into asking him for what I wanted. Free legal advice.

I dialled his office the next morning, a Friday, between my ten and eleven o'clock sessions. His secretary put me through.

'Can I pick your brain for a minute?' I asked. 'It's about a patient.'

'Whoa, it must be serious. You've never once told me anything about any of your patients. Not that I ever asked.'

'Well, consider this your lucky day,' I said. 'It's a woman who wants to divorce her husband. They have a two-year-old son. Before the kid was born, and before she was pregnant, she tried to commit suicide. An entire bottle of sleeping pills. Her husband found her and got her to vomit everything up. She ended up being fine. Physically, at least. Now here's the tricky part. Not only did they not go to the hospital after it happened, they never sought any professional counselling.'

'Why not?' he asked.

'Neither wanted to deal with the aftermath,' I told him. 'Now the husband is threatening to spill the beans to keep her from the kid. If she tries to divorce him. So if she goes through with it and files, what chance does she have at custody? How much of a role will her attempted suicide play?'

'First off, this is family law, and I'm not,' Parker said. 'So here we go. Will the suicide play a role? Yes. How much? It all depends. A custody case, as it should be, is geared entirely towards the well-being of the child. Anything that even hints at jeopardising that well-being is fair game. Do you think your patient is still a threat to herself?'

'Personally, I don't,' I answered. 'Professionally, though, I couldn't say for sure. We've only had two sessions. On the plus side, the suicide attempt was three years ago.'

'A point in her favour,' he said. 'Does the husband have money?'

'Yeah, why?'

'Quality of representation. A good lawyer won't be banking on some doctor saying she's unfit to be a mother. He'll assume she gets the medical thumbs-up going in and make it his mission to redefine the battlefield.'

'Which would be what?'

'The rest of her behaviour,' he said. 'Specifically, those things that either show or promote questionable judgment on her part. Does she drink, is she taking any antidepressants, has she ever been arrested? Nothing goes unscrutinised. Everything gets magnified. One speeding ticket, OK. Two speeding tickets, and she's got a death wish. From there, the husband's lawyer will be begging the court. The words won't be this but the message will be: "If we can't even let the kid be in the same car with his mother, how can we consider letting him live in the same house?"'

'Let's assume that my patient is otherwise a model citizen,' I said.

'Then she's got a fighting chance. Her lawyers will be digging up dirt on the husband. Even if he's a Boy Scout, they'll be nailing him for his lack of judgment when his wife tried to check out. It was his responsibility to get her to a hospital. That he didn't take her goes beyond stupid.' Parker laughed. 'Suicidal mother, idiot for a father. The kid's going to grow up to wish he was adopted.'

'Wonderful.'

'I can put you in touch with a guy who handles custody cases.'

'I might take you up on that later,' I said. 'One last thing, though. Absent of all the facts, give me her odds . . . ballpark.'

'Sixty per cent,' he said. 'Sixty-five if she's pretty.'

'Those aren't such bad odds. Thanks.'

I hung up the phone and thought of Sam Kent. She didn't have a marriage; she had an arrangement. I could hear the catching of her breath as Sam cried in my office that first day. It was the sound of suffocation. I wanted to help her, restore her confidence, and there was nothing wrong with that. I wanted to help all of my patients. That was my job. But this was different, and I knew it.

The wall was beginning to be chipped away, the separation between patient and doctor. Nothing was personal. Everything was professional. That's the way it had to be.

So put down the chisel, David. That's what I tried to tell myself.

Let the wall stand.

THE CHARITY FUNCTION. How the haves do for the have-nots without having to look at them. A cynical view of philanthropy and one that I was trying to shake. The Kesper Society cocktail party wasn't making it any easier.

The Kesper Society was started by Arnold Kesper. As in the Kesper Communications conglomerate. He, along with his wife, would throw huge, lavish cocktail parties twice a year and invite representatives from various causes. He'd mingle with them, listen to what they had to say, and then, after presumably giving it some thought, decide how much to bestow on each cause.

The good news was that being invited to one of these parties was to know you were getting some funding. The bad news was that the exact amount was a result of the impact you made in those pressure-filled few hours. Word had it that the more you kissed Kesper's ass, the more zeros were added on to your donation cheque.

Bennett Larson called two days prior to let me know he was going to be out of town for the event. I wasn't happy to hear it. Bennett Larson was an all-smiling, joke-telling, schmoozer and by far, Crescent House's top 'financial lobbyist'. Or, as he freely admitted, the Money Whore. Anything for a good cause, though.

Which was precisely what Crescent House was—a free psychotherapy and analysis clinic for the poor and uninsured that I'd recently been named a board member of, after having volunteered there for more than two years. With only one location, in Queens, Crescent House had set its eyes on expanding to the other boroughs and to other cities. There were plenty of therapists willing to donate their time. Some even their money. But securing the bricks and mortar, not to mention the real estate on which to break ground, required a much higher level of generosity. The Arnold Kesper variety.

So that Friday evening, *sans* Larson, I, along with some of the others filling out the Crescent House board, descended on the Great Hall at the Metropolitan Museum of Art, the site of the latest Kesper Society cocktail party.

WE WERE AN HOUR and a half into the party and were finally getting our audience with 'the man'. One of Kesper's minions, a petite and humourless-looking woman clutching a clipboard, had us all gather in a designated area before bringing over Kesper. 'Mr Kesper, may I present the representatives from Crescent House,' said the woman. Then, in a hushed tone, she introduced each of us to her boss. We might as well have been at the Vatican.

Given that, maybe the question he threw at me wasn't from so far out of left field. Up until that point, the conversation had been relatively innocuous. Kesper asked about what we did at Crescent House, and we answered the best we could. He expressed his admiration for our efforts and genuinely seemed to understand our objectives. Then Kesper spun on his heels and looked directly at me.

'Tell me, Dr Remler, did you think he was guilty?' he asked.

'I'm sorry?' I said.

'The rabbi in that trial,' said Kesper. 'Did you think he was guilty? Because I'm not so sure. I tend to think he was innocent. Though from what I understand your testimony sure did him in.'

I was slightly taken aback. 'I think it was certainly possible the rabbi was guilty,' I told Kesper. 'Though it was hardly a clear-cut case.'

The billionaire shook his head. 'That's far too diplomatic an answer,' he said. 'I'd have to believe that deep down, you have a very strong opinion one way or the other. Am I wrong?'

'You're not wrong,' I said. 'I just think it might be better if that strong opinion remained that way. Meaning, deep down.'

'Dr Remler,' Kesper said. 'I'd be dismayed to learn that your reticence is on account of not wanting to appear disagreeable with me. Maybe you'd like some assurance that speaking your mind will have no bearing on my intentions for Crescent House.'

'I don't think that's really necessary,' I said.

'Oh, come now, of course you do. I'd be lying if I didn't admit your not indulging me about that rabbi—not revealing your innermost thoughts on his guilt or innocence—would indeed adversely impact my feelings towards Crescent House. I agree it might not be fair. Nonetheless, it's honest. So I'm afraid that puts us at an impasse.'

The eyes of the other board members from Crescent House settled on me with a nervous, 'Don't blow it for us, Remler,' gaze. Damn integrity—there were more Crescent Houses to be built. I cleared my throat. 'Guilty as sin,' I crowed.

'What's that?' said Kesper, who no doubt heard me perfectly.

'I said I believe the rabbi was guilty. Guilty as sin.'

'That's what I thought you said.' He hunched forward and whispered, 'It's amazing what we'll do for money, isn't it?'

I said nothing. So Kesper continued, his voice now relentlessly cheerful. 'At least in your case it was for a good cause. With most people it's usually not. Thank you, Dr Remler. Thank you, Crescent House. Thank you very, very much.' He backed up a few steps before walking away.

I stuck around after that just long enough to polish off three bourbon and waters in ten minutes. Those, combined with the three I had prior to meeting Kesper, meant I was extremely good to go.

Out the front of the Met and into the brisk night air. I stood there under a street lamp for a moment, breathing it in. That's when I heard the voice over my shoulder. 'Fancy meeting you here.'

I turned round and saw a figure coming down the steps. A long black dress and a red shawl draped over her shoulders. A bag held in her hand. A familiar person in an unfamiliar setting. Then I realised. I was looking at Sam Kent.

'For a moment I thought you didn't recognise me,' she said.

'For a moment I didn't,' I told her. 'I think this is what you call "out of context."'

'I know, isn't this funny? The two of us being at the same function. Though I'm surprised I didn't see you inside.'

'Me too,' I said. 'So what wonderful cause were you shilling for?'

'I should be so lucky that this would be a one-time event for me,' Sam said. 'No, I'm afraid I'm a regular at these things. My husband's firm handles the charitable trust for the Kesper Society.'

'Where's your husband?' I asked somewhat warily.

'Singapore,' she said with a strained smile. 'He always manages to be away for these things, which leaves it up to me to represent the both of us. Any other event and I'd take a pass. But for all of Arnold Kesper's eccentric ways, he really has helped a lot of people. So is this uncomfortable for you? Bumping into a patient in public.'

'No,' I replied. 'Why do you ask?'

'I don't know. Woman's intuition?'

'A highly overrated sense,' I said. A wisecrack.

'Maybe for those who don't have it,' she countered.

Sam was sounding a little different that evening. More easy-going. Maybe she'd had a few drinks. Maybe it was our chance encounter.

She looked at her watch. 'So where are you off to now?'

'I guess home,' I said.

'That's what I hate about these parties. They ply you with booze, and give you just enough finger food to make you actually hungry before throwing you out onto the street without dinner.' She glanced around. 'Hey, you know what I should do? I should buy you dinner.'

'And why's that?' I asked.

'Because you've been helping me. I feel I owe you,' she said.

'Not with my rates, you don't.'

'Money well spent. Which is why you should let me buy you dinner. What do you say?' She was determined. I was hesitant. 'Wait, don't tell me,' she said. '*Of course*. You're thinking how that wouldn't reflect too well upon you, the two of us being seen together. Socialising with your patients must be a no-no.'

'It is frowned on by those who care about that kind of thing.'

'Does that mean you don't?'

'No, I do. I'm simply not as fanatical about it,' I said. 'But as far as going to a restaurant is concerned, I'm afraid appearances do come into play.'

'There you have it. That's our solution. Instead of buying you dinner, I'll cook it for you.'

'Sam, I'm not sure that—'

'It's pretty funny when you think about it. To avoid the suggestion of impropriety we're forced to do something far more suggestive.' She put a hand on her hip. 'So what will it be, David . . . your place or mine? Wait a minute, I just realised we can't go to my place. Celeste, our nanny, is there watching my son tonight. She's quite a blabbermouth. Her seeing you would *really* not be a good thing. So it looks like it's your place.'

At last, I had the chance to say something. It was the moment to give a deft explanation, make a graceful exit . . . alone.

Instead, I said nothing. I was too busy noticing the things I shouldn't have. The sheen of her hair. The snugness of her dress. The fact that I was seriously considering her offer.

Cool it, David. I was a man who knew better. But I was also a man who hadn't felt anything for another woman in quite some time. That man had also drunk six bourbon and waters on an empty stomach. The checkpoints were lax. The alarm bells temporarily out of order.

'There's really nothing in my refrigerator,' I said.

She smiled. 'Don't worry, I'll make do.'

Sam went to the kerb and began hailing a cab. Had it taken a few minutes for one to come along I probably would've got cold feet. Nixed the whole idea. But a cab rolled up within seconds. I did my best not to read too much into that. 'Fate' was such a big word.

THIRTY BLOCKS of pleasant conversation between the two of us and some spectacular rationalisation all on my own. I kept telling myself I hadn't done anything wrong. Nor would I.

Ten minutes later we arrived at my apartment.

Doormen in New York City can be counted on for two things. The first is saying what is pleasant and expected; the second is simultaneously thinking otherwise. 'Good evening, Dr Remler' was all the one on duty said as Sam and I walked into my building. But to read his mind? 'Hey, maybe that poor son of a bitch is finally going to get laid.'

Sam and I had the elevator to ourselves. 'I kind of miss not having them,' she said. 'Doormen, that is.'

'Your building doesn't have them?'

'No, we live in a town house,' she said. 'When I was single, though, I lived in a doorman building. Made me feel safer.'

'I'd say the same, but any time I happen to come home really late, the guy here has usually nodded off.'

'How long have you lived here?' she asked.

'About three years.'

She nodded slightly while appearing to put one and one together. It made three. As in how many years it had been since my wife died. Safe assumption that I would've moved in the aftermath.

Once in my apartment, I took off my coat and Sam handed me her shawl. I hung them up on a hallstand. While I went to turn on some lights, she disappeared on to a self-guided tour. I stayed in the living room, stacking newspapers and scooping up a few empty beer bottles.

Sam called out from my library. 'I pictured more wood panelling.'

'I hope you're not disappointed.'

'Quite the opposite,' came back her voice. 'I told myself that if I spotted a pipe rack I'd leave immediately.'

She walked out of the library and headed down the hallway to the bedrooms. First the guest's, then mine.

She reappeared. 'I like your place,' she said. 'No pretensions. She eyed a picture on a table. She picked it up. 'Are these your parents?'

'Yes.'

'They're adorable. Where was this taken?'

'On the back deck of their house in Santa Barbara.'

'That's nice.' Sam stared at the photo a little more.

'You told me your folks live in Arizona . . . Tempe, right?'

'Oh,' she said. 'Yes. Though my parents out in Tempe are actually my adoptive parents. I didn't mention it at the time because . . .'

'That's OK; you don't have to explain,' I said. 'You know therapists think everything has to do with parents. Mind if I ask you something?'

'It's about my birth mother and father, right?'

'Yes. Have you ever met them?'

'No. Apparently, my father died in some factory accident before I was born. As for my mother, all I know is her address and that she's really poor, which was why she had to give me up.'

'You've never wanted to make contact with her?'

'When I was younger I was far too angry about the whole thing. As I got older I thought it was too complicated—and as you well know, that's the last thing my life needs.'

'I can see why you'd think that, but taking care of one unresolved issue can often do wonders for working out another.'

'It's been so long, though. I can't help thinking I'd only be meeting a stranger and not my real mother.'

'Perhaps at first. In time that would change.'

This was turning into a session, and that was wrong. I was about to change the subject when she saw fit to change it on her own. She put the picture down. Next to it happened to be the phone.

'Do you mind if I call home?' she asked. 'To let Celeste know where I am.'

'Sure. No problem.'

Sam picked up the phone and dialled. I went into the kitchen to get rid of the beer bottles. I could hear her telling the nanny that she'd dropped by a friend's apartment and wouldn't be home for a bit. Sam called out to me. 'David, what's your number here?'

I walked to the entrance of the kitchen and told her. She repeated the number back to Celeste.

'I feel I've got to give her two ways to reach me,' said Sam after hanging up. 'She's got my cellphone number, but I don't trust those things. Half the time you can never get through to someone.'

'I know what you mean.'

She glanced over my shoulder. 'So is that the kitchen?'

'Ready and waiting,' I said.

'Good. Then let the magic begin.'

I followed her into the least-used room in my apartment and watched as she took a few seconds to size it up. 'You weren't kidding,' she said after opening the refrigerator and taking a look. Sam pivoted on her heels and eyed the cabinets. 'Pasta,' she said.

I opened a cabinet by the stove. On the top shelf, behind a couple of cans of soup, sat a box of linguini.

She took the box from my hands, went back to the fridge and grabbed eggs, butter, a jar of capers. She opened the freezer and started poking around.

I heard an 'Aha!' and she held up a package of chopped sirloin. 'Now I need a big bowl and half your spice rack.'

I got her the bowl and opened a cabinet littered with various seasonings. 'Do you want an apron?' I asked.

'Probably a good idea,' she said.

I dug one up and gave it to her. 'So, what are we making here?'

'It doesn't really have a name.'

'Interesting. The "no-name linguine". I like the sound of that.'

Sam tilted her head. 'Me too,' she said. 'It implies no responsibility on the part of the chef.'

Smiling, I leaned back on the counter and watched as she got busy. Meat in the microwave to defrost. Egg whites, spices and some capers in the bowl. 'Can I help in some way?' I asked.

She thought about it for a moment. 'You can open up some wine. You do have a spare bottle lying around, I hope?'

'I think so,' I said. I went to the dining room to fetch a bottle.

I brought back a Cabernet, uncorked it, and filled two glasses. 'To the no-name linguine,' I said, toasting.

Sam raised her glass. 'And to better days ahead,' she added.

It was a natural opening.

'Listen, Sam, normally I'd be discussing this with you in my office, but, given the circumstances, it makes sense to bring it up now. I spoke to a friend of mine about your situation. He's a lawyer and—'

Her face flushed with concern. 'You didn't mention my name, did you?' she asked, her voice nearly panicked.

'No, no. Not only wouldn't I do that, I couldn't. There's nothing I told my friend that could betray your privacy. I wanted to get some professional advice about your husband using your suicide attempt against you to get full custody of your son.'

'You mean, if I try to divorce him?'

'Exactly.'

'What'd your friend say?'

'Well, while he's a very good attorney, he doesn't practise family law. So this isn't definitive by any means. His take was that you stood a decent chance of winning if you went to court.'

'Based on what?'

'A few things. The amount of time that's passed since the attempt, your not being a mother when it happened, and the most important factor—that you *are* a mother now. And a good one at that, right?'

She nodded slightly. She seemed somewhat dazed.

'What is it?' I asked.

'The prospect of having to be judged, of having everything dragged out in a courtroom. I don't know if I can handle that.'

'I think you can. What's more, I think you have no choice. What you *can't* handle is your life as it is now. Wouldn't you agree?'

We were interrupted by three loud beeps. The microwave over the stove. The meat had defrosted, and I walked over to take it out. One hand pulled the door of the microwave open while the other—*shit*! I grabbed my left hand, writhing in pain.

'What happened?' she said, then she quickly realised. The burner was on. 'Oh my God, I forgot to put the pot on it.'

I looked down at the inside of my throbbing hand. I'd been branded by a GE Profile Range.

She rushed to the freezer and got some ice. 'I'm so sorry,' she said as she began gliding a cube in circles on my palm. 'I am so, so sorry.'

'It's OK,' I told her. 'I'll be all right.'

We were standing six inches apart. Facing each other. Our hands touching and our eyes locked. Staring. She was beautiful skin. She was full lips. She was so close I could hear her breathing.

I wanted to kiss her. Badly. And who knows, maybe I would have. Maybe I would have forsaken my professional responsibilities and done exactly what I shouldn't have. But at that moment, I looked down and noticed the embroidered words on Sam's apron. *Kiss the Chef!* It was the same apron I'd originally given Rebecca.

I backed away. Sam let go of my hand.

'Are you OK?' she asked. 'You look like you've seen a ghost.'

I had.

IT COULD'VE been awkward after that. It wasn't. Instead, Sam finished cooking. We ate, talked, drank the wine, and acted as if nothing had happened. Which it hadn't.

After heaping praise on Sam's no-name linguine and insisting I'd take care of the cleaning up, I watched as she tried to suppress a yawn.

'I think it's past my bedtime,' she announced. 'Would you do me a favour and see me into a cab downstairs?'

'I'll go one better,' I said. 'I'll see you all the way home.'

'Don't be silly. You don't need to do that.'

'But I do. In the name of gentlemen everywhere.'

She cocked her head. 'OK. But I live on the Upper West Side.'

'Oh, *now* you tell me!'

She laughed and grabbed her bag. I fetched my coat as well as her shawl. Out the door, down the elevator, up to the street corner, and into a cab.

'Fifty-six West Eighty-first. Right off of Central Park West,' Sam told the driver. I added that we'd be making a round trip. We were off.

We talked about movies. She'd seen a lot; I'd hardly seen any. Then I asked, 'When does your husband get back from Singapore?'

She turned to me. 'He gets back tomorrow night.'

We stopped at a light. I looked out of the window at some sign for a yoga studio.

'I really do hate him, David,' she said as the light flashed green and we turned.

'Which is why you've got to seriously consider what we talked about. You can win. You can get out . . . with your son.'

'You make it sound so easy.'

'It won't be; I know that. But I can help you through it.'

The cab came to a stop. Fifty-six West Eighty-first street. 'Home sweet home,' she said sarcastically.

I looked out of the window at her town house. Brick with columns. Tall windows. Flower boxes. Right over the entrance was a gigantic stone eagle with its wings spread.

'Yeah, the bird is huge,' she said, 'I'm not the one who picked it out.'

She turned back to me. And there it was. Close together, face-to-face. Temptation all over again. Though it was easier this time to turn it down. I had practice.

'So I'll see you Thursday, right?'

'Yes, Thursday,' she said, reaching for the door handle.

I reached for mine. 'Wait, let me walk you to your door.'

'No,' she said, 'the way Celeste's radar operates she probably has the curtains open to see if it's me. Best if we make sure it's *only* me.'

'Beware the nosy nanny. I'll wait until you get inside, though.'

She smiled and put her hand on top of mine. 'Thanks, David. Thanks for everything.'

I watched as she stepped out of the cab and walked up to her house. She reached into her bag, found her keys and waved. That was good enough for the cabbie. He sped off, but not before I got one last look at her. Sam Kent. Beautiful. Vulnerable. My patient.

TWO NIGHTS LATER, at around 2.30 a.m., I was awakened by a phone call. My eyes half closed, I answered it. 'Hello?'

I heard nothing on the other end.

'Hello?' I said again.

Finally, a voice, Sam's. 'I did it,' she said faintly.

'What are you talking about? What did you do?'

Silence.

'Sam, talk to me. What did you do? Did you leave your husband?'

'No, David,' she said. 'I killed him.'

I shot up in bed, jolted by what she'd just said. But there was something else. How she sounded. Drained. Listless.

'Sam, where are you?' I asked.

I could hear soft crying. 'Home.'

'Listen to me. Have you taken sleeping pills?'

No reply.

'Damn it, Sam. Answer me!' I yelled, wanting to know if she was trying to kill herself . . . again.

'It was the only way, David,' she whispered. 'The only way.' Then I heard a thump. It was the phone hitting the ground.

PART II
five

P ants, sweatshirt, socks, sneakers. I reached for my wallet on the bureau and instead knocked it to the floor. I knelt down to pick it up and smacked my head hard against an open drawer. I felt nothing. There was no time to feel pain.

Could she really have done it? Of course she could've done it. She told me she wanted to. 'It was the only way, David,' Sam had said on the phone. Sleeping pills. She was dying with each passing second.

I yanked an overcoat off my hallstand, grabbed my keys and left, slamming the apartment door behind me. Down twenty-two floors and a sprint past the doorman who—big surprise—was asleep behind his desk. Out on the street I didn't so much hail a cab as jump in front of one.

'Eighty-fifth and Central Park West,' I barked at the driver. No, wait, that wasn't the address. 'Actually, make that Eighty—' I stopped. Eighty-what? I couldn't remember. 'Just head to Central Park West in the Eighties as fast as you possibly can,' I said. He flipped the meter and we were off.

Up ahead the light turned yellow. If the driver had hit the gas we could've made it. Instead, he slowed to a stop before it went red. Clearly some additional incentive was in order.

'I'll give you two extra bucks for every red light you don't stop for.'

'No, not worth the risk,' the driver groused.

'Make it five bucks then,' I said.

That seemed to alter things a bit. 'I'll see what I can do.'

Two blocks later, he swerved into the bus lane to dodge a line of cars stopped at a light, and made his first five bucks. His head whipped back and forth through the intersection to check for crossing traffic. Not to mention cops.

The police. I'd neglected to call them. That was a mistake. The fact was, I'd reacted as David Remler, the guy who'd been with Sam in his apartment two nights prior. Not David Remler, the psychologist, who had a professional obligation. To inform the 'proper authorities'.

I quickly checked my pockets. Sure enough, there was something else I'd neglected to do. Bring my cellphone.

We zipped past two pay phones, and I thought about yelling for the guy to stop. I would get out and call the police. Tell them what had happened and to send an ambulance, that I would meet them at Sam's town house.

Sure, David, if you could only remember where the hell it was.

'You're bleeding,' the driver said. I watched in his rearview mirror as he pointed. 'There, on your forehead.'

I reached up above my eyes and felt around. Dry, dry . . . then wet. Mushy and warm to the touch by my right temple. I brought my hand down and saw the blood. With my other hand I checked my pockets for a tissue or napkin. There was nothing.

'Here,' said the driver. I looked up to see him passing back a crumpled ball of paper towel. I pressed the paper towel against the gash to try to stem the bleeding.

We were getting close. North on Central Park West in the Seventies. I peered out my window, waiting to see something other than that eagle that would jog my memory. A store. A building. Some type of sign.

I saw it. Right before the corner of Eighty-first Street, an actual sign, tucked inside a first-floor window. GO YOGA! I remembered seeing it that night riding back with Sam. We'd turned immediately after.

'Turn on Eighty-first!' I yelled at the driver.

Three seconds later he did, screeching left on red. 'What's the number?' he asked as we straightened out.

'I'll know it when I see it,' I told him. Then: 'There! On the left, past the streetlamp; that's it.' The statue of an eagle.

The driver hit the brakes and flipped the meter off. A total of $8.50, it read. 'Plus nine red lights,' he reminded me.

It was really only seven, but I wasn't about to argue. I was already halfway out of the cab, and tossed sixty bucks over the partition. He sped off the moment my door closed.

Sam's town house was completely dark. I rushed up the steps and reached the double doors. I pounded on them with my fist. I abused the knocker. It was wishful thinking. The prospect of getting Sam to let me in seemed altogether nonexistent.

I grabbed the cold brass of the doorknob and was about to—*What the . . .?* Around went my wrist. The spring latch snapped. No resistance. The door had been open the entire time. Sam had called me. She'd wanted me to come save her. The front door had been left open on purpose. In I went.

The only light was filtering in from the street—creating a few shadows, nothing more. I groped for a light switch, finding a round knob some ways in on the wall. A crystal chandelier lit up above me.

'Sam?' I yelled out. No answer.

I yelled her name again, louder. Nothing.

There were rooms on my left and right. A huge, curving mahogany staircase in front of me. I ventured to think. *Where would I be if I'd just killed my husband and tried to commit suicide?*

Upstairs, my gut told me. I ran, screaming Sam's name, nearly tripping as my shin slammed into the lip of one of the stairs. I reached the upper floor and hit another light switch. There was a wide hallway with two doors on each side, another door at the end. All were closed.

First up, a guest room. It had that minimal, barely used look. I darted across the hall and barged through door number two. It was a small study. A couch, a chair, a lot of books and a desk. But no Sam. No husband. The next door over—another bedroom. Larger, though no more lived in. I yelled out Sam's name. There was sweat running down my forehead, and I went to wipe it. Instead I was wiping blood. A wide red smear left on the back of my hand.

Across the hall again. I stormed in on an empty bathroom. Four doors down; one to go. It was the one facing me when I got to the top of the stairs. Presumably the master bedroom. I breathed in, exhaled, and reached for the knob, turning and pushing at the same time. But the door was locked.

'Sam!' I called out. I pounded with my fist. Nothing.

She had to be in there. Then another thought—they were *both* in there. Sam and her husband. A murder-suicide? Or a murder with an attempted suicide.

I took a few steps back and steeled myself. Time to find out.

Over and over I kicked. The wood shuddered with each kick until the door finally ripped open, flying on its hinges and slamming against the wall. I stepped in. An immediate rush of cold air hit me as I stood amid shadows of bellowing drapes. Every window was open.

The light from the hallway spilled in over my shoulder. I flipped a lone wall switch. Frantically, I scanned past a dresser and a night table. Across an unmade bed, thick with covers. Too thick, I realised.

That's when I began to see. The shape of a head . . . possibly an arm . . . what looked to be a pair of legs. I approached the bed, gripped the corner of the duvet, and gave a swift yank.

Lying there face down on the bed was a man. A very dead man. There was blood all over and all around him. He was wearing a pair of sweatpants and a T-shirt. The T-shirt was riddled with tears. Each one being where a knife had entered his body. It didn't matter that there was no knife to be seen. It was that obvious.

I killed him, Sam had said. *I killed my husband*.

I stared at the back of Sam's husband, unable to see his face. I felt I needed to see his face. As if none of this was really happening until I did. I reached down under his right shoulder and began to lift. So that's what they mean by dead weight. Finally, the body rolled over.

I had my pick of things to make me shudder. The excess blood that had gathered on his chest, thick and sticky. The fact that his eyes were open, fixed with fear and panic, and seemingly boring into mine. But the most unsettling was this: when I looked at the face of Sam's husband, I couldn't help thinking, I somehow know him.

I had this feeling that it wasn't the first time I was seeing this guy. Not in a picture but in person. I couldn't remember when and where exactly. Only that it felt very real.

That thought immediately took a back seat. It had to. I'd found Sam's husband but not Sam. There were more rooms to search. An entire first floor.

I bolted out of the bedroom and down the stairs. I bounced from room to room, going everywhere.

The library off the hall, over to the living room and the dining room off of that. To the den, then into the kitchen. On the far side of the refrigerator I saw a narrow door. When I opened it, there were stairs, steep and descending into darkness. The basement.

An exposed bulb beckoned with a pull chain a few feet in. I grabbed it and was rewarded with just enough light not to fall and break my neck. Down I went.

I reached the bottom. The air was musty, damp, and smelt of pine-scented laundry detergent. I could make out a washer and dryer, a boiler and a water heater. Yet no sign of Sam.

Where the hell is she?

The possibility sank in. She'd left the house. Maybe she didn't want me to save her after all. Perhaps she'd walked out of the house and neglected to lock it. If it were true, the front door's being open had nothing to do with me.

Truth was, I hadn't a clue. The one thing I was sure of was that Sam wasn't in that house. She could've gone anywhere. I had to call the police.

I turned and climbed back up those narrow stairs as fast as possible. Reaching the kitchen, I saw a cordless phone sitting on the counter. I took a step towards it. That's as far as I got, though.

'Freeze!'

I spun round to see two cops at the entrance of the kitchen. One was short, the other tall. Both had their guns drawn, and both barrels of those guns were pointed directly at my chest.

'Thank God,' I said, with a deep exhale.

'Put your hands up!' the short cop barked in response.

Up went my hands. 'Officers, I—'

'Do you live here?' the second cop, the tall one, asked me.

'No, I—'

'Who are you, and what are you doing here?' he asked rigidly.

'My name is Dr David Remler, and I'm a psychologist here in the city,' I said. I started to reach for my wallet.

The two officers cocked their guns. 'Keep your hands in the air!' was the gist of what they both shouted.

'Sorry! Sorry!' I raised my hand back up and swallowed hard. 'I only wanted to show you some ID.'

'Just tell us what you're doing here,' said the first cop.

'I got a call . . . one of my patients . . . Sam Kent,' I began. 'Actually, Sam is short for Samantha. She's a woman. Anyway, she told me she'd killed her husband and—'

First cop: 'Wait a minute, *who* said this?'

'Her name is Samantha Kent. This is her home,' I said.

'She told you she killed her husband?'

'Yes.'

'Where is she?' asked the second cop.

'I don't know,' I said. 'I thought she was here. That's why I'm here. But I've searched everywhere in the house, and I can't find her.'

Second cop: 'What about the—'

'He's upstairs,' I said with a grimace. 'I'm afraid she was telling the truth. It's pretty bloody.'

I saw both cops look at the blood on my forehead and right hand.

'How'd you hurt yourself?' the first cop asked.

'Oh, this . . . ,' I said. 'This is from my hitting my head back at my apartment in the rush to get over here. It's not what you think.'

'What would that be?' asked the first cop. 'What would we think?'

'Maybe that I had something to do with—'

The second cop jumped in. 'What'd you say your name was?'

'David Remler,' I answered. 'Dr David Remler.'

He nodded. 'Dr Remler, show us that ID, slowly.'

'Yes, sir,' I told him. I pulled out my driver's licence. My business card. My American Psychological Society card. I nearly pulled out my gym membership card. The second cop approached me, his gun still aimed at my chest. He looked everything over and gave a quick 'he is who he says he is' head bob to his partner.

'There's something else,' I said. 'It's why we've got to hurry. I'm pretty convinced that wherever Samantha Kent is right now, she's got a handful of sleeping pills in her.'

'What makes you say that?' said the first cop.

'Number one, the way she sounded on the phone,' I said. 'Number two, I'm her psychologist.'

First cop: 'You sure she's not here in the house?'

'Almost positive,' I said. 'Can we check the neighbourhood?'

'First,' said the second cop, 'show us where the husband is.'

THE RHYTHM and routine of a murder in Manhattan.

Or at least what happens after the murder. When the victim is found. When the system kicks in. When a bunch of people show up who make their living off of other people dying.

But for a time it was just me and the cops. At their request, I'd led them to Sam's husband. Up the stairs and down the hallway to the master bedroom. 'It was locked,' I said in response to their curious looks at the smashed-in door. 'I had to kick it open.'

We went in. The room felt even colder than it had before. They checked the bathroom and the walk-in closet. All clear. They hovered over the bed and took a good long look.

'Yeah, he's pretty dead,' said the first cop.

The second one looked at me. 'Is this how you found him?'

'Actually, he was under the covers,' I said. 'I pulled them back.'

'What about the body itself?' he said. 'Did you touch him?'

'He was face down. I rolled him over,' I said.

'Why?' asked the first cop, not terribly keen on my answer.

'I guess to see his face,' I said.

'Why?' he asked again. 'Did you know him?'

I still had the feeling I did, yet I couldn't figure out how. Saying *maybe* seemed like a really bad idea given the circumstances. 'No,' I said. 'I didn't know him.' And like that, I was on record.

There was no follow-up question, nothing that suggested they didn't believe me. Instead, procedure took over. The second cop called in to his precinct and reported that there'd been a homicide.

'The kid . . . ,' I said. 'Where's the kid?'

The cops turned to me, waiting for me to say something. I started to explain that Sam had a son, a two-year-old. I didn't get into why his mother would want to turn him into an orphan overnight. I did, however, press the issue about trying to find her.

'All right,' said the second cop. 'What does she look like?'

I described Sam Kent. Five foot six. Thin. Blonde hair.

'Any idea where she might have gone?' he asked next.

'No.'

'Any idea what she might be wearing?'

'No.'

'And you think she's taken sleeping pills?'

'I do,' I answered, 'though, I can't know for sure.'

The second cop called his precinct again and made what amounted to a 'be on the lookout' request for anyone on patrol. He also asked that all the emergency rooms in the area be checked. He relayed the information about Sam, right through the part about the sleeping pills.

'C'mon,' I was told.

The cops had to see for themselves that there was nobody else in the house. While the first one took me downstairs and kept a watch on me in the hall, the second went room by room.

As I stood there waiting with the cop, I heard the sound of gunshots out in the street. I spun on my heels towards the front door and was about to hit the deck. The cop didn't flinch.

'Firecrackers,' he said calmly. 'It's Hacker's Night.'

It took me a moment to get my calendar and jargon in order. I realised it was October 30, the night before Halloween.

The silence settled back in. I was growing increasingly impatient. 'Isn't there something I can do to help?' I asked the cop.

'There's going to be plenty you can do,' he replied. 'Just not with us. In a few minutes the detectives will get here, and you can give them your full cooperation.'

'Of course,' I said. Another question occurred to me. 'There's one other thing. I was about to call 911 when you guys showed up there in the kitchen. How'd you know to come—did a neighbour call?'

'An alarm,' the cop said. 'Silent. You must have tripped it.'

'But the front door was open,' I said.

'It wouldn't matter so long as the system was on.' He motioned with his head up to the ceiling. 'Motion detectors,' he said.

We were joined just then by the second cop. 'Nothing,' he said, referring to his search of the house.

'Good,' said the first cop. He glanced at his watch. As if on cue, the homicide detectives arrived. Two of them. They were followed by a couple of Emergency Medical Technicians and two detectives from the Crime Scene Unit. Then two guys from the morgue showed up, and a young Irish-looking kid from the District Attorney's office.

After checking out the bedroom upstairs and huddling for a few minutes with the two cops, the homicide detectives approached me and introduced themselves.

'Dr Remler, I'm Detective Joseph Trentino, and this is my partner, Detective Frank Lopez.'

I looked at the two of them. Trentino, fortyish, was average height, stocky and square-jawed. He wore thick-rimmed glasses and was losing his hair. His partner, Frank Lopez was slightly taller, thinner, and—thanks to his full head of hair—younger looking.

'Why were you here?' asked Trentino.

I told them everything I could about why I was there. How Sam was my patient. The phone call from her. Rushing to the house and frantically searching. Everything right up until I was told to freeze.

The two detectives took a few notes. Then came their follow-ups. Trentino fired off the first few.

'At what time did you say Ms Kent called you?' he asked.

'It was around two thirty.'

'How do you know?'

'At some point in the cab ride over here I looked at my watch for the first time. By then it was a little before three,' I said.

Trentino scribbled in his pad. 'You say the front door was open?'

'Yes.'

'The door to the master bedroom was locked, though?'

'Yes.'

'You kicked it in?'

'Yes.'

'Once inside you saw the victim there on the bed, right?'

'Actually no,' I said. 'I saw what looked like a body underneath the covers. As I told the officers, I pulled them back.'

'And the guy was staring up at you?' said Detective Lopez.

'I rolled him over. He was originally face down.'

Lopez grimaced. 'You rolled him over because . . .'

I shrugged. 'I'm not sure, to be perfectly honest.'

Trentino flipped back a page in his notes. 'I see you told the officers that you don't know the victim,' he said.

'No, I didn't know the guy,' I said.

And like that, I was *really* on record.

More questions followed. Mostly about what Sam had said to me on the phone. From there the focus shifted to my forehead. The gash. No sooner had I explained again about hitting my dresser drawer than Detective Trentino flagged down an EMT who was walking by.

'Let's see if we can't clean away the blood there on Dr Remler,' said Trentino.

The EMT obliged. With some damp cloth and a cotton swab on a stick he wiped and dabbed away the blood. Once the wound was clear, two butterfly bandages were applied.

'Good to go,' said the EMT when finished.

What a great idea, I was thinking. Being able to leave. Going home, going to bed. I looked at my watch. Quarter to four.

'Guys, can I have a word with you for a second?' One of the cops pulled the two detectives aside. I watched and waited as he filled them in on something. A minute later I was told what it was.

'We've had a chance to confirm some facts,' Trentino said. 'For starters, as you claim, a Samantha Kent does indeed live here. Though it turns out Kent is her maiden name. Did you know that?'

'No, I didn't.'

Trentino continued: 'Her husband's name is Conrad Birch. Or should I say *was* because that's him upstairs all right.'

Conrad Birch . . . Birch . . . Birch. I repeated the name over in my head, relieved it didn't immediately ring a bell.

'Finally,' said Trentino, 'it looks like you are who you say you are, Dr Remler. Your practice and your home address check out. So, for the time being, we've only got one other thing to ask you. Which is, you're not planning on leaving town any time soon, are you?'

'No,' I said. 'I have no plans to leave town.'

'Good,' he said. 'Then why don't you go home and get some sleep.'

I stood there . . . not going. 'What about Samantha?' I asked.

'We've got people looking for her,' said Lopez.

'Just the same, I want to stick around for when you find her,' I said. 'Better yet, I'd like to help in the search.'

'We appreciate that,' said Trentino. 'But the best thing you can do for everyone's sake is to go home, get some rest, and be available for us. When we find Ms Kent, you'll be among the first to know.'

'Maybe we could get a sketch drawn,' I said. 'Better yet, there's got to be a picture of her around here somewhere.'

All of us looked around the hall. Artwork but no pictures.

'We'll look around the house again. I'm sure we'll find something,' said Lopez. 'Even if we don't, your description will be good enough.'

I said good night to the detectives. Good morning would've been more accurate. Walking out of Sam's town house I could see the first hint of dawn illuminating the sky. A new day. Halloween, actually. But also a Monday. In about three hours I was supposed to be sitting in my office listening to someone talk about their problems.

I walked Sam's neighbourhood anyway. A few blocks in every direction, including a brief foray into Central Park. I couldn't go home without at least giving it a shot, long as it was. I held on to the hope but gave up on the search. A needle in a big city. The streets belonged to the cabs at this hour, and I raised my hand to hail one.

Back home at last. I checked the answering machine. Maybe Sam had tried to call me again. It wasn't blinking. I picked up the phone.

Mila once told me that the older she got the less sleep she needed. 'It's my body's way of telling me there'll be plenty of time for that soon enough,' she'd said. It only rang once before she answered.

'Mila, it's David,' I said.

I told her nothing of what had happened or where I'd been. What she heard was that I wasn't feeling well. My appointments would have to be cancelled. Dr Remler was taking a sick day. She didn't pry. Still, she could read between the lines. It wasn't a head cold; it was something else. Something I couldn't explain right then, but later when I was ready.

'I hope you feel better,' she said.

'Thank you, Mamka.'

I hung up and poured myself a finger of bourbon. Then another after that. I knew it was the only way I'd ever get any sleep.

I thought about the detectives, Trentino and Lopez. The questions they asked and the questions they didn't. They'd concerned themselves strictly with the events of the evening. Not once had they asked about Sam as a patient or what her motive might have been. They only wanted to know what had led up to Conrad Birch's getting killed. Again, I was left wondering. Where did I know him from?

No nearer to an answer, and having achieved the proper numbness from the bourbon, I was ready to sleep. I shuffled off to the bedroom.

six

Again, it was the phone that woke me. Ringing in my bedroom. Ringing in my head. I rolled over to the nightstand. A clumsy reach for the phone and a groggy hello.

'Dr Remler?' the voice said. This is Detective Trentino. We met—'

'Yes . . . last night.'

'We were wondering if we could have a few minutes of your time.'

'Ah, sure,' I answered. 'Is there any news about Sam?'

'That's what we want to talk to you about,' said Trentino. 'We're outside your apartment. We tried knocking and ringing the bell but—'

'I was asleep. I'm sorry.' I looked at my watch. It was almost noon. 'Give me a minute; I'll be right with you,' I said.

I put on the same clothes I'd had on the night before. The only addition was a baseball cap for the bed head. I went to let the detectives in. 'Sorry about that,' I said as I opened the door.

'No problem,' they both replied.

We stood there in the entryway for a moment. 'So, what is it? Did you find her?' I asked, bracing.

'We found her, all right,' said Lopez.

I exhaled. 'You mean she's OK?'

'Not exactly,' he said. 'Her husband's dead.'

Granted. 'But she's alive?'

'Very much so.'

'So where was she found?' I asked.

'That's the thing, Dr Remler,' Trentino said. 'She found *us*. When she returned home this morning . . . from a trip to Boston.'

My face probably said it all. Perplexed. 'I don't understand.'

'Neither do we,' said Trentino. 'However, she was definitely in Boston last night. All weekend, in fact.'

'That doesn't make any sense,' I said.

'No, it doesn't. Certainly not in relation to what you've told us. But here's where it really gets weird,' said Trentino. 'Samantha Kent says she's never even met you before.'

What were they talking about? What did they mean Sam had been in Boston? And what was this about her saying she'd never met me before? 'We're talking about Samantha Kent, right?' I said. 'Five foot six. Thin. Blonde hair, past her shoulders?'

'Actually, the Samantha Kent who we met, the one who lives at Fifty-six West Eighty-first Street, is a little taller,' said Trentino.

'Do you have a picture of her?'

'No, not on us,' he said.

'But she's blonde and thin, right?'

'Yes, she is.'

'OK, so I was off a bit with her height.'

'That depends,' said Lopez. 'The Samantha Kent we talked to—the Samantha Kent married to Conrad Birch—is five foot ten, easy.'

'That's impossible. There's no way she's that tall, and what is this stuff about Boston?'

'Samantha Kent was checked in at the Ritz-Carlton on Friday, Saturday and Sunday night. She was there for some conference—'

'The Children's Aid Society,' said Lopez.

Trentino nodded. 'We've got people from the conference, as well as hotel employees, confirming they saw her there. Hey, do you think I could have a glass of water?'

As segues went, that one was pretty strange. 'Huh?' I uttered.

'I'm sorry,' said Trentino. 'It's been a long night. I'm very thirsty; would it be possible for me to get some water?'

My answer was 'Sure.' My look at him was 'You've got to be kidding'. 'I'll be right back,' I said, heading for the kitchen. I pulled a glass from the cabinet and began filling it up at my cooler.

'Nice kitchen.' From over my shoulder. Lopez's voice.

I turned to see that the two detectives had decided to keep me company. I handed Trentino his glass of water. 'Detectives, in light of everything you've told me, I think I should see for myself this woman you're talking about,' I said.

'You mean, the real Samantha Kent?' asked Lopez.

I ignored the inference that I was either crazy or lying or both. 'Don't you agree we should arrange a meeting?' I asked.

'Yes, that meeting should happen,' said Trentino. 'Though, she's pretty shook up right now and not exactly taking visitors.'

'Particularly someone she doesn't know,' added Lopez. 'Excuse me, *claims* she doesn't know.'

'That's kind of the whole point now, isn't it?' I said. 'To clear up all this confusion.'

Trentino ran a hand through what little hair he had left. 'Like I said, Dr Remler, we'll arrange for you to see her.'

'Good,' I said.

'Hey, did you know you're missing a knife?'

I turned to Lopez, who'd asked the question, and followed his gaze to the thick wooden block by my stove. There were seven knives for eight slats in the block. I was about to answer 'No, I didn't know that' when, in a flash, I realised what was going on. 'What are you saying?' I asked.

Lopez walked over to the block and pulled out one of the knives. 'I was asking whether you knew there was a knife missing from your set. That's all. Why, what are *you* saying?'

I eyed them both. Really seeing them for the first time.

'Detective Lopez, you and I both see a knife block with seven handles protruding out of it, plus an empty slat,' I began. 'But you don't know it was a set to begin with. You also don't know if a set isn't made up of seven knives and the folks at J.A. Henckels saw fit to bestow a bonus slat upon their customers. So when you ask me if I know I'm missing a knife, my question to you is do you really know that I am?'

'Dr Remler, there's no need to be angry,' said Trentino.

'Or defensive,' said Lopez.

'You're right. The only need I've got right now is for you both to quit with the innuendos. If you've got something to say, say it. If you don't, then don't. I've answered every one of your questions and offered to help in any way possible. If what I've told you isn't matching up with what you think you've learned, then let's figure out who's in error.'

'I'm sorry if you've got the wrong impression,' said Trentino. 'We appreciate your candour, and we're well aware you've cooperated fully with us. The last thing we want to do is jump to any conclusions. Rest assured, we'll get to the bottom of all this soon enough.'

The two detectives thanked me for my time and told me they'd be in touch. I showed them to the door.

'Happy Halloween,' Lopez said.

Alone again in my apartment, I returned to the kitchen to make some coffee. There on the counter sat the glass of water Detective

Trentino had asked for. It was as full as when I'd handed it to him. The man who'd claimed to be very thirsty hadn't taken a single sip.

Sam Kent. Samantha Kent. Mrs Samantha Kent.

I picked up the phone and dialled. His secretary put me through.

'Hey, what's up?' came Parker's voice.

'Plenty. I need to talk to you. Can I come by your office?'

'Yeah, no problem. You OK?' he asked.

'I'm not sure.'

PARKER WAS IN HIS OFFICE, waiting for me. 'What happened?' he asked, looking at my forehead and the two bandages holding it together.

'It's a long story,' I said.

There was so much to tell, and I hadn't really given any thought about how to tell it. Where was I supposed to begin? I started with Sam's phone call to me and her confession, her enervated tone and my suspicions—another suicide attempt. I ended with the detectives dropping by my apartment unannounced. In between, I reconstructed the order of events, pausing a few times to question if I'd got it right or left anything out.

Parker wanted to know the who, what, when, where and why. And if at any point I wasn't giving it, he'd pepper me with questions.

'Here's the thing,' Parker said ultimately. 'There are two sets of facts: what you know and what you've been told. The first set—what you know—includes only what you can prove. What you've been *told*, on the other hand—the second set—is what's making up most of your story. Especially the confusing parts. You've got your sessions with this Kent woman and you've got the detectives, notably the curveballs they were throwing at you this morning. Again, it's just stuff you've been told.' He flung out his hands. 'So right away, you know what you have to stop doing, right?'

I looked at him, unsure.

Parker leaned in. 'You've got to stop treating both sets like they're the truth. Take the detectives, for instance. They're accountable for the truth only on the witness stand. Until then it's all a game. They think you're hiding something, and they want to find out what it is.'

'But I'm not.'

'Irrelevant. So that's the first thing. Being able to discern what's for real and what's merely bait.'

'The stuff about Sam Kent's being out of town, her saying she doesn't know who I am—you're telling me it might not be true?'

'No. I'm telling you not to believe it simply because you're told it,' said Parker. 'Example. You said the detectives claimed Sam was definitely at the Ritz-Carlton up in Boston. She *may* have been there, but there's no way the detectives have got around to proving that yet. Until they do, they'll act as if they have, even tell you they have witnesses. It turns up the heat on you.'

'That's legal?'

'It's all relative. Somebody was murdered, which happens to be extremely far down on the list of things that are legal. I think the word for what the detectives have, is leeway.'

'So, what am I supposed to do?'

'Exactly this. Talk to a lawyer,' he said. 'The visit the detectives made to your apartment—that charade about a glass of water to get into your kitchen—was all about one thing. What's more, it's the one thing I'm sure they didn't tell you.'

'What's that?'

'They found the murder weapon.'

'The knife?' I asked.

'Yep. Now they want to know if it could belong to you. That's your prize for being in the wrong place at the wrong time last night.'

'It probably didn't help that I lost my temper with them.'

'Don't worry about it. Who wouldn't be upset in that situation? What you've got to focus on from here on out is everything you know for sure, the stuff you can prove. And it all revolves around your patient. What you want to do right away is gather everything that establishes Samantha Kent as your patient. For starters, did she pay you by cheque or credit card?'

'She paid me in cash,' I said, barely above a whisper.

'She did?'

'Yeah, she said she didn't want her husband to know she was seeing a therapist. She told me he saw all the cancelled cheques and credit card bills.'

'Did one of your other patients see her in your office?'

I thought about it. 'No, I don't think so.'

'Wait—she would have to go through Mila to get to you, right?'

'Email. She exchanged emails with Mila after first contacting my service. They never actually talked.'

'David, how could—' Parker stopped. 'Sorry,' he said.

'It's all right,' I assured him. 'Let me explain.'

I told him about my first session with Sam. Her going on about not giving a phone number because she was moving. Then the supposed truth. Sam's fear of her husband. Her fear that she might kill him.

'How serious did you think she was?' he asked.

'Not enough to report her, if that's what you're asking.'

'So, what do we got?' said Parker. 'You were treating a woman who claimed to be Sam Kent. She's not. You don't know who she really is, nor can you prove she even exists.'

'My notes,' I said. 'What about my notes?'

'That's the problem. They're *your* notes. It proves nothing.'

I thought of something else. 'What about her phone call to me at home; can't we trace the number?'

'Did she call you on your cell?'

'No, landline.'

He shook his head. 'LUDs only cover outgoing calls.'

'Lugs?'

'LUDs,' he said. 'Local Usage Details—otherwise known as your phone records.'

Then a click in my head, the spark of remembrance. 'The party,' I said. 'The Kesper Society cocktail party. I told you I was going for Crescent House, right?' He nodded. 'She was there.'

Bingo, said Parker's eyes. 'You mean a roomful of people saw the two of you together?'

'Not exactly,' I said, deflated. 'She approached me outside on the sidewalk as I was leaving. She was dressed to the hilt and came down the steps of the museum as if she'd been inside.'

'But she never was.'

'So it would seem.'

'How'd she know you'd be there?' he asked.

'I have no idea.'

'She could've read it in the paper. The Kesper people put out a press release naming the organisations invited—it makes the gossip columns. She could've seen Crescent House listed somewhere.'

I nodded.

'She had to give you a reason for her being there, right?'

'She told me her husband managed the charitable trust for the Kesper Society.'

'Her husband being Conrad Birch?'

'She never referred to him by name.'

'She was alone, though?'

'Yes. She said her husband was travelling.'

Parker shook his head slowly. 'It's pretty damn incredible when you think about it,' he said, almost impressed. 'I mean, what that implies. The planning, the manoeuvring, the—'

'There's something else,' I said.

I told him what happened after the Kesper party, her coming back to my apartment and making me dinner. How fitting—the no-name linguine prepared by the woman using someone else's name.

Parker listened intently to the details of that night, the sexual underpinning being quite obvious.

'Tell me you didn't . . .' His voice trailed off.

'No, I didn't,' I said. 'She just cooked me dinner.'

'Was she ever by herself in the kitchen?'

I thought for a second. 'At some point I left to get a bottle of wine.'

'I wonder where she put it.'

'The wine?'

'The knife,' he said. 'She had to get it out of your place somehow.'

'You think—'

'More than think. You're missing a knife, all right. The same knife used to kill Conrad Birch.'

Parker leaned back in his chair and folded his arms. 'Congratulations, David; you're being framed for murder.'

ON THE BRIGHT SIDE, I didn't have to rush back to work.

'Take tomorrow off too,' Parker told me.

'I can't cancel another day,' I said. 'If you're worried about my mind-set, Parker, don't. I'll be fine.'

'That's not why,' he said. 'You need to be available for me all day tomorrow in case I decide to set something up with the detectives.'

'What for?'

'To air everything out. Otherwise you're a sitting duck,' said Parker. 'There are a couple of things you've got to do first. Try to figure out how you know Conrad Birch, if at all. If this woman has really done a number on you, the odds are there's a connection to be made. If we know what it is, I'm confident about going to the detectives.'

'And if I can't figure it out?'

'Then we wait. They've got you at the scene with an alibi that, so far, you can't prove. They've got the murder weapon, which may belong to you. The one thing they don't have is any inkling of a motive. My bet is the detectives will be paying you another visit.'

'Do I cooperate?'

'Not any more,' he said. 'You're on record as claiming you don't know Birch. You can't give them the chance to pin you as a liar. If they come to talk to you again, don't say a word—call me and we'll take it from there. In the meantime, I'm going to make a few calls. A couple of friends of mine in uniform might know something about the investigation.'

'What else do I have to do?'

'Go over your session notes you took on the woman,' he said. 'The fake Samantha Kent.'

The fake Samantha Kent. It would've been funny if it wasn't happening to me. 'What am I looking for?' I asked.

'Clues, a mistake, something she said that shows her hand. No matter how clever she's been, nobody's perfect. Buy one of those minirecorders in case she's foolish enough to call you again.'

'OK. What else?'

'I think that's it,' he said. 'On second thoughts, you should have your forehead checked out. You might need a stitch or two.'

'The EMT thought the butterfly bandages would be enough.'

'What EMT? You mean at the town house last night?'

'Yeah. The detectives had one of the medical guys look at it.'

'And he cleaned it for you?'

'Yeah, why?'

Parker thought for a second. 'It's nothing. Everything's going to be fine,' he said. 'Just hang in there, OK?'

'Do I have a choice?'

Parker shook his head, and let out a laugh as I walked out of the door to the cab. 'I'll talk to you later, all right?'

'Sure.'

I started to walk back uptown to my office. Every other block seemed to bring a new revelation. Another piece to the puzzle that was the fake Samantha Kent. My Mystery Patient.

The bit about her nanny. What was her name? Celine? Celeste? I was pretty sure it was Celeste. Celeste was the reason that dinner had to be cooked at my place. Then, at my apartment, she was supposedly on the other end of the phone taking down my number. My *unlisted* number. It would be needed two nights later when I got the call.

The favour she asked me. Escorting her down from my apartment and into a cab. She knew it was no favour at all. It was my obligation. As a *gentleman*. She had worked out a very crafty way of telling me her address. All very natural, intended to make sure I'd remember when the time came. When I had to rush to her rescue.

Oh, how easy I'd made it for her. She didn't have to tell me anything. I joined her in the cab and went along for the ride.

My Mystery Patient. She must have killed Conrad Birch. She must have had a key to his house. She must have known the real Samantha Kent would be out of town. I glanced down at my left hand. There was the coil mark from the stove on the inside of my palm. If that didn't sum it up, nothing else could. I'd really been burned.

What were her motives? Why did she want Birch dead, and why was I being set up to take the fall? I was becoming more convinced that I knew Birch somehow. It would mean she and I both knew him without knowing each other. Yet, there still had to be a connection between the two of us. For some reason she'd sought me out. Why?

I took a few more steps and stopped. I raised my hand, and marched out into the street looking for the first available cab. I had a feeling I knew where a few more answers were waiting, and it was exactly where I was heading. But the time for walking was over. I was now in a hurry.

seven

It was almost creepy. The darkness, the stillness of my office. I'd spent hours there alone so many times, and yet this time somehow felt different—as if I were trespassing on my own property.

I flipped on some lights and approached my credenza, pulling out a drawer. I went straight to the Bs. Baxter . . . Bernstein . . . Bibby, until . . . there it was. Birch, Conrad.

I'd known the guy from somewhere, all right. My office. I removed his file, took it over to my desk, sat down and opened it. As soon as I did I knew why my memory of him was so hazy. There was only a single page in his folder. It was from our first, and our last, session together. Conrad Birch had been a foot dipper. One of those people who, for any number of reasons, decided not to continue with therapy after their initial exposure to it.

My eyes immediately went to the date. It had been just over a year since Conrad Birch had sat in my office. I tried to picture him. It was no use. Any remnant of that day had been deeply buried. Mostly by the horrific image still fresh in my mind. A man drenched in blood and frozen in fear. Conrad Birch, dead in his bed.

I raced through my notes. It seemed Conrad Birch was having an affair, and he was worried. He said he couldn't leave his wife and understood he had to end it with his mistress. However, he feared how she'd take the news. She had a temper. She had a mean streak. He wanted to know how he should handle it.

That was it. The gist of what I'd written . . . other than a single last bullet point: *discussed how best to break with mistress*.

I probably told Birch what I'd told a lot of people before him. He needed to be sympathetic to the feelings of his mistress but also firm in expressing his own. I wasn't advocating cold-heartedness or deceit, just realism. There was going to be some hurting. The goal was to minimise it. Do that and both sides would end up OK.

Of course, in the case of Conrad Birch, he ended up at the morgue.

Was there a connection? Was his mistress my Mystery Patient? A jilted lover seeking revenge? While that suggested a motive for murder, it left unclear why she'd want me to take the fall.

She had a temper. She had a mean streak. That's what he'd said.

I went to my credenza and flipped through the Ks. My forefinger came to a stop on the newest name tab. Kent, Samantha.

I returned to my desk and went over what I'd written. Three pages representing two sessions. I was looking for a mistake, a slip-up. As Parker put it, something she'd said that showed her hand.

The problem was everything was about showing her hand. She made me think she was in a disastrous marriage, wed to an emotionally manipulative man. A mother of a young son stuck with no way out because of the taint of a suicide attempt.

'I'm here because I want to kill my husband,' she'd confessed.

It wasn't possible to lay down your cards any more than that. And all for one purpose. So when she called me telling me that she'd gone through with it, I'd *believe*. I'd jump to, a puppet on a string.

I closed the file. Slammed it, actually. The more I read, the more I came to realise what a dupe I'd been. It could've happened to anyone, I tried to tell myself. But it had happened to *me*, and I felt disgusted. Worse than that, I felt helpless.

THE SLENDER MAN with silver hair was putting on his Burberry coat while talking to someone. I saw him as I spun through the revolving doors. Then he saw me. Immediately, he turned on his heels to face me. 'Thank God you're here, Dr Remler,' he called out.

I had left the office with the two files and cabbed it back to my apartment. There in the lobby was Robert Gordon, the building's owner.

'I came down as soon as I was called. This has never happened before in any of my buildings, so I wasn't sure about all the legalities. I called my attorney to see if they could do such a thing without your being here.'

'Mr Gordon, I'm afraid I don't—'

'Turns out a search warrant entitles them to free rein.'

'A what?'

'A search warrant,' he repeated. 'It happened a little while ago. Two detectives arrived, along with a policeman, to search your apartment. They ordered the super, Javier, to open your door. Javier called my office immediately and . . . Dr Remler, wait!'

I was already gone, heading straight for the elevators. As I hit the UP button, Mr Gordon stationed himself next to me.

'When did you say this happened?' I asked.

'About an hour and a half ago,' he said, catching his breath. 'They were in your apartment up until ten minutes ago.'

The elevator arrived. I stepped on, and pressed for the twenty-second floor. As the doors started to close, Mr Gordon said, 'As you might imagine, Dr Remler, the building committee will have to conduct its own enquiry regarding this situation.'

At the twenty-second floor the elevator doors opened. For some reason, I expected to see a web of yellow tape around my apartment. Instead, when I reached my door there wasn't anything to indicate I'd had company, welcome or not. Somehow, that almost made it worse.

The door was locked. How thoughtful of the police. God forbid anyone else be afforded the chance to take stuff from my apartment. I reached for my keys and opened the door. The place looked pretty much as I'd left it. *Pretty much.* When I stepped in the signs were there. Cushions were rearranged, wall hangings slightly askew. That was just the living room.

The room to check after that was a no-brainer. I walked into my kitchen and immediately saw what I expected. Which is to say, I didn't see it at all. It was gone. I no longer possessed a knife set. They'd taken the entire block of J.A. Henckels. *They.* Who was I kidding? I had little doubt Detective Lopez was the one gleefully wrapping the thing up in an evidence bag. Not that Trentino didn't also have his fun. That full glass of water I'd given him—the one he never took a sip out of—was sitting in the exact same spot on the counter. Only now it was empty.

I was really starting to dislike these guys.

I poured myself a drink. Then another. After that I picked up the phone and dialled. It was Stacy who answered.

'Hi, David,' she said. 'He's right here.'

He got on the line. 'Hey, buddy.'

'The bastards came and searched my apartment.'

'I know,' said Parker. 'I caught wind of it about twenty minutes ago. A friend of mine from downtown.'

'They took the knives.'

'Makes sense, considering that they did find the murder weapon.'

'Where'd they find it?'

'In the alley next to the house. The knife was clean—no blood and no prints—but it was found directly beneath one of the windows of the master bedroom.'

'So they can march into my apartment and take my knives?'

'Among other things.'

'What do you mean?'

'I don't know yet, but they found something else implicating you,' he said. 'What does it say on the property voucher?'

'The what?'

'It's a piece of paper they're required to leave behind. It lists what was removed.'

'I haven't seen it,' I said. 'Where would it be?'

'It's supposed to be readily visible, but sometimes they like to have a little fun, like taping it to the toilet seat.'

'Hilarious.'

I checked in my bathrooms. I checked in my bedrooms. In the library on the seat of the chair behind my desk was the property voucher. Holding it in place was a book-cum-paperweight taken from my shelf: Dostoyevsky's *Crime and Punishment*.

I read Parker what was on the voucher. Indeed, there were two things listed, except the second item—after the knives—wasn't what you'd call specific: *Misc. Paper*.

'What's that supposed to mean?' I asked. 'It could be anything.'

'That's the point; they don't want us to know yet. Take a look on your desk there. Do you notice anything missing?'

I thumbed through a few stacks of papers. 'Offhand, I don't.'

'We'll find out soon enough. Did you learn anything at your office?'

'I did. I checked my files. Conrad Birch had come to me for a single session a little over a year ago. He was having an affair and wanted to end it. Birch was worried about how his mistress would take the news. He described her as having a mean streak.'

'You think—'

'It's a possibility,' I said. 'My Mystery Patient was his mistress.'

'That would explain a lot, wouldn't it?'

'Yes, except why I had to be involved.'

'Right,' said Parker. 'And that was your only involvement with Birch? One session?'

'That was it.'

'OK, now just tell me he didn't pay for the session in cash.'

'Wouldn't that be something?' I said with a half-laugh. 'But I'm sure it was either by cheque or credit card. I'll have Mila look into it.'

'Not that we're rushing to prove any connection,' he said. 'I mean, the good news is we know how you know him. The bad news is you told the police you didn't.'

'Couldn't we simply explain the circumstances?'

'We could, though I've got to think about that one. They can't subpoena your patient files, so it's a question of how they'd find out.'

'I don't want to lie, Parker.'

'You also don't want to go to jail.'

I took a deep breath. 'This is really happening, isn't it?'

'I'm afraid so.'

'When does it begin to get better?'

He didn't say anything. There was an ominous silence.

'Parker, what is it you're not telling me?'

Now it was his turn to take a deep breath. 'It's like this,' he said. 'But before you freak, trust me, it's not as bad as it sounds. Tomorrow, you're going to be arrested for the murder of Conrad Birch.'

I started to freak. He let me go on for a bit. I ranted. I raved. I exploded with anger. Only when I started to ramble on about prison did my best friend decide to reel me in.

'This is what I've been able to negotiate so far,' he said. 'I spoke to the D.A.'s office, and the cops are in line with this. They're not going to come and get you. We're going to go to them. That way, there'll be no flashbulbs going off. Turns out, Conrad Birch was a pretty big deal on Wall Street. Did you know that?'

'A big deal on Wall Street?' In a flash, the first session I had with Samantha Kent came back to me. Make that, the fake Samantha

Kent. She'd claimed her husband was a venture capitalist downtown. I'd even asked her if that meant Wall Street. I remembered because of the way she answered. It was a phrase she claimed her husband had often used. *That's where the money is.*

Like that, her duplicity became all the more staggering. She'd commingled fact and fiction. I explained this to Parker, and we agreed: the idea of my Mystery Patient being Conrad Birch's mistress was gaining momentum.

'Back to my impending incarceration,' I said.

Parker continued, 'We're going to make this as civil as possible. I've promised the D.A.'s office your cooperation, and they've promised a meeting. The arrest is going to happen, but the meeting gets us an up-close look at what they think they've got on you. It also means you'll be processed faster.'

'Is that supposed to cheer me up?'

'Yes, because you'll get a same-day arraignment and won't have to spend a night in lockup. You'll thank me later.'

'They've agreed to all this?'

'It wasn't easy. Now let's talk about posting bail. How much are you worth? Stocks, bonds, savings. You rent now, but there had to be profits from the sale of . . .' Parker was about to mention the apartment and the lake cottage I'd owned with Rebecca. I knew why he stopped. I could tell what he was thinking. *Probably not the best time to bring up the dead wife.*

But it was too late. I'd started to think about her, and I began missing her in a way I never had before. It had nothing to do with the places we called home. I simply realised that none of this would've been happening if Rebecca were still alive.

'Anyway,' said Parker, 'try roughing out a number.'

I started doing the maths in my head. Royalties from *The Human Pendulum* had proved a windfall. 'Three and a half million,' I said.

'How much of that is liquid?'

'Close to two.'

'Good,' he said. 'Push comes to shove, I can always secure a bond for you if necessary.'

'Thanks.'

'Hey, that's what friends are for.'

'I always knew you'd be my friend. Who would've thought you'd also be my lawyer?'

'I'm not going to be your lawyer.'

'What are you talking about?' I asked. 'Is it one of those conflict things?'

'No, it's not that,' he said. 'I'm a really good criminal defence attorney. But part of what makes me so good is that I know when a prospective client needs something different from what I can offer. Or, in certain situations, something better.'

'I think you're selling yourself short, Parker.'

'Not in this case. This one's going to be high profile. Talked about and written about. Which means you need someone with an equally high profile leading your charge; someone who's more used to playing in that arena. That's what I mean by better.'

'Are you sure?'

'Never more so,' he said. 'I've already made the arrangements. Meet me in the lobby of the Chrysler Building tomorrow at nine.'

'You're going to introduce me to the guy who's better?'

'No,' said Parker. 'I'm going to introduce you to the guy who's the best.'

BEFORE GOING TO BED that night, I called Mila to tell her I'd be out another day. At least. I also confirmed what she'd already suspected. It had nothing to do with my being sick and I apologised for being less than honest and further apologised for not being able to give her the whole story. I did reveal that the problem related to my newest patient, Samantha Kent. Or, as I told Mila, a woman posing as Samantha Kent.

I asked Mila if she could dig up the billing paperwork on Birch.

'Is there some sort of connection?' she asked while going through her files.

'Quite possibly,' I said, leaving it at that. She didn't press me.

'Here it is,' she said. 'He paid by cheque. June of last year.' Mila made a copy of all incoming cheques before depositing them.

'Do you want me to get it over to you?' she asked.

'No, hold on to it for now. I'll let you know when I need it.'

'No problem. Anything else?'

There was one more thing. I asked her about those initial emails sent by my Mystery Patient. 'Any chance you still have them in your computer?'

Mila's silence was answer enough. She'd deleted them.

I wasn't surprised. Nor was I terribly disappointed. Given the lengths gone to by my Mystery Patient to live up to her moniker,

I highly doubted she would have left an electronic trail.

'Sorry, David,' said Mila.

'Don't worry about it.' I hung up the phone and stared blankly at the wall. It was my word against the world.

That night, I got a good, solid, twelve minutes of sleep.

At a little past nine the next morning, I met Parker in the lobby of the Chrysler Building. As we rode the elevator up to the forty-fifth floor, Parker gave me a little background about the man we were on our way to see.

'His name is Victor Glass.'

He was the managing partner of Edwards, Vode, Isadore & Locke. It was one of the oldest firms in the city, as revered as it was feared. 'The founders were ruthless,' explained Parker. 'Dog kickers, candy from a baby, you get the idea—and just in case you don't, consider the firm's acronym.'

He waited as I strung together the first letters of the founders' names. Edwards, Vode, Isadore & Locke. I smiled, amused.

'Of course, that was a long time ago,' he said. 'They're all dead now. In-house counsel for Hell, Incorporated, if I had to guess.'

Which brought him back to Victor Glass. Parker described him as a tough-talking, charismatic guy's guy, who could go from turning the screws to turning on the charm and back again in a heartbeat. Throw in the fact that he possessed a brilliant legal mind and you had a criminal defence attorney who'd managed to win more than 70 per cent of his cases.

We got off the elevator and entered the spacious, ultramodern reception area of Edwards, Vode, Isadore & Locke. Not what I expected given the firm's long history. The space was a melding of curves and harsh angles, set off by minimalist furniture, sleek lighting and bizarre artwork.

'They've redecorated,' said Parker, looking around.

We approached a sharply dressed receptionist who pressed a button and announced our arrival into a tiny wraparound headset.

'OK, thank you,' she said into the headset. She looked at us with a pleasant smile. 'Mr Glass will be with you in a couple of minutes.'

We had a seat on what was a park bench made out of leather. Scary thing was, it was pretty comfortable.

Parker reached into his briefcase. 'Here,' he said, handing me a glossy folder.

'What's this?' I asked.

'Victor's press kit.'

I took the folder and stared at Parker with a raised eyebrow. 'The man has a press kit?'

'Yep.'

I opened the folder and began thumbing through tear sheets and reprinted articles. Victor Glass had been featured in everything from the *Harvard Law Review* to *Playboy*. As I looked at his photo in an article from *Esquire*, I realised I'd seen him before. Probably on TV.

'Just so you know, we fired the decorator,' he said.

I looked up to see Victor Glass standing in the reception area. His suit jacket was off, his shirtsleeves rolled back to the elbows. He hadn't sent his secretary, choosing instead to greet us himself. It was a nice touch.

'Aw, it's not so bad,' Parker said, getting up.

'Yeah, if you're Ray Charles,' said Victor.

The receptionist tried to contain a laugh as Victor walked over and gave Parker a hearty handshake. Each expressed how good it was to see the other. I stood up, and Parker made the introduction.

'Victor, this is David Remler.'

'I understand this isn't one of your better weeks,' he said.

'And it's only Tuesday,' I said.

Victor flashed a smile. His teeth were whiter than white. Suddenly, I understood the notion of someone having 'movie-star good looks'. Trim and fit, his hair combed back, he was the guy you'd normally see playing the part of a lawyer in some big movie. Only Victor was the real thing and, if Parker was right, one of the best there was.

And he couldn't have been more than forty.

'Why don't we head back to my office,' he said. 'We'll talk about what luck we might have with the rest of the week.'

We followed Victor down a long corridor. We took a right and walked along another corridor to Victor's office. He had two gate-keepers. Both sexy librarian types. One blonde, the other brunette.

'Hold my calls, Ashley, will you?' he said to the blonde. The brunette got up and followed us into Victor's office.

'You guys want coffee?' Victor asked.

We both declined. Secretary No. 2 smiled and left us.

'All right, then,' said Victor. He motioned us over to a seating area that included four oversized club chairs. I sat in one and looked around. In the corner, in front of a panoramic view of the East River, was Victor's massive desk. No wonder the guy seemed larger than life.

We were all seated.

Parker had already given Victor the big picture. Nonetheless, Victor wanted to hear it all from me. Start to finish. Beginning with the very first time a woman came into my office and introduced herself as Samantha Kent. I spoke as clearly and calmly as I could.

Along the way Victor cut in with a few questions. On the surface, he was filling in the gaps but below the surface, he was putting my story to the test—asking me about the details. What was she wearing at such and such a time? What wine did you drink at your apartment? Things like that. He didn't seem so concerned with my answers as with the way I gave them. Meaning, was I remembering or fabricating?

'And that brings us to our being here this morning,' I said.

Victor reviewed the notes he'd made. Then he looked up and stared right into my eyes. 'So, did you kill Conrad Birch?'

'I just told you I didn't,' I said with a note of defiance.

'No,' said Victor. 'What you told me was everything that supports the *argument* you didn't. That's all right. The question has been asked and answered. Your body language says it all. You didn't kill him.'

'Well, it's nice to have my lawyer at least believe me,' I said.

'Yeah, except I'm not going to be your lawyer,' said Victor.

I looked at Parker, who looked as confused as I did.

I threw my hands up. 'Doesn't anyone want to represent me?'

'What I mean is, I won't be lead counsel,' Victor said. 'That is, if we do indeed go to trial.'

'Why not?' I asked.

'Because I'm a guy, that's why.' He was about to explain when Parker jumped in. He'd caught on fast.

'Because you'll be standing trial for killing a guy, and in your defence, you'll be blaming it on a woman,' said Parker.

'A woman who we, as yet, can't prove exists,' Victor said. 'The prosecutor will stack the jury with chicks and make sure they all have a clear view of the grieving widow sitting in the front row.'

'Oh,' was the best I could muster in response.

Victor continued: 'So the last thing you need is some slick guy like me standing up to argue for the entire trial. I'll be there. I won't be silent. And I'll be making sure everything goes as planned. But day in and day out, what you really need defending you is a pair of tits.'

'And a great pair at that,' came a voice.

We all turned to look. She was leaning against the doorway dressed in a white blouse and a black skirt that came right above her knees.

But the most notable thing she was wearing was her confident smile. My lead counsel had arrived.

'Speak of the devil,' said Victor as she walked in the room. The three of us got up.

'No, Victor, *you're* the devil,' she said. She reached Parker first and put out her hand. 'I'm Terry Garrett.'

'Parker Mathis,' he said. They shook hands.

She turned to me. But instead of extending a hand, she simply looked me over. 'Oh, good, you're attractive,' she said. 'Maybe we'll want a jury stacked with chicks after all.'

Parker shot Victor a look. *A jury stacked with chicks?* It was the same phrasing Victor had used.

'Am I mistaken, or do the walls have ears?' said Parker.

Victor shrugged. 'Sorry. It's just that men in trouble talk more self-consciously when a woman is in the room. Given the specifics of David's predicament—his possible involvement with a female patient—I wanted to make sure we didn't have any filtering up front. I also didn't want to make you have the same conversation twice.' Victor pointed at the speakerphone device on a nearby table. 'This way Terry's up to speed.'

'Big Brother lives,' said Parker. 'Or, should I say Big Sister?'

'Hey, I just work here,' said Terry.

The four of us sat down.

'Terry is the latest addition to our family. She came to us from Weiss, Stone and Wilcox out in Los Angeles.'

'Excellent firm,' said Parker.

'Yeah, well, Weiss still isn't talking to me,' said Victor.

Terry smiled. 'I think Victor would prefer to think he stole me away. Truth is, I was always an East Coast girl at heart.'

'Second in her class at Harvard Law,' said Victor.

'Yes, and all my mother wanted to know was who was first,' said Terry.

'I think we had the same mother,' said Parker.

Terry laughed. Parker laughed. Victor cracked a follow-up joke. I gazed at all three with a face that said 'I hate to break up all the fun, but I'm about to be *arrested* later today!'

They all picked up on the look, and quickly got back to business. Were there any security cameras in my building that might have recorded my recent comings and goings, and with whom. If so, were the tapes saved and for how long?

I threw out another idea—finding the cab driver who took me to the town house that night. Surely he'd remember a guy who paid him an extra five bucks for every red light he ignored.

'I'm afraid it fails as an alibi,' said Terry.

What ruled it out was the fact that every window in Conrad Birch's bedroom had been left open. The cold temperature that night had chilled his body to the point of preservation, effectively extending the time-of-death estimate by a few hours. That would've given me ample time to kill Birch, go home, and come back again via the cab under the pretence of helping my patient.

Eventually, my legal troika moved beyond the facts of the case to strategising how the rest of the day should play out. First up would be our meeting with the detectives and the D.A.'s office. After that, I'd be processed and there'd be the arraignment.

'Are you OK, David?' Terry asked after a bit. I obviously didn't look it.

'As a matter of fact, no,' I answered. 'I've been sitting here for over an hour, waiting to hear one thing. Why a woman would want to pose as Conrad Birch's wife and frame me for his murder.'

'*Why?*' said Victor. 'David, this might sound strange, but that question really isn't relevant. Especially when it comes to keeping you out of jail. So don't worry about why. Making a jury believe it was possible in the first place—that's what we have to worry about.'

'Just the same, I'd still like to know. It doesn't make any sense.'

'I don't blame you,' said Terry. 'But that's the problem with irrational behaviour. Everyone always approaches it looking for a rational explanation.' She gave me a slight smile. 'I think I got that from a book called *The Human Pendulum*. Ever hear of it?'

'Rings a bell,' I told her.

'In everything you and this Mystery Patient talked about, I bet she never mentioned your book, right?'

'No, I'm fairly certain we never discussed it,' I said.

'It's just a hunch, but I'll bet you a million dollars she's read *The Human Pendulum* front to back. If not a few times over.'

Victor nodded and peeked at his watch. 'I think it's time,' he said.

'You're right,' said Parker. He turned to me. 'Are you ready?'

'As ready as I'll ever be,' I answered.

We all stood up.

'OK then,' said Victor, walking over and putting a hand on my shoulder. 'Let's go get you arrested.'

PART III
eight

I think it was David Byrne and his group, Talking Heads, who summed it up best with a simple lyric: *How did I get here?*

The 'here' was New York Supreme Court, specifically a chair at the defendant's table. To my right was Terry Garrett. To my left, Victor Glass. It was a lawyer sandwich, and I was the meat. Dead meat, perhaps. It had been seven months since that initial meeting in Victor Glass's office. Seven months since I'd been introduced to Terry Garrett. From that point on it had been a crash course in the American legal system.

Lesson 1: Beware of free medical attention.

From Victor's spacious office that first morning, we travelled to a cramped metal interrogation room at the Twentieth Precinct. Strictly by the numbers, the teams were evenly matched. On one side of the table were Detectives Trentino and Lopez. They were joined by an assistant district attorney by the name of Glenn Hemmerson. He was a thin man, roughly forty, with dark eyes, big ears, and a haircut that suggested either he or his barber had served in the military.

On the other side of the table was my team. Parker, Terry and Victor. Three-fifty, three-fifty, and five hundred an hour, respectively. Parker was reducing some of the sting by giving me the best-friend discount—100 per cent off. I was still looking at a serious legal tab in the making. When Victor excused himself for a few minutes to go to the bathroom, I couldn't help doing the maths. The guy was taking a thirty-three-dollar pee.

Not that I wasn't getting my money's worth.

Parker had placed me in very capable hands. Terry was razor sharp and possessed an unflinching poise. She also, for lack of a better phrase, knew how to 'work it'. While the two detectives seemed to care less that she was very attractive, Hemmerson, the assistant D.A., couldn't get past it. His was a libido on the loose. So whenever Terry talked, her eyes—long lashes and all—always fixed on Hemmerson. He was too busy loving it to question it.

Then there was Victor. Never had I seen a guy who could control a room like him. For sure, he didn't kill 'em with kindness. Victor was arrogant, bellicose and unreasonable. How much of it was an act I didn't know. What I did know was that he was able to keep the other side on their collective heels and therefore dictate the meeting's flow.

But as much as I derived some pleasure from watching Detectives Trentino and Lopez perform with a little less swagger, there was no denying the evidence they'd gathered. It was worse than I thought.

I was at the scene of the crime for a reason I couldn't prove. Strike one. The murder weapon had belonged to me. Strike two. Were Trentino and Lopez keeping a checklist, the box next to 'Did he have the means and opportunity?' would've been heavily shaded in.

Then came this development: motive. And where did it come from? The library in my apartment. The *Misc. Paper* of the property voucher finally defined.

It was a typewritten letter—hand signed—that Conrad Birch had apparently sent me a month earlier. As Hemmerson placed a photocopy of the letter on the table in front of me, I replayed that evening with my Mystery Patient. Our bumping into each other after the Kesper cocktail party. Her self-guided tour of my apartment. The playful quips shouted out from my library; how she expected more wood panelling and how if she spotted a pipe rack she'd be making a quick exit. Buying her the time she needed to plant the letter. To deliver strike three.

I leaned over the table and read it. Victor, Terry and Parker gathered behind me and did the same. Conrad Birch was writing to let me know he didn't appreciate the way I'd threatened him. He couldn't wire me the money right away because of a banking error. There was nothing sinister going on, he stressed in all caps. He'd soon clear everything up. He asked that I remain patient.

'Can you tell us what this letter is all about, Dr Remler?' asked Hemmerson.

'No, he can't,' said Victor quickly before I could respond. 'Not until we get a handwriting analysis on the signature.'

Hemmerson smirked. 'Fair enough,' he said. 'But perhaps this is a good time to give Dr Remler a second chance at a question he's already answered.' He turned to me. 'Did you know Conrad Birch?'

'Mr Birch had been a patient of Dr Remler's,' Victor said. 'Albeit for only one session.' He reached into a folder and pulled out the copy of Birch's cheque courtesy of Mila.

Hemmerson glanced at it. 'Why did your client lie to the police?'

'Not revealing the identity of a patient is Dr Remler's professional prerogative.'

'Barring unmitigating circumstances, yes. But the guy was dead. Murdered, I might add.'

'That doesn't change a thing.'

Hemmerson rolled his eyes. 'Then what about Dr Remler's so-called Mystery Patient? Why didn't he extend her the same privilege? Why did he so easily offer it up that he was treating her?'

Victor came right back. 'Because it was a life-or-death situation.'

'You mean, the life or death of someone he can't prove exists.'

'How quickly we forget who actually has the burden of proof.'

Hemmerson smirked. 'It's hardly shaping up to be a burden.'

The subject was dropped, if only for the time being, which pretty much underscored the reality of that meeting. The certain inevitability of everything that would follow.

'One last thing,' said Hemmerson. 'Would you care to discuss how and why your client's blood was found on the victim?'

Parker wasted no time. 'First off, you know that Dr Remler admitted to incidental, after-the-fact contact with Mr Birch,' he stated coolly. 'And as for how you even have a sample of Dr Remler's blood, well, that was illegally obtained evidence.'

'Am I supposed to understand what you're talking about?' asked Hemmerson.

'Why don't you ask your detectives,' Parker answered. 'When they had an EM technician clean a cut on Dr Remler's forehead I'm sure they asked permission to retain his blood for analysis, right?'

I remembered Parker's original hesitation when I told him about the EMT.

The assistant D.A. glanced at Trentino and Lopez, who weren't about to admit to anything. 'It's perfectly good evidence,' Hemmerson said.

Parker shook his head. 'Perfectly inadmissible is more like it.'

Terry interceded. 'Gentlemen, why don't we move on,' she said, while locking eyes with Hemmerson. His hard edge immediately softened, and he enthusiastically agreed. He was absolutely smitten. *Lesson 2: Don't slouch.*

Fingerprints. A mug shot. The requisite paperwork. I was read my rights and officially arrested. Murder in the second degree. By the time I was transported to central booking down on Centre Street, the clock on the wall said half past one. I'd left my watch with Parker at the precinct. I gave it to him to hold, along with my wallet and key chain. The alternative was having the police put them in some over-sized envelope for purportedly safekeeping.

At a little before two I was in a holding area waiting for my arraignment. Up until that point, the confusion of what was happening to me had been neutralised by a quiet confidence that everything would be cleared up. That 'justice' would prevail. Now I wasn't so sure. And it was scaring the hell out of me.

I looked up in the corner to see a security camera staring back. It reminded me that Terry had learned that none of the security cameras were the kind that recorded.

At around four thirty I was led out of the holding area by a grey-haired, potbellied officer, who guided me down a long hallway into the courtroom and over to a bench along the wall.

I saw Parker first. He was seated in the aisle on the other side of the courtroom. Next to Parker sat Terry. She looked up and caught my eye. She gave me the quick smile and reassuring nod. Then came a signal I didn't understand at first. Terry placed the back of her hand underneath her chin while slowly pushing back her shoulders.

Huh? She pushed her shoulders back a little more and I got it. *Sit up straight, David.* I was getting my first bit of coaching on being a defendant. Look good. Look sharp. Look innocent. In other words, good posture mattered. To judges and juries alike.

But at the arraignment it was just a judge. A relatively young one at that. Blond hair, square jaw and glasses. He talked fast and when someone didn't respond quickly enough he'd prompt them with even faster talking. Within five minutes he scolded three different attorneys for not answering his questions as soon as they were asked.

A few minutes later I was the next contestant. It was my gang of three and me again, but before our feet even came to a stop before the judge, he began firing away. 'Do you wave a—'

'Yes, we wave a reading, Your Honour,' fired back Victor.

Right off the bat, there were a few exchanges between the judge and the assistant D.A., Hemmerson. He was all business and barely glanced in my direction when summarising the People's case against me. Hell, he wasn't even stealing glances at Terry.

The judge asked Victor a few questions. A lot of it was legalese. At the rate that it was being thrown around, it might as well have been Portuguese. I simply stood there and concentrated on my posture.

The only disarray arrived with the request from Hemmerson that I be remanded. Victor immediately began singing my praises as a model citizen. He implored the judge to set bail and at a reasonable amount. Hemmerson pointed out the severity of the crime I was charged with. The public interest *required* that I remain incarcerated.

Victor was about to respond when Parker jumped in. 'Your Honour,' he said, 'Dr Remler is a psychologist with numerous patients who very much depend on his counselling day in and day out. As you well know, he's guilty of nothing at this moment, so as you make your decision I would ask that you weigh the adverse effects of removing Dr Remler from the lives—'

The judge interrupted. 'You don't think, Counsellor, that the patients will flee their doctor once they learn of his predicament?'

Parker smiled. 'With all due respect, sir, I imagine it will be quite the opposite.'

'Why's that?'

'Simple,' he replied. 'Misery loves company.'

Call it a minor miracle. The judge leaned back in his chair and chuckled. He grabbed his gavel and lifted it up. 'Bail is set at a million dollars,' he announced. Bang. The gavel came down.

My gang of three and I made a hasty exit from the courtroom. Out in the hallway I thanked Parker for his timely sense of humour. Terry echoed the sentiment and referred to an article she'd once read that said more than 60 per cent of judges have been in therapy. As for Victor, he wanted to know if Parker was currently 'happy enough' at his present firm. A pretty nice compliment, I thought.

Lesson 3: A grand jury will indict a ham sandwich.

I was out on bail. It was a seven-figure reminder of how that extended trip to South America was probably not a good idea. Nevertheless, freedom with a big asterisk attached to it was still freedom. While I didn't know if it was only temporary, it sure beat the alternative.

Fallout. A quasi-known person accused of killing another quasi-known person equalled full-scale media coverage in the city. By the time I got home from my arraignment after posting bail, there was a throng of reporters and camera crews camped outside the lobby. I had the cab driver pull round to the service entrance. I ducked in unscathed.

When I got to my apartment I had messages from the *Times,* the *Journal*, the *News*, the *Post*, the *Observer*, the *Voice*, and *Newsday.* CNN, CNBC, MSNBC, FOX, and all the local network affiliates had also tried to contact me. 'The best thing to do is let your machine pick up everything for a few days,' Parker said. 'After that, no one will bother you again until the trial.'

'Until', not 'if' there's a trial. There were now three—not two—

absolute certainties in the world. Death, taxes, and a grand jury indictment of David Remler.

The hearing was scheduled for three weeks after my arraignment. It was my assumption I'd testify. I assumed wrong. Victor explained that no matter how eloquent and persuasive I thought I could be, at the end of the day I'd be a liability to myself.

I asked why.

'Memory,' said Victor. 'Right now you may or may not be able to recall what's happened in the past month with one-hundred-per-cent accuracy. Six months from now something will be blurry if not lost completely. And that's all they need. Say one thing before the grand jury and another at the trial and—Pow!—the prosecutor's got you on an inconsistency. After that you're Pinocchio.

'Besides,' he added. 'A grand jury will indict a ham sandwich if presented with one.'

And there it was. Lesson number three delivered.

THE TRIAL, fast-tracked because of its high-profile status, got under way about seven months after the arrest. It was the beginning of May, but what had been an extremely cold and damp spring wasn't done yet, and summer seemed like a long way away.

Who are all these people? That was my first reaction walking into the courtroom. The aisles on either side of me were packed with spectators who, almost in unison, turned to stare. Parker was already seated in the first row directly behind the defendant's table. It was a location that very much represented his involvement in the case—always hovering in the background. He never strayed from the thinking and planning that led up to my trial.

Parker nodded as Terry and Victor came over. They wanted to discuss a final detail regarding the opening statement.

A few minutes later a door opened to the right of the bench. The jury was about to be let in. Parker returned to his seat, and the rest of us headed to the defendant's table. We sat down. Terry to my right. Victor to my left. Me in the middle. In the middle of it all.

And you may ask yourself, well, how did I get here? That's how.

I SIGHED. 'We're not doing very well, are we?'

Terry looked up at me from the notes she'd been poring over on her desk. The two of us were back in her office. The trial was three days old. 'David, we haven't even stepped up to the plate yet,' she said.

'But they sure have. I feel like we're getting hit really hard.'

Terry's mouth curled up at the corners. 'This Mystery Patient of yours did a serious number on you. She gave the prosecution a whole lot to work with.'

'Then why are you smiling?' I asked.

Her eyes narrowed. 'Because it's our turn now.'

That it was. The prosecution had rested. With their exhibits A through what felt like Z, their serology reports, their handwriting expert who verified Conrad Birch's signature on the letter planted in my library, and their detailed testimony from Detectives Trentino and Lopez, even I was wondering if maybe I did actually kill Birch. I could only imagine what the jury must have been thinking.

The jury. Terry had explained her approach to me on the eve of jury selection. 'I look at it this way,' she'd said. 'By and large, authors are viewed with a fair amount of reverence. One of our objectives in picking a jury, therefore, would be to select as many people as possible who've read *The Human Pendulum* or have at least heard of it. The prosecution would have the opposite objective. But the actual message of *The Human Pendulum* turns all that thinking right on its head. Your book is about the unpredictability of human nature; it maintains exemplary behaviour isn't cumulative and that we're all susceptible to evil given the right circumstances. No one is immune.'

I nodded. 'Including the author.'

'*Especially* the author,' said Terry. 'You can't be familiar with your book without considering the tantalising possibility that through the murder of Conrad Birch you've managed to prove your point.'

'So we shoot for a jury of nonreaders; those who aren't familiar with the book, right?'

'Right. We sacrifice reverence for ignorance. We want smart, just not *Book TV* smart. And, unless I'm giving Hemmerson too much credit, he will be gunning for exactly that crowd.'

She was right. Come jury selection, one of the first questions Hemmerson asked the candidates was whether they were familiar with *The Human Pendulum*. Those who were became his instant best friend. Meanwhile, those who weren't became Terry's best friend.

The challenges flew, but reality won. The people who made me a best-selling author were few and far between among the jury pool. Of the seven women and five men picked—five of them white, three black, three Asian, and one Hispanic—none had ever read *The Human Pendulum*. Only two had ever heard of it.

Still, Hemmerson had a grand old time with the book just the same. As he liked to remind the jury, I'd put my premise into practice. I'd engaged in a wicked bit of foreshadowing and showed the violent streak that burned within me. On the trial's second day, he stood in front of the judge's bench and announced to the courtroom that he'd contacted the Guinness World Records people. For with *The Human Pendulum* I'd written the world's longest confession.

Quipped an on-air reporter that evening, 'You might say they're really throwing the book at Remler.'

nine

I was still in Terry's office lamenting the efforts of Hemmerson and the prosecution when Victor strolled in. 'So does he or doesn't he?' was his first question.

Does he or doesn't he testify? That's what Victor was asking.

The risk was that Hemmerson might trip me up, make me contradict myself. But if I held my own—or better yet, appeared sympathetic—the reward could be a veritable fountain of reasonable doubt.

'Tough call,' said Terry. 'Particularly because Hemmerson has been given a really long leash. I swear, it's like Lomax has never met a defence objection he couldn't overrule.'

She was referring to Barton Lomax, the judge, an old and rigid man who didn't seem to sit on the bench as much as grow out of it. In his near thirty years of presiding over cases in Manhattan, he'd proved himself to be caustic, impatient and wholly intolerant of anyone who dared challenge his authority.

Terry regarded me for a moment. 'Let's wait and see,' she said. 'We'll take a measure of how things are going in a couple of days and decide then.'

Victor didn't hesitate. 'OK, you're the boss.'

She put her hand to her ear. 'What's that?'

'Cute,' said Victor. He turned to me. '"You're the boss." That's by far her favourite expression.'

'Only when you say it, Boss,' she added.

He chuckled. 'OK, so what else?'

'Witness list,' she said. 'Let's go over it.'

For the next twenty minutes we discussed the array of people who I hoped would be saving my butt.

Next up: damage assessment. It started first and foremost with Detectives Trentino and Lopez. Big hitters for the prosecution. They came across as very cool customers. Selective in their choice of words, levelheaded in their delivery. Hemmerson had both detectives recount all of their conversations with me. Trentino first, followed by Lopez. While it bordered on redundant, the echoing of their testimony furthered the notion that what both men were saying was fact and not merely opinion.

Hemmerson made sure to include a few damning titbits that went beyond the facts. It was like slow-pitch softball. He'd lob a loaded question at Trentino or Lopez, and they'd have a field day.

Example: 'Tell me, Detective Lopez, did you notice anything strange about the defendant when you visited him at his apartment the morning of the murder?'

'I did,' began Lopez. 'Dr Remler appeared a little out of it. Both Detective Trentino and I could smell alcohol on his breath.'

'Do you think he was intoxicated at the time?'

'I couldn't say for certain without administering a Breathalyser. But Dr Remler was inconsistent in his behaviour. At times cooperative but at other times quite abusive.'

Hemmerson acted shocked—shocked!—by this development. 'Did you feel threatened?' he asked.

'That's a relative term for me since I carry a firearm,' said Lopez. 'Suffice to say, I don't believe he was acting in a very rational manner.'

Terry hit back hard on her cross-examinations. By the time she was done with both Trentino and Lopez, the jury had been made aware that my being 'out of it' maybe, just maybe, had something to do with the two detectives having just woken me up. Then she trapped Lopez a bit with his implication I'd been drinking. She asked if he thought it was possible he had smelt alcohol on my breath the night before at Conrad Birch's town house. She'd stressed the word 'possible', and Lopez seized on it as if he'd been given a loophole from the truth.

'Possible?' he repeated. 'Yes, I think it's possible.'

'Then why didn't you administer a Breathalyser or have Dr Remler's blood drawn? Your mere suspicion in that situation would've satisfied any court's definition of just cause.'

Lopez didn't really have an answer for that. But the accusation had been made. The suggestion planted . . . The doctor was a drunk.

I realised I *was* drinking too much. First came Rebecca's death, then this trial. I was relying on the bottle to dull the pain. The problem was that it threatened to dull everything.

I'd seen too many patients not to know there was a significant chasm between alcohol abuse and alcoholism. Nonetheless, the lesser of two evils was still evil. So I decided that I'd go on an alcohol-free diet for a while.

Now, three days later and sitting in Terry's office discussing the detectives, I'd yet to have a drink.

From that issue to another: Mila. The poor woman wanted to help me. But she'd been a helpless pawn in my being framed and, as a result, was a key witness for the prosecution.

Said Hemmerson in the courtroom, 'Ms Benninghoff, you never actually talked to, or saw, this woman whom Dr Remler was calling Sam Kent, right?'

'I'm sure she—'

'Just yes or no, please, Ms Benninghoff.'

'No, I never saw this woman,' Mila said to Hemmerson.

'Or talked to . . .'

'No. But what I was trying to—'

'Thank you, Ms Benninghoff. Did you ever see any payment from her other than the cash Dr Remler gave you?'

'No.'

'Which means that she very well could've been a fabrication on the part of Dr Remler, correct?'

'No.'

'No? Why not, Ms Benninghoff?'

'Because I don't believe David would ever do such a thing.'

'Precisely,' said Hemmerson. 'You trusted him. And he knew you trusted him. Which made it all the more easy for him to accomplish his deception.'

That's when Terry objected for what was probably the third time in three minutes. The latest was to point out that Hemmerson hadn't actually bothered to ask Mila a question in that last exchange. Judge Lomax was quick to respond—small miracle—sustained.

Said Lomax, with more than a hint of sarcasm, 'Here's a yes or no for you, Mr Hemmerson. Do you actually have another question for the witness?'

Hemmerson took the talking-down-to in his stride. He'd made his point. 'No, Your Honour. No further questions.'

'Your witness, Ms Garrett.'

Terry stood up to cross-examine, but the facts were what they were. Mila couldn't prove any more than I could that the only mystery about my patient was who she was, and not, as the prosecution would contend, whether she existed. So when Terry walked up to the witness box and smiled at Mila, I had no idea what questions she'd ask. Turns out there was only one.

'Ms Benninghoff, the prosecution would have us believe that it was Dr Remler who sent the initial emails to you under the guise of Sam Kent. But if Dr Remler's objective was to create the appearance of a patient whom he could later claim was Conrad Birch's mistress, why would he make you first believe his patient was a man?'

'I have no idea.'

'Neither do I,' said Terry before turning to the judge. 'No further questions, Your Honour.'

At the time, I didn't know what she was getting at. Now, back in her office, she was about to let on.

'They're painting you as a criminal mastermind, David. You not only fooled strangers, you fooled people who knew you very, very well. You were cunning, imaginative, brilliant. You know what we have to do?'

'What's that?' I asked.

Terry grinned. 'We've got to show them they're right. That you are in fact a criminal mastermind.'

Confused, I looked at her, while Victor laughed out loud.

'I like it,' he said. 'I like it a lot.'

'What do you think, David?' she asked.

'I think I have no idea what you're talking about.'

'You got caught!' she said.

Victor chimed in. 'It's the one thing the prosecution hasn't delivered on. If you're so clever, how come you were dumb enough to get caught so easily. Approach it like that and the jury starts to wonder if maybe the real mastermind isn't on trial.'

'Don't you see, David? If we can make them wonder, we can make them believe,' said Terry, her intense look returning. 'That your Mystery Patient is very much for real . . . and very much at large.'

THE NEXT NIGHT I was eating Chinese takeaway in my kitchen when I flipped on the late local news. The top story was about a murder in Queens. The second story was about a suicide in Upstate New York.

I sat there bewildered as the anchorwoman spoke of the 'rabbi murder trial that had riveted the city' the previous year. 'Tonight,' the anchorwoman said, 'that rabbi is dead.'

It was an apparent suicide. Lest there be any doubt, 'sources' reported that the rabbi had left behind a suicide note in his cell. In it, he confessed to his crime. He had, in fact, murdered the woman. He'd killed himself in the very same fashion that his defence lawyers had tried to pin on his victim. Suicide by self-garroting. With a shoelace and a spoon, the rabbi was off to make peace with God.

I continued to watch the news up through the sport and the weather. When that same anchorwoman told me to stay tuned for *Saturday Night Live*, I turned off the television and went to bed. I didn't know exactly how to feel. So, in the end, I felt nothing.

'ARE YOU SURPRISED to see me?' she asked.

I'd just come out of the men's room at the courthouse that Monday morning. It was a little before 9 a.m. In a matter of minutes the first witness for the defence—*my* defence—was going to be called. I felt a tap on my shoulder. When I turned round, there she was. Smiling.

'Actually, I'm delighted to see you,' I said.

It was Emily Morgan. Fittingly, my Monday, nine o'clock. She was a seventy-four-year-old widow who had been coming to me for the past four years. If anyone threatened my premise for *The Human Pendulum* it was her. She was a genuine sweetheart.

'Do you realise, David,' she said, looking around, 'that in all my years in this city I've never once set foot in this building?'

'Consider yourself fortunate,' I replied.

'You know, come to think of it,' she said, 'I've also never eaten at Tavern on the Green.' She was just getting warmed up. For the next minute I heard about the one and only time she rode in a horse-driven carriage around Central Park.

I discreetly glanced down at my watch. Endearing as Emily was, I was about to be officially late to my own murder trial.

A quick goodbye and thank you for her support was followed by a near sprint to the courtroom. I pushed through the doors and fixed my eyes on the empty chair between Victor and Terry. I took a seat and, like a schoolboy, apologised to them both for running late.

After twenty seconds I was back on my feet again, standing as Judge Lomax was announced. Then, out of the corner of my eye, I saw her. Sam Kent. Samantha Kent. Mrs Samantha Kent. The real one.

For the first time, I was seeing her in person. There'd been a couple of pictures in the papers, and I'd gained a sense of what she looked like. Yet, as much as our lives had suddenly intersected, I didn't really know much about her.

What little I did know came from the brief stories accompanying those newspaper pictures. That and what was relayed to me by Terry based on Samantha Kent's statements to the police. Taken together, one thing was clear: my Mystery Patient had done her homework. Posing as Samantha Kent, she appropriated far more than a name.

Being an only child. Growing up in Larchmont, New York. Attending Brown. Even the former job as a buyer for Bergdorf's.

How she knew all this could've stemmed more from pillow talk than research. Over the course of their affair, Conrad Birch could've told her things about his wife. Either way, my Mystery Patient had really got into her role.

One thing she didn't appropriate was the family business. It didn't play into the sympathy card. Samantha Kent was the only child of Archibald Kent, founder of Kent Oceanic. They made most of the world's cargo ships and a hell of a lot of money in the process. At the age of seventy-seven and a widower, 'Archie' Kent supposedly had a net worth of $4 billion. That made Samantha one serious heiress.

But it was what my Mystery Patient flat-out made up that proved most pivotal. Two things in particular.

One was the nanny, Celeste. Samantha Kent and Conrad Birch never had a nanny. Because, two, there was no kid. The two-year-old boy at the centre of everything—the pending custody battle and, ultimately, the desire to kill Birch—was a complete fabrication.

Which meant that along with the pictures I'd already seen of the real Samantha Kent, I was able to add one more. A portrait of a woman in a state of disbelief. Especially when it came to my alibi.

She'd said she didn't know her husband had ever seen a psychologist. Considering what Conrad Birch told me in that one session we had together—that he was cheating on his wife—I was inclined to believe her. So what *did* Samantha Kent know?

The answer was this: all the things that guaranteed Terry would never call her to the stand. Samantha Kent knew that she came home from a trip to Boston to learn her husband had been brutally murdered. She knew that the knife used to stab him repeatedly was a knife I once owned. She knew that a letter signed by her husband had been found in my apartment and that it suggested I had a motive.

I was now staring at her. The real Samantha Kent was more blonde than she appeared in any picture I'd seen. Her hair was now different too. It fell straight to her shoulders, parted on one side and angling across her forehead. She was also thinner in person, with pronounced cheekbones. She was forty, forty-five at the outside. In total, she was attractive, although in a way that suggested she was once far more so.

That was what I saw. But it wasn't what I was staring at. What caught my attention, and held it, was something more. Something . . . intangible. A certain poise, a stoic demeanor, a chin held high. A reserved nature that set her off without appearing cold. What I was looking at in Samantha Kent was real wealth.

Then, she turned my way, staring right at me. And if the weight of her gaze was any indication, she didn't like what she saw. Could I blame her? A lot of people had been telling her that I was the guy who murdered her husband. Now here I was to prove them all wrong. Or at least create enough reasonable doubt to that effect. And the kicker? For my defence, I was pawning everything off on a heretofore nonexistent woman who was having an affair with her husband. If I were Samantha Kent, I'd hate my guts too.

'YOU MAY CALL your first witness, Ms Garrett.'

Terry stood from her chair to my right and adjusted her suit jacket with a slight tug. 'Thank you, Your Honour,' she said. 'The defence calls Dr Hans Lenbakker.' And so began Operation Brilliant Idiot.

A succession of witnesses would be called in strategic order. One to show my uncompromising genius in plotting a complex murder. The next to show how utterly stupid I was in trying to pull it off. Then back to someone for my genius. Followed by another one for my stupidity. And so on. Brilliant and idiot. Repeated enough times to make the jury get the point. I was neither smart enough nor dumb enough to commit this crime.

Dr Hans Lenbakker was sworn in and took a seat in the witness-box. While his grey beard was neatly trimmed, he had just enough of that Einstein rumple about him to suggest formidable intelligence.

'Thank you for being here today, Dr Lenbakker,' said Terry.

'You're very much welcome,' he answered.

Terry had the doctor give a brief history of his educational background and professional credentials. His specific area of expertise was the dating of paintings, along with paper- and parchment-based writings. By the time he got to his current stint as director of the

Smithsonian's Artifact Authentication Board, I could tell the jury was suitably impressed.

Terry strode back to the defence table, opened a folder and removed a page of loose-leaf notepaper that was sheathed in clear plastic. She approached Dr Lenbakker with it.

'I'm showing you what's been marked defence exhibit A,' she said to him. 'Do you recognise it?'

'Yes. I've examined it.'

'That was a couple of weeks ago, correct?'

'Yes.'

With that, Terry began reciting aloud my notes on Conrad Birch. Our one session together. The admission that he was having an affair. The feeling that he couldn't leave his wife and the fear of having to break it off with his mistress. 'Fear,' Terry repeated. She listed off my bullet points that said the mistress had a temper. A mean streak. Terry looked up at the jury. 'Dr Remler then writes that Conrad Birch had, and I quote, "overwhelming concern for how mistress will react".'

She handed the plastic-covered page to Dr Lenbakker.

'As you know, Doctor, these are notes that my client has offered as being a record of his one and only session with Conrad Birch,' she said. 'Based on your examination of the document, and in your expert opinion, when were they written? Last month? Last year?'

'Much longer than a year, closer to two years. The breakdown of the ink particles alone would heavily support that. The oxygenation would all but guarantee it.'

'So, Dr Lenbakker, if Dr Remler had intended to fake the fact that he once treated Conrad Birch in order to construct an alibi, what you're saying is that he was brilliantly planning to kill Mr Birch for nearly *two* years?'

'Objection!' shouted Hemmerson. 'First off, the murder itself was over seven months ago. More important, Dr Lenbakker has been called to verify ink, not the intentions of the defendant.'

'Sustained,' said Judge Lomax.

'I'm sorry,' she said. 'I just thought Dr Lenbakker might have an *ink*ling.'

Most of the jury giggled, along with the rest of the courtroom.

'Thank you, Dr Lenbakker.' He handed Terry back the page, and she entered it into evidence. 'I have no further questions, Your Honour.'

'Your witness,' said Lomax with a nod towards Hemmerson.

The assistant D.A. got up. 'We have no questions for Dr Lenbakker.'

'Very well, then. Ms Garrett, your next witness.'

'Your Honour, the defence has some additional questions for Detectives Trentino and Lopez. Given their presence in the court-room today, I'd like to call them back to the stand.'

'I'll allow it,' Lomax said.

Terry had told me it was common for detectives to attend the trials of their cases beyond the days they were testifying. A vested interest sort of thing. Nonetheless, neither she nor Victor were about to bank on it. So they let drop to a reporter the day before that they had a sur-prise witness lined up. Predictably, that reporter later asked the detectives if they knew who it was.

'The defence calls Detective Joseph Trentino,' announced Terry.

In the back of the courtroom, the detective lumbered to his feet and sidestepped past his partner, Lopez, out to the aisle. As Trentino began walking up, Terry pivoted on her heels to face the bench.

'Your Honour, I'd like to ask that Detective Lopez not be present in the courtroom for Detective Trentino's testimony. The reason is that I want both of their recollections as opposed to a joint one.'

Hemmerson was up on his feet objecting. 'Your Honour,' he said, steaming, 'this request by the defence amounts to an accusation of collusion by the detectives and, therefore, perjury. Not only do I ask that you deny the request, but I also demand an apology.'

The brief chortle in the courtroom was from Victor. First day of the defence's case and Terry had quickly got under Hemmerson's skin.

Lomax mulled over Terry's request and Hemmerson's objection. A few seconds later, he was asking Detective Lopez to go and stretch his legs for a bit.

As Trentino sat down, Terry did a little recapping. 'Detective Trentino, you've got a psychologist at the scene of a crime who explains he's looking for a patient of his. He tells you his patient has confessed to killing her husband. Only it turns out the husband is not her husband—he's someone else's husband. What's more, the patient has been pretending to be that someone else, that is, the husband's real wife. Sounds confusing, doesn't it? Almost hard to believe.'

'Yes.'

'I mean, if I were trying to make up an alibi, I certainly wouldn't choose one as far-fetched as that. Would you?'

Hemmerson objected on the grounds that it called for speculation. Terry countered that the detective had heard many alibis in the line of duty and that he was uniquely qualified to comment on the viability of the one put forward by her client. Lomax instructed Trentino to answer the question.

Said the detective, 'As alibis went it didn't seem very plausible. No, it wouldn't have been my choice.'

'In other words, if Dr Remler were fabricating his alibi, he'd been pretty stupid about it, right?'

'Those are your words, not mine.'

Terry nodded. 'What if I said Dr Remler could've been smarter about making up an alibi if that was indeed what he was doing? Could those be *our* words, Detective Trentino?'

'Sure, OK . . . yes, he could've been smarter.'

'Good. Thank you,' she said. 'Now let's go back to that fateful night in the Birch home when the police first found Dr Remler. He was coming up from the basement, correct?'

'I wasn't there, but that's what the initial two officers on the scene reported.'

'Do you know what Dr Remler was doing in the basement?'

'No, I do not.'

'You never asked him?'

Trentino's forehead was starting to crease. 'No, I didn't ask him that directly, because he'd told us he was searching for his patient.'

'Ah, the alibi,' said Terry, a finger raised in the air. 'And you believed it—what Dr Remler was telling you?'

'At first.'

'He said that he had searched every room in the house, right?'

'Yes, he said that.'

'And do you still believe that?'

'The answer is, I don't know,' he snapped.

Terry, incredulous: 'You don't know if you believe him?'

'That's right. I don't know.'

'Maybe this will help,' she said, turning to the jury. 'Dr Remler's fingerprints were found in practically every room in that house— *every* room—including the basement. That would be consistent with someone who was looking for someone else, wouldn't it?'

Hemmerson objected. 'I fail to see the point of this line of questioning.' The toss of a life preserver to his flailing detective witness.

Judge Lomax squinted at Terry. 'Ms Garrett, could you either get to your point or move on, please?'

'Your Honour, my point is simple. The prosecution would have us believe that my client plotted and carried out a complex murder. But if that were the case, it would've been pretty stupid of him to leave his fingerprints all over the place. Unless, of course, my client is telling the truth, which is what I'm trying to prove—that Dr Remler truly was looking for his patient that night, and that she truly did kill Conrad Birch.'

'Hell, you can't even prove she exists.'

Terry froze for a moment. Trentino had let his emotions overtake his brain. He'd blurted out something without thinking, and while it may have been true, it also played right into Terry's hands.

'You're right, Detective. And why can't we prove she exists? Because that's exactly what she wants. It's how she intends to get away with this murder. You think she's make-believe, but that's what she's *making* you believe. She's manipulating you just like she did Dr Remler. But, as opposed to my innocent client, you're helping her get away with it!'

'Detective Trentino is not on trial here!' Hemmerson shouted.

Lomax promptly scolded Terry for her tactics. He also reminded Trentino that he was on the stand to answer questions and not to inject commentary. Then, 'Do you have any further questions for the detective, Ms Garrett?'

'No, I don't,' she said.

Lomax asked Hemmerson if he wanted to re-question Trentino. He didn't. He was in damage-control mode, the best move being to get his detective off the stand as fast as possible.

'You can step down,' said Lomax.

Trentino did, but not without casting a cold stare on his least favourite woman in the room. Terry returned the stare and then some. Victor turned to me with a smile. 'That's my girl,' he whispered.

The proud boss was reflecting on the prowess of his recent addition to the firm and his decision to make her lead counsel on the case.

As soon as I had that thought, I had another. *What if there was more to it than that? 'That's my girl'*. My mind raced with the idea that Victor and Terry were an item. He was a good-looking guy; she was a good-looking woman. He was recently divorced; she was single. They worked together and knew each other to be smart and talented. It was more than conceivable. And I didn't like it.

The reason should've been because of the possible complications. I was on trial for murder and could ill afford a lovers' spat or quarrelling of any nature jeopardising my defence. Yet that was the last thing I was thinking about. Truth was, I simply didn't want Terry to be seeing someone. Not Victor. Not anyone. You'd think the prospect of spending the rest of my life in jail would've made all other interests a distant second. But there I was. A crush had crept up on me.

I told myself I was crazy. It hadn't been that long since I'd taken an interest in a woman, and she ended up framing me for murder. Now I was having thoughts about my attorney. Had the absence of companionship finally caught up to me? Was I that starved for attention?

The day continued. Terry didn't call Trentino's partner to the stand. Getting Lopez booted from the courtroom was a way of distracting the jury. She was making them consider the possibility that the two detectives were indeed in cahoots, railroading the defendant regardless of the facts. Between the nightly news and practically every prime-time cop show, one could hardly rule it out.

Instead, Terry continued with her strategic list of witnesses. There was the coroner who testified that Conrad Birch was definitely asleep before he was stabbed. This meant less of a struggle for the killer, if any at all. Very smart of me.

Then there was the policeman who had found my knife, the murder weapon, in the alley directly below Birch's bedroom. I obviously must have thrown it out the window to get rid of it. Very stupid of me. Unless it wasn't me. Unless *she* wanted the knife to be discovered.

Terry proceeded with her witnesses, sowing the seeds of doubt with a deft and efficient hand. My Mystery Patient seemed to be coming to life in that courtroom.

Operation Brilliant Idiot was rolling right along. Brilliantly. But then the wheels fell off.

ten

The defence had rested, my case made. And without my having to assume the risk of testifying. The time was a little before three on Friday. Hemmerson stood from his chair and announced, 'Your Honour, the prosecution calls Gabrielle Dennis.'

I could hear Victor and Terry utter in unison: '*Who?*'

We all turned and saw a bombshell of a young woman get up from her aisle seat in the back of the courtroom. She looked to be in her mid-twenties, with auburn hair and a top-heavy figure that left little doubt as to where she stood on the issue of breast implants.

The young woman walked past our table and up to the witness stand. As she was sworn in, Victor said, 'Get ready to pounce.'

Terry nodded and began to jot down a note. Victor opened his briefcase and took out his BlackBerry. He began to quickly type. Presumably an email to someone.

Hemmerson approached the young woman. 'Could you please state your name for the court?'

She leaned in to the microphone. 'My name is Gabrielle Dennis.'

'You're here today, Ms Dennis, because you knew the victim, Conrad Birch, correct?'

'Yes, that's right.'

'And in what capacity did you know Mr Birch?'

She didn't hesitate for a moment. 'I was his mistress.'

The courtroom launched into a collective murmur with a few scattered gasps. That's when Terry pounced. 'Your Honour, we've had no advanced notice of this witness and, given her claim, the timing of her appearance is dubious at best.'

Hemmerson jumped right in. 'Your Honour, the timing is not only genuine, it's also quite logical. Ms Dennis only became known to the D.A.'s office yesterday evening. She heard news reports of what the defence was claiming and believed it was her duty to come forward.'

'Is the prosecution claiming that they themselves haven't had time to vet this witness?' Terry asked incredulously.

'Justice is a twenty-four-hour-a-day operation,' said Hemmerson with a smirk. 'We've had ample time.'

'But not enough time to inform the defence. How convenient.'

Hemmerson threw a nasty look at Terry before addressing the judge again. 'Your Honour, if you let me proceed, you'll discover this is a legitimate witness. Ms Dennis has information that I believe will alter the course of this trial.'

Lomax raised his hand and declared that the questioning of the witness could continue.

'When did you first become involved with Conrad Birch?' Hemmerson asked.

'About two and a half years ago.'

'How did you meet?'

'We worked out at the same gym, Max Fitness,' she said.

'Do you remember who initiated your meeting each other?' Hemmerson asked her.

'It was kind of mutual. We were on treadmills next to each other one day. I was having a problem with setting a programme and he offered to help.'

'In terms of a sexual relationship, did he initiate the affair?'

'We were two consenting adults, but I'd say that's accurate.'

'Did you know he was married?'

'Yes, I knew he was married. He told me he was.'

Right then, I realised Samantha Kent was sitting through all this. It was bad enough for me. Her level of discomfort had to have been something else entirely. I stole a quick glance to confirm she was indeed sitting in the same seat she'd been in for the past week.

She wasn't in that same seat or any other. I was relieved. She certainly didn't need to hear the testimony of Gabrielle Dennis.

Hemmerson continued the questioning of his surprise star witness. 'How long did the affair last, Ms Dennis?'

'About nine months.'

'So you became involved with Conrad Birch about two and a half years ago, and the relationship lasted for about nine months, correct?'

'Yes, that's right.'

'The reason you're here today is because of news reports that told of how the defence was blaming the murder on a supposed Mystery Patient who was Conrad Birch's mistress, and that—'

'Objection!' shouted Terry.

'Sustained,' said Lomax. 'Mr Hemmerson, let's refrain from hearsay and the suggestion of blame in the media or by anyone else.'

'My apologies, Your Honour.' He turned back to his witness. 'Ms Dennis, you became aware of the defendant's claim that Conrad Birch had been a patient of his and told him of having an affair, correct?'

'Yes.'

'According to the defendant's handwritten notes, this affair took place roughly two years ago, which would seem to coincide with the time in which you were involved with Conrad Birch, right?'

'Yes.'

'Furthermore, you've read and heard in news reports that the defence is suggesting this mistress was Dr Remler's Mystery Patient, is that correct?'

'Yes, that's right.'

'So I have to ask you then,' he said with a bit of dramatic pause, 'have you ever been a patient of Dr David Remler's?'

She looked at me, her face nearing anger. 'No, I have not,' she said.

'Have you ever even met him before?'

'No, I have not.'

'Which is why you came forward, isn't it?'

'Yes. I didn't think it was fair.'

'Ms Dennis, you've displayed real courage in coming forward, so let me try to wrap this up. Tell us, how did the affair end?'

'Not very well. At least as far as I was concerned. Conrad told me he couldn't leave his wife. So what was the point?'

'You ended the affair, then?'

'Technically, yes. The way I saw it, I didn't have much of a choice.'

'Thank you, Ms Dennis,' said Hemmerson. 'No further questions.'

Judge Lomax: 'Your witness, Ms Garrett.'

Instead of getting up, Terry asked her first question from her seat. 'Ms Dennis, where did you and Conrad Birch usually do it?'

'Objection!' shouted Hemmerson. 'She's trying to demean the witness!'

'I'll rephrase the question,' said Terry. She stood up and walked in front of the defence table. 'Ms Dennis, where did you and Mr Birch conduct the affair?'

She answered, not very loudly, though. 'Mainly in hotels.'

'I'm sorry, could you please speak up?'

Gabrielle Dennis glared at Terry. 'I said, mainly in hotels.'

'Could you name one of them for us?'

With barely a beat in between, she did. 'The Wall Street Inn.'

'Did you ever pay for a room there?'

'No, Conrad did that.'

'Did you ever see him pay by credit card?'

'I never saw him pay at all,' she said. 'I know he paid. We just—'

Terry interrupted. 'You didn't want to be seen together in public. I understand. So it's not like anyone ever saw you together, right?'

'We were discreet, yes.'

I glanced at Victor, who was reading something on his BlackBerry. Terry looked at her watch. She was quite deliberate about it. 'Now, Ms Dennis, let's talk about your breakup with Conrad Birch. You said he told you he wouldn't leave his wife, is that right?'

'Yes.'

'Did that make you angry?'

'I was upset.'

'Were you perhaps more than that?'

Hemmerson objected. He wanted to know what Terry was getting at. So did Lomax. He asked her to get to the point.

'Let me put it this way,' she said. 'Ms Dennis, would you consider yourself to have a temper?'

'I can get mad about things, if that's what you mean.'

'No, what I'm asking is that if someone described you as having a mean streak, do you think it would be an accurate assessment?'

She mulled the question over. 'No, I don't think it would be.'

Terry nodded. 'Would it surprise you then that Conrad Birch told my client he thought that's exactly what his mistress had?'

'No, actually, it wouldn't.'

'Why's that?'

'Conrad had a tendency to exaggerate. Sometimes even lie. He was having an affair, after all.'

'I see,' said Terry, looking at the jury, specifically, the women. 'So someone having an illicit affair is more likely not to tell the truth. That's interesting, because you were also having an illicit affair.'

'But—'

'At least, that's what you're claiming here today.' Terry had talked right over her. 'Tell me, Ms Dennis, what do you do for a living?'

'I'm an actress.'

Terry paused. The answer was an unexpected windfall. The implication of someone playing a part. 'Are you currently working?'

'No, I'm not.'

'When's the last time you did work?'

'Well, I'm also a waitress.'

'I see. But in terms of the acting, when's the last time you got paid to do that?'

'Maybe six months ago. It was for a commercial.'

'As for other acting, is there anything we might have seen you in?'

Hemmerson objected. 'Is this a courtroom or the Bravo channel?'

Lomax agreed. 'Keep it moving, Ms Garrett. It's getting late.'

Terry's face lit up. It was as if Lomax had said the magic words. 'I agree, Your Honour, it is getting late. Given that, combined with the surprise nature of the witness, I'd like to request that we adjourn until Monday morning.'

Lomax looked at his watch. The clock on the wall was behind him. It was ten to five. Close enough for a full day, he apparently thought. 'Court is in recess until Monday morning at nine.'

Gabrielle Dennis stepped down as the rest of the people in the courtroom gathered their things and stood. Terry walked over to Victor and me.

'Did he email you back yet?' she asked Victor.

'Yeah. He's starting on it right away.'

I looked at the two of them. 'Starting on what? Who's "he"?'

'You'll see,' said Victor.

HIS NAME WAS Anthony Magnetti, but Victor called him 'The Magnet'. The reason was simple, he explained. The guy could pull almost any information about anyone right off his computer. Or perhaps more accurately, he could pull it off everyone else's computer.

'There are hackers, and then there's The Magnet,' said Victor to me. He seemed unaware he was talking about the guy the way a kid talked about a superhero.

The man who showed up at Victor's office after we returned from court was not about to inspire a Saturday-morning cartoon. Anthony Magnetti, aka The Magnet, was around five-and-a-half-feet tall, and easily three hundred pounds. The guy was somewhere between geek and hip. His thick black glasses were countered by a black leather biker jacket. And there was a ponytail hanging down his back.

'The Magnet has arrived!' exclaimed Victor, getting up from behind his desk. The two hugged like old friends.

Victor made the introduction. 'David, meet The Magnet.'

'Anthony Magnetti,' he said, sticking his hand out.

'Hi, Anthony,' I said, shaking it. 'David Remler.'

Victor returned to his desk for a moment. 'Let me just buzz Terry.'

Terry arrived from her office, where she'd been checking her email. 'Hey, Anthony,' she said. 'Three cases since I've been here and three dates with you. People are going to start talking.'

'Good,' he said. 'I'll be able to tell you what they say—a buddy of mine is teaching me wiretapping.'

Terry warmly shook hands with The Magnet and we all sat down. Let the briefing begin.

From the moment Victor first emailed him, The Magnet had been busy digging up everything he could find on our surprise witness. Gabrielle Dennis, the woman claiming to be Birch's mistress.

'OK,' said Terry. 'The possibilities are as follows. One, she's the real deal and is telling the truth. Two, she's a plant—'

'Or, should we say, *im*plant,' cracked Victor.

The Magnet put his coffee down and flipped a page on his notepad. 'Gabrielle Dennis's breast enlargement surgery was performed here in Manhattan four years ago on January 14 by Dr Rueben Stolzmier at a cost of six thousand four hundred and eighty-seven dollars.'

I couldn't help asking, 'Anthony, how could you find that out?'

He looked at me. 'Trust me, you don't want to know.'

Terry continued: 'As for the third and final possibility, it's this: Gabrielle Dennis is trying to jump-start her career.' She turned to The Magnet. 'Anthony, what's the deal with the gym?'

He flipped back to the first page of his notes. 'She and Birch were both members during that time,' he said. 'Gabrielle Dennis was much more of a regular than Conrad Birch.'

'And in terms of overlapping?' asked Terry.

'Only eighteen times from the first date you gave me.'

'OK, so Gabrielle Dennis and Conrad Birch could've met as she claimed they did,' said Victor.

'Or that's just the way she knew about him,' said Terry. 'What about the Wall Street Inn, Anthony? Or any other hotels?'

'Birch had four credit cards, plus a corporate card from his firm,' he answered. 'None showed any Manhattan hotel.'

'He would've paid cash. Credit cards are an infidelity trail,' said Victor. 'Not that I'm the voice of experience on that.'

'Of course not,' said Terry.

Damn. There it was again. That nagging feeling Victor and Terry were involved.

'What about the girl's finances?' asked Terry.

'What finances?' said The Magnet with a smirk. 'Gabrielle Dennis gives new meaning to "struggling actress". She has one cheque account with Chase, with three overdraws in the past three years. No lump-sum payments or steady increase in deposits during the time she claims she was with Birch.'

'What about any run-ins with the law?' Terry asked.

The Magnet shook his head. 'Nothing. She's hasn't owned a car for five years, so there's not even an outstanding parking ticket.'

Victor stood up and walked over to his windows. 'So, what I'm hearing is this,' he said. 'Nothing that's out-and-out suspicious on the one hand, versus on the other hand—'

Terry jumped in. 'Nothing in her testimony today that she couldn't have picked up from television or the newspapers.'

The Magnet reached for his coffee. 'Have you checked the autopsy report on Birch to see if he had any moles or beauty marks you could call her on?'

'I thought about that,' said Terry. 'I checked, and he didn't.'

Victor turned round. 'What else, Mag'?' he asked.

'I got into most every drugstore chain. She had a prescription for Xanax a year back with three refills, but who hasn't, right?' He scoured his notes some more. 'There is one other thing,' he said. 'It's far from a smoking gun, but it does make you wonder a little more about her real motivation.'

'What is it?' asked Terry, sitting up in her chair.

'Her phone records,' said The Magnet. 'Two days ago, Gabrielle Dennis placed three calls to EpicOne Media.'

'Who or what are we talking about?' I asked.

'Sorry, David,' said Victor, sitting back down. 'EpicOne Media publishes the *National Tabloid*.' No further explanation was needed. The paper they were talking about made the *Enquirer* and the *Star* look like the *Times* and the *Journal*. A monkey and a keyboard got it right more times than they did.

'The notion that she's trying to sell her story hurts her credibility,' said Terry. 'But it doesn't prove the story wrong .'

'Like I said, I didn't think it was your smoking gun.'

'Though it's not bad as far as ammo goes,' said Victor. He looked at his watch and then up at Terry. She nodded.

'On that note, why don't we let you go, Anthony,' she said.

The Magnet pushed off the arms of his club chair with a slight grunt and stood. As we shook hands, I thanked him for his efforts. Victor gave him another hug, and Terry volunteered to walk him out of the office. 'Back in minute,' she said.

Victor and I sat down again as they left.

'Did I tell you he's done work for the CIA and the Mossad?' said Victor. 'For all I know, Magnetti's not even his real name.' He stood up and headed for his bar. 'You want a drink?'

'No, I'm all set,' I lied. Few things sounded better than a drink at that moment. Fortunately, one of those things was the sound of my mental pen crossing off another day on my mental 'how long it's been since I've had a drink' calendar.

Terry returned. She sat back down, kicked off her heels and put her feet up on the glass table. Victor finished pouring what, of course, had to be my poison of choice—bourbon—and joined us.

'So, what are we thinking?' asked Terry.

'Fifty-fifty Gabrielle Dennis is telling the truth,' said Victor. 'Though if she's lying, I'd put my all money on you making her crack on Monday.'

'That's a big "if",' she said.

There was a rap on the door. Victor's two secretaries were standing there. 'All right if we head out, Victor?' asked the blonde.

Victor nodded. 'Yes, thank you,' he told them. 'Have a good night.' They wished us all the same before turning on their heels to leave.

When they were out of earshot, Terry kidded, 'Do you *really* need two secretaries, Victor, or is it the male-power-trip thing I think it is?'

'Oh, it's definitely the male-power-trip thing,' he said, grinning. 'Sometimes one woman just isn't enough.' He started to laugh.

'Of course!' exclaimed Terry.

Victor and I both looked at her. *What?*

'I just figured out what we have to do on Monday,' she said.

Terry stood up from her chair, rubbed her temples, and began to explain. When she was finished, Victor had only one thing to say.

'What the hell are you two still doing in my office when you should be rehearsing?'

ON MONDAY MORNING, Terry stood up in the courtroom and informed Judge Lomax that she had no further questions for Gabrielle Dennis. 'Instead, Your Honour, I'd like to call Dr David Remler to the stand.'

Does he or doesn't he? 'I do,' I told the clerk with my right hand raised. The whole truth and nothing but.

Lomax motioned for me to be seated. Terry approached and, despite her game face, managed to give me a reassuring nod.

'You begged me to put you on the stand, didn't you, Dr Remler?' she started.

I smiled like I was supposed to. 'I don't know about begged,' I replied. 'It was more like *strongly urged.*'

The quip brought a smattering of laughter from the courtroom.

'Either way,' said Terry, 'I had no intention of having you testify. I mean, we've all seen those television law dramas where those crafty prosecutors trip up the innocent defendant.'

'Objection!' cried Hemmerson. 'That's a gross mischaracterisation.'

'That my client is innocent or that you're crafty?' cracked Terry.

'That's enough, Ms Garrett,' said Lomax.

'My apologies, Your Honour.' She walked a few steps towards the jury while still talking to me. 'The point I was trying to make was that up until Friday I felt we'd done a pretty good job of proving your innocence. That's why I made the decision not to have you testify.

But then we heard from a young woman named Gabrielle Dennis.'
She paused. 'Had you ever seen her before, Dr Remler?'

'No, I hadn't,' I said.

'There's no way she's the woman who became your patient—the
one claiming to be Samantha Kent—is there?'

'No, it's not the same woman.'

'So, seeing Gabrielle Dennis testify on Friday that she was involved with Conrad Birch during the time he told you he was having an
affair . . . well, that must have come as quite a shock,' she said. 'If
Gabrielle Dennis was not the patient who framed you, then who are
we supposed to believe? You or her?'

Terry sounded as if she was turning on her own client. It made my
response sound that much better. 'Actually, I think the logical choice
is to believe both of us.'

Terry cocked her head. 'How do you figure that?'

'I think the prosecution has done me a favour. They've treated me
as if I've been lying through my teeth from the very beginning. But
with Gabrielle Dennis, they proved I was telling the truth about
Conrad Birch, that he was, in fact, an adulterer.'

'Yes,' said Terry. 'But they're trying to suggest that because his
mistress wasn't your Mystery Patient, you have been lying.'

I looked at Terry. 'Really, the only thing the prosecution has proved
is that *one* of his mistresses wasn't my patient,' I said calmly.

'What are you suggesting, Dr Remler?'

I reminded myself of the advice Terry had given me. *Talk as if
you're at some shrink conference, David, instead of a courtroom.*

'As a psychologist,' I began, 'I've seen examples of both men and
women who've had more than one extramarital affair at the same
time. In the case of Conrad Birch, therefore, I'm not surprised by
Friday's developments.'

Terry pursed her lips and nodded. 'So, in other words, once you're
not a one-woman man, who's to say you're a one-*mistress* man?'

'Exactly,' I said. 'But what's also key is that, at least with the
patients I've treated, there's an utter reluctance to admit it.'

'Why do you think that is?'

'I see it as a societal boundary. While we frown on those who have
affairs, we have come to accept it as commonplace. To hear that
someone has cheated on a spouse rarely shocks us.'

'But the prospect . . .'

'Of two affairs simultaneously? The stigma is more than double.'

'But Conrad Birch sought your counsel. He told you about his affair. Are you saying such a stigma would prevent him from telling you about an additional affair?'

'The short answer is yes,' I said. 'Although in the case of Conrad Birch we have to remember the purpose of our meeting in the first place. He was concerned about ending a relationship with a woman who had a mean streak. Guilt never really came into play.'

'But again, the prosecution has claimed you've fabricated this whole story right down to your patient notes written nearly two years ago. What do you make of that?'

'It would mean I not only had tremendous patience in plotting a murder but was also the recipient of tremendous luck. I somehow guessed that Conrad Birch was having an affair.'

Terry again walked towards the jury box. This time she went all the way to the far end of it and turned round—as if she were the thirteenth juror. 'In other words,' she said, 'you're not only a psychologist but, unbelievably, a member of the Psychic Friends Network.'

There was a smattering of laughter from the courtroom. Terry looked at Judge Lomax. 'I have no further questions, Your Honour.'

Before she could even get back to her seat, Hemmerson had stood up and fired his first shot. 'Dr Remler, tell me, the knife used to fatally stab Conrad Birch over fifty times, who did that belong to?'

'If you're asking whether it was in my possession at the time of the murder, the answer is no.'

'That's not what I'm asking. Was it your knife, yes or no?'

'Yes.'

'Yes, it was your knife,' Hemmerson repeated. 'And the letter that clearly stated how your relationship with Conrad Birch was more than doctor and patient, and signed by Conrad Birch—a signature that no one in this courtroom disputes—where was it found?'

'I'm told it was found in my apartment,' I answered.

'I'm sorry, Dr Remler, is it now your contention that the letter was not found by the police in your apartment?' he asked.

'That's not my contention. That letter was found in my apartment.'

'You also don't deny you were at the scene of the crime, correct?'

'Correct.'

'That your alibi for not being the murderer is that you were coming to the aid of a patient—a woman you cannot prove exists, correct?'

I tried to keep my composure. 'Yes, that's right.'

Hemmerson did his own walk towards the jury. 'Now, if I understand you correctly, you'd like us to believe that Conrad Birch was the Don Juan of Manhattan, that he had a whole harem of women.'

'That's not what I said.'

'You're right, you suggested he was having more than one affair at the same time. That's an awfully convenient argument, don't you think?'

Terry objected. 'Argumentative, Your Honour.'

'Sustained,' said Lomax.

'Withdrawn,' said Hemmerson. 'The fact is, you can't prove Conrad Birch was involved with more than one woman any more than you can prove your Mystery Patient exists. Do you disagree with that?'

'No, I don't.'

'Dr Remler, are you aware that of the seventeen hundred and eighty-four stabbings reported in New York City last year, seventeen hundred and three of them were committed by men?'

'No, I didn't know that.'

'Yet, you claim it was a woman who must have stabbed Conrad Birch, correct?'

'Yes.'

'Despite the fact that over ninety-five per cent of all stabbings are perpetrated by men.'

'No, not despite. I've simply explained what happened the night Conrad Birch died—my version of the events that took place.'

'You certainly have, Dr Remler. And it's quite an *unbelievable* version at that.' He turned to Lomax. 'Nothing further, Your Honour.'

QUESTION: when is a tie the same as a win?

Answer: when your attorney says it is.

That's what I was hoping. Terry seemed pretty sure about it.

The two of us were sharing a cab heading back uptown. Terry was returning to her office and I was going home.

As the buildings passed my window in a blur, I couldn't figure how Terry managed to sound so upbeat in the wake of my testifying. Sure, I came across decent enough when she was asking the questions. She'd prepared me well, and I'd managed to remember my lines. But any twinge of optimism had all but disappeared with Hemmerson's cross-examination. I thought the guy had me for lunch.

'Not so,' said Terry. 'He rubbed your nose in the evidence, but there was nothing new to be learned. The jury's already heard it all.'

'What about that little statistic about men and stabbings?'

'It may be true, but it also plays right into our hand. You're being framed. Your Mystery Patient chose a murder method that points the finger at you and away from her. It's one more dot to connect in our closing argument.'

'I suppose that makes sense.'

'It definitely makes sense. More important, what stood out today was how Hemmerson didn't really go after you on the multiple-mistress angle. He danced around the thing but didn't touch the psychology of it. He knew it wasn't his turf. That means what we've got is a jury contemplating the very real and *reasonable* possibility that Conrad Birch had more than one affair going on.'

'So Hemmerson didn't have me for lunch?'

'Light snack, maybe,' she said. 'But you scored points too. That's why I called it a tie. And, let's face it, a tie is as good as a win.'

I looked at her. 'I was with you right up until "let's face it",' I said.

'It's all about expectations, David. When jurors watch a prosecutor go after a defendant, they're looking for the knockout. It's all about absolutes. You're either innocent or guilty, and in either case, the verdict has to be unanimous. By holding your own with Hemmerson, it's as if he's the one who failed.'

We'd had a full thirty blocks of conversation about the trial. I decided to change the subject.

'Is this was what you always wanted to do? Practise law.'

'I knew I wanted to be an attorney since I was twelve.'

'Sounds like you remember the exact moment.'

'I do. It's when I saw Paul Newman in *The Verdict*.'

I started to laugh. 'That's so weird.'

'Why?'

'Because I wanted to be a psychologist ever since I saw Judd Hirsch in *Ordinary People*.'

'Wow,' said Terry. 'Two impressionable young people letting Hollywood dictate their entire future.'

'What's pretty amazing is that we both followed through on it.'

'You have, perhaps. I've still got a ways to go.'

'What do you mean?'

'The big plan was that I was going to represent the poor,' she said.

'What happened to your plan?'

'Nothing. It's still there—just revised. As much as I want to do "low-income law", I realise I don't want to live like the people I'm representing. So the revised plan has me doing "high-income law" for about ten years. That should pay the bills for happily ever after.'

'I'm impressed.'

'Don't be. I haven't done it yet.'

'You will.'

Terry gave me an appreciative look. Eyes that said thank you in a very real way. In that moment we weren't lawyer and client.

The cab pulled up in front of the Chrysler Building.

'It's time to be brilliant,' Terry said. She was referring to the crafting of her closing argument.

'How much of it have you written?' I asked.

'About two-thirds.'

'That's good. You're almost done.'

'Yes, except the one-third remaining is the part that's supposed to make twelve people say "not guilty". Piece of cake.'

I went home, later climbing into bed that night without having a drink. At seven forty-five the next morning, my phone rang.

'Hello?'

'David, it's Terry.' Her voice was anxious.

'Is something wrong?'

'I'm not sure,' she said. 'I got a call five minutes ago from Judge Lomax. He wants all counsel to meet in his chambers at nine thirty. And he specifically asked that you be there as well.'

'What do you think the reason is?'

'I don't have a clue. I called Victor to let him know, and he has no idea either. The only thing Lomax would say was that something highly unusual has happened.'

PART IV
eleven

Judge's chambers. Nine thirty on the dot. All were assembled. I'd met Terry and Victor out in the hallway first. 'So, what's our best guess?' I asked.

'Can't imagine what it would be,' said Terry.

Victor glanced at his watch. 'Neither can I. But it's time to find out.'

We walked to Lomax's chambers. His door was open, and the three of us stepped inside. Lomax wasn't there, but already seated and waiting were Hemmerson and the two other prosecutors who'd been assisting him. A young man and woman.

'Hello, Glenn,' said Victor.

'Morning, Victor. Morning, Terry.'

Hemmerson turned to me with a slight nod. I took a seat on the couch to the side of Lomax's desk.

Judge Lomax entered his office. In one hand was a coffee mug, in the other an ominous red folder. He took a seat behind his cluttered desk and began making room for the folder. 'Are we all here?' he asked, head down and shuffling some papers.

'Yes,' said Hemmerson.

'Yes,' said Terry.

Lomax looked up. His eyes were searching, and immediately it became obvious who they were searching for. The defendant. When they found me, I tried to gauge his expression, but the old man was wearing one serious poker face. He hit a button on his phone and leaned in to the speaker. 'Eunice, could you come in here, please?'

A slender, grey-haired woman entered the office with a stenograph machine. She took a seat behind Lomax.

Said Lomax, 'I want there to be a transcript of this meeting due to the unorthodox nature of what's about to occur and the impact it will have on this case.' He tapped his fingers on the red folder.

What the hell does he have in there?

After giving Eunice a glance over his shoulder, Lomax began. 'For the record, the defendant, Dr David Remler, is present in addition to his counsel. Also present is the prosecution team.' He turned to me. 'Dr Remler, what I'd like you to do right now is describe for us physically the woman you claim was your patient. You've stated that she introduced herself as Samantha Kent, correct?'

'Yes,' I answered. 'Though she went by "Sam" with me.'

'And her physical description?' asked Lomax.

'She was around five foot six. Thin. Blonde hair, past her shoulders if worn down,' I said.

That's when Lomax opened the red folder. Barely. He slid his hand in and pulled something out. A colour Polaroid. He held it up to me. 'Dr Remler, is this the woman you described?'

'Your Honour!' exclaimed Hemmerson. 'With all due respect, what the hell is going on?'

'It will all become clear in a minute or two,' Lomax said.

I leaned forward and studied the photograph. It was of a woman standing on a street corner in daylight. She was thin, medium height, with blonde hair about shoulder length. Everything matched the description of my Mystery Patient except for one thing. It wasn't her.

'No,' I said. 'That's not the woman.'

'Are you sure?' asked Lomax. 'Take a good look.'

I already had. 'Yes, I'm sure that's not her.'

I could tell Victor and Terry didn't know how to react to my answer, though disappointment appeared to make the most sense. Had the woman in the photograph been my elusive Mystery Patient, my defence would've taken a considerable turn for the better.

Hemmerson's smile was more shaky than confident. Nevertheless the prosecution had obviously dodged a bullet.

But wait. There would be another shot.

Lomax returned the photograph to his red folder and took out a second one. This one wasn't a Polaroid. This photograph was square, maybe five by five. He held it up to me as he'd done the first time. I stared in disbelief.

Eureka. There she was. My Mystery Patient. Thin, medium height, blonde hair about shoulder length. Except this time it was definitely her. The fake Samantha Kent. Although the shot was taken at night, there was plenty of light around her. She was wearing a long black dress and a red shawl draped over her shoulders.

'Dr Remler?' Lomax tried again. 'Dr Remler?'

I needed to say something if only for Eunice and her stenograph machine. The transcript had to make official what everyone watching me had already gathered. 'That's her. That's definitely her,' I said.

The shock of seeing the photo quickly gave way to the perplexing realisation of where it had been taken. There she was, standing under a streetlamp before the steps leading up to the Metropolitan Museum of Art. Venue for the Kesper Society cocktail party. Which meant . . .

'What is it, Dr Remler?' asked Lomax. He was staring at me.

He obviously had picked up on my expression—a look of putting one and one together in my mind. Turned out, he knew exactly what I was thinking.

My Mystery Patient wasn't standing alone. Lomax revealed that the photograph in his hand was only half a photograph. The other half had been folded back. With a flip forward, the picture became complete. My Mystery Patient and me. Standing side by side.

How did Lomax get ahold of this? It was surely everyone's first question. There'd been a flip-flop in circumstances.

Hemmerson was no longer smiling. Cut to Victor and Terry. Their disappointment was now the look of marvellous opportunity. The defence of Dr David Remler had taken a turn for the better.

'Your Honour, I demand an explanation!' barked Hemmerson.

'First of all, calm down, Counsellor,' Lomax said. 'Second, listen to what I'm about to tell you without interrupting me.' He swung his eyes over to Victor and Terry. 'That goes for all of you.

'When I returned here to my chambers yesterday after court was adjourned, there was a FedEx envelope waiting for me. Judges don't normally open anything they're not expecting. However, the sender was listed as NYU Law School, where I'm a guest lecturer, so I opened the envelope. Inside was a photograph and a typewritten note.' Lomax pulled a piece of paper out of the folder. 'There was only one sentence, and it read as follows,' he said. '"Dr Remler is telling the truth."'

He continued: 'Naturally, the contents of this envelope gave me considerable pause, first and foremost because of where the envelope came from. Or at least where I thought it came from. I went about contacting several people I know at NYU Law School, none of whom had any knowledge of the envelope. Nor were they able to trace it to anyone on campus.

'That's when I called FedEx. According to the tracking number, the envelope was mailed from one of their midtown locations. Paid for in cash. Beyond that, there was nothing more they could tell me. So, at this time, I have no idea who the mailer of this envelope is.'

'Excuse me, Your Honour.'

Lomax threw Hemmerson a cold stare. 'What did I tell you about interrupting?'

Hemmerson apologised, and Lomax went on. 'Putting aside the anonymity of the sender, the primary issue for me, as it relates to the trial, is the consequence of my having seen this picture. Which is what I'm sure Mr Hemmerson wanted to interrupt me about. I showed two photographs to Dr Remler. Yet, I stated there was only one in the envelope sent to me.

'The reason for this is simple albeit unconventional. Before I can entertain a host of conspiracy theories, the law requires that I first assume Dr Remler is innocent. I also have to assume he had nothing to do with sending me this photograph. But if that's the case, what I can't rely on as proof, is Dr Remler's word.' Lomax picked up the first picture he showed me. The Polaroid. 'Which is why there's another photograph. In other words, I needed a control group.'

The guy had been testing me.

'Yesterday, not long after receiving the envelope, I had Eunice here go out on the street with an instant camera we keep in the office. I asked her to find and take a picture of a woman who fitted Dr Remler's description of his alleged patient. This way, I could know that Dr Remler, a man whose freedom lies in the balance, wasn't simply being an opportunist.' Lomax stopped and examined the shot briefly. 'I think Eunice did a very nice job, by the way.'

I glanced at Eunice as she recorded Lomax's compliment. She gave the slightest of smiles.

'You've now seen how I've utilised that photograph, as well as the one sent to me. You've also seen how Dr Remler responded. For some of you, my actions might challenge your sense of a judge's prerogative. While I'll give both sides an opportunity to register their opinion, please keep one thing in mind. From a legal standpoint, I've already done my homework on this.'

The judge leaned back in his chair and put his hands behind his head. It was the body-language equivalent of 'Bring it on'.

Hemmerson brought it first. He fired off question after doubting question. The key one was this: 'How do we know the defendant himself or someone representing him didn't mail you the picture?'

Terry gave me a quick stare to make sure I kept my mouth shut. While my instinct was to defend myself, we had the best possible person to defend us. The judge.

Said Lomax, 'While it's conceivable Dr Remler and/or his counsel sent me the picture, it begs the question as to why they waited until now. Because if you look closely, you'll see it wasn't taken recently. In fact, it was taken many months ago. Right around the time of Dr Remler's arrest.'

'Is there some kind of date printed on it?' asked Hemmerson.

Lomax shook his head coyly.

'Then how could you know that?'

'Because I happen to be a fan of Mark Rothko,' he said. 'You see that swath of red in the background? That's the banner for what was the Rothko exhibit. I know because I went to it—last October.'

And like that, Mark Rothko became my favourite artist of all time.

A stymied Hemmerson cut his losses on that angle and moved to another. 'Your Honour, be that as it may, your leeway as a judge in this situation also permits you to ignore the contents of the envelope.'

'It does indeed,' replied Lomax. 'The problem with that, however, is twofold. First, someone out there knows I received the picture. If I choose to disregard it, it doesn't mean everyone else will.'

Hemmerson squinted. 'Who else are you referring to?'

'The press, for starters. Who's to say they won't get the same anonymous envelope in the mail. Then what?'

Hemmerson was dumbfounded. 'How on earth could you let the threat of media exposure dictate your actions?'

Lomax shook his head. 'It's not the press that has me concerned. I said the problem with ignoring the envelope was twofold. It's the second fold that has me concerned.' He picked up the picture again. 'If this woman was indeed Dr Remler's patient, it means she's still at large. Hell, even if she wasn't his patient, she's still out there. Only by finding her will we know for sure. Whether she's a material witness, suspect, or innocent bystander, we need her to be found. Ignoring her doesn't make her go away.'

So much for dumbfounded. Now Hemmerson looked panicked. 'Are you suggesting what I think you're suggesting?'

'Yes, I'm suspending the trial. A further police investigation is needed. They might want to start by showing this photograph to Samantha Kent. The real one. Maybe she'll recognise the woman.'

'And if it turns out this whole damn thing was a hoax—or worse, some desperate attempt to prevent a guilty verdict, what then?' Hemmerson asked.

'Then we start again,' said Lomax.

'But don't you see? That's a win-win for the defence.'

'That's odd,' interjected Terry, clearly unable to resist at that point. 'I thought this was about justice, not who wins or loses. You don't win if you put the wrong person behind bars.'

Victor cleared his throat. 'Your Honour, I don't know what your intention is regarding the dismissal of the jury, but I'd like you to wait at least a couple of days.'

'What for?'

'So Samantha Kent can see the photo before the news media gets wind of the suspended trial,' said Victor. 'I'd hate to think this mystery woman would know something was up before we got a positive ID on her.'

It was a good point, and the judge knew it. 'I see,' he said. 'Does the prosecution have a problem with that?'

Hemmerson rubbed his temples. 'With all due respect, sir, on my list of current problems relating to this case, that one kind of pales in comparison.'

'I'll take that as a no,' said Lomax. He proceeded to act out a cough. 'I'm feeling a bit under the weather.' He turned to Eunice. 'Would you please instruct the bailiff that today's session will be cancelled due to illness?'

IT WASN'T QUITE a celebration that night, though it shared many of the same telltale signs. Smiles, jokes, laughs, drinks, and even a toast.

'To the Phantom Photographer!' said Victor, raising his glass.

We all readily drank to that. My drink happened to be of the Diet Coke variety. Victor, Terry and I had been joined by Parker and Stacy. We were camped out in the very swank Bar and Books down on Hudson Street.

In listening to Victor, I couldn't help saying the words over in my head. *The Phantom Photographer*. I speculated on who took the picture. And *why*? I had no doubt that sending the picture to Lomax was an attempt to help me, but it seemed unlikely that that was the purpose of taking the picture in the first place. What, then, was the motive for tailing me like that? Or was it even me who was being tailed?

Naturally, I wasn't alone in pondering these questions. From the moment we left the courthouse that morning, Terry and Victor were equally stumped. By dinner, the list of confounded included Parker and Stacy.

'So, how did Hemmerson react to today's events?' asked Parker.

'Not very well,' said Terry.

'Parker, you should've seen the way Terry and Hemmerson got into it towards the end,' said Victor. 'It was beautiful.' He picked up his glass. 'To Terry Garrett and her excellent work in "People versus Dr David Remler".'

'Hear, hear!' we all said. As we clinked glasses, I couldn't help watching Victor's hand give Terry's shoulder a squeeze. It immediately became the most overanalysed squeeze in history. Was it sexual? Just friendly? Sexual disguised as just friendly?

I was staring at Terry's shoulder—postsqueeze—when I felt something. It was her eyes. She was looking at me looking at her shoulder. I looked up and our eyes met. She smiled briefly, and I looked away like a nervous schoolboy.

We continued to talk, tell stories and laugh for a while longer. Stacy got Victor to pledge money to her women's crisis centre on behalf of his firm. In addition, Terry offered to throw in some pro bono work.

After joking that he and Stacy should leave before anyone changed their mind, Parker looked at his watch. 'Seriously, though, it is getting late.' He and Stacy stood up, and we said our goodbyes.

Then there were three. We continued to have a good time. Certainly there was nothing outwardly awkward about the situation, but I'd be lying if I said there wasn't a part of me that was determined not to leave the two of them alone.

As it turned out, it was Victor who left Terry and me alone. He'd spotted someone he knew towards the front of the bar. In his words, an 'old chum from law school'. 'Be right back,' he told us.

Then there were two.

'We're not, by the way,' Terry said.

'Excuse me?'

'Oh, *puleeeze*, Victor and me. We're not an item.'

'OK, maybe I was wondering a bit,' I admitted. 'So why are you telling me this, that you and Victor aren't an item?'

'I thought you wanted to know. Turns out I was right. Though now that I think about it, if Terry Garrett were to marry Victor Glass, I wouldn't have to get new monogrammed towels.'

'Do you actually have monogrammed towels?'

'No.'

'You also don't strike me as the type who would take another man's name.'

'Ah, that's where you're wrong.'

'Really?'

'If only for the children. A mommy and daddy should have the same last name.'

'So you want kids?'

'I do,' she said. 'Do you mind if ask you a personal question?'

'Go ahead.'

'Did you and your wife want children?'

As soon as she finished the question, she regretted it. All because of my expression. There was no way I could hide my discomfort.

'I should've known better,' she said. 'I'm sorry.'

'Don't be,' I told her. I took a breath. 'It's just that when my wife died, she was four months' pregnant.'

Terry grabbed her forehead. 'Oh God. David, I didn't . . .'

'Really, it's OK. How could you know?'

Still, she clearly felt awful. Her eyes began to well up. 'That was stupid of me.'

'C'mon, Garrett. Don't go Jell-O on me!' The line got a smile out of her.

'That's better,' I said. I was about to take another shot at levity when I happened to look down at my hand. To think I didn't even feel it. Her hand was on top of mine.

'Sorry,' she said, slowly lifting her hand. 'That was stupid of me.'

'What if I said it wasn't?'

She blinked slowly. 'Then I'd remind you that you're my client. It's like you and one of your patients. It's not ever supposed to happen.'

I immediately slouched. 'It almost did happen with me.'

'Your Mystery Patient? That was different,' she said. 'For all intents and purposes, you were seduced. She knew it would work because you were vulnerable, having lost your wife. She took advantage of you emotionally.'

Terry's last sentence launched a flashback. That guy. His theory. Tangible versus intangible—the true difference between men and women. I could see him so clearly. Pompous Nathan looking at me incredulously at Cassandra Nance's party. His question. *Can you honestly say that you've never been taken advantage of emotionally by a woman?* I guess I no longer could.

'Still,' I said to Terry. 'I feel like some pathetic guy who falls for any woman who gives him the time of day.'

She rolled her eyes. 'Wow, that makes me feel really special.'

'You know what I mean. Besides, you're the one telling me you're not interested.'

A coy smile. 'I never said that.'

'Oh, really?'

'I was merely pointing out the circumstances of our relationship.'

'You mean, attorney and client.'

'Exactly,' she said.

'You're right,' I said. 'It would be wrong. But maybe the only thing wrong is the timing.'

'Maybe. But I can't think about that—or, more specifically, you in that way—and represent you at the same time.'

'That settles it,' I said. 'You're fired.' I laughed before she could think I was serious. 'How about this? We'll make a deal. When this thing is over and, hopefully, I'm not heading off to jail, you and I have dinner.'

'I think we have a deal,' she said.

I extended my hand. 'Then we'll shake on it.'

Terry glanced over at the bar and put her hand in mine. When I squeezed, she pulled me forward.

'What are you doing?'

'Taking a chance,' she said.

We were face-to-face, inches apart. Terry leaned in and we kissed. I was stunned that she'd just done that. But I couldn't have been more happy about it. 'You do realise your boss is twenty feet away?'

'Keenly aware of it,' she said.

We both looked over at Victor, who had his back turned to us. His 'old college chum' turned out to be a fetching young blonde.

Terry shrugged. 'Well, there go my monogrammed towels.'

twelve

Limbo. There was no better way to describe the feeling. A measure of relief trying to fend off a greater measure of apprehension. As nice as it was not having to go to court, I couldn't help thinking how much harder it would be if I eventually did have to go back. Priority number one: not getting my hopes up too high.

Resuming some semblance of a life in the meantime—that was priority number two. The key to doing that was going back to work. Take my mind off my problems by focusing it on the problems of others. Fact was, I'd left all of my patients in limbo.

Which was why a good number of them had decided to leave me. While there were certain things New Yorkers could abstain from for a while, a weekly mental-health fix didn't seem to be one of them. So when the doctor was away, some of the patients did stray.

On the flip side, my remaining patients expressed a stronger faith in me than ever before, and I actually picked up a few new ones. Go figure. Despite returning to the Swiss-cheese schedule of appointments that had marked the early days of my practice, I was heartened that there weren't more holes than there were.

ON THURSDAY, at four o'clock, I looked up to see Mila poking her head into my office. Right on time. Instead of meeting every other Tuesday at five as we usually did, she'd asked if we could make a switch. She also wanted to turn it into a weekly meeting for a while because with my being out of the office, the bills and other business-related issues had piled up.

'No problem,' I'd told Mila. 'When do you want to do it?'

'How about Thursdays at four?'

'Sounds good.'

Her motive couldn't have been more transparent but I didn't care. Mila obviously thought that filling the hour my Mystery Patient had occupied was in my best interest. Maybe it was.

I waved her in. '*Rád te˘ vidím*,' I said.

She nodded with approval. 'It's good to see you too,' she said.

Ever since her testimony at the trial, Mila had felt terrible. She so much wanted to help me, and the mere thought that she couldn't drove her crazy. Worse, with the cutthroat and manipulating questioning by Hemmerson, her testimony had managed to hurt my case.

After I assured Mila a dozen times that she'd done nothing wrong, her guilt began to subside. She was able to ask me for an update without getting emotional. Until the update became news of my trial's suspension. There was no stopping her tears of joy on hearing that.

'What's going to happen now?' she asked.

'First, the police are showing the picture to Samantha Kent to see if she recognises the woman. Obviously, we hope she does.'

'What if she doesn't?'

'The police release the picture to the press. It's printed in every local newspaper and gets shown on every newscast. Odds are somebody out there will recognise her.'

'You would think so.'

'Of course, finding out who she is—that's one thing. Catching her might be another,' I said. 'She might be someplace far away.'

I looked at my watch. I realised that for the second day running I hadn't heard from Terry. She had told me she'd call once the police had visited Samantha Kent. They were going to show the picture to her at her new apartment. It was no surprise she'd moved to a new address, given what had happened at the old one.

In the meantime, there were some cheques to sign with Mila. In addition, there were some of my books to sign. *The Human Pendulum* had become a hot commodity for collectors. Scary to think how many were hoping that I'd be sent up the river. A guilty verdict would do so much more for the value of a signed copy than an acquittal.

At about a quarter to five, Mila left my office. As I started to pack up for the day, the phone rang.

'Good, you're still there.' It was Terry.

'I was starting to wonder if—'

'Yeah, I know,' she said. 'Apparently things took a little longer than planned.'

'But Samantha Kent was shown the picture, right?'

'Yes, she saw it. She didn't recognise the woman.'

'Damn,' I said. 'So, how come it took so long?'

'Your buddies, Trentino and Lopez decided they wanted to show it to some of the neighbours from the old town house as well as some of Birch's coworkers. I couldn't really argue with that.'

'No, it makes sense.'

'Unfortunately, no one recognised your Mystery Patient.'

'What now?'

'You're going to see the picture of her on your eleven o'clock news tonight. I wouldn't be surprised if it's the lead story.'

'Can I ask you a silly question?'

'No, David, you won't be in the picture.'

'How'd you know I was going to ask that?'

'Woman's intuition,' she answered. 'The photo will be cropped like it was when Lomax first showed it to us. The only difference is that it will be magnified and computer enhanced so it's clearer.'

'The police are doing that?'

'At our insistence, yes. Trentino and Lopez are still convinced you're guilty and that you're somehow behind the picture. But starting tomorrow the phone tips should start pouring in.'

'You really think so?'

'You'll see. The public loves a manhunt. Kidnappers, snipers, you name it. The fact that in this case it's a woman—and a good-looking woman at that—only makes it sexier.'

We ended the call by agreeing to speak the following morning. The last thing Terry explained was the wording the police were providing for the news media. My Mystery Patient was not to be labelled a 'possible suspect'. Rather, 'the authorities believe she might have valuable information regarding the death of Conrad Birch'. Yeah, like maybe why she killed him.

That night, sitting on the couch in my apartment, I tuned in to the late local news. There was a full-screen picture of my Mystery Patient with the phone number to call.

I undressed for bed, embracing the possibility that this was the beginning of the end. A happy ending. That's when I got the call.

'DID YOU MISS ME, David?' I stood there, stunned. It was my Mystery Patient. Late at night and calling me again. Only this time she sounded a lot more awake. 'Because I certainly missed you.'

I wanted to scream and curse, unleash my rage. She'd played me for a fool, and I'd played right along. Which was why I remained calm. Because I was being given a golden opportunity—to learn something about the fake Samantha Kent. And to get it on tape.

The minirecorder that Parker suggested I buy was right there in the drawer of my bedside table. I grabbed the recorder and lifted it to the top of the phone by my ear. I pressed my thumb and we were rolling.

'I take it you watched the news tonight,' I said.

'Oh, c'mon!' she scoffed. 'You're not going to scream at me?'

'It's tempting.'

'But let me guess, the shrink in you says not to, right?'

'Something like that.'

A sigh. 'Yes, I watched the news tonight,' she said. 'I've got to tell you, if I'd known I was being photographed, I would've smiled more.'

'I doubt you're smiling now, though.'

'David, you're either smarter than I gave you credit for, or you're the recipient of some incredibly dumb luck. I think it was the latter.'

'Call it what you want. The fact remains, you're going to have a hard time shopping at your local supermarket tomorrow.'

'I know, what a shame,' she said, laughing.

'You really think this is funny?'

'Why, you don't?'

'Actually, in a way, I find it kind of ironic,' I said. 'Being framed only to be saved by a picture.'

She snickered. 'Is that what you think you are? *Saved?*'

'Let's put it this way: I'd much rather be me right now than you.'

'I wouldn't be so sure, David. Life is full of surprises. People never know as much as they think they do.'

'Starting with your real name, in my case. You could fix that right now.'

'What, and spoil the mystery?'

'At least tell me this. Why me? Why set me up?'

'That's easy. Murder one-oh-one. The best way to cover your tracks is to lead everyone to somebody else. And who more *deserving* than the smug psychologist who turned Conrad against me?'

'What are you talking about?'

'You know what I'm talking about.' She lowered her voice, making it deep. '*My therapist thinks this affair is destructive. My therapist thinks I really should end this and try to fix my marriage.*'

This was an avalanche of revelation. The suspicion all along had proved right; my Mystery Patient was the mistress. Or at least one of two mistresses, if a certain witness was telling the truth at the trial.

What she'd told me was at once startling and familiar. It seemed that Conrad Birch had done what so many before him had done—pawned off the guilt of a difficult decision by blaming the therapist. The poor patient who's rendered powerless. Pushed into it. It was so common in my profession that we had a name for it, the Shrink Rap.

My Mystery Patient wasn't the only one who'd set me up. Conrad Birch had as well. And they'd both done an awfully good job of it.

She continued: 'Tell me, David, what's it like to have so much power over people's lives?'

'I should ask the same of you.'

'No. What I've done is simply give you a taste of your own slick medicine. I saw how you work first-hand, remember?'

'What? That I tried to help you, at least the "you" you pretended to be?'

'You were playing God, and a self-serving one at that,' she shot back. 'Do you move in on all your vulnerable female patients?'

'That wasn't part of your plan? To make me attracted to you?'

She snickered. 'Yes, it was very much part of the plan, but it worked because of something else I knew—that you're either too arrogant or ignorant to consider the consequences of what you do for a living. The oh-so-sacred advice you dispense as you sit in your little cocoon of an office, shielded from the real world. That's why you had no problem telling Conrad what you did.'

'I didn't turn him against you,' I insisted. 'He used me as his foil. He was trying to take the easy way out. I never told him those things.'

She snickered again. 'I love that you actually expect me to believe you.'

'You'd rather believe the guy who left you and went back to his wife? Think about it,' I said. 'Can you honestly tell me he never misled you up until that point?'

'He lied to me plenty of times. That's why I killed him.'

I glanced at the recorder in my hand, the tape spinning.

'That's right. He lied to you. Perhaps even more than you knew,' I said. 'You followed the trial, didn't you?' She didn't respond. 'Another woman came forward claiming she was the mistress. If she was telling the truth, it means he was lying to you that much more.'

'Even more of a reason to kill him then.'

'Yet you'd still take his word over mine?'

'It looks that way, doesn't it?'

'But what about—' I stopped. I realised I was trying to make a rational argument to someone who completely embodied the irrational. What was the point? I had what I needed. She'd basically admitted to everything. Irrational, yes. But the thought occurred to me quickly: *After being so clever, could she suddenly be so dumb?*

It was as if she'd read my mind. 'So, did you get all of it?' she asked.

'All of what?'

'You've got a lousy poker voice, David. You were recording the conversation, weren't you?'

'No,' I lied. 'I wish I were, though.'

She laughed. 'Even if you're lying, you're still telling the truth.'

'What's that supposed to mean?' I asked.

'It's like I told you, life is full of surprises. Want one more?' She paused. 'I'm not done yet. First, I took care of Conrad. Now it's time for that bitch of a wife he ran back to. Tonight, she dies.' *Click.*

So much for remaining calm. The last time I was on the phone with this woman, she told me she'd killed Conrad Birch. She may have lied about being married to him, but she sure was telling the truth about the killing part. Now she was telling me Samantha Kent was next.

The threat was real. It was as real as she was. Something the tape would prove once and for all. I pressed rewind and waited a few anxious seconds. I pressed Play and listened for the sound of her words. What I heard was a sharp, piercing whistle amid static.

In a fumbling panic, I rewound the tape further. I got the same sound; nothing of our conversation. I checked the batteries. Fidgeted with the volume. Ejected the tape and put it back in. I was running out of remedies. *Funny thing is, even if you're lying, you're still telling the truth.* I told her I hadn't been recording the conversation. I thought I was lying. I wasn't. The truth was, I hadn't recorded anything.

And she'd made damn certain of it. As to how, I didn't know yet.

I had asked myself the question: after being so clever, could she suddenly be so dumb? The answer was no. It was me who couldn't have felt more dumb.

'Nine-one-one emergency,' the operator said.

As soon as I made the call, I wondered: what the hell was I going to say? That a woman's life had been threatened by another woman, only I didn't really know who the second woman was, let alone the address of the first?

I hung up and ran to my kitchen, where I had Terry's home number written down on a pad. I looked at the clock on the stove. It was past midnight. After four or five rings, Terry answered. She'd been sleeping and was barely awake when I started to tell her what had happened. She was wide awake by the time I finished.

'Stay there by the phone, and I'll call you back.' She hung up.

Terry was off and running. Still, I felt little relief. Someone's life was in jeopardy and there was only so much I could do to help. Worse, what if it was already too late? What if Samantha Kent was already dead?

I sat on the bed. Five minutes passed. I leaned back against my headboard. Twenty minutes passed. I looked at the phone and willed it to ring. It didn't. A half-hour had gone by without hearing back from her. Good enough reason, I thought, to give her a call. I dialled and waited. She didn't answer. I got her machine. She'd gone to Samantha Kent's apartment.

I pushed back the thought—the fear, really—that Terry would be so foolish as to go alone. I left a message on her machine just in case.

Finally, the phone rang. I answered in a heartbeat.

'David, it's Terry. I'm at Samantha Kent's apartment building,' she said. 'Get over here.'

'Where is it?'

'Ten-thirty Park Avenue, on the corner of Eighty-fifth.'

'Terry, what happened?'

'I'll explain when you get here. Come as fast as you can and bring the tape recorder.' She hung up before I could say another word.

AT LEAST TWO BLOCKS before reaching Samantha Kent's apartment building, I saw the red-and-blue dance of flashing lights and assumed the worst. The lights belonged to a total of two police cars. As I got out of the cab, Terry and I saw each other almost simultaneously. She was inside the lobby, visible through the glass doors. Before I could go in, she came out and took me by the arm, pulling me to the side.

'Good news and bad news,' she said. 'The good news is nothing happened. No one tried to kill Samantha Kent tonight.'

I did a quick exhale. 'What's the bad news?'

'The same thing. No one tried to kill Samantha Kent tonight, and you've got two detectives inside thinking you cried wolf.'

'Trentino and Lopez think I fabricated this? How could they believe I made up that phone call?'

'The same way they believe you killed Conrad Birch,' she said. 'Did you bring the tape?'

'Yeah.' I reached into my pocket and pulled out the recorder. 'Like I said, she must have done something—used a device, maybe—because she knew I couldn't record her. All you hear is a high-pitched whistle.'

I pressed Play so Terry could listen to it. I watched her grimace at the shrill sound. 'She did something, all right.'

'Any idea what?'

'I don't know, but, generally, where there's a will there's a gadget.'

'Maybe the police will have an idea.'

She shook her head. 'This tape is strictly between us for now. It's the only copy. You never hand cops the only copy of anything.'

'We need to have it checked out though, don't you think?'

'Definitely. Tomorrow we'll get The Magnet on it. If he can't figure out what happened with the tape, he'll know someone who can.'

I handed it over. 'Why couldn't you fill me in over the phone?'

'Sorry about that,' she said. 'When I called you, Trentino and Lopez were over within earshot. I didn't want them to hear anything, good or bad.'

'How'd you get in touch with those two in the first place?'

'I didn't. Victor did.'

'You called Victor?'

'Didn't have to. He was lying right next to me.'

I froze. Terry laughed. 'Oh, you should've seen your face,' she said. '*Yes*, I called Victor—right after I hung up with you. I wanted him to be the one to call the police.'

'Why?'

'Because he's a better alarmist when need be. In fact, he's upstairs in Samantha Kent's penthouse trying to get her to consent to police protection.'

'Do you think she needs it?'

'Probably not. Given our killer's star turn on the eleven o'clock news, she's probably en route to a faraway place. That said, better safe than sorry.'

'I agree.'

'Yeah, except Kent has refused the protection.'

I was about to ask why, but I knew why. *I* was why.

'She thinks I killed her husband.'

'Yeah, the Mystery Patient idea was never really a big hit with her,' said Terry facetiously. 'Hence, her nixing the protection.'

'Still, can't the police do it anyway?'

'Not without consent. If anything, they'd rather keep an eye on you.'

'Let 'em.'

She smiled. 'You have to give a statement. Tell them what happened minus the part about you recording the conversation.'

'What if they ask if I did?'

'If they do, say yes. They'll ask if you have the tape with you and you can say no.' Terry patted her pocket where she put the recorder. 'This way you won't be lying,' she said. 'At that point, I'll step in and tell them we'll have to make a copy before we can hand it over.'

Two seconds later, Victor came outside. 'There you guys are,' he said. He looked at Terry. 'You holding the recorder?'

'Yep.'

'We'll get to the bottom of that tomorrow,' he said. 'I'm thinking The Magnet could probably help us.'

'I'm thinking the same thing,' said Terry. 'Any luck with Samantha Kent agreeing to the police protection?'

'That's a big no-go,' said Victor. 'Though the woman wanted to press charges for harassment, David.'

'That's ridiculous,' said Terry incredulously.

'No kidding,' he said. 'Though our detective friends were considering it. Speaking of which, if we're out here any longer, they'll think we're plotting something sinister.' He turned back towards the entrance. 'C'mon.'

Terry and I followed Victor inside the lobby of the building, where Trentino and Lopez were waiting. They looked extremely unhappy.

'Let's make this quick,' said Trentino with a pronounced scowl.

'If you'd like to make it really quick, Detective, we can skip it altogether,' Victor said with a sarcastic grin.

Lopez glared at me. 'You mean pretend the phone call never happened?'

'Oh, that's good,' said Terry. 'Because you certainly wouldn't want to reveal your bias in the investigation now, would you?'

I stood there watching the sparks fly. I knew it was late. So I began telling Trentino and Lopez what happened. The phone call and what was said—her wanting to kill Samantha Kent as well as why she set me up.

As the detectives listened, with Trentino taking notes, there was no snickering. Not a single expression of disbelief. When Lopez asked me whether or not I'd been drinking prior to getting the call, neither Victor nor Terry jumped down his throat. I answered that I hadn't been, and that was the end of it.

Then all hell broke loose. It started with the doors of the elevator opening, though that's not what everyone heard first. Rather, it was the yelling, her yelling. 'You son of a bitch!'

Samantha Kent was coming at me, finger pointed, screaming, calling me a murderer.

She was wearing a long robe, only socks on her feet. She yelled, 'I swear to God I'll kill you!'

Trentino and Lopez cut her off before she could reach me. The screaming became louder. '*Police protection? Ha! The only protection I need is from you!*'

I was shocked. We all were. The poised, stoic Samantha Kent from the courtroom had succumbed to raw emotion. The night's events had triggered her breaking point.

Trentino and Lopez began forcing her back towards the elevator. She disappeared into it with them and a hushed quiet resumed.

I walked home. I needed the air. I needed some space. I tried to focus on what I really needed. Some answers. More than ever, my Mystery Patient had left me wondering. Why did she call? Why did she tell me what she did? Why did she say she was going to murder Samantha Kent that night and not do it?

Given that her picture had been plastered on the local news, our killer wouldn't likely stick around the city. Perhaps the threat against Samantha Kent was just a reminder of how much control my Mystery Patient still had over me. Even in her absence, I remained her pawn.

The mere thought of that word brought me back to my days at Columbia and one of my psych professors, Dr Alvin Wexler.

An avid chess player, Dr Wexler held the game up as a metaphor for practically everything. Our hopes, our dreams, our fears, could be better understood through a better understanding of chess.

As I walked those last few blocks to my apartment, I found myself recalling something Dr Wexler had told me. I'd received a B minus on a case-study analysis I thought I'd nailed. I approached Dr Wexler, wanting to know why I hadn't received a higher grade.

'That's easy,' he told me. 'You only saw what was in front of you.'
When I asked what he meant, he asked me if I played chess.

'A little,' I lied.

'Ultimately, chess is played in your head and not on the board in front of you,' he said. 'If you only play what you see, you'll never win. The point is, to excel in chess, and in anything else for that matter, you have to imagine. You have to see beyond what's in front of you.' He eyed me closely. 'In other words, Mr Remler, your paper proved only that you'd read the case. But those who scored higher proved something more. That they'd read *into* the case. They used their heads and saw beyond the facts presented.'

I pushed through my building's revolving door and into the lobby. Walking by the doorman, who was fast asleep at his desk, I stepped onto the elevator and hit the button for my floor. All along, I'd been staring blankly at the chessboard. It was time to start using my head.

thirteen

A little over fourteen hours. That's how long it took. From the moment I stepped off the elevator to the moment I made that fateful determination.

The first three were spent copping barely enough sleep to get me through the day at the office—six sessions I didn't dare cancel. It wasn't until the end of the day that I managed any answers. One big answer, really. I was being set up again.

My Mystery Patient had every intention of killing Samantha Kent. She'd merely lied about when. She also had every intention of making me the prime suspect. Again. The night before was all about laying the groundwork. She calls. I cry wolf. Everybody comes. The wolf's not there. Everybody goes home.

Those were the facts. That was the chessboard—there for everyone to see. Except now I was on to her game. I saw the move to come. It was the one in which Samantha Kent turns up dead . . . and everybody comes looking for me.

No, I told myself. I wasn't going to let it happen.

All along I'd done the expected. The right and rigid mind of a psychologist. That's what made me an easy mark. I was so predictable.

Except this time I'd come up with a crazy idea. Something I'd never normally do. Which was exactly why I decided to do it.

I DIALLED from my office. The phone rang a half a dozen times before someone picked up. 'Ten-thirty Park Avenue,' said the man.

'Yes, hi, this is Fiorillo Florist over on Madison,' I said. 'We've got a delivery for one of your residents, her name's Kent . . . Samantha Kent. Could you please tell me if she's at home right now?'

The question threw the guy off balance for a second. He cleared his throat. 'This is the doorman. Whatever you've got for her, drop it off and I'll make sure she gets it.'

'My customer insisted that this be hand delivered.'

'We don't give out information on our residents.'

'Sure, I understand,' I said. 'Here's the thing, though. This customer of mine plopped down three hundred bucks on the bouquet, and he doesn't want it sitting around. So, I tell you what, just let me know if she's home right now. If so, I'll send someone over, and you can take it from there.'

A heavy sigh. 'Yeah, she's here,' he said.

It was all I needed to know.

The next call was to Hertz. Early evening on a Friday meant limited availability. Fifteen minutes and a ridiculous day rate later, I was behind the wheel of a beat-up white Hyundai Accent.

My destination was Ten-thirty Park Avenue. Home to Samantha Kent and her penthouse apartment. Where I knew she was.

The rest was simple. Find a parking space, across the street from her building, that offered a good view of the entrance. Then sit, watch and wait.

Actually, there's never been anything simple about finding a parking space in Manhattan. The one I got took forty minutes of being double-parked with my hazards on. The car leaving happened to be the one I was blocking.

With the engine off, I made a quick call from my cellphone to the doorman. Chances were slim that Samantha Kent had left while I was in transit, but I had to make sure she was still there. She was.

My weekend plans were settled. If Samantha Kent was heading out, I was following her. If she wasn't, I was staying put. Either way, I'd still need to eat, but I was in the takeaway capital of the world. With a little explaining over the phone, the city was my menu.

All the same, I ate light. The last thing I wanted was to be off searching for a bathroom when Samantha Kent decided to go out. Or, worse, when my Mystery Patient decided to drop by. I was betting that she would come to kill Samantha Kent.

After eight hours in the Hyundai, that aching, no-sleep joint pain had settled in, as had the boredom. Worst of all, I was beginning to question what the hell I was doing.

Part of it was stubbornness, part of it a gut feeling. Mostly, it was because if I wasn't doing this, I'd be doing nothing.

Dawn. With it came a calculated risk. A nap. Two hours to try to offset the effects of the previous twelve. The word 'refreshed' didn't really come to mind when I awoke. However, I was in good enough shape to carry on.

At nine thirty a cab pulled up. Cabs were tricky. It was difficult to see who was getting out of them. I craned my neck to get a glimpse of the new arrival. It was a man. I watched as he—

Out of the corner of my eye. Walking towards the entrance. Big black sunglasses. Large shoulder bag. A long raincoat with a high collar. She was looking straight ahead. Inconspicuous. Incognito.

No one would've recognised her. Including me. Were it not for one thing. The Yankees cap. Grey flannel. The same cap she had on in my office that first day. My Mystery Patient had come to make her move. And I was going to stop her.

My hand swung towards the Hyundai's door, blindly reaching for the handle. I barrelled out of the car, my eyes fixed on her as she was turning into the building's entrance. She was all that I saw. Until it was too late.

I had tunnel vision. What I really should've had was oncoming-traffic vision. I heard the screeching skid of tyres, and the rest was a blur. The front of the van, the impact, the road. When I opened my eyes again, I was flat on my back looking up at an overcast sky. Then came the pain, in a continuous loop from my knees to my hips. A couple of people came rushing over, no doubt asking me if I was OK. But I couldn't hear them. Another person joined the circle hovering over me. A young man, the driver of the van.

My muddled gaze travelled down from his face to something he was wearing. It was a smock, 'Maxine's Bouquet' written across the chest. Irony of ironies. I'd been hit by a florist.

I saw the person standing next to him. The doorman from Samantha Kent's building had come out to see what had happened. Like the others, he was staring down waiting for me to move.

The sight of him sucked the fog out of my head in an instant. The woman in the Yankees cap. My Mystery Patient. She was on her way to Samantha Kent's apartment. And I wasn't. At least, not yet.

Faster than you can say 'TV evangelist', I jolted up and climbed to my feet. *Hallelujah.* Not really. It may have looked like a miracle, but it sure didn't feel like one. The pain was excruciating, yet I was off just the same, pushing past people and straight into the entrance of Ten-thirty Park Avenue.

'Hey!' I heard behind me. While everyone probably wanted to know where I was going, there was one man who *needed* to know. The doorman. Between a sprint and a hurried walk was my limping jog—right through his lobby.

I reached the elevators and smacked the Up button. Call it a break, one of the doors opened immediately. I took a glance over my shoulder. The doorman was heading right for me. I pressed PENTHHOUSE and the door began to close. In the last second, I caught a glimpse of the doorman arriving too late. His face was very pissed off.

Up went the elevator. A moment to catch my breath—and to realise again how much pain I was in. The elevator door opened.

I saw a square hall, sparsely decorated. No one there. I got off the elevator and listened. There were two apartments, three o'clock and nine o'clock. Hearing nothing, I started left, when over my shoulder I heard a crash. I turned on my heels and rushed to the opposite door.

It's going to be locked. But it wasn't. A twist of the knob and I was in. I heard a scream, raw and guttural. There was grunting and what sounded like gasping for air. It was coming from down the hallway in front of me. As fast as I could, I ran past a kitchen and a dining room. The noise—the struggle—getting louder as I got closer. Until it was right in front of me.

What I saw first was the knife. The long, steel blade, raised in the air and angled straight down. It was trembling. *They* were trembling. Standing toe to toe, Samantha Kent fending off the downward thrust of my Mystery Patient. Their arms were extended, locked at the elbows, but only Samantha Kent's legs were buckling. She was fighting a losing battle.

Do something, David. Head down, I charged across the room and tackled high. Her Yankees cap went flying. So did the rest of her. As we tumbled and headed towards the ground, I tried to spot the knife. Had it dropped? Was it still in her hand? I couldn't see it.

I also couldn't see the wall. I careened into it. On the heels of being knocked by that delivery van, the feeling was agony. The knife was lying on the ground maybe a yard away. But so was my Mystery Patient. She rolled left, then right, woozy from our collision.

Get the knife, David. I pushed off the wall and onto my knees. I was dizzy. The room was spinning. Wait—there were *two* knives in front me. Two of everything, double vision. Two knives—one real, the other not. How fitting. Unfortunately, it was the fake Samantha Kent who knew which one was real.

Her body stretched, and her hand reached. I couldn't stop her. She started to get up. Like a punch-drunk fighter, I did the same. I was back to seeing one of everything again. My Mystery Patient was standing before me with the knife gripped in her hand.

She lunged, but it wasn't a lunge. It was a bullet ripping through her. Fired from a gun held tightly in the hands of Samantha Kent.

The body of the woman I'd once known as my patient went rigid. Then it went limp. She fell to the ground as the blood seeped from her stomach. It was soaked up like a sponge by a beige carpet, and for the first time, I noticed we were in the living room.

My Mystery Patient was dead.

As soon as Samantha Kent pulled the trigger and quite possibly saved my life, she collapsed to the floor. I thought maybe she'd been stabbed while defending herself, the loss of blood finally taking its toll. But as I rushed to her side there was no blood to be seen. My best guess was that she'd fainted.

'Freeze!' Man, did that ever sound familiar. Slowly, I turned to face two cops with their guns drawn, and slowly I put my hands up—and kept them there.

Right behind the two cops were two paramedics. They all thought they were responding to an accident, a guy hit by a delivery van. They didn't expect to arrive on the scene and learn from a ticked-off doorman that said guy had decided to make a mad hobble up to the penthouse. Of course, that was nothing compared to their hearing the gunshot while stepping off the elevator.

So there I was. One dead woman, one unconscious woman, and me. *I can explain everything, officers . . .*

Luckily, I didn't have to. As one paramedic confirmed the death of my Mystery Patient, the other waved some smelling salts under Samantha Kent's nose. She came to. She was shaky, groggy, and a little dizzy, for sure. But she was also something else. Thankful.

Samantha Kent rose gingerly to her feet. As tears began to trickle down her cheeks, she walked over to me. I lowered my arms while the cops lowered their guns. The woman who earlier had screamed that she wanted to kill me, now wanted to hug me.

'Thank you,' she said softly.

I hugged her back. 'Thank *you*.'

She squeezed a little tighter, and I nearly fainted from the pain in my rib cage. The paramedics made it clear there was a hospital and an X-ray machine in my immediate future. But even more immediate was the cops' need to figure out what had happened.

We went into a study, away from the grizzly image of death sprawled on the beige carpet. That's where Samantha Kent did her best to explain. Beginning with the phone call she'd received the day before.

It was from a woman claiming to work in the Human Resources Department of Conrad Birch's firm. The woman said she needed the spousal signature on some documents so the final dividends from Birch's 401(k) money could be paid out. She offered to come by Samantha Kent's apartment the next morning since she herself lived not too far away. A time was set. Nine thirty, Saturday morning. Like that, my Mystery Patient was in.

'She looked so normal when I opened the door,' said Samantha Kent. 'I led her back to the living room and offered to make coffee.' She started to tear up again. 'I never even made it to the kitchen.'

Prompting her to turn round was what she described as a rustling noise. 'It wasn't loud or anything, yet for some reason it made me glance over my shoulder. Thank God I did.'

What she saw was the woman pulling a large knife out of her shoulder bag. 'Then the next thing I knew she was charging right at me.' Samantha Kent shuddered as if reliving the moment. 'The rest was a blur. Somehow I was able to grab her arm as she tried to stab me. Reflexes, I guess. It wasn't like I had time to think.'

She described the way she tried to fight off the woman. She remembered thinking she was going to die. 'I wasn't as strong as she was. I didn't know how much longer I could hold her off. And then . . .' She couldn't finish the sentence.

I finished it for her. 'That's when I showed up, I guess.'

The cops turned to me. Up until that point they hadn't made the connection. 'You're that psychologist,' said one of the cops, his finger pointing. I watched the other cop as he looked at Samantha Kent. He didn't say anything, though I could tell what he was thinking. *And you're that murdered guy's wife*.

Putting it together, both turned in the direction of the living room, where the paramedics were assisting the guys from the morgue. Almost in unison, they asked the same question. 'And is she . . . ?'

I nodded. 'Yes,' I said. She was her. My Mystery Patient.

I began to explain how it happened that I was there. Hearing myself talk, I realised how unbelievable it must have sounded. When I finished, the looks were priceless. They knew I had to be telling the truth. Who on earth could ever make something like that up?

One of the cops cracked a joke to that effect, and in the first real moment of levity, everyone allowed for a brief chuckle. Laughing hurt like hell, and there was no way to hide it.

'You should really go to the hospital,' Samantha Kent said.

The cops agreed, saying they could fill in their report later. They called to the paramedics in the living room, who came to the study.

'We'd like you to go as well, Ms Kent,' said one of them.

She'd have nothing to do with it. 'I'm OK,' she said. 'What I'd really like is to answer any further questions you might have, officers. Then I'm going to pack a suitcase, check into a nearby hotel and call my estate agent. Would any of you gentlemen like to buy an apartment?'

Her tone, calm yet determined, left little doubt that she was OK. Despite her brush with death, what was clearly evident was a desire to put not just the events of that morning behind her but everything that had led up to it. She'd lost her husband and had to contend with a murder trial in which his infidelity was discussed openly. If finally getting on with her life meant having to pull the trigger herself on his killer then so be it. One thing for sure, I was incredibly grateful she owned a gun.

'Sorry, sir, it's mandatory.' That was the response to the expression on my face as a stretcher was brought into the apartment for me. I climbed aboard and let the paramedics strap me in.

'Can you do me a favour?' I said to one of the guys as we wheeled towards the ambulance. 'See that white Hyundai over there, can you grab the keys from the ignition?'

'No problem,' he said. 'Lock it up, too, right?'

'Sure, thanks,' I told him.

X-rays at Lenox Hill Hospital showed three broken ribs. 'A hat trick,' claimed the doctor who examined me. 'Avoid comedy clubs, Shiatsu massages, and all middleweight title fights.'

'There's nothing that you can do?'

'Nothing the body doesn't do better and faster by itself.'

'What about the pain?'

'That I can do something about. Wait here and a nurse will get you a Percodan prescription.'

'Here' was a curtained-off area of the emergency room. I realised I should probably get in touch with a few people and fill them in. That's when I realised I'd left my cellphone back in the Hyundai. Good thing the car was locked after all.

The need to pester a nurse for a phone was instantly abated by a familiar voice right outside the curtain. 'Paging Dr Remler . . . '

'C'mon in, Parker.'

And Stacy right behind him. They manoeuvred round the curtain. 'What the hell were you thinking?' asked Parker, only half kidding. Stacy kissed me on the forehead. 'My hero!' she gushed.

I filled them in on what had happened. They could hardly believe it. Then I asked how they'd heard.

'Terry called me,' said Parker. 'She should be here in a moment.'

'How'd she know?'

'A reporter buddy of Victor's was monitoring the police band looking for tomorrow's story. He found it. He called Victor, who's in Connecticut playing golf. Victor got in touch with Terry.'

As if on cue, she poked her head round the curtain. 'Thank God!' she said. She was clearly more than my lawyer at that moment, and I watched as Parker and Stacy pretended not to notice.

I told the story over again to Terry. Parker and Stacy hardly minded. Even after hearing it for a second time, they still couldn't get over it. Neither could I. It was one thing to have the idea, to think I'd finally got inside the head of my Mystery Patient. It was another to find out I was right.

'So after all this, who was she?' asked Stacy.

I'd been wheeled out of Samantha Kent's apartment before the determination could be made. 'You'd think she'd have some identification on her,' I said. 'Maybe not.'

'Either way, we'll know soon,' said Terry. 'I'll make some calls in a little bit.'

Half of me wanted her to make those calls right away. The other half reassured me that after waiting this long, a little longer wouldn't kill me. An interesting choice of words given the morning I'd had.

So, for a bit more time, my Mystery Patient would remain a mystery. The difference now being that I was certain she had no further moves to make. It was a terrific feeling that I could sum up in one word. Checkmate.

There was just one problem, though. Something I didn't know.

There was more than one game being played.

fourteen

Her name was Haley Morgan. Age thirty-two. Only child of Adam and Shirley Morgan. Both deceased. Lived by herself in a studio apartment in Chelsea. She did a few small acting jobs and some modelling, mainly catalogues. In lean times—which was most of the time—she worked as an office temp. That was the hook. A little over two years before, she'd been assigned for a few months to a Wall Street investment firm. The same firm where Conrad Birch worked.

End of story. At least as far as the papers were concerned. In the twenty-four hours after my leaving the hospital—and in between a steady diet of Percodan and sleep—I took it all in.

'But there's more, isn't there?'

I looked across the table and watched Terry react to my question with a knowing smile. Two days after the fact, and we were having our agreed-to 'when this whole thing is over' dinner.

'Yes, there's more. The press haven't got ahold of her rap sheet yet. Two priors. One for cocaine possession, the other for theft of a doctor's prescription pad,' she said. 'Sad thing is, Haley Morgan was a smart girl. Graduated from Vassar.'

'Did you get all this extra stuff from The Magnet?' I asked.

'No, from her actual police file. As you might imagine, those guys are pretty tail-between-the-legs on this one. The more they feed us, the less we'll rub their noses in it publicly.'

'Any chance you'll hear from Trentino and Lopez?'

'The same chance you will,' she said. 'Somewhere between slim and none. That reminds me, though. Victor mentioned he was going to call you. Did you hear from him?'

'Yes, a congratulatory call. He told me what I did took guts, and I told him that "stupidity" was probably a better word. We settled on "tenacious". In the end, however, it was semantics. As Victor put it, all that mattered was the result.'

'He wrote Samantha Kent a note on behalf of the firm. I think that was a nice touch.'

'I agree. What did the note say?'

'I don't know. She almost didn't get it. Victor had it messengered, only to find out she's not living in her apartment any more. After some coaxing, a doorman revealed she'd checked into the Drake.'

'She did say something about going to a hotel. Can't blame her.'

The restaurant was the Blue Water Grill down in Union Square. Live jazz and fresh seafood. I went with the pan-roasted mahi mahi, while Terry opted for the lobster. She filled me in on her recent chat with The Magnet. She'd asked him how Haley Morgan was able to prevent me from recording our telephone conversation.

Explained Terry, 'It's called a sprayer. It's this small device that emits a high-frequency pitch preventing the magnetic recording of any fibre-optic transmission. Anthony said that while they're relatively new, they're available on the Internet.'

'What isn't? Nonetheless, it strikes me as odd that Haley Morgan would know about a device like this, let alone have one,' I said.

'There's something else,' Terry said. 'Apparently Anthony did a little checking on his own into Haley.'

'So, what did he turn up?'

'Perhaps a better understanding of her motivation. About a year ago, Haley had an abortion.'

It might explain why Haley hated him so much. Also, why she chose to make a child the centrepiece of her deception.

Still. 'It might not have been Conrad's kid,' I pointed out.

'There's always that possibility,' said Terry. 'The far greater possibility, however, is that it was.'

'This is something Samantha Kent should never know.'

Our plates were cleared and the table brushed free of crumbs. A touch of symbolism, perhaps, since it was about then that Terry and I realised this was supposed to be a date and not a debriefing session.

She was no longer my lawyer. I was no longer her client.

The conversation moved from the past to the future. The two of us.

Terry tackled my widower status head-on. She had no problem discussing my emotional connection to someone else, and what could've been a minefield in our relationship turned out to be the most meaningful exchange we'd had so far. For the first time I was able to talk about Rebecca without going on autopilot. I was sharing with Terry the one event in my life that had affected me more than any other.

Watching her listen to me and then follow up with the right questions, I knew she understood this was a part of who I was. I knew I was finally ready to move on with my life.

I held Terry's hand as we walked a few blocks after leaving the restaurant. I didn't let go during the cab ride back to my apartment. We kissed in the elevator. We kissed outside my door.

We stood facing each other in my bedroom. 'I haven't done this for a few years,' I said.

She started to unbutton my shirt. I started to unbutton her blouse.

She undid my belt and said, 'Would you like me to draw a diagram or something?'

I unzipped her skirt. 'No, the mechanics I remember. It's the nuances I might be a little rusty on.'

She reached back and unfastened her bra. It fell off her shoulders.

She was beautiful. Radiant. She gently pressed her body against mine, whispering in my ear. 'I think this is going to be good,' she said.

THE WORD HAD GOT OUT, and out of the woodwork they came—the people from my not-too-distant past who'd kept their distance.

There were the former patients who wanted to return. There were the tenants in my building who no longer had to look away when walking by me. Then there was my esteemed literary agent, Debra Walker Coyne. To be fair, she'd had no aversion to talking to me during the whole ordeal. She'd phoned to discuss business and each time she'd asked how I was doing and expressed her support. Nonetheless, I couldn't help harbouring a cynical suspicion that she had it all worked out in her head. Guilty or innocent, I was a good book in the making.

Cut to the Grill Room at the Four Seasons. Her usual table.

'So, how's my favourite best-selling and now truly famous author doing?' said Debra, standing up to give me a kiss on the cheek.

While there'd be no jail-cell memoir, my next project would still fetch a handsome advance. Supremely conscious of my six-figure legal tab, I grudgingly accepted her offer of lunch that Friday.

'Good to see you, Deb.' I sat down and unfolded my napkin.

She leaned in. 'I knew there was no way you could've stabbed someone fifty times over,' she said matter-of-factly. 'That's why your next book has got to be about this whole experience.'

'I'm not sure this is something I really want to capitalise on.'

As if to change the subject, while making sure to stay right on it, she asked me about some of the players involved. The detectives, my lawyers, the grieving widow. Most notably, she was curious about Haley Morgan, my Mystery Patient.

I told her what I knew, which wasn't much. Even less, given that I kept the information about Haley's abortion to myself.

Debra frowned. 'Did you at least find out if the police discovered anything where she lived?'

'Like what?'

'If you want to know the truth about a woman, all you have to do is rummage through her closets.'

'I don't think that's an option.'

'Maybe, maybe not. But you really should enquire with the police. I'll bet you they've gone through her apartment.' Debra continued, 'This woman nearly ruined your life, David. Just from a professional standpoint, aren't you the least bit curious about her?'

We ordered and ate, and all along Debra kept up the pressure on my writing about the ordeal. As she paid the hefty bill for lunch, I figured the least I could do was promise her I'd think about it.

After saying goodbye, I began walking uptown along Park Avenue. *Just from a professional standpoint, aren't you the least bit curious about her?*

The more I walked, the more Debra's words echoed in my head. She'd asked a good question. I'd asked the same question myself. Repeatedly. Only to suppress the answer every time.

But no longer. As much as I wanted to leave Haley Morgan behind and get on with my life, I now realised I couldn't. She may have been dead, but like it or not, her impact was living on. And it didn't take a rocket scientist to figure out why. No, it took a psychologist.

Haley had singled me out and made me her victim. The incredible anger I felt because of that had blocked any other emotion I might have felt for her. With her gone, however, the anger was starting to dissipate. Regret was creeping in.

If only she'd been my patient for real. If only Haley Morgan had come to me as Haley Morgan. Maybe she couldn't have been helped. All I knew was I'd never know for sure. Which was precisely what was consuming me at that point. Because I wanted to know something more. Until I did, there'd be other words echoing in my head as well. *No one can have more control over your life than you do.*

What happened to me from the moment Haley walked into my office had proved otherwise, to put it mildly. Sure, on the surface, I'd assumed control again. But deep down my grip felt tenuous. As tenuous as my understanding of Haley.

She was *still* my Mystery Patient—and until I changed that, there'd always be a part of me that felt helpless.

I came to a corner and a DON'T WALK sign. As I stood there waiting,

I happened to glance over at some benches in front of an office building. Sitting on one were two older men staring at what was between them. A chessboard. I took out my cellphone and dialled Ethan Greene in the D.A.'s office.

ETHAN GREENE looked at me as if I had three heads.

'Do you realise what you're asking me to do?' We were at a bar near Rockefeller Center.

'Yes,' I said. 'A favour.'

'No, you're asking me to break the law.'

'It's a small fracture at best.'

'Since when did you become the legal expert?'

'Since you dragged my ass into court to help you win your case.'

Ethan took a sip of his beer. 'Assuming for a second I get you into her apartment, what is it you intend to do?'

'I just want to look around for something that can help me better understand what motivated this woman.'

'Her own words weren't enough for you?'

'I just have a feeling there's more to know.'

'What are you telling me, this is a hunch?'

'Not quite that random. I spent a lot of time with her,' I said.

'Yes, as she was pretending to be someone else.'

'I realise that, but I have to believe parts of her—the real her—managed to slip through. I just want to know what those parts are.'

'But what if you're wrong? What if there's nothing more to know?'

'If that's what I find out, fine,' I said. 'It's the not knowing either way that's bothering me.'

'OK,' Ethan said. 'But you didn't get the key from me. You'll have it, but it won't touch my hands at any time.'

I thanked him profusely and asked when I could be expecting it.

'Tomorrow, two days tops.'

The next morning, a little after nine, there was a loud knock on my door. I opened it to see a bike messenger with dreadlocks. He asked me if I was Dr Remler. I told him I was. He gave me a small manila envelope and was off.

Inside the envelope were two keys and an address. One key was for the entrance to Haley's brownstone and the other for her apartment.

The cab dropped me off on Eighteenth Street, between Ninth and Tenth avenues. I unlocked the brownstone's heavy glass door and strolled in as if I lived there. I headed up the stairs.

Arriving on the second floor, I saw a web of yellow tape. The message was loud and clear: keep out. Quickly, I took out a pair of latex gloves from my pocket. It wasn't as if anyone had any reason to be taking fingerprints. Still, on they went.

I walked up to Haley's door, manoeuvred round the yellow tape and slid the key into the lock. With one twist I entered her apartment. It was a small studio.

I stood in the middle of the room and did a three-sixty. A bed, a bookcase, a chest of drawers, a sofa and a kitchen. Scattered clothes, magazines and a shelf of books. All novels, beach reads mainly.

I checked Haley's closet. Suitcases and shoeboxes crammed the shelf above the crush of hanging clothes.

I began to think of my conversation with Ethan. *But what if you're wrong? What if there's nothing more to know?*

Word for word, I remembered my answer. *If that's what I find out, fine. It's the not knowing either way that's bothering me.*

I wondered if I could just walk away now and never look back? To my surprise, the answer was *yes*.

I took a breath, and headed for the door. I was simply going to walk away. But just for the hell of it, I took one look back.

The next thing I knew, I was on an airplane.

THE SEAT-BELT sign lit up, and the captain announced that we were starting our descent. The temperature in Atlanta, he said with typical cockpit-calm, was seventy-two degrees.

On the way to the airport I'd made the call on my cell, posing as a telemarketer. I asked if her name was Evelyn Stark. She said it was. She also said she wasn't interested in whatever it was I was selling, and hung up.

I'd got what I needed. Confirmation. The knowledge it was her, Evelyn Stark. *Haley's birth mother*. Haley was indeed adopted, just like she told me. Only when she told me, she was posing as Samantha Kent.

It had become clear with a card. A Hallmark card with flowers and the words 'For My Daughter' on the front. It was inside a yellow envelope, a corner of which was peeking out from beneath a jewellery box on Haley's chest of drawers. When I was looking from a few feet away, it was barely visible. When I was looking back from the doorway of her apartment, it was practically neon.

The message inside was brief.

To my daughter Haley,
   It means so much that you've found me after all these years.
Thank you for forgiving me. I won't tell anyone what you've
told me.
   Love, Evelyn

Immediately, I'd flashed back to the conversation with Haley about
her mother, my describing how making contact could be a good
thing. Again, real advice for a real situation in an otherwise complete
lie. But what amazed me was the idea that it was such a paradox. The
warmth of reconnecting with her birth mother amidst the brutally
cold murder of Conrad Birch. Not to mention my being framed for it.

Then there was the last line on the card. *I won't tell anyone what
you've told me.* Had Haley really discussed what she'd done? It
seemed so unlikely. Then so did her taking my advice. All I knew for
sure was I'd be leaving Haley's apartment the same way I arrived.
Wanting to know more.

And pointing me in the right direction was the front of the envelope in the upper left-hand corner, a return address sticker.

Ms Evelyn Stark, 114 Traeger Mill Road, Griffin, GA 30224.

Three-plus hours and one Delta Shuttle later, I was renting a car at
the Atlanta airport. The free map at the counter got me to Griffin. A
gas station attendant got me right to the house, a tiny ranch.

She opened the door. 'Ms Stark, my name is Dr David Remler.' It
took only one look at her to know the woman standing before me in a
worn, faded blue robe had the hardened gaze of someone who had
nothing left to fear. This was the woman who'd put Haley Morgan up
for adoption. 'Ms Stark, I'm here about your daughter, Haley.'

She squinted. 'What kind of doctor?'

'I'm a psychologist.'

'Haley never said anything about a psychologist. Is she a patient of
yours?'

Present tense. She had no idea Haley was dead.

'Ms Stark, I'm afraid I have some horrible news for you.'

A cold stare remained fixed on me as I told her. Initially, there was
no reaction. She stood still, unblinking. Finally, she asked when it happened and where. 'Last week and in Manhattan,' I said. She nodded
and fell silent. I expressed how sorry I was, and she nodded again.

'I'm going to make some coffee,' she announced.

She only managed one step before she collapsed. I caught her just
in time, and she clung to me as if I were her capsized boat. The tears

418

started and she cried, the sound muffled against my shirt.

'Come, let's sit down,' I said. I practically carried her to a couch in a wood-panelled room to my right.

After a few minutes, Evelyn Stark began to compose herself. I knew she was going to want the details of her daughter's death. I'd have to edit, but there was only so much I could leave out. Conrad Birch became far less the victim and far more the villain.

I decided to steer the conversation more to Haley's life as opposed to her death. My motivation wasn't a hundred per cent altruistic. I was looking for some answers of my own.

'So you obviously got to know Haley,' I said.

'Only since last year.'

She explained how she'd always wondered about her daughter. She wanted to try to find her, except she knew if they were meant to meet up one day, it would have to be Haley who initiated it. And she did.

'Last fall she called me,' said Evelyn. 'A few weeks later, she came for a visit. I haven't had many happy days, but that's one of them.'

'Did she say anything about being involved with a married man?'

'No.'

'Did she seem angry about anything?'

'Not really.'

With each shake of Evelyn's head, I became more disheartened. I'd felt so strongly about tracking down this woman and talking to her, so strongly that there was something to learn.

'Ms Stark, what *did* you and your daughter talk about?'

'We talked about a lot of things, trying to make up for the lost time. It sounded like she was raised by a good family. She went to college, and she told me about the modelling she'd done. She was very pretty.' Evelyn stopped. 'Would you like to see the picture?'

'What picture's that?'

She explained that Haley had brought a camera down with her, and they'd taken some pictures using that 'thingy where you could press a button and then hurry into the picture.' A week later, she said, Haley mailed her a copy of one of the shots.

Evelyn got off the couch and went to a cluttered bookcase. She pulled down a small box from the top shelf. 'I keep it in a special place,' she said.

She opened the box and took out a picture. She handed it to me, and I saw two women smiling, a mother and daughter reunited, sitting on the same couch I was.

'This is really nice, Ms Stark,' I said. I was about to give the picture back when my hand froze. That's when I saw it. A simple date printed in the bottom right-hand corner of the picture. The same date Conrad Birch had been stabbed more than fifty times. Hackers' Night.

I asked Evelyn if the date was right. Perhaps the camera had been programmed wrong, the internal calendar never set correctly.

'No,' she said, looking at the picture again. 'That's when Haley was here. It was the night before Halloween. I remember because the next day, before she left, she went to the market and bought me some candy to give out to the kids.'

The next day? 'You mean Haley spent the night here with you?'

'Yes, why?'

My head was dizzy. If Haley was down in Georgia, she couldn't have been up in Manhattan. Then again, whoever said she was? Certainly not her. She could've called me the night of the murder from anywhere. Now it was all making sense. Haley Morgan wasn't working alone.

'Ms Stark, I have to ask you a favour,' I said, trying to remain calm. 'I need to borrow this picture for a day.'

'Where are you going with it?' she asked.

'Home to Manhattan. I promise I'll overnight it back to you on Monday.'

She hardly looked convinced. 'It's not that I don't trust you—'

'No, I understand,' I said. 'But what I haven't told you is why I need the picture. I'm going to be showing it to the police.'

'Why?'

'Because I think it proves your daughter didn't kill anyone.'

The change in her face said it all. I represented a shot at redemption for Haley. Never mind that the picture proved her daughter was an accessory to murder as opposed to an actual murderer.

'You say you promise to send it back?'

'Yes, Ms Stark. You have my word.'

I apologised again for having to be the bearer of such bad news. Then I hustled out of there. Picture in hand.

I hurried back towards the airport. There was a plane to catch, but, more important, there was a phone call to make. To Terry. I'd tell her what had happened and she'd tell everyone else, beginning with the police. They needed to know right away that the case wasn't closed. There was a killer at large. Which meant that Samantha Kent might still be a target.

I grabbed my cell and glanced at my watch—six twenty-five. I dialled Terry at her apartment. Three rings . . . four rings. *C'mon, Terry, be there.*

She wasn't. I left a message on her machine to call me as soon as possible and tried next to reach her on her cell. Not picking up at home; not picking up on her cell. *Damn, where is she?*

I next tried Victor. I called his home and his cell, both with no luck.

I drove another mile thinking of what to do. The knee-jerk move was to call the police, maybe even try to get ahold of Detectives Trentino and Lopez. They never believed me before. Now they had to. In my mind I went over what I'd tell them. That I'd gone to see Haley Morgan's birth mother and—I could see their faces. Hear their questions. Why was I visiting the mother? How did I find out who she was and where she lived? I'd have to give them answers while at the same time protecting Ethan.

I'd have to lie.

Or better yet, I'd call Samantha Kent directly. She'd undoubtedly start to panic once she heard what I had to say. But I'd do my best to calm her down.

'What city, please?'

'Manhattan . . . the Drake Hotel.'

I got the number and called, asking for her room. It rang eight times before switching to voicemail. I gave my cell number and told her to call as soon as she could. As I hung up, a horrible thought. What if Haley's partner had already got to her?

At least Delta Airlines was home. I called to reserve a seat on the next New York flight. 'There's a seven thirty, but that's in less than an hour,' said the agent.

I hung up and my cell rang. 'Hello?'

'Dr Remler?' It was Samantha Kent. Thinking she might have called in for her messages, I immediately asked where she was.

'I'm here at the Drake. I was on the other line,' she said. 'Is there some sort of problem?'

'Not yet,' I said. 'But something's happened. It's a long story, but the bottom line is that Haley Morgan didn't kill your husband.'

It took her a second. '*What?*'

'The night Conrad was murdered, Haley was in Griffin, Georgia. That's where Evelyn Stark lives—she's Haley's birth mother. Haley was staying with her that very same night.'

'How do you know?'

'Because I just came from Georgia.'

'If Haley Morgan didn't kill Conrad, who did?'

'That's the question. She must have been working with someone.'

'Oh my God, David. That woman from the trial. Gabrielle Dennis.'

The other mistress. Maybe. Deluded publicity hound, the real thing or accomplice. Somehow working with Haley, she came forward *posing* as the mistress to try to derail my defence.

'What do you mean? Did you talk to her?' I asked.

'She called me yesterday,' said Samantha. 'She was crying, telling me how awful she felt about everything. She said she wanted to tell me in person how sorry she was.'

'You didn't—'

'No, I told her that couldn't happen. I obviously want nothing to do with her. Except she was so persistent. Now I'm afraid.'

'Does she know where you're staying?'

'Yes,' she said, her voice quavering. 'What should I do? This is the last place I want to be.'

I was about to tell her to call the police when I heard a beep on the line. It was my call-waiting. 'Hold on a second, OK?'

I switched over. It was Terry. 'We're still on for dinner, aren't we?' she said.

'Not exactly,' I said. 'Where are you right now?'

'Walking out of the gym. Why? What's wrong?'

I told her as fast as I could. I also told her I had Samantha Kent on the other line. 'She's scared to death,' I said. 'I was going to have her call the police.'

Terry interrupted. 'I have an idea. I don't want you to call the police until you're back here with that picture. In the meantime, she should go to my place. Give her my address and tell her I'll be there myself in fifteen minutes.'

'Good, thanks,' I said. 'I'll come straight there after I land.'

I got back to Samantha and filled her in on the plan. Then I had to floor it to make that seven-thirty Delta flight.

A few hours later, I arrived at Terry's brownstone in the West Village. I buzzed and heard the return buzz of the front entrance unlocking. Hers was the top floor of the three-storey walk-up. I took the steps two at a time.

As I approached the door, I saw it had been left open for me slightly. I walked into the apartment and saw Terry sitting on the couch in her living room. I started to smile. Then everything went black.

422

fifteen

'You couldn't leave well enough alone, could you?'
Those were the first words I heard when I opened my eyes. They were being spoken by Samantha Kent.

'No, you had to go ahead and play junior detective.' She was sitting at a small table in Terry's kitchen. Legs crossed, lit cigarette in hand. 'And look where it got you.'

On the floor, to be exact. Face down, arms and legs tied together with duct tape. Next to me was Terry in the same position. A gash on her forehead was caked with dried blood. No telling how long I'd been knocked out.

'So, what do you have to say for yourself, David?'

It was a rhetorical question. The strip of duct tape over my mouth made sure of it. Terry's mouth was covered as well.

I was still groggy, but the big dots were easy to connect. Haley Morgan had been working with someone, all right. A confounding partnership. A man's mistress and the wife he was cheating on.

I tried to lift my head to get a better look at Samantha. I cringed in pain. If the piece of cookware sitting atop the table next to her was any indication, I'd taken quite a blow to the head from a saucepan.

'*Mmmmph,*' I said.

It was the best I could do through the duct tape. But that was the point. To get Samantha to remove it. I was borrowing from the psychology of hostage negotiations. First establish a dialogue.

She looked at me with a pensive smile. 'Got something to say, David? Of course you do. So many questions.' She leaned forward. 'You're not going to do anything stupid, like yell, are you?'

I shook my head.

Samantha got up from her chair. Before walking towards me, however, she picked up the saucepan. Just in case. She grabbed the tape and ripped it off my mouth. For a moment she stood there, hovering with the saucepan. But I wasn't screaming. Not from pain, not for help.

'Are you OK?' I immediately asked Terry.

She nodded.

Samantha sat back down. 'Now, what would you like to ask?'

I summed it up in one word. 'Why?'

'That is the question, isn't it—why? Why did I want Conrad dead? Why would I seemingly team up with the woman he was cheating with? And *why* were you the fall guy?' She looked at her watch. 'As much as I'd like to stick around and fill you in, I'm afraid I'm a little short on time.'

I glanced at my bound hands and feet. 'Funny, I was thinking the same thing.'

'A morbid sense of humour; I like that. Conrad had one as well.'

'Before you killed him.'

'Yes, before I killed him.'

'All because he cheated on you.'

She drew off her cigarette. 'You think this was a crime of passion?'

'What else could it be?'

'Try money.'

I didn't follow. She was an heiress. 'You mean, like an insurance policy?'

'You could call it that,' she said. 'The problem is it expired early last year. Right on our tenth wedding anniversary.'

I now followed. She was talking about a prenuptial agreement. Clearly, as successful as Conrad was, his bank balances were no match for the Kent fortune. 'There was no infidelity rider?' I asked.

'Ah, you mean a "bad-boy clause"? Yes, it was in there, but it didn't carry on. I wanted it extended past the ten years, but that was the give for getting the ten years in the first place. His lawyer had been pushing for seven.'

'How much did he stand to make off you?'

'About seventy million,' she said coolly.

'So instead of paying Conrad, you preferred to kill him?'

'First off, we're talking about *seventy million dollars*. Second, there are more sympathetic figures than Conrad hanging on the wall in the post office. Were she still alive, Haley Morgan would've backed me up on that.'

Now we were really getting into it. And the longer we talked, the better chance I had to think of a way out.

'You and Haley—a strange partnership, don't you think?'

'Actually,' she said, 'that was the beauty of it. There's something more dangerous than a woman scorned. *Two* women scorned.'

'In Haley's case, because Conrad broke off the affair, right?'

'Haley was angry all right, and when she showed up on my doorstep, her intent was to turn my world upside-down. But all I could do was stare at her black eye. Conrad hit her right after she confronted him.'

'About what?'

'The drug he secretly slipped her for a few days after she told him she was pregnant. The bastard. I know you're not *that* kind of doctor, but I suspect you've heard of mifepristone.'

I had. It was now more commonly known as RU-486. *Christ.*

Samantha continued, 'The doctor found traces of it in her blood. Right after she lost the baby. Needless to say, she was ripe for revenge.'

OK. 'But murder?'

'Admittedly, it wasn't her first impulse. That's why I supplied her with an additional five hundred thousand reasons to go through with it. Half up front, half on the back end, and all payable in cash. It was a lot of money for someone who didn't have any—especially with her sugar daddy having left.'

'So, what went wrong?' I asked. 'Haley ended up wanting to kill you.'

'No, the only thing she wanted that morning in my apartment was the balance of her money. I, naturally, had other plans.'

'Killing her, you mean.'

I could envision it. Samantha going after Haley. Using a knife—Conrad's murder weapon—so it would appear to be the other way round. But Haley sensed the ambush. She turned just in time. A struggle ensued. Then I came rushing in.

Samantha clapped her hands. 'You saved the day, David.'

I could see Haley's face now. I could see her eyes. They were staring into mine at the moment she picked up the knife from the living-room carpet. I was sure she was going to lunge at me. Now I knew otherwise. What I was really looking at in that split second was a woman trapped.

In the promise of a lie.

And when the bullet ripped through her body another split second later, Samantha had made sure it would stay that way.

'Given what you've said about Haley's being pregnant, I'm beginning to think Conrad never used me as a foil with her.'

'You're right. She never knew Conrad had seen a psychologist. But I did.'

'How?'

'I happened to stumble across the cheque Conrad had written you for his first session. Problem was, I never saw another.'

'Because there never was another session.'

'Exactly. Only I couldn't know that for sure. There was no telling the things you knew. Were Conrad suddenly to die, I could ill afford to have you coming forward and somehow implicating me. As it was, he ended up saying plenty in just your one session.'

'He intended to break off the affair.'

'No, what he really intended was to establish that *impression*. If I was to find out about the affair while the prenup was still enforceable, his lawyers would drag you into court to show his conflicted state of mind. Maybe instead of seventy million he'd end up with thirty-five.'

'So I was being used by everybody.'

'Nothing personal on my part. I didn't even know you.'

'Which was instrumental to your plan.'

'Yes, but that paled in comparison to your book.' She laughed. 'What a premise—good people doing bad things for seemingly no apparent reason. Hell, David, it was like you were asking for it.'

'So you had no problem framing me? It was that easy for you?'

Samantha looked at her watch again. 'I'm afraid I've indulged you long enough.' She rubbed her chin. 'What am I going to do with you two? Can't use my gun now, can I? They'd trace the bullets for sure. A knife? Not with Haley no longer around.'

She stood up and walked over to me, the strip of duct tape in her hand. She slapped it back on my mouth. She turned a knob on the stove. From the corner of my eye I could see a blue flame. She blew it out. The pungent smell of gas began to fill the kitchen.

'Yes, we're going to have to keep the hands squeaky clean on this one.' She proceeded over to one of the lower cabinets and opened it. She knelt and reached in. Out came a square, metal baking pan.

She stepped over Terry and me to the sink and turned the tap on. She hummed while filling the pan up with some water.

The gas, the metal baking pan, the water. There was only one place Samantha was heading next. The microwave. She slid the pan in, slammed the door shut and punched a few buttons. The microwave lit up with a soft glow.

Samantha looked down at us with a sick grin. '*Bon appétit*, guys.'

Out of the door she walked. She was gone. And in about five or six minutes Terry and I would be as well. We were smack in the middle of a time bomb. That metal pan was destined to spark and catch fire, turning the microwave into a pressure cooker. Aided by the boiling water, the latch would eventually give, blowing the thing open right into the gas-filled room. Boom.

I looked at Terry. We couldn't talk, but we needed to communicate. More than that, we needed to think fast. Somehow we had to get free and out of that kitchen. That's when I saw her eyes go wide. She thought of something and, with a jerk of her head, tried to tell me. She motioned again towards the cabinet next to the stove. Vertical from the ground up. There was something in there, she was trying to tell me.

With a rocking motion I began to inch closer to the cabinet. Hands behind my back, I stretched and leaned, my fingertips just catching the front panel of the cabinet. Except the handle was too high. I dug my nails into the edge of the door until I could get a grip on it. I pulled it open. Inside were dish towels, oven cleaner and tinfoil.

I turned back to Terry. *What am I looking for?*

She rolled her eyes around in circles. *Huh?*

The tinfoil. The *roll* of tinfoil. Specifically, the serrated metal edge on the box. The next best thing to a knife.

I'd started to reach for it when I heard a loud popping and looked up to see the first spark. Time was running out.

I fixed on the tinfoil box again. It was propped on a shelf, midway up the cabinet.

I got it and pulled, clinging to it while I rocked back to Terry. She tried to meet me halfway. We were back to back. She pushed her hands out, exposing as much of the tap round her wrists as possible. I angled the box, serrated edge down, until I had it aligned. Then I sawed. Above us the microwave groaned, its walls beginning to feel the inexorable push. It was only a matter of seconds.

Frantically, I kept sawing as Terry tried to force the cuts in the tape with all her might. It wasn't working fast enough. I dropped the box and grabbed her wrists, feeling for the tape. If I could turn the cuts into tears we had a shot. If not, we were surely dead.

I gave it everything. All I had and all I had to live for. Until, with a sticky rip, the tape gave. Terry's hands were free. She immediately pushed herself up, rising to her bound feet and lunging for a drawer. She pulled out a pair of scissors and cut between her ankles, dropping back down on the floor to do the same for me. I looked over at the microwave, its clock ticking away. Smoke was billowing out from the edges, thick and black. The pan was completely on fire.

With one last yank, the rest of the tape gave and I sprang to my feet. We sprinted out of the kitchen into the living room and headed into the hallway. As for the rest, it was a blur. The floor, the walls, the ceiling, they all shook. The noise was deafening. The sheer force of the explosion slammed into our backs, practically lifting us off the ground. Were it not for Terry's last-minute pull on my arm, we would've been engulfed in flames.

The pull led to a dive and a crash-landing in the bathroom. Amid the toppled walls and shattered glass, it was probably the thick porcelain tub we fell next to that saved us. We were bruised and we were bloody. But we were alive.

I held Terry tight in my arms. Our bodies intertwined and our eyes locked.

'*Mmmmph*,' she said. The duct tape was still on our mouths. We both ripped the strips off, easing the sting with a long kiss.

THERE WAS ONLY ONE other person who knew Haley Morgan hadn't killed Conrad Birch, and that was her mother. And there was only one other person who knew she knew. Samantha. I'd conveniently supplied the name, the town, the state—everything she needed to track the mother down. So after bidding Terry and me a fond farewell, Samantha was no doubt off to Griffin, Georgia, to pay a visit to Evelyn Stark. She was going to make sure the secret died with her. That very night.

She never made it on the plane. With one phone call from Terry to the police, patrol cars were dispatched to Kennedy and LaGuardia. They nabbed her at LaGuardia.

AFTER BEING CAUGHT, Samantha had the right to remain silent, but she chose to talk. Her lawyers weren't about to stop her. Their angle was criminal insanity and, despite the premeditation, they felt it was their best shot. I couldn't help marvelling at what this meant. She immediately had to be evaluated by a shrink.

Don't ask me how I got my hands on the report. While you're at it, don't ask Ethan Greene either. His days of owing me were over.

In the course of two sessions, Samantha managed to be very forthcoming. According to her, she felt no remorse. Rather, she believed she was completely justified in doing what she did. And what she did was pretty crazy.

Samantha explained how she slipped out of the Ritz-Carlton in Boston and made the drive down to Manhattan and back undetected.

It was a round-trip that fell neatly between the time she placed her wake-up call and when she received it.

There was also her getting Conrad's signature on the letter planted in my apartment. She simply caught him as he was rushing out to work and thrust in his face a stack of things for him to sign. 'He doesn't bother to read anything,' she claimed. 'He just scribbles his name and barks out, *Next!*'

Meanwhile, there was Haley. On the night of the murder she had one job. Calling me. What she obviously didn't tell Samantha was that she'd decided to do it from Griffin, Georgia. Maybe it was happenstance. Or maybe it was the shrewd move of someone who didn't trust her partner. Visiting her real mother for the first time doubled as an alibi for Haley. If it ever came to that. It never did. Only because she shouldn't have trusted Samantha at all.

Having Haley call me after my trial got suspended was Samantha's idea. The 'sprayer' device belonged to Conrad. He apparently was paranoid about people taping his business dealings over the phone.

Threatening to kill 'the bitch Conrad ran back to' would further insulate Samantha from any suspicion. At least, that's how she explained it to Haley. In reality, the call was all about her getting away with murder for a second time. *The mistress strikes again.* Were there to be any doubt, Samantha knew I'd gladly come forward and, seeking my own vindication, tell of the phone call I'd received.

Of course, how fast I came forward was of considerable surprise to her. She obviously had no idea I'd be staking out her apartment.

Still, she turned that miscalculation to her advantage. What's more, my showing up that morning most likely saved her life. Her effort to kill Haley had been met with considerable resistance. Who knows what would've happened if I hadn't come bursting in. Haley Morgan. With a knife. In Samantha Kent's living room.

And I had no *clue* what was really going on.

One morning I was walking from my office to the corner deli when a limousine pulled up. The rear-seat passenger called my name. It was Arnold Kesper. His tinted window was half down, and he was peering out at me. I walked over to the kerb.

'It's nice to see you again, Dr Remler.'

'You as well, Mr Kesper.'

'Can I give you a lift to wherever it is you're going?'

'It would be a very short ride,' I said. 'I'm just going to the corner.'

'In that case, can I delay your arrival there for a few minutes?'

He opened the door and began to slide over. I got in.

He continued: 'On the subject of rides, you've had quite a wild one in the past year or so. First the rabbi trial and then one of your own.'

'What did you think?'

'What did I think? To be perfectly honest, at first I was rather indifferent to your plight. Guilty or innocent, you seemed to face a predicament that was similar to the rabbi's. Two men asking to be taken at their word. Except you didn't believe the rabbi, did you, David? So perhaps it would've made sense if I didn't believe you.'

'Mr Kesper, I'm not offended if you had your doubts.'

'You were right; I was wrong. The man was indeed lying. Guilty as sin, as I think you put it.'

'Lucky guess, perhaps.'

'No, you saw the situation for what it was, while I saw it for what I hoped it wasn't. Your vision proved to be far more enlightened than mine.' He nodded at his minion, who reached to her side and picked up an envelope, handing it to me.

'What's this?' I asked.

'Something I no longer need.'

I opened the envelope. Inside were pages of contact sheets plus their negatives. In every picture was the same person. Me. Me walking into my office. Me hailing a cab outside my apartment building. Me exiting a Starbucks.

'One of the trappings of preposterous wealth, David, is the ability to do almost anything you want. Including finding out almost anything you want to know about anybody. There are people who, for one reason or another, fascinate me. You were such a person because of your role in the rabbi trial and the book you'd written. It made me curious about the kind of man you really are.'

'You mean whether I have any skeletons in my closet.'

'That's one aspect, yes. Though I can assure you I'm not one to root for skeletons. I don't get my jollies from observing human weakness. Rather, I simply think it's better to know than not know.'

'In other words, it gives you leverage.'

'You could say that.'

I sat there groping for a proper reaction. I wanted to be angry, wanted to lay into Kesper for his arrogance and disrespect. But most of all, I wanted to thank him. Because I knew what he'd done.

Behind the last contact sheet was an enlargement of one of the shots. It had been taken the night of the Kesper Society cocktail party—my

Mystery Patient and me standing outside the Metropolitan Museum of Art. I continued to stare at the picture, flashing back to that night as well as to when I saw it for the first time. In the chambers of Judge Lomax.

Said Kesper, 'After I heard about the rabbi's confession note my indifference to your situation changed. That's when I took a second look at the pictures I'd arranged to be taken. Miracle of miracles, there you were with the woman who fitted your description.'

'How did you know Judge Lomax would do what he did?'

'I didn't. But I figured sending him the photo would be a good first move. As it turned out, it was the only one needed.'

'It certainly turned things around,' I said. 'For that I can't thank you enough.' I slid the pictures back into the envelope. I started to hand them to Kesper.

'No, those are yours to keep. Or dispose of, whichever you prefer. I no longer have a need for them. I know what kind of man you really are.' Arnold Kesper extended his hand. We shook. 'Good luck, David.'

'Thank you,' I said. 'Thank you for everything.'

I reached for the door handle.

'Oh, I almost forgot,' he said. 'I have something else for you.'

He nodded at his minion, who opened a file next to her on the seat. She took out small envelope, and handed it to me. I began to open it.

'Actually, why don't you do that outside,' he said.

'Oh . . . OK, sure.' I stepped out of the limo, which promptly took off. I watched it disappear into the traffic. I opened the envelope. Inside was a cheque made out to Crescent House. It looked like the one for a million dollars that Arnold Kesper had already given us. Except this one had an extra zero attached.

THREE YEARS LATER. It's got all the trappings of happy ending but forgive my reluctance to call it that. Life, for all its wonders, has a nasty habit of reminding you that you're never *really* in control.

I'm still a practising psychologist. I've got a full load of patients again. Mila remains my *Mamka*.

Samantha Kent got life without the possibility of parole. Not a single one of the jurors in her trial bought into the insanity plea.

Much to the consternation of Debra Walker Coyne, my agent, I never wrote a first-hand account of what happened to me. Instead, I let Kevin Daniels, back from the belly of the beast, Hollywood, take his crack at the story. I must admit he wrote a pretty good script, which a studio finally bought. But after floundering in development for a time, the project is now in turnaround.

'Them's the breaks,' said my new bride.

Normally, Terry's falling for a guy she'd represented in a murder trial would've been an extremely bad career move. Except she always knew her career was changing. As of a year ago, she said goodbye to the world of criminal law to oversee the expansion of Crescent House to other cities. Owing to Arnold Kesper's additional ten-million-dollar donation, there have already been a few ribbon-cutting ceremonies. With more to come.

However, Terry won't be able to make the next one, which takes place in Chicago in a few weeks. You can't fly when you're beyond seven months' pregnant.

We don't know if it's a boy or a girl. But we have the name picked out. In an effort to come up with a more kid-friendly unisex name, while still giving a nod to Terry's favourite book, we've decided on Harper Lee Remler. The nursery is ready.

Which brings me to one final thing. A little while back, Terry found a safe-deposit-box key. She asked what it was for and I told her the story of the list my first wife, Rebecca, had made when she was pregnant, and how I'd found it after she died. Terry asked what was on the list, and I told her. I still had it memorised.

When she asked me if I'd get the list from the bank, I didn't know why she wanted it. Two days after I gave it to her, I found out. That's when I walked into the nursery and saw the list framed and hanging on the wall. 'It's what *every* child should be taught,' she said.

To love.
To laugh.
To laugh some more.
To listen and learn.
To say please and thank you.
To have opinions.
To respect those of others.
To be honest.
To be a friend.
To be yourself.

HOWARD ROUGHAN

Not many people have the daily grind of commuting to thank for their success, but Howard Roughan says it worked for him. After ten years living in New York, he and his wife moved to Connecticut to start a family. 'Truth was, we didn't want to raise a kid who would be more clever and hip than his parents by the age of five,' he says, explaining the move. The downside was that it meant a long daily commute to and from his job as creative director for an advertising agency in Manhattan. To pass the time he began to jot down notes for a story. 'I found myself to be really productive. On a train there's a strange kind of silence that you only get with a large crowd who are not talking to each other. I don't know if it was that or the motion of the train, but I started writing.'

Eventually he sent what he had written to an agent, who sold the unfinished book to a publisher. Roughan quit his job and kept writing at home—until he hit a problem with the novel. 'One weekend I thought I'd try to finish a chapter but I was getting nowhere, so I decided to take action. I grabbed my wallet and laptop, drove to the station, got on and just wrote. Sure enough, by the next stop, I had it figured out.' He continued his trips in and out of the city until he finished the book, *The Up and Comer*, which is about a slick New York lawyer living life in the fast lane.

Inspiration for his second novel, *The Promise of a Lie*, came from a converation with a woman who was seeing a psychologist. 'She spoke of how important trust was in her therapy,' he recalls. 'It got me thinking and plotting. What if the doctor could be trusted but not the patient? Could a psychologist ever be fooled by someone pretending to be someone else? Before I knew it I was outlining *The Promise of a Lie*.'

And does he still ride the trains? 'As I no longer commute, and my wife has refused to allow me to build an actual train car outside our house, I now maintain an office in the town where I live. However, when the occasional writer's block sets in, I've been know to make up any excuse to take a train somewhere. Old habits die hard.'

The Death and Life
of Charlie St Cloud

BEN SHERWOOD

What do you do if you make
a promise to the person you
love most in the world? You
never break it.

So, for thirteen years, Charlie
St Cloud has been true to
his word, without thought
for his own life.

But you can't live in the past
for ever. Sometimes you just
have to open up your
heart and let go . . .

INTRODUCTION

I believe in miracles.

Not just the simple wonders of creation, like my new son at home nursing in my wife's arms, or the majesties of nature, like the sun setting in the sky. I'm talking about real miracles, like turning water into wine or bringing the living back from the dead.

My name is Florio Ferrente. My father, a fireman, christened me after St Florian, the patron saint of our profession. Like my pop, I worked my whole life for Engine Company 5 on Freeman Street in Revere, Massachusetts. I served as God's humble servant, going where the Lord dispatched me, saving the lives He wanted rescued. You could say I was a man on a mission, and I'm proud of what I did every day.

Sometimes we arrived at a fire too late to make a difference. We threw water on the roof but the house still burned down. Other times we got the job done, protecting lives, whole neighbourhoods.

Most folks have a picture of us loaded with gear rushing into flaming buildings. That's right. This is serious business. But in the quieter moments we also have our share of laughs. Above all, we tell stories. What follows is my favourite. It's about what happened thirteen years ago on the General Edwards drawbridge not far from the red-brick station I call home. It wasn't the first time we had raced there to prise people out of wrecks.

My first trip to the bridge was back in the blizzard of 1978, when an old man missed the warning light that the ramp was going up. He crashed through the barrier, flew right off the edge and was submerged in his Pontiac for twenty-nine minutes. We knew because that was how long his Timex had stopped when the divers cut him out from under the ice. He was frozen blue with no pulse, and I went to work breathing life back into him. In a few ticks, his skin turned pink and his eyes blinked open. I was about twenty-four years old, and it was the most amazing thing I'd ever seen.

The *Revere Independent* called it a miracle. I like to think it was God's will. In this line of work, the truth is you try to forget most of your runs, especially the sad ones where people die. But there are some cases you can never get out of your mind. They stay with you for your whole life. Counting the old man in the ice, I've had three.

When I was just a rookie, I carried a lifeless five-year-old girl from a hellish three-alarm on Squire Road. Her name was Eugenia Louise Cushing. Her pupils were pinpoint and her blood pressure was undetectable, but I kept trying to revive her. Even when the medical examiner pronounced her dead on the scene and began to fill out the paperwork, I kept going. Then, all of a sudden, little Eugenia sat up on the stretcher, coughed, rubbed her eyes and asked for a glass of milk. That was my first miracle.

I picked up Eugenia's crumpled death certificate and put it away in my wallet. I kept it as reminder that anything is possible in this world.

That brings me to the case of Charlie St Cloud. Like I said, it starts with a calamity on the drawbridge over the Saugus River, but there's a lot more to it than that. It's about devotion and the unbreakable bond between brothers. It's about finding your soul mate where you least expect. It's about life cut short and love lost. Some folks would call it a tragedy, but I've always tried to find the good in the most desperate situations, and that's why the story of these boys stays with me.

You may think some of this seems far-fetched, even impossible. Believe me, I know we all cling to life and it's not easy in these cynical times to cast off the hardness and edge that get us through our days. But open your eyes and you will see what I can see. And if you've ever wondered what happens when a person close to you is taken too soon—and it's always too soon—you may find other truths here, truths that may break the grip of sadness in your life, that may set you free from guilt, that may even bring you back to this world from wherever you are hiding. And then you will never feel alone.

The bulk of this tale takes place here in the snug little village of Marblehead, Massachusetts, a wedge of rock jutting into the Atlantic. It is almost twilight now. I stand in the ancient town cemetery on a sloping hill where two weeping willows and a small mausoleum overlook the harbour. Sailboats tug at moorings and little boys cast their lines from the dock.

Nearby, I see a fuzzy old man put a fistful of hollyhocks on his wife's grave. A history buff makes a rubbing from a weathered stone. The tidy rows of monuments drop down to a cove on the water.

We'll start by going back thirteen years to September 1991. In the rec room at the firehouse, we were polishing off bowls of my wife's famous *spumone*, screaming about the Red Sox, who were chasing the Blue Jays for the baseball pennant. Then we heard the tones on the box, rushed to the rig and took off.

I

RACING THE MOON

Charlie St Cloud wasn't the brightest boy in Essex County, but he was surely the most promising. He was junior-class vice president, shortstop of the Marblehead Magicians, and co-captain of the debate club. With a mischievous dimple on one cheek, nose and forehead freckled from the sun and caramel eyes hidden beneath a flop of sandy-blond hair, he was already handsome at fifteen. Yes, Charlie St Cloud was quick of mind and body, destined for good things.

His mother, Louise, cheered his every achievement. Indeed, Charlie was both cause and cure for her own life's disappointments. Those troubles had begun the moment he was conceived, an unwanted pregnancy that pushed the man she loved—a carpenter with good hands—right out of the door. Next came Charlie's obstructed journey into the world, requiring surgery for him to be born. Soon a second son arrived from another father, and the years blurred into one endless struggle. But for all her woes, Charlie erased her pain with those twinkling eyes and optimism. She had grown to depend on him as her messenger of hope, and he could do no wrong.

He grew up fast, worked hard at his books, watched out for his mom, and loved his kid brother, whose name was Sam, more than anyone in the world. Sam's father—a bail bondsman—was gone, too, barely leaving a trace except for his son's curly brown hair and some bluish bruises on Louise's face. Charlie believed that he was the only true protector of his little brother. The boys were three years apart, and best friends, united in their love of catching fish, climbing trees, a beagle named Oscar and the Red Sox.

Then, one day, Charlie made a disastrous mistake, one the police could not explain and the juvenile court did its best to overlook. To be precise, Charlie ruined everything on Friday, September 20, 1991.

Mom was working the late shift at Penni's market on Washington Street. The boys had come home from school with mischief on their minds. They had no homework to do until Sunday night. They had already jumped a fence and sneaked onto the property of the Czech refugee who claimed to have invented the bazooka. At sunset, they played catch under the pine trees in their yard on Cloutman's Lane, just as they had done every night since Charlie had given Sam his first Rawlings glove for his seventh birthday. But now it was dark and they had run out of adventures.

Sam might have settled for crashing and watching Chris Isaak's *Wicked Game* video, but Charlie had a surprise. He pulled two tickets from his pocket. Red Sox tickets. They were playing the Yankees.

'No way! Where'd those come from?' Sam asked.

'I have my ways.'

'How we gonna get there? Fly?'

'Don't you worry about that. Mrs Pung is on vacation. We can borrow her wagon.'

'Borrow? You don't even have a licence!'

'You want to go or not?'

'What about Mom?'

'Don't worry. She'll never know.'

'We can't leave Oscar. He'll freak out and mess up the house.'

'He can come too.'

Sure enough, Charlie, Sam and their beagle were soon driving to Boston in Mrs Pung's station wagon. Without their neighbour Mrs Pung, that is.

The journey took thirty minutes, and Charlie was especially careful on Route 1A where the cops patrolled. The boys listened to the pre-game show on the radio, talked about the last time they'd been to the ballpark, and counted their money, calculating they had enough for two frankfurters each, a Coke and peanuts.

Now, with its red bricks and shimmering glass, Boston was waiting across the Charles River. They turned down Brookline Avenue and could see the hazy lights of Fenway Park stadium. Biting at the chilly air, Oscar leaned out of the window.

In the parking lot, the boys stuffed Oscar into a backpack and took off for the bleachers. Their seats were in right field, directly behind a guy who must have been seven feet tall, but it didn't matter. Nothing could ruin the spectacle of the grass, the chalk lines, the infield dirt and the Green Monster—the stadium's famous left-field wall.

One of their heroes, Wade Boggs, sat out the game with a sore right shoulder, but Jody Reed took his place and delivered, with a run-scoring double and home run off the left-field foul pole. The boys ate two hot dogs each with extra relish. Oscar got some CrackerJacks from a woman in the next row. A big bearded guy next to her gave them a few sips of Budweiser.

Roger Clemens shut out the Yankees, allowing only three hits and striking out seven. The crowd cheered, and Oscar howled. With the final out and a 2–0 victory in the books, the fans scattered, but the boys stayed in their seats, replaying the highlights. The team was now miraculously within striking distance of Toronto.

'Some day, we'll have season tickets,' Charlie said. 'Right there behind home plate in the first row.'

'The bleachers are good enough for me,' Sam said, eating the last of the peanuts. 'I don't care about the seats. As long as it's you and me, that's what makes baseball great.'

'We'll always play ball, Sam. No matter what.'

The stadium lights began shutting down. The ground crew had just about spread the tarp over the infield.

'We better go,' Charlie said.

The boys headed for the parking lot, where the white station wagon was all alone. The trip would take half an hour. They would be home by 10.30. Mom wouldn't be back until midnight. Mrs Pung in Florida would never know.

They drove silently for a while, then Sam asked out of the blue, 'How long will it be until I'm grown up?'

'You already are,' Charlie answered.

'I'm serious. When do I stop being a kid?'

'When you're twelve, you're a man and you can do what you want.'

'Says who?'

'Says me.'

'I'm a man and I can do what I want,' Sam said, enjoying the sound of it. A great moon floated on the Saugus River, and he rolled down the window. 'Look,' he said. 'It's bigger tonight. Must be closer to us.'

'Nah,' Charlie said. 'That's just an optical illusion. It's always two hundred and twenty-five thousand, seven hundred and forty-five miles away.' Numbers were easy for him. 'At our speed right now, it would take about a hundred and seventy days to get there.'

'Mom wouldn't be too crazy about that,' Sam said.

'And Mrs Pung wouldn't be happy about the mileage.'

The boys laughed. Then Sam said, 'It's no optical delusion. It's closer tonight. I swear. Look, you can see a halo just like an angel's.'

'No such thing,' Charlie said. 'That's a refraction of the ice crystals in the upper atmosphere.'

'Gee, I thought it was a refraction of the ice crystals on your butt!' Sam howled with laughter, and Oscar barked.

Charlie checked his mirrors and took one quick glance to the right. The moon was flickering between the iron railings of the drawbridge, keeping pace with them as they sped home. It sure seemed closer than ever tonight. He turned his head for a better look. He thought the bridge was empty so he pushed down on the gas.

Of all his reckless decisions that night, surely this was the worst. Charlie raced the moon, and in the final second before the end, he saw the perfect image of happiness. Sam's innocent face looking up at him, the Rawlings glove on his hand. And then there was only fracturing glass, metal and blackness.

With a cold wind rushing through the spans in the General Edwards drawbridge, Florio Ferrente snatched the Jaws of Life from the back of his rig. The Hurst tool weighed forty-one pounds and its serrated blades could chop through steel, but he wielded them like kitchen scissors.

Florio knelt for a moment and offered the fireman's prayer that came to his lips every time he went to work. *Give me courage. Give me strength. Please, Lord, through it all, be at my side.*

Then came the blur of action. He evaluated the spilt gasoline and the chance of a spark or explosion. He assessed the fastest way into the wreck—through the windshield, hood or doors? And he did the maths on how much time he had for this rescue. Time, precious time.

Florio ran past the jagged skid marks and jackknifed tractor trailer. He didn't bother to stop for the truck driver leaning against the centre divider. The man reeked of beer and blood. It was one of the rules of rescue: heaven protects fools and drunks. The guy would be fine.

The instant licence-plate check on the white wagon had revealed that the Ford belonged to Mrs Norman Pung of Cloutman's Lane, Marblehead. Age: 73. Vision-impaired. Perhaps the first clue.

The vehicle was crunched and tossed upside-down, its front end smashed into the railing of the bridge. He could tell from the trail of glass and metal that the car had rolled at least twice. Florio peered through a squashed window. There was no noise inside. No sound of breathing or moaning. Blood trickled through cracks in the metal.

With swift movements, he jammed a power spreader into the narrow space between the hood and door. A quick flick of his thumb and the hydraulics surged. The car frame groaned as the machine drove the metal apart. Florio pushed his head inside the wreck and saw two boys, upside-down, unconscious, tangled in seat belts. Their twisted arms were wrapped round each other. No sign of Mrs Pung.

'Two traumatic arrests up front,' he shouted to his partner, Trish Harrington. 'A dog in back. Scoop and run. Priority One.'

He slid out of the wreckage and shoved the Hurst tool into the hinges of the door. Another jab of the thumb, and the blades took two powerful bites. Florio pulled the door off.

'Gimme two C-spine collars,' he yelled. 'And two backboards.'

He crawled back inside. 'Can you hear me?' he said to the smaller boy. 'Talk to me.' No response. No movement. The kid's face and neck were wet with blood, eyes and lips swollen.

Florio wrapped a brace round the boy's neck, strapped on a backboard, then cut the seat belt with his knife. He lowered the patient gently and pulled him out onto the pavement.

'Pupils are blown,' Florio said, checking with his flashlight. 'He's posturing. Blood from the ears.' Bad signs, all. Time to go after the other victim. He climbed back inside. The teenager was pinned beneath the steering column. Florio wedged another spreader into the foot space and hit the hydraulics. As the metal separated, he collared the boy quickly and tied the back brace into place, then pulled him out and carefully set him down on the road.

'Can you hear me?' he said. Not a word.

'Squeeze my hand if you can hear me,' he said. Nothing.

The two young victims were now lying side by side on backboards. The little dog on the back seat was hopeless, crushed between the rear axle and the trunk. What a waste. 'St Françis,' he whispered, 'bless this creature with your grace.'

Florio checked his watch. This was the golden hour: less than sixty minutes to save their lives. If he could stabilise them and get them to the trauma surgeons, they might survive.

He and his partner lifted the first boy into their ambulance. Then the second. Trish ran round to the driver's seat. Florio climbed into the back and leaned out to pull the doors shut. Then the ambulance lurched forwards and the siren screamed. For an instant, Florio's fingers found the well-worn gold medallion round his neck. It was St Jude, patron saint of desperate situations. He put his stethoscope to the chest of the younger boy. He listened and knew the simple truth.

This was a time for miracles.

A mist shrouded the ground, muffling the sounds of the world. Charlie, Sam and Oscar huddled in the damp and dark. There was no one else around. They could have been anywhere or nowhere. It didn't matter. They were together.

'Mom will kill us for this,' Sam said, shivering. He smacked his fist into his mitt. 'She's gonna be mad.'

'Don't worry, little man,' Charlie said. He pushed the curls from his brother's face. 'I'll take care of it.'

He could imagine his mother's disappointment: her forehead turning red, the veins in her temples pulsing.

'They'll send us to jail for this,' Sam said. 'Mrs Pung will make us pay, and we don't have any money.' He turned his head and focused on the jagged shape of the station wagon. What hadn't been destroyed in the crash had been cut to pieces by the rescuers.

'You won't go to jail,' Charlie said. 'They wouldn't punish a twelve-year-old that way. Maybe me, I was driving; but not you.'

'But it was my fault,' Sam said. 'I distracted you with the moon.'

'No, you didn't. I should've seen the truck and got out of the way.' Charlie looked around, trying to make sense of the landscape. There was no sign of the bridge, no curve of the river, no outline of the city. The sky was a blanket of black. All he could see were shapes moving in the distance, solids in the fluid of night.

And then, through the gloom, he began to realise where they were. Somehow, mysteriously, they had been transported to a small hill with two drooping willows overlooking the harbour. He recognised the curve of the shore with its huddle of masts bobbing on the water.

'I think we're home,' he said.

'How'd that happen?'

'No idea, but look, there's Tucker's wharf.'

He pointed, but Sam wasn't interested. 'Mom's going to ground us,' he said. 'We better make up a good story or she'll use the belt.'

'No, she won't,' Charlie said. 'I'm coming up with a plan right now. Trust me.'

But he had no idea what to do or how to get them out of this jam. Then he saw another light in the distance, faint at first, but growing brighter. Maybe a flashlight or a rescue party. Oscar began to bark, friendly at first, then he let out a long yowl.

'Look,' Sam said. 'Who's that?'

'Oh shit.' Charlie never swore, and Sam tensed up.

'Is that Mom?'

'No, I don't think so.'

'Then who? Who's coming? I'm scared.'

The light was warm and bright, and it was getting closer.

'Don't be afraid,' Charlie said.

They were dead and gone.

No pulse. No breath. Hypoxic. Dead and gone. Florio flashed his light stick one more time into the blown pupils of the older boy. They were black and bottomless.

He stuck leads on the kid's wrists and left chest, then punched the button on the monitor. The line on the six-second ECG strip was flat.

'This is Medic Two,' he said into the radio. 'I've got two crunch cases. Pulseless nonbreathers.'

Florio grabbed his intubation kit and slipped the curved steel blade of the laryngoscope into the boy's mouth. Pushing aside the kid's slack tongue, he aimed for the entryway to the trachea, a small gap between the vocal cords. He pressed the instrument into position. With a whirl of motion, he inflated the cuff and began to ventilate.

The vehicle hurtled towards the North Shore ER, and Florio pulled out the Zoll defibrillator paddles, pressed them to the kid's bare chest and blasted him with 250 joules.

Damn. The monitor showed no cardiac conversion. In rapid mechanical movements, Florio clamped a tourniquet on the kid's arm, found a vein, jabbed a needle, plugged in an IV line, and pumped adrenaline. Then he dialled up 300 joules.

He pressed the button and the body convulsed. Again, no luck. But Florio had been here before. He had saved countless diabetics in hypoglycaemic seizure and rescued dozens of heroin ODs. He never gave up. It was never too late for miracles.

So Florio dialled up 320 joules on the Zoll and hit the button. The body in front of him heaved from the shock. This was the last chance. Unless he could get the boy back into cardiac rhythm, it was over.

The gloom was gone and the light had almost encircled them.

Sam was shaking now and had wrapped his arms round Oscar. 'I'm afraid,' he said. 'I don't want to get in trouble. I don't want Mom to yell. I don't want strangers to take us away.'

'It's gonna be OK,' Charlie said. 'Trust me.' He felt the warmth of the light reach all the way inside and the pain began to go away.

'Promise you won't leave me,' Sam said, reaching for his hand.

'Promise.'

'Cross your heart and hope to die?'

'Yeah,' Charlie said. 'Now, promise you won't leave me either.'

'Never,' Sam said. His eyes were wide and clear. His face was tranquil. He had never looked so peaceful before.

They hugged each other, then stood side by side, feeling the light come over them, a brilliant blur of white and gold.

'Don't worry,' Charlie said. 'Everything'll be OK. I promise.'

FLORIO HEARD the monitor beep.

Perhaps it was St Florian. Or St Jude. Or simply God's grace. The ECG strip showed the boy's heart had suddenly flipped back into a regular beat. Then, incredibly, his eyes opened slowly. They were the colour of caramel and surrounded by exploded capillaries. He coughed and stared straight up.

'Welcome back,' Florio said.

The boy seemed confused and worried. 'Where's Sam?' he muttered. 'I was just talking to Sam.'

'What's your name?'

'I promised Sam I wouldn't leave him.'

'Tell me your name, son.'

'St Cloud,' he said faintly. 'Charlie St Cloud.'

'You're gonna be OK, St Cloud. I'm doing the best I can for Sam.' Florio crossed himself and prayed silently.

Then he heard Charlie say again, 'Where's Sam? Where's my brother? I can't leave him . . .'

THE WORDS DIDN'T MAKE much sense, but Charlie understood the urgency in the man's voice. It was a tenseness that adults always showed when things weren't going well. The paramedic was working on Sam right beside him.

Then Charlie felt a wave of pain in his back and neck. He grimaced and cried out.

'I'm here with you,' the paramedic said. 'I'm giving you something that'll make you sleepy. Don't worry.'

Charlie felt warmth spreading through his shoulders, down his legs. Everything grew blurry, but he knew one thing for sure. He had given his word to his little brother. A promise to take care of him. Their fathers may have come and gone, but no matter what happened, he would never leave Sam.

In Charlie's numbed mind, his neck in a brace, an IV in his arm, he somehow pictured the days and years ahead—the days and years with his brother at his side, always together, no matter what. There was no alternative. Life without Sam was simply unfathomable.

He reached out across the narrow divide of the ambulance, past the thick waist of a paramedic. He found Sam's skinny arm, the IV, the baseball mitt wedged next to his body. He felt his brother's hand, all limp and cold. And Charlie held on as hard as he could.

II

DIVE FOR DREAMS

The flags on the wharf whipped in unison as Tess Carroll pulled her banged-up '74 Chevy Cheyenne to a stop. She got out of the truck and studied the snapping shapes in the wind. She knew this was a calming southeasterly breeze, no more than four knots. It began up in the ice floes of Nova Scotia, blew down with the trades over New England and would meander all the way to the Caribbean.

Tess walked to the flatbed and tried to open the tailgate, but the darn thing wouldn't budge. She had bought the old pick-up from a junk yard, and her dad had put life into it with a used engine. When it needed another motor, he told her to trade it in. She didn't listen, and years later, when he died without warning, she knew she would never get rid of that Chevy.

Tess reached over the side, grabbed hold of a big nylon sail bag and hauled it out. She was tall and lean with dark straight hair in a pony-tail that poked through the back of a Patriots' cap. She balanced the bag on one shoulder, turned and walked towards the dock. Up ahead, a few old wharf rats were playing cards. They were retired fishermen who lounged around by the water every afternoon.

'Hey, princess!' an old-timer rasped.

'How you doing, Bony?' Tess said.

'Losing my shirt,' he said, throwing down his cards. 'Need a crew for the afternoon?'

'Wish I could afford you.'

'I'll work for free,' he said. 'I can't take another minute here.'

'He can't take another losing hand,' one of the guys cracked.

'Please, Tess, let me sail with you.'

'You really want another heart attack?' Tess said, adjusting the sail-bag. 'You know I'll give you one.' She winked. 'See ya later.'

'Watch out for the weather,' Bony called out, as Tess headed down to the dock.

'Will do, and try not to break any hearts while I'm gone.'

The fishermen laughed as she walked on. She was wearing khakis with flowery patches on both knees, a white tank top and an over-sized, blue button-down shirt. Her eyes were a soft shade of emerald green, and her nose came to an impossibly fine point, the kind women in New York paid plastic surgeons thousands to create.

Tess strolled along the dock towards her gleaming thirty-eight-foot sloop, an Aerodyne with a slate-blue hull, an immaculate white deck and QUERENCIA painted in gold on the stern.

'You going to help or just sit there?' she said to a massive mound of a man who was dangling his feet over the side of the yacht.

'You're doing fine without me,' Tink Wetherbee said, standing up. He was six foot four inches tall, with a chest as puffed out as a spin-naker, a bearded face, and shaggy brown hair that he chopped him-self. Tess liked to joke that if Tink strapped a barrel round his neck he would look exactly like a St Bernard.

'You know,' he was saying as she stepped aboard with the sail bag balanced on her shoulder, 'you're pretty strong for a girl.'

'You mean, pretty strong for a girl who signs your pay cheque and could kick your sorry ass,' Tess said, heaving the bag towards him. It hit squarely in his prodigious stomach and he stumbled back.

'What's sorry about my ass?' He held onto the sail bag and craned his neck for a look.

'Trust me, Tink. It's a sorry sight.' Tess hopped into the cockpit of the boat, elbowing him in the ribs as she went by. 'Just one more week,' she said as she untied the wheel. 'One more week and I'm gone. Think you'll miss me?'

'Miss you? Did the slaves miss their masters?'

'Funny,' she said, taking the covers off the navigation instruments. 'So how's our mainsail? Ready for the big trip?'

'The best we've ever built,' he said. 'You'll be the envy of the world.'

'I like the way that sounds.' She stretched her arms and back. Her body ached from all the preparations of the past few months. She had done thousands of military presses and biceps curls. She had run and swum hundreds of miles. Every step and stroke had been carefully calculated so she would be ready to lash sails in Force 10 winds, stand long watches in high seas, and haul anchors.

Next week, with the blast of the starting cannon, Tess would set sail on a solo race around the world and, if lucky, ride the wind more than 30,000 miles. It was the greatest adventure—the dream of a lifetime—and an enormous opportunity for her sail-making business. Fewer people had circumnavigated the world alone than had climbed Mount Everest, and Tess's goal was to become one of the first ten women to make the journey. So far, eight had succeeded.

The whole community was rooting for her, holding bake sales and lobster cookouts to raise money for the quest. Starting in Boston Harbor, the race itself would be covered by every TV station in New England, and journalists around the globe would track her progress.

Tink knelt on the deck and pulled the mainsail from the sail bag. The sheet was folded like an accordion and he began to spread it out. Tess bent down to help. 'It's gorgeous,' she said, stroking the green taffeta outer layer. This wasn't any old piece of sailcloth; it was a state-of-the-art laminate with Kevlar fibres, built to ride out the worst weather in the world.

'Sure hope we spelt my name right,' she said, pulling the corner of the sail to the mast, where she unscrewed a shackle and attached the tack. She knelt on the deck, turned the winch and began feeding sail to Tink. Inch by inch, the green sheet began to climb the mast.

Tess smiled as the triangle emblazoned with her company name— CARROLL SAILS—took to the sky. Mariners on five continents would see it and, with any luck, they would want one for their own.

She turned the winch more slowly now, and the mainsail was almost two-thirds up the mast. Without checking the weather vane, she knew the wind was from the northeast, and the tickle on the back of her neck told her it would be rough later on the water.

Tess loved the wind and its ways. She had mastered the air in every form, flying hang-gliders and sailplanes, racing windsurfers and catamarans, and thrilling to the free fall of parachutes. Indeed, she had made the wind her livelihood.

Straight out of university with a physics degree, Tess had gone to work for Hood Sails in Newport, immersing herself in the advanced science of modern sail design. She worshipped Ted Hood, a Marbleheader and America's Cup skipper, who knew more about striking a curve on a spinnaker than anyone on earth. But after a couple of years, she realised she just didn't like spending her days running computer models on lift and drag ratios. So with $186.40 in the bank, she quit.

Dad went in on a bank loan with her and she opened her own sail loft on Front Street in Marblehead. Within a year, she had hired a dozen of the smartest designers, cutters and sewers in the area. She paid them better than anyone around, and encouraged them to dream up ways to make boats go faster.

Now the wind was picking up and Tess cranked the winch, but the sail suddenly seemed to jam. She pushed hard on the handle, then Tink gave a hand, but the sail wouldn't move.

'Better get up there to take a look,' she said.

'Want to hoist me?' he said, patting his belly.

'Nobody's that strong.' She walked over to one of the lockers, pulled out the boatswain's chair, fastened it to another halyard and positioned herself on the wooden seat.

'Up, up, and away,' she said, and with a few good tugs of the line, Tink lifted her in the air.

A seagull wheeled overhead as Tess soared to the top of the forty-seven-foot mast. She grabbed hold of the pole and reached into her pocket for her army knife, then she inserted the point under the jammed halyard and lifted it back into the sheave.

'We're clear,' she yelled to Tink. 'Just give me one more second. I love it up here.' She looked down on the town curving along the waterfront. She saw fishermen on the rocks casting for stripers. Across the harbour, kids were flying kites on Riverhead Beach. In the distance, she made out the mausoleums and obelisks of Waterside Cemetery sloping down to the shore. Her dad was buried there under a Japanese maple.

Marblehead was definitely her favourite place on earth, a world unto itself. But much as she loved it, Tess believed there was more for her out there beyond the rocks. There was a world to see and, God willing, great love to find. Over the years, she had given a good look at every eligible guy in town, all seven of them. She had dated fellows from Boston to Burlington, and now she dreamed of meeting a dashing millionaire, in somewhere like Australia or New Zealand, who spoke three languages, restored fifty-seven-foot classic boats and was tall enough to twirl her around in her heels.

'Hey, girl, you're not getting any lighter up there,' Tink shouted from below.

'Sorry,' she yelled. 'Just trying to memorise how everything looks.'

Back on deck and out of the harness, Tess made for the cockpit, where she pulled out a clipboard with her checklist. This weekend trip was her last chance to make sure everything was shipshape. She would inspect the sails, autopilots, electronics and survival equipment. Then she would take a few days off with her family and friends, and try to relax before the starting gun next week.

She could feel Tink's breath on her cheek as he peered over her shoulder at the list.

'You sure you don't want me to come along?' he asked. 'You know, in case it gets lonely or cold out there?'

'Nice offer, but I don't need any more ballast on board.'

'Who's going to hoist you when the main gets stuck again?'

'I'll figure something out,' Tess said. 'Now, tell me about that low-pressure front. What's the deal?'

'It's not good,' he said, pulling a computer print-out from his pocket and unfolding it. 'It looks like a lot of low pressure coming down from Maine. You can see the isobars on the back side of the depression.'

'That means more wind,' Tess said, grinning.

'Wish you weren't going out at all, but you better head southwest and get ahead of the storm. Don't want you to break anything on this boat before you have to.'

'See you Sunday, big guy.'

'Radio if you need me,' he said, going to the rail.

Tink jumped down to the dock as Tess turned the key and the onboard engine rumbled. She put one fist on the throttle and was ready to push off when she heard a voice call out.

'Hey, sailor,' a woman said from the wharf. She was in her late fifties, with fluffs of grey hair poking over a sun visor. 'Got a goodbye kiss for an old lady?'

Grace Carroll was every inch as tall as her daughter, and she moved up the gangway with forceful steps. 'I was in the kitchen looking out of the window and I saw you on the mast,' she said. 'Thought I'd come down to say hi.'

'Aw, Mom,' Tess said, 'I'm sorry I didn't call. I've been so busy—'

'Don't worry about me,' Grace said, stepping aboard. 'I've been running around getting the fundraiser ready for next week.' For years, Grace had been on the board of the Female Humane Society, which was founded after a gale turned seventy-five Marblehead women into widows in the early 1800s. 'Just be careful out there,' she was saying. 'I'm counting on you to entertain all the old ladies.'

'I'll be there,' Tess said. 'Don't worry.'

Her mother looked up and down *Querencia*, then said, 'Dad would be so proud, and darn jealous too.'

It was true. He would be proud *and* jealous. He had taught her to tack in a little tub with a broomstick mast. He had cheered when at the age of five she won her first race week series in a Turnabout. Above all, he had encouraged her to live boldly and to see how far she could go in the world. He used to quote the e. e. cummings poem: '*dive for dreams . . . and live by love.*'

When the heart attack hit him two years ago, a gaping hole opened up in Tess's universe. She had tried everything to fill the void, but it was futile. So she had decided to do what he had told her: push the limits and see how far she could go. Her race around the world was in honour of him.

'When will you be back?' Grace asked.

'Sunday for dinner, or maybe sooner. Depends on the wind.'

'Want me to make chowder?'

'More than anything in the world.'

Grace ran her hand through her hair, then said, 'Tell me something. Who am I going to feed every Sunday night when you're gone?'

'That's easy,' Tess said. 'Tink and Bobo.'

'Bobo? That old hound! He'll eat me out of house and home! You sure you can't take him around the world?'

'Wish I could, but it's against the regs. No companions allowed.'

'Silly rules. What's the point without a companion?' Grace's pale eyes managed somehow to ask questions without words, and Tess knew exactly what her mother was wondering: Why haven't you found one yet? Why haven't you settled down? Then Grace's expression changed, and she was back in the moment. 'Love you,' she said. 'Have a good sail. And don't forget you need to go see Nana when you get back. She could use a hug from her granddaughter.' She turned to go back down the gangway, but Tess stopped her with a hand on the shoulder.

'Come here, Mom,' she said, opening her arms. She pulled her tight, the way Dad always did, and thought for a moment her mother might break in her arms. It was as if Grace's body had shrunk from the lack of physical contact and the absence of her life companion. Tess could feel her mom's arms round her, too, squeezing as if she didn't want to let go.

After a few moments, they released each other. Grace pinched Tess's cheek, kissed her and walked down to the dock.

Tess leaned forwards on the throttle. The boat glided away from the slip, moved into the channel and passed the other vessels moored in the harbour. She inspected the clipboard with the weather map and the course Tink had charted. It was the easy route, away from the low pressure bearing down from the north.

But Tess wanted action. She wanted to tense the sails and feel the speed. On the horizon, she could see a vast expanse of grey altocumulus clouds with small ridges underneath like fish scales. She thought of the mariner's rhyme, 'Mare's tails and mackerel scales make tall ships carry low sails.' It would be blowing hard in a few hours, just the way she liked it.

When she cleared the harbour mouth and passed the light, she aimed the boat on an unlikely course. Her compass indicated a 58-degree heading straight for the Eagle Island Channel and the Powers Rock buoy. For Tess, the easy route was never an option. If she couldn't make it through a little low pressure, how would she ever get all the way around the world? So she eased the sheet to a broad reach and filled the mainsail with wind.

She watched her instrument dials leap as *Querencia* gained speed and rode a rising wind straight into the storm.

The woman in the black dress wept. She knelt beside a gravestone and clutched the granite slab with one hand. Her frail body jerked with every sob, and her grey hair, wrapped in a careful bun, seemed to shake loose strand by strand.

Charlie St Cloud watched from behind a boxwood hedge. He recognised the woman but kept his distance, respectful of the pain. There would be a time to offer a helping hand, but not now.

He had opened this very grave that morning, carried the coffin from the hearse, lowered it into the ground and backfilled the job when the funeral was done. It was the only burial of the day in Waterside Cemetery. Work was pretty quiet. One of Charlie's men was out trimming hedges. Another was pressure-washing monuments. A third was collecting branches that had come down in a storm. September was always the slowest month of the year in the funeral business. Charlie wasn't sure exactly why, but he knew December and January were definitely the busiest. Folks passed away more often in the coldest months and he wondered if it was the frost or a natural response to the excess of the holidays.

Thirteen years had gone by since Charlie had first come to Waterside. Thirteen years had passed since the paramedics failed to revive his little brother. Thirteen years had vanished since Sam was buried in a small coffin near the Forest of Shadows. Thirteen Octobers. Thirteen years keeping the promise.

Charlie was still a handsome young man with a flop of sandy hair. That mischievous dimple in one cheek always flashed when he smiled, and his caramel eyes melted just about everyone he met. With each passing year, his mother insisted he looked more like his father—a compliment of sorts because the only picture he had ever seen of his dad showed a rugged man on a motorcycle.

Charlie now stood six foot three inches. His shoulders were square and his arms well muscled from hauling coffins and stone. The only legacy of the accident was a barely noticeable limp.

After the crash, he had finished high school, spent a couple of years at Salem State College and had graduated with a degree in emergency medicine. He was a licensed paramedic, but he would never go too far from Waterside.

The cemetery was his world: eighty acres of grass and granite encircled by wrought iron. He lived in the caretaker's cottage by the forest and ran the whole operation—interment, mowing and maintenance. Now twenty-eight, Charlie had spent his adult years looking after the dead and the living of Waterside. He had sacrificed a great deal to keep his word to Sam.

Today, like every day, he watched someone weep, and his heart ached. It was always this way. Young, old, healthy or infirm: they came, they coped, and they moved on.

The woman tried to stand but wobbled in her heels, then fell back to one knee. This was the moment to offer a hand. Charlie moved towards her. He was dressed in the Waterside uniform: a pale blue polo shirt with the cemetery logo, pressed khakis and work boots.

'Mrs Phipps?' he said.

She looked up, startled, and seemed to stare right through him.

'It's me,' he said.

She shook her head, puzzled.

'It's me, Charlie St Cloud. Remember? Tenth grade English?'

Ruth Phipps wiped her eyes, then nodded. Back then she was known as Ruthless Ruth, the terror of Marblehead High, renowned for ruining grade-point averages with her impossible final exams.

'I came by to offer my sympathies,' Charlie said. 'And to say that you picked one of the most beautiful spots in the cemetery.'

She shook her head. 'It was so sudden. So unexpected. I never even had time to say goodbye.' Mrs Phipps wiped the tears from her face. Her arms were as frail as a willow's branches, her eyes as brown as bark.

'I'm so sorry,' Charlie said.

'What's going to happen to me now? What will I do?' Her body was still shaking. 'What about my sweet Walter?'

'Trust me,' he said. 'It's going to be all right. It just takes time. You'll see.'

'Are you sure, Charlie?' Her voice was a whisper.

'Not a doubt in my mind.'

'You were such a bright boy. I wondered what happened to you.'

'I live over there in that cottage by the forest,' he said. 'You're welcome any time.'

'That's good to know,' she said, pushing a loose strand back in her bun. 'Thanks for your help, Charlie.'

'My pleasure. That's why I'm here.'

Then Mrs Phipps walked slowly down the hill towards the great iron gates on West Shore Drive.

IT WAS CLOSING TIME, and Charlie zoomed the utility cart up and down the narrow paths, taking the turns like a Grand Prix racer. In his early days on foot, it had taken more than an hour to cover all the acres, looking for mourners lost in thought, picnickers asleep on the lawns, teenagers hiding behind headstones. To speed up this routine over the years, he had modified the little vehicle, secretly adding horsepower. Now he could secure the grounds in twenty minutes.

He always started at the north end, high on the hill, and made his way south across the fields of stone packed in tidy grids. Every pound of granite, every begonia blossom, Charlie thought, was proof of the enduring human need to be remembered. Now he drove along the Vale of Serenity and gazed down at the harbour, where a vintage schooner was sliding into a slip. Then he stopped to greet an elderly gentleman wielding a red watering can.

'Evening, Mr Guidry,' Charlie said.

'Well, hello, Charlie!' Palmer Guidry said. His hair was wavy and white and his face was stubbled with an old man's uneven shave. He was one of the regulars who came every day to pull weeds from his wife's grave and wipe dust from her stone. An old cassette recorder playing Brahms was propped against a tree.

'It's closing time,' Charlie said. 'Can I give you a lift?'

'Why, thank you. So good of you.'

Charlie stepped from the cart and walked towards Mr Guidry. 'Here, let me give you a hand with your things.'

It was a conversation repeated almost word for word every evening. Charlie had looked up Mr Guidry's condition. It was called early-onset Alzheimer's and it afflicted his short-term memory.

Mr Guidry folded his duster neatly and tucked it in his bag. He switched off the cassette machine and made one last inspection.

'I love these hollyhocks,' he said, running a hand along the crimson bloom of one plant. 'You know, they were Betty's favourite.'

'I think you told me once,' Charlie said, picking up Mr Guidry's bag and cassette recorder.

'Did I ever tell you about the time Betty planted the back yard with hollyhocks?' he said, tucking the red watering can under his arm and shuffling towards the cart. 'They grew seven feet high!'

'I think you mentioned it once.'

'Night, Betty,' he said, climbing into the front seat. 'Sweet dreams, my love. Be back soon.'

As they headed down the hill, Mr Guidry recited the story of the hollyhocks for the thousandth time. Charlie loved the way Mr Guidry twinkled with each word and how the tears always fell as they passed through the iron gates and made their way onto West Shore Drive.

'Thanks for the story, Mr Guidry,' Charlie said, as the old man got out of the cart.

'Want to come over for dinner tonight? I'll cook one of Betty's favourites. Finest meat loaf on God's green earth.'

'Thanks,' Charlie said. 'But there's somewhere I have to be.' He watched Mr Guidry get into his gold Buick and slowly pull out onto the road. Then he checked his watch. It was 6.12 p.m. Sundown was exactly thirteen minutes away. The iron gates creaked as he pushed them shut. It was definitely time to squirt oil in the hinges. Then again, there was something reassuring about the familiar sound.

He turned the big skeleton key in the lock. Waterside was now closed for the night, not to reopen until eight the next morning. He walked back to his cart and sat down in the seat. He looked out across the grounds, where sprinklers were shooting mist into the air. The serenity around him was palpable. Now he had this paradise to himself—fourteen hours until the world returned. Time for himself. Time to be. Time to think. But, most of all, time for his most important activity, hidden deep in the woods.

The Forest of Shadows was the last undeveloped section of Waterside: twenty snarled acres of oak, spruce, maple and cypress, and very valuable property. Charlie regularly heard rumours that one developer or another was panting to snap up the land. But this enthusiasm had cooled a few months ago when a real-estate agent died mysteriously and a prospective buyer collapsed from a brain haemorrhage. Now folks whispered that the woods were haunted.

Charlie knew better. The forest was the most perfect place in Waterside and it suited him fine that no one dared venture into the gloom. On this night, he steered the cart along the bumpy trail and stopped next to the blue spruce. A squadron of Canada geese honked overhead. The light was low, speckling the undergrowth. He checked over his shoulder, a matter of habit. Of course no one was following, but he had to make sure. Absolutely sure.

Then he quickly changed out of his uniform and put on an old sweatshirt, jeans and running shoes. He reached under his seat, pulled out his baseball glove and ball, and stepped into the woods. No one else would have spotted the footpath between the trees. It began on the other side of a rotting log, then widened into a trail that had been tramped down from his walk every night for thirteen years. It followed the line of a little hill to its crest, past a copse of maple trees, then dropped down beside a waterfall and swirling pool.

Charlie, who knew every bump, every vine underfoot, could have run it with his eyes closed. He hurried on past the pool and through a cypress grove, which gave way into a clearing. Here was surely the greatest secret of Waterside: a special place he had created with his own hands. Back then, he had decided to make it the exact replica of the yard at their home on Cloutman's Lane. There was a lawn ninety feet long with a pitcher's mound, rubber and plate.

He walked over to a swing hanging from a sycamore tree and plunked himself down on the wooden seat. He kicked his feet up and began to glide. With the breeze beneath him, it felt like flying. Then he leaped from the seat, landed on the ground and grabbed his mitt. He tossed the ball into the darkening sky. It touched the treetops before dropping back down again. Then he hurled it up once more. Just as it was about to land in his glove, the wind suddenly gusted and the ball went flying across the field, rolling along the grass, stopping on the edge of the woods. And then a little miracle happened, just as it did every night at sundown.

Sam St Cloud stepped from the gloom of the forest and picked up the ball. He was unchanged after all these years: still twelve years old with untamed brown curls and a Rawlings baseball mitt under his skinny arm. He wore a Red Sox cap and jersey and baggy shorts. Oscar sprinted from the undergrowth, tail held high. With soulful eyes and his distinctive yowl, he, too, was the same as before. The dog nipped at Sam's scrawny knees, then yelped at Charlie.

'C'mon, big bro,' Sam said with glee, 'let's play catch.'

A thirty-foot wall of water crashed into the cockpit, knocking Tess from her foot cleats and sweeping her into the lifelines. She gasped for air as the cold ocean wrapped itself round her, sucking her to the brink of oblivion, and then, thank God, her harness and jack line held fast. Moments before, she had zipped into her orange survival suit, essentially a one-person life raft designed for sailing in dangerous weather, enabling her to survive for up to a week in the ocean.

Tess coughed up a mouthful of sea water and pulled herself back to the wheel. *Querencia* was pounding through the howling darkness under bare poles. The mainsail was lashed to the boom.

Giant breaking waves were raging in twenty-second sets, hammering the hull, sending great blasts of spray in the air. Splotches of phosphorus streaked the sky in a stormy fireworks show. The ocean ahead looked like an endless range of mountains and cliffs rushing towards her at forty miles an hour, and monstrous peaks collapsed with the force of a landslide.

Tess didn't worry about the blistering wind, the confused sea or the salt stinging her eyes. She didn't care about the numbness in her hands or the pain in her hip from the last fall. She wasn't alarmed by the radar showing another deep depression building behind this low. All her attention was focused on one nagging problem: the sloshing sea water in her new nonslip boots. 'Damn,' she raged. 'Five hundred bucks for this gear, and the damn stuff leaks.'

Tess braced for the impact of the next breaker. Even as it slammed *Querencia*, washing her sideways, she held fast to the wheel. Yes, she thought, this was definitely good practice for the Southern Ocean above Antarctica, where she would face snow squalls and icebergs. That is, if she ever got there. All night, the crests had been breaking into spindrift, but now they were toppling, tumbling and rolling over. That meant only one thing: the storm was gathering strength.

Dangerously close to pitchpoling, *Querencia* was hurtling down the face of a giant wave now at a near-vertical angle. Tess held her breath as she plunged into the trough with the next huge wave rising before her. She heard a loud crack over her head, looked up, and saw that the wind-direction indicator and masthead instruments had blown off. Then the boat broached as the wave smashed the starboard side. She lost control of the wheel, slipped away from the cockpit and skated to the very edge of the boat, now heeling at an extreme angle. Her body was wrapped in the lifelines and she felt the ocean whooshing inches from her face.

Querencia seemed to be going sideways faster than forwards. The rigging was screaming in the wind. The ocean was almost entirely white and Tess knew it was time to go below. Hand over hand, she climbed uphill to the cockpit. She flipped on the autopilot and adjusted the course to run before the storm. Then she waited for a break in the attacking ocean. She would have only ten seconds to make it inside.

She raced forward to the companionway hatch, slid open the cover and pulled up the washboard. She put both feet on the first rung of the ladder, then fumbled to unhook the tether from the jack line. Her gloves were thick, her fingers deadened by the cold. The stern began to rise, and there were only seconds before impact. As a marauding wave overtook the boat, she unfastened the harness and slid inside the cabin, accompanied by a torrent of sea water. With a swift and practised motion, she jammed the washboard back in its slot and slammed the cover closed.

Tess waited for a moment in the darkness, listening to the roar outside, the dripping and creaking inside, and the pounding of her heart. *Querencia* was groaning from the relentless attack. Tess shimmied to port, sat down at the navigation station and flicked on a light. She unzipped her hood and pulled off her gloves.

She checked the map on her laptop monitor and guesstimated she was a good three hours from landfall in New Hampshire. She reached for the radio. It was probably time to give Tink an update. She called the marine operator, gave him Tink's number and waited for the connection. Damn, she would have to admit she had ignored his advice. She had sailed straight into the low. Tink would give her hell.

Unless she lied.

Tink's voice crackled on the speaker. 'How's my girl?' he asked.

The boat lurched violently, but Tess stayed cool. 'Everything's great,' she said. 'Smooth sailing.' The truth would only make him worry. 'Just checking in,' she went on, trying to sound unfazed.

'How's the weather?'

'Plenty of wind,' she said, listening to the hammering waves.

'What about the mainsail?'

'It fits perfectly, with a beautiful flying shape. Tell everyone they did a great job.'

'Will do.'

'I better run,' she said, as the boat pitched forward and plummeted down a steep wave. 'I'll call tomorrow.'

'*Adios*, girl. Take care.'

Her white lie wouldn't hurt him, she thought. She'd be back in time for supper on Sunday, and he'd never have to know the truth. She shoved the mike back in its cradle, hopped across to the galley and strapped herself in with the safety belt. She was tired and a bit queasy from the thrashing, but she knew she needed energy. She pulled a PowerBar from one of the lockers. Her fingers could barely get a grip on the wrapper. She tore it with her teeth and ate it in four bites.

There was nothing to do now but wait. She unhooked herself, made her way forwards to the main cabin and unzipped the top of the survival suit. She climbed into her bunk, cocooned by mesh that held her snugly in place, and began to make a list of all the things she would do when she got back home. Food was uppermost on her list. On her expedition around the world, she would have to subsist on freeze-dried rations, and would probably lose fifteen to twenty pounds. During her last week on land, she wanted to splurge. Caramel popcorn and peppermint candy at E. W. Hobbs in Salem Willows. Burgers at Flynnie's on Devereux Beach. Calamari and lobster at the Porthole Pub in Lynn. She grinned at the gluttony. To work off the guilt, she would go on long runs around the lighthouse and take walks with Mom along the Causeway.

And of course, she would visit Dad's grave at Waterside. She had gone there almost every week since he had died two years ago. Sometimes she stopped by on a morning jog with Bobo.

Tess didn't believe in ghosts or spirits. All that psychic stuff was a bunch of hooey for desperate people. It was the feeling of stability that kept her going back, and the serenity. It was a quiet place, and beautiful, too. Somehow, she felt centred there.

This time, when she got back, she would sit on the bench under the Japanese maple and tell him about her stupid decision to sail into the storm. She knew, wherever he was, he would scold her. Hell, he might yell. But he would never judge her, despite all her flaws and foolishness. His love had always been unconditional.

Her eyes began to feel heavy and she was tempted to take a cat nap, but suddenly her bunk dropped out from beneath her as the boat plunged into a hole. She floated for a second, then slammed back into the berth. Then *Querencia* broached, lurching violently to one side. Tess was thrown hard against a porthole. She feared that the boat had been knocked down flat with its mast in the water, but the weight of the keel rolled the craft back upright. She stepped from the berth and started moving towards the ladder. She needed to see if there was damage to the mast. She zipped up her suit and hood and began to climb up to the hatch.

Then the world turned upside-down.

It had been their ritual for thirteen years. And their secret too. Every evening they came together to play.

Thwack.

Sam caught the ball in his mitt and threw it back—a two-fingered fastball. It had started long ago on the evening of Sam's funeral. As the sun set, Charlie had stayed alone by the grave. And then, incredibly, impossibly, Sam had appeared, his body banged up from the crash, still holding his mitt and ball. Oscar was there too.

'What now, big bro?' he had said. 'C'mon, let's play catch.' The moment had rendered Charlie so distraught, so inconsolable, that doctors gave him powerful drugs to ward off the visions. At first the experts called them dreams, then delusions. They never believed what he could see. But see he could, and they were not illusions or hallucinations. He had been dead and had been shocked back to life. He had crossed over and then come back. He had made a promise to Sam and had been given the power to keep it.

A few months later, when yet another grown-up refused to believe what he could see, Charlie pretended it was over. He professed the apparitions were gone. So the doctors pronounced him healthy and took him off the drugs. Charlie swore he would never tell another soul about Sam. It would be his secret for ever.

From that day forward, Charlie and Sam played ball each and every evening. Their game at dusk, Charlie believed, was the key to his gift, and he feared that if he missed a single night it would be gone. As long as they threw the ball every night, he could see Sam and Sam could see him. Their time together was confined to the Waterside grounds, for Charlie swiftly realised his gift did not extend beyond its walls or gates. It had worked this way for thirteen years.

Over time, he realised his gift had grown, as he began to notice other spirits passing through the cemetery on their way to the next level. They came in all shapes and for every reason, but they each shared one telltale trait: they shimmered with an aura of warmth and light. Helping these glowing souls with their transition, he came to think, was his purpose and his punishment.

'So?' Sam asked. 'How was work today?'

'Pretty good,' Charlie said. 'Remember Mrs Phipps? Ruthless Ruth?'

'Yeah, your English teacher?'

'Exactly,' Charlie said, floating a knuckleball. 'Saw her today, hanging around her grave.'

'No way!' Sam said, firing a fastball. *Strike one.* 'What happened to her?'

'Heart attack.'

Sam's throw sailed high and Charlie leaped to catch it. *Ball one.* For his next pitch, Sam kicked his leg up and zinged a fastball. *Strike two.*

'So how's she doing?' he said.

'She's taking it hard.'

Curveball, low and outside. *Ball two.* 'When is she crossing over?'

'Not sure. Her husband Walter is on the other side.'

Fastball in the dirt, *ball three.* Full count. Two blue jays shot across the field in little loops.

'C'mon, Sam,' Charlie said, smacking his mitt. 'It's three and two, a full count. Give me your out pitch.'

They played ball until it was almost too dark to see, telling each other stories about their day. As a spirit, Sam could have roamed anywhere he wanted, travelling in the Milky Way, shimmering with a rainbow over the Lakes of Killarney, catching the sun over the Great Barrier Reef and riding the moon over Machu Picchu. The possibilities were truly infinite. The known universe with its hundred billion galaxies could have been his playground.

But Sam had sacrificed all that. He spent his days and nights on Marblehead adventures, sitting behind home plate at Seaside Park for Little League games and skateboarding down Gingerbread Hill.

'C'mon,' he said. 'Let's go swimming before it's too late. Tag, you're it!'

Then he sprinted in the direction of the pool, with Oscar and Charlie giving chase. It was the most comforting feeling in the world—the three of them flying through the trees without a care—just as it had been all those years ago on Cloutman's Lane, and just as it would always be.

Tess found herself pinned to the ceiling of her boat with bilge water surging round her head. Radio equipment slammed about and pots and pans clanked. Chaos resounded inside the cabin. Outside, the ocean and wind roared. Then the lights flickered out.

She heard the sea rushing into the boat, but fear was not foremost in her mind. *Querencia* was built to capsize and right herself. There were pumps on board to expel the water.

She huddled on the ceiling, up to her knees and elbows in water, and muttered to the boat, 'Please turn back. Come on, come on. Get upright, please?' But nothing happened, so she crawled towards the nav station and found the emergency position-indicating radio beacon in its bracket. She hated needing to ask for help, but she pushed down on the yellow power switch, breaking the safety seal, and saw the LED flash. The device was now sending a distress signal via satellite that would ping on every Coast Guard screen in New England. Suddenly she did not feel so alone.

But wait, she reminded herself, *Querencia* wasn't sinking, and there was no real need yet for an SOS. If the boat started to go down, there would be plenty of time to call the Coast Guard. So Tess flicked the toggle off and the Mayday light stopped blinking.

A minute went by, then another. She was sickened by the sulphuric stench of battery acid leaking from the power units. What was taking the boat so long to roll back over and right itself? The weight of the keel was supposed to pull *Querencia* upright.

Tess was not an especially religious woman. She went to the Old North Church on Sundays largely because it was important to her mother. She was friendly with Reverend Polkinghorne and had built him a sail or two. But she didn't like the conventions of organised faith and she preferred doing it her own way. She considered herself a spiritual person with her own relationship to God.

Now, upside-down in the Atlantic, she found herself praying in the darkness. She began by apologising for her arrogance. She knew she had taken too big a risk. She had been careless, and now she felt ashamed. This wasn't how she wanted it all to end, all alone on a weekend sail in a storm that could have been avoided. She prayed to God to be merciful. And then she summoned her father. 'Dad, please help me. Tell me what to do.' He had always bailed her out of desperate situations. She closed her eyes and promised that if she got back to the harbour she would never do anything so rash again. She would play it safe in the race around the world, even if it meant going slower. Yes, when she got out of this mess, she would go straight to Waterside and take an oath: she would change.

'Show me the way home,' she whispered into the roiling darkness. 'Dad, please help me.'

The day was grey as granite and the ground was soggy from a night of hard rain. The storm had blown a riot of leaves and branches all over the lawns. Charlie hid under his yellow hood and looked into the hole where one of his gravediggers was shovelling. It was backbreaking work on a normal day, but when the ground was drenched and the backhoe couldn't manoeuvre in the muck, it was especially miserable. Now, compounding the gloom, Elihu Swett, the cemetery commissioner, had stopped by for a spot inspection.

'The Ferrente funeral party will be here any minute,' Elihu was saying beneath his great umbrella. He was an elfin man in a tan trench coat, royal-blue corduroy suit and rubber galoshes. 'How much longer till you're done?' he asked, taking a sip from a Mountain Dew bottle that seemed half his size.

'Don't worry, we'll be ready,' Charlie said, kneeling down and looking into the opening. 'How are you doing, Joe?'

'Just fine,' Joe Carabino said from the bottom of the grave. 'But it's Elihu that I'm worried about.' He winked.

'What's the matter?' Elihu asked, stepping gingerly towards the hole.

'A lethal dose of caffeine is ten grams,' Joe said, leaning on his shovel. 'A few more of those Mountain Dews and you'll be pushing up daisies.' He paused for dramatic effect. 'You feel all right? You seem a little pale.' Before Joe could even razz him about his bloodshot eyes, Elihu stuffed the bottle in his coat pocket and took off for his Lincoln Continental.

With a swift movement, Joe jumped up from the grave and high-fived Charlie with a muddy hand. 'The old lethal-dose-of-caffeine trick,' he said. 'Poor Elihu, works every time.'

Joe was in his early thirties and built like a bull. His blunt face was darkened by the sun and his thinning hair was teased into a few proud, well-gelled spikes. By day, he worked with the dirt and the dead. By night, he chased women up and down Cape Ann with a shameless repertoire of strategies and tactics. His only other great devotion was to his own brand of evangelical atheism. That was just fine as long as he kept his missionary work outside the iron gates, but once or twice Charlie caught him grumbling 'There is no heaven!' at a graveside service or griping 'What a waste!' when a gilded ten-foot cross was brought in by crane to stand atop a mausoleum.

'What's your story tonight?' Joe was asking as they finished dressing the job. 'How about coming out with me to happy hour? I'm taking the *Horny Toad* up to Rockport. I know these gals who run a bar there. The things they do, man, you wouldn't believe.'

'Give me a hand with the lowering device,' Charlie said, walking towards the panel truck on the service road. In every cemetery around the world, this stainless-steel contraption was used to lay the dead to rest. With nylon straps and a simple switch, one man could do the work of many and lower a thousand pounds into the earth.

'The Dempsey sisters. You ever heard of them?'

'No, never.'

'You'd like Nina and Tina. Trust me.'

'Let's see how it goes today,' Charlie said.

'Yeah, yeah. "Let's see how it goes." But when it's quitting time, you'll disappear. Same old story. You know, you should live a little.'

THE FUNERAL DIRECTOR'S HELMET of black hair was as shiny and sleek as the paint job on her brand-new Cadillac hearse. 'How you guys doing?' Myrna Doliber said, slamming the front door shut.

'Better than most,' Charlie answered. He had tucked in his shirt and jammed his work gloves in his back pocket. 'How 'bout you?'

'Peachy,' she said. 'Two kids with chickenpox and a third with a busted arm.' Myrna's ancestors, the Dolibers, had been the first settlers to arrive on the peninsula back in 1629. Somewhere along the way, they had got into the funeral business and ran a monopoly all the way north to Beverly and south to Lynn. On busy days, every Doliber was put to work, even Myrna, who was known as the most superstitious person in Essex County and who kept a running list of ill omens.

'Hey, Myrna, I counted thirteen cars in your funeral procession,' Joe said with a mischievous grin. 'That mean someone's going to die today or something?'

'Knock it off,' she said, walking to the tail end of the hearse. She opened the door and stood back. Charlie reached in, released the latch, grabbed a handle of the coffin and rolled it onto the cart.

The two men pushed the coffin across the lawn and stopped beside the grave. Charlie lifted the foot of the box, which was always lighter, and Joe took the heavier head. It was a point of pride: Joe was the strongest worker in Waterside and he liked to show it. They carried the coffin and positioned it on the lowering device. Everything was now ready for the funeral.

'OK,' Charlie said. 'Break time. I'll catch you down by the water.'

'Ten-four, boss.' Joe reached behind his ear for a Camel and strolled down the hill.

Charlie walked up the rise and stood under a weeping mulberry for the best view of the proceedings. Car doors were slamming, and men and women were coming up the hill. Dozens of fire-fighters in dress uniform stepped from their vehicles. Bagpipes played a wailing song. Charlie watched the tears wash down so many faces, then looked over the job one last time. He and Joe had done good work dressing the site, camouflaging the pile of earth beneath the carpet of Astroturf and spreading a canopy of roses and carnations around the hole. Now, where was the dead man in the crowd? Often Charlie would see the departed walking the aisles or weaving among the tombstones while the mourners sniffled into their Kleenexes. With their familiar glow, the deceased might sit under a tree or lean against the coffin to take notice of who had managed to come for the burial. Insincere eulogies and phoney tears could provoke the dead to scoff vociferously. But more often than not they would be touched, even surprised, by what their lives had meant to others.

Charlie could always spot the luminous new arrivals. Those who died violently sometimes had scrapes or limped from broken bones. Those who passed away after a long illness were weak and hobbled at first but soon regained their strength. Charlie remembered how banged up Sam had looked after his own funeral, but within days he was back to his old self.

For some, of course, attending their own funeral was too much. At first, they stayed away. Then after a day or two they'd appear at Waterside and make peace with the end. Finally, they'd fade away to heaven, the next level, or wherever they were headed for eternity.

It all depended on how quickly they wanted to let go.

Charlie listened to Father Shattuck begin the ceremony. His few remaining hairs were as white as his collar and had been meticulously spun round his head like a halo. His dramatic performance was identical every time—all the way to the climactic pauses in Psalm 23 as he walked through the Valley of the Shadow of Death.

I shall fear no evil . . .

Then he read from Ecclesiastes. '"There is a season for everything,"' he intoned. '"A time for every occupation under heaven. A time for giving birth, a time for dying . . . a time for tears, a time for laughter; a time for mourning, a time for dancing . . . a time for searching, a time for losing . . . a time for loving, a time for hating . . .'''

And, Charlie thought, a time for new material . . .

Father Shattuck finished, and Don Woodfin, the chief of the Revere Fire Department, stepped forwards. He was a gaunt man with a thick moustache that bridged two hollow cheeks. 'In our one-hundred-and-nineteen-year history,' he began, 'we have suffered six line-of-duty deaths. We gather here today to mark our seventh.' He bowed his head. 'We thank you, Lord, for the life of a great man. We are grateful for his devotion to a fireman's duty, for his dedication to the preservation of life, and for the way he faced danger.'

In the front row, a woman and her baby boy wept. 'We ask the comfort of your blessing upon his family,' the chief said. 'May they be sustained by good memories, a living hope, the compassion of friends and the pride of duty well done. Amen.'

A man came and stood beside Charlie under the tree. He was wearing a fire-fighter's dress blues and he seemed lost in thought. There was a faint glow around him that made it clear: he was the dead man, and this was his funeral.

'Can you see me?' the man asked after a while.

'Yes,' Charlie whispered.

'Are you dead too?'

'No.'

The man scratched his neck. 'You look so familiar,' he said. His face was grizzled and his voice was as rough as gravel. 'Wait,' he said, 'you're the St Cloud kid, right? Charlie St Cloud? I'm Florio,' he said. 'Remember me?'

'I'm sorry,' Charlie said. 'My memory's fuzzy.'

Near the grave, the chief was invoking the fireman's prayer. Florio folded his arms and bowed his head. Then the chief gave his cue, and Charlie stepped forwards. He flipped the jam break on the lowering device and the coffin began its dignified descent.

Charlie looked at the name carved on the stone.

FLORIO FERRENTE
HUSBAND—FATHER—FIREMAN
1954–2004

And then he realised: Florio was the fireman who'd saved his life.

The coffin bumped gently to the bottom of the grave. Charlie pulled the straps and tucked them beneath the Astroturf. Then he stepped back to the mulberry tree as mourners threw roses onto the coffin.

'I'm so sorry I didn't recognise you,' he said to Florio.

'Don't worry,' Florio said. 'It was a long time ago, and you weren't in very good shape.'

'What happened to you? I had no idea—'

'It was an easy two-alarm in a residential unit,' Florio began. 'We breached the front door with the battering ram. Rescued a little girl and her mom. Kid was screaming her head off about her cat and dog. So I went back in to get them, and the roof fell in.' He gave an uneven smile. 'That's it, lights out.'

Firemen were wiping their eyes with their sleeves. Some crouched in silent prayer. A woman stepped forwards, cradling her baby boy.

'My wife, Francesca, and our new son,' Florio said. 'We tried for years for her to get pregnant, then it finally happened. No better woman on this earth, and Junior is my pride and joy.' His voice began to break. 'God knows what I'll do without them.'

'It's too soon to think about that,' Charlie said. 'Give it some time.'

They watched as his wife and baby left the grave, passed the other mourners and got into a limousine. Then Charlie began filling the hole, and Florio watched. Shovel after shovel. *Dust to dust.*

'You know,' Florio said after a while, 'I've thought about you a lot over the years. I felt so bad I couldn't save your brother. And I always wondered what happened to you. You married? Kids? What have you done with your precious life?'

Charlie kept his eyes to the ground. 'No wife, no family. I work here and volunteer at the fire station.'

'Oh, yeah? You a fireman?'

'I got qualified as a paramedic. I put in a few nights a month. I'd do more, but I can't go too far from here.'

'You know, I was a medic for more than twenty-five years. Seen a lot, but I only saw two other people come back from the dead like you did.' He paused. 'That was a gift from God, son. God had a reason for saving you. He had a purpose. You ever think about that?'

A long minute passed as Charlie shovelled more earth into the hole. Of course he had thought about that. Every single day of his life, he wondered why he hadn't been taken instead of Sam. What on earth was God's reason? What purpose did He have in mind? Then Florio broke the silence again.

'Don't worry, son,' he said. 'Sometimes it takes a while to figure things out. But you'll hear the call. You'll know when it's time. And then, you'll be set free.'

The corners of her eyes and mouth were flaky with dried-up salt from the ocean. Tess brushed away the deposits, remembering the last time she had looked like this. Then, the white residue had been left by the flood of tears after her father's funeral. Her mother had wiped the grains from her face, saying they were a reminder that tears and sea water had mixed together for thousands of years.

Tess also had a whopper of a headache and her body was black and blue from the battering she had taken. But the welts and bruises didn't seem to matter just now. What was foremost in her throbbing brain was that she was back on solid ground exactly where she wanted to be: Waterside Cemetery, near her father.

She sat in the mottled shade under the maple next to his grave. The lawn was damp, but she didn't mind. She was relishing just being there in one piece. She stretched her legs and looked at the granite headstone. She knew she owed her life to her father. After that miserable storm, he had guided her home to safe harbour. 'I never stopped talking to you out there all night,' she said. 'You must've heard me.'

Of course, she didn't actually believe that Dad was lolling around the cemetery, waiting for her to show up. No, he was out there somewhere, a force of energy, or something like that.

Tess stared up at the rust-coloured leaves. This was the one safe place in the world. The wind was gusting from the north now and big cauliflower clouds filled the sky, making it one of those rare afternoons in New England, impossibly crisp and fresh, like an apple.

Then an image from last night grabbed hold of her mind: *Querencia* flipping over, the world inverting. 'Jesus!' she said out loud. She rubbed a bruise on her forearm. She'd learned her lesson. Three hours capsized without electricity or radio had scared the hell out of her. Now she had to make good her promise to her father.

She scooted across the grass and leaned against his headstone. It was cool against her sore back and felt good. She turned her head and ran her fingers along the engraving.

GEORGE CARROLL
1941–2002

'I knew you'd come through for me,' Tess said, with tears welling up. She wiped her eyes. She had a simple rule about crying. Weeping was for wimps. But in front of Dad it was different. He had comforted her through heartbreak and disappointment. He had been the only person who really understood her. No one else came close.

'I promise that I'll change,' she said. 'No more crazy stuff on the water.' She paused. 'I finally scared myself to death.'

She ran her fingers through her hair and felt a bump on the back of her head. *Ouch*. It was sensitive to her touch. When did that happen? Must have been when she capsized. The details of the night were a blur, and she still felt rotten from the pummelling waves and noxious diesel fumes. She needed a shower and some sleep.

Tess ran through the list of all the things she needed to do before the starting gun next week. Her first stop on Monday morning would be at Lynn Marine Supply on Front Street. She would give Gus Swanson an earful. Those leaking boots were inexcusable.

Next, she would have to face Tink. She dreaded the moment. He would give her the full inquisition, and then they would go stem to stern and tally the damage. Of course, the rigging would need tuning. The mainsail would have to be resewn. Her team would have to work overtime to make the repairs in time for the race.

'I know,' she said aloud. 'It's a waste of hard work and money.' That was what really made her feel the worst. Dad had left her a chunk of dough and had urged her to spend it seeing the world. It wasn't much, but he had broken his back saving it, and he wouldn't be happy watching her blow it on repairs.

She sat silently for a few moments and she could hear his voice. It was only a distant sound in her mind now, grey cells rubbing together, but the memory made everything all right. And then suddenly she heard the gunning of an engine and an awful drone. It sounded like a buzz saw. It was coming from just over the hill.

Tess jumped up and stomped off to see what on earth was causing the ruckus.

WHAT HAVE YOU DONE with your precious life? Florio's words had lingered in the air long after Charlie had gone off to the fire station to partake of the wine and cheese reception in Florio's memory. No matter what chores were there to distract Charlie, the question followed. In the Dalrymple family plot, he poured the cement foundation for a new headstone and searched for answers. On the Mount of Memory, he chopped up an oak that had fallen in the storm and he wondered. What had he done with his second chance?

He watched a squadron of geese take flight in a tight V-formation, honking as they cleared the treetops, circling once over the grounds, then winging across the harbour. One thing was for sure: he had spent far too much of his precious life battling those evil creatures. They chomped on grass, devoured flowers, dirtied monuments, and even attacked mourners.

On this fine afternoon, Charlie sat on a bench by the lake with Joe the Atheist, who had invented an ingenious method of scaring off the loathsome birds. It involved deploying an armada of remote-controlled toy motorboats.

'PT-109, ready for attack,' Joe said.

Charlie's mind was elsewhere. 'You think you'll ever do anything important with your life?' he asked.

'What are you talking about? This is important,' Joe said. 'We've got a job to do.' He looked through a pair of army field glasses and positioned a metal box with a joystick in his lap.

'I'm serious. You think you'll ever amount to anything? You think God has a plan for you?'

'God?' Joe said. 'You kidding me? I believe in luck. That's all. You've either got it or you don't. Remember last year? I was one digit away from winning thirty-four million in the Massachusetts lottery. You think God had anything to do with that? No way.' He smiled and leaned forwards. 'Look! One more squadron of geese at two o'clock by the Isle of Solitude,' he said. 'Requesting permission to attack.'

'Permission granted,' Charlie said.

Joe jammed the control stick forward. A grey patrol boat zoomed straight for the birds. The engine blared and a horn hooted. 'Two hundred feet and closing,' he said, peering through the binoculars.

As always, the boat worked perfectly. With much panic, the last remaining birds scooted along the water, took flight with a few flaps and soared over the trees. The little boat banked hard, swooping close to the shore, kicking up a wave of spray. And then Charlie saw a young woman standing on the far side. She was tall and beautiful, and she was waving to him. She seemed to be shouting, but her words were drowned out by the droning engine. It was Tess Carroll.

'I'll catch you later,' he said to Joe, who was focused on manoeuvring PT-109 back to its little dock.

'Ten-four,' he said.

Charlie jumped in his cart and steered round the lake towards Tess. She was a minor celebrity in town and, truth be told, he had long admired her from afar. They had gone to high school around the same time but she was a couple of years younger. Two years ago, Charlie had buried her father, and she had come just about every week since to pay her respects. She was always alone or with her golden retriever. She never wanted to be disturbed.

But there she was now, stunning in jeans and a button-down shirt, marching along the gravel path towards him, her ponytail sashaying behind. He ran his hands through his hair and slowed to a stop.

Before he could say hello, Tess let loose. 'God almighty!' she said. 'Do you really need to make such a racket? A person comes here for some quiet and what does she get? The invasion of Normandy!'

'Actually, it's our geese-management programme,' Charlie said, but as the phrase left his lips it sounded funny.

'Geese-management programme?' Tess barely contained a guffaw.

'Yes,' he said, 'the Canada geese population—' He stopped mid-sentence. She was smiling at him with the most remarkable smile.

'No, go on,' she said. 'I'm mesmerised. Tell me more about the Canada geese population.' She twiddled her ponytail with one hand and tilted her head. A fizzy mixture of attraction and awkwardness was rising in Charlie.

'Let me start over. I'm sorry about the noise. We get a little carried away here sometimes.' He grinned. 'I'm Charlie—'

'St Cloud,' she said. 'I remember.'

'You're Tess Carroll, the one going around the world,' he said, a smidge too enthusiastically. He had read about her just the other day in the *Reporter*. A front-page feature had described her solo race, and a colour photo had shown her in the cockpit of an Aerodyne 38. 'That's some boat you've got,' he said.

'Thanks,' she said, pushing a wisp of hair from her eyes. 'You sail?' she asked. 'Don't think I've seen you on the water.'

'Used to. You know, Optimists, 110s. Nothing fancy. Look, I'm sorry we disturbed you. Won't happen again.'

'Don't worry about it.' She scrunched her face. 'I'm just being a pain in the ass today. I've got a killer headache.' She rubbed her forehead and the sun glinted in her eyes.

Charlie lived in a verdant world surrounded by every imaginable shade of green, but her eyes were perfection. Light as lime on the outer edges, rich as emerald towards the centre. Transfixed, he found himself saying the opposite of what he intended: 'I better go now.'

'What's the rush? Another attack on those poor geese?'

Charlie laughed. 'Thought you wanted a little quiet, that's all.'

'It's better now.'

Charlie felt her eyes looking him up and down, and he was embarrassed about the mud on his boots and the stains on his trousers.

'You know,' she said, 'my dad's buried here. Just on top of that hill.' She pointed. 'The view's pretty nice up there.'

Without another word, she took off, her ponytail bouncing behind her. Charlie wasn't sure whether to follow. Was she inviting him for a look? Or was she finished with the conversation? Every instinct told him to go back to work. But he found himself racing up the hill. When he reached the crest, Tess had already plopped down on the grass. Her legs were stretched out and she was looking down towards the harbour, where the boats pointed northeast on their moorings. In the distance, a fisherman was hauling a lobster pot from the water.

'Looks like Tim Bird had a good catch today,' she said. 'His stern sure is riding low.'

'Your dad was a lobsterman, wasn't he?' Charlie said, sitting down not far from her.

She looked at him. 'Yeah, how'd you know?'

Charlie wasn't sure whether to answer. He didn't want to seem strange, but he remembered every job he had worked in the cemetery.

'How'd you know about my dad?' Tess asked insistently.

'I was working the day he was buried.'

'Oh.' Tess rubbed her forehead and smoothed her hair back. 'I was in such a fog. Barely remember a thing.'

But Charlie recalled the entire funeral and the fact that her dead father hadn't shown up in the cemetery. It wasn't too surprising: many folks chose to move on immediately to the next level.

He studied Tess's face. She was lovelier, more real than anyone he had known in a long time. He was beginning to feel emboldened. 'This may sound weird,' he said, 'but I loved that poem you recited.'

'You remember?'

'It was "dive for dreams" by e. e. cummings.'

'My dad's favourite,' she said.

'I looked it up afterwards.' He paused, then recited a few lines:

> 'trust your heart
> if the seas catch fire
> (and live by love
> though the stars walk backward)'

'. . . *and live by love,*' she repeated, '*though the stars walk backward.*'

'It's great,' Charlie said, 'but I'm not really sure what it means.'

'Me neither.'

Her face relaxed, her eyes twinkled and her lips curled up in a bow. She leaned back and let out a laugh that echoed across the grounds. Charlie was sure it was the best sound he had heard in ages.

Then she fixed her eyes on him and said, 'So tell me, Charlie St Cloud. What's a guy like you doing in a place like this?'

IT FIGURED SHE WOULD spot a cute guy the week before leaving town. That's what had always happened. Her timing was either impeccably off or the guys she liked turned out to be deadweight.

She was lying in the grass and she was kind of liking this guy Charlie. It was strange. She had lived in this town all her life and had never really noticed him until today. Back at school, everyone had known about the St Cloud boys. They were the most promising brothers in Essex County until the elder had killed the younger on the General Edwards drawbridge. It was an accident, a real tragedy, and folks whispered that Charlie had never got over it.

But here he was and he seemed perfectly OK. All right, he worked in a cemetery and that was a bit odd, but he was funny, kind and great-looking in that rough way. His hands were a little muddy, but there was a gentleness to him, a sweetness. And then there was the way he was looking at her.

'Charlie?' she said. 'Quit staring and answer my question.'

He blinked. 'What question?'

'What are you doing here? Why work in the cemetery?'

'Why not? Beats having an office job. I get to be outdoors all day, plus, it's fun being the boss, you know?' He pulled a blade of grass from the ground, put it between his fingers, cupped his hands and blew. It made a strange whistle and suddenly the trees seemed to come alive. This guy was too much. Even the birds sang to him.

She pulled a few blades and held them to her face. 'Love that smell.'

'Me too.'

'You'd think they'd bottle it and sell it.'

'All you need is some hexanol, methanol, butanone and—'

'OK. You talk to the birds. You know the chemicals in grass. Are you for real?'

Charlie laughed. 'Of course I am. Real as you are.'

Tess studied the dimple on his cheek. The shock of hair flopping down over his eyes. He was real, all right. 'So what about all the dead people? Isn't it a little creepy, you know, working here every day?'

He laughed again. 'Not at all. Hospitals and nursing homes deal with death. Funeral homes too. But this is different. This is a park. When folks get here, they're in coffins and urns.'

Tess pulled the rubber band from her ponytail. She let her hair fall around her shoulders. Her headache was still there and she was groggy from the lack of sleep, but she wanted to know more. 'What about your brother?' she asked.

'My brother? What about him?'

It was almost imperceptible, but she sensed him pulling back.

'He's buried here, isn't he? Is that why you're here?'

Charlie shrugged his shoulders. 'It's my job,' he said. 'Pays the bills and beats selling insurance in an office, know what I mean?'

Tess watched his eyes. She knew his answer was just camouflage.

'Listen,' he said, getting to his feet. 'I've got to get back to work. It's been really nice talking.'

'I'm sorry, that was none of my business. Me and my big mouth.'

'Trust me, there's nothing wrong with your mouth,' he said. 'Maybe we can talk about it another time.'

Tess stood and looked up at Charlie. Suddenly the intrepid sailor didn't know which way to tack. 'I'd like that,' she said at last.

'Hey, good luck with that trip of yours,' he said.

'Thanks,' she said. 'Hope I see you again when I get back.'

'Get back?'

'You know, I'm sailing in a few days.'

She watched his face closely. His brow furrowed and then he surprised her. 'Listen, if you don't have plans, how about dinner tonight? I'll throw some fish on the fire.'

'You cook, too?'

'Nothing fancy.'

Tess smiled. 'I'd love to,' she said.

'Great. I live over there by the forest,' Charlie said, pointing to the cottage nestling against the trees. 'I'll meet you at the front gates. Eight o'clock work for you?'

'It's a date.'

Charlie waved, then strolled off towards his cart, leaving Tess alone on the hill. For months, she had walled herself off from the world with preparations for the race. She was the last person in Essex County who was supposed to have a date tonight.

The splashes of purple and pink painted across the sky meant trouble. For years, Charlie had organised his life around the sundown meeting with Sam, and he knew that tonight he had until exactly 6.51 p.m., the precise moment of civil twilight when the centre of the sun's disc dropped six degrees below the horizon and the hidden playground was dark. That gave him twenty-one minutes to race around in his old '66 Rambler to pick up swordfish steaks at the Lobster Company in Little Harbor, and then whip over to the other side of town for salad and dessert ingredients at Crosby's. It was going to be very close.

He thought of Tess standing up there on the hill and couldn't believe his gumption. He had actually asked her to dinner at his place, and her green eyes had lit up when she'd said yes.

Charlie aimed the Rambler into a parking place on Orne Street, glanced at the sky and checked his watch. Seventeen minutes to go. He got out of the car and saw from the low light reflecting on the water that the sun had already dipped below the tree line. He rushed down the street and opened the door to the Lobster Company. Once inside he was accosted by the smell of brine and fish. Big tanks filled with lobsters gurgled in the middle of the room. The concrete floor was wet from water splashing over the edges.

Bowdy Cartwright stood behind the counter. He had owned the Lobster Company for ever. He was a jowly fellow, with at least three chins, who had amused generations of kids with his uncanny imitation of a puffer fish. 'What are you looking for today?' he asked. 'We've got good haddock for chowder and clams for steamers—'

'I'll take two swordfish steaks, half a pound each,' Charlie said.

'You got it. Just off the boat from the Grand Banks.'

A young woman stepped out from one of the back rooms of the store. Margie Cartwright flipped her long blonde hair to one side and flashed a red lipsticky smile. She went straight to the cash register, leaned over and thrust her cheek towards him.

'Come on, Charlie. Give one up for your old gal.'

Way back, before he ruined everything, Margie was his sweetheart. She was a year older, and they had met one freezing Thanksgiving at the big game against Swampscott. She was a cheerleader who had insisted on wearing a little skirt and sweater whatever the weather.

Their romance was innocent enough, with nights spent immersed in conversation at the House of Pizza. Then came the accident, and Charlie had retreated. Margie had tried to bring him back, but he'd pushed her away.

Charlie leaned forwards and kissed her.

'Thatta boy,' she said, batting long eyelashes. Charlie smelt her Chloë perfume. In many ways, Margie hadn't let go of her glory years. Her long blonde hair was unchanged, and she wore a tight pink sweater, short black skirt and high boots.

'So? Whatcha cooking tonight?' she asked.

'Oh, nothing much.'

'Here ya go,' Bowdy said, handing Charlie a paper bag. 'That's two swordfish steaks, Margie. A little more than a pound.'

'Fish for two?' Margie said, arching a well-plucked eyebrow. 'C'mon, Charlie! Who is she?'

Charlie threw a $20 bill on the register. 'Sorry, Margie. I gotta run.'

'What's the big secret? You know I'm going to find out anyway! Might as well tell me.'

Charlie thought for a moment. She was right. Her network of spies would report back within days. What was the harm in telling? In fact, maybe she could help.

He checked his watch—eleven minutes to go—and decided to skip Crosby's for salad and dessert. He leaned forwards conspiratorially, and said, 'Swear you won't tell?'

'Cross my Catholic heart.'

'All right,' he said, lowering his voice. 'What do you know about Tess Carroll?'

'Nana, can you hear me? Nana?'

Tess leaned forwards and peered into her grandmother's soft green eyes. The old woman was sitting in a brown recliner near a window in her room in the Devereux House nursing home. Tess had walked over on her way home from the cemetery.

'Nana, it's me,' Tess said. 'You won't believe it. I think I just met a great guy!'

Her grandmother blinked and stared out of the window. Her wrinkled hand fumbled for an orange-juice carton with a straw. She lifted it up, and took a sip. Some days, she recognised Tess. But on occasion, it seemed as if she didn't even see her granddaughter at all.

'What are you searching for out there?' Tess asked. The window looked out onto a parking lot, where Tess saw a bird on a fence. 'Are you looking at that sparrow? Is that what you see?'

Nana smiled, closed her eyes for a moment, then opened them again.

'Listen, Nana, I came to say goodbye,' Tess said. 'Remember? I'm going on a big sail all the way around the world.' She paused and looked at her grandmother's beaded necklace. Every day she insisted on being dressed in a colourful hat and cheerful jewellery. 'I'll bring back jewels from the Orient. How does that sound?'

Nana's lips curled up. There was a little twinkle in her eye. Tess wondered what she was thinking. Could she even hear any of this?

'You know I'm here, don't you?' Tess said. 'You know I'm right next to you.'

The room was silent. Then Nana finally spoke in a firm voice: 'Of course I do.'

Tess was speechless. It was the first time in months that her grandmother had acknowledged her presence.

'You all right, honey?' Nana said.

Tess still couldn't find words.

Nana's eyes focused and she said, 'It's OK, dear. Everything's going to be all right, and I'll see you very soon.' Then her lids closed, and her head began to tilt. Soon she was snoring softly.

Tess got up and kissed her grandmother's cheek. 'Love you,' she said. 'See you soon.'

Charlie let go of the rope and flew through the air. He tucked into the cannonball position, held his breath and splashed into the cool water. With a few good kicks, he swam to the mossy bottom, grabbed hold of the big boulder to keep himself down and listened to the sound of crackling air bubbles and his pounding heart.

He had made it to the forest before sundown with only seconds to spare, but now he faced unfamiliar feelings about being there. When his lungs began to burn, he let go of the boulder and pushed off the bottom. He broke the surface with a great splash and, when the ripples had settled, he heard Sam's voice on the bank: 'One minute and

twenty-two seconds! Charlie St Cloud shatters the Waterside record!'
His brother was sitting shirtless on a log with Oscar.

It was just past sundown in the Forest of Shadows, and soft streams
of violet light filtered through the trees. Charlie climbed out of the
pool and wrapped a towel round his shoulders. His dripping cut-offs
touched his knees, where scars from the accident crisscrossed in
fading stripes. He glanced at his watch. Tess would arrive at the iron
gates in sixty minutes.

'Time for one more dive,' Charlie said. 'Go for it, little man.'

Sam jumped up and, with a gangly arm, reached for the rope. He
wore jean cut-offs, too, just like his older brother, and was so skinny
he seemed to be all knobs and joints. 'Give me a push,' he said.

Charlie obliged, and Sam swung low across the water, then arced
upwards. At the perfect moment, he let go. Like a leaf on the wind, he
soared up and up, defying gravity. Then he tucked into a front somersault with a 540-degree spin.

Sploosh.

Sam disappeared underwater for the longest time, and when he
finally surfaced he had a big smile. He climbed out of the pool and
grabbed his towel. 'You want to try a misty flip?' he asked.

'No way. Too hard.'

'Chicken.'

'Chicken? You've got a few advantages in the flying department.'

'Don't be a wimp,' Sam said. 'It's easy. I'll show you how.'

'Nah, I'm done.' Charlie pulled a sweatshirt over his head.

'What's up with you tonight?' Sam asked. 'We barely even threw
the ball around and now you're splitting.'

'Nothing's up.'

'Yeah, right. You're acting all freaky.'

'No, I'm not.'

'Are too.'

'Enough, Sam.'

Charlie sat down on the log, slipped on a running shoe and began
to tie the laces. He hated being impatient with his brother, but tonight
he was tired of the same old routine.

Sam's eyes widened. 'Wait a minute! It's a girl, right? You met
someone. You've got a date tonight!'

'What are you talking about?'

'Liar!' Sam said. His brown eyes were full of glee. 'Tell the truth.
Resistance is futile. What's her name?'

Charlie pulled on the other shoe and made a quick calculation. He figured he would get home faster if he just surrendered to the cross-examination. 'Her name is Tess Carroll,' he said finally. 'She's a sail-maker. Her dad died a couple of years ago from a heart attack.'

Sam sat down beside him on the log. 'Does she like the Sox?'

'Don't know yet.'

'So what's the matter? What are you so afraid of?'

'Not afraid of anything.' Another lie. He was petrified.

Sam smiled and put on his T-shirt. 'I can do recon, if you want. See if she has a boyfriend.'

'Margie Cartwright says she's single.'

'So how can I help?'

'Stay out of it.' Charlie checked his watch again. 'I better get going.' He stood up from the log. 'Remember,' he said, 'no monkey business. Stay away from Tess and keep clear of the cottage tonight.'

'Relax, you're too uptight,' Sam said. He stood up, reached for the rope. 'Give me a push, big bro.'

Once more, Charlie obliged and Sam swung out over the pool. He glided back and forth a few times, picking up speed, and then, at the perfect moment, he let go. 'See you later.'

Charlie blinked, Sam vanished, and all that was left in the Forest of Shadows was the fading light and the whoosh of the wind.

Tink had already ploughed through a pint of Ben & Jerry's Chunky Monkey and was halfway through a triple-decker baloney, Swiss and slaw sandwich. A giant bottle of Diet Dr Pepper, his only nod to weightwatching, sat with the remains of his trencherman's snack on the bench in Crocker Park. Tess's dog, Bobo, lazed in the grass nearby, chomping through a bag of sourdough pretzels.

Tink had come to hang out here on the bluff above the harbour as day turned to night. An hour earlier, he had swung by Lookout Court to check on Tess's place while she was away and to make sure every-thing was all right. He had let himself in the front door that was always unlocked and had seen the usual mayhem of her whirlwind. Running shoes strewn in the living room, dirty dishes piled in the sink and Bobo whimpering to go outside.

So he had taken the golden retriever to the park, as he often did.

Now Saturday night was already upon him, and again he had nothing much to do. Some weekends, he managed to score a meal off Tess by dropping by and pleading hunger. If she was home, she always took him in and they wound up cooking together, renting a movie and lazing on her sofa. She managed to burn everything she ever touched in the kitchen, but he didn't mind. He just liked being near her.

On one hand, Tess was like his kid sister. She was the type of girl who needed a big brother to keep her on the straight and narrow. She was smarter than everyone else and as strong a sailor as anyone he had ever met. But she'd also needed an anchor since her dad had died, and he was trying his hardest to fill that job.

Since the moment they'd met he had wrestled with a wicked crush on her. At the time, he was a small-time celebrity, doing the weather on TV, and had volunteered to sit in the dunking booth to raise money for charity. A stunning woman with long dark hair had fired three footballs at the target. Each spiral had found its mark, plunging him into the murky tank. Once he'd dried off, he'd been determined to meet the girl with the killer arm.

That was four years ago, before he was run off the air for calling the emaciated anchorwoman on the eleven o'clock news a 'skeletal gasbag'. Tess had written to the station on his behalf; they had become fast friends, and he had gone to work for her in the sail loft. When it came to men, though, she was a mystery. There was no holding on to her. She was a free spirit, and he lived uncomfortably with his longing.

Bobo was eyeing his triple-decker now, and Tink pulled out a slice of baloney and tossed it to him. 'So what's the girl up to?' he asked. 'She got a hot date tonight?' The dog woofed. 'Figures.'

Tink hated that this would be his life for so many months while Tess was sailing around the world. He got up from the bench, wiped the mustard from his beard and tucked in his flannel shirt.

'Time to go, boy,' he said, snapping the leash on Bobo. He tossed the trash in the can and they lumbered down Darling Street.

CHARLIE HAD PULLED OUT all the stops for dinner and Tess was enjoying every moment. His grilled swordfish with tomato and capers had been sublime, and the salad of beetroot and oranges was heavenly. She had no room left for dessert. But she would find a way.

They were seated at a little round table on the edge of his living room. The lights were low, a log crackled in the fireplace and two candles framed his face. He was telling her a story about his surname, which came from St Cloud, Minnesota, the Mississippi River town where his mother had been born. The original St Cloud, he explained, was a sixth-century French prince who renounced the world to serve God after his brothers were murdered by an evil uncle. Tess watched his mouth move and listened to his beautiful deep voice. Then, seamlessly, he was delving into something called nephology, the scientific study of clouds.

Charlie was a gentler, more sophisticated breed than the critters she had grown up around, Tess thought. There was also something effortless about the evening. For starters, there wasn't a cookbook in sight. He did it all himself—sautéing, flambéing and all those other activities in the kitchen that she had no idea about.

'I love the name of your boat,' he was saying. '*Querencia*, right?'

'Yes,' she said. 'You speak Spanish?'

'No, but I read a book about bullfighting once. Isn't that the spot in the ring where the bull feels protected and secure?'

'Exactly,' she said. 'Sometimes it's a place in the sun. Other times it's in the shade. It's where the bull goes between charges. It's like an invisible fortress, the only safe place.'

'Just like your boat.'

'Yeah, and just like Marblehead.'

Soon, Tess found herself wanting Charlie to know everything about her. And she wanted him to know more about her dad, who for some reason tonight felt closer than ever.

Yes, Tess felt a rare connection to Charlie, and it was at once exciting and frightening. With every passing moment, she knew that she was losing a little bit of control, and that wasn't good. Everything about him was like a gentle undertow pulling her deeper and deeper.

'Want dessert?' he asked all of a sudden.

'Do I look like a girl who ever says no to dessert?'

'Coming right up,' he said, gathering the dishes.

'Better be good.' She sat back in her chair. 'You sure I can't help with anything? I feel like a lump just sitting here.'

'Make yourself useful and change the CD.'

'Any requests?'

'Nope, it's a test.'

On a stand in the corner, the stereo was playing the blues, something vaguely familiar on the guitar. Looking over his stacks of CDs, she felt a twinge of pressure. What if he didn't like what she chose?

She thumbed through a few, then she saw the Jayhawks and slipped *Hollywood Town Hall* into the machine. The Minnesota band felt just right: not too predictable or noisy, with a few jangly ballads.

'Not bad. You can stay,' Charlie said, emerging from the kitchen with a chocolate cake and candle.

'Wow! What's the occasion?' she said.

'Your birthday.'

'But it's not till February.'

'September, February, whatever. I thought we should celebrate early because you're going to be away.' He held the cake forwards so she could blow out the candle.

In that moment, Tess almost melted, but something inside told her to be on guard. She carefully took his measure. He was standing there all tall and handsome, with the candle flickering in his eyes. His dimple danced on one cheek, and the cake itself seemed miniature in his large hands.

'Go on,' he said. 'What are you waiting for? Make a wish!'

Was he pulling her leg? No one on planet Earth was that sweet. She took a breath, wished for him to be as perfect as he seemed, and was about to puff out the candle when he busted up laughing. 'You totally fell for it, didn't you?' he said.

Tess couldn't help giggling too. 'Yes, I did,' she said. She poked one finger into the icing. 'Tell the truth. Why the cake?'

'It's the anniversary of Ted Williams hitting .406.'

'You're kidding.'

'Nope,' Charlie said, setting down the cake. 'This week in 1941, Teddy Ballgame played a doubleheader and went six for eight. The guy was only twenty-three years old.'

'Oh, no,' she said. 'A Red Sox fan.'

'You?'

'Hate baseball. It's so boring. I call it standball. You know, they just stand around for nine innings. Football is more my speed, and the Patriots are my guys.'

'Really?' he said, a bit incredulous. 'I didn't figure you going for guys with no necks.'

'Oh, yeah, big time, and the hairier the better.'

With that, Tess suddenly felt relieved. The bubble had burst. They didn't agree on everything, and that brought a curious comfort.

Charlie handed her a piece of cake and she took a bite. She closed her eyes and said nothing.

'It's OK?' Charlie said. 'I ran out of time and threw it together.'

'It's edible,' she said, rolling the chocolate over her tongue. She was working it, and Charlie, which she enjoyed. Finally, she smiled. 'Actually, it's wonderful. Like everything tonight.'

'You like to cook?' Charlie asked.

'No, I like to eat,' she said, slowly savouring another bite. 'The worst part of solo sailing is the food. Miserable freeze-dried rations.'

'Slow down,' he said. 'I only made one cake.'

She grinned. 'So where'd you learn to cook?' she said. 'Your mom?'

'Yup. I called her in Oregon to get some ideas for tonight.'

'So what's she doing in Oregon?'

'She moved out there right after the accident,' Charlie said. 'She didn't want any reminders. She's got a new life now. She's married with stepkids.'

'You mean she just left you here?'

'No, I refused to go. So I lived with the Ingalls family till I graduated. Since then, I've been on my own.'

Tess got up from the table, walked over to a darkened corner of the room with charts on the wall and switched on a lamp. The charts showed the roads and waters of the Eastern seaboard. She noticed strange concentric circles drawn neatly on each of them. They spread out from Marblehead and reached to New York and Canada. Next to the charts there were tables listing the times of sunrise and sunset.

'What are these about?' she asked Charlie. She put a finger on one of the loops. 'I know it's got something to do with distance, but I can't figure it out.'

'It's just a project of mine,' he said, standing up and moving towards a big antique map that was framed behind glass. 'Tell me more about this trip of yours.'

'What about it?'

'For starters, your route?'

'OK, I start in Boston Harbor on Friday, then head south to the Caribbean, and eventually go through the Panama Canal.'

'Show me.' He watched as Tess walked across to him.

'You're limping.'

'Just a few knocks from my last sail.'

'That where you got those bruises?'

'Yeah, I got tossed around pretty good.'

They stood there, just inches apart, as Tess traced her route across the Pacific. She could feel his breath on her neck as she pointed to distant stops like the Marquesas, Tuamotu Islands, Tonga and Fiji. Then he brushed against her for a closer look as she traced the course over the top of Australia, across the Indian Ocean to Durban, around the Cape of Good Hope into the South Atlantic, where the winds would push her home.

'That's a long way by yourself,' he said. 'Don't think I'd be brave enough to do it.'

'You're just smarter than I am.'

They were side by side, staring at the whole wide world that she was going to circle. She turned to Charlie and looked into his eyes. 'Where do you dream of going, Chas?' She heard herself call him by a nickname—it just came out, but she liked the sound of it.

'Zanzibar, Tasmania, the Galapagos. Everywhere . . .'

'So why don't you?'

He pushed his hands into his pockets and sighed. 'Too many responsibilities here.'

'All work and no play?'

He didn't answer. For the first time this evening, there was a twinge of discomfort. Despite his smile and twinkle, this man was hiding something. But instead of wanting to run from his secrets, she just wanted to be closer.

'So,' she said, 'what's stopping you?'

His eyes dodged her and then he flashed that smile that must have got him out of most tight spots. 'Let's take a walk.'

'In the cemetery? It's the middle of the night.'

'C'mon,' he said, grabbing their coats. 'Anybody who'd sail solo around the world can't be scared of a cemetery. I want to show you something.'

IT WAS MIDNIGHT in Waterside, and fog oozed between the monuments. As Charlie led the way across the lawn, the moon was invisible behind the clouds and walls of darkness closed in on every side. Marble angels and granite nymphs appeared from nowhere as his flashlight slashed the gloom.

It was the witching hour, and Charlie was under a spell. Everything about Tess had thrown him off balance in the best possible way. From the moment she had come strolling down West Shore Drive, he had tried to memorise every detail about the evening. Her hair had been blowing wild, and when he'd greeted her with an outstretched hand, she'd ignored it and kissed him hello on the cheek.

'Dinner ready?' she'd said. 'I'm starving.'

Sure enough, she'd eaten two portions of everything and had been lavish with her praise. He loved the way she'd seemed to devour life, savouring every bite. He'd told real stories, not the canned ones that usually came out on dates. Tess had drawn out the real Charlie, the one with dreams of breaking free of everything that reined him in.

He'd even wanted to tell her about his charts on the wall, the sunset tables, and how those concentric circles governed his life. The rings on the charts showed the ambit of his world, demarcating exactly how far he could go from Waterside and still get back for Sam. A trip to Cape Cod. A drive up to New Hampshire. The outer circle was the absolute farthest he could go. Beyond that line, there was no chance of making it home in time. The promise would be broken and his brother would be gone.

It could be dangerous sharing all this with Tess, but now, with the night winding down, he was feeling ready to reveal a little more.

'Where are we going?' she asked as they tramped up the hill.

'Trust me, it's special.'

They walked on, and the moon finally poked through the clouds, gently touching headstones in every direction.

'We used to sneak in here all the time when we were kids,' Tess said. 'I made out with my first boy behind that obelisk over there.'

'Who was the lucky guy?'

'Tad Baylor. I think he was in your class.'

'The human fly?' Tad had been caught stealing final exams from the copy room after scaling the wall of the administration building and climbing through a window. 'You have excellent taste.'

'I was fourteen,' she said, 'and he was a great kisser.'

They kept on going across the lawns. An owl hooted from the tree-tops. The air was cool and Charlie buttoned up his coat.

'So how long have you worked here?' Tess asked as they passed through a plot of Revolutionary War graves.

'Thirteen years,' Charlie said. 'Barnaby Sweetland gave me my first job here when I was in high school. He was the caretaker for thirty years. Remember him? The guy had a voice like an angel, and he ran the chorus at the Old North Church. Every day in the grounds, planting, cutting, sweeping, we could hear him singing to the skies.'

They had reached the crest of a hill where two willows hovered over a small, square stone building above the harbour. Guarding the entrance were two columns and a pair of crossed baseball bats. Tess walked straight to the front steps. Charlie aimed the flashlight at the name St Cloud carved on the lintel.

'Your brother,' she said.

'Yes, Sam.' Charlie traced the sharp outline of the structure with his beam.

Tess touched the smooth stone. 'Is it all marble?'

'Imported from Carrara. They spared no expense. The driver of the eighteen-wheeler that hit us was drunk. His company paid for every inch of this. It was all about public relations.' He ran the flashlight down one of the columns. 'They gave the guy five years, but he got away with three for good behaviour.'

'I'm so sorry.'

'Don't be.' He shook his head. 'It was my fault. I never should've taken Sam to Fenway, and we never should've been on the bridge in the first place. If I'd been paying any attention, I could've avoided the crash, you know, gotten out of the way of the truck.'

And so, without noticing, Charlie broke one of his cardinal rules. He began talking about Sam. With everyone else in the world, he had always dodged the topic.

He sat down on the steps of the mausoleum and said, 'You were right this afternoon. Sam is why I work here. I promised I'd always take care of him.'

'So you think he's around?'

Charlie looked up at her. 'As sure as I am of anything.'

'If only I had that same certainty about my father.' She sat down beside him. He could smell her shampoo, feel her warmth. 'I wish I knew Dad was close by.'

'What makes you think he isn't?' Charlie asked.

'There'd be some kind of sign, don't you think?'

'I think those signs are all around if you know where to look.'

He made an absent-minded looping motion with the flashlight beam, and as it swept the darkness he saw the most unexpected sight: Sam was hanging upside-down from a hemlock branch and making a funny face. Charlie shut off the beam and leapt to his feet.

'What's wrong?' Tess asked.

'Nothing. Just got a chill.' He flipped the flashlight on again, turned it in the direction of the branch, but Sam was gone.

'You were telling me about Sam,' she said.

He focused on her emerald eyes. Did she really want to hear the answers? He was about to speak, but with his peripheral vision he saw something move. Over her shoulder in the light of the emerging moon, there was Sam racing across the lawn with Oscar.

'What do you miss most about him?' Tess asked.

'I miss punching him on the nose when he was a brat,' he said in a voice that he hoped Sam would hear. 'He liked to spy on people even when it was totally inappropriate.' Charlie checked over Tess's shoulder again, and now Sam was gone. 'Most of all,' he continued, 'I miss that feeling when you go to sleep at night and when you wake up in the morning. It's the feeling that everything is all right in the world, that you aren't missing anything. Sometimes when I wake up, I get it for a few seconds, but then I remember what happened.'

'You think that'll ever go away?'

'I doubt it.' He found himself opening up even more. 'Some days are better than others. You know, it feels like it's gone, and I'm just like everyone else. Then, without warning, it comes back and lodges in my mind. That's when I don't feel right being around anyone. So I stay here behind the gates, listening to music and reading books. I never really know when it'll hit me. It's like the weather. Blue sky one day, thunder and rain the next.'

'Same for me,' she said, her voice almost a whisper. 'But it's strange. Tonight's the first time in two years that I haven't missed Dad so much it hurts.' Then she smiled and did the most incredible thing. She reached over and squeezed his hand.

A hemlock branch snapped behind Tess. She spun round, surprised by the noise. A fistful of needles landed on her shoulder. She turned to Charlie with one eyebrow arched. 'Did you just see something? What was that?'

He laughed. 'You wouldn't believe me if I told you.'

'Go ahead, try me.'

'Maybe it was your dad.'

Tess scoffed. 'If Dad was here, he wouldn't pussyfoot around making tree branches snap. He'd really let me know.' She stood up. 'Tell the truth, do you really believe in that stuff?'

'Absolutely. I've seen too many things that defy explanation.'

She chuckled. 'You mean like twigs falling from a tree?'

'No,' he said. 'Like meeting you. Like dinner tonight.'

She looked at him for a long moment. Her eyes seemed full of feeling. Then she abruptly changed the subject. 'Charlie, do you think your brother and my father are here somewhere?'

'Maybe.' Charlie looked for Sam in the darkness, and he popped up behind a gravestone. 'But I don't think spirits stay here for very long unless they want to,' he said. 'I bet your dad has moved on to a better place.'

'You mean heaven?'

'Sure, heaven. Or someplace else. Wherever it is, death isn't the end. It's an elevation, really. It's like catching the moon.'

'Catching the moon?'

'It's hard to explain,' he said. 'I read somewhere that seventy-five billion human beings have lived and died since the beginning of history, and I believe their souls are out there somewhere.' He looked straight up into the sky. 'It makes me think of that John Lennon song. You know, "We all shine on in the moon and the stars and the sun."'

Tess stared into the opening between the clouds. The Milky Way spread out in a great swath. 'I like that, Charlie,' she said. 'I need to know he's out there somewhere. You know? That he's OK.'

'He is,' Charlie said. 'Trust me. It's hard to explain, but I'm sure.'

'You've got a feeling?'

He smiled. 'Yeah, a feeling.'

Then she turned to Charlie and said, 'I'm glad you brought me here tonight. It really means a lot.'

'Me too.'

They were so close together now that Charlie thought he could actually feel an electrical charge. They stayed there in each other's glow for what felt like forever, until she looked down at her watch and said, 'I better go.'

For a moment, Charlie felt defeated, but then he decided to be daring. Without saying a word, he reached for her waist and pulled her close. To his surprise, she came to him without resistance. He kissed her softly and tumbled into the most incredible feeling. The warmth reached all the way inside and filled him with the most exhilarating sensation he had ever known.

'Tad Baylor, eat your heart out,' she said when they pulled apart. Then she grabbed his flashlight, twirled around and marched off towards the great iron gates.

THE STREETS WERE ALMOST entirely deserted as Tess hurried past Five Corners and the Rip Tide Lounge, a fancy name for the rough dive where she had waitressed on breaks from college. She walked up Washington and Middle Streets, past Abbot Hall, where the clock on the tower gonged one, then turned into Lookout Court. She jumped the three steps up to her green colonial in a single bound and let herself in the unlocked front door.

'Hey, Bobo!' she said. 'Where are you, boy?' She had forgotten to leave a light on and was surprised her retriever wasn't waiting at the door for her to return. 'Bobo?'

She flipped on the lamp in the living room and saw her dog on the big couch. He was lying with his head on a cushion and was staring right at her, but he didn't move an inch.

'What? No love for your girl?' she said. 'I bet you're hungry.'

She went into the kitchen and found a note from Tink by the toaster.

Hey, Girl,
 Took Bobo out & ate your leftovers. I was tempted to try on your clothes, but not my size. Too bad. See you mañana at your mom's dinner.

She chuckled. It was too late to call, so she got out some dog food, scooped it into Bob's bowl and set it on the floor. 'C'mon, boy. Chow time.' She went back into the living room. 'Hey, what's the matter, boy?' The dog shook his head, let out a sleepy woof and buried his nose in his paws. 'OK, I'll take you on a big run tomorrow, all the way to the lighthouse. And I'll make you scrambled eggs and bacon for breakfast. How's that?' He snorted.

Tess saw the light flashing on her answering machine. One message. She walked over and hit play. She heard her mother's voice: 'Tessie, it's me. Just a reminder. Dinner at six tomorrow. If you're back earlier and feel like brunch with the old ladies, swing by church in the morning. It would be nice for everyone to see you before you go.' There was a pause. Then she said, 'Love you.'

Tess climbed the slanting stairs to the first floor. 'C'mon, boy,' Tess said. 'Bedtime for Bobo.' She turned on the television and switched to the Weather Channel. A reporter was finishing a story about the damage from that nasty storm. It had slammed some tuna boats returning to Gloucester, sunk a tug somewhere near Providence and was moving down to Delaware and Maryland. 'Yeah, and it almost killed me,' she said, shaking her head.

She slipped off her shirt and jeans and changed into her tattered football jersey and some thick woollen socks. She hopped onto the four-poster bed, threw her head back on the pillows, and knew she was never going to get to sleep. She felt wired, like she could fly. It was Charlie St Cloud and that incredible kiss.

So why had she run? It was a reaction born of experience and disappointment. She couldn't remember when, but somewhere along the way, she had turned off those emotional taps and they were rusty from disuse. It was better that way. She had once calculated that there had to be someone out there in a world of 6.3 billion people who would love her well and long. She had even planned to sail out to find him. It was a romantic idea, but deep down she knew the truth. She would spend four months all alone on the water, never docking long enough to get attached.

She got out of bed, pulled on her red bathrobe and stepped onto the landing. Then she climbed the steep ladder up to the widow's walk at the top of the house. It was a small square room enclosed in glass, which looked onto the harbour below and the twinkling lights of Boston to the southwest. For hundreds of years, women had climbed these rungs to watch their men return from the sea.

She lit the candles on the window ledge, then curled up on a banquette and pulled a blanket round her. She leaned her head against the cold glass. There was Waterside in the distance. For the first time, she noticed a light in the black patch of woods. It was surely Charlie's cottage. What a strange and magical place, surrounded by sad reminders of his loss, and yet so warm and safe.

She fought the feeling as long as she could, but then she remembered his hands on her waist, pulling her towards him, and the exhilaration of pushing up against his body. She wanted to kiss him again, and she closed her eyes to imagine the possibilities. First light was just hours away and she could hardly wait. Tomorrow would be an unforgettable day.

Charlie sat on the dock in the Waterside cove, leaned against one of the old wooden posts and sipped his morning coffee. He was still sleepy from staying up so late replaying every detail of the evening and hoping Tess was doing the same.

Now, as wriggles of steam rose from his mug to vanish in the bluish grey of the morning, he listened to the boom of the cannons at the yacht clubs across the water signalling the arrival of the sun.

There was no official business in the cemetery on Sundays, so Charlie could take his time. The gates opened to the community at

8 a.m., but there were no burials. Joe would come by soon in the *Horny Toad*, and they would shoot across the harbour to the Driftwood for breakfast. Then they would hang out with the wharf rats who were burning off the hours till the football began.

'Heads up!' a voice cried out. Charlie turned just in time to see a tennis ball fly by his head, with Oscar chasing at full speed.

'Morning, big bro,' Sam said, stepping from the mist onto the dock. He was wearing a grey sweatshirt with its hood pulled up over his head. Messy curls drooped over his eyes. Even though playing catch at sunset was the key to renewing their promise, sometimes Sam dropped by at daybreak before taking off on his adventures.

'Morning,' Charlie said.

'Soooooo?' Sam said, plopping down beside his brother.

'So what?'

'Don't play dumb! How was the action last night?' Oscar had captured the ball and was back, wagging his tail, ready for more.

'None of your business,' Charlie said, hurling the ball onto the rocky shore. 'If you weren't dead, I'd beat your brains in for spying.'

'Gimme a break. I followed the rules. I kept my distance.'

'You were pushing it. You were right up against the line and you know the code.' When folks had begun whispering that Charlie was losing his mind and talking to the ghost of his brother, Sam had agreed he wouldn't interfere when others were around.

'I like her,' Sam said. 'She's OK, even if she roots for the Patriots.'

Charlie didn't answer.

'Look at you, playing Mr Cool. So what happened?'

'Nothing.'

'Why'd she take off so fast last night? You kissed her, then she split. Bite her tongue or something?'

'It was getting late, I guess. It was only our first date.'

'You think she got spooked by the cemetery?'

'No, she doesn't scare easily.'

'Maybe you bored her to death with all your stuff about clouds.'

'Very funny.'

Sam poked at one of the nails in a post. Oscar brought the ball back and sat down for a rest, his tail thumping the boards. 'What's a real kiss feel like?' Sam asked. He plopped down on the dock next to his beagle. 'You know, a kiss with all the works.'

'All the works?' Charlie smiled at his kid brother. Even though all those years had gone by since the accident, Sam remained twelve years old, forever asking innocent questions about the things in life that he would never know. He could have moved on to the next level and opened himself up to all the wisdom and enlightenment in the universe, but he chose to stay.

'There's nothing like it,' Charlie said, 'and there are a zillion different kinds. Some are exciting and sexy and—'

'Slippery?'

'I can't do this.'

'C'mon. I wanna know!'

Charlie had to think. A kiss? How do you explain a kiss? 'Remember that Little League game when you played the Giants?'

'Yup.'

'Tell me the story.'

Sam grinned. 'We were down four to one in the last inning. I came to the plate with two outs, the bases loaded, and Gizzy Graves was on the mound. I missed the first two pitches by about a mile, but I smashed the next one over the left-field fence for a home run.'

'And how'd it feel?'

'Best thing in the world.'

'That's a kiss, minus the bat.'

Sam laughed. 'And minus Gizzy Graves.'

'Exactly.'

Charlie watched his little brother and felt the hurt. In the abstract, Sam understood the concept of the perfect kiss, but experiencing one was entirely different. Charlie was suddenly swept up in all the amazing things Sam was going to miss. He had been cheated of so much.

Suddenly, a horn hooted on the water. Joe was steering his boat into the cove. 'Ahoy,' he said. 'Top of the morning to you.'

Charlie waved, then mumbled to his little brother, 'Gotta go.'

'See you at sundown,' Sam said, scooping up Oscar.

Charlie jumped onto the boat, and Joe pushed forwards on the throttle. He aimed for the wharf across the harbour. 'Look at you!' Joe said. 'You're all happy today.'

'What are you talking about?'

'You've got a bounce in your step. A grin on your face. Tell the truth. You get laid last night?'

'No comment.'

'You snake! What's her name?' He spun the steering wheel hard, narrowly avoiding a moored catamaran.

Charlie leaned into the wind and shook his head. He zipped the front of his navy fleece. Tess was his secret, and he was going to hold on to it as long as he could. The last thing he needed was Joe meddling or making a play for her himself. 'Nice day, huh?'

'Nice day, schmice day. The truth will come out,' Joe said, idling the engine and letting the boat drift towards the wharf. The dock was already crowded with other vessels, and he deftly steered into an open slot. Charlie climbed out, tied up and headed for the Driftwood, a small wood-frame shack with peeling red paint. Joe caught up with him and the two stepped through the screen door.

Fish netting and harpoons dangled from the ceiling and a lacquered sand shark grimaced from one wall at a barracuda over the kitchen door. Most of the little tables were already crowded.

Hoddy Snow, the harbourmaster, and his two deputies were huddled in a corner by the jukebox. Tink and a crew of sailors sat at their regular table in the front. Hoddy stood up. 'Can I have your attention, fellas?' he said in an urgent voice. He was a hulking man, and his shiny hair was combed neatly in law-enforcement style. 'Your attention please.' The room fell silent. 'Sorry to interrupt your breakfast, but we've got a serious situation and we need everyone's help. We just got a call from the Coast Guard in Gloucester. They want our help putting together a search. A fisherman picked up a life ring and a rudder floating off Halibut Point. They think it's from Marblehead.'

'What boat?' Charlie asked. 'Whose is it?'

Hoddy's eyes narrowed. His voice choked up for a moment, and there was no doubting his seriousness. 'It's *Querencia*,' he said. 'Tess Carroll's boat is missing.'

Bobo galloped like a dog possessed down Devereux Beach.

Tess stood on the cool sand and called out to him, but he ignored her, charging ahead, splashing through the surf. From the moment she had opened the door at dawn, he had bolted into the street and taken off without her. He was old, deaf and arthritic, but they still ran together every Sunday morning. Normally he stayed on the leash, lumbering along beside her. But not today.

Tess felt the wind rising off the ocean as she watched Bobo bound up to a fisherman sitting on a deck chair. He was about 150 yards away, but she could tell it was Dubby Bartlett with his prized casting poles planted in the sand, lines spinning out into the surf. He always fished there on Sunday mornings.

'Dubby!' she called out. 'Hold on to Bobo! I need to get him on the leash.' He petted the dog, then looked up and down the shore, like he was expecting her to be right behind.

'Dubby!' she shouted again. 'Over here!'

The wind was blowing pretty hard, sending up a spray of sand, and Tess's voice must have got lost in the swirl. Bobo jumped up on him, nuzzled his face, barked, then took off again. For a moment, Dubby watched the dog go, then he went back to his reels.

Tess gave chase again, shouting for the retriever to stop. She was getting angrier. What on earth had got into him? He was like a puppy again, totally uncontrollable.

'Bobo!' she yelled. 'Come back here!' But the dog trotted along the trail that ended on the rocky banks of Waterside cove and ran up the sloping embankment through the back gates of the cemetery.

Tess lost sight of him but knew he was heading to the top of the hill speckled with tombstones. She climbed after him, and was soon strolling between rows of markers. When she reached her dad's grave, Bobo was sitting by the headstone, as she'd expected.

'You're a bad dog!' she said. 'What the heck has got into you?' Bobo rolled over and scratched his back in the grass. 'Don't think you can charm your way out of this,' she said. 'I'm really mad. That was crazy!' She sat down beside him and ignored his yelps.

Instead, she looked out on the harbour and was amazed by the strange brilliance of the day. The blue of the ocean seemed more vivid than ever, and the sails on the boats shone like mirrors against the sun. *Querencia*'s mooring was hidden from view by a gorgeous forty-two-foot schooner that had probably come into the harbour to pick up gear from Doyle Sails. Tess inhaled the unmistakable odour of herring bait from the lobster traps stacked on the wharf. Even her sense of smell was more acute today. Then she heard laughter and shouting behind her. She turned and saw a beagle sprinting from the woods, chased by a gangly boy in jeans and a grey sweatshirt.

'I'm going to get you!' the kid was yelling, his Red Sox cap askew on the dark curls spilling from its brim.

Tess stood up and called out, 'Hey! You need a hand?'

The boy saw her and stopped running. A puzzled expression crossed his freckled face, and he approached slowly. His beagle was growling at Bobo and the kid asked softly, 'Does he bite?'

'No,' she said. 'He's an old guy. Lost most of his teeth.'

The kid dropped his mitt, knelt down and gave the retriever a big scratch on the belly. Then he looked up at Tess with curious eyes.

'He likes that,' she said. But the boy didn't answer. He just stared.

'What?' she said.

'Nothing.'

'Nothing? Nobody looks at someone like you're looking at me and it's nothing.'

'You can see me?'

'Of course I can.'

'But that's impossible.'

Tess assumed the kid was playing a game. 'Are you invisible or something?'

'Yes.'

'Wow. That's pretty cool. What's your secret?'

Sam didn't answer. The boy and his beagle just stared. It was beginning to unnerve her a little. Then, after a long moment, he finally said, 'What's your story? When did you get here?'

'Just a few minutes ago,' Tess said. 'My dad's buried here. So are my grandparents and great-grandparents.'

'That makes sense,' Sam said, picking up his glove and ball. 'You feeling all right?'

'Definitely,' Tess said. 'Hey, you play for Marblehead?'

'Obviously not any more.' There was an awkward silence. Then he said, 'You're Tess, right?'

'How'd you know?'

'I heard about you from Charlie,' he said. Oscar barked at the sound of his name.

'Charlie?'

'He'd kill me for saying anything. Swear you won't tell.'

'Cross my heart.' She smiled.

'I think he likes you,' Sam said.

Tess felt a twinge of embarrassment. 'Well, I like him too. You know where I can find him right now? Is he home?'

'Did he know you were coming?'

'No. I didn't tell him.'

'What else didn't you tell him?' Sam asked.

'I'm not quite sure what you mean.' The kid was starting to get to her again. 'Do me a favour, OK? Give Charlie a message?'

'Sure.'

'Let him know I came by.'

'Will do.'

The kid threw his ball and the beagle took off after it. 'Hey, Tess,' he said. 'You play catch?'

'Sure.'

'You throw like a girl?'

'Not on your life.'

'Then come back tonight. Charlie's always here at sundown. See that forest over there? The big blue spruce?'

'Yes.'

'Follow the trail on the other side of the old log.'

'And then what?'

'You'll find us in the clearing. We'll throw the ball around.'

'Sounds fun,' she said. 'I'll see you later.' She took a few steps down the hill. She was liking the thought of playing catch with Charlie and the boy. Then she spun round. 'Hey, what's your name?'

He hesitated for an instant before he answered. 'I'm Sam St Cloud.'

III

IN BETWEEN

The ocean had never looked so massive. Whitecaps streaked to the horizon, and the thirty-five-foot lobster boat careened through the waves. With one hand, Charlie steadied himself on the dashboard; with the other, he peered through binoculars and swept the confused seas. He and Tink were running a track leg in a search pattern on Jeffreys Ledge, an area not too far from where the fisherman had picked up debris from *Querencia*.

That morning in the Driftwood, he had absolutely refused to believe the news about Tess. At first, he had erupted: 'No way. It's not possible.' Then all eyes in the restaurant had focused on him.

'You know something we don't?' Hoddy had asked.

Charlie had wanted to tell them about her visit to her father's grave and their dinner in the cottage. He had wanted to describe their midnight walk and even their first kiss. But he had suddenly felt afraid. It was an unconscious reflex. Maybe something terrible had happened to *Querencia* on the water and it was Tess's spirit that had come to the cemetery. It wasn't impossible, and in that instant he knew he had to protect himself. 'She's got to be around somewhere,' he had mumbled, trying to mask his confusion. 'Don't you think?'

'What are you talking about?' Tink had said, stepping forwards. 'They found her rudder and a life ring. There's been no word from her in more than thirty-six hours. What more do you need?'

Charlie had felt himself scrambling. 'What about her house? Anyone look there?'

'Of course,' Hoddy had said. 'No luck. Dubby Bartlett saw her dog running on the beach without a leash this morning. Her mother was expecting to hear from her by now, but there's been no word.'

And so the men had paired off to start the search. Charlie joined up with Tink, who had borrowed a lobster boat. The two had known each other only casually from the local beer-and-clam circuit, but they were both hell-bent on finding Tess. Around midday they had spotted a life raft that was partially inflated and blackened with smoke. Hauling it aboard, Tink unravelled when he realised it belonged to *Querencia*. First he unleashed a gut-wrenching scream, then he shouted: 'No!' That single, simple syllable stretched into an agonising wail until he ran out of breath, and great tears coursed down his cheeks.

The boat had vanished. Tess was nowhere.

In the outer reaches of his mind, Charlie began to wonder what had really happened. Was it Tess in the cemetery last night or her spirit? He had seen thousands of souls come and go and he had never before been fooled. They all gleamed with an aura of light. The old no longer hobbled. The infirm were restored with vigour. At first, their edges would soften and shimmer, then they would begin to look the way they had always imagined themselves. When they were ready to go on to the next level, they would fade away like mist in the sun.

But Tess was different. He had gazed into her eyes. He had stood right next to her. He had even felt himself falling a little in love. No, she couldn't have been a spirit. There was nothing diaphanous about her. She was too real, too substantial, too alive.

In the western sky, Charlie saw splashes of rust and plum. The angle of the sun was low on the water, and he suddenly realised that for the first time in thirteen years he hadn't thought about Sam all day. Now his heart began to pound. There was only an hour of light left to find her—and an hour of light to get home.

Just then, Tink turned the wheel sharply. 'Tank's almost empty,' he said. 'We're losing the sun. I hate to go back to port, but we don't have much choice.'

Charlie nodded but felt no relief. He went to the stern and sat down. He put his head in his hands and closed his eyes. He replayed every moment in his mind, trying to make sense of it all. Maybe Tess's beauty had overwhelmed him. Maybe the sparks had distracted him from the signs. How could he have been so wrong?

He stood up again and moved forwards to the cockpit beside Tink. The low light of dusk was slanting off the water and he knew the sun would be gone at 6.33 p.m. He glanced at the speedometer. Fifteen knots. 'Can we speed up a bit?' he asked gently.

'What's your problem, Mario Andretti? Why the big hurry?'

'I just need to get back.'

Tink turned the wheel five degrees to starboard. 'You got something more important to do? A hot date?'

Charlie didn't even bother to answer. He stood listening to the thud of the waves against the boat.

After a while, Tink reached out a hand. 'Look, I'm sorry. My nerves are fried.' Charlie thought he saw tears in the man's eyes. Then Tink said, 'So how do you know Tess again?'

'We only just met.'

But Tink wasn't really listening. He seemed lost in his own fears. 'I never should've let her go out into that storm,' he said.

That was strange. Tess hadn't mentioned bad weather. 'Whatever happens,' Charlie said, 'she's going to be OK.'

Tink looked over with sad eyes. 'You think?'

'You just have to believe.'

And that was exactly what Charlie was forcing himself to do— believe Tess was OK. But, of course, with every passing moment, with every empty stretch of ocean, his growing fear was that she wasn't. He knew all about the middle ground between life and death and how spirits separated from their bodies. He had been there briefly himself, only to be shocked back to life. But he had to accept the possibility that Tess's soul had come to the cemetery to find her father without realising what had happened to her body. Folks often showed up bewildered by their own heart attacks or aneurysms. Sometimes they didn't even comprehend that life was over and had to spend a few days figuring things out. Others knew right away what had brought them down, and they screamed at God and the world from the moment they arrived. They were the ones who held on to family and friends. And then there were the folks who had it the easiest of all, letting go quickly and moving right on to the next realm.

Up ahead, Charlie saw the mouth of the harbour. The sky was dark grey, and the lighthouse flashed its familiar green beam. Tink steered towards the wharf and glided in smoothly.

Charlie jumped out. As he tied up, he heard the blast of the sunset salute cannons. 'I've got to run,' he said.

'You sure you're OK?' Tink asked. 'You don't look so good.'

'I'm fine. Call me later if you hear anything.'

'Will do,' Tink said.

He had a stitch in his side and his lungs ached as he made the last turn down West Shore Drive. When his fists closed at last round the heavy wrought-iron bars of the gates, he rested his forehead for a moment against the cool metal, then hurried inside.

He found the utility cart beside the Fountain of Youth and aimed the little vehicle towards the Forest of Shadows. He steered along the bumpy trail and stopped under the low branches of the blue spruce. He was in such a hurry that he didn't even bother to check over his shoulder. Instead, he reached under the front seat and patted around until he found the glove holding the ball in its firm embrace. Then he leapt over the old rotting log and dashed through the woods. A sliver of grey graced the canopy of the cypress grove as he tore into the clearing. In the twilight, he could just make out that the pitcher's mound, rubber and plate were empty.

'Sam!' he yelled. 'Sammm?'

The swing was empty.

'Sam!'

But there was no answer. Charlie could feel the dread begin to rise—first in his stomach, then his chest. His head began to pound. It certainly didn't help that he was so tired. Fear flooded through him. He knew he had to stop himself from thinking the absolute worst. So he crossed a few yards of grass and settled onto the swing.

'Sam!' he tried again. *'Sammm . . .'*

And then, as his voice trailed off, a little miracle happened. Charlie heard a sound—so faint at first that he wasn't sure it was anything more than his own imagination.

'Charlie!'

There was Sam coming from the forest. Oscar pranced behind him.

'Where've you been?' Charlie said, jumping from the swing. 'You scared me.'

'I'm here. Relax.' Sam smiled. 'Want to play catch?'

'No, I need to talk about something.'

Sam walked over to the picnic table and sat down. 'What's going on?' he said. 'How was your day?'

'Miserable,' Charlie said.

'What happened?'

'It's Tess.'

Sam's eyes were wide. 'So you found out.'

Charlie felt his stomach clench. What did Sam know? How did he know it? 'Have you seen her?' Charlie asked. 'Has she been here?'

'She came looking for you.'

'You saw her?'

'I saw her.' His voice was soft, like he was cushioning the blow. 'And she saw me.'

Charlie felt himself deflate. There was no denying it any more. In all his years in Waterside, he had never met a living person who could see his brother, or any other ghost for that matter. He looked up into the darkness. All day he had hoped she was alive, but now he understood she was a spirit in the middle ground.

Sam was sitting right next to him, but for the first time it wasn't enough. Charlie knew he wanted more. He needed more.

'Does she know yet?' Charlie asked.

'I'm not sure. I think she's figuring it out.'

'Is she fading already? Is she moving on?'

'I can't tell. But it's going to be OK, big bro,' Sam said softly.

'How can you be sure?'

'Don't worry,' Sam said. 'She's coming here tonight.'

What had begun as the strangest day of her life had morphed into the most frightening. It had started with that headache that refused to go away and it had ended in despair back at her father's grave.

After meeting Sam St Cloud in the cemetery, Tess had spent the day in a thick soup of confusion. The kid was Charlie's brother, but he was dead, killed thirteen years ago in that terrible car wreck. How was it possible to have a conversation with him? Maybe it was true what they said: hang around a graveyard too long and you start to see ghosts. Was the boy an apparition? Or was she hallucinating? Or was it some punk playing stupid tricks? She had to see Charlie again, and she would ask him about his brother.

As the sun rose over Marblehead and the weekend sailors made their way from the harbour, Tess walked Bobo back home to Lookout Court. No one greeted her on the street, not even her old friend Tabby Glass, who was jogging on the far sidewalk.

'Want some chow?' Tess asked when they finally reached her house, but Bobo just plunked down on the front steps.

'All right, suit yourself,' she said. 'I'm going down to check on *Querencia.*'

She jogged down the steep public steps that descended the hill from her little street, then strolled along the waterfront. The colours of the hulls and the sails seemed brighter. The smell of salt in the air was sharper. She walked along the dock, stopped at her mooring and, in that instant, knew something was really wrong.

Querencia wasn't there.

Tink would never have taken her out without asking permission. She felt a little woozy and her head seemed to spin. She knelt down to get her balance, bracing herself with one hand on a weathered plank. She thought she might be sick, leaned over the ledge and peered into the water below. She adjusted her eyes and gasped.

Her reflection was missing. Only the sky and the clouds looked back at her. A sudden numbness overwhelmed her and Tess finally understood. She wasn't there at all.

Her mind raced back over the puzzling events of the last day. Bobo paying no attention to her commands. Dubby Bartlett ignoring her on the beach. No one had acknowledged her because no one could see her. No one except Charlie St Cloud and his dead brother Sam.

What on earth was going on?

She leapt up and spun around. She grabbed her waist and then her hair. She rubbed her jeans. She rolled a button on her shirt between her fingers. Everything felt as normal as ever. And yet it wasn't.

She called out to Bony and the other old guys sitting under the tree, but they kept on chatting. Her soul filled with dread. Something terrible must have happened. She tried to remember the boat and the storm. She could see herself capsizing, then fighting her way onto the deck after *Querencia* righted herself. But then what? Had she made it back to port? Her memory was a fog.

When did she die?

The question seemed impossible. Tess felt the terror and turmoil inside. She desperately needed an anchor. Then she realised she only had to do one thing: find Charlie. If anyone could explain what was happening, he could. But what if something had changed and now she had become invisible to him too?

Anxiously, she made her way back to the cemetery, but Charlie was nowhere to be found. Finally, Tess all but threw herself on her father's grave under the Japanese maple. If this was death, she thought, then Dad would come to be with her. Or maybe he would be waiting for her somewhere else. Where was she supposed to go? What was she to do? She began to cry and didn't stop until she fell asleep, exhausted.

When she woke, gasping with fear that she would never find Charlie, the sky was almost dark. As she pulled herself up from the grave, she remembered Sam's instructions: find the blue spruce in the forest and the trail on the other side of the old log. She shuddered. The woods had been so creepy last night. Could she do it alone?

To her surprise, the forest was peaceful and calm. She followed the path past a waterfall and pool, then threaded her way through a cypress grove. Suddenly, she heard voices up ahead and a beagle's yowl. When she came into the clearing, there was Charlie on a log.

The very sight of him lifted her spirits. At least she could be certain that part of her life was real. She just wanted him to tell her it was all some big mistake. She wanted to kiss him and start up exactly where they had left off last night.

As she approached, she prayed Charlie would still be able to see her, and when he leapt up and smiled at her, she felt an incredible wave of relief. She wasn't alone any more. She heard his deep voice: 'Thank God you're here. I was afraid you were never coming back.'

'Where have you been?' she asked. 'I was looking all over for you.'

'Been looking for you too,' he answered.

'HI, SAM,' SHE SAID. They were the two sweetest words ever. Charlie had never thought he would hear a woman greet his brother that way.

'Hi,' Sam said. 'Shame you got here so late. It's too dark to play catch.' He turned to Charlie. 'She says she doesn't throw like a girl! You believe her?'

'Now's not the time,' Charlie said. He looked at Tess. Her eyes were full of feeling. She was just standing there—as real as anyone.

There wasn't a single sign that she was fading. And yet, in his brain he knew she was. He wondered how much she understood. He decided to start with a simple question. 'How are you doing?'

'I was fine until I couldn't see my reflection in the water,' she said. 'Now I'm just confused. Tell me what's going on, Charlie.'

She obviously didn't know what had happened, and he knew he would have to be the one to break the news.

'I'm not sure where to start,' Charlie said.

'How about the beginning?'

'All right,' he said. '*Querencia* has been missing for forty-eight hours. The whole town is worried sick. The fleet went out to search.'

'Missing for forty-eight hours?'

'A fisherman found a piece of your hull off Halibut Point. Tink and I found your life raft in Sandy Bay.'

'Where?'

'Sandy Bay, off Rockport.'

'That's strange. I wasn't anywhere near Rockport. Must've been the wind and the current.' She walked over to the swing and sat down.

'Do you remember what happened?' Sam asked.

'Not really,' she said.

'You've got to try to remember,' Charlie said. 'We need to know where you were when it happened.'

Tess jumped down from the swing. 'Look, I know exactly what happened. The storm was force ten, and I spent the night upside-down on the water. It was freezing.'

'Then what?'

'Next thing, I was at Dad's grave.'

'Do you know how you got to the cemetery?'

'No, Chas. It's a blur.'

'That's OK,' he said. 'Sometimes, when it happens suddenly, you don't even realise what's going on. It takes time to sink in.' He watched her carefully, weighing the impact of his words.

She seemed dazed, then said, 'What's going to happen to me?'

'Everything will feel better soon,' he said, his voice choking on the words, 'and you'll realise you're going home where you belong.'

'Home? What are you talking about? Home is at Lookout Court with Bobo. Home is with my mother and my friends.' There were tears in her eyes now. She brushed them away and tried to force a smile, but it came off a little crooked. Then she said, 'And I was even beginning to think home might be with you.'

NIGHT WAS FALLING on the forest. The moon was up, the stars were out, and Tess sat with Charlie and Sam in the clearing. She was trying to hold herself together. But little by little, the reality of it all was locking into her consciousness.

Life was over.

She would never get to know this Charlie St Cloud, who had appeared from nowhere in her life and was instantly snatched out of reach. Why had she met him now? God must have had a reason.

She tried to concentrate on what Charlie and Sam were saying, taking turns to describe the afterlife and the road ahead. They made it all sound like the most natural transition in the world. After a while, she interrupted Charlie. 'I need to understand how this works. How can you see Sam?' She hesitated. 'And how can you see me?'

'When our accident happened,' Charlie explained, 'I crossed over too. It was a classic near-death experience, and when they shocked me back to life I was graced with this gift. I could still see people in limbo between life and death.'

'That's where I am now?'

'I think so,' he said, 'but you threw me off a little. You don't really look like most spirits.'

'I'll take that as a compliment,' Tess said. 'Now, what about touching? How did we kiss last night? How can I open doors and change clothes and feed Bobo?'

Charlie smiled. 'Right now, you have one foot in both worlds. You're here and not here. You're literally in between.' He reached out and took her hand. 'Folks who die very suddenly, or who don't want to let go, can exert a very strong physical presence. They're the ones who make lights flicker and things go bump in the night.'

'How come I haven't seen any?'

'Besides Sam, there aren't any around right now,' he answered. 'Mrs Phipps from the high school moved on this morning. And I haven't seen a fire-fighter named Florio in a while.'

'See, God picks when you live and die,' Sam added. 'But when you're here in between, you have a choice. You can stay here as long as you want, like me. Or you can go to the next level right away.'

Tess felt a wave of worry. 'Why hasn't my dad come to see me?' she asked. 'I always thought he would be here waiting.'

'Don't worry,' Charlie said. 'He'll be there for you, but you haven't crossed over to the other side yet.'

'I thought *this* was the other side.'

'That's what everyone thinks,' Sam said. 'Everyone tells you that when you die, you see the light and you pass on. Period.' He smiled and lowered his voice to a whisper. 'It's actually more complicated. There are lots of levels and places on this side.' He drew a circle in the air. 'Imagine that this is the land of the living. Marblehead is right here in the middle of everything. Your mom, your friends, Bobo.' Then he traced another circle round it. 'We're right here. One level beyond. This is the middle ground.'

'Think of it as the way station between life and death,' Charlie said. 'It's like a rest stop on the highway. I was actually there for ten minutes before the paramedic shocked me back.'

'I don't get it. If this is a rest stop, what's Sam still doing here?'

The brothers looked at each other. Sam hunched his shoulders and was about to speak when Charlie cut in. 'We made a promise.'

'What kind of promise?'

There was a long silence. 'Fine,' Tess said. 'Don't tell me. But am I right, Sam? You can stay here as long as you want?'

'Yes.'

'Can I stay here too?'

'You're getting ahead of yourself,' Charlie said.

'Yeah,' Sam said. 'There's time for all of that later. Right now, you've got a lot to learn.'

'Go ahead,' Charlie said. 'Show her how it works.'

'My pleasure.' Sam looked up at the sky, waved his hands in a small circle, and suddenly the wind soughed through the trees. A shower of leaves swirled around them. 'Not bad, huh?' he said. 'And we can dreamwalk too. We can go right into people's dreams and we can tell them stuff.'

'You mean when I dream of Dad—'

'Exactly,' Charlie said. 'Spirits at any level can dreamwalk, even after they've crossed over.'

Tess shook her head. She was overwhelmed. She had dreamed of her father almost every night for a year after he died. Was he visiting in her sleep? She didn't know what to believe any more. And then a spark of anger ignited in her soul. She knew one thing for sure: she didn't want to spend eternity making the wind blow or wandering through people's dreams. She wanted her life back. She wanted to sail. She wanted to live. She wanted to love.

'What happens if I don't want to cross over?' She reached her hand towards Charlie. 'What if I just want to stay here with you?'

'There's no rush,' Charlie said. 'You have all the time in the world.'

Sam got up and went to her side. He put his hand into hers and he pulled. 'Come on, Tess, let's go.'

'Go where?'

'I'll show you around. It's like orientation. It won't take long.'

Tess wasn't sure what to do. She didn't want to go anywhere. She just wanted to hold on to this place and this moment lest it never be the same again. Then she heard Charlie's calming voice. 'Don't be afraid. When you're finished, come back to my cottage.'

She looked into his eyes and couldn't believe her misfortune. She had been ready to sail around the world to find her mate, and he had been waiting right here at Waterside.

She felt Sam tugging. 'Come on,' he was saying, and she found herself walking hand in hand into the Forest of Shadows with a dead boy and his dead beagle. It boggled her mind. After a few steps, she turned back and saw Charlie silhouetted alone under the moon.

'Promise you'll be here when I get back?' she called out.

'I promise,' he answered.

'Don't worry, Tess,' Sam said. 'He always keeps his promises.'

TESS WAS A NATURAL at flying. Actually, 'flying' wasn't quite the word. It didn't look anything like Superman with his arms outstretched and cape flapping. It was called spirit travel, Sam explained, and it was controlled by the mind. You only had to imagine the possibilities and you could run, swim, dive or glide through any dimension. You just had to think of a place and you were there.

For Tess, it felt like the ultimate extreme sport, with no limits on how fast or far she could go. She had never believed in any of this supernatural stuff, but soon she was soaring over downtown, circling the gilded weather vane atop Abbot Hall, then shooting down to the harbour to check out the boats.

'Sure beats PlayStation 2, huh?' Sam said as they materialised near the top of the Marblehead lighthouse.

'Blows my mind,' she said, watching the powerful green beam slice right through her.

'Where do you want to go now?' Sam asked.

Tess thought for a moment. 'How about my mom's?'

'OK, lead the way.'

And just like that, they found themselves near Black Joe's Pond on Gingerbread Hill. The family home, a colonial with opposing brick chimneys, sat like a toy house overlooking the pond. It had barely changed since it was built by her ancestors in 1795. The downstairs lights were on in the living room, and in the window on the first floor she saw a shaggy face. It was Bobo, looking down blankly on the grass where she was standing.

A car pulled into the driveway, and Tess noticed a jam of vehicles near the house.

'Wonder who's here,' Tess said.

'They're your friends.'

'Oh my God. What are they doing?'

'I guess they really liked you.'

Once more, Tess had that overwhelmed sensation. Then she said, 'Come on, let's go and look.'

She recognised most of the cars, including Reverend Polkinghorne's red Subaru, and she hesitated. The last time he had been over to the house was when her dad had died. Would her mother have the strength to go through it all again?

Then she resolutely started across the grass, covering the ground in twenty steps. The side door to the mudroom was open. Her father's boots were arranged neatly on the floor. He had been gone for two years, but her mother left them there as a comfort.

Grace was in the kitchen stirring the old chowder pot. Her face was long, her eyes were red and her blue blouse and brown skirt didn't belong together.

Tess walked over and stood right beside her. She wanted to hug her so badly, but just as she reached out, Sam cut between them. 'I'm sorry,' he said, 'but you really shouldn't.'

'Why not?'

'It freaks them out.'

'What do you mean? It's just a hug.'

'Trust me, it just makes things worse. Eventually, you'll see there are much better ways to let her know you're here.'

Tess stepped back and watched Grace finish preparing the chowder, then heard the kitchen door swing open.

It was Reverend Polkinghorne. 'You're working too hard,' he said. 'Won't you let me do anything? I'm very handy in the kitchen.'

'You can bring some dishes into the other room.' Grace churned the chowder a few more times, picked up the pot with oven mitts, and headed into the dining room. Tess and Sam followed.

The Four Seasons was playing softly on the stereo and the room was filled with friends. Tess moved around, eavesdropping on conversations, not surprised by what she heard. These moments were always awkward and uncomfortable, and folks carried on about the darnedest things. Myrna Doliber, the funeral director, was relaying one of her superstitions: 'If three people are photographed together, the one in the middle will always die first . . .'

Then, in a flat, strained voice, Grace called out from the dining room: 'Come 'n' get it.' She stood at the buffet table ladling chowder into bowls. When everyone had been served, Reverend Polkinghorne led them all in prayer. 'Let us thank God for food when others are hungry, for drink when others are thirsty, for friends when others are lonely,' he began. 'And may God's light surround our beloved Tess, wherever she is, and may He bring her home safely to us.'

'Amen.'

Grace was obviously doing her best to hold it together. Her lips were pinched, and her eyes were slits. A few visitors ooh'd and ahh'd over the chowder, and then Grace began to crack. Her fragile smile crumbled and her eyes filled with tears. With a quick flick of her hand she wiped them away.

Tess was desperate to do something, but Sam put his hand on her shoulder. 'Don't,' he said. 'She has to go through this.'

Then the bell rang and Grace hurried to the door, where Tink's bulk filled the frame. He bent down to give her a big hug and followed her into the living room. The crowd quietened down to hear the latest on the search. 'The last boat is back,' he began. 'They found some more junk and debris. Could be trash from *Querencia*.'

'No sign of her yet?' Bony asked. 'No radio signal? No flare?'

'Not yet, but we're going out at first light and we'll find her.'

'Why wait for tomorrow?' Grace asked. 'What about now?'

'There's no point. We've got thick overcast and the moon's gone.'

Grace walked over to the window and stared out into the distance. Tess moved closer. How could it not calm her to touch her? Carefully, gently, she laid her hand on her mother's shoulder. Grace stiffened, then shuddered, whirled round, and with a look of fright in her eyes, hurried back to her guests.

'I just got the worst chill,' she said to Reverend Polkinghorne. 'It was just like when George died. I could swear this house is haunted.'

Sadness overwhelmed Tess. 'I can't stay here any more,' she said to Sam. 'I've got to go. Now.'

She rushed out onto the lawn under a black sky. She wanted to run as fast and as far as she could. She had never felt so powerless in her life. There was nothing she could do for her mom. There was nothing she could do for herself.

If only her father were still there. Then a terrifying thought filled her mind: what if Dad had gone through this same hell, forced to watch them suffer? Had he been there in his chair at the dining-room table for those agonising, silent dinners? Did the dead grieve right alongside us? Did they feel our pain?

She had always been taught that they were in a better place, that they were embraced by the light, that they were with the angels. But what if that really wasn't what happened?

Tess went down to the pond and sat on a rock. Sam joined her, and after a long silence she asked, 'Will it always feel this way?'

'No,' Sam said. 'It starts off pretty bad, but it changes. You'll see.'

'What was your worst moment?'

Sam skipped a stone on the water. 'It was right after the accident,' he said. 'Charlie and I were together. It was scary. Charlie had just made a promise to stay with me for ever and then suddenly he began to disappear. I was stranded all alone in this weird place that turned out to be the cemetery.' His voice choked up. 'We figured out later what had happened. The paramedic had shocked him back to life and he was gone. I thought I'd never see him again.'

'Then what happened?'

'It turned out all right. We still hang out every day and play catch.'

Tess watched him for a moment and felt more sadness. How many boys like him were out there in the ether, holding on to their big brothers and sisters who were still alive? How many husbands were floating between life and death, clinging to their wives in this world? And how many millions of people were there in the world like Charlie, who couldn't let go of their loved ones when they were gone?

They sat silently by the pond and listened to the bullfrogs. In the distance, a boat engine rumbled. She heard noise on the lawn and turned to see the guests leaving. Then the lights went off in the kitchen and living room. Through the window, she watched her mother's silhouette climb the stairs. She saw her come to her bedroom window, scratch Bobo behind the ears, look out for a few moments, then close the curtains.

Tess pulled her knees close to her and wrapped herself in a ball. She desperately wanted to be comforted by the only person who could help her through this lonely night.

The charts were strewn all around. So were the print-outs from the Weather Service and the National Oceanic and Atmospheric Administration. With ruler and calculator, Charlie was reckoning where to search at dawn. He didn't care that the Coast Guard's supercomputer had crunched all the data on tides, currents and water temperature and concluded that Tess's chances of survival were slim to none. In fact, he conceded that the situation appeared hopeless, especially since Tess's spirit had already alighted in the cemetery. But he knew of plenty of miracles on the ocean: sailors subsisting for days, weeks, or even months on life rafts or lashed to wreckage. And Tess's survival suit was rated for freezing temperatures. In theory, she would have been wearing it when *Querencia* sank, so she could still be alive.

The logs in the fireplace had burned down to embers. The time on the VCR said it was almost midnight. How did it get so late? At first he didn't notice the tree branches rustling against the window, but then they grew louder. That was strange. He stood up, went to the door, opened it and looked outside.

Tess was standing in the shadows. Charlie's heart leapt. 'God, am I glad to see you,' he said, grabbing her hand and pulling her inside.

She looked at him with the saddest eyes. 'Something's happening to me,' she said. 'I couldn't even knock on the door. There wasn't any sound when I tried, so I had to make the wind jostle the tree branches.'

Charlie tensed. She was losing her physical connection to this world. It was the first clue that she was fading, but he still couldn't believe it. He couldn't detect a single sign that she was a spirit.

He tried to put his arms round her, but she stopped him. 'I wish we could, but Sam says it's against the rules. He says it's too much for people to handle.'

'I'm willing to take that risk.' His hands circled her and he pulled her close. There was no mistaking it. She was real.

When they let go of one another, she moved towards the couch, plopped down in the middle and buried herself in the cushions. 'I can't believe this is happening,' she said. 'I just can't . . .'

'Tell me about tonight,' Charlie said, sliding in beside her.

'I went to my mom's with Sam,' she said. 'I couldn't take it. It was just too sad. I can't believe I put her through this again.' She pulled a cushion into her lap. 'My crazy friend Tink thinks he's going to

512

rescue me tomorrow. God bless him. Poor Mom is clinging to that hope.' She threw the cushion down.

Charlie put his arm round her. He could feel her shaking with every breath. And that was what seemed impossible to explain. She was a spirit and yet she was shuddering right there in his arms.

'What about you?' she said. 'Where've you been tonight?'

'I went down to the dock to see what was going on.' He stroked her shoulders and her hair. 'Coast Guard says *Querencia* was destroyed by fire. They think there's no way you survived.'

'Do you believe that?' she asked.

'No,' he said, trying to convince himself. 'Not until we find your body.'

Tess was staring at the burning log. 'A fire . . .' she whispered. Then suddenly her eyes sparked and she said, 'Charlie, my God. I think I remember what happened . . .'

THE BOAT HAD BEEN upside-down for ever. It was pitch-black in the cabin and the floodboards were floating around her. She was doused with diesel fuel and battery acid. The water was rushing in, but she couldn't tell how much or how fast. And, most frightening of all, the boat was making the most horrible noises. *Querencia* was in agony. Tess was praying to her father to guide her through the ordeal. She was too proud to activate the emergency beacon or radio for help. She would tough it out until there was absolutely no other choice.

Then, like a miracle, the boat righted herself.

Thank you, Dad, wherever you are . . .

Tess feared that the boat had been dismasted in the roll-over. She crawled through the galley, pushing pots and pans and gear out of her way. She zipped up her suit, fastened her mask and climbed up the ladder of the companionway. At the top, she stopped for an instant to listen. She could hear the fury of the storm, but she needed to check the rigging. She held her breath and opened the hatch.

The pressure changed instantly as the wind burst inside along with a gush of sea water. She quickly hooked her tether onto the jack line and pulled herself on deck. The sky and sea had merged into one great wall of white and it felt like she was flying.

She wasn't sure she could stand upright in the high winds, so she stayed in a crouch as she scanned *Querencia* for damage.

Sure enough, the mast had been sheared like a toppled tree from the deck, leaving a jagged stump. The remains of the pole, fastened by halyards, were swinging from the boat and slamming into it like a battering ram with every ransacking wave. Tess knew she had to chop them loose or they would pierce the hull.

The boat was pitching violently. She scooted to the cabin locker and pulled the bolt-cutters from the bracket. It took all her strength to slice through the stainless-steel rod rigging and to sever the mainsail and two jibs. Instantly, a massive wave swept the mast away.

Then she duckwalked to the cockpit and surveyed her instruments. *Damn!* The autopilot was off. Must have happened when she lost power. She punched the button to get it going again, but it was out. She tried the back-up. It was gone too. Now there was no choice: she would have to steer her way through this. But where the heck was she? She peered at the compass, trying to get her bearings.

Before she could finish, a wave smashed into the rear deck, slamming her hard against the wheel. It knocked the wind out of her, and she bent over, gasping for breath. A thunderous boom overhead made her stand right up. She looked to the heavens and saw a brilliant flash, then a zigzagging web of lightning. It spread out like lace across the sky. Even in the maelstrom, she appreciated its beauty. But she also knew the lightning rod had been swept away with the mast and with it her only protection.

She leaned back towards the controls and tried to calculate her location. She had been running without steering for a few hours. It was hard to tell which way the wind and current had carried her, but she estimated that she was somewhere between—

Tess never finished the thought. The boat breached violently, and she toppled towards the lifelines. She skidded along the deck, slammed into a stainless-steel stanchion, then felt her safety harness cutting hard into her ribs. Now she was lying flat on the deck, staring up into the darkness. Her side ached, and she wondered how long the boat could take this beating. She pulled herself back to her feet, inched towards the cabin, and peered inside. The water had already swallowed the bunks and was rising fast.

Tess recognised that it was time to abandon ship. *Querencia* was going down. So she pulled the cord on the thick bundle strapped in the back of the cockpit and the raft began to inflate.

She had two choices: hurry below and activate the distress signal, or stay above and contact the Coast Guard on Channel 16, the emergency frequency. The radio in the cockpit was faster and, incredibly, it was unscathed. She reached for the mike.

Before she could even say 'Mayday', without any warning of thunder, a lightning bolt slammed into the deck. Tess felt the blast of heat from an explosion, then saw fire on the starboard side of the boat where the fuel tank was stored. Suddenly, the boat pitched to starboard, Tess lost her footing, and she felt the full force of her body slam against the jack line. For an instant, she was dangling upside-down over the transom. Then she felt the safety wire snap and the tension release on her harness. Now there was nothing keeping her on the boat. She began to slide into the churning ocean.

In that instant, dragged away by the waves, she looked back at her beloved boat, and those were the last images she could remember: *Querencia* on fire and the white sky and sea closing in all around.

'WOULD YOU EVER LEAVE the cemetery?'

Tess's question lingered in the glow of the fireplace. Perhaps they were simply in denial, or maybe they were swept away by each other, but they had abandoned the gloomy subject of the shipwreck and were dreaming out loud about what life would be like together.

'I mean, would you ever come with me around the world?' Tess asked. Her face was tucked into Charlie's neck.

'You've never seen me sail,' he said. 'Be careful what you wish for.'

'Don't joke. I'm being serious.' Her next question seemed almost too direct: 'Are you going to stay here for ever with Sam?'

Charlie stroked her hair. 'I couldn't face life without him.'

He kissed her softly on the forehead, and she felt safe enough to ask, 'So what about us? What's going to happen to you and me?'

He pulled her closer and kissed her gently on the cheek. Then he whispered, 'Come with me.' He slipped from the couch and stood up.

Tess watched him beckon and she didn't know what to do. One candle was still burning on the coffee table. The fire was out. The room was silent. 'We can't,' she said as the sadness returned. 'It's impossible. I couldn't even knock on the door. I'm not really here.'

'Can you feel this?' he said, leaning forward and kissing her on the corner of her eye.

'Of course.'

'Can you feel this?' he said, running his hand across her shoulders and down to her breasts.

'Yes.'

'You're still in between. Anything is possible.' He took the candle from the table and crossed the living room. 'This way,' he said.

Tess followed him up a steep staircase. His room was small and cosy, with a vaulted ceiling and exposed beams. A big bed took up almost all the space. He set the candle on the nightstand.

In the low light, Tess could see Charlie take off his T-shirt and dive onto the bed. She began to unbutton her shirt. Suddenly she noticed. The lines of her hands were softer. Her skin was fainter. Even the feeling of her clothes was different. Everything was less substantial. It took a moment to process, but then she realised.

She was beginning to fade away.

It filled her with pure terror. This was really, truly the end. It made no sense. Sam had promised the timing would be her decision. She had made up her mind: she didn't want to go yet. She wanted to stay right here with Charlie. She finished the last buttons of her shirt and kicked off her shoes. She dashed over to the bed and blew out the candle. She didn't want him to see her this way. She didn't want him to know it was happening.

Their fingers touched and they were together, his arms encircling her waist and her hands moving round his neck. Their kiss was deep, connecting, like a familiar story with a beginning, middle and end. They caught their breath, and then she kissed his forehead, face and shoulders. After kissing for the longest time, they began to fold into each other slowly and smoothly. For the first time ever, venturing deeper, Tess lost her sense of where she ended and he began.

Afterwards, with Charlie resting his head on her stomach, she felt the tears begin to well up, then spill.

'Please don't cry,' he said.

'I can't help it. I want to stay here with you. I don't want to go.'

'Don't worry,' he said. 'There's no rush.'

But in the shadowed bedroom, he still had not seen her fading form. She ran her hands through his hair and rubbed his sinuous back. She pulled him towards her once more. She didn't want to waste a single moment. There was no time to rest or sleep, for in her heart and soul she knew they would have only tonight.

THE TRADE WINDS rocked them gently in the hammock. The flag on the mast of the Catalina 400 rippled. They were anchored somewhere in the cays off the coast of Belize. Sipping from a coconut, Tess was nuzzled up against Charlie. She offered him the straw, he took a sip, and then kissed her lips and throat. He could smell the tanning lotion, sea salt and that unmistakable scent that was just hers.

'I love you,' she said, her eyes reflecting the sun and sky.

Just as he was about to swear his love, Charlie heard clanging. He lifted his head and looked down the length of the boat. An American flag fluttered at the stern. They were all alone, but there was more clanging, like someone beating a pan.

He struggled to make sense of the noise. 'What's that?' he asked, but Tess didn't answer. She suddenly seemed far away. He opened his eyes and reached out for her . . . but she was gone.

'Tess?' His heart ached as he leapt from the bed to the window. Outside, silver sheets of rain obscured the cemetery. That racket had to be Tink down on the dock, clanging the bell on the post. A century ago, the clamour was the fastest way to summon the gravediggers when a coffin from the North Shore had arrived by boat.

'OK, OK!' he grumbled. 'Give it a rest! I'll be right there!' He turned and grabbed his clothes from the chair. And there it was.

A note on her pillow.

His pulse quickened as he unfolded the piece of paper.

My dearest Charlie,

As I write this note, I can barely see my hands or hold this pen. By the time you open your eyes in the morning, you won't be able to see me any more. That's why I must go before you wake.

I'm sorry to leave without saying goodbye, but it's easier this way. I don't want you to see this happening to me . . . I just want you to remember our time together.

I had hoped to stay longer. There's so much we could have done. But I'll never forget how you opened my heart and made me feel more alive than I ever dreamed possible.

Sam told me that the timing of moving on was my decision. But apparently it's not. I hate the thought of leaving, but I'm hopeful about what's to come. I'm not afraid. You see, I think we were destined to meet. Some day, we'll be together. I believe that with all my heart.

Until then, I want you to dive for dreams. I want you to trust your heart. I want you to live by love. And when you're ready, come find me. I'll be waiting for you.

With all my love, Tess

Charlie felt the numbness spread from his fingers up his arms and all the way through his body. Dammit. When had he fallen asleep? How could he have let her go?

He threw on his clothes, folded the note and put it in his pocket. Tink was still clanging the bell on the dock. Charlie ran down the stairs and straight out of the door. He didn't even bother to grab a coat. When he got to the dock, Tink was in a lather.

'What took you so long?' he asked.

'I'm sorry,' Charlie said. The rain was cold, and he was shivering.

'You ready? Forget your coat?'

'It's too late,' Charlie said.

'Too late? For what? You're the only one who's late.'

'There's no point any more.' The water was streaming down his face and arms. 'Tess has gone. You won't find her out there.'

'Dammit, St Cloud. Last night you were the one who said we can't give up on her.'

'I know,' he said, brushing the rain from his face. 'I was wrong.'

Tink gunned the boat engine. 'I'm going without you. And screw you for wasting my time.' He pushed away from the dock and cursed as he steered into the channel.

Charlie watched Tink's boat disappear into the mist. Slowly, he felt himself steeling inside. It was Monday morning. The week was starting. His workers would be arriving soon. There were graves to dig. And when the day was done, his little brother would be waiting.

Nothing had changed. Everything had changed.

It was a miserable day, even for a funeral. Abraham Bailey, one of the richest men in town, had died in his sleep, and Charlie, bundled against the wind, was dressing the grave. With every action, memory fragments exploded in his mind: Tess's eyes, her laugh, her legs . . . Stop! Pay attention to the job, he admonished himself. Put out the chairs. Arrange the floral tributes.

He peered into the muddy ground that he had opened. It wasn't his most careful work. He brushed away a few stray clumps of dirt and smoothed the surface around the opening.

Then he stopped.

His will was broken. His edge was gone. He had lost his drive. The tape-recorded bells in the Chapel of Peace began to ring. He listened. And remembered. Walking under the moon. Making love by candlelight. The images rolled on, merging with the murk in his head and blurring grey like the cloud cover. For thirteen years he had been inured to the pain and drudgery of this place, but did he really want to spend his whole life here, only to be buried near his brother?

His eye caught sight of a big man moving between the tombstones. The afternoon light filtered right through him. It was Florio Ferrente, the fire-fighter, and he was fading.

'Greetings,' he said.

'Hey, haven't seen you in a few days.'

'Been real busy,' Florio said, 'trying to look after the wife and son.' Charlie put down his shovel. 'How are they holding up?'

'Not so good. It's been real rough. Francesca isn't sleeping. The baby won't stop crying. So I got a question for you, Charlie.' Florio seemed ten years younger and twenty pounds lighter. He was ready to move on. 'I need to know. How long does this last? You know, the pain? When Francesca hurts, I hurt too. It's like we're connected.'

'You *are* connected,' Charlie said, 'and it lasts until you and your family release each other.'

'What about you?' Florio asked. His eyes were serious. 'You think you got everything figured out?'

'I guess so. Why?'

'Just wondering.' Florio looked Charlie up and down, then put his hat on his head and adjusted the brim. There were tears in his eyes, and he wiped them away with a shimmering slab of hand. The light flowed through him as he looked across the vast lawns studded with granite. 'Remember the end of my funeral? Father Shattuck said, "May he rest in peace." I don't want to rest. I want to live.' He shook his head. 'But there isn't time for that. Know what I mean?'

'I do.'

'I guess I better get going.'

'You sure you don't want to stay?'

'No,' Florio said. 'Just watch out for my family, OK? Keep an eye on Francesca and the boy.'

'I promise.'

They shook hands, and Florio pulled him into an embrace. When they let go, Charlie saw the sparkle of a gold amulet round Florio's neck and recognised the engraved figure of St Jude, patron saint of desperate situations.

Florio grabbed Charlie's arm. 'Remember, God chose you for a reason.' Then he walked away, a gleaming mountain of a man, disappearing among the monuments.

AFTER HIS LAST EMPLOYEE clocked out, Charlie drove the little cart to the cottage by the forest. He went straight to his armchair, plunked himself down with a half-bottle of Jack Daniel's. He stared at the wall right in front of him with the maps and circles that defined his life. Twilight tonight would come at 6.29 p.m.

He guzzled one shot and poured himself another. This wasn't like him. He rarely drank and certainly not alone. But he wanted the pain to go away. He drained the second glass and poured a third. Soon his head was swimming and swirling through wild thoughts.

He thought about Sam and the promise. At first, the gift had seemed the greatest blessing. But now he understood. He and his kid brother were both trapped in the twilight. They were mirror images, clinging to each other, holding each other back from what awaited them beyond the great iron gates.

This was the end. He was finished with waiting for sundown every night to play catch with a loving ghost. He was through with the boundaries of those circles on the charts. And most of all, he was done with being alone. Florio was right. He had been given a second chance. And he had wasted it . . .

At first, the solution came to him as a faint glimmer. Something like it had crossed his mind thirteen years earlier when Sam had died. Back then he had pushed the answer into the dark caverns of his mind where it had belonged. But now the idea made another dramatic entrance. This time it seemed almost irresistible.

Come find me, Tess had written in her note. The answer was right there in her letter. If he couldn't be with her on earth, then why not join her out there somewhere? Why not give up this world for the next? It would be over quickly. It would put an end to all the pain. Most important, he and Tess would spend forever together. And he could keep his promise by bringing Sam along to the next level.

So what was he waiting for?

He got up and ripped the charts from the walls. He wouldn't need them where he was going. The room was spinning fast now. He reached out for a lamp to steady himself, but he lost his balance and fell to the ground, his head slamming against the wooden floorboards. He lay there stunned for a few moments and tried to focus his bewildered mind.

Then the thought came back to him again. It was the perfect solution to his problems, and only one question remained to be answered:

How would he take his own life?

WHEN CHARLIE CAME round, his body ached and he had an awful taste in his mouth. He sat up and rubbed his head. What time was it? He checked the clock over the fireplace: 5.35 p.m. Wow, he had been out for almost an hour. The last thing he remembered was ripping everything from the wall. Then he must have passed out.

He scooped up the torn scraps on the floor. Surprisingly, one chart had survived his attack and lay apart with a ray of sunlight glancing across the Isles of Shoals. His mind was racing. Was this a message? Or was this flat-out drunken craziness? He turned the chart round. It showed the area from Provincetown to Mt Desert Island, Maine, and the stretch from Cape Ann all the way across Bigelow Bight.

He studied the contours of the coast and ran his finger over the islands five miles offshore. As a boy, he had sailed every inch of that rugged coastline. He had explored the nine rocky outcroppings of the Isles of Shoals and had climbed to the very top of the old White Island Light. He knew where the waters were shallow and the ledges were hidden at high tide, and on countless fishing trips there he had caught bushels of mackerel and bluefish.

Come find me . . .

These desolate islands off the border of New Hampshire and Maine were nowhere near the Coast Guard's search area. In fact, the first wreckage had been picked up eighteen nautical miles due south off Halibut Point, and the burnt life raft had been floating even farther away. It was incredible: they had been searching in the wrong spot! Tess was waiting for him. And he had already wasted a day.

Charlie knew exactly what he had to do. He grabbed his coat, flew out of the door and took off across the cemetery.

IV

THE WIND

The bow of the *Horny Toad* scudded along the waves. Charlie stood on the tower of the twenty-eight-foot sportfishing boat and steered into the gloaming. The twin diesel engines were cranked up at full thrust, and in the cockpit Tink bounced along with his stomach jiggling and his shaggy hair blowing wild in the wind. Below on the back deck, Joe the Atheist shivered and sobered up faster than he would have liked.

When Charlie had finally found Joe at the Rip Tide, he was wobbling on a stool, well into his fourth shot of Jim Beam. The place was clogged with happy-hour regulars. Charlie had managed to elbow his way to the bar. He had grabbed Joe's stool and spun him round.

'I need a favour,' Charlie had said.

'Bartender!' Joe had shouted. 'A drink for my friend!'

'I need the *Horny Toad*,' Charlie had said.

Joe had lurched back and yelled, 'Hey, fellas! The boss wants my—'

Charlie had grabbed him by the collar. 'I don't have time for this. Tell me where your boat is. I'll have it back tomorrow morning.'

'You're going out all night without inviting me?'

'Just give me the keys. If anything happens, I'll pay you back.'

'Where you going? I want to know.'

'Please, Joe.'

'Answer's no,' he had said, crossing his tattooed arms.

Charlie's heart had sunk. He didn't have time or options. Who else was going to lend him a speedboat? And then, he had lost control. He had grabbed Joe by the collar and pulled him in so close he'd been able to smell the bourbon and tobacco. The room had stood still.

'Goddammit, I'm taking your boat!'

'Goddammit?' Joe had hissed. 'Who do you think you're talking to? I don't buy that baloney, remember?' Nobody in the bar had moved. Then Joe had burst out laughing. 'C'mon, St Cloud, let's get out of here. Wherever you're going, I'm coming with you.'

Joe had slammed his glass on the counter, lunged off the stool and stumbled towards the door. On the way to the boat, Charlie had grabbed his foul-weather gear from the back of his Rambler, while Joe had rummaged around in his Subaru and unearthed a party-size bag of Doritos and a pint of Old Crow.

On the dock, Tink had been dejectedly coiling his lines after a day of futile searching. His only sightings—some melted shards of fibreglass and charred seat cushions—were bad omens that the fire on *Querencia* had burned all the way through the hull.

'You were right,' Tink had said. 'It's too late.'

'No, I was wrong,' Charlie had answered. 'It's not too late. She's still out there. She's waiting for us.'

'Don't screw with me, St Cloud.' Tink's face had filled with anger. 'I'm not in the mood.'

'I'm serious, Tink. I think I know where she is. Come with us. What've you got to lose?'

'My sanity, but it's probably too late for that . . .' Tink had lifted his duffle and cooler, and hopped onto the *Horny Toad*.

Now Charlie aimed the prow on a fifty-five-degree heading towards the Gloucester sea buoy. They were doing twenty-five knots, and if the wind stayed behind them, they would be able to pick it up to thirty once they got round the tip of Cape Ann. At this speed, Charlie calculated it would take an hour. He checked the compass, then looked back over his shoulder. A flock of herring gulls was following in their wake. He checked his watch. It was already 6.20 p.m. He turned to Tink. 'Take the wheel for a minute?'

'You bet.' Tink stepped forwards and put both hands on the wood. Then Charlie climbed down the ladder and went to the stern. He stood there staring towards the west. Water and land merged in the twilight, a wedge of grey against the sky. The sun had slumped below the horizon. He imagined his little brother showing up and waiting all by himself on the swing, and felt the tears well up.

The view before him was changing colours, like slides on a screen. There were great strokes of purple on the horizon mixed with slashes of blue and white. He tried to savour the magnificence of the moment. For all those years, he had only seen the sun disappear between the trees in the forest. Now the whole world was before him, and he gasped at the vast beauty of it all. He breathed the damp and salty air, and the sky dissolved once more into bands of blue and grey until everything was black.

'Goodbye, Sam,' he whispered. Then he turned and climbed the ladder back to the bridge. There were stars in the sky ahead, and he knew one thing for sure. Tess was out there waiting for him, and he would not let her down.

THEY WERE SMACK in the middle of the Isles of Shoals, between Smuttynose and Star Islands. Charlie reached for the searchlight and hit the switch. The beam sliced the darkness and its white point glanced off the water. A night of desperate searching stretched ahead.

He and Tink took turns at the wheel, sweeping the emptiness with the light, calling out until their voices were hoarse. Joe woke up around 3 a.m. and pitched in for an hour, steering while Charlie and Tink stood watch. With each brush of the searchlight, with every advancing second, Charlie's heart sank even further. 'Give me a sign, Tess,' he prayed. 'Show me the way.'

There was only silence.

As dawn came at 6.43 a.m., the east began to glow with stripes of orange and yellow. But the arrival of this new day meant only the worst for Charlie. He had risked everything and he had lost. His back ached from standing watch. His stomach growled from lack of food. His head hurt from a night of crying out into the gloom.

Then he heard Joe down below, grumbling and grunting as he climbed the ladder. 'I'm sorry,' he said. 'I must've nodded off.' His voice was raspy from sleep. 'Any luck?'

'None.'

'Well, you did your best,' Joe said, reaching for the wheel and shoving Charlie aside. 'I'm the captain of this boat and I say we go home.'

'It's just getting light,' Charlie protested. 'Maybe we missed her last night.' He turned to Tink. 'What do you say?'

Joe interrupted: 'Face it, Charlie. I know you had to get this out of your system, but she's gone.' He started to turn the boat around.

'No! She's alive.' Charlie barely recognised his own voice. 'Cold water slows your metabolism. It's the mammalian dive reflex. Your body knows how to shut down everything except for essential functions and organs.' It was the only thing left to hold on to. 'Remember those climbers on Everest a few years ago? They were above twenty-seven thousand feet in the death zone. But they managed to survive.'

'Those climbers were lucky, that's all,' Joe said.

'It wasn't luck. It was a miracle.'

'How many times do I have to tell you? There's no such thing.'

Joe pushed forwards on the throttle and the boat leaped for home. Charlie knew it was over. Numbly, he made his way down the ladder to the stern, where he sank down on one of the benches. As he stared at the wake spreading out behind him, the sun bathed the ocean in a soft glow. But Charlie felt an aching cold inside. He wondered if he would ever be warm again.

Sam was wind. He whooshed across the Atlantic, skimming the wave tops. He was liberated from the in-between, and the parameters of his new playground were dazzlingly infinite—the universe with its hundred billion galaxies and all the other dimensions beyond consciousness or imagination. No longer constricted by his promise, he had moved on to the next level, where he could morph into any shape.

Sam was now a free spirit.

But there was one more thing he had to do on earth. He swept over the bow of the *Horny Toad* and swirled around his brother, trying to get his attention, but to no avail. Then he twanged the guy wires of the boat, making an eerie, wailing song, but Charlie didn't hear.

Last night, Sam had felt annoyed and betrayed by Charlie's abrupt departure from the cemetery. At sundown, he had hung around the Forest of Shadows, waiting. Loneliness had overwhelmed him as the purple light vanished from the sky, and the hidden playground had grown dark. Soon anger began to creep in as he realised his big brother had ditched him for a girl and had broken their promise.

Then Sam was struck with an amazing notion. He had never really thought about moving on before. Life in between—making mischief in Marblehead and playing catch at sundown—had always suited him and Oscar just fine. But if Charlie was willing to risk everything to venture out into the world, then maybe Sam should do the same.

And so, without trumpets or fanfare, without a blinding flash of light or chorus of angels, he had simply crossed over to the next level. The transition was as smooth and effortless as his fastball.

From that moment forward, everything had changed for Sam. He was filled with the wisdom of the ages and all the knowledge and experience that had eluded him when his life was cut short.

With this new perspective, more than ever Sam wanted to comfort his brother and make sure that everything would be OK.

ABRUPTLY, THE WIND changed to the southwest, pushing the white-caps in a new direction. Absorbed in his thoughts, Charlie paid no heed, until a bracing splash of spindrift hit him in the face.

Through stinging eyes, he recognised the sea was in turmoil and the wind was gusting. He jumped to his feet and sprang up the ladder into the tower, where Joe was struggling to stay on course and Tink was studying the charts.

'Need some help?' Charlie offered eagerly.

'Sure,' Joe said, 'how about driving while I take a leak?'

'No problem.'

Charlie seized the wheel and fastened his sight on the white tufts of the waves and their spray, adjusting his steering to every subtle change in the wind's direction. Soon a jagged shape, small and shrouded in grey fog, began to take form in the distance. What was it? A boat? An island?

Suddenly it became clear. It was an outcropping in the water. Through binoculars, he could see its eroded slopes and surface spotted with seaweed and guano. The boat was bouncing now, and he fought to keep his focus on the rock. For an instant, he thought he spotted a fleck of colour. Doggedly, he repositioned the lenses.

Then he saw something truly extraordinary: a glimpse of orange, the unmistakable colour of an ocean survival suit.

THE HOWLING ROTORS from the Coast Guard Jayhawk blasted Mingo Rock with wind and spray. An aviation survivalman dropped down in a sling on a cable to the ledge where Charlie cradled Tess's head in his lap, her face covered with his jacket to protect her from the downwash. She was still bundled in her survival suit and lashed with a rope to a banged-up watertight aluminium storage container. Her makeshift raft, he guessed: she had probably floated on it until she had found this rock and somehow pulled herself onto it.

His exhilaration had been eviscerated by the reality of her condition. Her skin was almost blue. Her pupils were pinpoint. She had a contusion on the back of her head. She had no detectable pulse.

He had got there too late.

His heart was filled with alarm as the survivalman unpacked his emergency kit. The guy didn't waste a word, moving with urgency and efficiency.

'She's hypothermic,' Charlie said. 'I've been doing CPR for twenty minutes.'

'Good,' the man said. 'We'll take it from here.' Deftly, gently, he began to cut Tess from the rope, and Charlie admired his skill. Any sudden movement of the patient's arms and legs could flood the heart with cold venous blood from the extremities and induce cardiac arrest.

Then the survivalman radioed the helicopter that he was ready, and a rescue hoist litter dropped from the air.

'Where you taking her?' Charlie asked, praying the answer would be a hospital and not the morgue.

'North Shore ER. Best hypothermia unit around.'

Charlie watched the survivalman lift Tess into the stretcher harness and strap her in. He hooked his belt to the cable, gave the thumbs-up sign to the winch operator and watched them lift off from the rock. Charlie stared straight up into the pounding rotor wake as the basket swayed and was finally pulled inside the helicopter. Then the Jayhawk tilted forward and climbed into the west.

CHARLIE HATED the emergency room. It wasn't looking at these ill and anxious people that unnerved him. He was uncomfortable because of what he couldn't see but had always sensed. His gift had never extended beyond the cemetery gates, but he knew the spirits were there in the hospital.

Was Tess's spirit here now? he wondered, as he sat on the hard Formica chair and listened to the fish tank bubbling across from him. He closed his eyes to rest, but his mind would not stop. He had spent the last two hours in a frantic race to the hospital, desperate to get to Tess and find out her medical status. But no news. Tink sat on the other side of the room. Big fingers poking at his little cellphone, he was dialling numbers all over Marblehead, letting folks know Tess was in the hospital.

Charlie tried to calm himself, but his thoughts kept circling. Why were they taking so long? Maybe it wasn't just hypothermia. Perhaps her head injury was more serious than he imagined. Suddenly the revolving doors spun round and Charlie saw Tess's mother enter. He recognised her immediately from the oval shape of her face and the angle of her nose. He jumped up.

'Mrs Carroll,' he said, 'I'm so sorry I didn't get to Tess sooner.'

She shook her head. 'Bless you for finding her,' she said, reaching out to touch his arm. 'Please call me Grace.'

'I'm Charlie,' he said. 'Charlie St Cloud.'

'St Cloud. Like an angel from the sky,' she said.

Tink approached and put a burly arm around her.

'Have the doctors told you anything about Tess yet?' Charlie asked.

'No, I got here ten minutes after the helicopter landed, and the Coast Guard wouldn't tell me anything.' She stared into Charlie's eyes. 'How'd she look when you found her? Did she say anything?'

Before Charlie could answer, the ER doors opened and a nurse came out. 'Mrs Carroll?' she said. 'Please come with me. The doctor is waiting to see you.'

'Oh, good,' Grace said.

Charlie, however, was crushed. His stomach clenched. Doctors always showed up with good tidings but dispatched the nurses to bring families in when things had gone wrong.

Grace turned to Charlie and said, 'Come on, let's go. You, too, Tink. I'm not setting foot in there by myself.' The three marched forwards into the ER, and the nurse showed them to a consultation room.

The doctor began with a few banal pleasantries and introductions.

Charlie watched her carefully for clues. Her face expressed compassion, but the muscles in her neck were taut. Next she dived into the facts. Her speech was staccato. 'Tess suffered acute head trauma and extreme hypothermia. She's in critical condition. She's unable to breathe on her own. We have her on a respirator now.'

Grace put her hand to her mouth.

'I can assure you that she isn't in any pain,' the doctor said. 'She's in a deep coma. She's not responsive in any way. We measure these things on something called the Glasgow Scale. Fifteen is normal. Tess is at level five. It's a very grave situation.'

Grace was shaking now, and Tink put his arm round her. 'What's going to happen?' he asked. 'Will she wake up?'

'No one knows the answer to that question,' the doctor said. 'The only thing we can do is wait.'

'Wait for what?' Grace asked. 'Why can't you do anything?'

'She's a very strong and healthy woman,' the doctor said, 'and it's quite extraordinary she survived this long. But the cranial trauma was severe and her exposure to the elements was prolonged.' She paused. 'There is a theoretical chance her injuries will heal themselves. And there are coma cases that defy explanation.' Her voice lowered. 'But I believe it's important to be realistic. The likelihood of a reversal is remote.'

There was a long silence as the words registered. Charlie felt solid ground collapse beneath him. Then the doctor said, 'If you want to have a moment with her, now would be a good time.'

'**I** quit.'

They were two words that Charlie never imagined uttering, but he was stunned by how easily they came out. He was standing on the shoulder of Avenue A, the asphalt lane that bisected Waterside.

Elihu Swett, the cemetery commissioner, had been making rounds in his Lincoln Continental and had pulled over to the side of the road. From his capacious front seat, he peered up through the open window. 'You sure I can't make you reconsider?' Elihu asked.

'I'm sure.' Charlie smiled. 'It's time for me to go.'

Elihu scowled. 'Maybe you'll change your mind,' he said. 'You'll always have a place here if you want to come back.'

After shaking his hand, Charlie jumped into his cart and scooted off along the paths. He had decided to treat his last day like every other, so he did his chores, made his rounds and stopped to say good-bye to his pals. Joe the Atheist hugged him hard and confided that he was rethinking his relationship to God.

Then, back in the cottage, he threw his few good things into a duffle bag and packed his favourite books and CDs in another. He would leave the inherited furniture from Barnaby Sweetland, his pre-decessor, for the next caretaker. He looped the keys on the hook, set his bags out on the step and closed the door behind him. Then he loaded the cart and headed north, to the small mausoleum on the hill shaded by two willow trees.

He got out of the cart, took an old-fashioned skeleton key from the glove compartment and opened the door. In the semidarkness, he sat on the little sarcophagus and swung his legs. He chucked the ball into the mitt. Then, with a smile at the blue angel in the stained-glass window, he put them down on the smooth Carrara marble. Right where they belonged.

The sun was going down and Charlie locked the vault. He stood looking down on the harbour below. God, he would miss Sam and their mischief. Then the wind picked up, the trees in the forest began to shudder and a flurry of crimson oak leaves floated down, twirled in front of him and blew away.

Sam was there, Charlie knew right away. His brother was all around him in the air, the sky, the sunset and the leaves. On his last day at Waterside, there was just one more place to go.

The hidden playground was silent. No fussing birds, no frantic squirrels, no spirits drifting. It was 6.51 p.m. Charlie drank in the sylvan setting, memorising the colour of the leaves and the angles of the light. He knew he would never return. Soon the forest would overrun the ball field, and no one would know it had ever existed.

The thought brought tears to his eyes. This had been the most important space in the world to him, but he had made his choice and now there was somewhere else he needed to be. He took a deep breath, inhaling the musty fragrance of autumn, and was about to go when he was startled to see a young man walking across the grass.

The intruder was tall, at least six foot three inches, and his shoulders were square and broad. His face was narrow and long, his hair was curl and his shining eyes were unmistakable.

Charlie gasped in astonishment.

'Hey, big bro,' Sam said with a smile.

'Look at you!' Charlie managed to say at last. 'You're a man.'

'Yes,' he said, 'I'm finally a man and I can do what I want.'

They were face-to-face now, and Charlie realised that his brother was glimmering like a hologram with luminous surfaces. Sam was now a reflection of the past and the present and a projection of the future—all he had been and all he wanted to be.

'You crossed over,' Charlie said.

'I did.'

'And how is it?'

'Beyond anything we ever imagined, Charlie. It's mind-blowing.'

'So how did you get back here? I didn't realise you could return.'

'There are lots of things you don't understand,' Sam said. 'But don't worry. That's the way it's supposed to be.'

They wandered into the forest and sat on the log by the pool.

'You mad I broke the promise?' Charlie asked.

'No,' Sam said. 'It was time. We were holding each other back.'

In that moment, Charlie realised what he had truly lost in those thirteen years. They had never shared an adult conversation. Sam had not grown up, and their relationship had been frozen in time.

Charlie wished he could wrap his arm round Sam's shoulders. 'That was you out there on the water the other morning, wasn't it?' he asked. 'You know, with the spray and the wind?'

'Sure took you long enough to notice!'

Charlie studied the translucent outlines of his brother who had grown so much and yet was still the same.

'I guess I have only one regret,' Charlie said. 'I'm sorry I held on to you for so long.' He wiped tears from his face.

'It's OK,' Sam said. 'I held on just as much as you.'

There was a long silence, then Charlie asked, 'You think we'll ever play catch again?'

'Of course,' Sam said. 'We'll be back together in the blink of an eye. And then we'll have forever.'

'Promise you won't leave me,' Charlie said.

'Promise.'

'Cross your heart and hope to die?'

'Hope to die,' Sam said. 'I love you.'

'I love you too.' The brothers stood up.

Sam went to the tree at the foot of the pond. There was a thick rope hanging from a lower branch. 'One last push?' he said.

With a whoop, Charlie pushed, and Sam began to swing out over the water. 'Bye, big bro,' he shouted, letting go and reaching for the sky. He tucked into a tight forward somersault with a twist. Then Sam was gone, vanished, and the clearing was silent except for the swinging rope and a flurry of crimson oak leaves on the wind.

THE LAST CLOSING TIME, the last zoom around to collect an elderly gentleman in a seersucker suit in the Vale of Serenity.

'Good evening,' Charlie said.

Palmer Guidry poured the last drop from his red watering can, his old cassette recorder played Brahms.

'Well, hello, Charlie!'

'We're shutting down for the night. Can I give you a lift?'

'Why, thank you. So good of you.'

Mr Guidry made a final inspection of the crimson bloom of a tall plant. 'Hollyhocks were Betty's favourite,' he said.

'I think you told me once.'

'You know, Betty planted the whole backyard with pink hollyhocks one time. They grew seven feet high!'

'Oh, really?'

'Night, Betty,' he said. 'Sweet dreams, my love. Be back soon.' He climbed into the cart and tucked the watering can and cassette recorder underneath his legs.

'Want to come over for dinner tonight?' Mr Guidry asked as they approached the iron gates. 'I'll whip up one of Betty's favourites. Finest meat loaf on God's green earth.'

'Yes,' Charlie said. 'I'd like that. In fact, I'd like that a lot.'

Mr Guidry hesitated for a moment. Even with Alzheimer's he knew something was different. Something had changed. His eyes twinkled, and his face displayed a hint of recognition. 'Don't you have someplace to be?' he asked. 'Isn't that what you always say?' It was another little miracle, one of those mysterious moments of clarity in a confusing world.

'Not any more,' Charlie said. 'I'll follow you home.'

As he pushed the great iron gates shut for the last time, he smiled. Then he turned and hefted his two duffles into the back of his

Rambler. Mr Guidry pulled out onto West Shore Drive in his Buick, and Charlie followed him down the road. He looked out of the window and waved goodbye to the rows of monuments, the acres of lawns, and his world within a world. And Charlie St Cloud, dearly departed caretaker of Waterside Cemetery, never looked back.

Marblehead hummed with Thanksgiving week contentment. The chilly air carried the comforting scent of burning logs. Hibernating boats huddled on winter dry docks and dreamed of warm weather. Twinkling Christmas decorations made their merry debut. Around Engine Company 2 on Franklin Street, life was especially good. There hadn't been a big blaze since the School Street fire.

Charlie was wearing the uniform of a full-time paramedic at the station, now also his home until he found a place of his own. On this utterly uneventful Friday, as the clock in the rec room chimed six, Charlie grabbed a coat from his locker and headed out to the Rambler. With a few turns of the key, he brought the old car to life.

Tonight Charlie had only one place to go. He headed down Pleasant Street and within minutes pulled into the parking lot of the North Shore Medical Center. He walked right through the lobby, waved to the admission nurses and went straight to Room 172.

Tess was alone and asleep in her coma. Bandages and ventilator gone, she was pale, but was breathing on her own now. Her hands were folded on her chest, and she seemed completely at peace. He had memorised every detail of her oval face, her pale lips and her long eyelashes.

In eight weeks, Charlie had studied all sorts of books and articles on brain injury. The longest, best-documented complete recovery from a coma was two and a half years, but he knew something miraculous could also happen for Tess, and, in a way, it already had. God had answered his prayers. She hadn't vanished from the cemetery because she was moving on to the next realm. She had disappeared because she was trying to return to this life.

Hanging over her bed, an autographed poster of Tom Brady, the Patriots quarterback and Super Bowl hero, said, *Get well soon*. Photos of her dad fishing on his lobster boat and of *Querencia* in sea trials crowded the bedside table.

'Big weekend for your boys,' Charlie said, sitting down beside her. He pulled the *Boston Globe* sports page from his coat pocket and read her the highlights. 'Looks like the Jets plan to challenge your linebackers with some new tight end they drafted.'

This was Charlie's ritual now, but he did not want to slip back into his old habit of following a fixed routine. Sometimes he stopped by in the morning. On other occasions he dropped by after work. One week he would skip a few days, then another he would show up steadily for a stretch. He wanted to be there for her, but he also wanted to live his life.

Charlie believed that Tess was listening to every word of every story. He tried to make things quick and funny. He wanted to amuse her, even in her sleep. Sometimes he imagined her throwing her head back in laughter. Other times he pictured her giving him grief when he went on for too long.

It was dark now. The hospital was silent. It was time to go. 'Night, Tess,' he said. 'I sure miss you.' He kissed her on the cheek and had started through the door when he realised he had forgotten to say something. 'I'm having dinner with Tink tonight,' he said, going back to her. 'We're heading over to the Barnacle. I wish you'd warned me how much that guy could eat. There aren't enough clams in the ocean to fill him up.' He reached forwards and pushed her curls away.

Then Charlie saw her lashes flutter and her incredible emerald eyes open, and he wondered if he was imagining them.

MIST SHROUDED THE GROUND, muffling the sounds of the world. She couldn't see anyone else around. She could have been anywhere or nowhere. It didn't matter. Charlie was gone, her father had never come to greet her, and she was all alone.

Ever since leaving the cemetery, she had been in this same place. It was like the deep ocean on a moonless night. The sky was a blanket of black without familiar stars to give her bearings. In the distance, vague shapes like thunderheads seemed to shift about. Sometimes voices emerged around her, then went away.

She had tried to call for help but no one answered. She wanted to cut through the gloom but couldn't seem to budge. And so she had waited, watching for the moment to make her move.

Now was the time.

At first, with darkness slowly giving way to light, everything was blurry. Her brain, the room, and the man looking down at her. 'Tess,' he kept saying. 'Tess, can you hear me?' Of course she could hear him. She wanted to form words in response, but she couldn't make sounds. How strange. She tried again, but her mouth and throat were parched. When at last she found her voice, it was raspy and barely audible. 'Tess,' she said. 'Tess.'

'Yes, Tess!' the man said. He was so excited.

'Yes, Tess,' she repeated.

'You're back! My God, you're back!'

'You're back,' she said. She knew she was just repeating his words, but it was the best she could do.

'How do you feel?' he was saying. 'Does anything hurt?'

In fact, she couldn't feel a thing. Her body was numb and her head groggy. She moved her eyes around the room. 'Where?' she began tentatively. 'Where am I?' That wasn't bad, she thought. *Where am I?* A complete sentence. She smiled faintly, and the skin on her cheeks felt tight.

'You're in the hospital,' he said. 'North Shore Medical Center.'

The words didn't register entirely. 'Where?' she asked again.

'The hospital. You had an accident. You were injured. But everything's OK now.'

Hospital. Accident. Injured.

'What accident?' she asked.

'You were sailing,' he said. 'Your boat caught fire in a storm. Do you remember?'

Fire. Storm. She didn't recall. 'Boat?' she said. 'What happened?'

'I'm sorry,' he said, 'but *Querencia* burned and sank.'

Querencia. She liked the way that sounded, and the lilt of the syllables brought back fragments of memory and meaning. '*Querencia.* Spanish, safe place.'

'Yes!' the man said. 'You're right. It's Spanish.'

She was trying to focus. More thoughts were taking shape.

'Water,' she said. 'I'm thirsty.'

The man hurried to the sink and poured her a glass. Gently, he held it to her lips, and she took a sip, swirling the cool liquid in her mouth. She squinted towards the window, where the branches of a tree were blowing in the wind. 'Window,' she said.

'Yes, window.'

'Open it, please.'

The man rushed over, threw the bolt, and slid it up. 'There you go.'

An amazing breeze wafted into the room, and Tess closed her eyes as it rustled her hair. Water and wind. Yes; she loved them both.

The man reached for the phone. 'I'm calling your mom. OK?'

'OK,' she said. 'Mom.'

The man punched the numbers and began to speak rapidly. She couldn't follow what he was saying. When he put it down, she asked, 'Who are you? Doctor?'

'It's me, Charlie. Remember?'

She didn't remember. Her memory was blank.

'Tess, please, try to think back,' he was saying. 'It's me, Charlie.'

She shook her head. 'I'm sorry, I just don't remember . . .' Then she saw tears streaming down his face. Why was he crying? 'What's wrong?' she asked.

'Nothing's wrong. I'm just so happy to see you.'

Tess smiled, and this time her face didn't feel so taut. 'Your name?' she said. 'What's your name?'

'Charlie St Cloud.'

Charlie St Cloud. She crinkled her nose. Things were coming back faster now. Files were opening in her brain. 'St Cloud,' she said. 'Not a Marblehead name.'

'You're right,' he answered. 'Minnesota. Long story, too.'

'I like stories,' she said.

And then Charlie sat down beside her and explained that his name came from a Mississippi River town where his mother had grown up. The original St Cloud was a sixth-century French prince who renounced the world to serve God after his brothers were murdered by an evil uncle.

Tess liked the deep timbre of his voice. It reminded her of someone but she couldn't place it. When he was done telling her the story, she reached out and touched his hand. It felt so warm and strong.

'The Patriots have a big game this weekend,' he was saying. 'You love football, remember?' She studied his gentle face with a dimple in one cheek. There was something different about this man.

'Tell me another story, Charlie.'

'Anything you want,' he said, and he began to talk of sailing around the world to distant places like the Marquesas, Tuamotu Islands, Tonga and Fiji.

Every word came like comfort, so she eased back into the pillows and basked in the warmth of Charlie's caramel eyes. She wondered how it was that she already knew she could listen to this man for a very long time.

IT WAS PAST MIDNIGHT. The doctors had finished checking Tess and, incredibly, had determined that her physical and cognitive functions were intact, and her memory would probably return to normal.

A writer and photographer from the *Reporter* had rushed over to ask questions and snap pictures for a special edition of the paper. Tink and the crew from the sail loft had paraded through with encouragement and news from the company. Her joy exceeding her energy, Grace had finally gone to sleep in the next room.

Now all was quiet.

Wide awake in the waiting room, Charlie stared at the fish tank. Grateful as he was that she was back, his mind stuck on one question: Would she remember him?

Their first kiss . . .

Their night in each other's arms . . .

As friends and family surrounded Tess that evening, Charlie had watched as she gradually recalled *Querencia*'s struggle against the storm. Whenever her gaze turned to Charlie in the back of the room, and it was often, she had smiled but seemed unsure who he was or why he was there. Who could blame her?

Now the doors opened across the waiting room, and a nurse beckoned in a hushed voice, 'She's asking for you, Charlie.'

'What?'

'She wants to see you.'

He covered the distance to her bedside in what seemed like five steps. Amazingly, she was sitting up, her face softly illuminated by the nightlight. 'I'm glad you're still here,' she said.

'I'm glad you are too,' Charlie answered.

She was studying him intensely. Finally she said, 'So you're the one who found me.'

'I guess that's true.'

'After everyone had given up?'

'Pretty much.'

'I need to know something,' she said. 'It's important.'

'Yes, I confess, I'm a Red Sox fan,' he said with a smile.

She threw her head back and laughed. 'I can forgive that,' she said, 'but there's one thing I can't remember.'

'What's that?'

'How we met.'

'You wouldn't believe me if I told you.'

'Try me,' she said. 'Tell me our story.'

'Well,' he recalled, 'it starts in Waterside Cemetery where a brave and beautiful sail-maker complained to the caretaker about a disturbance of the peace.' Charlie smiled. 'The charming fellow tried to explain the importance of his geese-management programme, but the unimpressed sailor only laughed.'

And so Charlie tenderly described their first encounters, from a candlelit dinner with a Ted Williams cake to a midnight walk with weeping willows and a marble mausoleum. As her eyes registered every detail, he was filled with hope. He had let go of the past and reclaimed his life. And now, the greatest blessing of all, he and Tess were starting over.

AFTERWORD

I believe in miracles, and now you know why.

I stand on a sloping hill in Waterside Cemetery, a place Charlie loved and shaped with his own hands. The iron gates stand open. A fuzzy old man puts a fistful of hollyhocks on his wife's grave.

That's the world you know. It's the one you can see when you pass by the cemetery in your town. It's the one that's real and reassuring. But there's another world here too. I'm talking about what you and Charlie can't see yet, the level beyond the in-between. It's a place called heaven, paradise, or nirvana—they're all the same, really—and it's where I came when I crossed over. It's where Mrs Ruth Phipps can once again hold hands with her beloved Walter. And of course, it's where Sam and Oscar can explore the universe.

From this vantage point, I see everything now. My voice and thoughts are wind, and I send them towards Charlie. He's with Tess in North Shore Medical Center, where she gets stronger every day.

Yes, that's one of our abilities on this side—to glimpse, hear, and know all. We are everywhere. We experience everything. We rejoice when you rejoice. We're sad when you're sad. We grieve when you grieve. And when you hold on too long, it hurts us the same way it hurts you. I think of my wife, Francesca, and our son. I know it will take time and many tears, but I want them to move on. Some day she'll marry again and find new happiness.

Charlie knows what's important now. First and foremost, he and

Tess will fall in love again. They'll kiss for the first time. They'll sail the coral cays of Belize on their honeymoon. They'll settle down on Cloutman's Lane in the same house where he grew up. They'll have two sons. He'll build his boys a playground with swings under a pine tree. He'll play a good game of catch with them every night, and he'll encourage them to race the moon and go on great adventures.

Charlie's gift of seeing the spirit world faded away just as soon as he and Sam released each other for the last time. But every day, he'll try to live with his eyes open to the other side, letting the possibility of miracles in. That's death and life, you see. We all shine on. You just have to release your hearts, alert your senses and pay attention. A leaf, a star, a song, a laugh. Notice the little things, because some-body is reaching out to you. *Qualcuno ti ama.* Somebody loves you.

And one day—only God knows precisely when—Charlie will run out of time. He'll be an old man, floppy hair turned grey. He'll look back on his quietly remarkable life and know he made good on his promise. And then, like the seventy-five billion souls who lived before him, each and every one a treasure, he, too, will die.

When that day comes, we'll be waiting. Waiting for Charlie St Cloud to come home to us. Until then we offer these parting words . . .

May he live in peace.

BEN SHERWOOD

The themes of loss and love that Ben Sherwood explores in *The Death and Life of Charlie St Cloud* grew out of a painful personal experience. 'When my father died eleven years ago—very suddenly, at the healthy and vigorous age of sixty-four—it was a crushing loss . . . Only recently did I realise that I was in the grip of that loss without being aware of it. We all lose someone at some point—parent, friend or sibling—and we all have this choice whether to stop, to freeze, or to move forward. One of the ideas in the story that is very important to me is that holding on doesn't just hurt us and damage us, but that maybe it hurts them [the people we are mourning] too.'

In the interests of research into Charlie St Cloud's job, Sherwood spent time as a gravedigger in a rural cemetery, and says it was a life-affirming, if back-breaking experience. 'One becomes intensely aware of the fragility of life when one sees the gravestones of children, or witnesses the cemetery familiars who come back every day to be with their wives or husbands.'

On a happier note, it was while developing the second theme of the novel—the love story between Charlie and Tess—that Sherwood found a deep, healing love of his own. He met Karen Kehela, producer of the film *A Beautiful Mind,* and in August 2002 proposed marriage to her on bended knee on the 102nd floor of the Empire State Building. The couple married in Los Angeles the following March, beneath the sycamore tree where the author and his sister had played as children. For Sherwood, as for Charlie St Cloud, finding love brought liberation from guilt and sadness.

Sherwood wrote his first best seller, *The Man Who Ate the 747*, when he was working as a network news producer for NBC and ABC. It was around the time of President Clinton's impeachment and the war in Kosovo, and Sherwood believes that his novels came partly from a desire to escape the cynicism and political machinations he saw around him. 'There is a certain innocence in the way *The Death and Life of Charlie St Cloud* is told, which is very much the way I want to write. Besieged by a world that is grim and bleak, I think people want a story that is life-affirming and hopeful.'

THE ZERO GAME. Original full-length edition © 2004 by Brad Meltzer. British condensed edition © The Reader's Digest Association Limited, 2004.

THE FIRE BABY. Original full-length edition © 2004 by Jim Kelly. British condensed edition © The Reader's Digest Association Limited, 2004.

THE PROMISE OF A LIE. Original full-length edition © 2004 by Howard Roughan. US condensed edition © The Reader's Digest Association, Inc, 2004. British condensed edition © The Reader's Digest Association Limited, 2004.

THE DEATH AND LIFE OF CHARLIE ST CLOUD. Original full-length edition © 2004 by Ben Sherwood. British condensed edition © The Reader's Digest Association Limited, 2004.

The right to be identified as authors has been asserted by the following in accordance with sections 77 and 78 of the Copyright, Designs and Patents Act, 1988: Brad Meltzer, Jim Kelly, Howard Roughan and Ben Sherwood.

ACKNOWLEDGMENTS AND PICTURE CREDITS: *The Zero Game*: pages 6–8: illustration: Curtis Phillips-Cozier; Getty Images; page 153: © Jackie Merri Meyer; *The Fire Baby*: pages 154–156: Corbis; Getty Images; *The Promise of a Lie*: pages 292–294: Getty Images; page 433: © Suzanne M. Sheridan; *The Death and Life of Charlie St Cloud*: pages 434–436: illustration: Andrew Gawne; page 539 © Kara Baker.

DUSTJACKET CREDITS: Spine from top: illustration: Curtis Phillips-Cozier; Getty Images; Corbis; Getty Images; illustration: Andrew Gawne.

Printed by Maury Imprimeur SA, Malesherbes, France
Bound by Reliures Brun SA, Malesherbes, France

230/04